LONG MAY SHE REIGN

LONG MAY SHE REIGN

ELLEN EMERSON WHITE

Feiwel and Friends New York

A Feiwel and Friends Book
An Imprint of Holtzbrinck Publishers

 For information, address Feiwel and Friends, 175 Fifth Avenue, New York, N.Y. 10010.

Library of Congress Cataloging-in-Publication Data Available

ISBN-13: 978-0-312-36767-1
ISBN-10: 0-312-36767-8

First Edition: November 2007

10 9 8 7 6 5 4 3 2 1

www.feiwelandfriends.com

For

JAN PRICE

Thanks

LONG MAY SHE REIGN

1

THE WORST PART—although it was hard to choose—was that she still cried. A lot. Mostly at night; always alone. Which was risky, because her parents inevitably came in to check on her, and she'd have to pretend to be asleep.

But now, it was going on to two in the morning, and she was by herself in her room, and she sort of wished that one of them *would* come in. See how she was. Have a conversation about nothing in particular, maybe. But, it was the middle of the night. Normal people were already asleep.

Meg pushed away from her desk. Her chair was on rollers now, which was one of the many changes in her life that they didn't really discuss. At least she wasn't using the actual wheelchair anymore. Just a brace and a cane. And her hand, gosh, she could almost move two of the fingers now, and—yes, it was time for Nightly Self-Pity.

For that matter, it was also time for some more ibuprofen. At this point, the doctors only gave her prescription painkillers as a last resort, and she couldn't quite bring herself to tell them how much she still needed the god-damned things.

She reached for her cane, then changed her mind. The thought of making her way across the room to the bathroom was too tiring. Hell, even the concept of getting up and limping the few steps over to her bed was exhausting to contemplate.

"Hey, you," she said to her cat, Vanessa, who was asleep on the rocking chair by the fireplace. "You want to fetch me some water?"

Vanessa stretched out one paw slightly, but otherwise didn't respond. Didn't even open her eyes.

Of course, this was the White House. All she had to do was pick up the damned phone, and someone would appear within seconds, and—except that it was too late to bother them. Too embarrassing. Too *pathetic.*

Christ, she was tired. Using her good hand, she dragged her chair back to the desk and looked at her books. Even though it was only two courses, the work was still too hard. She should have just taken the semester off. Maybe the whole year. But then, she would spend even more time alone in this stupid room, and what? Sleep twenty, twenty-two hours a day? Wake up for the occasional meal, or physical therapy session? Oh, yeah, that'd be productive.

Which didn't change the fact that even her truncated version of college was too much pressure. Having to leave the house—having to leave the second floor, for that matter—accompanied by three times as many Secret Service agents as she had had before, while everyone *everywhere* stared, and took photographs, and—well, nothing like getting kidnapped by terrorists to guarantee ending up being the center of attention. To become permanent public property.

All the more so, because she had ended up with a few battle scars.

To say the very least.

Yup, Self-Pity Time was kicking into high gear.

"If you do something well, do it often," she said to Vanessa, who didn't even stretch this time.

So, she picked up *Winesburg, Ohio*, the book they were currently reading in her Twentieth Century American Fiction survey course. The other class she was taking was Introduction to Astronomy. Mainly, because it was taught in a darkened auditorium, and she could keep a low profile. Unfortunately, the class was pretty hard—or else, she had become very dense—because retrograde motion and parallax seemed to be beyond her. She'd never exactly been Miss Wizard, but before—last spring—at least she hadn't been a *cretin*. Now, just opening the book made her hands shake.

Hand.

Whatever.

There was a soft knock on the door, and Meg turned in her chair, feeling instant relief and annoyance. Definitely the President's knock. Her father's knock would be both higher on the door, and louder.

Less guilt-ridden.

"Come in," she said.

The door opened, and her mother stepped into the room, her glasses—she always wore contacts, so she must be tired, too—in one hand, a couple of thick leather binders under her arm.

"I didn't mean to disturb you," her mother said. "I just—I saw the light."

Meg knew perfectly well that the lamp was on, but glanced at it, anyway. "Yeah."

"Lots of studying?" her mother asked, her expression more worried than she'd probably intended.

Meg nodded. "Yeah."

"Pain okay tonight?" her mother asked.

No. But, Meg just shrugged.

Her mother shifted her weight, and then moved the briefing books to her other arm. "Do you—need anything?"

Other than a new life, say? Meg shrugged, and looked at her mother, who seemed pretty exhausted and shaky in her own right. "Are you up because you have work, or because you can't sleep?"

"I can always find work to do," her mother said, wryly.

There was no such thing as a direct answer from a woman who held regular press conferences. But, it was also more than slightly possible that her mother was staying up until her father went to bed first, since the two of them weren't exactly skipping through meadows together these days.

Yet another situation which loomed over all of their lives, but was never mentioned.

"You're sure you don't need anything?" her mother asked.

A serious dose of painkillers. "Could you—" She felt stupid asking someone, particularly the damn *President*, to— "I was, uh, just going to get some water."

Her mother moved so swiftly to the bathroom that Meg felt even more stupid, and she picked up her cane, then eased her way over to the bed. She couldn't work the childproof lids on pill bottles with one hand, so everyone always left them open for her.

Cut her meat into bite-sized pieces.

Checked—far too often—to make sure that she didn't need help with what the occupational therapists tactfully called "personal care."

Just generally made her feel like a strong, proud, and independent adult.

She shook two ibuprofen out and waited for her mother to come back. "Um, thank you," she said, and gulped the pills down, trying to make it look as though her hand *wasn't* trembling.

"Would the heating pad help?" her mother asked. "Or some ice packs? Or we could hook up your TENS unit?"

Doubtful, in all three cases. "I'll try it, maybe," Meg said, then finished the water and set the glass carefully on the bedside table. "The heating pad, I mean."

"Would you like some more?" her mother asked, poised to move.

She was always thirsty now. *Always*. She nodded without making eye contact.

Her mother went to refill the glass, and then reached for the phone. "Why don't I have them bring in a pitcher of ice water for you?"

God, no. Meg shook her head.

Her mother hesitated, withdrew her hand, and looked uncomfortable. No, *unhappy*. Completely, utterly, *miserably* unhappy.

"I'm fine," Meg said. "Just kind of tired."

Her mother nodded, and they avoided each other's eyes.

"You're sure there's nothing else I can do for you?" her mother asked finally.

A question they all asked her about seven hundred times a day, and she never really had an answer. "No," she said. "Thanks."

Her mother nodded, and took a step towards the door. "Well. I'll let you get some rest."

Except that naturally, now that she was leaving, Meg couldn't help wanting her to stay. "I—" She stopped. No. It was way too late to start a Conversation. And her mother, what with being the leader of the Free World and all, unquestionably had a much more pressing day ahead than she did.

"What," her mother said, moving Vanessa—who hissed and leaped onto the bureau, knocking over a stack of prescreened unanswered sympathy letters from strangers—so she could sit down in the rocking chair.

She looked so eager, that Meg couldn't bring herself to say, "Never mind." "I just—I keep thinking—" Meg stopped again. Kept thinking *what*? "The semester's going to be over soon."

Her mother nodded.

"I mean—" Christ, she really had no idea what she meant. Even when she was trying as hard as she could to concentrate, her mind seemed to fumble things. "I don't know."

Originally, she would have been going off to Williams for her freshman year, but then, when her plans were—interrupted, they—she?—had decided that she would commute to George Washington University, instead. Warm up, sort of. Then, second semester, maybe she could—only now—

"Whatever you want to do, we'll arrange," her mother said.

Whatever she *could* do would be a better description. Meg swallowed. "I don't know if I, um, you know—well—"

"So, stay here through the spring," her mother said. "Williams isn't going anywhere."

No. Probably not. "I don't really like it," Meg said. Actually, she hated it. "GW, I mean."

"Well." Her mother frowned, and used her glasses to move her hair back. "How about Georgetown? Or—"

"I don't like *school*," Meg said. Or, she didn't like going out. Then again, she didn't like staying *in*, either. "I mean—" God, she didn't have the energy for this. "I'm sorry, forget it. This isn't a good time to get into it."

Her mother sighed. "Meg—"

"I really can't talk about it right now," Meg said, starting to feel panicky.

"Just remember that you don't have to make any decisions until you're ready," her mother said. "You're not on a timetable."

Oh, yeah, right. It wasn't like the whole god-damn world was watching every single move she made. Not like that at all.

"Okay," Meg said, and hoisted herself onto her cane. "I, uh, think I'll get ready for bed."

Her mother stood up, too. "If there's anything—"

Right. Meg nodded.

"Sleep well," her mother said.

Highly unlikely. For both of them.

"Yeah," Meg said. "You, too."

IT TOOK A couple of hours for her to fall asleep, during which she made a significant dent in *Winesburg, Ohio*, but she woke up after what felt like only about ten minutes, terrified and confused, and out of breath.

A nightmare. Just another nightmare. Okay. She reached for the glass of water on her bedside table, her hand shaking so badly that she spilled most of it across the front of her t-shirt. Then, she waited. If she'd screamed—which she did more often than not, apparently—one of her brothers or her parents would show up to see if she was all right, and she would have to go through the whole polite "No, no, I'm fine, don't worry" routine.

After five minutes, she figured she was safe. The dream had either been silent this time, or quiet enough so that Steven, whose room was right next to hers, hadn't heard her.

Instead of trying to go back to sleep, she just lay there, watching the grey light through her draperies gradually get brighter. It would be nice to stay in bed and skip her classes, but if she did it once, she would be tempted to do it again—and again, and again, so she forced herself to sit up.

She was tired, and her head hurt, and—well, most people had problems, right? She should just grow up, and get on with it already.

How cheering. She swung her bad leg over the edge of the bed, the normal jolt of pain jarring through her entire body in response. Just to make things seem worse, she took off her nighttime splint, and tried flexing her right hand, which was full of pins and wires and metal plates and so forth, where the bones wouldn't heal properly. Her middle and ring fingers could only flex about an inch—sometimes—and the pinky occasionally twitched. For all intents and purposes, her index finger and thumb had turned into a rigid little claw.

All of which hurt like hell.

Yes, that was probably her cue to sing "Oh, What a Beautiful Morning." Being as she had such a jovial outlook on life and all.

Showers required standing in the tub with a cane and leaning against the wall, wearing a special waterproof knee brace—a process which wore her out so much that she usually took baths, or sat underneath the spray on a small plastic bench, instead. It also always took forever to get dressed, using various assistive gadgets the therapists had given her, along with the cloth loops, hooks, and Velcro tabs someone or other had sewn into most of her clothes—including her bras, which was mortifying. Her parents' former rule that sweatpants were to be solely reserved for sports and hanging around at home, not for going to school, was now tacitly ignored by one and all, since they were easier for her to put on than anything else. Her brother Neal, who was ten, rarely took advantage of this unspoken change in policy, but Steven—big, tough ninth grader—did constantly.

When she was finally finished, she packed her knapsack with the books and notebooks she would need for her two classes. Like wow, big day ahead. But even though she would be home by lunchtime, she was already so tired that she—

"How you doing this morning?" her father asked from the doorway.

Terrible. Rotten. Lousy. "Fine," she said. Swell. *Nifty*.

He came over to carry the knapsack for her, and they walked very slowly down the Center Hall towards the Presidential Dining Room. Meg wasn't hungry in the morning—or really ever, anymore—but in her Quest for Normalcy, she usually made an effort to sit at the table and fake it.

Her brothers were already eating, and her mother was sipping coffee and glancing at her watch.

Great. Now she and her brothers could watch her parents pretend to be civil to each other, until her mother took advantage of the first possible opportunity to escape to the West Wing.

"Good morning," her mother said, looking so chic and perky—and overly thin—in her burgundy houndstooth designer suit that most people weren't even going to notice that she clearly hadn't slept much.

"Hi, Meggie," Neal said. He was so god-damn respectful to her these days that it kind of drove her crazy.

"Hi," Meg said, and sat down, dropping her cane on the floor.

Steven grunted—sort of—and kept eating.

Their father frowned at him. "You can't manage 'good morning'?"

"What?" Steven put his spoon down, his eyes widening. Much wider than necessary. "I mean, yo, I am like, totally sorry. I was just, you know, sitting here, and thinking all the stuff I think, and just like, all caught up in it, and—I am *totally* sorry."

Meg grinned. "I'm still not hearing a 'good morning' in there."

"Oh. Well, I meant to," he said. "I was just—you look so fat and ugly, I was like—I was *dumbstruck*."

Neal mouthed the word "dumbstruck," and laughed.

"I am just so sorry," Steven said, then looked at their father, who was still frowning. "What?"

Their father motioned towards his head, and Steven whipped off his Red Sox cap.

"Oh my God," he said, putting the hat on Neal. "*Every* day, you tell me, and *every* day, I forget."

The kid had to be mainlining testosterone—there was no other explanation. By the time he was sixteen, one, or both, of her parents was going to be in a Home for the Extremely Tense. But, Christ, at least he was funny.

"Miss Powers?" one of the butlers, Jason, asked, standing by her chair.

"Oh." Her mind was a blank. "Just some—toast, please. Whatever you have."

"Are you sure you don't—" Her father started, then apparently thought better of the idea and busied himself with his coffee.

"I think she ought to have some eggs," Steven said. "In fact, I think everyone at the table ought to—"

"Steven," their mother said, very sharply, and he returned to his cereal. Since their father was generally the strict one, when their *mother* said something, they were more apt to listen.

Jason served her, and Meg nodded her thanks, then picked up one of the toast quarters, self-conscious about the crunch it was probably going to make when she bit into it. Somehow, breakfasts on Mondays, Wednesdays, and Fridays were even more uptight than the other days. Like they all assumed she wasn't going to make it home again.

"Sleep all right?" her mother asked.

Meg nodded, losing interest in what was left of her toast piece and putting it down. "Did all of you?"

Steven put his hand to his forehead. "I—I was a little restless," he said, making his voice quaver.

Throw the kid a straight line, and he never missed. "I, too," Meg said, and drank some orange juice. Sometimes—not too often, of course—she considered letting her sense of humor come back.

Considered it.

"Are you coming home after your Astronomy class, or—?" her father asked, too casually.

Or what? Have lunch with her many new college friends? Run out to Bethesda or Rockville for a few rousing sets of tennis, and maybe a round of golf? Obviously, he was worried, but it was pretty god-damn suffocating. Especially since she didn't have anywhere to go. Her stomach hurt, and she pushed her plate away. "I should be home at about quarter to twelve," she said. Through her teeth.

"You don't need to be on a schedule," he said, glancing at her mother, who was glaring at him. "I just meant—"

"No problem." Her stomach was starting to ache so much that it was definitely time to leave. "I'd better get going."

Her father was already up, handing her the cane and her knapsack.

Meg nodded and took them. "Thanks." Every time she said goodbye now, it seemed so damned ceremonial.

So ominous.

"Where's your jacket?" her mother asked, looking away from the papers Frank, her personal aide, had just brought in. "I think it's pretty chilly out there."

Her coat, which was unusually heavy, because of the Kevlar—or whatever the hell it was—lining it just happened to have. These days, regardless of the weather, they were *all* expected to wear terribly heavy outer garments, whenever possible. Presumably, helmets would be next.

Neal went to get her jacket, and then tried, ineptly, to pull it on over her splint, which made forcing her hand through the sleeve that much more painful.

"Do you want it zipped?" he asked politely.

Jesus, how old did they think she was? "*No,*" she said, and then sighed. "I mean, thanks, anyway."

"Have a good day," her mother said.

A good couple of hours was more accurate. Meg nodded. "Yeah. You, too."

"Yo, wait up." Steven took his hat back from Neal, then picked up his own knapsack and coat from the floor. "Later," he said to everyone else.

"You'll be home after basketball?" their father asked.

Meg limped out to the hall so she wouldn't have to listen to Steven getting grilled about *his* itinerary for the day.

"Maybe," Steven was saying. "Gotta stop on the Mall first, see if I can score some coke."

When he finally came out, they rode down in the elevator together, leaning against the polished wooden wall on either side of the mirror, Steven significantly more subdued now.

"Maybe you *should* zip up," he muttered.

Okay. She looked at Mickey, the elderly operator, and Garth, the head of her Secret Service detail, both of whom were pretending they couldn't hear their conversation. "If you do, too," she said.

Steven nodded, zipped his jacket, and then helped her with hers.

Meg looked over at him—as tall as she was now, slouched in his Red Sox cap, bullet-resistant Spyder ski jacket, New England Patriots sweatshirt, jeans, and high-tops. Out of nowhere lately, he'd been growing, and his voice was much deeper. Hard to get used to.

When the elevator stopped, they all waited for her to go first. Meg limped out into the Ground Floor Corridor, where the rest of their Secret Service agents were waiting to meet them. She and her brothers all had full details now, with at least six agents, and sometimes, eight. And God only knew how many unmarked cars and so forth. Their agents were also a lot more overt and aggressive than they had been six months ago. Although two of her three daily shifts had one female agent each, she was mostly surrounded by hulking armed men, which was more than a little unnerving. And not even slightly discreet.

They went through the Diplomatic Reception Room, Meg acutely aware of the degree to which she was slowing everyone else down, and out to the South Grounds, past the ever-alert and expressionless Marine guards. Their respective cars were waiting for them, parked along the driveway, and she could see some press people standing around, too.

She hadn't been surprised when they had followed her the first few times she left the White House, but it had taken her a while to figure out why at least a couple of reporters and camera people were almost always close by—more often than not these days, she had a death watch. Journalists who wanted to be sure they were on the scene to record the event when and if something bad happened. Her mother, of course, had one, the Queen of England had one, the Pope had one, and for the time being, ridiculous as it was, *she* seemed to have one. It went without saying that it was expensive to send reporters out to do nothing—with luck—so, to be cost-effective, press organizations only set up body watches on people who had a very good chance of making news—or getting knocked off. Comforting to know that she now fell into that category.

Although, so far, their efforts had only been rewarded by one morning when a man threw an egg at her—which was, bizarrely enough, hard-boiled, and another day when some lunatic ran across H Street screaming weird accusations about a massive cover-up and black helicopters, plus the time she fell on the stairs going into Corcoran Hall, and the days when protestors and demonstrators of various kinds were all over the campus, armed with signs and taunts, and the afternoon when some paparazzo guy on a motorcycle had tried to—actually, considering how rarely she went out, arguably, the press was getting its money's worth.

"Well." Steven looked around, and then zipped his jacket a little higher. "Okay, then."

Christ, the poor kid was only fourteen. "No one's going to shoot us, Steven," she said.

"Hell, no," he said. "Later."

She watched until he was safely inside his car—because, yeah, some god-damn maniac with a rifle *might* be perched somewhere with a good view of the South Lawn, then put on a pair of very dark sunglasses and turned to go to her own car. Her left foot flopped unexpectedly—it happened pretty frequently, because of the nerve damage in her knee—and she lost her balance to the degree that even one of the stolid, unmoving Marine guards jumped towards her. But, she caught herself with her cane and a quick crouch on her good leg, waving everyone off with her splinted hand, although Garth and one of her other agents, Kyle, stayed significantly closer to her than they had been before.

And, damn it, she could hear cameras clicking. Christ, she couldn't even *trip* without having it documented.

There was no question in her mind that she would have been much better off if she had just stayed in bed today.

2

GW WAS PRACTICALLY next door to the White House, so it wasn't much of a drive. Meg sat in the back, with Garth up front in the passenger's seat, and another agent, Paula, driving. These days, she had so many conflicting feelings about the Secret Service, that there was never much conversation when she was with them, although she did, at least, always try to be courteous.

"Do you have plans today, or just your two classes?" Garth asked. Although he was wearing a tie and a grey suit, he mostly looked like a burly Irish former offensive tackle from Boston College—and, in fact, he *had* gone to BC, but he had been a defensive lineman.

He already knew the answer; why ask the question? "Just my classes," Meg said stiffly.

He nodded, and Paula—who was tall and lithe, and had been headed for the WNBA before the Secret Service snagged her—nodded, too, glancing at her for a second in the rearview mirror, Meg quickly looking away.

The two primary agents who had been guarding her the day she was kidnapped had both been killed—a guy named Chet whom she'd really liked and felt very guilty about, and Dennis, who had sold the crucial information that had enabled the terrorists to get her in the first place. So now, she didn't *trust* her agent, but she also couldn't help worrying that they would get hurt, and it would be her fault.

She spent so much time in the family quarters of the White House, anyway, that she didn't see these new agents much, or know them very well. At this stage, she kind of wanted to keep it that way. They took her to class three times a week, they brought her home, and other than the occasional doctor's appointment or medical procedure which needed to be done in a hospital setting, that was about it. Once, in October, she had gone to the movies with Steven and Neal, and her father's chief of staff, Preston—who was easily one of her favorite people in the world—but that had pretty much been the extent of her social life.

They were at the university now, near the side entrance of the building where she had Astronomy. Classes were changing, so it was crowded, and she took a deep breath, hoping that no one would be able to tell that she was afraid to get out of the car.

Another agent, Martin, was holding her door open, and she slid out, awkward with the cane, keeping her head down. Okay. Fifty feet. She had to walk maybe fifty feet to get to the entrance. People were looking at her—they always did—and she felt very exposed, especially when a couple of them aimed cell phone cameras in her direction. She didn't really worry about being kidnapped again—how likely was *that*?—but it was too easy to imagine some nameless psycho lunging towards her, or one of those cell phones *actually* being a gun, or someone waiting avidly by a window in one of the other nearby buildings, like the man who had shot her mother early in her term, or—Jesus, no wonder her family was paranoid. They'd earned the right.

And no wonder the press sat around waiting to see who was going to be next.

Once she had made it up the steps and they were inside the building, she relaxed a little. At least now, if anything bad happened, it would be *off*-camera, and not replayed on television endlessly. Sometimes, she felt as though every single time she turned on the news, there was a story about gun control or crime rates or something, and they would show the same relentless clip of her mother crumpling to the sidewalk. She'd seen it so many times by now that it had—almost—lost its horror. Which was horrifying in and of itself.

Her agents all looked uneasy, and she realized that she'd stopped walking. They hated that, because she was *never* supposed to stop in transit, if at all possible. So, she continued down the crowded hallway towards the little amphitheater where her Astronomy class met, limped up a few more damn stairs, and sat, as always, off to the left, in the last row, where she had a good view of the entire auditorium—and both exits. A lot of people skipped on a regular basis—the class was considered a complete gut—and she never had to worry about having to sit next to anyone. Except during the midterm, and there had been a seat between every person. She had gotten an eighty-two—and was, privately, very ashamed of having done so badly.

People were still filing in aimlessly, but the professor started his lecture, anyway, and she reached for her notebook and pen. He seemed like a nice enough man, but he was very boring. If she were an ordinary student, she would blow off the class, too. He was talking about Kepler's Laws, and she took notes, her good hand shaking just enough to make it difficult.

Maybe thirty people had shown up, and she looked around for anyone who seemed out-of-place, or too old, or—during the first class session in September, she had noticed two students who didn't appear to be the right age, but she found out later that they were undercover security. Knowing that had yet to make her any less vigilant, since—theoretically—she was the one who had the strongest motivation to keep herself from getting killed.

Some days, more so than others.

There was one guy, earlier in the semester, who she had caught glancing at her one time too many, and she asked the Secret Service to run a check on him, in case he was some kind of plant from an angry militia group or whatever. He'd turned out to be a sophomore sociology major from Delaware. "I think he *likes* you," one of her agents had said. "Oh," she'd said. With near-total disinterest.

Once she'd finished her scan of the room—she recognized everyone, for whatever that was worth—she went back to taking shaky notes and waiting for class to be over. Then, her agents hustled her out to the car, and drove her to the building where her English class met. Not that it was much of a walk.

This class was much smaller, and it was a lot harder to hide. A couple of times, she'd even had to make comments about whatever book they were reading. The professor, Dr. Raleigh, almost always wore peasant blouses, long gathered skirts, and brown leather sandals. Very Bennington. She appeared to be good-natured, if overly fond of literary symbolism. Dr. T. J. Eckleberg as God, and all of that.

There were windows in this classroom, so she always sat in the middle of the back row, so that she could keep an eye on them *and* the door, without really having to turn her head.

Jesus, her hand hurt today. She should have taken some damned ibuprofen but she had left the Residence in such a hurry, that she had forgotten. But there might be some inside her knapsack, or one of her jacket pockets, and she could just swallow them dry, without—

"What do you think, Meg?" Dr. Raleigh asked.

Meg straightened up. "What?" Oh, Christ, they were all staring at her. She looked at her notes, trying to remember what they had been discussing. "I guess—I don't know, I—" Were they still staring at her? Yes. Great. They probably thought she was really dumb. Like her parents had paid off the school to have her admitted part-time. *Winesburg, Ohio*. Okay. Odds were, they were talking about small-town America. Her notes said something about "grotesques," but she had absolutely no memory of anything else her professor had said.

They were all still looking at her.

"Well, I—" Oh, hell, she might as well go for it. "I was thinking about what a human comedy it was," she said. Oh, yeah, right. All she thought about was comedy. Joy. Excitement. Laughter. *Fun*. "I mean, of course, their emotional shortcomings are tragic, but—" Yes, they were staring even harder now—"It's very—Balzacian, really."

Damn, the room was quiet.

"I don't suppose that's what you were looking for," Meg said, pleasantly, "but that's what I was thinking."

"Well, no," Dr. Raleigh said, after a pause, "but it's an interesting idea. You've obviously given this a great deal of thought." She turned towards the guy with the goatee, who always slouched, half-asleep, by the windows. "Terence? How about you?"

Everyone's attention now focused on Terence—poor sucker—and Meg let out her breath.

There was some more discussion—a very pretentious girl from Chattanooga even started drawing parallels to *Père Goriot*, like the Balzac thing had been her idea in the first place—and then, class was over. Amid the zipping of jackets and knapsacks—and the ringing of suddenly liberated cell phones, their professor asked them to have the first twelve chapters of

Main Street read by Wednesday, and to remember that their final papers were due a week from Friday.

Once she was back in the car, she felt very—sadly enough—tired. Drained, even. Other than a couple of "pretty warm for December" remarks, they rode home in silence. Her agents saw her inside to the First Family elevator; she thanked them and rode up to the second floor.

Quite an eventful day. *Morning.*

It was quiet in the family quarters, although she thought she could hear a vacumn cleaner off in the distance. Generally, the White House staff seemed like a bunch of little magic fairies, who cleaned like crazy, but were rarely visible to the human eye.

A butler—Felix—came out of the kitchen. He was a very sweet older man, with nine grandchildren, whose latest pictures he always carried, and enjoyed showing, given even the slightest bit of encouragement.

He smiled at her. "May I get you some lunch, Miss Powers?"

"No, thank you," she said. "I'm fine."

Although he probably didn't want to look deeply concerned, he did, anyway. "We'll fix anything you want."

Amazing how damned nice everyone was to her. "I know, I just had a really big breakfast," she said. "But, thank you." She smiled back at him, and turned to go down the hall.

"Would you like me to bring you a Coke?" he asked. "Or maybe—"

Usually, it was easier just to agree. "Sure," Meg said. "Thank you."

She had barely made it to her room, when he appeared with a large, well-iced crystal glass and a small plate of assorted cookies on a silver tray, a linen napkin draped over his arm. She thanked him again, and then, as soon as he left, sank onto her bed. Now that she was home safely, she was completely worn out.

She had only been lying there for a few minutes, staring at CNN—just long enough for their dog, Kirby, to come galloping in to greet her, and Vanessa to hiss and flounce out of the room—when her phone rang. Ten to one, it would be her father. Make that, a thousand to one.

She picked it up. "Hello?"

"Hi," her father said. "I thought I'd check in."

Right. She knew he was just being thoughtful, but Christ, it was oppressive. Meg closed her eyes. "I just got back."

"Classes any good?" he asked.

Engrossing. Unforgettable. *Glorious*. She shrugged. "They were all right, I guess."

"Good," he said, rather heartily. "Would you like to come to a luncheon?"

Her father, being the First Gentleman, got stuck going to a hell of a lot of luncheons. "Who've you got today?" she asked.

"It's an NAACP thing," he said. "It should be nice."

Since she couldn't even face the prospect of having lunch in the privacy of her bedroom, the odds of her going *out* again were pretty slim. "Thanks," she said, "but I think I'll take it easy this afternoon."

For a change.

"Okay," he said, almost without pausing first. "Well, I should be back around two, two-thirty. We could play some chess, or—whatever you want."

She was tired of chess. Tired of books. Tired of television. Tired of movies. Tired of the Internet. Just plain god-damned tired. "Yeah, maybe," she said. "I'm pretty—tired."

"Well, if you need anything—" he started.

"Yeah," she said. "I mean, thanks."

After hanging up, she slumped back down on the bed. Her leg hurt. Her hand hurt. Her *stomach* hurt. She was too exhausted to go over and close the curtains, so she covered her eyes with her left arm to make it seem dark. If she was lucky, she could fall asleep until dinner-time.

If she wasn't lucky, it was going to be one hell of a long afternoon.

THEY GOT HER on her way home from school. On her way *out* of the school, to be precise. One minute, she was joking around with her friend Josh; the next, she was inside a van, reeling from having a gun butt slammed into her face, and being punched by a group of masked men until they managed to knock her out. Unknown hours later, she woke up missing a few teeth, dizzy and sick, handcuffed to a metal bed in a small dark room somewhere.

It was never clear exactly who they were, or what they wanted, except that they were Americans, hired to do the job by some damned Middle Eastern fundamentalists. One of the men kept coming into the room, and—well, he came in a lot.

Which was pretty much all she ever felt like remembering about that. He hadn't actually *physically* raped her, but—it was safe to say that he hadn't been kind.

On the fourth day, they panicked, and came in to kill her—except that, for reasons she still couldn't understand, she ended up in an abandoned mine-shaft. Alone, without food or water, her left knee destroyed, her right wrist chained to a rock wall. She liked to think that they were giving her a chance—hoping someone would find her, maybe—but the simple truth was, they had left her to die.

The only way out, she'd finally realized, after a few very long days—she was pretty foggy on time—was to shatter her right hand. She used a rock. Repeatedly. Her logic had been, better crippled than dead.

Sometimes, she still felt that way.

Once she got through the boards nailed across the entrance—only a really sadistic son-of-a-bitch would have added *that* touch—she was in the middle of the mountains. North Georgia, she found out later. She spent the next week—maybe?—staggering, falling, drinking from streams, crazed from hunger, and in so much pain that she could damn near *feel* herself losing her mind. And, as far as she could tell, most of it was still out there somewhere.

It was, historically speaking, a Tuesday afternoon in June, thirteen days after she'd disappeared, that she crawled into a backyard. Scaring the hell out of the teenaged boy who happened to be *standing* in it at the time.

And now, here she was, enjoying a life of physical therapy, isolation, and constant nightmares.

Which made her wonder, all too often, why the hell she had gone to the trouble of surviving. At this point, it seemed—ill-considered. At best.

There was a knock on the door, and she took a minute to decide whether to answer it. Usually, when she didn't, whoever it was would assume she was asleep, and go away.

Leave her alone.

"Who is it?" she asked, finally.

"Just came up to say hi," a voice said. Preston. "You busy?"

Since he was one of the very few people she could stand to be around, she picked up her cane and limped over to open the door.

"Hey," he said. "Feel like hanging out for a while?"

Not even remotely. "How come you're not at the lunch with my father?" she asked.

He shrugged. "We're back. Come on."

Preston rarely took no for an answer, so she followed him down to the West Sitting Hall, one of the only places in the White House decorated with furniture from their house in Massachusetts. As a result, they all found it comforting to spend time there.

She sat down on the yellow paisley couch, moving a pillow over to the coffee table and propping her leg up on it.

"Looks like it hurts today," Preston said, sitting in one of the matching arm chairs.

Just for a change. But she shrugged, instead of answering. After the first several thousand times, complaining became tiresome.

"I could do with some lunch," he said. "How about you?"

Well, that wasn't transparent, was it. "You just *had* lunch," Meg said.

"You know how it is, you never really eat at those things." He got up. "Any requests?"

"Spam," she said. Haggis. Jellied eel.

He laughed, and disappeared into the kitchen, where, in all probability, the on-duty upstairs chef would leap to attention. Not that the White House was—regimented, or—militaristic.

Despite his official position on her father's staff, more than anything else, Preston was probably her entire family's best friend. He and her father were a quirky pair—the tall, ever-cool young black guy, and the uptight, conservative tax attorney who never saw a plain white Oxford shirt and dark Brooks Brothers suit he didn't like. It had the makings of a very banal, big-budget buddy movie, frankly.

When he came out of the kitchen, she examined his outfit: grey windowpane-plaid wool suit, black and white pencil-striped shirt, and a golden silk tie with diamond patterns.

"Well?" he asked, pulling out his handkerchief to show her that it was gold, too.

"I don't know about this tie business," she said, imitating her father's inflections. "It's a little bold."

Preston just laughed.

"Did you see the President today?" she asked. "She's looking pretty bold herself."

He nodded. "I keep waiting for her to bring back pillbox hats."

Meg grinned, picturing that. Her mother was nothing if not elegant, but hats did not always favor her. This had presented problems, now and again, during poorly-advanced photo ops on the campaign trail.

"So," Preston said. "Learn a lot about the solar system?"

"Kepler's Laws." About which, she had retained nothing. "You know," she said, tentatively. "I'm *way* stupider than I used to be." Her diction wasn't so terrific, either.

Preston looked worried. "I think you're just having trouble staying focused."

Maybe.

"It's very common," he said.

She raised an eyebrow at him. "Still reading Post-traumatic Stress Disorder books?"

"Passes the weary hours, Meg," he said.

Well, so it would.

"Try to remember to cut yourself some slack," he said. "It hasn't been that long."

It sure as hell *seemed* long.

There was the sound of a helicopter outside on the South Lawn—Marine One, about to go somewhere or other. She'd have to be sure and turn on CNN, find out what excuse her mother was using to skip dinner tonight.

"What?" he asked, looking at her.

Where to begin? "All we had were the meals, Preston," she said.

He sighed. "I can see how it might feel that way, but you had a lot more than that."

Yeah, they'd had skiing, too. And now, they weren't anything resembling what they had been. Just five repressed people who rarely found themselves in the same room together, and when they did, avoided looking at one another.

Ten words—from a speech which was now considered iconic enough so that snippets were still regularly being broadcast at unexpected moments, spoken by a world leader with an unrecognizably cold and fierce expression on her face—had essentially been all it took to destroy her family.

Can not, have not, and will not negotiate with terrorists.

And, by all reputable accounts, the world leader *did* not negotiate with terrorists. Or allow any other country or third party to do so. Strong rumor had it that a couple of well-meaning, highly-placed officials, who made tentative back-channel overtures, had been gone from the administration, permanently, within a matter of hours.

Ten words. Damn. They might have been *necessary* words, but—damn.

One of the stewards, Pete, was setting the shiny mahogany table where they had casual Sunday breakfasts, and late-night snacks, and things like that. Informal things. Once she and Preston were sitting down, her leg resting on a footstool, Felix brought out glasses of lemonade, small salads, and two cups of vegetable barley soup which had been sent up in the elevator from the main kitchen downstairs.

"Would you like your hamburger medium-well, Miss Powers?" he asked.

Christ, she wasn't even hungry. "Sure," she said. "I mean, thank you." After he and Pete had returned to the kitchen, she looked at Preston. "Little snack?"

He pushed the basket of crackers and breadsticks in her direction. "Can't stand to see you looking so frail."

"I'm not frail," Meg said, somewhat crankily. "I'm not fat, but I'm not frail."

He nodded, helping himself to a few breadsticks without further comment.

Fine. Whatever. She managed two spoonfuls of soup, before losing interest in it, and moving the bowl away.

Preston didn't say anything, but there was something so god-damn judgmental about the way he glanced at her, that she had to swallow and close her eyes to keep from snapping at him.

"At least try the salad," he said.

What little appetite she'd had was now gone, and she clenched her good fist, resisting the urge to storm—stagger—down to her room and slam the door.

"Meg," he started. "I'm not trying to—"

"Then, don't," she said.

He nodded, reaching for his salad fork, and it was unpleasantly silent.

Meg moved her jaw, fighting to keep her temper under control. "Look. I'm sorry. I don't meant to be rude to you."

Preston shrugged. "I think if you're angry, you should *be* angry."

Oh, yeah. Like she wanted to open Pandora's god-damn box.

"Delicious dressing," Preston remarked, eating his salad.

"I'm not angry!" Meg said.

He nodded. "Okay."

She scowled at him. "All anyone does is fucking humor me."

He nodded.

"I'm sick of it," she said. "I'm sick of *everything*."

There was another—short—silence.

"Well," he said. "As long as you're not angry."

For a second, she was furious; then, she relaxed. "Yeah," she said.

Because she wasn't angry at all. Not at anyone, or anything.

Hell, no.

3

"SO, WHAT'S THE word from *People*?" she asked, while they were waiting for their hamburgers. The last she had heard, they were threatening to put her in their 25 Most Intriguing People of the Year issue.

"Not too good," Preston said. "I think they're going to lead off with you."

Oh, swell. "You can't stop it?" she asked.

He shook his head. "Sorry. Their feeling is that it was such a major story that they're not about to ignore it."

Bigger than Patty Hearst, the media was always saying. Bigger than—well, big. Very big. No wonder she couldn't escape from the damned thing, with everyone writing about it all the time. "I'm not giving them any kind of interview," she said.

His grin was ironic. "That has been indicated."

She laughed. Indicated very strongly, in other words. "What pictures are they using?"

"The usual, I assume," he said.

Meaning some kind of "before" photo—probably from one of her tennis matches, or else, on a ski slope; a view of the school exit where it had all happened; another of her just home from the hospital, gaunt and battered; and finally, one of her forlornly limping around GW. Or they might also pick one of the photos of the mammoth piles of flowers and cards and candles and other remembrances which people had placed along the White House fence while she was gone, mostly directly in front of the North Portico, and at the foot of the South Lawn. Those shots always gave her the creeps, because they were so blatantly funereal and meant as a memorial—except for the little detail that she hadn't actually been *dead*.

Technically, anyway.

Felix and Pete carried over trays with hamburgers, condiments, French fries, and onion rings, as well as another pitcher of lemonade.

"It'll die down soon," Preston said, when they were alone again. "It's just going to take a while."

Right. She tasted her hamburger. It was very good—but she still wasn't hungry. "Before I know it, I'll be a trivia question," she said. A "Whatever happened to . . . ?", which would leave people faintly disappointed if it turned out that she hadn't been trundled off to rehab, had a nervous breakdown, found God, or done something otherwise predictable and life-altering.

"A trivia question everyone gets *wrong*," he said, and grinned at her.

In the best of all possible worlds, yeah.

After that, he shifted the conversation to the Patriots, the unseasonably warm weather, and how hilarious and adorable Neal had been when he flipped the switch during the official White House Pageant of Peace holiday tree-lighting ceremony. In fact, there were cynical types who referred to him as a walking vote machine, although Meg's feeling was that he was probably just a nice kid. She nodded, and agreed, and shook her head at appropriate moments, happy to let Preston do most of the talking.

She didn't want dessert, but when he decided to have cake *and* coffee, she stayed in her seat.

"When's Josh get back?" he asked conversationally.

Meg shrugged. She and Josh had broken up right before everything happened, but they were still trying to maintain a friendship, with only modest success. It had pretty much been reduced to emails here and there—he had gone to Stanford, and seemed to be loving college, but going out of his way not to rub it in, to her relief. She'd lost touch with most of her other high school friends, too, both the ones from Massachusetts, and the people she'd met in Washington.

"Beth going to come down?" Preston asked.

Meg shrugged again. She and Beth had been almost inseparable since kindergarten, but even their friendship was a little strained lately—mainly because Meg was embarrassed about being such a basket case, while Beth was off at Columbia, enjoying effortless success.

"She taking the city by storm?" Preston asked.

Meg nodded. New York was, unquestionably, Beth's kind of town.

"I wouldn't be surprised to see you end up there, too," he said.

How tiresome. "Your books tell you to initiate discussions about the victim's future?" Meg asked.

"Just an observation," he said.

Yeah. Sure.

Preston tasted his coffee, then added some sugar. "What are you going to do this afternoon?"

Sit in the nearest window, and sing happy songs to herself. "I'm probably going to read," she said. After doing her god-damn physical therapy. The White House physician, Dr. Brooks, wanted her to have formal, supervised PT and OT sessions six days a week, but their current agreement was three days, and other than that, she did the exercises by herself.

Most of the time, anyway.

"Want to come downstairs, help answer some of the animals' letters?" he asked.

Yes, people actually wrote letters to their dog, Kirby, and to Vanessa, and their other three cats, Adlai, Humphrey, and Sidney. So *many* letters that she really had to wonder about the mental health of a large number of Americans. "I think I'll pass," she said.

He shrugged. "Okay. How about we—"

"I'm doing my best, Preston, okay?" she said. Snarled, actually. She took a deep breath. "I'm sorry. My best just sucks these days."

He smiled, but his eyes were sad. "It won't always, Meg."

She looked at him, quite close to smiling herself. "What could be nicer, than having lunch with Annie."

"Mr. Rogers," he said.

She laughed. "That *would* be nicer." To get one of her exercises out of the way, she unstrapped her splint, took a rubber band out of her pocket, and fit it around the fingers on her right hand. "Do you mind if I do this in front of you?"

"I think it's great if you do it," he said.

Mr. Rogers probably would have, too. She could flex a couple of the fingers, slightly, but none of them would really extend at all—and trying to force them was beyond excruciating. Not the surgical outcome she'd anticipated, and they had been in there three times so far. She stretched the rubber band a fraction of a millimeter, concentrating on not yelping or gasping. "I don't mind the hand so much, but I can't god-damn stand not being able to walk."

He nodded.

It hurt like hell, and she shut her eyes. "I mean, if I can't get around, I'm going to be stuck in this god-damn house forever." Or, at any rate, until her mother left office. At which point, she'd be trapped in the house in Chestnut Hill, presumably.

"We need to figure out a way to help you past that," he said.

She nodded. The pain was actually starting to make her feel faint, so she slipped the rubber band off and put her splint back on, keeping her eyes closed until she was sure she wasn't going to cry. Her putty exercises were going to have to wait until later. *Much* later.

"What's your feeling on next semester?" he asked.

"I don't know," she said. "What do you think?"

He looked at her thoughtfully. "Truth?"

That was a moronic question. Meg frowned at him. "No, Preston—*lie* to me."

He grinned, then looked serious. "My feeling is that you should get the hell out of here. Maybe you're making some progress with the PT, but the rest of you is going way downhill."

She'd asked for honesty; she got honesty. "*Way* downhill?" she said.

He sighed, and put down his coffee cup. "Meg, you're eighteen years old, and you're practically a shut-in. You don't eat, you don't sleep, you don't see anyone your own age, you suddenly think you're stupid—" He shook his head. "I'd like to see you go away before it gets even worse."

She couldn't really contradict him, but it wasn't quite that easy. "How many people do you think there are out there who cut my picture out of magazines, hang them up on the wall, and—make plans?" she asked, looking right at him so he wouldn't avoid the question.

He did, however, avoid her eyes. "I don't know. I hope there aren't any."

The man was a cockeyed optimist. She leaned forward to steal a bite of his cake, remembered that she didn't want any, frowned, and put her fork down. "Care to put money on that?"

He pushed the plate closer to her. "Well, for sanity's sake, let's assume they don't exist."

She shook her head, and pushed the plate back to him. "They got to my mother; they can sure as hell get to me again." Or her father, or her brothers—which was too awful to imagine, in all three cases.

"Unfortunately, your mother makes some kind of twisted sense as a target," he said. "You don't."

Christ, was he really that naive? Or just trying to sound reassuring? "We're dealing with maniacs, Preston," she said. "I don't think they're real *logical* about these things."

He glanced down at his plate, and set it aside.

She looked at the remaining cake, then decided that she would have—what the hell—just one bite.

"It's good," he said.

She nodded. Maybe two bites wouldn't be the worst idea she had ever had.

"You know what I think?" he asked.

Three bites would be pushing it. She lowered her fork. "This isn't going to be more honesty, is it?"

He nodded. "I think it's worth the risk."

Jesus, what was this, Bluntness Day? Maybe he should try reading his trauma books more carefully. "Yeah, well, you're not the one they're going to blow away," she said. Bluntly.

He nodded.

"So, you can afford to be sort of—free and easy—with advice," she said.

He nodded again, and this silence lasted longer than any of the others had.

"I'm often very rude to you," she said.

He grinned at her. "Actually, I figure it's a compliment."

She really *was* having lunch with Annie.

"Maybe a little backhanded," he said.

She laughed. "Maybe."

They sat there.

"So," he said. "Sure you don't want to hang out downstairs for a while?"

She nodded.

"Some other time, then," he said.

She nodded.

HER MOTHER DID not, in fact, make it home in time for dinner, although after checking the White House closed-circuit television feed, Meg caught ten minutes of a speech she was making in Detroit to some auto workers who had just begun production on a new, much more energy-efficient line of hybrid minivans—and that was *almost* like being in the same place together.

Or, maybe not.

After supper, her father went wherever the hell it was he went—usually, they found him reading in the Yellow Oval Room, or out on the Truman Balcony—and her brothers headed up to the solarium to watch some action movie, while she stayed in her room, finished *Winesburg, Ohio*, and started *Main Street*.

At about nine-thirty, her phone rang. She didn't feel like talking to anyone, but she sighed and picked it up.

"Good evening, Miss Powers," a White House operator said. She had *all* of her very few calls routed through the switchboard these days, instead of the direct line, so that she didn't have to answer them. "Miss Shulman for you?"

Beth. "Okay," Meg said. "I mean, thank you."

There was a clicking sound, and then Beth came on. "Meg?"

"No, this is her secretary," Meg said. Who did she *think* it was? "Can I take a message?"

"You may," Beth said cheerfully. "Tell her to get up here and visit me—this town is great."

Jesus. Meg grinned in spite of herself. "You're already calling it 'town'?"

"Well, hey," Beth said, somewhat self-consciously.

Another month, and she'd be a native. Pick up an accent and everything.

"So. How's it going?" Beth asked.

"Super," Meg said. "It's kind of like a carnival."

"You hate carnivals," Beth said.

It was nice to have someone appreciate the subtext in a joke. "Yeah," Meg agreed. Circuses, too. She—and, oddly, her entire family—particularly despised clowns. The Moscow Circus had once come to the East Room to perform after a state dinner, and they'd had to sit there in the front row and look happy. It was very hard. Even Neal hated every second of it, and later that night, had actually thrown up. Naturally, they all blamed the clowns.

"How are you, really?" Beth asked.

Meg shrugged. "Well, you know."

"I *don't* know," Beth said.

Upon which, Meg decided to change the subject. "How about you? Things are—okay?"

A month or so earlier, Beth had been completely freaked out when her period was three days late, and Meg had come up with a wildly impractical and potentially politically inflammatory plan wherein she would get herself admitted to the hospital, under the auspices of another surgical revision of her hand or knee, and Beth would conveniently come down to visit—and instead, they would take care of the situation somehow, as quietly and privately as possible. Maybe not the most ideal stratagem in the world, but it had been her first, and best, suggestion. Of course, Beth had promptly gotten her period the next morning, and neither of them had brought it up again.

"Fine," Beth said, sounding embarrassed. "I mean, things are good, except for finals. What about you?"

"Well—I have finals, too," Meg said. Defensively. Especially since she *didn't* have a sex life about which to fret, or celebrate, as the case might be. And, of course, she had only two finals, instead of the normal four or five other people had.

"You worried about them?" Beth asked.

What, because she was psychologically delicate? "No more than anyone else," Meg said.

"Well, since I've missed like, every other class, *I* sure am," Beth said.

Hmmm. Beth hyperbole, or reality? Meg thought about that. "Do you really miss that many?"

"Yeah," Beth said, and then laughed. "Don't tell anyone."

"What do you do instead?" Meg asked.

"I don't know." Beth paused. "Sleep. Go to movies. Drink coffee in disreputable cafés."

Often, she very much wished that she were Beth. If she went off to college and did any of that, the wire services'd probably pick it up.

"How's physical therapy?" Beth asked.

"The same." Which sounded kind of self-pitying. Although Beth had sat in on a few sessions, so she knew what it was like. "I mean, you know," Meg said. "Um, how's Ramon?" Beth had pretty much joined the Man of the Month Club since she'd been away at school, and Ramon was the replacement for Jimmy, who had been her not-particularly-gentlemanly cohort in the pregnancy alarm.

"He's okay," Beth said. "Hear that noise?"

Meg listened, hearing indistinct, but monotonous, music. "Is that a bass?"

"Yeah," Beth said. "Catchy, hunh?"

Oh, yeah. Terribly. Even so, it was hard to suppress a flash of envy.

"I'm being careful this time," Beth said. "I mean, I'm not—well, anyway, he's all right. But, I don't know. I don't think we're going to make it through winter break."

Not exactly a ringing endorsement. Meg frowned. "I thought you said he was really cute."

"He is," Beth said. "I mean, he could give Preston a run for his money, but—oh, I don't know. I'm bored."

"As cute as *Preston*?" Meg said. No small feat.

"In a different way, but yeah. He's just—he sort of walks around trying to be this real hip inner-city guy, but he's actually from Shaker Heights, you know?" Beth said. "Not your type."

Beth had not, to Meg's knowledge, ever spent time with anyone who was even vaguely her type.

Whatever the hell her type was.

Emphasis on the past tense.

"You're still not telling me anything about your life," Beth said.

And, gosh, there was so much to tell. "Where should I start?" Meg asked.

"Anywhere," Beth said, sounding just the tiniest bit too supportive.

She knew everyone was just trying to be nice to her, but *Christ*, it was patronizing. Meg gritted her teeth, the implants on her left side—yet another one of her many physical souvenirs—still feeling unfamiliar in her mouth. "Before or after the strip-tease at the Washington Press Club?"

"Oh, during," Beth said. "Definitely during."

The bass had stopped playing, and Meg could hear a very deep male voice saying, "You done yet?"

"No," Beth said, sounding impatient. "I'm on the phone."

"*Still?*" the male voice said.

"Wait a minute, Meg," Beth said, and Meg could hear her covering the receiver with her hand. "I'm on the phone, Ramon, okay? Jesus."

"Look, it's not a big deal," Meg said quickly. "I kind of have to go, anyway."

Beth sighed. "Meg, I'm not—"

"I really do," Meg said, even more quickly. "I mean—uh, talk to you later. Or, you know, sometime." She hung up, feeling unexpectedly shaky and upset. In case Beth was going to call back, she disconnected it, holding the plastic cord tightly in her good hand. So, she wasn't away at school, or having a social life, or—it wasn't a big deal. She should just sleep. It was the easiest—the *only*—way to get through the—but first, some ibuprofen.

As she reached for her cane, she heard someone at her door and turned, angrily, to see who it was.

"*What*, for Christ's sakes?" she asked, and saw her mother standing there.

Naturally.

Her mother spoke as carefully as ever. "I just wanted to let you know that I was back."

"Good," Meg said, not looking at her. "Fine."

Her mother hesitated. "Is there anything—"

Jesus! "No," Meg said. "Give me some god-damn space, how about?" For *once*.

Her mother nodded and withdrew, and Meg limped over to close the door behind her. Slam it, really. Christ, her room was about as far from a sanctuary as—she swung the cane, *hard*, at her dresser, hoping to chip the antique wood. To smash it. But the cane glanced off the side and down, knocking her off-balance. She landed on the rug, groaning as her knee buckled underneath her. It hurt so much that she wanted to cry, but someone would probably open the god-damn door to check on her, and—oh, Christ, it really hurt. And she'd managed to bang her hand pretty badly, too.

She stayed on the floor, eyes closed, fighting off an absolute *torrent* of tears. If only they would prescribe some real painkillers again, instead of just useless over-the-counter stuff. But, she'd better take some now, so maybe, in an hour, her leg would feel less—she pulled in a couple of deep breaths, trying to get under control. She was tired of hurting. Beyond tired.

She took one more deep breath, rubbed her sleeve across her eyes—she was probably god-damned entitled to cry, but she still hated doing it—and reached for her cane, slowly dragging herself to her feet.

Her life was a complete and total fucking nightmare.

4

PHYSICAL THERAPY WAS awful. And she had to do it day after day, week after week, month after month. Tuesdays, Thursdays, and Saturdays, without fail, and then, more often than not, occupational therapy on Sundays.

Although she had had to deal with so many different medical and dental professionals during the past six months that she had, frankly, lost track of who most of them were, a hand rehabilitation specialist named Carlotta came to the White House regularly, and a somewhat shy woman named Edith was the physical therapist who usually worked on her knee, as well as her balance and general conditioning, often under the supervision of one or more of the military nurses who were assigned to the White House Medical Unit. The occupational therapists were almost always from Walter Reed or the NNMC, and instead of worrying about names, she just called them by their ranks. None of them ever talked much during the sessions, by Meg's choice. She would just sit there quietly and let them hurt her, cooperating when it seemed to be indicated.

For her knee, mostly they did range-of-motion stuff, and very few weight-bearing exercises. Like, she would sit on an examining table, with her leg hanging over the side—painful in and of itself—and Edith would make her raise it. Or she would lie down on the table and try to straighten her leg, tighten her quadriceps, or flex and extend her foot. Sometimes, she would have to lift a light weight or pull against some Thera-Band, which hurt so much that it was always a struggle to keep from slugging whoever was asking her to do it. Instead, she would grip the edge of the table with her good hand, her teeth pressed against her lower lip, attempting not to bite right through it.

Once, she'd had a male physical therapist—Edith was home sick, maybe—and he'd been so critical about the "results of her therapy thus far," exhorting her to "dig in," that she'd told him to get the fuck away from her, or she'd god-damn well make him regret it.

Since then, she'd always had female therapists, she'd noticed. Although the guy's gender hadn't been nearly as much of a problem as the Nazi-coach attitude.

Not that men in their thirties were her favorite people these days. Particularly tall, muscular Caucasian men with dark hair.

Be interesting to see how that PT guy would feel if some son-of-a-bitch had kicked *his* god-damn knee apart.

And then stood there, smiling faintly, afterwards. Making her literally *crawl* down that filthy hallway, back to the room with the metal bed, handcuffed the whole time, and—Christ, talk about degrading. Even among the many bad memories, that one ranked pretty high.

It had been a few months after she got back before one of her orthopedic surgeons had told her, hesitantly, that such a severe traumatic dislocation of the knee could actually have been fatal, because if there had been significant vascular injuries—in other words, if the bastard had managed to shred her arteries, along with the ligaments, cartilage, and nerves—she probably would have bled to death. No one had said anything at the time, but for several weeks, they had also been very concerned about the prospect of having to amputate her leg, because of possible necrosis or some damned thing. Apparently, her instinct in the mountains, to try and force the joint back into place and rig up an incompetent splint with sticks might have saved her life.

During physical therapy—usually at the beginning, while she still had some energy—they also made her do weight-resistance and strengthening exercises with her good arm and leg, to "keep them well-toned." Like she really gave a damn. But she did all of the stupid repetitions, allowed them to shoot the dumb electro-stimulus and ultrasound stuff into her, got grimly into the White House swimming pool when they asked her to do slow-motion versions of the same movements in the water, let them strap ice or heat packs all over her, afterwards—oh, yeah, it was a great way to spend a few hours.

Day, after *day*, after god-damn day.

Bright and early the next morning, she sat in the little physical therapy room which had been set up near the White House Medical Office on the ground floor. Personally, she didn't see why she couldn't do it in the family quarters—maybe up in the third-floor gym, or in the little room where President Eisenhower used to paint landscapes, and where the current occupant of the Oval Office got her hair done—but she had a feeling that Dr. Brooks wanted the sessions to be held downstairs just to make her leave the second floor more often.

With luck, it *wasn't* because the President was afraid that someone might notice a faint scent of ammonia in the tiny second-floor cosmetology room, and suspect that all of that thick auburn hair was actually, deep down, getting pretty god-damned grey.

"How is it today?" Edith asked, unfastening the knee brace, one Velcro strap at a time.

It was ice cream in the spring. "It's okay," Meg said evenly, trying to prepare herself not to wince as Edith helped her ease her leg over the edge of the table.

It *hurt*. It hurt a lot. Fuck. She pressed her teeth together.

Edith smiled at her. "You're making much more progress than you think you are."

Well, that was good news, seeing as she was shooting for the Olympics and all. Edith was moving her knee around gently, and Meg clenched all of her muscles—she was supposed to try and keep her leg relaxed—waiting for it to be over.

"Do you want to try now?" Edith asked.

More than she wanted world peace. Meg set her teeth into her lower lip, and then raised her leg so that it was mostly straight—she was still at least twenty degrees short of full extension—which seemed to take an incredibly long time. Then, very slowly, she lowered it. She was supposed to do *ten* of these. Christ.

"Okay?" Edith asked.

Oh, yeah. It was a day at the beach. An afternoon in the Green Monster Seats. A devil-may-care night gallivanting on the town. Meg nodded. She was supposed to concentrate on lowering her leg as slowly as she had lifted it—and not arching her back, and not holding her breath—but mostly, she had to focus on not groaning or crying.

"Let's try a weight," Edith said, when she was done.

Meg nodded, not looking at her.

Lifting the weight—was it three pounds, maybe? five?—hurt so much that she couldn't stop shaking.

"Only four more," Edith said, her voice encouraging.

Meg finished the set, trembling so hard that the whole table seemed to be vibrating. The whole *room*. She brushed her sleeve—surreptitiously, she hoped; yeah, right—across her eyes. "Should I do a couple more?" she asked, hearing her voice quiver. "Sets, I mean."

Edith looked uneasy, moving a blond wisp of hair back behind her ear. "If you think you can."

Of course she couldn't. But, then again, she *did* have those Olympics looming ever closer. Wanted to nail her compulsories and such.

"Take your time," Edith said.

Well, true, it wasn't like she had any place to go. So, she pushed herself through ten more leg lifts, but when she started the last set, the pain was so severe that she felt sick to her stomach. She closed her eyes, forcing herself to continue. To keep the third of a glass of orange juice and half piece of raisin toast she'd had for breakfast down in her stomach, where they belonged.

"Good job," Edith said, when she was finished. "A month ago, you couldn't even do five of those."

Gee, maybe the *New England Journal of Medicine* would write her up. *JAMA*. Meg hung on to the table, out of breath, her t-shirt feeling damp against her back. Yeah, that was progress, all right. A tiny little weight, and she felt like passing out.

After working on her hamstrings, and getting her to tighten and relax her quads for a while, Edith strapped her up with ice, spread a light fleece blanket over her, and left the room.

Meg sank back against the pillows at the end of the examining table. Jesus. Now, she would probably go upstairs and sleep for the rest of the day.

She was dozing, right there on the cold, thinly-padded metal table, when there was a knock on the half-open door, and Dr. Brooks came in. Technically, he was a Navy Admiral, and they were probably supposed to address him that way, but he, and her family, all preferred "Dr. Brooks." He was such a kindly and sympathetic man that she always made sure not to be surly, or swear in front of him—no matter how much she felt like it.

He smiled at her in his grandfatherly way. "Edith tells me that you did extremely well today."

Yeah, she couldn't be prouder. Meg nodded. "I lifted five whole pounds." Or possibly only three.

"Progressing to weights is a very big step," he said.

Unh-hunh.

"Getting a little more movement in the hand, too," he said.

Unh-hunh. Emphasis on, a little. She nodded politely.

"We'd like to start weaning you off that, over the next couple of months—" he indicated her cane—"and see how you do with just the brace."

Meg looked down at the bulky ice packs. "So, I'll put my full weight on it?"

Dr. Brooks nodded. "It'll improve your mobility, and should accelerate your progress."

No point in asking how much it was going to hurt. "Will I always need a brace?" she asked. "Just to walk?"

"Well, the extent of—" He hesitated. "I think you're coming along very well so far, Meg."

None of the medical people ever directly answered her questions, especially when bad news was involved. Meg looked at her ice packs. Hard to believe that tennis and skiing had once been such major parts of her life. Two of her favorite reasons for getting up in the morning. And now, presumably, *walking* was going to be an achievement. "I, um—I'm having a lot of pain, sir," she said. "Lately."

He frowned. "The ibuprofen isn't doing anything for you?"

It probably wasn't making things worse, but that was about it. She shook her head. "Not really."

"Well, why don't we put you back on the Tylenol-3 for a while," he said. "I'd like to avoid the stronger medications for now, if possible."

So much for more Percocet or Vicodin. Ultram, Hydrocodone,

Tramadol Hydrochloride, Darvon, Lortab, Dilaudid, Fioricet, Voltaren, Toradol, Anaprox, Lodine, OxyContin. She knew all their damned names, at this point. But, Meg nodded. The last thing she needed was a trip to Hazelden or someplace. Not that she was an addictive type, but Christ, chronic pain was a whole different ballgame.

Dr. Brooks picked up one of the ice packs, checking for swelling, maybe. He examined her knee, frowned again, and then replaced the ice pack. "Is it unbearable?" he asked, his expression noticeably more concerned.

Well, it hadn't *killed* her yet. Although not, she suspected, for lack of trying. "I guess not," she said. Doubtfully.

"Well, I think I'll give you something stronger for the next week or so," he said, "and we'll see how you respond, okay?"

She wanted to nod eagerly, but that seemed too close to the reaction an outright junkie would have.

"I'm also going to have one of the orthopedists come over later today, and give you a look," he said.

Christ. That sounded ominous. Meg looked at him nervously. "Is something wrong?"

Dr. Brooks shook his head. "No. I just think it's a good idea if we stay on top of things."

Which didn't *sound* all that good.

"There's no need for you to be alarmed, Meg," he said, with his very kind smile. "You know how careful we like to be around here."

And how.

"Do you have any questions?" he asked.

None that he was going to be able to answer. In all likelihood, she would need a damned theologian, or something, for *that*. So, she shook her head.

"Can we get anything for you? Some juice, maybe?" he suggested.

She shook her head. "No, thank you."

"Well." He smiled at her again. "Edith will be back in a minute to get rid of all that ice, and then I'll send Carlotta in, so you can finish up for today."

Meg nodded. All she had to do now, was stay awake that long.

When she finally got back upstairs, she went right to bed. After calling the switchboard and asking them not to put any calls through, and unplugging her phone again, for good measure.

It was just past seven o'clock when a knock on the door woke her up. She looked around the darkened room, tired and confused, as Vanessa yawned and stretched next to her.

The knock came again, very quietly.

"Who is it," she said.

"I just, uh—" Steven cleared his throat. "Dad said to ask if you want dinner."

Did she? It seemed like an inordinately complicated decision.

"Meg?" he said through the door.

She sighed, and reached over to turn on the light. "I don't know. I mean, you can come in, if you want."

He opened the door, walking partway into the room.

"So, uh," he stared down at his high-tops, "how you doing?"

Sometimes she forgot that all of this must be pretty hellish for her brothers, too. Okay, *most* of the time. Suddenly, she wasn't really part of their lives anymore. Not the way she had been.

She sat up, her neck very stiff. "I'm all right. I was just—reading." Not that there was an open book nearby, but she knew he wouldn't contradict her. "How was school?"

Steven shrugged, reaching out to pat Vanessa, who swiped at him and jumped off the bed. "Friendly, that cat," he said.

"Fickle," Meg said. "How was basketball?"

"Okay." He glanced at her for a second. "Got a game tomorrow."

"Well—that should be good," Meg said, trying to sound enthusiastic. Or, at least, *interested*.

He nodded, glancing at her again, and then away.

Oh, Christ. He never asked any of them—never had—but she knew that he loved it when people came to his games. That he played better. "Steven, I—" She sighed. "I get really tired."

"Hunh?" He looked up. "I mean, yeah, I know. That you need to rest and all."

"Yeah," she said.

He shoved his hands into his pockets, still not meeting her eyes. "Do I tell Dad you don't feel good, or—"

She sighed again. "I don't know." Was she hungry? No. "I should probably eat."

He nodded.

Jesus, if the thought of *dinner*, just down the hall, safe inside the White House, was daunting, how could he expect her to go to a crowded gymnasium and watch a noisy basketball game?

He headed for the door. "I'll tell Dad you'll be there in a while."

Feeling guilty, she took a deep breath. "Steven. I *want* to go to your game. But—it's kind of scary."

He shrugged. "Hey, no big deal. I just thought—it like, totally doesn't matter. I only meant if you weren't busy and all."

Busy sleeping. "Is Dad going?" she asked.

Steven shook his head. "He can't tomorrow. Mississippi, or something."

No point in even asking if their mother was planning to show up. She would always try to make it to at least one game of whatever sport Steven was playing that particular season, but weekday afternoons were the worst possible time.

"Neal'll be there," Steven said. "He always comes."

Had she known that? In fact, did she have any idea what her brothers did with themselves lately? Probably not. Would it be enough to have Neal with her, or would she still be afraid? Christ, if she couldn't manage this, how the hell was she going to go away to school? Go anywhere. *Ever*.

Steven went out to the hall. "Dad said we'll eat around seven-thirty."

Meg looked at her clock. Quarter past. "Okay, I'll get cleaned up."

Steven nodded, closing the door behind him.

She used her good hand to guide her leg over the side of the bed, then leaned down for her cane. Seven-fifteen. That was early. She plugged her phone back in, and dialed Preston's office extension. He was on another line, the staff told her, but they put her right through, anyway.

"Hey, what's up?" Preston asked, sounding as though he had all the time in the world.

"Were you talking to someone important?" she asked, feeling incredibly intrusive.

"No one I can't call back," he said. "What's on your mind?"

"Nothing." Oh, yeah, like she called him up every other minute. "I mean, I don't want to bother you when you're working."

"I'm not doing a thing," he said.

Sure. "Well, it's just—" She let out her breath. "Are you busy tomorrow afternoon?"

"No," he said, without hesitating.

Yeah, right. *No one* who worked in the White House ever had a free afternoon. She had to smile. "You liar. Aren't you supposed to go to Mississippi with Dad?"

"Louisiana, actually," he said. "And Maureen—" who had been hired to be her father's press secretary, after Preston officially took the chief of staff position— "is going, so no problem."

She was a complete jerk even to have picked up the phone; she *knew* better than to get in the way of White House events.

"For that matter, your father's a pretty big kid," Preston said. "He could probably handle a day care center and a community housing construction site on his own."

There was a good chance of that, yeah.

"What'd you have in mind?" Preston asked. "Maybe some Christmas shopping?"

On the one hand, she hated it that they all dropped everything whenever she said a word; on the other hand, thank God they did. "Steven has a game," she said. "And I thought—well—"

"You want some company, maybe," he said.

Yeah. Only now, she felt—weak. Incompetent. Halfway to fulfilling the wimp acronym. "Do you mind?" she asked.

"No, sounds fun," he said. "The little guy coming, too?"

Neal was the Little Guy; Steven was the Big Guy. "Yeah. But, can you, um—" Christ, this was humiliating. She sighed. "Leave with me? Instead of meeting us there?"

"Sure," he said instantly. "No problem."

Which was such a relief that she was all the more embarrassed. "I—I'm sorry to ask," she said. "I know how busy—"

"Wouldn't miss it for the world," he said.

THE GAME WAS at three-thirty. Leaving her just enough time to go to her classes, come home, do her exercises, then rest for an hour. She was supposed to meet Preston downstairs at two forty-five, and at two-fifteen, she actually found herself standing in her bedroom, leaning on her cane, worrying about what to wear. To a junior varsity basketball game, for Christ's sakes.

So, she put on a clean pair of sweatpants, a blue Lacoste shirt, an old V-neck tennis sweater, and Saucony running shoes with one of the pairs of special elastic laces Carlotta had given her. That way, each shoe would expand enough for her to put her foot in, and then snap back into place for a fairly tight fit. The laces looked goofy, but it was preferable to going around in orthopedic Velcro shoes or slip-ons. She had to use a long plastic hook to pull her left sneaker on, since her knee couldn't even take the pressure of pushing her foot into a shoe, but at least she could get into it without having to ask for help from anyone.

Preston was waiting for her near the Diplomatic Reception Room, surrounded by several staff members and aides, who—judging from the tenor of the conversation—all seemed to be very anxious about the logistics of several upcoming holiday parties and receptions the White House was holding. And her father was going to have to host the unveiling of the official White House decorations in a couple of days, an annual chore which, she knew, did not thrill him.

"Just use your best judgment," Preston said to Ginette, the deputy press secretary. "I should be back around five-thirty, six."

As the staff members moved off towards the East Wing, Meg nodded a self-conscious hello in response to the various nods and "how are you today"s.

"So." Preston slung on his coat—a long, quite smashing, grey duster. "We ready to go?"

Meg nodded, putting on her sunglasses.

"Maybe we should work up an endorsement deal for you," he said.

Meg flushed, and straightened them. There was presumably something extremely nonegalitarian about overpriced designer sunglasses. She had several pairs of glasses with clear lenses, which she wore sometimes when she was trying very hard not to be recognized, but it never seemed to make much difference, and she felt much safer behind sunglasses. The darker, the better.

When they got outside, there were a few reporters—and civilians—hanging around, some of whom shouted questions, to which she responded with a smile and a vague, friendly wave before getting into the car.

"Are my little friends coming?" she asked.

Preston nodded. "Looks that way. Sorry."

Swell. They hadn't even pulled out of the driveway yet, and she was already exhausted. She sat back, keeping her sunglasses on, her fist tight in her lap.

"Okay?" Preston asked.

She nodded, pretending to look out the window, but keeping her eyes closed. Then, as they drove towards the Southwest Gate, she started having trouble getting her breath.

Oh, Christ. Oh, Christ, oh, Christ, oh, Christ. She was going to lose it, right here in the car, and when they got to the school, she wouldn't be able to—

Preston's hand came onto her shoulder. "You're all right, Meg. I'm not going to let anything happen to you."

Which gave her another reason to panic. What if they were attacked, and *Preston* got caught in the cross-fire? Or her brothers. Or a bunch of innocent bystanders. Or—

"Count to ten," he said. "Do it a couple of times."

She looked at him, hoping like hell that he couldn't see the tears in her eyes behind the sunglasses.

"It's okay," he said. "We're the only ones here."

She wanted to sob, and throw up, and just generally fall apart. Make the car turn around, hurry inside, and huddle in her room for the rest of the day and night. The rest of her *life*, if possible.

The gates had opened, and they were on the street now, and it occurred to her that her all-too-quiet agents were witnessing this silent meltdown, too. It was bad enough to make a fool of herself in front of Preston, but she really didn't want her agents to see how cowardly she was. So she sucked in her breath, counted to ten, counted to twenty, and then—just to be sure—counted to fifty.

Preston gave her shoulder one last squeeze, took his hand away, and pulled a small tin out of his inside coat pocket. "Altoid?" he asked.

Why the hell not. With an effort, she opened her fist, and then clumsily helped herself to a couple of mints. "Thanks."

"I have LifeSavers, too," he said.

Good to know.

"This is going to make your brother very happy," he said.

It damned well better.

5

WHEN THEY GOT to the school, she saw a lot of extra Secret Service agents milling around, indicating that Neal had gotten there ahead of them. Which made sense, considering that he was only coming over from the Lower School. Although security was much heavier on game days, regardless. With all three of them in the same place, there would be at least twenty-five agents in and around the school. Probably not the most efficient use of the taxpayers' money—but, as far as she was concerned, the more, the merrier.

She moved as quickly as she could, very aware of the size of her entourage. The deathwatch didn't help matters any. Once they got to the gym, everyone—a pretty sparse crowd, luckily—turned to stare, and she stopped short, not sure if she could go through with this.

"Come on, there's Neal." Preston steered her towards the bleachers, where Neal, his friend Ahmed, and three Secret Service agents were already watching the action on the court.

Carefully, she climbed—hopped, sort of—up several rows and sat down next to Neal. "Hi." She nodded at Ahmed. "Hi."

Ahmed nodded gravely, peering at her through his very thick glasses.

"Steven made like, the last four in a row," Neal said, pointing at the lay-up drill.

"It was *ex*-cellent," Ahmed said, in his precise, clipped little voice. He was a Foreign Service child, and had picked up a British accent somewhere along the way.

Meg looked across the huge gym—it had been built quite recently, and was quite state-of-the-art for a high school—at the far basket, searching for Steven. He was wearing his usual number 9—the number he tried to be assigned in all sports, because of Ted Williams. Her family had always been partial to Ted Williams. And Carl Yastrzemski, of course. Jim Rice. David Ortiz. The usual suspects.

The other team, in blue and white, looked taller, and Meg glanced at Neal. "Are they good?"

Neal nodded.

"Is Steven's team going to win?" she asked.

Neal and Ahmed shook their heads.

Oh. Meg scanned the whole gym, including the jogging track up above them, still wearing her sunglasses, looking for anything out of place, or suspicious, or—fortunately, the most unusual phenomenon was the number of men lurking around in suits and earpieces. Her body-watch had filtered in, the cameraman and photographer wandering down to a spot near the scorer's table to join three other photographers and videographers, who might be professionals—or simply overly-involved parents.

"Do you think Steven minds the cameras?" she asked Preston.

He grinned, loosening his tie—purple and black-striped, and quite flashy. "I think Steven *loves* the cameras."

That was probably true, when it came to sports. Not that he would ever admit it.

The scoreboard buzzer sounded—making her flinch—and both teams trotted over to their respective benches. Or, more accurately, two lines of white folding chairs. All of the players pulled off their warm-up pants as their coaches gave them last-minute instructions. Steven saw her and shook his head, pointing to his own eyes.

Meg sighed and took her sunglasses off, and he nodded, obviously amused. Then, his team gathered in a tight circle, each stuck a hand forward, and they all shouted, "One, two, three, let's win!" The circle broke up, and the starting five ran out to the court, where the other team, the Panthers, joined them.

Her high school had actually played both of these schools in tennis; neither of their number one players had been terribly impressive, in Meg's opinion.

Before, of course, she had had to drop off the team for security reasons, after her mother's shooting. She'd been undefeated in singles at the time, and so, even though there were a couple of matches and the ISL Tournament left, she was still picked All-League, and as the team

MVP—which, she suspected, had resulted in a certain amount of legitimate grumbling from other players.

And now, it seemed like a hundred years ago.

The game started off rough, and only became more so. Lots of loose balls, plenty of traveling and double-dribbling, fouls galore. Both teams seemed to be pretty well-coached, moving in and out of zone and man-to-man defenses, but they missed many more shots than they made. Steven's team, the Hoppers, had cheerleaders, of assorted sizes, who were waving green and white pom-poms, and breaking into little routines every so often.

Neal and Ahmed kept jumping up every time Steven got the ball, and when he spun down the lane and flicked it in with his left hand, Meg was kind of excited herself.

"The kid has some pretty moves," Preston said, as Steven stole the ball from the boy he was guarding and passed ahead to one of his teammates for an easy lay-up.

Meg grinned. "Did you teach him that little pump-fake?"

Preston shook his head and pointed at one of Steven's agents, who was posted outside the entrance to the locker rooms. "That one came from Billy, I think."

Only Steven would have an agent named Billy. Bud. Scooter. He tended to get along very well with his agents, who gave him constant sports advice. "If they teach him a breaking pitch, my father will kill them," she said. Her father had a rule that none of them could throw curve balls until they were at least sixteen and their arms were fairly mature. In Meg's case, she had not found this sanction particularly confining. Steven, however, complained about it constantly. "Location," their father would say. "Work on your location."

Steven's coach, an Hispanic guy in his late twenties, paced up and down as though it was the seventh game of the NBA finals, while the assistant coach just sat in one of the folding chairs and yawned a lot. "Open man!" the head coach kept yelling. "Look for the open man!"

Look for the knobby-kneed little boy, more accurately. It was funny to watch them play, all energetic and uncoordinated, their hands and feet seeming to have grown much faster than the rest of their bodies. Sort of like German shepherds.

At half-time, Steven's team was down twenty-eight to nineteen. And not happy about it, as their coaches herded them off to the locker room, for strategy and pep talks, she assumed.

"It's an *ex*-cellent game," Ahmed said.

Neal nodded. "Way more excellent than usual."

"You guys always come?" Meg asked. Which she was probably supposed to know.

They both nodded vigorously.

The cheerleaders were—prematurely—doing a "victory, victory, that's our cry!" cheer, finishing with what had to be unintentionally staggered jumps. One girl managed a split, though, which was reasonably impressive.

"Did you ever do the cheering?" Ahmed asked.

Neal almost fell off the bleachers laughing, and when Meg checked Preston's expression, he was laughing, too.

"No," Meg said. "I never did."

"Victory, victory, our god-damn cry," Preston said, just under his breath.

Meg grinned at him. "What, you don't think I'd be a good cheerleader?"

"No comment," he said.

Which was aptly timed, because a print reporter—Meg was pretty sure she worked for one of the national weeklies, or maybe *The Washington Post*—was coming over. The various photographers had been shooting away throughout the game, taking far too many pictures of *her*, but Meg had been doing her best to ignore them.

"Enjoying the game?" the woman asked.

Meg nodded. "Yes. Thank you."

Neal and Ahmed were watching the cheerleaders and giggling—in all likelihood, it was the beginning of the end of the old latency period.

The reporter gestured towards her leg. "How's the knee coming along?"

"Very well, thank you," Meg said. Just in case this was for attribution.

"Are you enjoying the game, Hannah?" Preston asked.

"Yes," the reporter said, although her smile looked less than genuine. "A great deal." She looked back at Meg. "Will you be staying on at GW next semester?"

If she had to have a death-watch, it would be nice if they didn't *speak*. "I haven't made a decision at this time," Meg said, relieved to see Steven's team hustling—with a vengeance—out of the locker room. "It goes without saying that I have numerous options under consideration."

"Well," the reporter said, "do you expect to—"

"Why, look," Preston interrupted, amiably. "I think the game's about to start again."

"So, it is," the reporter said, and nodded at Meg. "It's good to see you looking so well."

Meg nodded back. "Likewise."

Once she was out of hearing, Preston shook his head. "Well, no one will ever accuse you of not being a pro."

Meg shrugged. Not exactly a skill that made her proud.

"Want a LifeSaver?" he asked.

She wanted one very much.

Steven's team started off well in the third quarter, going on a seven-point run that Steven capped off with a driving lay-up, getting fouled on the play.

"Powers, Powers, he's our man! If he can't do it, nobody can!" the cheerleaders chanted, and two girls turned cartwheels.

Steven missed the foul shot, and did not look pleased. Especially when, despite throwing a couple of elbows, he missed the rebound, too.

"He's mad," Neal said.

Meg nodded. And Steven mad was rarely a pretty sight.

There was a time-out, and Meg watched Steven's coach scribbling wildly on a small chalkboard, drawing a comprehensive series of plays. Steven and his teammates watched with ferocious concentration, but most of them looked puzzled. Baffled, even.

"Now, go *do* it!" their coach ordered, as the scorer's horn sounded to resume play.

The game continued. Sloppily. And the other team was still winning. There was a loose ball, and Steven and one of the Potomac players went scrambling out-of-bounds for it, ending up tangled together, in the second row of the bleachers. The referee blew the play dead and went to fetch the ball.

Getting up, Steven and the other player exchanged words—and then, shoves. As both benches cleared, and the referee and coaches waded in to break it up, Preston sighed.

"Here we go," he said.

Steven had always been one to get in fights, to the degree that it was barely newsworthy anymore. However, he probably shouldn't have chosen a day when her death-watch was there, to capture it on film.

Indeed, the press had moved in, en masse, and Preston sighed again.

"Damage control," he said, and went down to join the melee.

Neal shook his head. "Dad'll be really upset."

Meg nodded. "I think I'm skipping dinner tonight." Despite the fact—or more likely, *because* of the fact—that her father had been known to throw a punch or two himself when he was younger. At least, so Meg had heard. She had only *seen* once, when her mother broke her leg, and he did not react well when he confronted the drunk guy who had skied in front of her.

The two boys had, by now, been hauled apart, and Meg could hear Steven protesting to his coach, "Did you hear what he said to me? *No*body gets away with saying that to me!" His fellow pugilist was complaining just as vociferously, on the other side of the court.

Upon which, Meg saw the reporter who'd come over during halftime heading in her direction. Her agents must have noticed, too, because Kyle—yet another beefy ex-jock type, and easily the most belligerent and quick-tempered guy on her entire detail—moved to block her path.

"Excuse me," he said. "I'm afraid that seat's taken."

But, no point in having word get out that she was too scared to face people, no matter how accurate it might be. And, what the hell, maybe it would be a good test. Coping and all. "It's okay," Meg said. "He'll be right back. Thanks, though."

Kyle nodded, but posted himself only a few feet away.

In her straight skirt and high heels, the reporter wasn't really dressed for a JV basketball game. But since she was only about twenty-six, she was probably trying to look older.

And not succeeding very well.

"A little excitement," the woman—Hannah?—said, motioning towards the court as she sat down.

Her mother had always told her to count to three before she answered questions from the press. Just long enough to plan an answer; not long enough to look daft. End quote. "They play hard," Meg said. "Nothing wrong with that."

The reporter had a small notebook and pen in her right hand, but didn't appear likely to use them. Unless, of course, Meg said something *really* stupid. "Your brother gets very angry, though, doesn't he."

Oh, please. It wasn't like he was going to grow up and be a Hollywood bad boy. "He plays with intensity, that's all," Meg said.

The reporter nodded, then abruptly switched topics. "How is the investigation going?"

Bringing her captors to justice and so forth. Tracking them to the ends of the earth. As if they were ever going to find them. Especially the one guy. The *smart* one. Not bloody likely. "I'm sure it's coming along very well," Meg said, "but I really don't give it much thought."

The reporter nodded. Hannah Goldman. That was her name. *Newsweek*, maybe? *The Times*? No, it was *The Post*. Meg was almost sure it was *The Post*. Not that it mattered, really. "Are you disappointed by their progress so far?" she asked.

No, she was overjoyed that the guy, and his fellow thugs, were still running around loose six months later. Maybe even, if she was *really* unlucky, stalking her. Getting ready for Round Two. "I have complete confidence that the investigation will be brought to a successful conclusion," Meg said.

The longer she lived in the White House, the more she sounded like an official spokesperson. An unnamed top-ranking official in the Administration.

The game had started again—Steven's coach put him on the bench to cool off—and Meg could see Preston deep in conversation with one of the photographers. A wire service guy.

"Is the President—" Ms. Goldman began.

"I'm sorry," Meg said, cutting her off. Automatically. "You'd have to ask the President."

Ms. Goldman nodded, and glanced down at her notebook. "The way your public and private lives have intersected must be very difficult for you."

Christ almighty. Talk about tenacity. Which was probably a good quality in a reporter, but still. "I'm not sure I understand what you mean," Meg said. Lied.

Ms. Goldman wasn't fooled, but kept up her end of the charade. "I just imagine that all of this has put a strain on your relationship with your mother."

"No, that hasn't been my experience," Meg said. There was a grain of truth to that—most of the strains in her relationship with her mother were of many years' duration, had—more or less—been dealt with, and now just lingered below the surface, rarely mentioned or acknowledged.

Of course, the thing about reporters was that, especially when it came to personal matters, it was easy enough to flat-out lie to them, and unless they had incontrovertible evidence to the contrary, there wasn't a damned thing they could do about it.

"Well," Ms. Goldman said, and glanced over at Neal, Meg glaring at *her*. "Well," she said again, apparently thinking better of including him in any of this. "Who do you think will win the game here?"

Good. A softball. Meg shrugged. "Winning is secondary." Which was *such* a whopper, that she half-expected lightning to come searing through the gymnasium roof. "I just like to see both teams enjoy themselves." And, in addition, red, white and blue were her favorite colors.

Ms. Goldman nodded, clearly not buying a word of it. "Right." She stood up. "It was nice talking with you, Miss Powers."

Unh-hunh. "Yes, you, too," Meg said.

When the reporter was gone, tentatively making her way down the bleachers on her high heels, Meg looked at Kyle, who had a wide smile on his face.

"If you don't mind my saying so," he said, "you can sling it with the best of them."

Meg laughed. "Thanks. I think."

While Steven was on the bench, his team fell ten points behind again, and by the time he got back in, the game was pretty well lost. The final score was forty-three to thirty-eight, the Hoppers losing, and the two teams lined up to exchange handshakes. Or, anyway, hand *slaps*.

Preston stood up, stretching. "Well, *that* was relaxing," he said.

Meg looked over at the reporters, who were gathering their coats and other paraphernalia. "Think you stepped on it in time?"

He shook his head.

Oh.

Steven bounded up the bleachers, his face flushed, his hair damp and rumpled.

"Stupid game, hunh?" he said, and gave Neal and Ahmed smacks on the head. "Hey, you little twits."

Neal hit him back; Ahmed adjusted his glasses and punched Neal, who pushed him, and then, all three of them laughed.

Little boys. Christ. Meg reached for her Kevlar jacket, and then put on her sunglasses to prepare to go outside. Face the world again.

Steven shook his head. "Yo, Meg, it's dark out there." Then, he looked at Preston, slightly quelled. "You know, he started it, not me."

"Well, you could do some work on the old temper, maybe," Preston said. Pointedly.

Steven shrugged. "I always fight with that guy. It wasn't any big deal."

"Well, someday it might be," Preston said.

"I hear ya, I hear ya." He grinned at Meg. "Glad you came, ugly." He smacked Neal on the head again, then jumped down the bleachers to join his team. "Later!" he called back, then grabbed one of his teammates, and they went scuffling to the floor.

Meg laughed. "What a jerk."

Preston was smiling, too. "That's for sure."

Once they were in the car—Neal and his agents were giving Ahmed a ride home, and Steven was "hanging out to mess around with the guys"—Meg was so exhausted that she wasn't sure if she was going to be able to stay awake. And her knee hurt. Her hand hurt even more.

The most logical route home would go right past her old high school—but her agents didn't drive in that direction, and they hadn't on the way over, either.

Thank God.

"Enjoy your sojourn with Ms. Goldman?" Preston asked, after taking and making several brief calls on his cell phone.

Meg opened her eyes. "She was really fishing."

"Just doing her job," Preston said. "Any problems with her?"

Meg shook her head. Unless lying was a problem.

"Good." Preston pulled some papers out of his briefcase to study, squinting in the very dim light. "I always forget how much you like reporters."

Meg frowned at him. "I hate reporters."

"You hate the concept," Preston said, glancing at the top sheet. "But you've always seemed to enjoy dealing with them in person."

Meg took her sunglasses off. "What, is that bad?"

He fumbled inside the briefcase for a penlight and his reading glasses. "Makes *my* life easier."

Meg kept frowning, still not sure if she should be flattered or insulted.

"It was just nice to see you having fun," he said.

Okay. She *guessed*. Then she leaned over to see what he was reading. "That's *policy*, Preston." Not East Wing stuff at all.

He turned off the penlight, looking a little embarrassed.

Well, hell. "You and Dad are just bored out of your minds, aren't you," she said.

He shrugged. "I can't speak for your father."

Her father, who had had to take an indefinite leave of absence from his law firm, to avoid any possible conflicts of interest—and had been chafing, unhappily, at the protocol requirements of being a Presidential spouse, ever since. He couldn't even fool around with the stock market—which he loved—because all of their money had been put into blind trusts for the duration of her mother's time in office.

And she assumed that Preston was being offered lucrative non-government jobs right and left; sooner or later, he would probably take one.

Which would be bad for her family, but great for him.

"I know *I'm* tired," she said, "but you look pretty tired yourself."

He nodded. "We lead high-pressure lives, Meg. Know what I'm saying?"

And then some. Preston wasn't one to discuss his private life—with anyone, as far as she knew—but she did know that his long-time girlfriend, Rachel, had recently moved out, and that he was unhappy about it. Not that it was something she could really bring up.

They were on Pennsylvania Avenue now—almost home.

"Are you going to come upstairs and have dinner with us?" she asked.

He shook his head. "Sorry. Too much work."

Since he probably averaged eighty or ninety hours, if not more, at the White House during the average week when nothing went horribly wrong—not that there was *ever* an average week—his job probably had a lot to do with why he and Rachel had broken up. Maybe everything to do with it.

And she hadn't helped much today, by making him take the afternoon off, so that now, inevitably, he would have to stay much later than usual tonight.

"Thank you," she said. "For before, I mean. I don't know why I did that."

"I saw your hand clench, Meg," he said. "That was about all that happened."

What a nice man. "Thank you, anyway," she said.

They pulled through the Northwest Gate, and up to the North Portico. Her knee had stiffened pretty badly, and it was a struggle to get out of the car. But, in case there were any photographers around—and she could see some of the news correspondents doing their early evening stand-ups on the lawn, off to her right, she was careful to keep a smile on the entire time.

In the bright light of the Grand Foyer and Entrance Hall, she could see that Preston really did look worn out.

"At least come up and get something to eat," she said. "Instead of take-out, or whatever."

He grinned at her. "You suddenly sound just like Beatrice Fielding."

His mother. Great. Meg flushed, and looked down at the very shiny, diamond-patterned floor, which was so incredibly well-polished that she could almost see her reflection.

"Although it *is* the most coveted invitation in Washington," he said.

That was the rumor. The President so rarely allowed anyone to eat privately with the family—because, yeah, all they *had* were the goddamn meals—that it had become a much sought after, and almost never achieved, political goal. The current Beltway Holy Grail. "If they only knew," Meg said, wryly.

Preston laughed, and walked her towards the elevator, adjusting his stride to match hers.

"Um, thank you for coming with me," she said. "I wouldn't have been able to do it, otherwise."

"Yeah, you would," he said. "You just don't know it yet."

Be nice if he were right.

6

DINNER WAS EVEN more tense than usual. Steven had the good sense to tell their parents about the fight, instead of their having to hear about it elsewhere—like the network news, say—but they were both pretty mad. Meg's father, more so. Her mother had been in Chicago most of the day, and was now fielding calls about a massive earthquake in Indonesia, and an apparent new rebel insurgency in Sudan, and so, was too distracted to pay much attention to anything else.

"How many times are we going to have this conversation?" their father asked, as they all ate—or tried to eat—their salads. "If this keeps happening, you aren't going to be allowed to go out for sports anymore."

Steven scowled. "I get in fights at school, too. You gonna make me not go to school?"

"The idea, is for you not to get in fights at all," their father said. "For you to start behaving more responsibly."

Steven slouched down, his arms folded across his chest. "He called me a pussy," he said sulkily. "*No*body calls me a pussy."

Now, their mother stepped in. "Steven, I recognize that you swear, but I *really* don't like that word."

"I don't either," Steven said. "That's why I hit him."

Meg laughed. Christ, this conversation was predictable.

"It's not funny," Steven said, glaring at her.

"Yeah, it is." Meg took a bite of her corn bread. Carl, one of the chefs, made genuinely *fabulous* corn bread. "I mean, Christ." She glanced at her mother. "Sorry."

Her mother shrugged a "my life is a heavy burden" shrug.

"I had a fun time," Neal volunteered. "I'm totally glad we went."

Since the rest of her family was not prone to spontaneous utterances, they all thought about that.

"Did you win?" their father asked.

Steven shook his head, still sulking.

"How many points did you score?" their mother asked.

Steven shrugged. "Sixteen. And seven rebounds."

"He was really good," Neal said. "Like, when the coach took him out, they were losing and stuff."

"How about you?" their father asked. "How was school?"

"Boring," Neal said, sounding as happy as can be. "Can you pass the milk, Meg?"

Before doing so, Meg paused to wait for the inevitable.

"*Please*," their father said.

"Please," Neal said.

Meg passed the milk.

"Was school all right for you?" her mother asked.

Meg looked up. "Me? I mean, yeah. I guess so. How was Chicago?"

Her mother frowned. "Cold," she said finally.

"Metaphorically speaking?" Meg's father asked.

Her mother smiled a little. "It's a tough town, Russ. Very tough town. How was your trip?"

"It's a *warm* town," he said. "And I had some absolutely delicious iced tea."

Her mother's face relaxed into a full smile. "Your day beats mine, then."

"Did you get to hammer, Dad?" Neal asked. Since a visit to a building site, especially down on the Gulf Coast, inevitably meant that her father would bring along a pair of work boots, take off his jacket and tie, and pitch in, using tools with both skill and abandon.

Their father nodded. "I did. Along with some drilling and sawing."

Which might explain why he seemed more cheerful than usual.

Now that the tension had been broken, Meg felt hungrier, and was glad to see Jorge and Silvio coming in with the main course. Chicken, in what smelled like some kind of mushroom and wine sauce, rice pilaf, baby carrots sauteed with honey and dill. Okay by her.

Her mother started getting ever-more-frequent phone calls, and she left a few minutes later to go back downstairs to the West Wing. After the rest of them had dessert—or, at any rate, her brothers had dessert, while her father drank coffee, and Meg ate half a chocolate chip cookie, she went down to her room. She *wanted* to go straight to sleep, but steeled herself to work on her English paper, instead.

Religious Imagery in Selected Twentieth-Century Fiction. Fun.

She could order anything she wanted from the White House librarian, who would have it sent over from the Library of Congress or someplace—a service which had gotten Charles Colson, among others, in trouble, as she recalled—but asking the librarian to get her "you know, holy stuff" wasn't going to be much help.

After answering her email—one from Beth, who was obviously upset about the way their phone call had ended the other night, although Meg just wrote "*no big deal, don't worry about it*" in response; as well as emails from Josh and a couple of people she knew from various newsgroups and forums, who had no idea they were corresponding with the President's daughter—she ran a quick search for information which might be germane to her paper, but didn't come up with much. At any rate, nothing which seemed terribly reliable.

Her parents had set her up with several special keyboards designed for one-handed typing, but she was so accustomed to a traditional layout that the adaptive ones were too complicated to use. She also had all of the latest versions of voice recognition software, but they seemed like more trouble than they were worth, and she couldn't get excited about head-movement controlled, or wand mouse, technologies, either. So, she had gone back to a regular laptop, and sometimes a foot pedal, and just typed far more slowly than she once had, using her left hand.

She forgot, at one point, and tapped the space bar with the heel of her bad hand, which sent a jolt of such intense pain reverberating through her entire body that she had to stop and huddle over her splint until she could absorb the spasm. If she hadn't been afraid that someone would come in and see her, she might even have let herself rock back and forth and groan pathetically for a while. But she just swallowed, *very* hard, shook her head a few times, and went back to what she had been doing.

By eleven, she was so tired that she decided to watch CNN for a while to clear her head. The lead story was the earthquake in Indonesia, with videos showing a distressing amount of devastation. Entire villages appeared to have been wiped out, and rescue and relief teams from the United States were already en route to the region, with the White House—well, okay, the *President*—also issuing a statement expressing great sympathy for the Indonesian people and pledging a very large sum of money to help with the rebuilding and recovery.

Her mother, of course, was in a number of the other news stories—among other things, there was a G8 summit coming up soon—and Meg found watching a clip of her responding to questions, during a press availability on the South Grounds, after she got back from Chicago, more eerie than usual. Despite the warm smiles and light humor here and there, she looked so sad. Haggard. Listless. As though she neither swashed, nor buckled, anymore. Had the changes happened so subtly that no one who didn't know her well would notice—or did people just feel better picturing their President a certain way, regardless of reality?

The door was open, but her father still knocked.

"How's the paper coming?" he asked.

Meg turned away from the television. "I'm just taking a break," she said quickly. Although, really, she was old enough to make the choice to goof off, if she wanted. She should have grown out of all those years of having him—or Trudy, who had been their housekeeper in Massachusetts, but had morphed into being their adopted grandmother—say sternly, "Is your homework done yet?" Her mother, often foolishly, assumed that her children were honorable enough to turn off the television if they still had studying to do. Except, maybe, for Steven, who took great pride in never doing anything until he was forced.

Her father sat down in the rocking chair, then indicated the television. "Not much good news."

Was there ever? "The earthquake looks pretty bad," Meg said.

Her father nodded. "I'm afraid so."

Earthquakes, typhoons, hurricanes, tsunamis, floods, fires, plane crashes, bombings—all too often, current events just seemed like an endless stream of tragedies. The news anchors must have wanted to spend time on something less dire, too, because now they were discussing the Congressional squabbling—oh, yeah, *there* was some red-hot information—over the pending selection of the new Senate Minority Leader, after the former one had stepped down, due to health issues, or an ethics problem, depending on the source. The President had yet to indicate her official preference, but one of the proposed leaders had, very recently, very conveniently, been invited to a private luncheon meeting with her, while the *other* two had attended a group breakfast. Much was being made of this, and probably with good reason. Publicly, her mother had been saying that they were all fine men, with whom she'd served for many years.

Her father sighed. "All that politicking."

Meg nodded, glad that neither he, nor she, had added, "And, for what?" She had *thought* it; maybe he had, too. "Funny they don't notice," she said.

"Notice what?" he asked.

She pointed at the screen, even though it was a commercial now. "How different she looks."

He shrugged. "Some of the more astute ones do."

"To me, she looks like someone going through the motions," Meg said. Hesitantly.

"Well, you know her better than they do," her father said.

Not exactly a contradiction.

"Besides," he said, "they're probably hoping she'll get her second wind back."

Wasn't she on her fourth or fifth wind by now? "Do you think she will?" Meg asked.

His glance at her knee brace was, she knew, inadvertent. "I hope so."

Right. The whole family was being dragged down by *her* lack of well-being. She unfastened the top two straps on her splint, and lightly rubbed the scar tissue below her pinky and ring finger, on the off chance that one of these days, some of the fascia might release.

"It's feeling better?" he asked. "Lately?"

Since it wasn't, Meg shrugged in lieu of answering, and they watched as the network cut to a grimy, and just a shade too chipper, field reporter giving a live report from the scene of the earthquake, standing in front of mud and rubble, which had been a thriving marketplace less than ten hours earlier.

The next time a commercial came on, Meg let out her breath.

"I'm in the way here," she said.

Her father looked up, startled. "What?"

"I'm in the way," she said again. "In the White House."

"Of course you're not," he said. "You could never be."

Meg shook her head. "I'm supposed to be away at school. And as long as I'm here, limping around, and hiding, and sleeping a lot, things can't get back to normal."

If, of course, they'd ever been normal—but, that was a different issue.

"Meg, you could never be in the way," her father said, sounding very upset. "I don't know why you would think a thing like that."

Was he being dense, or just trying not to hurt her feelings? Or was he so clouded by guilt that he wasn't really listening? "Dad." She stopped, afraid that she might be going to lose her temper, and took a minute to pick up the remote and flick off the television. "Just—pretend I'm an adult for a minute, okay?"

"I know you're an adult, Meg," he said. "I didn't mean to suggest otherwise."

What was too bad, was that he had done it automatically. "Every second I'm here is a reminder that I'm not supposed to be. That everything's wrong." She went on before he could interrupt, or contradict her. "I don't just mean all of you. I mean me, too. I mean, *everyone.* It's like—advertising—that something bad happened. That our lives changed." That the son-of-a-bitch had beaten her down.

That she was a god-damn *victim.*

"I don't—" Her father frowned. "Meg, recuperation is bound to be—"

"Dad, listen to me," she said, trying not to lose patience. "I'm not doing a pity thing, I'm making sense. Everyone's spending their time being so god-damn careful and nervous, and I just end up feeling—I don't know—omnipresent."

Her father sighed, and rubbed his hand across the back of his neck. "It's only been a few months. You shouldn't expect—"

Meg shook her head so that he would stop. "She can't even look me in the eye," she said quietly. "Neither of you can."

Her father—right on cue—didn't quite look at her. "Naturally, we both feel responsible."

Yeah. They never looked at her, and for the most part, they never looked at *each other* anymore, either. "As long as my life's a disaster, no one can get beyond it. I feel like—I don't know," she said. "Like everything's revolving around me, and I hate it."

He nodded.

"I mean, Christ, I feel—" It all seemed so damned hopeless. She had managed to hold off on her pain medication earlier, but now, she took one, with the dregs of a glass of Coke on her bedside table. "I don't know what to do."

"You're already doing it," her father said. "You get up, you go to your classes, you study—you're taking it as it comes. We're very proud of you."

He just plain wasn't hearing her. "I can't even talk to Beth anymore," she said. "I feel—" Stupid. "Embarrassed." And left out. Left behind. *Lost.*

He nodded.

"I just—I don't know. I didn't expect my life to turn out this way." She glanced over to see him watching her intently. "I hate it *here*, and I don't belong anywhere out there. I'm like a—pariah."

Her father sat back in his chair, rubbing his temples this time.

"What," she said, amused in spite of herself. "Stumped for an answer?"

He smiled faintly. "This is a tough one, Meg. The only thing I can tell you is that it's going to get better. And that you're doing all of the right things."

Be nice to be back to the days when her parents had had no trouble answering her questions. She, personally, could think of only one possible solution here. "I—I want to leave next semester," she said. "Go to school for real."

Her father blinked. "Next *month*?"

She nodded.

"All right," he said, after a pause. "Then, we'll arrange it. The Secret Service has already been spending time up there, just in case."

Now, it was Meg's turn to be surprised. "So, that's it? I mean, just like that?"

"If that's what you want," her father said.

Jesus, *was* it? Maybe she'd better give this a little more—no. If she thought about it, she would back out. "Well—okay, then," she said. "That's what I'd like to do, if it's okay with you."

Her father nodded. "We'll get to work on it first thing tomorrow."

Somehow, she'd expected him to put up more of an argument. Tell her all the reasons why she wasn't ready, and should wait until next fall, or her junior year, or—

"This doesn't have to be final," he said. "I mean, you can always—"

Meg shook her head. "No. I'd really like to try it. I think I—yeah, this is definite." Christ, she hoped she wasn't going to regret this.

Actually, she already did.

ON FRIDAY, SHE handed in her English paper, and also finished up the last assignment for her Astronomy online laboratory section. She studied all weekend for her finals, both of which were scheduled back-to-back on Monday afternoon. That morning, she was so nervous that she couldn't manage to eat breakfast, and by the time she got to the campus, she felt weak and dizzy enough to regret not making more of an effort to force something down.

The auditorium was more crowded than it had been all semester. Amazing to see how many people never bothered coming to class. Either they were all smarter than she was, or they were all taking it Pass-Fail. Or maybe both.

There were no aisle seats available in the back, so she had to cross awkwardly in front of a few people, trying not to bang any of them with her cane. A girl who was reading *People* looked up at her, blushed, and put the magazine away.

Oh, Christ, it was Monday. The magic week of the 25 Most Intriguing

People of the Year issue. Terrific. Plus, so many seats were already taken—since they had to leave one between each person—that she didn't have much choice other than to sit here. Next to her Big Fan.

She moved her jaw, sat down, took out a pen, and then shoved her knapsack under her seat, never looking to her right where the girl was.

"I wasn't reading about *you*," the girl said defensively.

Meg uncapped the pen, staring straight ahead. The pen actually had the Presidential Seal on it, which probably made her look arrogant, but—too late now.

"I just like to read *People*, okay?" the girl said.

Meg glared at her. "I didn't tell you not to."

The girl glared back. "Maybe you're too exalted for me to sit next to?"

Anyone who treated her normally—was rude, say—won points in her book. "Sorry," she said. "It's none of my damn business what you read."

The girl shrugged. "It didn't occur to me that you'd be sitting right next to me."

That *would* be kind of a nightmare, to be reading peacefully, and have one of the very people walk by and get all offended. The professor was just beginning to hand out blue books, so there was still time before the exam began.

Curious, Meg tried to see the magazine, now hidden under the girl's notebook. "Am I on the cover?"

The girl, who was wearing a tight black midriff-baring tank top—in December—nodded and pulled it out to show her.

There she was, nestled right among the movie stars, athletes, and, of course, British royalty. Although she herself was partial to the notion of a Queen, Meg had always had her doubts about whether the American public was quite as monarchically-fond as the media seemed to think.

The shot of her was the same damned one they always used—in a wheelchair, the day she came home from the hospital, looking small and damaged, her eyes hidden behind sunglasses.

"I knew they'd pick that stupid picture," she said aloud.

The girl studied the cover. "It isn't very good of Brad Pitt, either."

True. Meg laughed. "No, it really isn't, is it?" She knew without checking that this girl was a high-top Converse All-Stars type, and her guess was—purple. She looked down, and saw that her guess was correct. On the left foot, anyway. The girl was wearing a green one on her right foot. "Did they make me out to be this pensive, delicate sort of recluse?"

The girl nodded. "I think they said that we cried for you, we laughed with you, and throughout it all, we admired you."

"Oh, Jesus." Then, Meg raised an eyebrow. "That's pretty good recall for someone who didn't read the article."

The girl's face turned red. "I might have skimmed it."

Just maybe. "Is that horrible picture of me lunging for the volley in there?" Meg asked. To illustrate, vividly, the tragic physical decline from able-bodied athlete to pathetic cripple.

"I think so, yeah," the girl said. "I mean, I don't know, but it shows you playing tennis."

Before the kidnapping, the one she saw constantly was a photo someone had snapped of her slumped forward, with her head in her hands, sitting on a bench in the hospital hallway after her mother was shot. The damn thing had been in just about every Year-in-Review magazine that came out. The President's daughter, caught in a moment of private grief. Grief that got splashed all over every supermarket checkout line in America. Overseas, too, for all she knew.

The boy on her other side passed her a stack of blue books, and she took one, then handed the rest to the girl.

"Did you study for this?" she asked.

The girl shook her head.

Oh. "Do you think it will be hard?" Meg asked.

The girl shook her head.

Oh. Meg frowned. "Did you take this Pass-Fail?"

The girl nodded.

Which she should have done herself, but if she had, she wouldn't be able to transfer the credit. Since she was now committed to leaving.

Maybe.

Probably.

Almost definitely.

She looked over at the girl again. "Do you understand parallax?"

The girl shook her head, quite nonchalant about the whole thing.

"Neither do I," Meg said, and reached over to take the small pile of exams from the boy next to her and pass them along.

"You may begin," the professor said, once everyone was reasonably quiet.

Meg turned over her test and read the first question. Parallax.

Naturally.

7

AFTER THE EXAM was over, she felt so shaky that she wasn't sure she was going to be able to make it through another two hours of test-taking. There wasn't enough time to get anything to eat, but she stopped at a vending machine and drank a Coke in about five big gulps. Maybe the combination of sugar and caffeine would be enough to do the trick.

She must have looked unsteady on her feet—God knows she *felt* that way—because her agents seemed to be worried, and she had the sense that they were exchanging glances, especially when she had a small dizzy spell and had to stop for a minute.

"Do you need to sit down?" Brian—who was a stocky former Army Ranger—asked, suddenly right by her elbow.

Meg shook her head, feeling slightly invaded, and wishing he would just leave her alone.

Now, Paula was coming over, too, and Meg was going to tell both of them to back the hell off already—except that Paula was holding out a PowerBar.

"Eat this," she said.

Meg shook her head. "No, I'm fine, I just—"

"*Eat* it, Meg," Paula said. "Okay? You look like you're about to pass out."

She wanted to argue, but they both looked so concerned, that she nodded, said thank you—and ate the damn thing.

Which tasted pretty good, actually.

In contrast to Astronomy, everyone in her English class seemed anxious, and she couldn't decide whether that made her feel better, or worse. The black molded plastic chair felt even more uncomfortable than usual, and she hadn't been able to find an empty left-handed desk in the back row, so she was going to have to twist her body to one side in order to be able to write. The lights in the room seemed unusually bright, and she wished that she could put on her sunglasses, but she was afraid that it would look too weird.

"Good afternoon," Dr. Raleigh said. She was decked out in an ankle-length madras dress, the colors only bleeding slightly, and although her hair usually hung loose, today it was arranged in an ornate thick French braid, so she must be feeling celebratory about getting to give a major exam. "Please turn *all* of your cell phones off, and put everything under your desks, please."

"We can't keep our pens?" someone asked, and most of the class laughed.

"You may keep your pens," Dr. Raleigh said—big of her—and passed out the tests. "There are five essay questions. I would like you to choose three to answer, and you should spend equal time on each. Please be as specific as possible." She paused. "You have two hours."

All around her, Meg could hear paper rustling and blue books being opened. She picked up her test sheet, feeling sick to her stomach.

The questions were terrifying. The first one said: *compare and contrast Fitzgerald and Hemingway, in terms of both style and philosophy.* The second question was: *select four of the novels and discuss why each one has a uniquely American vison.* Oh, great, the vision thing. The third one read: *choose three of the novels, describe the roles that women and minorities play, and explain how each book is a product of its era.*

Jesus Christ. Meg put her test down, her hand trembling. At the moment, she couldn't even remember which books they had read.

Everyone else was writing; she could hear them. Was she the only idiot in the room? She heard a small flapping sound, and stiffened. Someone was turning a *page* already?

Two hours. She only had two hours. They were all scribbling away, and right now, she didn't know if she could spell her name right. Meghan did have an "h," right? Maybe her parents hadn't actually wanted the Gaelic form, after all, maybe—she gripped her pen, trying to stop shaking.

It was a test. It was only a test. It wasn't life or death—she *knew* what life and death situations were like, and this was only—but, Christ. She couldn't remember anything.

She bent over the paper, rereading the question. How was she going to choose three, if she didn't know the answers to *any* of them? Oh, God.

Something grazed her arm, and she damn near flew out of her seat. Then, she saw her professor bending down next to her.

"Relax," Dr. Raleigh said. "It's not that important."

Not that important? It was a *final*. Meg swallowed, horrified to find herself on the verge of tears. Yet again.

"You've done excellent work all semester," Dr. Raleigh said. "This won't affect that."

Meg looked around, and saw that everyone else was crouched over their blue books, writing industriously. "I don't want special treatment," she said, keeping her voice low.

"You've done A work," Dr. Raleigh said. "Just relax."

A couple of people glanced at her covertly as their professor returned to the front of the room, and Meg pretended not to notice.

A test. Only a test. Okay. Meg took a deep breath, read the questions one more time, and then picked up her pen.

They probably weren't the most sparkling and incisive essays ever written, but she managed to finish the exam, handing it in a couple of minutes before the two hours were up. After she turned her blue books in—she had gone through one and a half, Dr. Raleigh reached out to shake her hand. Her *left* hand, luckily, but Meg was still caught off-guard, and had to awkwardly shift her cane out of the way so she could return the handshake.

"I've enjoyed having you in class this semester," Dr. Raleigh said.

Yeah, what with all four oddball comments she'd made. "Thank you." Meg knew she should say something else, but her mind was as much of a tabula rasa as it had been all morning. "It was very interesting."

"I hear you're going to be transferring next semester," Dr. Raleigh said. "Good luck up there."

Which was very nice of her.

Especially since, odds were, she was going to *need* it.

BY WHITE HOUSE standards, they had a quiet Christmas. There were, of course, lots of parties—for the staff, the press corps, the Secret Service, the Foreign Service, members of Congress, and all of their respective families. There were also innumerable other receptions being held, including one for a group of homeless families who were enrolled in an ambitious job training program and also helping build new housing units for themselves—which had given her father a few chances to hammer *locally*, another for a highly-decorated Army unit which had just returned from a lengthy peacekeeping mission overseas, an afternoon tea for cancer survivors, and a party for handicapped children, featuring a jovial White House electrician dressed as Santa Claus and a lot of outrageously good-looking, mostly well-meaning, celebrities. Plus, her parents—her father, in particular—were making daily visits to veterans' hospitals, nursing homes, drug treatment centers, hospices, and the like.

Meg skipped all of the major public events, like the Congressional Ball, and the Kennedy Center Honors, but she steeled herself to make appearances at most of the parties in the Residence, especially the ones which included children, or anyone who was physically challenged. Seeing people who were small, and sick—and beaming away, or were completely crippled, but still full of joy and enthusiasm, really made her feel selfish for worrying so much about her own, relatively manageable problems. One little girl in a wheelchair *really* broke her heart by complimenting her cane prowess. And when a bright-eyed boy, about eleven years old, who'd recently undergone a liver transplant, asked her to show him where and how she had used the rock to break her hand, she found herself quite willing to do it, making the story—she'd had plenty of experience with little boys, after all—as harmlessly gross as possible, with just enough gore to keep him happy. His response was "*Cool!*", and she'd laughed, and said, "Yeah, well, don't try it at home."

The White House looked excessively festive, with wreaths and trees and garlands and ribbons and lights galore. The pastry chef had created the traditional towering homemade gingerbread house, and her father was a good sport about having to appear on all of the morning network news shows to talk about the history of White House Christmases past and present. He even read *The Night Before Christmas* aloud on a nationally televised holiday special, sitting in a rocking chair in front of the fireplace in the Blue Room, wearing bright-red suspenders, in what her mother generally described as his "Daddy Walton" mode.

Every year, Christmas at the White House had a different theme, and this year's was "Our Global Community," with exhibits explaining various traditions and customs, complete with handicrafts from countries all over the world, most of which had been made by children. It was all a little cloying, but also very well-intentioned.

The huge tree in the Blue Room had been donated by a family farm in Wisconsin, and smaller trees had been placed in strategic spots throughout the entire complex. The tree in the family quarters, from the same Wisconsin farm, was still alive, in a big plastic container, so that it could be replanted outdoors after the holidays were over. The First Family, being a Good Environmental Role Model. Vanessa and the other cats thought the dirt was great, and kept climbing into the planter, and scratching clods all over the floor in the Yellow Oval Room. Neal and Steven kept pretty busy sweeping the dirt up—no point in upsetting White House purists, or the staff, any more than necessary—and one night, very late, she even saw her mother bent down by the tree with a little broom and dustpan. She kind of wished she had a camera handy, so she could post the photo on the Internet, and caption it: What the President *really* does with her time.

They went up to Camp David early on Christmas Eve, which—because it was a secure, well-guarded military facility—meant that most of their agents, and as many members of the White House staff as possible, would have a chance to spend Christmas with their own families.

Of course, normally, they probably would have headed off to Stowe or someplace, and skied all week, and Meg insisted that they still should, but the rest of the family must not have wanted to remind her that she couldn't participate anymore. Although she *would*, admittedly, have felt envious, and maybe even bitter, the entire time, it didn't seem fair that everyone else had to suffer because of her misfortunes. And, in the wake of the holiday parties, she had to remind herself that they were pretty minor misfortunes, in the scheme of things.

Albeit, extremely major for her.

By New England standards, the weather was very warm—even up in the mountains, and on Christmas night, she sat on the patio outside Aspen, the First Family cabin. There were some lights around—other cabins and buildings, and that sort of thing, but it was also dark and woodsy, with trees everywhere. Very much, in a lot of ways, like the forest she'd dragged herself around for all those days—which was the main reason she had been avoiding Camp David ever since. But she must be doing better, because while the idea of being in the midst of so much nature made her feel edgy, she was able to sit outside by herself without falling apart.

Or, anyway, so far. It helped that it was getting foggy, and she couldn't see all that much.

The rest of her family was inside the cabin, and the sound of Christmas carols playing drifted through the open windows. Her mother was still probably making holiday phone calls to a long, carefully researched, staff-provided list of service members stationed around the world, and Meg wasn't sure what her father was doing, but her brothers were almost certainly busy trying out all of their new video and computer games. Right after dinner, they had screened one of the new Christmas movies—First Family fringe benefit—and they had more to watch later, if they wanted.

She hadn't been able to get very good gifts—just one quick Sunday afternoon shopping trip with Preston, but it was always hard to go into stores unnoticed, anyway. And even more difficult to keep gifts a surprise, what with photographers all over the place. She'd had to get Preston to leave her alone—except for several agents—in the Men's Department for a few minutes, so she could pick out the most outrageous, yet tasteful, tie possible for him.

The majority of the gifts she had been given—mostly, of course, from her parents—were different from any presents she'd ever gotten before. College stuff. Yet another new laptop computer, pens, pencils, highlighters, large plastic paper clips, legal pads, lots of software, a little voice-activated tape recorder, in case she wanted to record her lectures, an iPod with massive amounts of storage space, fancy headphones, a special tray with a handle to use in the dining hall, a folding rocker knife for the same purpose, a very thick terry-cloth bathrobe—because shrugging one on was often easier than trying to use towels one-handed, books, several pairs of sunglasses, and all kinds of other things. So many gifts, that it was more than a little obscene. Steven's present had been a sweatshirt with the slogan "The Queen Is Not Amused," which she was already wearing, and Neal had selected a video game for her that revolved around soldiers and many complicated missions behind enemy lines. Not her kind of thing at all, but she had been careful to act wildly excited about it, to make him happy.

She looked at the trees, her leg propped up on a small pillowed bench. The woods *were* dark and intimidating, no question about it, so maybe she should go inside. There were guards everywhere, so there wasn't much chance that anyone could infiltrate the compound, but what if—she heard the cabin door open, and stopped gripping the arm of her chair so that she would be able to appear calm, and relaxed, and full of holiday cheer.

Her mother came out, bundled up in a heavy cardigan, accompanied by a Navy steward, who was carrying a tray with mugs of cocoa and just-baked cookies.

"Hot chocolate?" she asked.

"Sure," Meg said. "Thanks."

After the steward had left, her mother sat in the rustic wooden lawn chair next to hers.

"You warm enough?" she asked.

Meg briefly considered taking umbrage at this—shouting that she was an adult, and bloody well old enough to decide whether she needed a jacket or not—but it was, after all, Christmas. Besides, if her mother *hadn't* asked, Meg would have been disappointed in her. So, she just nodded.

"Not much chance of snow with these temperatures," her mother said.

It probably wasn't the right time to bring up global warming. Meg stirred her cocoa with the candy cane adorning the mug, and then drank some. "Nice and quiet up here," she said.

"Good to get away," her mother agreed.

She kind of liked it when she and her mother spoke in terse, incomplete sentences. It seemed—slangy. Dashing. *Macho*. "Going back tomorrow?" she asked.

Her mother considered that. "Day after, probably."

Meg laughed. How brusque, and pithy.

"What?" her mother asked.

"Nothing," Meg said. She and her brothers were going to stay up here through New Year's, while her father would probably—it had yet to be determined—go back and forth at least once. "Thanks for all the stuff. I mean, you guys gave me way too much."

"Well," her mother said, and left it at that. She had always been a big gift-giver, and the reason was probably some complicated combination of guilt and generosity.

"Anyway, thank you," Meg said. "They were all really nice."

Her mother sipped some cocoa. "We'll have to make a list of whatever else you might need up there."

Beth, who was supposed to fly down to Washington for a few days before her winter break was over, would, without question, be full of advice. Most of it solicited. "I'm sorry Mrs. Peterson couldn't come," she said.

Her mother nodded, and looked worried.

Her mother's best friend—one of the only people around whom Meg ever saw her come close to relaxing—was in the midst of radiation and chemotherapy for breast cancer, and hadn't been feeling up to traveling lately. So, her mother had been flying to Boston every month or two—using various transparent, manufactured political excuses—to see her, instead.

Inside the cabin, there was a crash, then sounds of a scuffle, followed by a yelp. Human, not canine.

Meg looked at her mother. "*I* didn't hear anything."

"Neither did I," her mother said.

Being as it was Christmas and all.

There was another crash, and Meg heard her father shout, "Hey!", and Neal saying, "*Steven* started it!"

Yes, it was nice to be outdoors. "When's Trudy going to get here?" Meg asked.

"By the weekend, as far as I know," her mother said.

They didn't have any grandparents—hadn't, for many years—and Trudy had assumed the role by default. In general, since they didn't have much of an extended family, Trudy—and now, Preston—had always taken on extra importance. Her father's sister, and somewhat bohemian ne'er-do-well husband, were also supposed to visit for a couple of days later in the week, along with two of her much-older cousins, and some of her parents' friends would probably be around, too.

She could hear her father saying, patiently, "It isn't broken, I just think that *someone*—" "someone" had to be Steven—"took the batteries." "It's *broken*, Dad," Steven was insisting, "because, you know, it's foreign."

Meg looked at her mother. "So. How about that trade deficit?"

Her mother sort of laughed, sort of groaned. "Not on Christmas."

Right.

"You want to have Beth come down early?" her mother asked. "Be here for New Year's?"

Meg shook her head. "She probably has real plans." Which sounded incredibly rude. "I mean, you know, social stuff."

Her mother looked at her closely. "Do you want to go up there?"

God, no. The idea of having all the people she'd grown up with see her like this was—nope, no way. "I'd kind of rather be quiet," Meg said.

Her mother nodded. "Me, too, actually."

There was another loud crash inside, Kirby barked, and her brothers laughed wildly.

"Are you curious?" Meg asked.

Her mother shook her head. "Not even faintly."

Right.

8

WHEN SHE CALLED Beth the next day, dropping the idea of New Year's, Beth allowed as how coming to Camp David maybe wasn't the *worst* idea she had ever heard. Providing, of course, that there would be plenty of champagne available. But, of course, Meg said, although she had no idea.

Beth arrived right after lunch on New Year's Eve, a White House car having picked her up at the airport, and whisked her out to the mountains—much as Trudy had shown up a couple of days earlier. Without looking very happy about it, her father had headed back to Washington after breakfast, so that he and her mother could go to a couple of private parties with friends—political and otherwise—before returning to Camp David later that night.

Steven's friend Vinnie had also come up to visit, and so far—it would appear—he and Steven, with Neal trailing after them, had spent the entire day having a belching contest. Charming. They also went and shot skeet—Camp David had its own little range—which was going to displease her parents, if they found out. Trudy had managed to dissuade them from trying to take the secure elevator down to the bomb shelter beneath the lodge, and the last time Meg had seen them, they were careening along one of the paths through the woods in a golf cart, the usual mode of transportation at Camp David.

Although people normally drove them more cautiously.

She was sitting in the sun porch with Trudy, when a steward came and told her that Beth's car had just pulled in.

"Thanks." Meg put down her Coke and looked at Trudy, who was peering through her glasses as she crocheted a winter hat for Neal. Trudy made things for everyone she liked, scrupulously taking turns. "I'll be right back."

Trudy smiled up at her, plump in just the right way in her green wool dress. "Okay, dear. If you see the boys, tell them to come in and get something to eat."

"I think they're off being cretins somewhere," Meg said.

Trudy smiled again. "I'm sure they are."

Meg limped after the steward, getting to the door just as Beth came in, wearing a long black coat, red sunglasses, and a red beret.

"Why, hello," she said, and whipped off the beret, revealing a very short, very punk, very *blond* haircut.

Meg knew she wanted an explosive reaction, but decided not to give her one. "What, no purple streak?"

Beth took off her sunglasses. Her eyes were still brown. "You know, that's exactly what my mother said."

Meg laughed. Apparently, Mrs. Shulman was finally beginning to loosen up. "What did your stepfather say?"

"He just looked disgusted," Beth said, and thought. "Or maybe, it was appalled."

Flummoxed, perhaps. Meg squinted at her. "How many earrings are you wearing?"

"Five," Beth said.

Meg nodded. Not that she couldn't count, but she'd wanted to hear it for herself. "The feather looks dumb."

"Thank you, Meg," Beth said. "You always know just what to say. Besides, you're still wearing those same damn little hoops."

Okay, so she wasn't big on earring variety. Old news.

Beth shrugged off her coat to reveal a grey cashmere sweater, a silver necklace, and black slacks.

"How cutting-edge," Meg said.

Beth grinned. "My mother insisted. She said I wasn't going to Camp David looking like a she-didn't-know-what."

As long as Meg had known her, Mrs. Shulman had been endlessly dismayed by the fact that she had given *birth* to a she-didn't-know-what. As soon as they walked into the sun porch, Trudy went bustling off to bring them some of the brownies she'd baked that morning, even though Meg pointed out that the stewards would be happy—delighted, even—to do it.

Beth watched her go. "They must all be completely petrified of her."

A safe assumption. There was a very tough—and exacting—lady hiding behind that round, smiling face. Her foot did its sudden flopping thing, and she had to grab the edge of a table to keep from falling, dropping her cane in the process. She glanced at Beth self-consciously, and then lowered herself—carefully—into an overstuffed chair.

Beth started to say something, then just bit her lip and looked away.

They sat there, in nearly-deafening silence.

"Good Christmas?" Beth asked finally.

Meg nodded. "My parents gave me everything in sight."

"*We*, of course, don't observe those pagan rituals," Beth said.

Meg shrugged. "Then, I won't give you the present I got you."

"No, it's all right," Beth said, sighing deeply. "Just this once, I'll explore your wretched gentile traditions."

"Thought you might," Meg said.

Trudy came out with a platter of brownies and sugar cookies, while a steward carried a tray with a pitcher of milk and several glasses.

"Thank you, Brady," Trudy said, as he set it down on the coffee table. "Please have some brownies."

"Yes, ma'am," he said, but didn't touch them. He looked at Meg. "Will there be anything else, Miss Powers?"

Surely, he must realize that Trudy was completely running the show here. Meg shook her head. "No, thank you."

Just as Trudy sat down, her brothers and Vinnie—and Kirby—came noisily in, disheveled and out of breath. Judging from their clothes, they had either had a leaf fight—or the golf cart crashed. Or some combination of the two.

"Hey, excellent," Steven said, heading straight for the brownies.

Trudy looked very stern. "Not so fast, young man."

"She wants us to be clean and stuff," Steven said to Vinnie. "Wash up." Then, he noticed Beth's hair. "Yo, look! It's like—some weird alien!" He grabbed Neal and Vinnie, trying to knock them to the floor. "Take cover!"

Beth laughed, as all three of them flattened behind the couch. "Now, see," she said to Meg. "That's the kind of reaction I like."

"It talks *English*!" Neal gasped.

"Too weird, though, man," Vinnie said. "It has like, a feather coming out of its brain."

All three of them poked their heads up enough to study Beth's earrings.

Vinnie frowned. "It's, like, an antenna."

"No, it's a death-laser!" Steven said, and they hit the deck again.

"Boys," Trudy said, obviously no longer in the mood for such foolishness.

They got up, suddenly angelic and polite.

"Sorry, lady," Steven said. "Don't know what came over us." He looked at Neal and Vinnie. "Fall out, men! Double-time!"

"I'll get there first!" Neal said, and they all raced for the nearest bathroom, trying to shove each other out of the way.

Meg leaned closer to examine Beth's feather. "It does look like an antenna."

"It *is* an antenna," Beth said, and helped herself to a brownie.

Even after changing their shirts and combing their hair, her brothers and Vinnie's energy levels were still pretty high, and the rest of the afternoon was on the rambunctious side.

"All right, boys," Trudy said, when dinner was over. "I think it's time for you three to start calming down. Why don't you go watch a movie?"

"Soldiers!" Neal said enthusiastically. "They sent us that cool soldier movie."

"Excellent," Steven said, and the three of them left the room, wrestling and trying to trip one another the entire way. Kirby barked, and followed them.

"We do have a lot of good stuff," Meg said to Beth. "All the Christmas movies."

Beth shrugged. "Sounds like a plan."

The stewards had already cleared the table, and Meg could tell that Trudy was dying to go into the kitchen and clean up.

"They honestly don't mind," Meg said. "I mean, we almost never come up here." Anymore. "I think they get really bored."

"I know," Trudy said, looking fidgety. "I just feel funny about it."

Meg nodded. She felt funny about it herself. "Well, come watch movies with us."

"Something without soldiers, please," Trudy said.

That meant that car chases, cops, street gangs, and spaceships were probably out, too.

Which was going to limit their options.

"Chick flick," Beth said. "We definitely need a chick flick."

Yes, they very definitely did.

MEG'S PARENTS HAD wanted to be back by midnight, and Marine One landed just after eleven. Her father went into Steven's bedroom suite, where Steven and Vinnie and Neal were mesmerized by yet another action movie, and dragged them out to the living room. At midnight, like most other people in America, they were sitting in front of the television, watching the ball go down in Times Square. The stewards served champagne to everyone—her brothers and Vinnie were elated—and then they all went out to the patio to watch the fireworks display some of the Marines had put together.

"I think this is going to be a good year," her mother said, which she said every year.

Odds were, it would have to be better than the one that had just ended. Meg sipped her champagne, rather than make a crack to that effect.

"Bound to be an improvement," Beth muttered, next to her.

Since she was *already* mentally and physically crippled, yeah. "I hope so," Meg said quietly.

Once the fireworks were over, her brothers and Vinnie got bored, and went back to their movie. Trudy trailed after them, and Meg figured that she had decided to take on the thankless chore of trying to talk them into going to bed afterwards—and also, possibly, keep a little distance from her mother. Ever since—everything, Meg had noticed that there was a distinct hint of tension between the two of them, although it went without saying that no one ever mentioned it.

"Well." Her mother got up from her chair. "That was very nice. Thank you, everyone."

A steward appeared in the doorway. "Can we get you anything, Madam President?"

"I'm all set, thank you, Wilbur," she said, then looked at the rest of them. "How about all of you?"

"I'm pretty tired," Meg's father said. "I think I've about had it for tonight."

Meg nodded. "You're going to need lots of energy for all that football tomorrow." Her father, on New Year's Day, could not in any way, shape or form be blasted away from the television set.

"Right you are." He bent to give her a kiss on top of the head. "Happy New Year." He smiled at Beth. "Happy New Year, Beth." Then, he glanced at her mother. "Are you coming, too?"

Her mother hesitated, then checked her watch—although surely, she must have had some sense that it was shortly after midnight. "In a little while, maybe. I'm just going to go into the study, and—well."

Study, presumably.

Meg looked down at her splint, so that she wouldn't have to see whatever expression was on her father's face.

"Okay," he said, shortly. "Fine." He smiled at Meg and Beth again, but less convincingly this time. "Good night."

When her parents had both gone off, in different directions, Beth let out her breath.

"Damn," she said.

Meg nodded. "I told you. It's been—Christ, that was comparatively *friendly*."

Beth just shook her head.

Anyway. When it came to parents, and emotional turmoil, Beth had been there, and done that.

"Trudy doesn't seem to be too happy with her, either," Beth said.

Nope.

"Must be hard," Beth said, "when no matter what you do, all day, every day, it still pisses off *millions* of people."

Yeah. Regardless of where she stood in the polls at any given point in time, her mother's life was still pretty much a perpetual no-win situation.

Beth glanced at her. "Worse, though, when it's your own damn family."

Not the conversation with which she wanted to begin the New Year. "Yeah," Meg said, and leaned down to pat Kirby, who wagged his tail, and went back to sleep, his head resting on her right foot. "Um, anyway. What do you want to do now?"

Beth motioned towards the remaining champagne. "Be a shame to let that go to waste."

A terrible shame.

They were on their third glasses, mostly being quiet, when Beth coughed.

"Um, look," she said. "I really did appreciate it."

The pregnancy scare. "I didn't do anything," Meg said.

"No, but I know you would have, and—well, thanks," Beth said, and then looked over. "Did you tell your mother?"

Who would, naturally, have had to be involved with any possible subterfuge of that sort, had it come to pass. "Nothing to tell," Meg said.

Beth looked relieved, and finished off her champagne. "Good. I wasn't sure how embarrassed I should be in front of her."

Meg refilled their glasses. "Were you going to do better stuff tonight? I mean, you know, better than this?"

Beth shook her head. "Anne-Marie Hammersmith's having a party, and I think there was another one at what's-his-name, Kurt's house."

Neither of which sounded very enticing. "Do you mind missing them?" Meg asked.

Beth shook her head again. "The truth is, I've lost touch with a lot of people."

"Really?" Meg said. "What's that like?"

Beth laughed, and drank some champagne.

"How's Sarah, anyway?" Meg asked. She had known Sarah Weinberger since they were about eight years old, but Sarah—like most of the people she had grown up with—started treating her so differently after her mother got nominated, that their friendship had gradually fallen apart. Thinking about it made Meg sad, so she rarely did.

"She's okay," Beth said. "Pretty much the same."

Meg nodded. Strange to have grown up somewhere, and feel so far away from it. What with one thing and another, they had only gone back to Massachusetts a few times since the Inauguration, and Meg hadn't really enjoyed it, although it was great to be in their own house again. The last time had been almost exactly a year ago, and except for Beth, the conversations she had with almost everyone she saw were pretty much of the "How you doing" and "Where'd you apply to school" variety.

"You probably would have lost touch with most of them, anyway," Beth said. "I mean, I'm surprised how fast I did."

The difference, of course, was that Beth had moved on and met *new* people.

"Everyone thinks I have an attitude, because I hang out with you," Beth said. "That I think I'm too cool to live, and all that."

"You already thought you were too cool to live," Meg said.

"Well, yeah, that's what I said," Beth agreed, "but it didn't go over too well."

Meg grinned. No doubt. As she recalled, Beth had had an attitude in *kindergarten*. "What about people at school?" she asked, and gestured to indicate Camp David—and the White House, in general. "Do they care?"

Beth shrugged. "If they make the connection. And then, I don't know, everyone wonders if you're really all right, or if you've gone around the bend or something."

"Swell," Meg said.

Beth winked at her. "I just tell them that you were always crazy."

Oh, well, that was much better, then. Both of their glasses were empty—again—and Meg filled them with what was left in the last bottle.

"Do people drink a lot?" she asked, trying to sound very casual. "And stuff?"

Beth nodded. "Yeah. And Ramon and his friends like to get high. Just, you know, pot, for the most part. Making '420' jokes all the time."

And probably about "skiing," too, although Meg thought it was close to an atrocity to abuse the best sport in the world by turning it into drug slang. "Um, what about you?" she asked, careful not to look at her.

"Not really," Beth said. "I maybe take a bong hit or whatever sometimes, to be polite, but I'd rather, I don't know, sit in some jazz bar in the middle of the night, and get weird liqueur, and be kind of amused by it all."

Well, *that* was a tough one to picture.

"What are you going to do?" Beth asked.

With the exception of slugging scotch with a god-damned terrorist one long night—easily the single lowest and most disgraceful behavior of her entire life—Meg had never done much more than have a beer or two at a party, and even then, she'd always worried about publicity. She sighed. "I don't know."

"It's hard to avoid," Beth said. "I mean, if you're going to have any kind of a social life."

Definition of a dilemma. All of this was starting to make her feel pretty sorry for herself—which meant that she'd already broken her New Year's resolution. "I don't know," Meg said. "I'm guessing I probably won't have much of a social life, then."

Beth looked irritated. "I'm not saying you have to get knock-down staggering drunk every night, but I don't think it would kill you to cut loose a little."

Meg shrugged, thinking about the guy. About sitting there in that windowless little room, already groggy from pain and starvation, letting her share of his bottle of scotch blur her mind even more. They'd talked, and it had been strange and scary and civilized all at the same time. Like being on a date with Ted Bundy, or something. Sitting there, drinking, *handcuffed*, with a guy who'd torn her knee apart, who'd held a gun in her face—more than once, who'd punched and kicked her—also more than once, who'd laughed at her jokes—again, more than once. A guy who both enjoyed her company, and enjoyed hurting her. Enjoyed her company *while* he was hurting her. It wasn't anything she could really explain, and Beth was the only person with whom she'd ever tried.

She looked up, acutely aware that Beth was watching her.

"I know what's bothering you," Beth said.

Yeah, she probably did. For all her goofiness, Beth might be the most astute person she had ever known. "I liked him," Meg said. "What the hell's the matter with me that I *liked* him?"

Beth shrugged. "He was smart. You like smart people."

He was smart, and funny, and charming, and vicious, and sadistic—and she'd *liked* him. What kind of person was she, that she could like a sociopathic monster?

"Meg." Beth sighed. "So, you offered to sleep with him, so what?"

Meg looked around, afraid that someone might have heard. She knew that there were security people all over the place, but she thought—*hoped*—not within earshot.

"And even if he'd said yes, who cares?" Beth said. "I mean, Christ, you do what you have to do. Let go of it already."

They'd had this conversation before, and Meg had yet to be convinced. Had yet to be anything other than ashamed. She wrapped her good arm around herself, feeling cold suddenly. "It wasn't very—brave."

"Brave?" Beth said, *not* quietly, then lowered her voice. "Christ, Meg, you were a freakin' Amazon."

Meg frowned at her. "That's flattering."

"Don't twist it around—I hate it when you do that," Beth said. "You know what I mean. You were a complete *warrior*, okay?"

Hardly. Meg shivered, and looked out at the dark, shadowy trees. Scary trees.

"You still having nightmares?" Beth asked.

That was such a stupid question that Meg didn't bother answering.

"You're right," Beth said. "I'm sorry. Are they getting any better?"

Meg shook her head. The ones with the guy were always pretty much the same—she'd be somewhere normal, like in her room, or back in Massachusetts or something, and he'd appear, out of nowhere, giving her that crooked grin, then pulling out the gun. She usually woke up just before he fired it into her face. Freud would have a field day.

There were other nightmares, of course, most of them surreal, disorienting fragments she forgot before she even opened her eyes, but the one thing they had in common was that she was always completely terrified by them. "What do you think he thinks?" she asked. "About me not being dead?"

"I don't know," Beth said. "He's probably pissed off. And—bemused."

Sounded plausible. Meg looked at her. "You think he's planning to come after me?"

Beth shook her head. "No way. The one thing you *know* is that he's not stupid."

True. But, still. "What if he's really mad?" Meg asked. "I mean, you know, vengeance."

"I don't think so," Beth said. "As long as he hasn't gotten caught, what does he care? I mean, when you get right down to it."

Well, yeah. It wasn't like anything she'd told the FBI and counter-intelligence types had made much of a difference. "You know where I'd look?" Meg asked, and tapped her knee brace. "The guy's an ironist. I bet he's teaching skiing somewhere."

Beth laughed. "Do you really think that, or are you being a jerk?"

"I really think that," Meg said. "I think that's the way he'd operate. Big Sky, or someplace, or maybe over in Europe."

"Well—that *would* be ironic," Beth said.

Meg nodded. To put it mildly.

Beth looked at their empty glasses. "You know what I think? I think we need another bottle of champagne."

Even though her parents had probably gone to bed, Meg looked guiltily at the quiet cabin.

"I think you should get good and drunk," Beth said. "So you don't go up to school worrying that if you have one beer too many, you're going to—I don't know—ask half the football team to sleep with you."

Meg wasn't sure if she should be offended or amused, so she decided to be amused. "What if we drink more champagne, and I ask *you* to sleep with me?"

"I would be amazed," Beth said.

"Amazed, and dazed—and completely fazed," Meg said.

Beth laughed. "I think you're already drunk."

Meg nodded, quite seriously. "I'm a little buzzed, yeah. I'm just starting to notice this."

"So. You want to go for it?" Beth asked.

Absolutely.

9

THEY WENT TO the kitchen and liberated a magnum of champagne, leaving behind an uneasy, albeit sleepy, Navy steward. Whenever she and her brothers wanted to do something questionable, the staff wasn't sure whether they should *let* them—and risk getting into trouble, or *refuse* them—and risk getting into trouble. As a general rule, they erred on the side of letting First Family members do whatever the hell they wanted.

"Think he's going to report it?" Beth asked.

Meg shook her head. "Not likely. Except for it showing up on the expense sheet."

"Do you care?" Beth asked.

Hmmm. "Not much," Meg said.

The Secretary of State and his wife were staying over in Dogwood, and Meg was almost sure that there were guests in Birch, too—and probably most of the other cabins, so instead of trying to find someplace away from Aspen to drink undisturbed, they went back out to the patio. It would have been more private to sit down by the pool, but she wasn't up for attempting the stairs—or risking a late-night fall into the water, so they stayed where they were.

Beth opened the bottle, and the cork flew about ten feet away.

"*L'chaim,*" she said, refilling their glasses.

Meg nodded. "*A ta sante.*"

Beth grinned. "Which just about sums up the difference between us, don't you think?"

Yes, the argument could be made.

They sat outside for a long time, sipping champagne, and talking about nothing in particular. Their favorite very bad television shows, the dearth of decent modern rock-and-roll songs, things they had done when they were little, and the general state of the Boston Red Sox—the latter, pretty much being a rambling, unfocused monologue on Meg's part.

"Are the trees moving?" Beth asked.

Meg studied the trees. They were bobbing. Weaving. Tilting. "Yes."

"Thought so," Beth said, and topped off their glasses.

Meg picked hers up, spilling most of it in the process, and then looked down at the large splotch on her sweatshirt. "I think I'm maybe a little tired."

"I *know* I am," Beth said, and then laughed. "It's a Happy New Year, though."

Very happy. Meg fumbled for her cane, locating it with some difficulty. It took her several tries to stand up, and when she did, she found one-legged balance unusually challenging.

Which struck her as being terribly funny.

Beth got up, equally clumsy, and motioned towards their glasses and the bottles. "Do we take this stuff to the kitchen?"

Meg gestured so widely that she dropped her cane and lurched against her chair to keep from falling over. "The fairies," she said. "The fairies will come get it."

Beth picked up the cane for her. "What if the fairies don't come?"

In the White House, the fairies *always* came. "Hmm," Meg said. "I don't know."

Beth gathered up the bottles and glasses, and they made their way into the cabin, reminding each other to be very, *very* quiet. As a result, every sound they made—like trying to open the door—seemed extremely loud, and they would have to struggle not to laugh.

Beth pointed to a side table. "Will the fairies find them there?"

Meg shrugged. When it came to fairies and sprites, who knew how their minds worked?

Beth set the bottles and glasses down. One of the bottles started to topple onto the floor, and she caught it just in time, both of them laughing again.

"Shhh," Meg whispered.

"You're the one making the *ruckus*," Beth whispered back.

"No way." Christ, she sounded like Steven now. "I mean, you are, too." She stumbled against another table, knocking over two candlesticks.

"Shhh," Beth said.

"You're the one who—" Meg started.

"Hey." Beth picked up a pillow from the couch. "Let's have a horrific cat fight, how about?"

The image of the two of them brawling, right here in the Presidential cabin, was so funny that Meg started laughing again—and had trouble stopping.

"Shhh," Beth said.

Oh. Right. They were being quiet.

It was dark in the hallway leading to Meg's bedroom, and they felt their way along, Meg planting her good leg cautiously with each step.

Kirby came snuffling out from the room her brothers and Vinnie were sharing.

"Is that a fairy?" Beth asked, and Meg laughed harder, since Kirby was quite possibly the most indelicate dog in the world.

Then, suddenly, her father was standing in the hallway, tying the belt on his bathrobe and frowning at them.

"Is *that* a fairy?" Beth asked, and they both broke up completely.

Meg was the first one to get under control. "Hi, Dad," she said, making an effort to stand up very straight and look utterly sober. "You're up early."

He didn't smile, but he didn't really look mad, either. "Everything okay, Meg?"

"Absolu'ly, Dad," Meg said, then looked at Beth. "Damn, you hear me drop that 't'?"

Beth nodded. "Wait a minute." She bent down. "There it is, I see it."

This time, her father smiled. Slightly. "You two help yourselves to some champagne?"

Beth stood up and pretended to hand Meg a tiny object. "Your 't'."

"Thank you," Meg said, and looked at her father. "Absolu*t*ely, Dad."

Which she and Beth found pretty hilarious.

"Try not to wake up the whole house," her father said, "okay?"

So, would he mind if they woke up *half* of the house? Meg knew she should be worried about this—that he was going to yell at her or something, but it all seemed too funny.

"Well. We can talk about it another time," he said.

Meg nodded, and laughed. "Yeah." Whatever. "Good night."

"Right." He started to go back into the Presidential bedroom suite, then paused. "Just tell me one thing, Meg. Tell me you weren't in golf carts."

"We weren't in golf carts," Meg said, although now that he mentioned it, it would be really fun to—

"Don't get any bright ideas," her father said quickly.

"No ideas," Meg agreed, and limped towards her room.

THEY SLEPT LATE. *Real* late. In fact, Meg only woke up because she heard Beth groaning and saying, "Oh my God." She forced her eyes open, the inside of her mouth feeling as though she'd eaten about a bale and a half of cotton. Hulls and all.

"Jesus Christ," she said, once she'd noticed what a tremendous headache she had.

"Happy fucking New Year," Beth said, looking as though her headache was even worse.

Lifting her eyebrow would hurt, so Meg didn't bother. "*That's* a nice way to start off the year."

Beth mumbled something quite a bit more profane, then draped her arm over her eyes. "What time is it?"

Meg frowned at her clock. For a while. "Almost one."

"Oh." Beth lowered her arm, winced, and covered her eyes again. "I hate this year. I can already tell."

At the moment, Meg wasn't too fond of it, either. Vanessa stretched and walked up to her pillow, and Meg patted her, even though the sound of purring was too much for her ears.

"You think we're in trouble?" Beth asked.

Upon which, Meg remembered their late-night encounter with her father. "I hope not." She could be pretty sure that he was already occupied by the Bowl games, but that didn't mean that he wouldn't be able to find time to yell at them. At her, anyway.

"We probably are," Beth said grimly.

"Yeah." It took even more effort than usual to sit up, and once she managed it, she was tempted to lie right back down again. "God, I feel terrible."

"I bet I feel worse," Beth said.

"I bet you don't," Meg said. Her eyes hurt, her head hurt, *everything* hurt. But it had been a long time since the pain in her knee and hand weren't the first things she noticed on any given day—which was either progress, or a setback.

In the other twin bed, Beth lifted herself up onto her elbows. "I guess we'd better go out there looking god-damn bandbox fresh."

"Yeah." Best defense was a good offense. Meg rubbed her eyes. "You want to go first?"

"Gee." Beth stood up lethargically. "Thanks."

After Beth had showered and gotten dressed, Meg went in to take a bath. Even her good hand and leg felt uncoordinated, and when she finally made her way back out, it was past two.

Beth, her—blond—hair still wet and spiky, was lying on her bed, staring at the wooden beams running across the ceiling.

"Time to make our move," Meg said.

Beth sat up, slowly.

"There's aspirin and stuff in the medicine cabinet, if you want some," Meg said.

Beth nodded. "I found it before."

Out in the living room, one of the Bowl Games was on, loudly, and her father, brothers, and Vinnie were watching, along with Preston, and a bunch of White House staffers, Marines, and Navy stewards, mostly male. Trudy, who very much stuck out in the group, was sitting at the end of the couch with her crocheting. A fire had been lit in the fireplace, and the room was very warm. Hot, even.

Preston, who must have driven up bright and early, grinned when he saw them. "Good morning."

"About *time*," Steven said, through a mouthful of potato chips.

Beth shrugged. "Beauty sleep."

"Didn't help 'em much," Steven said to Vinnie, and they both laughed raucously.

Trudy moved her yarn to one side. "Let's see about some lunch for you two."

Meg's father was already on his feet. "Don't worry, Trudy, I'll take care of it."

Oh, great. Meg sat down in an empty chair, deciding that *far* too much light was pouring in through the wide windows. Something important must have happened in the game, because half of the room cheered, and everyone else groaned.

There was a lot of food spread out on a buffet table—chili and rice and salad and so forth—and Meg looked at Beth, who shook her head. Firmly.

"You two sleep all right?" her father asked.

Beth nodded. "Yes, sir. Thank you."

It might be a good time to change the subject. Meg looked around. "Where's Mom?"

"Laurel," her father said.

The cabin where most official meetings were held. She'd probably been giving a New Year's Day radio address or something, too. Consulting with her staff. Making decisions. Issuing proclamations.

Plus, of course, avoiding all of them.

"There's plenty of food over here," her father said, "if you—"

Meg shook her head. "We're going to start off with Cokes."

"*Small* Cokes," Beth said in a low voice. "Or ginger ale, if you have it."

"Come in the kitchen, then, Meg," her father said. "We'll see what we can find."

Time to get yelled at. Happy New Year. Meg lifted herself up onto her cane and followed him.

"I think we may be starting to run short on some of the food, guys," her father said to the steward and Navy cook who were on duty in there.

After the two men left the room to check—and replenish—the table, her father gave her a very penetrating look. "Feeling all right today?"

Meg nodded, hoping her eyes weren't as bloodshot as they felt.

"How about Beth?" he asked.

Meg nodded, keeping her eyes down, so that he might not notice.

He dropped ice cubes into two glasses, and then sighed. "Don't make a habit of it, okay?"

She nodded.

"Okay," he said, and patted her on the back, before filling the glasses with soda.

Meg glanced up. "That's it? I'm not in trouble?"

"Well, I think it was pretty harmless," he said. "In the scheme of things."

She agreed. One hundred and twenty percent. "Thanks," she said.

Once they went back out to the living room, she and Beth slumped in their chairs with their Cokes.

"I don't believe I care who's playing," Meg said, as more cheers and groans erupted.

"I know I don't," Beth said.

A touchdown scored—apparently controversial, as the quarterback might have been beyond the line of scrimmage when he passed the ball—and the reaction in the room went well past mere noise, crossing the line into vociferousness.

"Is it too soon to go back to bed?" Beth asked.

They had been out here for—maybe—twenty minutes.

"Yes," Meg said.

"Oh," Beth said, and they sipped their Cokes.

THE NEXT DAY, they both felt better, and by the time they went back to Washington, Beth was full of exhausting "shopping for college" and "going out to get some ice cream" plans. She even talked Meg into inviting Josh, and a couple of her other friends who were home on winter break, to come to the movies with them one night, which ended up being a somewhat stilted social encounter, but ultimately kind of fun. By doing small things like parting her hair on the side, or tying it up in a high ponytail, or wearing one of her pairs of clear glasses—subtle disguise tricks Preston had taught her—she even managed not to be recognized, some of the time.

Of course, the infamous combination of her hand splint and knee brace—and the fact that she maybe looked a hell of a lot like an eighteen-year-old version of someone world-famous—was generally a dead giveaway. To say nothing of her army of agents.

On Friday, Beth was flying to California to visit her father and his latest very young girlfriend, Jasmine, and Meg went downstairs with her to the South Portico to say good-bye. The Residence was going to seem painfully quiet now, especially since Trudy had already left, the day before, to go back to her condo in Florida.

"So," Beth said. "You're out of here in about three weeks."

Meg nodded. Just in time for the second semester, although that meant she would miss the entire January Winter Study program. With luck, were she to make it to her senior year, they would still let her graduate.

"Well, I'll come up and see you before Spring Break, maybe," Beth said, adjusting her—pink, this time—beret. "If you want."

Meg nodded, although that was too far in the very uncertain future to seem plausible.

Beth looked at her. "You're moving really well now, Meg. I can see the difference."

She didn't agree, so she shrugged and gripped her cane. "Maybe. I don't know."

"You're going to be skiing next winter," Beth said.

Now, she *heartily* disagreed.

"Well." Beth glanced at the car waiting to take her to the airport, and then grinned wickedly. "Off to see Jasmine."

Meg grinned back. God help Jasmine.

SHE WAS LYING on her bed that night, with post-exercise ice packs covering her knee and hand, watching C-Span, when her mother tapped on the already-ajar door.

Supposedly, her parents had been out for the evening. "You're back early," Meg said.

Her mother shrugged, looking tired in her long black and white gown, which—in Meg's opinion—had kind of a Cecil Beaton feel to it. A smashing, ribbon-bedecked hat would have improved it, though. "They like it if you show up, but they don't expect you to stay. In fact, I think they're relieved when I leave."

Meg nodded. Her parents often breezed through several social gatherings in a couple of hours. Smiles, posing for photos, handshakes, waves—and then, it was on to the next event.

With Beth around, it hadn't seemed as obvious that she had barely seen her mother at all lately—a fast good-night here and there, ten minutes at breakfast, that sort of thing. If she were, oh, say, *keeping track*, it would probably bother her that they hadn't spent any significant time together since Christmas night, on the patio outside Aspen.

Her mother came over to check the glass pitcher of ice water on her bedside table—which, go figure, was now being brought to her room at regular intervals, unasked—and refilled her glass. Meg picked it up without thinking and drained half of it, then felt stupid and put it down.

"Did you get enough supper?" her mother asked.

As usual, she had left considerably more on her plate than she finished, but Meg nodded.

"Okay," her mother said. "Good. That's good." She looked at the desk chair, and the rocking chair, but remained standing. "Do you have a few minutes?"

Hmm. Apparently, it had taken all this time for the other shoe to drop. Meg clicked off the television. "Is this about what happened at Camp David?"

Her mother looked puzzled momentarily, then shook her head. "No. I mean, yes, obviously, I hope that, in the future, you'll do your best to make, um, judicious choices, whenever possible, but, no. I was just hoping to discuss something with you."

Even by their current low standards, this had been an unusually unsuccessful conversation so far. Her mother seemed to have some sort of specific agenda here, but it was hard to assess what the—except then, she realized what was probably coming, and found herself gulping down a burst of dread. Her mother was going to say, "Your father and I have decided that it would be better if he took the three of you back to Chestnut Hill," and then—

"We need to talk about the State of the Union," her mother said.

Oh. Meg let out her breath, so close to tears that she had to blink a few times.

"What?" her mother asked, looking concerned.

No good could come from confessing that she'd expected a divorce announcement. As opposed to the State of the *actual* Union. "Nothing," Meg said. She rarely exaggerated about the degree to which the pain was bothering her at any given moment, but she would make an exception in this case. "It's just—" She gestured towards the ice packs— "you know. No big deal."

"I can call downstairs," her mother said, heading for the telephone. Meaning, in this case, the Medical Unit. "I have no idea who's on duty, but they can send him or her up here, and—"

A reaction she should have seen coming. "I'm *fine*, Mom," Meg said. "Really. Anyway, what about the State of the Union?"

Her mother hesitated. "If it's not a good time, we can—"

It was very disconcerting to see such an abnormally self-confident—in fact downright *cocky*, now and then—person act so god-damned unsure of herself. A person who, apparently, found it less stressful to run the country than to have a conversation with her own daughter. "Just, you know, *talk* to me, okay?" Meg said. For once.

Her mother sighed, and lowered herself into the desk chair. "I hate even bringing this up, but—frankly, we're in a difficult position. Much as I'd prefer to do so, I don't think I can just ignore what happened. I'm certainly not going to dwell on it, but—it can't go unremarked."

Terrific. With all of the things she found to worry about every day, the State of the Union address hadn't even made the list. Now, it was going to be somewhere near the top.

"I don't expect you to come," her mother said, "and I'll touch on it as lightly as possible, but—" She sighed. "I don't know, Meg. Unfortunately, a great many people feel very invested in the situation, and I don't see how I can avoid it."

Even more terrific, which could probably be raised to a "nifty." "If I don't show up, it'll make you look—" Like a worse mother than usual. "It won't look good," Meg said.

Her mother waved that aside. "I don't *care* how it looks. I'm trying to figure out the best way to handle things."

Was that really true? If so, it was another huge change. Not too long ago, she *would* have cared, even if she didn't admit it. Meg frowned. "Do you want me to come?"

"That's entirely up to you," her mother said, so swiftly that the answer was obviously yes.

Swell. So much for Presidents not passing the buck.

"Meg, you know I don't want you and your brothers *ever* to do anything you find too public, or in any way uncomfortable," her mother said.

Meg was feeling almost testy enough to remark that *handcuffs* were uncomfortable, but she made herself resist the impulse. Besides, it would be a cheap shot. However, she'd better come up with some response or other, before her mother kicked into the shopworn "I won't let you three be used as props" riff.

Which, in all fairness, she'd always been pretty scrupulous about observing, by politician standards.

"I'll be as brief, and oblique, as possible," her mother said. "There's going to be a short section on heroism, and—well, I can't overlook the obvious."

Oh, for God's sakes. She must have done something really awful in her last life, to get stuck with such a bizarre one this time around. "So," she said grimly, "the gallery's going to be seeded with carefully selected Americans, all of whom have heartwarming and courageous tales to tell?"

Her mother flushed, but nodded. "I'm sorry, but yes. Unless you have a better idea."

So, she'd be surrounded by *real* heroes, and look like a grasping wannabe, trying to usurp their genuine achievements—on national television. Picturing that made her head—and hand—start throbbing. "I'm going to look egotistical. Because they'll all be actual brave people, and I'll just seem—" Meg shook her head. "You're going to need to come up with something else." Or, better yet, leave her out *entirely*, as—frankly—a normal, caring parent would do.

Her mother smiled slightly, which was jarring. "Interestingly enough, I gather that some of the people we've approached have expressed the same concern."

And she still wanted her to go, and be undeservedly feted? Talk about hubris. "See," Meg said. "I told you."

"They seem to feel that they would have no business sitting in the same gallery with *you*," her mother said. "Which leads me to believe that you all are just wired a little differently from the rest of us."

Christ, this was going to be awful. And she really had no choice *but* to go. Meg scowled. "Oh, yeah, it'll look heroic as hell if they're all up there waving modestly, and I'm back here, hiding in my room."

"People might not even notice," her mother said.

Was it her imagination, or had the President's nose just grown a couple of inches? Time to return to the Land of Political Reality.

"All right, they'll notice," her mother conceded. "But, I promise I'm only going to mention it in passing."

Great. Just fucking great. "Even if you don't bring it up, my not being there would send a pretty bad message," Meg said. The State of the Union address being what it was. "And if I *am* there, everyone's going to be looking at me, trying to figure out how sane I am."

Her mother's shrug was reluctant, but affirmative.

Wouldn't it be nice to be able to recuperate without millions of people watching her do it? Or, more specifically, *fail* to do it?

Truth be told, though, her mother had been—and probably still was, even though she rarely mentioned it—in a similar situation. The last State of the Union address had been less than three months after the shooting, and while her mother had looked, and sounded, powerful and optimistic, she was so weak and exhausted afterwards that she'd almost passed out the second she was safely back inside her limousine, where—secretly—a medical team had been waiting the entire time. Because she'd been afraid she might slur her words, or that her eyes would look glazed, she hadn't taken any painkillers before the speech, but she'd sure as hell slugged some down in the car on the way home.

A more discouraging memory was the degree to which her father had been quietly frantic about her mother's well-being, before, during, and especially after, the speech. In fact, he'd hovered over her to such a degree that her mother had been quite snappish to him in the holding room, right up until it was time for her to go out and address the nation about how wonderful everything was.

A speech which, as it turned out, got glowing reviews, and was described as being, among other things, "inspirational" and "fiery." Later, when they were all in a better mood, they had been amused that part of the reason the speech had been so damned "fiery" was probably because of the vicious parental argument which had served as her mother's unofficial warm-up.

"Maybe you and your brothers should just stay home," her mother said. "You don't need the extra pressure."

Oh, *now* she thought that? Please. Meg gritted her teeth. "I also don't need the whole world thinking I'm too damaged to show my face in public."

"It really only matters what *you* think," her mother said, with almost no hesitation.

Except that there was at least one other person who lived in the White House who she assumed also had a pretty strong opinion about the prospect of all of this. Meg glanced over at her. "What's Dad think?"

Her mother's face tightened. "It's probably better if you ask him directly."

Yeah. God forbid they all be open and honest with one another. Act like a real, live family. "Completely against it," Meg said, "right?"

Her mother's jaw was rigid, which served as a more than sufficient answer.

"I know you're not asking me to do it for political gain," Meg said, since she was quite sure that that was going to be one of her father's main objections.

Her mother looked at her sharply. "No, I'm not. But, by the same token, I don't guess we can pretend that your sitting there, appearing calm and healthy and dignified, isn't going to be to my benefit."

Well—yeah. If she were less tired, she'd probably be angry about being put in such a difficult position, but mostly, she just felt resigned. Trapped, but resigned.

And her mother had to feel even *more* trapped. By ambition. By circumstance. By plain old bad luck. By the damning, crushing weight of hindsight.

By can not, have not, and *will* not.

"I'm never going to be able to tell you how sorry I am, Meg," her mother said, looking at her with great intensity. "About everything. If I'd ever dreamed that anyone would—"

Meg shook her head. "I—I can't do this tonight. I really can't." Didn't ever want to do it, frankly. "I said I'd go to the damn speech. Okay? Just—take it and be happy."

For a second, her mother looked as though she'd been punched in the stomach, but then she recovered herself and nodded. "Yes. Of course." She got up abruptly. "I'm sorry, I didn't mean to—" She stopped. "Anyway, I'm sorry. Please let me know if you need anything."

The albatross of other people's guilt was just—then, it occurred to her that maybe she had gone too far, and should apologize, but her mother was already gone.

So, she sat on her bed and stared at the blank television screen.

The State of the Union Address.

Great. Just *great*.

10

SHE HAD SUCH terrible dreams that night that whatever yelling she had done woke Steven up, and he came into her room to see if she was okay.

"You want me to get Mom or Dad?" he asked, once she was awake enough to have some idea of where she was, and what was going on.

Meg shook her head, fumbling for her glass of water and drinking some. "No, thanks, I'm fine. I'm sorry I was, you know, *loud* again."

He shrugged. "You, uh, you want like, more to drink?"

What she wanted was for her brother, never once in his life, to feel as though he needed to wait on her. Meg put the glass down unfinished, to prove that she wasn't thirsty. "No, I'm—"

"—fine," he said.

Yeah. Something like that.

Once she'd talked him into going back to bed, she watched C-Span until she fell back to sleep—which took about three hours, by which point she felt quite capable of going down to the press room and giving an extensive briefing about the state of economic development in emerging third-world nations.

By the time she made it to breakfast in the morning, everyone except her father was long gone. She found him on the couch in the West Sitting Hall, reading the morning newspapers, even though it was past ten o'clock. He certainly didn't go rushing joyously down to the East Wing lately, ready to Embrace His Day.

He stood up when he saw her. "Hi. Sleep all right?"

As ever. She nodded.

"Well, let's see about some breakfast for you, then," he said.

She had no appetite at all, but she had a double-session of physical therapy scheduled at eleven, and should probably have the good sense to get something into her stomach. If nothing else, it might help wake her up a little.

They sat quietly at the table in the West Sitting Hall, trading sections of the newspapers, while Meg did her best to eat an English muffin. The political coverage was less diverting than usual, and even the editorial cartoons were dull—although, granted, on any given day, they never had much hope of measuring up to her all-time favorite, which showed a group of stone-faced men in suits standing in a clump in the Oval Office, presumably just having shared some very grave news, while a—quite good—caricature of her mother, complete with one hand delicately extended as she examined her fingernails, was saying, "Yes, yes, that's all very interesting, but more importantly, do you think this dress makes me look fat?" Her father had liked it so much that he had had a copy blown up, signed by the cartoonist, and framed, and then given it to her mother for her birthday—and she had laughed and promptly had it hung in her private study.

And, for a few seconds, she wondered what, if anything, her father was going to get her mother for her birthday *this* year.

"I'm going to the State of the Union," she said.

Her father nodded. "So I hear."

Not exactly a ringing endorsement. But she really wasn't up for another stressful conversation, and since he was staring down at his coffee, he probably wasn't, either.

"Will you sit next to me?" she asked.

Now, he looked up and smiled gently at her. "Of course," he said.

Good.

SHE SPENT MOST of the next couple of weeks gutting her way through intense physical therapy sessions—trying to wean herself off the cane, which wasn't going very well, doing a certain amount of packing, and sleeping as much as possible. She also managed to make it to another one of Steven's games with her father and Neal—and with their father sitting there in the stands, this time, Steven *didn't* get into any fights.

One afternoon, while she was stretched out on the couch in the West Sitting Hall after physical therapy, trying to decide whether to try and summon the necessary initiative to take a sip from the glass of Coke which was sitting only about two feet away, her mother's very polished—and high-strung—press secretary, Linda, and the deputy assistant to the President for communications, Caryn, came up to talk to her about what she was planning to wear to the speech. Meg said, "Sweatpants," but after exchanging frowns, Linda and her cohort discussed the compendium of possibilities in far too much detail. They felt that black would be too funereal, but that pastels would send the wrong message, and downplay the gravity of what had happened.

Meg just sat on the couch, smiling stiffly, and trying to visualize herself in a pastel ensemble. A pantsuit, maybe. She was going to suggest bright, flaming red, just to be difficult, but that would inevitably lead to them worrying about whether that might convey a certain sexual licentiousness, or—possibly, even worse—a tendency towards bedrock conservatism.

Since she wasn't really participating, Linda and Caryn decided, of their own volition, that it would be best for her to select something which would subtly compliment her mother's choice, without reflecting it too closely, or upstaging her in any way—and on and on, it went.

When they finally left, Meg was so tired that she limped to her room and slept right through supper. Felix came in with a tray at about eight-thirty, and she finished half of the onion soup and ate a few carrot sticks. He returned to clear it away, looking rather crestfallen when he saw how little she had eaten, and a few minutes later, he was back with a pitcher of ice water, a tall frosted glass containing a vanilla milkshake, and a plate of peanut butter cookies.

So she lay in bed, sipping the milkshake and looking at the ceiling, with Vanessa purring on her stomach, and C-Span droning on in the background for company. There were nights when the pain was manageable—and there were nights when it was so severe that, on top of the throbbing and pounding of the pain itself, she would actually run a *fever*. But she couldn't bring herself to tell anyone how truly bad it was today, because if she did, her parents would get all upset, and a bunch of doctors would show up, and confer, and frown, and she would never get any damn sleep.

It was almost midnight before her mother came in to see how she was doing.

"Are you all right?" she asked. "Your father says you didn't feel well enough to get up for dinner."

Nope. She hadn't. Meg shrugged. Seeing her mother in person, as opposed to her dutiful emissaries, reminded her that she was mad as hell.

"Is there anything I can do?" her mother asked.

Meg shook her head.

"Okay," her mother said. "I just—wanted to see how you were."

Meg nodded, staring at the ceiling.

"Okay." Her mother folded her arms uneasily, then glanced at the television. "Anything interesting?"

"There are people out there who don't support your policies," Meg said. Some of them so much so that they flirted with apoplexy.

Her mother nodded. "Yes, that's the word around the office."

No doubt.

It was quiet for a minute.

"Well," her mother said. "If there isn't anything you want me to—"

"If you're so damn worried about what I'm going to wear to the speech, how come you can't say so *yourself*, instead of sending messengers?" Meg asked.

Her mother frowned. "I'm sorry. What are you talking about?"

"It's not like I was planning to embarrass you, anyway," Meg said. Or herself, for that matter. "So, why have them come up here and bug me about it?"

Her mother caught on then, and her expression darkened to an almost frightening degree. "Who was it?"

Oh. Meg frowned, too. "You mean, you didn't tell them to do it?"

"Of course not," her mother said. "You can wear whatever you want to wear." She stopped. "As long as it's—well—"

A dress.

"Who was it, Meg?" her mother asked. "I *really* want to know."

Would it be smart to get people on her mother's staff in trouble, or should she opt in favor of just—

"Never mind," her mother said, and scowled. "I know who it was." She strode towards the door. "Excuse me for a moment."

Meg thought about calling her back—but, the truth was, they probably deserved to get into trouble. After physical therapy, she needed to be able to rest, and try to get her psychological equilibrium back, without having anyone show up, uninvited, to interrogate her.

Ten minutes later, her mother came back in, still looking angry, but in a much calmer way.

"Did you yell at her?" Meg asked. Since Linda was, unquestionably, the instigator.

Her mother looked alarmed. "*Her?*" She spun around as though she was going to rush out of the room to correct her dreadful mistake, then grinned. "I yelled at both of them. They know perfectly well that you and your brothers are off-limits."

Good.

Her mother sat down on the edge of the bed, which made Vanessa hiss—and flee. "It won't happen again, but for God's sakes, Meg, if it *does*, don't just lie here and be angry—pick up the phone and tell me, so I can take care of it."

Meg nodded. As far as she could remember, she had never been one to go running off to her mother when things went wrong, especially with staff members or the press, but maybe she had, and she'd just forgotten.

"I know it was the right decision at the time," her mother said, "but in retrospect, I really regret agreeing to let your father lay claim to Preston."

Meg nodded again. In all likelihood, Preston—who had been indispensable during the campaign—had originally been destined for an influential position in the West Wing, but early on, the media treatment of her father had been so merciless and insulting, that Preston had ended up joining his staff, instead.

"Sit up for a minute, okay?" her mother asked.

She was too god-damn tired to sit up, but slowly did it, feeling shaky, and having to support herself with her good hand.

Her mother leaned forward and hugged her tightly. "I know you think you made an unbreakable promise, but I'm not holding you to it," she whispered. "If you decide you don't want to go, even on your way into the gallery, *don't*."

A firm hug was much nicer than a tentative one.

"Okay?" her mother said.

Meg nodded.

Her mother reached over to feel her forehead with the back of her hand, frowned, and then picked up the telephone. "Yes, hello, could you send someone up to my daughter's room with some ice packs? And a thermometer, too, please." She listened for a moment. "Thank you." She listened again. "No, I'd prefer that you didn't put it through here, I'll take it down in the Treaty Room." When she hung up the phone, she sighed. "I'm sorry, this is going to be a while. If your light's still on, I'll come in and see how you're doing?"

Meg nodded. The take-charge mother was so much easier to be around than the burdened-by-guilt one.

"Good," her mother said, hugged her one more time, and left the room.

IN THE END, she wore a green dress. Not lime or kelly, but not quite forest, either. Pine, maybe. Perhaps it dovetailed with her mother's blue one—a brightish indigo or midnight, which brought out her eyes to an amazing degree; perhaps it stood on its own.

Perhaps she didn't really care.

Either way, it was a nice dress. Simple, dignified, classic lines; went well with pearls. She couldn't manage even a low heel without stumbling, so she wore black flats. Since she would be sitting down just about the entire time, it probably didn't matter much, anyway. Although she *did* agree to have her hair blown out, and so forth, to prepare for the cameras.

She was incredibly tense—but, on State of the Union day, everyone in the entire White House was a nervous wreck. Even the usually unflappable Neal fell prey to the collective anxiety and had to come home sick from school. This caused a huge debate about whether he, and maybe Meg's father, should stay home, but Neal got so upset about the idea of missing all of the excitement that her parents finally agreed that he could go to the speech, as long as he ate—and kept down—his dinner.

The First Family was supposed to make their formal entrance to the gallery after all of the Senators and Representatives and the diplomatic corps, and right before the Supreme Court justices. It was considered de rigueur for everyone to clap when they came in, but as they made their way to their seats, Meg being extra-careful on her cane going down the steps, and worrying like hell that her foot might make one of its untimely flops, the entire chamber burst into such loud applause and cheering that she seriously considered throwing up right on the spot.

Which would not be ideal.

"It's all right," her father said, in her ear. "Just nod at them. You don't have to wave or anything."

Okay. Nodding was relatively easy. She nodded, politely, and the noise seemed to intensify. Everyone she passed, most of whom were complete strangers, seemed to be very happy to see her, and kept reaching out to try and clasp her hand—good luck to them and the Boston Red Sox, touch her sleeve, or pat her on the back. It was hard not to flinch each time, and she was relieved when her father quickly began shaking hands with almost all of the people they went by, preempting their attempts to greet her. Then, finally, they were sitting down, with her father on one side, and Steven on the other.

The applause seemed to go on endlessly, but it was probably just a matter of seconds.

Or minutes.

Or hours.

Months.

Then, the Supreme Court justices were announced, and everyone's focus—and the applause—shifted.

"Well, now, this isn't fair," a voice said, very quietly. "I paid good money for these seats, and it turns out that my view is blocked. By, granted, someone who looks quite extraordinary in her dress, but still blocked."

Meg smiled, in spite of herself. The only specific request she'd made was for Preston to be seated directly behind her, for moral support.

"And check out your tie, Little Guy," he said to Neal. "You *exude* power."

Neal, who was wearing a bright red tie, straightened it proudly.

There were more formal entrances—her mother's Cabinet, and the like—and she concentrated on trying to look relaxed and unruffled, since there was no way of knowing when television cameras would be pointed in their direction, and it wouldn't be safe to let her guard down for even a second. Then, she suddenly started getting scared that she might panic, the way she had in the car on the way to the basketball game that time, and what would happen if—

"I had a very bad blister," Steven said.

Where the hell had that come from? Meg looked over.

"Blood—actual *blood*—was dripping out of my finger," he said. "And Coach, like, wanted me to come out of the game, but I had a shut-out going, and we were only up by one run, so I said, no way, and kept pitching." He paused. "It was wicked brave of me."

Meg laughed. "You're an unbelievable cretin, Steven."

"Yeah," he said, "but a *brave* cretin."

And, for that matter, a funny cretin. "If you'd been doing paraffin treatments on your hand, or soaking in pickle juice—" as any sensible pitcher should— "you never would have gotten the blister in the first place," Meg said.

Steven shrugged. "Maybe. But that doesn't mean I didn't *suffer*."

Neal looked worried. "I thought we weren't supposed to talk in the gallery, Dad."

"*I* can talk," Steven said. "That rule is really just for you and Meg. Because, see, I'm—"

At which point, the Sergeant-at-Arms gave his clarion "Mr. Speaker, the President of the United States!" yell, and her mother, cool and confident, was being escorted into the Chamber to a standing ovation. People swarmed in her direction, and it was clear that it was going to take quite some time for her to work her way down the aisle.

Meg glanced at her father. "Do you think she's scared?"

He nodded once.

Well, it sure as hell didn't *show*. There was an unexpected burst of laughter from her mother's general vicinity, and Meg was wildly curiously about what she might have said to provoke it—and if she would even remember the joke, if any of them asked her later.

She finally made it up to the front of the chamber, greeted Vice President Kruger and the Speaker of the House, and handed them sealed copies of her speech, saying something which made both of them grin broadly. For someone who was supposed to be scared, the President seemed to be feeling pretty god-damned loose. Those who were completely not-in-the-know assumed that she and the quite conservative Speaker were fervent enemies, but, in fact, they had been freshman representatives during the same election cycle together, and had established a friendship so surprisingly solid that the Speaker and his wife were on the tiny list of Washingtonians who *had* been invited to private dinners with the family—on more than one occasion. He and her father watched football together sometimes, too.

Which didn't stop him from torpedoing the Administration's legislation on a regular basis.

The applause had yet to die down, and finally, the Speaker used his gavel to bring order to the chamber and proclaim his "great honor and very high privilege to present the President of the United States."

Predictably, there was another ovation in response, but finally, after one quick glance up at them in the gallery, her mother began to speak. Meg was too distracted to pay attention, but she clapped mechanically when other people did, although she thought the cheering and other unruly outbursts of support—some of them purely partisan; others appearing genuine—made Congress seem more like a bunch of rowdy, ungovernable frat boys than anything else.

At one point, her mother made a crack to the effect of "am I mistaken, or are only half of you pleased by that?," which got a pretty big laugh—and a full round of applause. With luck, America was amused, too.

The speech was the same stuff Meg had been hearing her practice for the last few weeks, pacing up and down the second-floor hallway at odd moments, muttering brutal criticisms to herself throughout—but, verve and style made all the difference.

One of her mother's pet projects was a national service program which, in lieu of solely targeting young Americans, was *retroactive*. The goal was to encourage all Americans to provide voluntary service to others, and to the nation, harnessing the brainpower, talents, and efforts of the entire citizenry in countless ways. This made a good segment of the chamber nervous—and noticeably silent—probably because they assumed that the plan would result in yet another bloated, overpriced bureaucratic agency, although her mother stressed that the plan would be localized in order to respond to the specific needs and interests of each individual community, and that said service could be rewarded by college tuition reimbursements, fixed-rate low-interest loans for small businesses and individual entrepreneurs, personal income tax deductions, and other "service-related" incentives.

Which seemed to leave most of the opposition entirely unsure of whether to applaud or not.

The other idea Meg knew was near and dear to her heart was for the United States to make a commitment—to its own citizens, as well as people all over the world—to make an all-out, full-time, soaring effort to end world hunger, once and for all. In fact, the President was, essentially, proposing a *war* against hunger. And she was very frank about the fact that simply providing food to the masses was only a short-term solution, to a far more complex problem. She talked about the necessity for the United States to share its good fortune with others, and to encourage every civilized country in the world to join together in the effort—and to continue to work tirelessly to foster democracy in lands which were less than hospitable to the notion of humanitarian ideals, so that their citizens would have the freedom to determine their own destinies. That eradicating hunger was a challenge the country could, and *would*, meet. That this was a battle America had a moral imperative to fight—and win. That to do otherwise would be an utter failure of leadership.

This segued into the need to put aside rigid ideologies and form bipartisan coalitions to serve the nation as a whole, and then, into a paean to the American spirit. Strength, and idealism, and empathy. Imagination, ambition, persistence. Of making mistakes, acknowledging them—and rushing right out to engage the world all over again. Resilience. Determination. Endurance.

Dreading the inevitable, Meg tightened her good hand in her lap, below the wooden railing, working to keep her expression pleasant—and immobile. Several other people were being officially recognized—a store security guard and single mother, who had been on her way home from work when she saw a tenement on fire and ran inside to evacuate all of the occupants, sustaining severe burns and smoke inhalation, clearing the entire building before rescue personnel arrived. A man whose life had taken some terrible and unforeseen turns, leaving him homeless and in despair—who had become an ordained minister and was now the beloved leader of a once-downtrodden, and now thriving, rural parish. A boy whose school bus had crashed through the side of a bridge and ended up submerged underwater, until he managed to force a window open and help lead all of the other students and the unconscious driver to safety. A Marine from a peacekeeping mission overseas, whose helicopter had been hit by ground fire, and even though he was gravely wounded, he managed to fly the chopper to safety, landing without sustaining any further casualties to the other soldiers aboard. A posthumous recognition of a police officer who, at the expense of her own life, had brought down three armed robbers single-handedly inside a crowded fast-food restaurant—and whose family was sitting proudly, and sadly, in the gallery in her honor.

Then, her mother spoke about the nature of heroism. Dramatic, awe-inspiring achievements—and the quieter, less recognized forms. The overburdened nurse effortlessly handling an entire ward alone on a busy night. The teacher who brought excitement and inspiration to every lesson, despite overcrowded and underfunded classrooms. Parents who were simultaneously raising children, taking care of aging relatives, and working full-time. Immigrants who brought fresh perspectives, hope and diversity to the nation.

Just as Meg was hoping that her mother had had a last-minute change of heart and was going to overlook her, she began talk about a year of turmoil and triumph. Of prayers answered. That there was a story they all knew—but also, a more mundane, daily struggle, met without bitterness or complaints. Of her astonishing good fortune to be able to watch not just one person, but *four* people, do just that, with honor and dignity, every single day. Of indomitable—by which point, Meg was so mortified that the words were just one big blur in her head.

Except that her mother must have wrapped up that section, because there was a veritable explosion of applause—*affectionate* applause—and everyone else seemed to be standing, while her mother smiled up at her, and ever so briefly put her hand over her heart instead of clapping.

It was overwhelming, but it was nice. As though people really did care, and that what had happened to her *mattered* to them. And there was such a sweetness in her mother's expression that Meg smiled back at her, shyly. Her mother held her gaze, then nodded, and quickly moved back into her speech, and the applause died down. Meg's heart was still thumping so hard that she couldn't really hear anything else, and her father reached over to squeeze her hand—below camera-level, and she was grateful enough to hang on for a minute.

"Okay?" he whispered.

Meg nodded, although she was still having trouble hearing, or thinking, clearly. But she could sense an exuberance and confidence in her mother's voice, as she finished the speech, and there was a final ovation. After one last glance up at them, she was out on the House floor, with a wave of people—from both sides of the aisle—proffering handshakes and congratulations.

"Just another boring Tuesday night," Preston said.

Meg smiled weakly. "Same old, same old," she said.

11

IT HAD BEEN decided in advance that her father would stay behind to wait for her mother, and that she and Steven and Neal would go back to the Residence with Preston. He led them through a veritable gauntlet of well-wishers, reporters, and cameras, moving them along as swiftly as possible, although she had to stop more than once to pose for the requisite photographs with all of the people who had been recognized in the speech, most of whom were as embarrassed and self-conscious as she was—with the possible exception of the kid who'd saved his classmates on the school bus, and seemed to be pretty damned pleased with himself.

Lots of other people wanted to be introduced to her—and Steven and Neal, too, for that matter—or have their pictures taken together, but Preston tactfully discouraged most of them, with inoffensive, and accurate, remarks about her brothers having to be up early for school the next day. A couple of times, though, he gave her one of his tiny eye-flicker nods, and she would immediately pause next to someone or other, for a photo or brief conversation, assuming that some unknown political debt was being repaid—or extracted. The party had pretty much held its own during the midterm elections, neither gaining nor losing a significant number of seats, but she knew Preston wasn't ever one to miss an opportunity to shore up a shaky ally.

Just about everyone seemed to be sneaking quick looks at her hand, and she also overheard more than a few "God, it's *uncanny*, isn't it?" exchanges, as though she had some control over whom she happened to resemble. A few reporters asked easy "were you proud when you watched the President tonight?" questions, but then, one of them wanted to know if she thought she would ever have any hope of leading a normal life, given her significant physical impairments and the fact that she was still a universally acknowledged terrorist target.

She could tell that Preston didn't like that one any better than she did—and was making an angry mental note about the guy, but before he could cut him off, she just smiled and said something off-hand about the fact that she thought normality was probably overrated.

After that, Preston and their agents were much more authoritative about moving them along, and when their car was on its way back to the White House, she finally let out her breath. Christ, it had been a long night. Preston was saying jocular things to Steven and Neal, but she could tell that he was still furious about the one reporter.

"I'm *fine*," she said, when they happened to meet eyes at one point.

Preston shook his head. "I'm sorry, I should have been faster."

"I'm fine," she said, again.

He didn't look convinced, but he nodded.

Once they were finally upstairs at the White House, in relative privacy, she sank down on a settee in the Center Hall. Steven went to check his email, while Preston sent Neal off to change into his pajamas, and then sat next to her.

"How you doing?" he asked.

Mostly, she was exhausted. It was extremely damned stressful to pretend to be completely healed and fit, with untold numbers of cameras—and commentators—poised to capture every potential tremor or twitch.

"You were just right," he said. "Even Linda couldn't have asked for more."

Hell, Linda was *always* capable of asking for more. Meg grinned at him. "She would if she had the nerve."

He grinned, too. "Well, maybe."

Left unsaid was that, for the time being, Linda would definitely *not* be inclined to risk the President's wrath again.

"I really am sorry I wasn't quicker, Meg," he said. "I know what that son-of-a-bitch is like, but he caught me off-guard by throwing you the little softball first."

Hmmm. Meg frowned at him. "Am I mad at you about that?"

He nodded.

Oh. She wouldn't have said that she was—but, he was probably right. Which made her quite passive-aggressive. "It's okay," she said. "It didn't bother me."

"You got ambushed," Preston said. "Go ahead and be angry about it."

Mainly, she was just tired.

"Good answer, by the way," he said. "You made him look even smaller than he is."

It would be nice if that were true.

To her brothers' delight, Jason brought hot fudge sundaes out to the table in the West Sitting Hall, and the four of them sat down to eat, although Meg mostly watched hers melt, and Preston took only three bites before turning to his cup of coffee.

"Mom was *good*," Neal said with his mouth full. "They *totally* liked her."

Steven transferred the whipped cream from Meg's dish onto his own sundae. "Yeah, right, like you weren't falling asleep the whole time."

"*I* was awake," Neal said, moving his arm to block Steven from stealing his whipped cream, too. "You were all bored and stuff, but *I* wasn't."

While they traded "You were more bored," "No, *you* were more bored" insults, Meg glanced at Preston. "How do you think it played?"

Preston lifted his hands as though he was holding a bat, swung them forward, made the sound of hitting a ball, then squinted as if he was watching it fly over the center-field fence.

"That was nice," Meg said. "Do you do shadow-puppets, too?"

He nodded. "I'm also very good with interpretive dances."

There was no question but that she would pay a *serious* admission price to see that.

She was too exhausted to wait up for her parents to come home, or bother checking her messages, of which there were apparently quite a few. She also didn't have the nerve to turn on C-SPAN or CNN or—God knows—Fox, on the fairly-likely chance that she might be forced to see *herself* being beamed around the world, and maybe even having her body language and demeanor analyzed by self-styled experts, and other such embarrassments.

But, thank God, it was over, and she hadn't cried, or panicked, or fallen, or—as far as she knew—looked rattled or intimidated.

Although she would have been a lot more impressed with herself if her last thought before she fell asleep hadn't been about the degree to which she did, indeed, have significant, permanent physical impairments—and the fact that she almost certainly still *was*, and possibly always would be, a target.

She made a point of avoiding all forms of media for most of the week, with the exception of the snarky articles about her mother's speech at the Alfalfa Club dinner, an event at which she was required to be witty and self-deprecating, and Meg's father had to sit there on the dais and smile and laugh and be unreservedly supportive. Naturally, they came home on the early side, both in foul moods. Apparently, it had not been her mother's finest performance, and although it was moderately well-received, it didn't seem to have gone unnoticed that many of the jokes had been ghost-written, and lacked the President's normal easygoing, friendly, off-the-cuff touch. But the coverage was minimal beyond the Beltway, luckily, since the dinner was traditionally considered off-the-record, and supposedly off-limits to the press.

Beth's verdict on the State of the Union Address—after commenting that, once again, Meg had selected one of the least interesting pairs of earrings ever assembled by human, or even mechanical, hands—had been that she looked appropriately mortified about being singled out, in a courteous, if somewhat patrician—and fortunately, *not* imperious—way. Which was a relief because, if caught on the wrong day, she and her mother were both capable of erring in that direction. Meg liked to think of that tendency as being regal, but ingrained imperiousness was probably closer to the truth.

Appearances aside, the people in Beth's dorm had been deeply disappointed that her mother had not, even once, used the phrase, "The State of the Union is strong," and their drinking game had suffered accordingly. However, one of the other cues had been to take a large gulp every time the cameras cut to the First Family, and as a result, they had all gotten smashed.

She spent the next few days doing last-minute packing for school—and trying not to think about how nervous she was. Downright scared, actually. It was almost impossible to sleep, and she had more nightmares than usual—which meant that the rest of her family wasn't sleeping very well, either. Unfortunately.

The plan, was for her to fly up to Albany with her parents in Air Force One; then, her mother would stay behind and have a not-wildly-necessary meeting with the governor, while Meg and her father, and maybe Preston, went over to the campus. After lengthy discussions, they had all finally agreed that having her mother make the entire trip would turn the whole thing into too much of a news event, and Meg wanted to slip in as unobtrusively as possible. Having the First Gentleman along wasn't exactly the route to anonymity, but it wouldn't compare to the utter madhouse, and massive entourage, which would accompany the President.

The night before she left, dinner was very quiet. Even Steven was subdued. The chefs have gone all-out, and they were having steak—her portion arriving presliced; something which *wasn't* going to happen in the dining hall, she assumed—and jazzy little potato baskets, along with an assortment of grilled vegetables and full soup, salad, bread, and dessert courses. Preston had come upstairs to eat with them, but he wasn't much more talkative than anyone else.

"So," her father said. "You all packed?"

Which he had asked her at breakfast, and then again during lunch.

"How come I can't come?" Neal asked, for about the tenth time.

Her parents looked at each other; her mother shrugged, and her father nodded.

"I guess you could miss a day of school," he said.

"All right!" Neal said happily. "Steven, too?"

Their father nodded again. "Sure."

"Okay," Steven said, without much enthusiasm. "If you want."

Knowing perfectly well that he had a basketball game, Meg wasn't sure if she should be amused, or hurt. "I think you should play in your game," she said.

He looked guiltily at their parents. "Hey, no big deal. I mean, you know, I want to come. Say good-bye and all."

What a liar. "It's not like I'm going off to *war*," Meg said. "I mean, Christ." She glanced at her mother. "I mean, shoot." Golly. Gosh.

"An ivory tower," Preston remarked, "but a battleground, nevertheless."

Now, they all looked at *him*. Meg, for one, was amused.

"How poetic," she said. "Do you have a special dance that goes along with that?"

He winked at her. "We few, we happy few," he said, and cut into his steak.

However, back to the matter at hand—before either of her parents took a committed position, from which they would be reluctant to back down. "Anyway," she said to Steven, "just play in the game. I'd rather not have it be such a production."

Neal looked hurt. "You don't want me to come, either?"

Jesus. Everyone was so damned touchy. "Of course I want you to come," she said. "Give me a break, okay?"

"Then, let's consider it settled," her mother said, no doubt anticipating the potential deterioration of this conversation. "Neal can come; Steven can stay here."

"What about Preston?" Neal asked.

Her mother grinned. "If he brings a permission slip, yes, he may come along as well."

"Okay, then. I shall call Beatrice Fielding at once," Preston said.

Did his mother know he did that? "Do you ever say that right in front of her?" Meg asked. She had been introduced to Mrs. Fielding several times, at ceremonies and functions, but couldn't remember him ever being anything other than extremely respectful towards her. And Mrs. Fielding, who had raised four daughters by herself—as well as Preston, who was the baby of the family—struck her as being cheerful and affectionate, but definitely also a formidable woman.

Preston shook his head. "I just say, 'Yes, ma'am,' 'Thank you, ma'am,' and 'No excuse, ma'am.' "

"I bet he calls her Mommy," Steven said with his mouth full.

Neal laughed. "Mommy *dear*."

"Only if I really, *really* want something," Preston said.

Dinner with Preston was definitely preferable to dinner without Preston—and she was fairly certain that, if asked, four other people at the table would be in complete agreement. "Just make sure to give your outfit some thought," Meg said. "I have a fashion reputation to uphold."

She hadn't seen it, with her own eyes, so she could neither confirm nor deny, but the word was that she had made more than one Ten Worst Dressed List this year.

He nodded solemnly. "I will select the finest pair of sweatpants I own."

Meg couldn't resist watching her mother, who was clearly dying to ask the obvious question, but forcing herself to remain silent. "Well, luckily," Meg said—just to be a little bit mean, "Linda and I spent a good chunk of the afternoon exploring my options, since it's vital to send exactly the right message."

Upon which, her mother came very close to dropping her fork—and quite possibly stalking out of the room to pick up the nearest telephone.

"That would be humor," Meg said.

After only a tiny hesitation, her mother nodded and resumed eating.

Not terribly good humor, but humor, regardless.

After dinner, she went to her room to finish up some final packing—and, what the hell, decide what she was going to wear.

She had just about settled on her red ragg sweater—Williams was, after all, deep in the New England countryside—when Steven showed up in her doorway.

"So, yo," he said. Christ, his voice was deep now. "You're out of here tomorrow."

Meg nodded. "Yeah." As far as she knew, her brothers had been up in the Solarium, watching the Celtics with their father. "Is it halftime?"

He shrugged, but she knew that meant yes.

"So, uh, look," he said. "You mad I'm not coming?"

She shook her head. "The fewer people, the better, as far as I'm concerned."

"You going to miss Stupid?" he asked, indicating Vanessa, who was asleep inside an open Camp David duffel bag.

She was going to miss Stupid very much. "Yeah," Meg said.

"Well—you'll be back lots," he said. "On, like, vacations and all."

"Yeah." She reached over to pat her cat, who woke up long enough to grab her hand between her paws and wrestle violently with it.

"You scared?" Steven asked.

Enough to destroy her capacity for rational thought. But, she shrugged.

"It'll be good, though," he said. "You know, college."

Either that, or a total, humiliating, very public disaster. Meg shrugged again.

"I'll pat her and stuff," he said. "So she isn't sad. I mean, you know, even if she bites."

And Vanessa was highly likely to bite. "Thanks." Meg unhooked a claw from her wrist. It hurt, but not enough to stop patting her.

"Be weird," he said. "You not being around."

Meg swallowed, feeling—already—a strong jolt of homesickness. "At least it's under better circumstances this time."

He nodded, not looking at her.

Intelligent of her to bring up the last time—the *only* time—she had ever been away from home for more than a couple of days.

"I guess there really isn't any comparison at all. I mean, it's not as though—" Nothing like compounding the issue. Jesus. "Anyway," she said. "What's the score?"

"Celtics up by three," he said.

"Well—good," she said, and it was quiet.

"So, uh, you're going to be really busy up there?" he asked.

Meg frowned, not sure what he meant by that. "I don't know. I'm taking four classes."

He nodded, rocking slightly on his heels.

"I guess it'll be pretty hard to make friends," she said. "I mean, you know how people always act."

He nodded, rocking.

What the hell did he want? "So, I'm guessing I probably *won't* be all that busy," she said.

He stopped rocking, but still didn't make eye contact. "So, it'd be okay if I, you know, call you up sometimes? If I like, want to talk to you?"

Meg smiled. She was quite fond of her brothers. In fact, excessively so. "Yeah," she said. "I hope you do."

THE PRESS POOL the next day seemed large enough to invade Normandy. And she had to do lots of waving and smiling, along with making tedious "yes, I'm certainly looking forward to it" and "this is an exciting new step" comments.

During the flight up, her mother enacted a closed-door policy for the Presidential suite—broken only twice, by Winnie, her deputy chief of staff—so that Meg and her parents and Neal could be alone together. Normally, her mother's flights tended to be gregarious and quite social, with people popping in and out to say hello, so there was probably some grumbling about the lack of access, but Meg didn't particularly care, and she was pretty sure her mother didn't, either.

They were served a very attractive lunch, which none of them really ate. Meg managed maybe three sips of her Coke, and then gave up.

When the plane landed, she said good-bye to her mother inside, rather than out in front of all those damn cameras. Her mother hugged her so fiercely that it was hard to breathe, and there was a lot of blinking going on.

"You're sure you don't want me to—" her mother started.

Christ, not again. Meg shook her head. Firmly.

"Right. Okay. You'll call tonight?" her mother asked.

Meg nodded. The easiest way to avoid crying was just to do as little talking as possible.

"I'm very proud of you," her mother said, and Meg nodded.

Outside, it was cold and windy and snowing a little, with plowed drifts running along the side of the tarmac. The Secret Service, along with what looked like most of the police officers in New York, was keeping the crush of journalists and civilians back, but it was still pretty intense. Her mother gave her one last hug, and then they went to their separate motorcades. Once she and her father and Neal were safely inside their car, Preston joined them.

"Imagine what it would be like if you *weren't* going to school in the middle of nowhere?" he said, and Meg smiled. Weakly.

The drive was less than an hour, even with the weather, but again, there wasn't much conversation. Mainly, her father kept going over details. Like the checking account and credit card that had been set up for her, the technical details of her upgraded encrypted satellite phone, and what to do if she ran into any one of a number of complicated and improbable situations.

"Russell," Preston said, very serious, "what if she can't find just the right kind of paper for her printer? You know, the perfect kind. What should she do?"

"The Marines, damn it," Meg said.

Preston shook his head. "It's domestic, Meg. I think the National Guard is the way to go."

Her father sat back, folding his arms. "Fine. I'm just trying to be practical."

"Check out these mountains," Neal said, looking out the window. "They're pretty neat."

Be a lot neater if she were going to be skiing down them—but, this wasn't the time to be thinking about that. She had a terrible headache, so she took off her sunglasses, rubbing them across the front of her sweater. She was carrying some ibuprofen in her pocket—she had decided to wear jeans and her now elastic-laced L.L.Bean boots, despite her mother's almost-invisible wince—and she pulled a couple out, borrowing Neal's orange juice to swallow them.

Naturally, she also had her cane, her brace, and her splint, as well as her laptop, and a knapsack full of things like tampons, a hairbrush, and a small collection of framed photographs. Saying good-bye to Vanessa had been very, very hard, and it was the only time all day she had—privately—cried a little.

So far, anyway.

She had taken a tour of the college—Christ, a *long* time ago—and suddenly recognizing a motel, she realized that they were almost there. She had been assigned to a dorm called Sage Hall, somewhere off this main street. They had given her a single room—the Secret Service had insisted—but, apparently, lots of freshmen had singles, so it might not seem like favoritism. The dorm was co-ed, and had vertical entries, although she wasn't sure what that meant. That guys lived nearby, presumably.

"Go, Ephs!" she said to her father, Ephs being the nickname of the Williams sports teams.

He smiled, although she knew that the fact that she had decided to enroll at the archrival of his undergrad alma mater, Amherst, was still something of a sore spot. And her mother didn't always remember to hide the fact *she* would have far preferred seeing her go to Harvard, or—at the very least—Princeton, or Yale. But even though she had been accepted everywhere she applied—unsurprisingly, given the prestige of admitting a Presidential child, regardless of his or her intellect—she had been so sold on the idea of going to an academic powerhouse which *also* happened to be in ski country, and have an excellent tennis team, that back in April, when her life still seemed promising, she had turned all of the other schools down without a second thought.

The campus was just about as New England picturesque as it was possible to be, and the snow only added to the effect. It was easy to tell where Sage Hall was, because there was a crowd. Exactly what she'd hoped there wouldn't be, but it was too late now. Most of the people seemed to be there intentionally—press and the like; and the rest seemed to be passing by and stopping to see what was going on. Although with all of the Secret Service agents and the motorcade, it couldn't be all that tough to figure out.

"Looks like we have company," she said, as the car slowed to a stop.

Her father frowned at Preston, who shrugged.

"What did you expect, Russ," he said.

Her father just frowned.

Some agent or other opened the car door, and Neal was the first one out.

"This is nice, Meggie," he said. "It's really pretty."

At least someone was thinking positively. Meg got out after him, gripping her cane, and trying to decide if she was going to use it or not. The sidewalk had been shoveled, but it was still icy, and she almost slipped—which was one hell of a way to start college. Her father put out his hand to help her, and she shook him off. Christ, he didn't have to *stress* the fact that she'd almost fallen, did he?

The President of the college was waiting out in front of a cast iron gate and two brick pillars to greet them, along with a bunch of deans and trustees and other officials, and there was a flurry of quick greetings and introductions. Luckily, it was starting to snow even harder, and cold as hell, and therefore, unlikely to be prolonged.

They walked through the gate to the edge of a snowy quadrangle, which was surrounded by three old brick buildings, and huge bare-limbed trees. Several paths had been cleared around and across the quad, although the snow was marked up enough to make it look as though a rowdy game of touch football or something had just ended. There were a fair number of students clustered nearby, most of whom were trying to look jaded—but they were, after all, hanging around to watch, so they couldn't be all *that* jaded.

Reporters were still shouting questions in their general direction, but Meg just nodded at them, trying to keep her balance on the slick walkway, assuming that Preston was going to take care of it. The god-damn cameras had almost certainly captured her stumbling out of the car, and the shot was probably going to be shown all over the place tonight.

It was maybe too soon to form a strong opinion—but so far, college *sucked.*

12

HER DORM WAS a large L-shaped building off to their right, and she set her good foot carefully with each step, dreading the thought of tripping again. Various flyers and notices were taped to the green-painted door to her entry, and she saw one of the deans frown, probably because the papers flapping in the wind looked pretty haphazard and messy. For her part, she kind of appreciated the fact that no one had bothered tearing them off or in any way tried to make the door look pristine for her arrival. One of her father's agents held the door for them, and the small foyer and inside stairs were very congested, predominantly by men in suits. Which was unsurprising, since she, Neal, and her father were at the same location, but had to be incredibly irritating for the people who actually lived here, so they had all probably already decided to dislike her, as a result.

There was a small Secret Service security desk just inside the main entrance, with a large room set aside as the command post up a small flight of stairs, and she had been told that one of the rooms on her floor was going to be used as an additional checkpoint. She'd also already seen more than one tiny camera and what looked like a couple of high-tech sensors of some kind, too. Christ. Maybe everyone in the dorm was getting a tuition rake-off or something to make up for all of this.

There were some more introductions—too many, really, for her to take in, although she tried to focus more acutely when she saw a couple of people who were her age, and one of the deans said, "And these are your Junior Advisors, Dirk Broadlund and Susan Dowd."

Junior advisors were the Williams equivalent of Resident Dorm Advisors, and Beth and Josh had both been giving her mixed reviews about *their* RAs, so she was uneasy about having to deal with these two strangers. But, it was safe to assume that they had each been so thoroughly vetted that neither of them was, for example, trying to make a point of sleeping with every single female freshman in the dorm, like the guy Beth had been doing her best to avoid ever since he had made an incompleted pass at her during the second week of classes.

Dirk was a big guy with light brown hair and a patchy beard, who was wearing hiking boots, baggy cargo pants, a t-shirt which read "*WOC. Get Outside and Play.*" and a blue blazer—the latter, presumably, in an effort to look presentable when he greeted the First Family.

Her other JA, Susan, was a good four inches shorter than she was, and quite thin, with chin-length dark hair and very blue eyes. She looked faintly familiar, for no good reason, but maybe her photo had been somewhere in the massive sheaf of housing and other paperwork she and her father had spent several hours filling out right after Christmas. In any case, she had on running sneakers, jeans, and a purple Williams sweatshirt, which meant that she had either decided not to dress up at all to meet the First Family, or that she had forgotten they were coming.

Almost certainly the former.

Realizing that she still had her sunglasses on, Meg pushed them up on top of her head, and tucked her cane under her elbow, so she could shake hands with them. Dirk, who had automatically put out his right hand, blushed and held out his other one, instead. Susan must have taken instant note of that, because when it was her turn, she led with her left hand, which made things much less awkward.

Although they both seemed very friendly, Dirk hung back to a degree, while Susan unhesitatingly went over to introduce herself to her father and Neal, so she probably served as the primary JA in the entry. Or, maybe, she just wasn't quite as shy.

"Is this where she's going to live?" Neal asked, looking at Susan, not Dirk, so he must have sensed the same supervisory hierarchy.

Susan smiled. "Yeah." Then, she glanced at Meg. "Come on, I'll show you your room."

Which was on the third floor. Meg looked up the stairs, not too eager to start climbing, but then Susan motioned her off to the left, past the security desk, instead, where there was an elevator. Which made her feel handicapped and pitiful—but, to hell with it. The damn thing would make life easier.

The elevator wasn't very big, so only Susan, and the head of her father's detail, Ryan, got on with them for the ride up.

"Do you prefer Meghan, or Meg?" Susan asked.

A thoughtful question, given the fact that most people she didn't know just went ahead and called her Meghan. "Meg," Meg said. "Uh, do you like Susan, or Sue, or—?"

"Definitely Susan," her JA said, and flashed a smile. "But, I answer to almost anything."

"Here, pup!" Neal said, immediately. "Come here, pup!"

Susan laughed, and Meg grinned, too, wondering when, exactly, he had started developing this unexpectedly amusing smart-ass streak. It also suddenly made her miss Steven terribly, but she didn't want to think about that, or the fact that she really wished her mother was here with them, or anything else that would make her feel homesick, like—oh, God, *Vanessa*. What was she going to do without Vanessa? How was she going to be able to get to sleep, or—she ducked her head, so she could close her eyes for a second, and make sure that there was no chance in hell that she was going to cry, or look, in any way, vulnerable.

The elevator stopped, and Susan got off, pointing out the bathroom, and then leading them down a cramped hallway. Grey floors, white walls, with a thin wooden strip running along them about waist high, blond wooden doors, round institutional lights placed every ten feet or so, and there was a gun-metal grey storage closet or something next to the elevator. Red and white exit signs, fire alarms, sprinklers and emergency lighting, what might be heating grates. Meg didn't see anyone other than Secret Service agents and aides, but the dorm seemed crowded. Or, at any rate, *sounded* crowded. Lots of noise, mostly rock and roll. Strange voices everywhere, both male and female.

Susan stopped in front of a room in the corner and opened the door. "Here you go," she said.

Meg took a deep breath, and limped inside.

Some of her stuff was unpacked, and some of it wasn't, but the first thing she noticed was the bed. An extra-long twin bed, with a sturdy wood and white metal frame, across from the door, exactly where the bed in the room where she'd been held for all that time had been. *Exactly.*

Feeling dizzy, she flipped her sunglasses down and turned to look in the other direction, at the utilitarian desk and padded wooden chair.

"This is an orientation packet for you," Susan said, holding out a manila envelope, "and it'll tell you a lot of the things you'll want to know."

Meg nodded, still so rattled by the bed that it was hard to pay attention to anything else. Susan was telling her some other stuff, and she nodded at the right times, resting her hand on the edge of the desk so that she could lean on it and take the weight off her knee.

"Well, tell you what," Susan said, looking increasingly uncomfortable. "Why don't I let you do some unpacking, and have a look around, and I'll stop by later to see how you're doing."

Meg nodded, managing—barely—to smile.

Once Susan had left, there was a short silence.

"Well," her father said. "How about we start out by—"

"Can we move the bed, Dad?" Meg asked, and heard her voice shake. "I *really* don't want it there."

Her father looked slightly alarmed, but then nodded and leaned out into the corridor. "Sammy?" he said to one of his aides. "Want to give me a hand here for a minute?"

Sammy came scurrying in—although, Christ, it wasn't his fault that he had a pale little rodenty face and big horn-rimmed glasses that overwhelmed his features. Although he probably could have chosen more flattering frames, had he been so inclined.

"We're just going to change a few things around," her father said, pulling the bed away from the wall. "Where do you want it, Meg?"

Anywhere else. "I don't—" Did her damned voice *have* to tremble? "Over here, maybe?"

Her father nodded, Sammy lifting with him. They hauled the bed to the other side of the room—where it didn't fit, and blocked the combination bureau-closet. So they moved it again, so it was in a different corner, near the window. It wasn't a very big room, and after some discussion—Neal was full of well-meaning, impractical suggestions—her father and Sammy shifted the desk and MicroFridge unit over to where the bed had originally been, and put the small bookcase near the foot of the bed.

While they did all of this, Meg went through her knapsack, looking for absolutely nothing. She'd asked the advance people not to unpack for her, but—not unexpectedly—books were already on the shelves and the bed had been made, with one of Trudy's crocheted quilts on top of it. Moved to the new spot, the bed didn't bother her quite as much, and she was relieved to see that it was lower than the other one had been, and the frame was different, too.

"Okay?" her father asked.

Sammy was breathing hard—and only in his late twenties—which, under different circumstances, she might have found funny.

She nodded. "Thank you."

"Okay, then." He looked at Sammy. "Thanks. When Preston gets through, you can send him in here."

Sammy nodded, closing the door behind him.

"They put away your clothes and everything," Neal said, checking inside the closet.

But, of course. The advance people would have been trying to be nice, but it made her feel—incompetent. Childish. Helpless. Suddenly very tired, she sat down on the bed, touching Trudy's quilt for reassurance.

"S-sorry you had to move stuff," she said. It wasn't anything she wanted to explain, but her father wasn't an idiot, so he had probably figured it out.

He sat next to her. "I like it better this way."

Right.

He put his arm around her for a minute, and she knew he understood. Thank God.

"It's a nice room," he said. "Especially once you put some posters up on the walls."

She nodded.

"You going to be all right?" he asked.

Doubtful. But, she nodded.

"Well. Let's get you the rest of the way unpacked," he said.

She shook her head. "No, let me finish up. So I'll, you know, have something to do."

When they were gone, and she was alone.

He kissed the side of her head. "Okay. But, how about I set up the computer for you?"

A fair compromise. She nodded. "Thank you."

Neal had checked each of the bureau drawers, as well as the small closet, where even her *jeans* had been neatly hung. After that, he sat at her desk and looked through those drawers, too. A small paper shredder had been set up—everyone in her family routinely shredded *everything* remotely personal, without thinking twice—-and he leaned over to make sure that it was plugged in. The WHCA people had installed a telephone with three different lines, and he lifted the receiver, then nodded approvingly, and hung up.

"Leave the drop-line alone, okay, Neal?" their father said, as he reached for the other, super-secure telephone, which would connect directly to the White House switchboard as soon as anyone picked it up.

Neal looked disappointed, but nodded. Then, he opened the MicroFridge, which was crammed full of groceries, and she also caught a glimpse of several gel ice packs in the tiny freezer. Finally, he used the remote to turn on the small television, which was on top of the bookcase, to make sure the prearranged cable service was working, and that the recorder had been set up properly.

"Everything seem okay?" Meg asked.

"Yep, so far," Neal said cheerfully. "Can I try the bed now?"

Why not? She lifted herself up onto her cane, and he took her place, lying down. When he saw her watching, he pretended to be asleep.

"It's that comfortable?" she said.

He nodded, laughing.

There was a knock on the door, and Preston came in, pausing to admire the room. "Looks good," he said. "Looks very good."

To her, it looked monastic—but, hey, America was a melting pot. She gestured towards the window facing the side street, and the waiting, lurking media. "Are they going to be out there constantly?"

Preston shook his head. "I think most of them'll leave once we take off."

Most.

"And Ginette will handle the rest of them," he said. "She'll be up here through Friday, or longer, if you want."

Her father's rather annoying and snippy deputy press secretary. But, Meg nodded.

Preston leaned against the bureau, slightly adjusting the crease in his slacks. "Looks like a nice place, Meggo. I think you're going to do all right here."

Oh, yeah. Without a doubt. Meg nodded.

"Russell-baby," Preston said, "need some help with the mechanics there?"

Her father, bent over the all-in-one printer, just grunted.

"It's something," Preston said to her. "Watching a fellow who's so handy."

As it happened, her father *was* quite handy, but Preston had explained to her more than once—at length—that in his worldview, reality and amusement rarely ought to be allowed to interfere with one another.

When her father was finally finished, and Neal had gone out to explore the hallway and bathroom, there didn't seem to be much left to say.

"So." Her father tucked his Swiss Army knife—which she knew he treasured—into the top drawer of her desk. "Would you like to—"

What she would like, would be not to have such a prolonged good-bye. "You guys should get going, maybe," she said. "So you can get back."

"Okay. You're probably right." Her father stuck his head out into the hall. "Neal, come on, let's get a move on."

"They seem really nice," Neal said, when he came in. "All those girls."

"What, did you go and meet everyone?" Meg asked.

Neal nodded. "There's lots of people around."

Lots of total strangers. And it was kind of demoralizing that her ten-year-old little brother was more socially adept than she was.

"Well, we're going to say good-bye now, okay?" their father said.

Neal nodded, and gave her a big hug. "Steven says we can call you up? When we want? And send lots of email?"

Neal loved email so much that he usually sent her several notes almost every day—despite the fact that his room was maybe forty feet away from hers. "Yeah," Meg said, her throat feeling constricted. "I hope you do."

Preston hugged her, too. "Don't *you* be afraid to call."

She nodded, although she probably would be.

He stepped back to look at her. "Take care of yourself, okay, Meg?"

She nodded again, keeping her eyes down, in case she was going to cry.

Then, Preston took Neal out to the hall, and she was alone with her father. Now, she *really* wanted to cry—and also wished harder than ever that she'd let her mother talk her way into coming along, after all.

"You sure you're going to be all right?" he asked.

She nodded.

"Well, you just do what you can do," he said. "Don't worry about trying to impress anyone else. If you need to—"

She interrupted him before he could say "come home." "No problem," she said. "I'm sure it's going to be great." Except that she really was going to cry, and she rubbed her hand across her eyes. "Don't worry."

He hugged her almost as tightly as her mother had. "If you're in any pain," he said, when he finally let go, "or it's too much—"

"I will," she said quickly.

He reached out to touch her face for a second. "Your mother and I love you very much."

Meg nodded, swallowing. He was about to leave, and she wanted, desperately, to go with him. To forget this whole stupid college idea. To go back where she would be safe, and protected, and—"You don't want to be late," she said, her voice trembling more than ever.

"Okay." He hugged her again. "I love you."

She went out to the hall with him, to wave good-bye like she was a normal, happy freshman, looking forward to the future. Then, when they were gone, she went back into the room, closed the door, and leaned against it.

Damn it. Damn it, damn it, *damn* it.

She took a few deep breaths, to make absolutely sure that she wasn't going to burst into tears, then stared at her new prison cell of a room, all of the furniture plain and generic and impersonal. And out there, beyond the door, on this huge snow-covered campus, were hundreds and hundreds of people she didn't know. Strangers who were going to be watching her every second, waiting for her to—but, she *absolutely couldn't* cry, because if she did, her eyes would get red, and everyone would be able to tell that she had fallen apart.

So she opened her knapsack, and pulled out the framed pictures she'd brought along. The photographs were mostly candids, although a couple of them had also been used for press releases. Steven, intent in his uniform, playing baseball. Neal and Kirby on the South Lawn, near the Children's Garden. Her mother throwing out the first pitch, somewhat ineptly, at Fenway Park. Her father in his East Wing office with Preston, both of them with their feet up on the desk, grinning. Her father again, hammering this time, at a housing project, wearing a flannel shirt, a tool belt, and a truly disgracefully ragged pair of jeans. Trudy, in their kitchen in Massachusetts, gesturing emphatically at the camera with a wooden spoon. Beth, wearing—big surprise—a flamboyant hat. Her mother and Neal—quite possibly the best picture ever taken of either of them, which was saying a lot, since they were by far the most photogenic members of the family—in the private study off the Oval Office, her mother working at her desk, Neal pointing at something he was apparently watching on television, the two of them smiling at each other and looking happy as hell. A shot of Sidney, Adlai and Humphrey, curled up asleep in the Lincoln Bedroom. Vanessa, sitting by her window in the sunshine, washing herself. Vanessa, sprawled across her pillow. Vanessa, lying on her computer keyboard. And, finally, a picture—an old one—of her whole family, near the gondola at Stowe.

She arranged the photos neatly on top of the scarred wooden desk, bookcase, and MicroFridge, then studied them, feeling very homesick. Even for the White House.

There was a knock on the door, and although she wanted to be alone, she limped over and opened it to find Susan standing there.

"Hi," she said. "Your family get off okay?"

Which made it sound as though they'd slipped out in the dark of night, as opposed to having their every step recorded by half the free press. "Yes," Meg said. "Thank you."

Susan noticed the pictures, and smiled. "First thing I did my freshman year, too."

Meg felt her cheeks redden. "Oh, yeah?" she said somewhat stiffly.

Susan nodded. "I was homesick before we even left my apartment."

"Oh, yeah?" It was important to be polite, and make a good impression, so Meg smiled back. Stiffly. "Where are you from?"

"Boston," Susan said.

Which was probably why she seemed familiar, since on further reflection, she had a certain kind of Boston Irish look. "Really?" Meg asked, interested in spite of herself. "Where?"

"Right in the city," Susan said.

Since people often said they were from Boston—and were actually from Methuen, or Waltham, or someplace. "Where'd you go to school?" Meg asked.

"Well, surprisingly enough, *Boston*," Susan said.

Which made sense. Feeling a little more relaxed, Meg leaned against her desk, so she could subtly prop her bad leg up on the chair. "I haven't been up there for a long time. I kind of miss it." *Kind of?*

Susan nodded, her expression hard to interpret.

"I mean, you know, like when the Red Sox come to Baltimore, we go there, and—well, we did last spring, anyway, and—" Meg stopped, feeling very dumb. She was sort of—babbling, here. "I guess I just mean I'd like to go to Boston again, sometime. Um, anyway," she looked in the direction of the hall. "I'm sorry about having so many agents. I know they're going to be in everyone's way."

Susan shrugged. "It'll be the safest dorm on campus."

Or the most dangerous, depending upon how one looked at it. "Well, I'm sorry they have to be here," Meg said.

Susan shrugged again. "They've been around for a while, so everyone's used to it."

She was probably just being kind, but Meg nodded.

"Dinner starts in about half an hour," Susan said. "Why don't you walk over with some of us?"

Meg shook her head more vigorously than she'd intended. "No, I—we had a late lunch." On Air Force One. With the President. Jesus.

"So, you can just have a salad or something," Susan said.

Meg could already feel her heart beating faster at the thought of having to go outside. Of having to leave the *room*. "I—I have a lot of unpacking to do."

Susan leaned back against the doorjamb, folding her arms. "The first time's the hardest. Once you get it out of the way, it'll be easier."

The hell did *she* know about it? In lieu of scowling at her, Meg concentrated on a rip in her jeans, up near the top of the brace.

"Look, I know it's a little more complicated for you," Susan said.

A *little*? Meg looked up just long enough to cock an eyebrow at her.

Susan nodded. "I know, but you also feel like every other freshman feels the first day. And in a lot of ways, I'm guessing you're better equipped to handle it."

If this girl thought that, then she must not look like quite as much of a basket case as she was afraid she did. "Well, I think it's probably just complicated," Meg said, aware that her voice was as cool and dismissive as it was when she spoke to reporters. And that wasn't fair—after all, it was this person's job to be friendly to her. "I mean, I appreciate your offering. Thanks."

Susan looked at her for a minute, then nodded. "It *is* complicated," she said. "If you were one of the other freshmen, I'd bully you into it."

Well, that was straightforward. "So, you're not going to bully me?" Meg asked.

"I thought I might—wheedle," Susan said.

Cajole. Placate. Coax. Meg grinned, pulling at the little tear in her jeans.

"Tell you what," Susan said. "We'll be by to get you for dinner. Got it?"

Which sounded altogether too much like an order. And—*we*? Meg frowned.

"I'm guessing you won't say no if there's a group," Susan said.

Good guess. Meg sighed. "Okay."

"Okay, then." Susan pushed away from the door. "See you in a while."

Meg nodded, and turned to open one of her few unpacked boxes. Then, it occurred to her that she'd better let her agents know that she would be going out, and just generally review the basic procedures with them again. On Sunday, she and her parents had had a long meeting with Mr. Gabler, who was the Special Agent in charge of the entire White House Presidential Protective Detail, and the main thrust of her new security seemed to be that everyone who came into the dorm would have to have their IDs checked at the first-floor guard post, and then *double*-checked, if they came up to her part of the third floor. There were also video cameras, built-in alarms, anti-bugging devices, and God only knew what else. Weapons caches, escape routes, safe rooms, and emergency contingency plans, probably.

Not much fun for the people who lived in her entry, who—no matter what Susan had said—must completely resent her.

The Secret Service room was next door, to her left, and two of her agents, Larry and Ed, were standing there, talking. When they saw her, they stopped and looked alert.

"Uh, hi," she said. "Is it okay if I—" No, that was the wrong way to start. "I mean, I guess they're going to dinner in a while, and Susan said for me to come, too."

"Sure thing," Larry said, and picked up his phone, presumably to let Garth, along with whichever agents were posted downstairs, know.

"Is it the same as it used to be?" Meg asked. Seemed like centuries ago. "I try to let you know as soon as *I* know I'm going somewhere?"

They both nodded.

Not that she was expecting to be doing much of anything, beyond the very basics of going to classes, physical therapy, and maybe the occasional meal.

"Okay." She felt so damned awkward around her agents now. "I mean, I will."

Larry and Ed nodded. Big, bulky guys, per usual, differentiated mainly by the fact that Ed had a mustache, and Larry looked as though he had gotten his nose broken a couple of times.

Not that she was one to talk, when it came to the latter.

Christ, she was pretty much going to be *living* with these people now, instead of being able to leave them downstairs and escape to the safety of the second floor of the Residence. She definitely didn't want to make friends with any of them, but it was going to be unpleasant for everyone concerned if she couldn't figure out a way to feel slightly at ease in their presence.

And vice versa.

"Your father showed you where your panic button is?" Ed asked.

Meg nodded. It had been wired into her room, and the cord was long enough so that she could either put it on her desk, or next to her bed, depending. As opposed to the portable one she was required to carry *with* her, at all times.

Unless, of course, it was forcibly torn away from her by—but, she wasn't going to think about that. And now, instead of having an unknown GPS microchip embedded in the back molar that had ended up being ripped right out of her mouth, along with two other teeth, she had some kind of high-tech tracking device implanted just under the skin on her left upper arm, and presumably, next time, terrorists would use knives or razors to slice it out of her, and then—

"There's one in the bathroom, too," Larry said. "Just above the sinks, on the left side."

Meg nodded. Another carefree reminder for the other people who lived on the floor.

"For the time being, your windows have been sealed," Ed said—meaning, Meg knew, bullet-proofed—"but when the weather gets warm, we'll see about making some other arrangements. If it gets too hot in there, let us know."

She liked fresh air, but she had gotten used to not having much in the White House. Whenever any of them felt like they couldn't breathe—which was a regular complaint of her father's, in particular—they would have to go out to the Truman Balcony for a while, or up to the more private area on the roof outside the Solarium.

They all stood there.

"Um, look," Meg said. "Just so you know."

Larry and Ed both tensed.

Christ, what were they expecting her to say? That she hated them, and what had happened to her was all their fault—even though they hadn't been assigned to her at the time? "I don't ever play games with this stuff," she said. *Ever.* Once, right after they'd moved to Washington, she'd decided to give her agents the slip, just for fun—and her parents had been so incredibly furious that she had never tried it again. Her mother had yelled at her on live television, even. And now, of course, there was no chance in hell that she would take any kind of unnecessary risks. "If I tell you I'm going to be somewhere, or doing something, that's where I'm going to *be*. You don't have to worry that I'll try to pull a fast one on you."

They nodded.

Okay. She nodded, too. With luck, they were always going to be where she expected *them* to be, too.

Except that she wasn't going to count on it.

13

SHE LIMPED BACK to her room, deciding that she should probably get cleaned up for dinner—and check the location of the panic button in the bathroom, while she was at it. So, she pulled a small hand towel and her toothbrush and toothpaste out of her knapsack.

The bathroom was definitely spartan, and unappealing—two stalls, one of which was wheelchair-accessible, white walls, blue tiles, overhead lights that were too bright, a grim dark shower, and a larger one with a handrail and a white plastic shower bench. There were two round sinks, with a mirror above each one, and small built-in shelves, overflowing with plastic shower caddies full of shampoo, toothpaste, face cream, makeup, and blow-dryers and so forth, and a couple of hand towels hung from nearby hooks.

Three tall, very narrow shelves on the left—right by the god-damn panic button—were empty, which she figured meant they had been reserved for her. Seemed logical, anyway.

It was hard to open toothpaste tubes one-handed, and she stuck it under her right arm, so she could maneuver the toothbrush over there with her good hand, and use her upper arm muscles to squeeze some out. More often than not, this was an imprecise process, and a large glob would end up spilling on the floor.

Pretty weird to see all of this feminine stuff around—her brothers weren't big on mousse and Noxema and all, and she had never really shared a bathroom with her mother, except maybe on ski vacations, and that sort of thing. And now, the idea of having to use this space along with a bunch of strangers was very unpleasant, indeed.

A blond, round-faced girl came in, and stopped short when she saw her.

Meg's mouth was full of toothpaste, and she figured—just a guess—that this wasn't a real good time to spit, so she nodded, instead.

"I, uh—" The girl backed up towards the hall. "I mean, I forgot my—excuse me." She left, the door swinging shut.

Great. Meg spit out the toothpaste. "Nice talking to you," she said to the closed door, and then finished brushing her teeth.

She didn't want to go back out to the corridor, and face people she didn't know, but Christ, she couldn't hide in here indefinitely. So, she limped out as quickly as possible and hurried into her room.

Jesus.

Susan was going to show up soon, to make her go to dinner, and she was so tired that she just wanted to lie down on the damn bed that made her think of being handcuffed and terrified and alone, and sleep for about a decade.

However. Odds were, college people didn't nap. Or sit in their rooms, fighting off tears every other minute, either.

She wanted to turn on CNN, for comfort, but there was too high a chance that she might see *herself*, which would hardly be calming. So, she used her new room key—Christ, it had been a long time since she'd needed *keys*—to slit open the carton where she'd packed her favorite CDs. MP3s were easier, and more fun, and she liked her iPod and all, but she always had to be extra-careful, since illegally downloading music might make the Administration look bad, and—well. Yet another tedious compromise in her life. Beth emailed her pilfered music files constantly, of course, but they had such utterly different tastes that Meg usually just thanked her and stored them in an unused folder on her desktop.

Since it sounded as though every single person in the entire dorm was playing some kind of loud music, she might as well join the trend. Damn, this place was *noisy*. But, if a headache was inevitable, it would be better to have one of her own making, so she pulled out the Doors and turned up the volume as high as it would go. Call her old-fashioned, but most of the music she liked had come out before she was born. Hell, some of it predated her *parents*.

When the dreaded knock came, "Twentieth Century Fox"—one of her all-time favorites—was playing. Blasting, really. She swallowed, and opened the door, to see Susan standing there with three other girls, all of them wearing coats and scarves, ready to go out into the snow.

"Want to head over for dinner?" Susan asked, as though this hadn't already been planned.

No. "Um, yeah, okay," Meg said, and coughed. "Let me, uh—I mean, I guess it's cold out there, so—" She moved clumsily over to her desk chair to pick up her Kevlar ski jacket.

"This is Meg, guys. And this is Tammy," Susan said, indicating the somewhat pudgy blond girl to her right—the same one who had darted out of the bathroom earlier, "and," she motioned towards a tall, solemn girl who had shoulder-length black hair and very white skin, "Mary Elizabeth. And this," she pointed at a somewhat furtive-looking girl with glasses, who didn't appear to have washed her possibly brown hair recently, "is Jesslyn."

They all nodded at one another, and then Meg turned off the CD and picked up her cane. Using the damn thing was only going to make her look more conspicuous, but it might help keep her from falling, so she couldn't leave it behind. Dr. Brooks had given her several easily-attached rubber cane tips with sharp, metal teeth, which she was supposed to use to dig into ice and snow, to make it easier to keep her balance. She even had crampons to strap onto her boots, if necessary, but that would probably be overkill for a short—she hoped—walk to the dining hall.

"You like the Doors," Mary Elizabeth said flatly.

She *loved* the Doors. "Yeah," Meg said. In all probability, Mary Elizabeth wasn't going to be enchanted by Joan Jett, either. Or the Stones. Or the Animals. Or even Julie Andrews. Looking at her in her thigh-length heavy peacoat and homemade wool scarf, Meg's guess was that Oberlin had been her first choice, but she hadn't gotten in—and was still pissed about it.

Tammy, on the other hand, her eyes wide and awed as she peeked into the room and saw all of the photographs, was wearing a puffy pink ski jacket, and gave every appearance of being delighted to be at this preppy Eastern school. Jesslyn seemed—well—weird, her movements abrupt and jittery, as though she had just taken a couple of handfuls of Ritalin, and chased them with a six-pack of Red Bull. She had on a badly-stained tan coat, what appeared to be an authentic, somewhat moth-eaten coonskin cap, black boots, black pants, and a black hooded sweatshirt which was about three sizes too big for her.

"Um, the stairs are fine," Meg said, when Susan headed for the elevator.

Susan hesitated.

"Really," Meg said. The five of them crammed together inside the elevator seemed like an experience worth avoiding. "At home, I always take the stairs."

Larry, who had joined them in the hall, *didn't* glance at her when she said that, but she had a feeling that it had been his first instinct. The schedule had been set up so that some agents would always be at the dorm, standing guard; others would be with her; and still others would serve as advance security teams and do surveillance, all of which had to be costing the taxpayers an offensively high amount of money.

She was never sure if she should introduce her agents to people or not, although it had been easier when she had fewer. "Um," she gestured towards him, "this is—"

"It's okay," Larry said. "We've met."

Meg nodded; her dormmates nodded; her agent nodded.

Swell.

The stairs took some effort—okay, a hell of a *lot* of effort—and she tucked the handle of her cane over her shoulder, so that she could grip the banister with her good hand, and make her painful way down to the first floor, having to go so slowly that it probably made the rest of them feel even more uncomfortable than taking the elevator together would have.

Only three agents—Kyle and Paula joined them down in front of the command post—were going to walk over with them, so at least a couple of the others must have gone on ahead.

When they got outside—it had stopped snowing, but it was really *cold*—a group of bored-looking reporters and camerapeople instantly perked up and came over to intercept them.

Oh, Christ.

Brian and Larry were trying to keep them at a distance, but there was an immediate clamor of questions, along with a disorienting number of flashbulbs and Minicam lights, and it was a struggle not to close her eyes—or look apprehensive.

"Are these your friends, Miss Powers?" someone shouted.

Now, how was she supposed to answer that? If she said they'd just met, it would sound as though she didn't *want* to be friends with them—but she couldn't claim to be their well-established chum, either. So, what the hell, she would answer the question she wanted to answer, instead of the one they'd asked. A simple tactic, taught to her long ago, by a powerful political figure of whom she was almost always fond.

"We're going to dinner," she said, and tried to get past them by staying behind her agents—the blocking backs—who had formed a little wedge, with Kyle in the lead.

But, the reporters kept trying to jostle their way closer, waving tape recorders and microphones and talking all at once. There seemed to be more still cameras than usual, so a lot of the independent paparazzi must have arrived in force today, too.

"What do you expect to—"

"Are you afraid that—"

"Why didn't the President come—"

"Hey!" Kyle said, sounding quite lethal. "Let's back it off, okay?"

"Look, buddy," one of the reporters said, "we're just trying to—"

"I'm doing *my* job, too," Kyle said, and without actually elbowing anyone, he managed to clear a space for her to limp through.

Two more agents, a few campus police officers, and her father's deputy press secretary—what the hell had taken her so long?—had worked their way over to them, and Ginette began giving some terse instructions about where everyone should stand for the statement she was going to read, and Meg was able to start following Susan and the others across the quad.

"Sorry," she said, too embarrassed to look at anyone.

"Wow, is it always like that?" Tammy asked.

Damn near. "Sometimes," Meg said. "I apologize if they bothered you."

"Wow," Tammy said, again. The others didn't say anything—Susan maybe looked a little tense, Mary Elizabeth a little annoyed, and Jesslyn a little puzzled. Maybe. It was hard to tell, with total strangers.

The main freshman dining hall was downhill on the lower part of the campus, in a huge dorm complex called Mission. It seemed like an incredibly long walk, but maybe she was just tired. She also hadn't thought to bring a glove along, and although she could tuck her splint into her jacket out of the wind, the hand gripping her cane was exposed. And it really was *extremely* cold. Considering that she'd grown up in New England, she bloody well ought to have known better. And, as always, she felt like a jerk because she was moving so much more slowly than anyone else, although Susan was taking her time—downright ambling, in fact. Probably not her usual pace.

There were a lot of people pouring in and out of Mission, and despite the snow, a couple of guys were playing Frisbee in an open area to the left of the building, gregarious enough to suggest that they were showing off. One of them, a tall Mr. California type, kept throwing the Frisbee to—at?—girls walking by, most of whom ignored him, some of whom flipped it back. Or flipped him *off*. His long-haired friend seemed to find any of these responses equally hilarious.

Predictably, the I'm-God's-Gift guy whipped the Frisbee in their direction. Her agents were not amused; Meg paid no attention to it whatsoever. Tammy bent down and tossed it back. Badly.

Inside, there were ski-jacketed people everywhere, and the noise level was even more oppressive than the dorm had seemed. In fact, it was so crowded that, for a second, she thought she might lose her breath the way she had that time in the car with Preston, or lurch against the wall from the sudden wave of dizziness which was destroying her ability to see clearly.

The nearby conversations and shouted greetings abated somewhat as people recognized her, but the majority of them were too busy being cool to outright stare. Mostly.

The dining hall was down on the lower level, and the line stretched up a long flight of stairs, everyone loud and jovial and post–Winter Study vacation-tanned.

"Don't worry, it moves pretty quickly," Susan said.

Meg nodded, clutching her cane and staying near the banister by the wall, wishing like hell she had had the nerve to bring her sunglasses along, or at least her Red Sox cap, so she could pull the brim down low over her face. She was trying to be unobtrusive, but since Garth was standing near the main door, and Kyle and Paula were spreading out in her general area, and Larry or someone was probably posted behind the food counters to watch out for rogue poisoners—all of them wearing their damned earpieces and looking much too old in their recently-donned college garb, anyone with half a brain would instantly know that she was someplace nearby.

It had been very windy outside, and she balanced on her good leg long enough to lift her left hand and move her hair to cover as much of the gun-butt scar running up the side of her forehead as possible.

Her stomach hurt. And what she could smell of dinner didn't really smell delicious.

"The food's good here," Tammy was saying—to her, it would appear—"but I guess you're used to *really* good food."

That seemed unanswerable, so Meg just shrugged. The menu board posted at the bottom of the stairs indicated that tonight's offerings included roast turkey with stuffing, something called Tofurky, and vegetarian lasagna. Mashed potatoes, vegetable du jour, cranberry fruit salad, marble cake, that sort of thing. All of which sounded reasonable enough—that is, if a person had an appetite.

The line did move quickly, and she handed over her new ID card, which had been sent to the White House in her registration packet—the advance team had handled all of that, but the photo, from her high school yearbook, was not attractive—to be swiped through some little machine. She'd had a student ID at GW, too, but the only time she'd ever had to produce it was during her lone visit to the library, and the woman at the front desk had thought it was just about the funniest thing ever to be asking her for identification.

"Can you carry your tray by yourself?" Tammy asked. "Do you need help?"

Oh, hell, a *tray*. Fuck. It hadn't even crossed her mind to bring along her adaptive, one-handed tray, and she probably wouldn't have had the nerve to use it in public, anyway. "No, thanks, I'm all set," Meg said, and draped her cane over her shoulder, hoping that people couldn't see how violently she was trembling, or how weak her knee was.

When she finally made it through the service line, her tray empty except for some vegetarian lasagna and a roll—she was too tired to attempt going over to the salad bar—some guy jumped up from his table, which made Kyle take three protective steps towards her.

"Can I take that for you?" the guy asked.

Take it where? Would he give it back? "Thanks," Meg said, but shook her head. It was going to be a challenge to carry the damn thing through a crowded room, but with her left hand doing most of the work, and using her right forearm for shaky support, she could probably manage it.

Unless she tripped, or her foot flopped, or her knee gave out, or—but maybe it was borrowing trouble even to let any of those things cross her mind.

The dining hall had a huge wall of windows, with a nice view of the snow and trees, and Susan glanced at Garth and then selected a table as far away as possible from them, which wasn't easy, given the design of the room. Meg quickly chose a seat which would put her out of viewing range of as many people as possible. Paula and Kyle were at an adjoining table, with Larry well off to the right by the windows, and Martin—where the hell had he come from?—was standing near the beverage area. She couldn't see Garth, but he was probably busy coordinating everyone else's positions, and getting updates about whatever was happening with Ginette and the media, back at the dorm.

The sounds in the room seemed deafening—cacophonous, even—with competing conversations, and plates and silverware clattering. It seemed that almost everyone had just gotten back from a Dead Week winter break, which had left all of them full of energy and joie de vivre. And it also felt as though every single one of them was checking her out.

God, did her stomach hurt.

Dinner conversation was strained. When it was going *well.* Dirk came over to join them for a while, which helped a little—but, not much. Meg, for one, didn't have anything she wanted to say, so she just pretended to eat, and occasionally answered yes or no to a direct question. She really wanted—*needed*—a Coke, but that would entail getting up and crossing the room in front of most of the freshman class, and trying to get it back to the table without spilling anything, so she tried not to think about how thirsty she was. Her throat *wasn't* dry; it was entirely her imagination. She was just—nervous, not dehydrated. It would be fine.

Maybe.

People kept coming over—ostensibly to say hi to someone else at the table—but, somehow, conveniently, ended up getting introduced to her. Like, big god-damn deal, but there wasn't much she could do about it.

"Think you're going to like our little school?" some guy asked, jocose enough for her to find him immediately off-putting.

"It seems very nice," Meg said, politely, not making eye contact. No point in encouraging him. Plus, everyone who approached the table stared at her bad hand, and she had to keep remembering to put it in her lap, out of sight.

Throughout most of this, Jesslyn was telling a very patient Tammy all about some incomprehensible math theorem, which had captured her imagination during their week off, and Meg decided to assume that she was eccentric, rather than disturbed—and also, possibly, some kind of prodigy, given her obvious passion for the subject.

An entire table of guys sitting nearby seemed to spend about ten minutes staring at her, then one of them said something, they all laughed, and a couple of high-fives were exchanged. Meg wanted to cringe, but she kept her face expressionless and made sure to display no reaction at all.

"They're a bunch of jerks," Susan said, softly enough so that Meg was almost sure she was the only one who heard her. "Just ignore them."

Easy for her to say.

"You know the Riemann Hypothesis, right?" Jesslyn said to Tammy, who bit her lip and shook her head—which Jesslyn seemed to find a shocking response.

Mary Elizabeth looked across the table at her. "So. Uh, what are you majoring in?"

Political science, in all likelihood, but she wasn't about to admit it. "I don't know," Meg said. "What are you majoring in?"

"I don't know," Mary Elizabeth said, somewhat defensive.

Meg shrugged. "Okay, then."

A bright light—yes, that inimitable television klieg brightness—came beaming through the windows, and Tammy gasped.

"Are they allowed to do that?" she asked, automatically reaching up to straighten her hair.

"No," Meg said, and frowned at her agents. Paula and Martin were already gone, and Kyle had jumped up to go after them. And Christ, now people were *really* staring. She was tempted to leave, and escape to the relative safety of the dorm, but then that, too, would be filmed for posterity. Or, at least, the next news cycle.

"I suppose they are going to take over the whole campus for the rest of the semester?" Mary Elizabeth asked, sounding hostile.

"I don't know," Meg said, resisting the urge to ask exactly how *big* the campus was. "I certainly hope not."

"I'm sure it's just because it's your first day," Susan said, frowning so slightly at Mary Elizabeth that Meg almost missed it. "It'll die down."

Unless, of course, someone tried to kill her, or something otherwise provocative.

"Oh, come on, Susan," Mary Elizabeth said. "Are you going to tell me that you don't mind—"

This time, Susan's frown wasn't subtle.

When the rest of them had finally finished eating, and they all headed back to the dorm, she was surrounded again, at the edge of the quadrangle. Mary Elizabeth, Jesslyn, and Tammy immediately went into the building, and Susan hesitated, but then followed them.

"How was dinner?" one of the reporters asked, as a lot of microphones came towards her face, and Garth scowled and lifted his hands, gesturing for all of them to move back.

Oh, for God's sakes. And where the hell was Ginette? Why hadn't her father had Maureen stay behind, instead? Or better yet, Preston.

Christ, it would be a treat to see *Linda* right about now. "The duck terrine was a little underdone," Meg said.

Which resulted in the exact reaction of mingled confusion and amusement she'd anticipated.

"You're saying the food is bad?" one of them pressed her.

Typical. Jesus. No god-damn sense of humor. "Absolutely not," Meg said. "The spinach timbales were on the money."

Ginette, who had finally forged her way through the crowd to stand next to her, cleared her throat.

"What?" Meg said. "I mean, you know, they asked."

Ginette raised her voice. "Miss Powers has had a very long day, and she isn't going to take any more questions."

"Good as it was," Meg said quietly, "a meal really isn't a meal without polenta."

The reporters who heard that laughed, and Ginette shot her a look.

"Excuse me," Meg said to the group in general. "I guess I'll see you all later."

Or, preferably, *not*.

"What are you going to be doing now?" someone called out.

Brushing and flossing. "Unpacking," Meg said. And writing them all "Bon Voyage" notes.

"Why didn't the President come here with you today?" one of them wanted to know.

Because of the god-damn media. And because, just possibly, she was busy running the country. "Well, there's our long-standing feud to consider," Meg said, and Ginette glared at her.

A noticeable flurry of excitement ran through the crowd, and they surged closer, with more questions, in an attempt to explore what too many of them were foolish enough to believe might be a scoop. Not a lot of big leaguers out there tonight, apparently.

"Really, I have to go inside now. Good night," Meg said, and ducked into the dorm, leaving Ginette to handle any further questions. Clean up the little mess she'd made.

A gawky guy on his way down the stairs mumbled an indistinct hello, which she returned just as ineptly.

She was just coming out of the bathroom, having, in fact, brushed her teeth, when she met Ginette in the hallway.

"I'll be here in town until the bulk of them leave," she said, tight-lipped and somewhat out of breath, "and from now on, you can just refer all questions directly to me."

Meg moved her jaw. "I don't need anyone to run interference."

"Well, yes," Ginette said, taking off beige calfskin gloves one finger at a time, "I realize that, but—"

But what? Meg looked down at her splint, considering—just considering—losing her temper.

"Sometimes," Ginette seemed to think that she was speaking with great tact, as opposed to being condescending, "people don't realize that the things they say are going to look and sound very different in—"

An Asian-American guy in a rugby shirt, and a much shorter, curly-haired Caucasian guy wearing a Seahawks cap came bursting out of the stairwell, laughing about something, although they stopped when they saw her, ducked their heads, and hurried past them into Sage D.

"I've been doing this for a pretty long time," Meg said, keeping her voice nice and calm. Since she was a damn *toddler*, in fact. "I think I've got it under control."

Ginette started to contradict her, but then nodded.

"But, if you'd feel better," Meg said, calm as can be, "you should run your concerns by Preston. We can go right in my room, and give him a call now, if you want."

Ginette didn't say anything, but she was clearly insulted.

Okay, okay, that was immature. Meg shifted her weight, slipped, and grabbed for the wall—and, to her horror, Ed pretty much *lunged* out of the security room to make sure she was okay. Meg nodded a polite thank you, but edged away so that she could stand on her own, without any support. "Look," she said to Ginette. "I'm really tired, my knee hurts like hell, my hand hurts even more, and I'm feeling a little short-tempered. I know that you—" she glanced at Ed—"all of you—are just trying to help, but I kind of need to figure out a way to live my life, you know?"

Which was going to include popping off to the press now and again.

Ginette nodded.

"Not that I don't appreciate your input," Meg said. No point in having her go back to Washington in a snit about what a bitch the President's god-damned daughter was.

Ginette nodded.

Duly quelled. But she shouldn't have given into the temptation to pull out the "*Preston* trusts me" trump card. "Are you staying at the Inn?" she asked, trying to move the conversation onto more friendly ground. Which was just down the street.

"For the next couple of days, yes," Ginette said.

"Okay," Meg said. "I'm not going to be going out again tonight, and tomorrow, my classes start. Then, on Friday, I have to go to North Adams for physical therapy. Other than that, it'll probably just be a couple of walks down to the dining hall."

All of which she was already dreading.

Ginette nodded.

Too quelled. "Do you think the ravening horde is going to want to come with me?" Meg asked. "To the hospital, I mean."

"Well—" Ginette looked unsure of herself. "I don't know. The ones who are still up here, perhaps."

"Maybe you should ride along with me, just in case," Meg said. Did that sound like an order, or an invitation? "I mean, if you want to, that is."

"Of course," Ginette said, regaining a trace of the normal efficiency in her tone. "Just have someone call over with your schedule whenever it's convenient."

"Okay," Meg said, and limped towards her room. "Good night."

The only thing she felt like doing now, was going to bed, and *staying* there.

14

AS SHE UNLOCKED her door, she was surprised to hear her phone ring. Except, of course, it would be one of her parents, checking in to see how she was. She had a line to use for routine school-related matters, another one for casual friends and acquaintances, and a third extra-secure number to give out only to her closest friends, while the drop-line was reserved solely for her family, and maybe Preston and Dr. Brooks. This seemed to be the third line ringing, which meant that, other than Trudy, it could really only be one person.

"So," Beth said, when she picked up. "*You* were all over the news. And what pretty earrings you had on."

Meg laughed, lifting her leg onto the bed and moving a pillow underneath it from force of habit. Also, because it was throbbing like crazy. "Yeah, I figured you'd notice."

"Instantly," Beth said.

The angle of the pillow made her leg feel worse, and Meg adjusted it.

"So, have you met people yet?" Beth asked. "Are they nice?"

"Well, they seem okay." Meg looked at the half-open door to make sure that no one was within earshot. "It's kind of weird—there's like, *girl stuff* in the bathroom. I mean—I don't know, it seems strange. And it's really loud, hearing voices all over the place."

"Have you told your doctors about these voices?" Beth asked.

Meg decided she was too tired to find that funny. "You know what I mean. I mean, *girls* everywhere."

Beth sighed long-sufferingly. "No one's given you the 'now we're in college, now we're women' speech?"

"No," Meg said. Thank God.

"Besides," Beth went on, "when you get right down to it, Meg, except for your mother and me, how many women do you actually know? I mean, like, to spend time with."

Not too many, now that she thought about it. Or even, any. These days. "Well, Trudy," Meg said uncertainly.

Beth sighed, more deeply.

"Okay, I guess I'm used to mostly men being around," Meg said. Or maybe it was because almost all of the women she knew were so unusually self-confident and overachieving.

"It'll probably do you good," Beth said. "You know, being forced to deal with them for once in your life."

Something about the way that sounded made her want to shudder. "Yeah," Meg said. Fun. "I guess."

Beth laughed. "The next thing you know, you'll be transferring to Smith."

Never happen. "Well, I'll keep you apprised," Meg said. "Anyway, what's going on with you?"

"Well, gosh." Beth paused to think. "The same constant stream of excitement and success."

"How nice for you," Meg said.

After they hung up, her parents called, too, but it made her too homesick to talk to them, so the conversation was rather abbreviated. Yes, they had a good flight home; yes, her dinner was fine; no, her knee was okay, in spite of the snow, and so forth.

It was only nine-thirty.

Maybe she should call Beth back.

No, that would be dumb. Although dumb was something she did very well. Did the *most,* anyway.

She could try lying down, maybe. Take out a couple of the advance-team-procured ice packs, and watch some ESPN or C-Span. Or, maybe—a girl wearing a bright, almost glowing, green Gore-tex jacket swung into the room, supporting her weight by hanging on to the door-jamb with one hand.

"Hi!" she said, like Meg knew her or something. "I'm Juliana."

If she left her door very slightly cracked open, she couldn't expect people to knock. Maybe. "Uh, hi," Meg said.

"I live next door," Juliana said, tossing long blond hair back over her shoulders. "I'm very noisy. I *never* study." She tugged a guy with rumpled brown hair and a sparse mustache into the room. "This is Mark." She pushed him back out. "See you around!" she said, and they disappeared into the room next to hers, Mark giving her a vague wave. Within seconds, some kind of techno-rock came blaring out into the hall, competing with numerous other thumping bass lines—and someone's mournful female folk singer drifting over from the Sage D entry.

"Nice to have met you," Meg said, even though Juliana had long since left. But, the encounter improved her mood, and she limped over to a box full of books and a few DVDs to continue unpacking.

She was organizing the top drawer of her desk, with the astonishing plethora of stationary supplies she'd received for Christmas—and looking, wistfully, at her father's Swiss Army knife, when there was a light knock on the door. Not, she was guessing, Juliana this time.

"You busy?" Susan asked.

Meg shook her head, and closed the drawer. "Not really."

Susan motioned towards the screeching music. "You meet Juliana?"

Meg grinned. "Yeah."

Susan grinned, too. "Every dorm needs one." Then, she tapped the orientation packet, which was still sitting on top of the desk, untouched. "You go through any of that stuff yet?"

Date rate and bulimia. Also, condoms. Meg nodded, although, of course, she hadn't.

Susan shrugged. "Some of it's worthwhile, some of it isn't."

Which she had figured out already, without even opening it.

"I'm guessing you're extra-informed on the various—social ills," Susan said.

And had even gone on-the-record with a number of them. Meg nodded.

Susan returned the nod, then put her hands in her pockets. "You'd be surprised by some of the things even smart people don't know. I think the school just wants to be sure its bases are covered."

Litigiously speaking, no doubt.

Susan, who seemed almost as uncomfortable as she was, leaned against the wall and folded her arms. "You're all set for classes?"

Thanks to the White House minions. They had even gone ahead

and purchased all of the textbooks she was going to need. Without having been requested to do so, of course. Meg nodded.

"Your advisor's name is in your packet somewhere," Susan said. "You should stop by to see him or her tomorrow, go over things. And you'll have to take the Quantitative Studies exam, and maybe some of the placement exams, if you want."

Meg nodded—since it seemed to be the only thing she still remembered how to do. For the time being, the college had waived her mandatory swim test, at least. Her advisor was someone in the English department. A woman, which was unsurprising, considering her recent negative encounters with male medical personnel, about which one and all would have been briefed. "Does it matter if it's not something I'm going to major in?"

Susan shook her head. "The assignments are pretty random. They figure everyone's going to change majors a few times, before they settle down."

"Did you?" Meg asked.

Susan nodded. "God, yes. Right now, I'm double-majoring in English and history, but I went through drama, political science, classics, and even psychology for a while." She paused. "I still sometimes think about going back to drama."

"So, that's normal?" Meg asked, tentatively.

"If it isn't, I'm in trouble," Susan said. She started to unfold her arms, hesitated, and refolded them. "What are you going to be taking?"

Which seemed awfully personal. "Do you have to approve it?" Meg asked.

Susan laughed. "No, I was just curious. You don't have to tell me."

Oh. Well, there wasn't really any good reason to keep it a secret, since Ginette was probably going to release some of the details to the press tomorrow. "Well, intro things," Meg said. Should she be more specific? Probably. "Uh, psychology, the political science one about democracy, Shakespeare, philosophy—you know. Basic stuff."

Susan nodded. "That sounds good. How early do you have to get up?"

"Well, political science is at eight-thirty," Meg said.

Susan winced.

She was having her own doubts about the wisdom of having signed up for a course about the three branches of government and policy-making, but she didn't want someone else to *share* them. "Why, is that bad?" she asked, worried.

"No," Susan said. "It's just—early."

Hard to argue with that, yeah.

Susan nodded towards the remaining boxes. "You need help unpacking?"

A genuine offer, or was she fishing for something? Trying to curry favor? Meg frowned. "No, I—" Christ, she was just trying to be *nice*. Hospitable. Neighborly, even. "Thanks, but I'm all set."

"Okay." Susan straightened up, her hands going into her pockets again. "It's none of my business, but do they bother you? The press, I mean. Or are you used to it?"

Meg shrugged. "Both, I guess."

"You have to wonder," Susan said, sounding almost as though she were talking to herself, "about the kind of person who would *want* to do that for a living. There's something very—savage—about it."

"I guess Woodward and Bernstein went to everyone's heads, back in the day," Meg said, grimly. "And, hey, the whole world wants to be famous, right?" God only knew why.

Susan nodded, looking preoccupied. "Seems that way, yeah."

Hmmm. There was something else going on here, but Meg couldn't figure out what it was.

"Anyway," Susan said. "Anything you want to ask? Or, I don't know? Talk about?"

It must suck to have to serve as an officially designated friend. "Are people going to hate me?" Meg asked, taking a guess about what might be bothering her—and was probably *infuriating* Mary Elizabeth. "Because of all the reporters and the disruption and everything?"

Susan shook her head. "Some of them have preconceptions, that's all. About what you're going to be like."

Status quo, then. "Do you?" Meg asked.

Susan blushed. "Yeah. But I'm trying to rise above them."

Okay. That was honest. She might as well be equally direct. "Am I living up to the preconceptions?" Meg asked.

"Well—my father would say you're a cool customer," Susan said.

Ouch. Meg narrowed her eyes. "What would he mean by that, exactly?"

Susan considered that. "I'm not really sure, when you get right down to it."

Still, it probably wasn't praise. "He seems really nice." Meg glanced at the hallway to make sure no one was out there within listening distance. "But what about Dirk? Does he always make you do all of the work?"

Susan smiled, and Meg suddenly wondered if she seemed familiar because she had something of a political smile, which didn't always make it up to her eyes. "Truth?" she asked.

Well, that wasn't exactly a political strategy. Meg nodded, uneasily.

"He was sort of intimidated, because you look even more like her in person," Susan said. "And he's shy sometimes, anyway."

An odd trait in a JA, but okay. And she *wasn't* so damn sure she looked that much like her mother, either. Certainly, she hadn't inherited the sense of style, or the élan.

The techno-rock stopped playing, and Juliana replaced it with a monotonous dance mix.

"She's happy to turn it down, if you ask," Susan said. "I mean, if it drives you crazy."

Meg shrugged. "My brother listens to rap and heavy metal most of the time—this seems pretty benign." Often, for multiple stereo effect, Steven would play the same song that was also being shown on MTV, both at top volume. When he couldn't get them synchronized right, which was almost always the case, it was very irritating. Especially to her father.

"Well, if it bothers you, don't be shy about telling her," Susan said. "Juliana is impossible to offend."

Suggesting that someone—or maybe, *many* someones—had tried. Meg nodded.

It was quiet.

"Are you a breakfast person?" Susan asked.

Meg shook her head. Never had been, never would be.

"Well—I'm not, either," Susan said. "But if you're up, and looking for someone to go with, come down and knock on my door."

An extremely unlikely scenario. Except, she *hated* that god-damn word. The guy had used it—"Worst scenario, I start *liking* you," the night they got drunk together—and ever since then, hearing it, or even thinking it, was—"Great," Meg said. "If I'm up, I'll do that. Thanks."

Susan must have picked up on the tension in her voice, because she retreated towards the door. "Okay, good. I'll, uh, maybe I'll see you later, then."

Meg nodded, aware that her face had started perspiring, and trying to repress the massive wave of fear she had just inflicted upon herself.

After Susan had—rather hastily—left, she stuck it out for another couple of hours, aimlessly unpacking and icing her knee and hand, until it seemed late enough for her to get away with turning her light off for the night. She felt shy about venturing out to the bathroom, especially since everyone else seemed to have visitors wandering in and out of their rooms, and to be having fun being back at school.

She was so tired that her toothbrush felt heavy. She'd stuck her tiny stash of remaining prescription painkillers in her knapsack, and she popped one while she was in the bathroom, hoping to hell that it was going to work. Quickly. She might have been lonely at home, but Christ, at least she'd had something resembling *privacy*.

Making her way over to the door was improbably exhausting, and she kept her eyes down, not wanting to have to talk to anyone, or—worse—meet anyone new.

Tammy was on her way in, but she stopped to look at her. "Are you all right?"

Did she fucking look all right? She wanted to be alone. She wanted to be *home*. "I'm fine, thank you," Meg said, and limped past her, having to use the wall as a guide, since she hadn't had enough energy to bring her cane along.

"D-do you need help?" Tammy asked.

"No. Thanks," Meg said, went into her room, and closed the door. Almost slammed it.

This stupid place was unbelievably noisy. She was surrounded by strangers. Everything hurt like hell. And if she were home, she would—absolutely, positively, without any doubt—be sobbing right now.

SHE LAY IN the dark, trying to sleep, for a very long time. Missing her family. Missing her *cat*. Even in its new position, she hated this bed. It felt—horribly familiar. The frame, the not very good mattress, the slightly dusty smell, all of it. When they had been on the phone, her mother had suggested that they arrange to have a new replacement bed delivered, and she wanted to say yes, but was afraid it would make her seem too much like the damn Princess and the Pea to the rest of the dorm. No point in measuring up to their worst expectations, if she could avoid it.

Trudy's quilt, at least, was familiar in a good way, and she pulled it closer. The room seemed musty, and she didn't like its shape, or the bare walls, or the way light came in underneath the door and at the edges of the extra-heavy—probably bullet-resistant—window shades. She was cold. Scared. She wanted Vanessa.

Finally, she was starting to doze off, when she heard low male laughter, very close to her door. She stiffened, feeling around for anything nearby that she could use as a weapon, trying to remember exactly where the new panic button was. Oh, God. Oh, God, he was here. Somehow, he had found out exactly where she was—probably just by turning on the damn television, and—a female voice was saying something now, and she realized that it was only Juliana and Mark saying good-night.

Okay. Okay. There were agents—and reporters—all over the place, and odds were, no one was coming up here to kill her. Not tonight, anyway.

She tensed and released her muscles, trying to relax. To go back to sleep. *Not* to cry nervous reaction tears.

And, at all three of these things, she was only modestly successful.

She had even more nightmares than she would have predicted in a moment of profound pessimism, and at one point, woke up crying very hard, sitting straight up in bed, putting much too much weight on her splint, and as she slowly figured out where she was—and *wasn't*—she hoped to hell that she hadn't screamed. Or, if she had, that no one had heard her.

Around daybreak, she gave up on sleep completely, and lay there, staring at the ceiling, the smoke detector, the ugly round light, and the empty walls, swallowing another pain pill dry—which made her miss the dependable pitchers of ice water she normally found on her bedside table. Here, she didn't even *have* a bedside table.

There was juice and milk and soda crammed into her little refrigerator, but she felt too sluggish and tired to give any serious consideration to dragging herself over to get a drink. So, she pressed her good arm across her face, to make the room seem darker, and to try and prevent herself from doing any more crying. As it was, she was going to be attending her first classes, and meeting her advisor—and dealing with the god-damn media—with red, swollen eyes, making the reality of her long, sleepless night, and pathetic loneliness, all the more obvious.

She stayed in bed until almost seven o'clock, then decided she might as well get up. The doctors had molded her a new waterproof plastic brace, complete with drainage holes, so she could take showers more easily now, but it was still a slow and painful ordeal, every single time. Not that the shower bench in the handicapped stall had much appeal, either.

The thing to do, was go out and make sure the bathroom was free. Her knee was very stiff, and her left hip was aching for some reason, too. All of those damned stairs, probably. When he saw her, Jose, the agent on duty in the security room, straightened up behind his desk, and they exchanged good mornings. Then, she established that the bathroom was empty, and hurried back to her room to get soap and shampoo and all.

She wasn't sure what people wore to the shower in college. In movies, they always seemed to have on flip-flops and artfully-draped towels. Her terry-cloth bathrobe would have to do. Her family had never been inclined to wander about casually in pajamas, forget towels. As a rule, they all liked to be *dressed*. Even in Chestnut Hill, with no witnesses around, they had generally been somewhat formal. And she hated slippers, so she always used an old pair of Top-Siders, instead.

As she limped back out to the hall, she ran into Mary Elizabeth, who was carrying a large towel and wearing a red corduroy bathrobe. They stopped, and looked at each other.

Meg took a step back, and had to catch herself against the wall, when her left foot refused to cooperate. "Uh, sorry. I mean, I don't know how it works."

"We take turns," Mary Elizabeth said, "how do you *think* it works?"

Yeah, she maybe should have figured out that one on her own. But this girl was certainly going out of her way to piss her off, wasn't she. "Sorry. Just trying to be polite." Meg turned to go into her room. On the other hand. She turned back. "Am I wrong, or do you seem to have a problem with me?"

Mary Elizabeth scowled. "I don't have a problem."

Right. "Good," Meg said. "Hope we keep it that way." Maybe her parents hated her mother or something.

Mary Elizabeth's scowl eased into—a mere frown. "Look. There are two showers in there, it's not like—"

Meg shook her head. "No, it's okay, I'll wait until later. I need to make a phone call, anyway." Yeah, right. At seven-fifteen.

It wasn't a very relaxing way to start the morning, and if her father had known that she was skipping breakfast, too, he would have said that that was no way to improve her day. A gaggle of reporters met her on her way to her political science class, but Ginette had come over from the Inn to deal with them, and her agents were working with the local and campus police to force them off campus property to whatever degree possible. Meg kept to herself, saying nothing more than a friendly "Good morning, nice to see you," while moving past them.

The class had about thirty people, all of whom seemed edgy—including the professor—about having her spend the next semester in a room where the Presidency was going to be discussed, and quite probably criticized, on a regular basis. She took a seat in the back of the room, and spent most of the class period wondering if she should drop the course, and take something else—except that she *wanted* to study political science, and hell, she was paying tuition, too. Or, at any rate, her parents were paying it.

So she just sat quietly and read the syllabus and took detailed notes—in a brand-new purple Williams College notebook someone on the advance team had purchased. They had to write their names, local phone numbers, and email addresses on the class roster sheet, and she left her phone number blank, because she couldn't actually remember which one she was supposed to use for things like that. When she passed the roster along, the people next to her noticed that she hadn't filled that section out, and exchanged glances, which might have been a sign of disapproval, or might just have been curiosity.

Once the class ended, she went to meet with her academic advisor, who was a literature professor, with a special interest in women's studies. Dr. Nyler was rather entertainingly gender-obsessed, and very disappointed that she hadn't signed up for any feminist courses, because she was sure Meg would have many fascinating insights to contribute.

Oh, no doubt.

It was barely eleven o'clock, and she wasn't sure she could make it any longer without lying down for a while, but she had to go to her Philosophy class, which was small enough to sit at a seminar table. To her horror, the professor went around the room, asking them each to say their names, where they were from, and tell a little about themselves.

When it was her turn, she just said that her name was Meg, she was from the Boston area, originally, and that she was a freshman. The professor, who seemed sweet, if a tad addled, nodded encouragingly, as though she might be inclined to share more, but Meg sat back and motioned for the guy next to her to go ahead and introduce himself.

One of her agents was in a chair in the far corner—in high school, they had always stayed outside in the corridor, or down in the command center—and the professor pretty much proved that he was a flake, when he turned towards him with an expectant look on his face, after everyone else had spoken. Her agent looked panic-stricken for a second—which she found funny, and also, alarming—and then said that his name was Brian, and he was from Washington, DC. "Splendid, splendid," the professor said, and began to hand out syllabuses. Brian must have wanted to avoid trouble, or long explanations, because he accepted one without a word, folding the paper neatly and sticking it in his pocket.

After that, she had to spend some time in the Dean's Office, being welcomed by a steady stream of college administrators and faculty members, and then sitting in an empty room to fumble her way through the requisite Quantitative Studies exam.

She hadn't had anything close to a full meal since that last dinner back at the White House, so she knew she had to *force* herself to go to the dining hall and get some lunch, even though she had no appetite at all. The student center, which was right near her dorm, was supposed to serve food, but she was too shy to go in there by herself, so she made the slow, snowy trek down to Mission, instead.

The place was mobbed, and without the buffer of a kindly JA and three reluctant hallmates, she almost left. Today, at least, she *did* have her sunglasses, and she kept them on as she waited in line. Made it a little hard to see but that seemed like a minor price to pay.

A few people said hello to her, and she nodded in response. It seemed—opportunistic. Or, possibly, friendly.

Her stomach hurt so much that she didn't feel safe taking anything more than a cup of mushroom barley soup and some crackers and a Coke—part of which she spilled as she made her way to an empty table. Brian sat there, too, with a cup of coffee, for which she felt pitifully grateful. Not that they were apt to have much of a conversation, but it was still a nice gesture. Hard to tell, at this point, if she was setting the tone, or if it was mutual.

"Pretty cold out there," she said, after a couple of silent minutes.

Brian nodded. "Sure is."

"I hear you're from Washington," she said, and he smiled, but didn't respond any further.

So much for that. Meg started eating her soup, the spoon wavering in her hand. She could feel that her shoulders were hunched—and likely to remain so—and wondered if everyone in the crowded room was staring at her. Surely not. But, it definitely felt that way.

So far, it seemed pretty clear that deciding she was ready to go away to college by herself had been one *hell* of a mistake.

15

TWO SPOONFULS OF the soup were enough to make her feel so sick that she decided to give up and retreat to the dorm for the rest of the day. People would notice that she had rushed out, alone, after only about five minutes—but, it was preferable to the dreaded notion of vomiting in public.

"Hi!" a very happy voice said. "Can I sit here?"

Juliana. Who put her tray down before Meg had a chance to say anything.

"Can my friends sit here, too?" she asked, and turned to summon them without waiting for an answer.

Mark and two other guys carried their trays over, boisterously selecting seats. The friends were scruffy in the same way Mark was—ripped jeans, flapping unlaced hiking boots, flannel shirts, shapeless old sweatshirts, wispy attempts at mustaches, and—in one guy's case—an actual full beard.

"This is Simon," Juliana indicated the guy with the beard, "and this is Harry," she pointed at the one who had only managed a thin mustache and a small patch of hair below his lower lip.

"*Skipper*," Simon corrected her. "Everyone calls me Skipper."

Mark laughed. "You wish everyone called you Skipper."

Simon looked at Meg. He was a brawny guy, with lots of bushy brown hair. "They do call me that," he said. "It suits me."

"Get yourself a little sailor's hat," Harry—long narrow face, pale blond hair, and inescapably preppy in spite of his best efforts—said. "And then we'll see."

"I crew boats all the time," Simon insisted. "Every summer."

Harry nodded, downing one of his three glasses of milk. "Yup. Sailboats galore in Indiana."

"You know it," Simon said, and turned to Meg. "Remember, it's *Skipper.*"

She nodded, tightening her hand around one of her little packets of saltines. Crushing them, as a matter of fact.

He motioned towards the soup. "That's all you're eating?"

"Not if you don't give her a *chance* to eat it," Juliana said. She had a pulled pork sandwich, a spoonful of succotash, and an orange on her plate, while the other three had each taken several sandwiches, along with huge portions of french fries.

"Well," Simon shrugged, "she looks very slim. Maybe bigger, and more balanced, meals are something she should be thinking about."

"Let her eat, for Christ's sakes," Harry said, already well into his second sandwich, dripping barbecue sauce everywhere.

Sitting there, so tense that the saltines were now powder, Meg tried to think of something she disliked more than being the center of attention. Luckily, Mark had started talking about some genetics course he was going to be taking, and whether it was too much work to be worth the trouble. It developed that he and Harry were both pre-med, and they discussed various science requirements and academic strategies, while Juliana made cracks about the twisted concept of being devoted to one's studies. This was, evidently, a conversation they had all had a number of times before.

Simon nudged her. "It's not, you know, bad, to be thin. I mean, like, I have sisters, right? And, all they eat are rice cakes, right? So, I was just commenting, not, you know, criticizing. In case, I don't know, you're sensitive or whatever."

"How did you get *in* to this school?" Harry asked. "What'd you get, four hundreds, maybe, on your SATs?"

Simon didn't even look slightly offended. "Diversity, man. The place wants diversity."

"Yeah, well, then, go to *Wesleyan,*" Harry said, and even Meg laughed.

She let them all talk, contributing nothing more than the occasional nod or smile, if it seemed to be indicated. Her soup, still barely touched, had gotten pretty cold, but when Juliana went up to the front to get a cup of milky, heavily-sugared coffee, and brought one back for her, too, she was surprised by how good it tasted.

"So, like, how bad's your leg?" Simon asked, eating french fries three at a time. "Ligaments, cartilage, the whole deal?"

Nerve damage and bone chips, too. Which Dr. Steiner, her primary orthopedic surgeon, had described as "troubling multiple avulsions." Meg nodded.

And this would be a really bad time to start thinking about how close the kicks had come to killing her.

"It hurts lots?" he asked.

She nodded. Hardly the proper, politic reaction, but—too late now.

"And you walked on that puppy?" he said. "In the woods and all?"

Walked, staggered, crawled. Entirely unaware that she was courting a fatal arterial rupture with every single movement. Meg shrugged, hoping he would change the subject.

Juliana was already frowning at him. "Eat your lunch, Simon."

"Yeah, but that was *hero* shit," he said. "That was pretty cool. And her hand and all? *Serious* hero shit. I mean," he gave Meg a wide, infectious grin, "way to go! It was something."

"Well," Meg said, and looked down at her coffee.

"I mean, maybe people aren't supposed to mention it," he said, "but *I* think it was cool."

Meg tried to smile, her face feeling very hot. "Well, that's very nice of you, Skipper, but I—I'd really rather—"

"She wants you to put a sock in it," Harry said.

Precisely.

"Okay." Simon shrugged, undaunted. "Just wanted to tell you."

Ideally, he would not feel the need to do so again.

But, it had been pretty nice to hear.

SHE WAS VERY pleased, the next morning, to find out that her psychology class was large enough to meet in a big lecture hall, and that the professor had no interest in having them introduce themselves. Unfortunately, the same did not hold true for her Shakespeare class—and when she told them her name was Meg, someone actually said, "Hey, wait, no, it's supposed to be Meghan," and most of the rest of the people in the room nodded. Since a guy named Jim hadn't described himself as "James," and another guy named Bill hadn't said "William," she wasn't sure why she fell under different rules, but merely said that they could all call her whichever one they preferred.

It was almost a relief when it was time to go over to North Adams for physical therapy, with Ginette in tow. A few reporters were following along, and advance word had it that others were waiting in a hastily assembled "media area," at the hospital, to film her arrival. Christ.

Once they got there, a number of hospital officials came out to meet and greet her, and "show her the facilities." Then, she met still more people—nurses and doctors and therapists, with everyone being "brought up to speed," in great detail, on her condition. Or lack thereof. Which, to her way of thinking, kind of violated patient confidentiality, in the extreme.

By the time she had to start doing the physical therapy itself—her new hand therapist was named Cheryl; her knee therapist was Vicky—she was too drained to want to have anything to do with the ever grueling exercises. But, the hospital was enforcing a "No Media" rule inside, much to her relief, so except for an audience of orthopedists, two neurologists, and a physiatrist, she was able to toil away in partial obscurity.

"I'm sure it won't be like that next time," Ginette said, after they had negotiated past the group of remaining press stragglers outside, and were riding back to Williamstown.

Better not be. Meg nodded.

"It—" Ginette hesitated. "It looked very painful. The therapy, I mean."

Meg nodded, and they rode the rest of the way without speaking.

She couldn't face the idea of going out again that night—so, she didn't, by simply telling Tammy a "no, thanks, I already ate" fib. Tammy didn't question this, even though the dining hall had just barely opened for dinner, and the odds of Meg already having been there and back were unlikely.

Later, Susan and Dirk each stopped by to see how, and what, she was doing—upon which she pretended she had been deeply engrossed by reading *King Lear*. Josh called from Stanford to say hello, and later on, Neal called, and her father came on the line to say hi, too. Meg lied to all of them, saying, "yeah, everything's fine, I'm having fun, I like it a lot." Then, she—fuck it—covered the telephones with a thick pillow, so she could ignore them if they rang again. If the Leader of the Free World couldn't reach her for a few hours, *too bad*.

She spent the weekend keeping a very low profile, mostly staying in her room and studying. On Sunday night, there was an entry meeting in the second-floor common room, complete with snacks, with attendance just short of being mandatory. So, she went, allowing Susan to drag her around for a few minutes to meet people, because it was easier than refusing.

The meeting dissolved into an impromptu party, but she made polite excuses and returned to her room to stare at CNN. It was a little unsettling, whenever her mother popped onto the screen for one reason or another, but also strangely comforting, too. Made her feel slightly less homesick.

Late that night, she had an incredibly bad dream about—well, she wasn't exactly sure of the details, but it had definitely been frightening. She had had nightmares every night since arriving on campus, but this was one of the wake-up-shouting ones. As usual, when she opened her eyes, she wasn't sure where she was, but she could tell from the raw feeling in her throat that she'd screamed. Loudly.

There was an urgent pounding on the door. "Meg?" a male voice said. "Are you all right in there?"

Agents. School. Oh, Christ. "I'm fine," she said weakly.

"You sure?" It sounded like Ronald. Or maybe Dave, or Larry. "I'm sorry, but can you open up for just a second?"

If she didn't, he would probably break the door down or some damn thing, so she hauled herself up, pulling on an old Stowe sweatshirt over her sweatpants and "In Bill We Trust" Patriots t-shirt. Then she opened the door to see a very concerned-looking Ronald.

"I'm all right." She realized that her face was damp, as though she'd been crying in her sleep, and quickly wiped her eyes with her sleeve. "It was a bad dream, that's all."

"I'm sorry," he said. "I'll just take a quick peek inside, okay?"

What, in case some evil person hiding behind the door had made her say that under duress? She moved aside to let him go past her, and saw—acutely embarrassed—that Mary Elizabeth and Jesslyn, and a couple of people from Sage D, the next entry over, were all in the hall. Then, Juliana's door opened, and she and Mark came out.

Juliana yawned. "What's going on?"

"I really apologize," Meg said, knowing how awful she must look, so humiliated that she thought she might die on the spot. "I—" she felt as though she might be running a fever, too—"I have nightmares sometimes. I hope I didn't disturb anyone." A pretty stupid remark, considering that they were all standing there—and now, Tammy was on her way out of her room, too, making it a clean sweep of the entire third floor.

"Did something happen?" she asked, looking confused when she saw how many people were in the corridor.

"It's a party," Juliana said. "Guess we should have invited you."

Tammy must have still been half-asleep, because she looked even more confused.

Ronald left Meg's room, patting her on the shoulder. "Excuse me," he said to Tammy, and moved past her, back to his desk.

Normally, she wouldn't have been too thrilled about having one of her agents touch her, but this situation was an exception. She needed a pat on the shoulder.

Hell, she needed a *hug*. And for one of her parents to pour her a fresh glass of water, and sponge her face off with a cool washcloth.

"So, you're okay?" Juliana asked.

Meg nodded, bright red.

"Well. Good night," Mary Elizabeth said, and headed back to her room, Tammy and Jesslyn following suit.

It made things worse to realize that they all knew she had been crying, and she limped towards the bathroom to wash her face. She stayed in there for quite a while, out of sheer embarrassment, and when she came out, Juliana and Mark were gone, but Susan was leaning against the wall, in raggedy cut-off blue sweatpants, Nikes, and a Falmouth Road Race t-shirt.

"Hi," she said.

Christ, had one of the others picked up the phone and asked her to hurry upstairs—or had the screaming been that loud?

"I just wanted to make sure you were all right," Susan said.

Meg nodded. "Perfectly fine, thank you." The fact that she felt lost and afraid and alone was really no one's god-damn business.

"Are you really?" Susan asked.

Meg nodded.

"Okay, as long as you're sure," Susan said, sounding as though she didn't believe her at all. "You going to be able to get back to sleep?"

Not a chance in hell, but Meg nodded. "Um, you couldn't actually *hear* me, could you?"

Susan hesitated, which answered the question.

Great.

"It's no big deal," Susan said. "I was already awake."

At four in the morning? Yeah. Sure.

"I was just—I usually don't sleep that much," Susan said. "So, I was reading. Anyway. Feel like hanging out for a while?"

God, *yes*. But, they barely knew each other at all, and what would they talk about? The vicissitudes of post-traumatic stress disorder? Meg shook her head. "No, that's okay. Thanks."

"Well, I'll see you later, then," Susan said.

Meg nodded, closed her door—and turned on C-Span.

OVER THE NEXT few days, it happened almost every night. Fortunately, it wasn't always screaming, but it *was* always crying. And if she yelled, her agents felt compelled to check things out—or at least have her open the door briefly, immediately destroying the tiny illusion of privacy she'd managed to create for herself by spending so much time in her room.

Maybe the thing to do, would be to make a habit of sleeping through dinner, so she'd be awake at night, and wouldn't keep bothering everyone else.

She *wanted* to pick up the phone, call her parents, and beg to come home. Say that it had been too soon, she wasn't ready, she'd try again next year. Georgetown, maybe. Not someplace so far away. On the other hand, she would just end up sitting by herself in her room in the White House—and she might as well sit alone here in Williamstown.

She figured out pretty quickly that breakfast was the least crowded meal, so she decided that it was her favorite, because she had to do *some* eating. Coffee was rapidly turning into her new best friend, and she'd even found the nerve to start venturing into Goodrich, where there was a coffee bar, to buy lattes once or twice a day. Then, when she had to go get some money out of the cash machine at her new bank on Spring Street—sort of a foreign experience—she discovered a coffeehouse nearby, and ducked in to get yet more caffeine to go—an impulse promptly recorded by a couple of bored photographers hanging out across the street.

A lot of people tried to start conversations with her—after class, in the dining hall, near the mailboxes, while other people would see her and promptly head in the opposite direction. Seemed excessive, in both cases. And the damned Frisbee boys somehow always managed to catch sight of her, and hurl the stupid thing in her direction. Her agents didn't like it much. The Mr. California guy was in her psychology class, and he invariably sat in the middle of a group of girls who didn't seem to realize that they were fawning over him. Frankly, she questioned their taste in men.

Jesslyn spent hours hunched over her computer in her room, playing poker and blackjack on the Internet, and rarely interacted much with anyone, and Mary Elizabeth, of course, had yet to be friendly, but lately, Tammy seemed to be avoiding her, and even Juliana was sort of keeping her distance, which was depressing.

She was lying on her bed, resting from physical therapy, an ice pack tucked inside her brace and another one on top of her hand, when there was a knock on the door. It would be nice if the person went away, but when there was a second knock, she grimly got up.

"Hi," Susan said, her hair wet from the shower, so she must have just returned from one of her daily runs, or a karate workout—Dirk had mentioned to her that Susan was a 2nd kyu brown belt, which was hard to picture, considering how small and, at first glance, unthreatening she was. "I'm going over to meet a friend of mine at Dodd—" another one of the dining halls, in one of the most desirable dorms on campus—"for dinner. Feel like coming along?"

Meg shook her head. "Thanks, but I've already eaten."

Susan looked at her watch. "The hell you did."

Oh. Meg frowned at her. "I had a late lunch."

"*During* physical therapy?" Susan said.

Exactly who did she think she was? "Is it any of your god-damn business?" Meg asked, making an effort to keep her voice civil. A weak effort.

"As a matter of fact, it is," Susan said. "This is what JAs do."

"Yeah, well, don't worry, I'll give you a good evaluation," Meg said.

Susan sighed, and ran a hand back through her hair. "Meg, I was only—"

"Who asked you to?" Meg said.

Susan didn't back down. "Thought it up *all by myself*."

Yeah, well, screw her.

"Look, I'm sure you're really tired," Susan said, sounding pretty tired herself, "but not eating isn't going to—"

"You don't know me," Meg said. "You can't tell me what to do."

Susan's expression tightened. "You don't know me, either. There's a chance I might know what I'm talking about."

Yeah, right. "And maybe you don't," Meg said. *Definitely*, she didn't. "I just want to be left alone. Okay?"

Susan raised her hands. "Okay. Fine. My mistake."

For a second, Meg felt guilty, but then she was just angry and exhausted, so she closed her door and went back over to lie down. And slap a pillow over the telephones. It would probably be best if she didn't speak to anyone else right now—or go near her email, either.

She was half-asleep when there was another knock on the door. She shook herself awake, and limped over to answer it.

Susan tossed her something wrapped in napkins, which Meg automatically caught left-handed. "Good hands," Susan said, and left without another word.

Meg didn't move for a minute, then opened the napkins to find a peanut butter and jelly sandwich. And Christ, she was pretty hungry.

Pretty ashamed of herself, too.

She put the sandwich on her desk, then went downstairs to knock on Susan's already-ajar door. She and Dirk had rooms right next to each other, which opened onto a large, generally occupied common room—which, at this very moment, had three of the guys from the entry gathered around the television, playing some loud video game with lots of flashing lights.

"Um, thanks," she said.

Susan, who was stuffing books into an old red knapsack, shrugged. "No problem. Make sure you eat it."

Meg shifted her position, forgetting that her leg was going to buckle. It promptly did, and she changed back to her right leg. "I, uh—" An apology was due here. "Funny thing, my ears were kind of burning while you were at dinner."

Susan grinned. "I bet they were."

Right. "Anyway, I'm sorry," Meg said. Which, on the whole, she was.

Susan put the knapsack down. "Meg, I know you're having a hard time, but I can't stand around and let you starve yourself, you know?"

Meg checked to make sure the guys were completely occupied by their video game, because she sure as hell didn't want anyone overhearing *that*.

"Go ahead and close the door," Susan said.

What, like she wanted to have some long stressful talk about Her Problems, or some damn thing? No way. "I'm just tired from physical therapy, that's all," Meg said. "It isn't any more complicated than that."

Susan shook her head. "Bullshit."

Even if all four of her limbs worked properly, it might not be a good idea to smack someone who studied karate.

Tempting as it might be.

Susan frowned, and then walked over to close the door herself.

Swell. Was she being imprisoned now? Time to pull out the fucking panic button, maybe.

"I'm not going to push you, Meg," Susan said. "Because—well, I don't like it when people do it to me. But if there's anything you feel like talking about, I want you to know that you always can. Anything at all. Any *time* at all."

What, she was suddenly going to spill her guts to someone she scarcely knew? Yeah, right. "Thanks, but I'm fine," Meg said. "I'm a little tired, and maybe a little homesick. Nothing too interesting. Just wanted to thank you for the sandwich, that's all."

Susan looked frustrated, but she nodded.

"Well," Meg reached back to open the door, "I have a lot of reading to do tonight, so I'd better get moving." Except, maybe she should smooth the waters, a little. "And even though it's entirely misplaced, I really do appreciate your concern."

A pleasantry which seemed to make Susan furious, although in a very repressed way, her lips tightening so much that they almost disappeared.

"What?" Meg asked.

Susan shook her head, turning away to sort through a few papers on her desk.

"You don't have to edit around me," Meg said. "What was it you *felt* like saying?"

Susan's eyes narrowed. "You really want to know?"

On second thought, maybe not—but, Meg nodded.

"I was thinking that she taught you well," Susan said, "didn't she."

Nice. Besides, it couldn't be taught; a person was god-damn *born* with it.

Although one thing her mother had, unintentionally, passed along to her was the ability to give someone an "if I didn't think it would bore me beyond description, I would arrange to have you blown off the face of the earth" look. She had almost never seen that look—and had used it herself even more rarely—but that didn't mean that she didn't know how. Maybe she couldn't do karate, or even stand on her own two feet, but that didn't mean that she was *entirely* without resources. "You have a problem with the President?" Meg asked.

Even though she had just been the recipient of a fleeting, but distinctly wintry and contemptuous stare, Susan didn't seem to be at all phased. "No," she said evenly. "Not with the President."

Okay. *That* was blunt. And it would be nice if they genuinely liked each other, but it certainly wasn't *required*. "Well." Meg opened the door. "I'm sorry if I offended you. It wasn't my intent."

Susan sighed. "Meg—"

"Excuse me," Meg said, and headed for the stairwell and back up to the third floor.

SHE HAD ONLY choked down half of her sandwich, when her father called, and after that, Trudy and Beth did, too. She kept the conversations on the usual optimistic, if fallacious, "everything's just peachy" level. Not that any of them bought it, probably.

There wasn't much to do, so she tried to study, but couldn't concentrate. She was pretty thirsty from the peanut butter, and went out to the bathroom to get some water.

Mary Elizabeth was already in there, washing her face. She saw Meg, nodded briefly, and kept scrubbing away.

Meg drank a full mug of water, and refilled it. "Hi."

Mary Elizabeth nodded, smoothing on some kind of expensive face cream.

Meg finished off the second mug. "Pretty quiet around here tonight."

Mary Elizabeth nodded.

Scintillating. She filled the mug a third time, so she would be able to make some instant coffee in her microwave.

"A lot of reporters still around," Mary Elizabeth said, washing and buffing away.

Okay, she'd had *just* about enough of that. Of everything. Especially since the press had mostly gone away, except for the odd stringer or feature writer here and there, and the ever-insatiable paparazzi, who never failed to pop up at unexpected moments in their endless attempts to capture her in potentially scandalous or newsworthy situations. "It's a death-watch," Meg said. "They want to make sure they're on the scene, in case I get killed." She paused—undeniably, for effect.

Mary Elizabeth stared at her.

"Doesn't really make you want to walk around near me, *does it*," Meg said.

Mary Elizabeth wiped her face with a towel, not noticing that she hadn't washed off all of the cleansing cream yet. "I didn't know that's what they were for," she said quietly.

"That's what they're for," Meg said. "Hope you aren't inconvenienced by them."

As she went back out to the hall, she ran into Juliana, who was bopping down the hall, not a book in hand.

"Hi, Bucko," she said, chipper as can be. "What are you up to tonight?"

"Trying to piss off the whole entry," Meg said. "I already got Susan and Mary Elizabeth, and I figured I'd go after you and Tammy next."

Juliana looked in the direction of Tammy's partially open door, where—judging from the sounds of animated, one-sided conversation, she was on the phone. Or else, she was deeply, irrevocably, psychologically disturbed. Then she looked back at Meg. "Takes a lot to piss *me* off."

Meg shrugged. "I could probably do it." *Easily.*

Juliana laughed. "Hey, go for it." Then she looked more serious. "How'd you manage to bug Susan? She's like, Miss Mellow."

Miss hot-blooded Irish temper Mellow. "I was rude and arrogant," Meg said. "Worked like a charm."

Juliana nodded. "Okay. I can see how that might." She started to open her door, then paused. "I can't picture Susan mad."

"She was polite about it," Meg said.

"Oh." Juliana nodded. "Well, that's all right, then."

There was no question but that Juliana operated on a different frequency.

However, if Beth's planet turned out to be full, she might not mind getting a visa to visit Juliana's for a while.

Both planets seemed to be a hell of a lot nicer than the one she lived on.

16

BEFORE SHE EVEN had time to turn on her microwave—some member of the advance team had left a generous supply of coffee, tea, cocoa and instant soups in a small wicker basket—Juliana came in. Meg was going to snap, "Can't you *knock*?" in an attempt to make her angry, but—well, it was already too late. She must have looked exasperated, though, because Juliana gave her a big shrug.

"In my life, an open door's an invitation," she said.

Clearly.

Juliana came bouncing the rest of the way into the room and sat down on the bed, making herself right at home by grabbing a pillow to put behind her head and leaning against the wall.

"Comfortable?" Meg asked.

Juliana nodded. "Yes. Thank you." She picked up the open philosophy book—Kant—and started flipping pages.

"Help yourself to the quilt, if you get chilly," Meg said.

Juliana laughed, and dropped the book. "You're a bitch on wheels, you know that?"

Jesus, even *Beth* didn't go that far.

"Don't get me wrong," Juliana said. "It can be a good quality. I mean, you're not at all like I expected you to be."

"Sorry to disappoint," Meg said, and stuck her mug in the microwave.

"I mean, acerbic?" Juliana shook her head. "Who would've figured? I thought you were going to be all noble, and—boring. Like living with a princess or something."

"Feel free to *think* of me as a princess," Meg said. "If it helps you."

Juliana laughed again. "Weird sense of humor, too. I thought you'd be no fun. Like, way too dignified and stuff. But, this is much better."

Speaking of weird, Juliana took first prize in *that* contest. "Well, gosh," Meg said, and then thought of something. "Did you call me 'Bucko,' before?"

"Yeah," Juliana said. "I thought you needed a nickname."

And she chose Bucko? Great.

"I'll have to think it over," Juliana said. "Maybe I can do better."

Hard not to.

"Are you going to offer me some of whatever you're having?" Juliana asked. "A specialty coffee, maybe?"

Apparently so. Meg handed her the little wicker basket.

Juliana, indeed, selected a tin of specialty coffee. "I'll get my mug."

"Do that," Meg said. "Hurry."

Juliana grinned. "I have Oreos, I'll bring them, too." She left, returning almost immediately with the cookies and a bottle of Baileys Irish Cream. "Now, we can sit and talk."

Didn't sound like she had much choice in the matter. Her cup was a Red Sox mug Neal had given her for her birthday once; Juliana's was blue, with "Wild Thing" splashed across it in red.

"Mark seems very nice," Meg said, as the water heated.

Juliana nodded. "I think being pre-med is a waste of time, but I like him a lot. Seen anyone you like yet?"

"Well—" No. Even though, tediously, guys sidled—or swaggered—up to her constantly, in the dining hall and library and so forth, to try their luck. Meg frowned. "I haven't really looked." In *months*.

"Simon'll probably ask you out, but you can say no," Juliana said.

It was always good to have permission. Meg took the mugs out of the microwave one at a time, using her right elbow to close it again.

Juliana stopped pouring liqueur into her coffee long enough to reconsider that. "Unless, of course, you want to go. Then, you should say yes."

"Well," Meg took an Oreo, "that's good advice. Thank you."

Without asking, Juliana leaned over and poured a shot of Irish Cream into Meg's mug, too. "The thing about Simon is, he'll always be nice. Not be a jerk to you."

"I get sick of that," Meg said, forgetting that she should just speak in her usual vague, noncontroversial generalities. "I don't like it when they let me push them around."

Juliana frowned. "You and Simon should probably just be friends, then."

Damn, and the invitations had already gone out to be engraved.

"Are the upperclassmen all over you?" Juliana asked. "I bet they are."

"Only the sycophants," Meg said, without thinking.

"Whoa." Juliana stopped crunching her cookie. "Does that mean me, too?"

Hmmm. "No," Meg said. "You probably would have been friendly to me regardless."

"Not if you were boring. Then—no way in hell." Juliana picked up another Oreo, looked at it, put it back, then picked it up again. "Although I was trying to decide if you were a royal bitch, or just shy."

"I'm shy," Meg said.

Juliana shook her head. "Nope, you're a big faker. People might *think* you're shy, but it'd be more you not being friendly."

"Would you be friendly, if you were me?" Meg asked stiffly.

Juliana shrugged, twisting her Oreo apart. "I don't know."

"I mean, Jesus Christ," Meg said. "I can barely function, and you want me to be charming? Jesus." She slugged down some of the liqueur-enhanced coffee. "I just—look, this isn't something I talk about, okay?"

Juliana nodded. "Okay."

Neither of them spoke for a minute.

"I know I'd have bad dreams," Juliana said. "Anyone would. I mean—"

"I *really* don't talk about it," Meg said through her teeth, "okay?"

"Fine." Juliana flipped what was left of her Oreo up in the air and caught it in her mouth. "But not even Mary Elizabeth thinks you're a jerk for having nightmares."

Meg flushed. Christ, she knew they'd all been talking about her behind her back, but it wasn't much fun to get verbal proof.

"They'll probably go away," Juliana said. "Once you're used to being here. I mean, I was like, crying and calling my mother every other minute during First Days, and everything."

This, from one of the most seemingly imperturbable people she'd ever met? Meg looked at her. "*You* were?"

"Sure," Juliana said, with a shrug. "I mean, you're living with like, strangers, and they never seem to shut up, and it's far away, and the food's all different—I was totally not into it."

Meg thought about that. "You seem extremely well-adjusted."

"So do you," Juliana said.

Yeah. Right.

"What are the dreams about, anyway?" Juliana asked. "If that's not too personal."

"Too personal," Meg said without hesitating.

Juliana shrugged again. "Okay. Want another Oreo?"

Why not?

LATER, AFTER EVEN Juliana had conceded that academic requirements were an inherent aspect of the college experience, and slogged off to work on her *Agamemnon* translation, Meg slouched against her pillows and tried to get through the next chapter in her psychology book without falling asleep.

"Studying?" Susan asked from the door.

Theoretically. Meg shrugged and underlined a sentence without bothering to read it, first.

Susan nodded, and stood in the hallway, looking indecisive.

She was going to have to stop leaving her god-damn door ajar, even though open doors were the dorm norm. "About to tell me it's very late, and I have to turn my light off now?" Meg asked.

Susan shook her head.

Good.

"I'm sorry about what happened before," Susan said. "I'm not supposed to lose my temper with any of you guys, and—well, it's the first time I've ever—I'm really sorry."

Making her, what, the exception to prove the rule? Except that that wasn't going to get them anywhere. "Well." Meg moved her jaw. "I, um, maybe have a little bit of a temper myself."

Susan grinned, for a second. "You don't say."

Meg was damned if she was going to blush—but had a feeling that she might be doing so, anyway. "My really mean look was supposed to completely intimidate you."

Susan nodded. "It was pretty scary, yeah."

Was she being serious—or sarcastic? Susan Dowd was very goddamned hard to read.

"It actually made me feel a little more comfortable with you," Susan said. "It was very human."

But not, perhaps, engaging, or appealing.

She realized that the half of the peanut butter sandwich she'd never finished was still on her desk—just as Susan noticed it, too.

Fuck.

Talk about a conversation killer.

"If we even *suspect* someone might have an eating disorder, we're supposed to be very proactive," Susan said.

Oh, for Christ's sakes. As it happened, she already had a headache, but increasingly, it was getting worse. "And if you suspect someone's just having a normal, rocky adjustment period?" Meg asked.

"Then, we try to be proactive about *that*," Susan said.

With stellar results, no doubt.

Susan sighed. "I'm trying to figure out the boundaries here, Meg, but you're going to have to help me out."

Like it wasn't already abundantly clear? "Well, it's pretty easy," Meg said, gripping her pen so hard that she felt it start to bend. "There are people who like having their hands held—and there are people who *don't*."

Susan nodded. "And you're one of the clingy ones, right?"

Something like that, yeah.

"Put it this way," Susan said. "The better you seem to be doing, the more space we'll be able to give you."

Then she was damned well going to have to start doing better.

THE NEXT MORNING, she woke up much too late to make it to breakfast, and when she got downstairs—agents in tow—to go to her political science class, the only people waiting outside on Park Street, behind the dorm, were a New England–based print person, and a local wire service photographer, plus the usual smattering of tabloid types. Even her old buddy from Steven's basketball game, the ever-persistent Hannah Goldman, hadn't been around at all for a week or two.

Oddly enough, Mary Elizabeth was there, too, by a weathered wooden bench, all bundled up in her peacoat and scarf and a light blue knitted hat. She saw Meg coming, and frowned at her watch. "Cut it pretty close, don't you?"

Meg frowned back. "What's it to you, if I cut it close?"

Mary Elizabeth didn't answer, checking through a battered olive green army surplus shoulder bag.

Very strange. It was almost time for class, and Meg started picking her way across the ice, Mary Elizabeth falling into step with her.

"Griffin?" Mary Elizabeth asked.

Extremely strange. Meg shook her head. "Hopkins, actually."

They crossed the quad in front of Chapin without speaking, Meg not sure if she should be amused, or unnerved. When they got to the front of the building, Mary Elizabeth stopped.

"Nice talking to you," Meg said.

Mary Elizabeth glanced behind them, and over at Spring Street, where one of the more industrious freelance photographers was already standing, and then lowered her voice. "Don't *ever* accuse me of being afraid to walk near you."

Meg laughed. So that's what this was all about. "Well, I'd love to see your expression if a firecracker went off right about now."

"I bet you'd be more scared," Mary Elizabeth said, unsmiling.

Meg laughed again. "I bet you're right." Bulletproof jacket or no bulletproof jacket.

Mary Elizabeth's face softened slightly. "I don't know. Maybe I'd be more scared."

"Maybe," Meg said.

"Maybe," Mary Elizabeth said, and walked away towards wherever her class was.

THE NEXT DAY was Friday, and Meg knew that everyone else in her dorm probably had plans. Everyone else at the *school*. The campus seemed—energized. Lots of people shouting to one another, music blaring, paper signs announcing various parties and films and performances tacked up on trees and telephone poles and bulletin boards.

The loudest music in the entry was coming from Juliana's room, and when Meg glanced through the open door, she saw her sitting at her desk, drumming on a textbook with two pens.

It *was* an open door. Meg stuck her head in. "Um, hi. I was just—what's happening around here tonight?"

"All kinds of good stuff," Juliana said, drumming away. "Don't tell me you're going to be *social*?"

Tough call. "Depends on what's going on," Meg said.

Juliana shrugged, picking up a can of cheese spread and spraying some into her mouth. "There's a whole bunch of parties. You going to go out?"

Safety in numbers. "Are you?" Meg asked.

"Yeah. Only, Mark's taking me out to dinner, first. Spending *money*, if you can believe it. But, that doesn't help you any." She put down the aerosol cheese and got up. "Come on."

Meg followed her, it developed, downstairs to Susan's room, where the music of choice was John Coltrane. This, in direct competition, with the predictable video game two of the guys were playing in the common room.

"Hey, JA!" Juliana said. "Are you going to rock and roll tonight?"

Susan, who was on the floor doing abdominal crunches, looked up. "Yeah. I know some people who are having a party over at Greylock. You guys want to go?"

"Well, I'm going to come late," Juliana said, "but I think Bucko here'll tag along with you."

Wait, that sounded like a really bad idea. Meg shook her head. "No, I—"

"Sure." Susan very slowly lowered herself with near-perfect form. "I think I'm going over around nine, nine-thirty."

"Okay, good," Juliana said, before Meg could think of a sufficiently plausible reason to decline. "That's a plan, then."

A terrible plan.

"Great." Susan raised herself, slowly. "Now, go away before I completely lose count."

One of the last things she felt like doing was heading off someplace alone with Susan. They didn't seem to get along that well, anyway, but even though she was almost always friendly and approachable, there was also something about Susan that—Meg couldn't quite put her finger on it. An alone-in-a-crowd quality. It was probably just garden variety New England reserve—but, still. It was there.

And she hadn't been to a party since—Christ—last May. A real party, with people her age, as opposed to official White House stuff. She assumed most people would be wearing jeans, and she also put on a blue silk shirt Josh had always liked, along with a pair of big, clunky, supposedly very hip earrings Beth had given her.

To her relief, when Susan showed up at her door, she was dressed pretty much the same way.

"We ready to go?" Susan asked.

Meg nodded, hoping she couldn't tell that she was nervous to the point of nausea. The arrangement she had made with her agents was that—after a fast walk-through—one of them would be posted outside the suite where the party was being held, while the others stationed themselves in and around various dorm entrances. She decided to leave her cane behind, in order to look less crippled—and hoped she wouldn't regret the impulse.

"I think it'll be mostly juniors and seniors," Susan said, "but I'm pretty sure Tammy's coming."

Meg nodded. At least she'd know one other person, then. "I'm not going to—well, cramp your style, am I?"

Susan shook her head. "No. But, if a guy named Keith comes over to talk to me, you can tactfully drift away."

Meg grinned. Keith. Fair enough.

The party was hot, noisy, crowded, and dark. Like most parties. The school policy seemed to be that if people were at an officially sanctioned party, they weren't supposed to drink if they were underage, but if it was more informal, it didn't seem to be an issue, unless campus security decided to do an unannounced inspection. Or, anyway, that was her best guess, judging from the amount of casual drinking she'd noticed around the entry, especially among the guys who lived downstairs—at least half of whom seemed to have huge crushes on Juliana and came up to flirt with her constantly.

This particular party was being thrown by a bunch of juniors, and the music was mostly Sixties standards, with a little rap thrown in. Almost everyone seemed to notice her come in, even if none of them acknowledged it, and once she was standing with Susan, holding a cup of beer, she wanted nothing more than to go back to her room.

Susan introduced her to a lot of people, and Meg smiled and nodded and sipped her beer. After a while, she was uncomfortable enough to detach herself from the group—mostly Drama and English majors—and walked around aimlessly, before stopping to lean against a wall.

She hated this. She hated this a lot.

Susan came over, about two minutes later. As ever, the mother hen. "You having an okay time?"

No. "Yes," Meg said, the beer cup clenched in her hand. It was better than—arthroscopic surgery, say.

Susan looked at her closely. "You want to come over here, and meet a bunch of rowdy rugby players?"

Meg shook her head. "Maybe later."

"Okay," Susan said. "Well, what about—"

Meg shook her head harder, beginning to feel panicky. "Later, okay?"

Susan hesitated, and then nodded. "Okay. Sure."

Meg nodded, too, and drank some of her beer. She should probably just leave. She'd made a good-faith effort to fit in; no need to prolong the agony.

Most of the people who walked by said hello to her—oh, yeah, like they didn't have ulterior motives—and she would nod back, careful not to make eye contact or initiate anything. Eerie to have stared into *gun* barrels before—and find this almost as scary. Different scary, but still scary.

What's it like living in the White House? What's your mother *really* like? Is it true you broke your own hand? Did it hurt? What about your leg?

She was almost finished with her beer, and she looked down at the cup, wondering if she should go get another one, or just take off.

A guy was heading in her direction, and she recognized him. Frisbee Boy. Swell. He was drop-dead good-looking, if one liked blond California boys; as it happened, she did not.

"So." He slouched against the wall, maybe a foot away from her. "Waiting for a bus?"

"Yeah," Meg said, and pointed. "There it is now. Excuse me."

He gave her a big grin that was probably supposed to be irresistible. Devastating, even. "What's your hurry? Hang out for a while."

Not bloody likely. "I'm sorry, I—" She gestured vaguely, and moved past him. "Someone's waiting for me over there."

"Yeah, well, fuck you, too," he said, and went over to a group of guys, who were all watching—and laughing. Maybe at him, maybe at her. She didn't really care, either way.

She limped over to the keg, where a guy who looked like a rowdy rugby player was sloppily filling plastic cups.

"You legal, miss?" he asked, and laughed.

She managed a small smile, took a fresh cup of beer, and limped away. Her knee was starting to hurt. A lot. Which was as good a reason as any to drink too much. Everyone else certainly seemed to be.

It was getting more and more painful to stand, and she wished there was somewhere she could sit down. Somewhere private. Which kind of defeated the purpose of going to a party, but—if only people wouldn't *stare* at her all the time. Watch every move she made.

Most of the suite rooms seemed to be filled with people playing Beirut or dancing or making out, although one room looked as though it might be empty. But when she got closer, she saw three guys and a girl over by the desk, passing around a joint. So much for the smoking ban inside buildings. Maybe only *cigarette* smoke counted.

"Oh." She stopped, flushing. "Excuse me."

They all exchanged glances, then one of the guys held the joint out. "Want some?" he asked.

She glanced, reflexively, over her shoulder to make sure none of her agents had come in to check on her. "I, uh—" She hesitated. Even if she *wanted* to, she really couldn't. "Thanks. I'd better not."

"They can't arrest people or anything, can they?" one of the other guys asked.

She didn't *think* so. It wasn't as if they were officers of the court or anything. Were they? Besides, presumably, they had more important things on their minds. So, she shook her head.

"Sure you don't want a toke?" the girl asked.

Meg nodded, and went back out to the main room. Christ, it was tiresome to have to avoid everything that might be fun, purely because of potential headlines. She really was going to leave, but then she saw Tammy, who waved her over.

Since it was better than fleeing alone into the night, Meg went.

"Hey, hi, Meg!" Tammy said. Overly enthusiastic, but harmless enough, considering that this was the same girl who had come into the bathroom once and gasped, "*You* use Crest, too?"

"She's just, you know, like regular, almost," she heard Tammy saying as she walked over.

Oh, great. But she pretended to be interested in being introduced, even though she forgot their names—two girls and a guy—almost immediately.

"She studies a whole lot," Tammy said to her friends, then looked at Meg for confirmation, "don't you?"

Was that rhetorical? No. "Heaps and heaps," Meg said, and drank some beer.

At which point, the conversation—if it could be legitimately described that way—pretty much died. She was going to tell them she was kidding, but—well, did anyone really care? Doubtful.

"So, uh, what're you majoring in?" one of the girls asked.

What *was* she majoring in? Meg shrugged. "I don't know yet."

Another little silence.

"She went to Buckingham Palace," Tammy said. "She met the Royal Family and everything."

The other three looked at Meg, but didn't say anything.

"They were very nervous," Meg said. "At first."

Tammy and her friends smiled uneasily.

She could tell they were trying not to look at her hand, and resisted the urge to hold the splint behind her back. "Interestingly, though," she said, feeling—perhaps—a little drunk, and therefore, less cautious, "my mother has taken to wearing tiaras constantly, ever since."

Now they all laughed, uneasily.

Meg swallowed some more beer. It was almost gone. *Damn.* "We told her the scepter was a little much."

The boy, and ones of the girls, laughed outright.

"What were you all talking about?" Meg asked. "Before I interrupted."

"Oh, just, you know, movies," Tammy said, and paused. "You've met like, lots of movie stars, right?"

She knew Tammy meant well, but Jesus. Meg shook her head. "Not really."

"Well, like who?" Tammy asked.

Going back to her room—and even flinging herself onto her bed and crying herself to sleep—would have been a much better choice. Live and learn. "Really, no one," Meg said, finished her beer, then held up the empty cup. "Excuse me for a minute."

The same guy was still working the keg, and he winked at her. "Back already?"

What was he, her father? "Just couldn't get enough of your smiling face," she said.

He refilled her cup, his hand lingering a little too long when he gave it back. "So, stick around."

Accepting an invitation from a very large jock—who was downing beer after beer from a huge stein, and probably had been for hours—was not necessarily a wise idea.

"Next trip, maybe," she said.

The people who had been smoking pot were back out in the main room, and she headed for the bedroom they had been in, hoping to find it empty. To her great relief, it was, and she sat down on top of the desk, easing her leg up onto a nearby chair. Her good hand was trembling almost as much as her bad one, and she took a healthy gulp of beer. The alcohol seemed to be making her more sad than anything else, and tears were starting to seem like a viable activity.

"You think you own the place or what?" a voice asked from the door.

Frisbee Boy. Naturally. Meg ignored him, drinking her beer.

"So," he said, and wandered the rest of the way into the room.

Be still her fluttering heart.

"Guess you think you're too important to talk to me," he said, without rancor. "That you're pretty hot stuff."

What an asshole. She looked up. "I think you've got that market pretty well covered yourself."

He grinned. "Just might."

She returned her attention to her beer.

Apparently not one to take a hint, the guy came closer. He had thick blond hair, with more than one rather sexy cowlick, and was wearing a faded UCLA sweatshirt with the sleeves pushed up, old Levi's with rips across the knees, and high-top cross-trainers.

Okay, he was cute. He was a god, even. Just not a god she would choose to worship.

"So," he said, again.

"I was kind of looking for some privacy," she said.

He shrugged. "That sounds good. Us, having some privacy."

Oh, please. She shook her head, and looked in the other direction.

He laughed, and sat down on the bed. Sprawled, actually. Too goddamned attractive for his own good. "Tough lady, hunh?"

Did the guy ever quit? She sighed.

"Just pretend I'm not here," he said.

Good idea. If she ignored him long enough, maybe he would go away, because she was too tired to get up. She didn't talk; he didn't talk. She drank her beer; he drank his beer.

"My brother blew his knee out," he said.

Automatically, she touched her brace.

"Playing football," he said.

She sipped her beer. "How is he now?"

The guy shrugged. "Pretty good. He limps sometimes."

Sometimes. "Does he still play football?" Meg asked. Did he *ski*?

"Well—" the guy avoided looking at her— "he's in law school now, so—well."

Sounded like a definite no.

"He wasn't all that good, anyway," the guy said. "I mean, it wasn't like he was going to go pro or anything, he just played for fun."

Meg nodded. "Still probably hurt, though."

"Well, yeah." He stood up, and she did sort of like the way he moved. Languid, athletic. Okay—cool. He was cool. Very, very cool. "Don't think we introduced ourselves." He put his hand out. His right hand. "I'm Jack Taylor."

Well, his name *would* be something like Jack, wouldn't it. Appropriately rugged and—phallic. "Meg Powers," she said, not bothering to put her beer down, or respond to the outstretched hand.

"Oh my God." His eyes widened. "Any relation?"

Jerk. But, she couldn't help smiling. "None whatsoever," she said.

"Whew." He leaned against the desk, right next to her. "It would've made me real nervous."

"I'm sure," she said. He was very close to her. *Too* close.

"Aren't you in one of my classes?" he asked.

Two could play at that. "I don't know," she said. "I never noticed."

He nodded. "I must be thinking of someone else. Could've sworn that was you, always waving and smiling at me."

What an active fantasy life he must have.

He reached out to touch her shoulder. "I'm ready for another beer. How about you?"

Saying yes was probably going to mean more than one thing. "Okay," she said, and finished what was left in her cup. "Sure."

17

WHEN THE GUY at the keg saw them walking over together, he looked disappointed—and not exactly friendly. So Meg decided to keep her distance, watching from across the room as they exchanged what appeared to be hostile words, and then the guy handed two beers to Jack somewhat ungraciously.

"What was that about?" she asked, when Jack damn near *strutted* back to her.

He shrugged. "Guy's a little wasted, that's all."

Their hands touched as he gave her her cup, Meg surprised to find herself repressing a shiver.

Well, okay, she wasn't surprised.

"Kind of crowded in here," he said.

Kind of *obvious.* "I guess," she said, and drank some beer. The first few had tasted pretty foul; this one was just fine.

"Well, you know," he said, "I live down in Armstrong, and—"

"Leaving so soon?" she asked.

He grinned. A fairly cute grin. She'd always liked a sort of wolfish look. She, herself, had raffish down pretty well. "Thought you might find it a little stuffy in here," he said.

In some quarters, Williams itself had a reputation for being a little stuffy. A Republican training ground. At least ten of whom seemed to be in her political science class. "No," she said, "but it's nice of you to think of me."

"I'm like that," he said. "Thoughtful."

Oh, yeah. Without a doubt. Actually, what he was, was very sexy. Although it had been almost a year since she—well, no time like the present.

"This is just way too crowded for me," he said. "I'm going to go into the other room."

Meg nodded. "I guess I'll see you around, then."

"Well, it's your call," he said. "I can either kiss you here, or we can go someplace else."

There was something to be said for being direct. "Here's okay," Meg said, and was amused to see him look startled.

He recovered himself, and bent towards her.

"Then again, privacy's okay, too," she said.

He grinned, and with his hand on her waist, they went back to the room where they had been before. Once they were in there, Meg started to feel as though this was a very big, drunken mistake—but, he was already kissing her, even though they were both still holding their drinks, and—damned if she wasn't kissing back. *Hard.*

Upon which, it occurred to her that this was something she had always enjoyed. Had really missed.

He was backing her up now, and despite the brace, her knee started to give out.

"Watch it," she said, much more snappishly than she'd intended.

"Oh." He stopped. "Right. Sorry."

Remembering that she also had a completely useless hand—to the degree that the most she could manage was to rest her splint ineffectually on his shoulder—she began to feel extremely self-conscious, and much less aroused.

Just as she decided to step away from him and sip her beer, he took the cup from her, sloshing some of the liquid onto her shirt in the process—which amused, and annoyed, her in approximately equal proportions.

"Aw, hell, I'm sorry," he said, and tried to brush the beer off the silk, although his hand wasn't anywhere near the spot where it had actually spilled.

Oh, yeah. A true Lothario. She started to pull free—write the whole thing off as a momentary, ill-advised, alcohol-fueled loss of common sense on both their parts—but, he was lifting her up onto the desk, and moving in to kiss her some more. It was actually a good choice, since she could rest her bad leg on the chair, and as things progressed, she found herself instinctively using her other leg to pull him even closer.

A reaction which seemed to please him very much, and the whole situation began escalating so quickly that, drunk—and intensely excited—or not, she tried to lean away from him. "Jack," she said, "I really don't—"

He didn't seemed to hear her—or, if he did, he either wasn't paying attention, or wasn't terribly interested in her opinion.

"Uh, look," she said, aware that she was having trouble getting her breath for all of the wrong reasons now. Specifically—fear. "Let's cool it, okay? I think things are getting, uh—"

"No, come on, this is good, Meg, this is really good," he mumbled against her mouth, one hand up underneath her bra, the other trying to work its way inside her jeans. "Just let yourself go with it."

She should have known better than to expect him to be content with simple making out, and it was her own damn fault for drinking so much, and for not breaking this off as soon as he had pulled off his sweatshirt and started unbuttoning her shirt. "Jack," she said. "I don't want to—"

"God, you're so hot," he said, kissing her even more deeply as he climbed up onto the desk and tried to move her down onto her back. "I can't believe how hot you are."

If she wanted, she could reach into her pocket for her panic button, or raise her voice a little, and her agents would come running in—but, to hell with *that*.

She pushed him away, violently, with her good hand. "I said, back off already!"

He stared at her. "What? We just got started."

"Yeah, well, now we're finished," she said, and laboriously slid out from underneath him, almost falling over in the process of trying to stand up. Her good hand was more uncoordinated than usual, but she finally got her shirt rebuttoned, then picked up her beer—or maybe it was his—and swigged some, although more alcohol was probably the last thing she needed.

He scowled, and put his sweatshirt back on. "What's your problem?"

"You," she said. "At the moment."

"What's wrong with you? One second, you're like, totally into it, and the next—" He shook his head, and then made such a quick move forward that, for a second, she was afraid he was going to hurt her. He saw her expression and scowled harder. "I'm getting my beer, okay? Jesus." He retrieved his cup—or, possibly, hers—and stepped away sullenly. "Believe me, touching you is just about the *last* thing on my mind right now."

It was mutual.

"You should go see a shrink or something," he said. "You're really screwed up."

As insults went, she found that one pretty god-damned dull. "Hey," she said, "you're the one who—"

"Oh," he said, nodding, "so now it's my fault that you got raped by terrorists?"

What? Where did he get *that* idea?

He must have realized how that sounded, because now he looked guilty. Horrified, even. "I, uh—I'm sorry. I didn't mean that, Meg, it just came out. I really didn't mean to—"

"Is that what you think?" she asked, very, very quietly.

"No," he said, looking even more guilty. "It just—I don't even know where that came from, I—"

"Well, here's where you missed the boat, Beach Boy," she said, angrier than she could—almost—ever remember being. "I wasn't raped by terrorists, I *stood up* to god-damn terrorists!" Which, somewhere in the beer-numbed fog that was her brain, she realized was true, even if she'd never quite thought about it that way before. "So, trust me, as far as I'm concerned, some little wannabe date-rapist is just boring."

His expression changed from guilt, to fury. "Hey, I didn't do anything to you—I stopped, remember? You said stop, I stopped. Period. Okay? Let's just agree we don't like each other, and forget about the whole thing."

"With pleasure," Meg said, and splashed what was left of her beer across the crotch of his jeans before shouldering past him to the door.

"If you were a guy, I'd knock you down for that," he said, his fist clenching.

She stopped abruptly and turned to face him. "Go ahead, Beach Boy. *Try* it."

Instead, he finished his beer, dropped his cup on the floor, too—pointedly—and walked out of the room.

She was right behind him, but instead of veering towards the keg, she headed straight for the suite exit, the stairwell—and out of the dorm.

Away from the god-damn party.

Kyle caught up to her within a few seconds, slightly out of breath. "Leaving?" he asked.

She was in no mood to answer exceedingly obvious questions.

Three of her other agents fell into step once they got outside, and she didn't bother explaining herself to them, either. It was extremely cold without her jacket—to say nothing of potentially physically risky—but she wasn't about to go back for it.

"You want to borrow my coat?" Paula asked, already starting to take it off.

"I like the fresh air," Meg said. "It's *bracing*." So what if it was snowing. That, and being drunk, and not having her cane, made it hard to walk without stumbling, but—to hell with it. After all, she was *already* crippled. What difference would it make if she fell down and broke a few more bones?

They must have caught on to the fact that she was kind of enraged, because none of them spoke again until they had made it back—unscathed; *quelle bonne* luck—to Sage, by which time Meg was having trouble keeping her teeth from chattering.

"Uh, are you in for the night?" Kyle asked.

"Haven't decided," Meg said shortly. Although it wasn't like she had any friends here. Any kind of normal social life at *all*.

He nodded. "Okay. But, if you do want to go out again, we'll need to—"

"Don't worry. You'll be the first," she said, and limped into the building.

THERE WERE A lot of people around, mostly guys from the entry, hanging out on the landings, with some of the stairwell doors illegally propped open, and she hoped that she didn't look as angry as she felt. With luck, she just looked—distant. Unapproachable.

She was hoping to be able to escape into her room, but unfortunately, just as she got off the elevator, her knee so swollen that her brace was now too tight, Juliana and Mark came out of Juliana's room. Mark had his arm draped around Juliana's shoulders, and it looked as though they had had a very nice time at dinner.

"Hey, we were just heading over," Juliana said cheerfully. "Was it really boring or something?"

Meg shrugged, avoiding her eyes. "It was okay. I'm kind of tired, that's all." She dug around inside her pocket for her keys, and promptly dropped them, having to bite back a deeply-felt "*Fuck*" in response.

Mark bent down and picked them up for her. "Come back with us. Maybe we can all liven it up."

Meg shook her head, unlocking her door with some difficulty. "No, thanks. I, uh, I'm really wiped out. But, I hope you guys have fun."

Before she could close the door, Juliana stopped it with her hand and came in after her.

"You all right?" she asked.

Christ, would it be too hard for all of them just to leave her *alone*? It was way past time to give up, call her parents, and ask them to arrange to have her brought home for the rest of the year, so she could at least have some privacy, maybe. And she was god-damn well going to do just that, first thing in the morning. Meg shrugged. "A little too much to drink, maybe. So, I'm going to sleep it off."

"Where's Susan?" Juliana asked.

Oh. Right. Susan. Fuck, and double fuck. "Um, still over there, I think," Meg said. "I couldn't find her before I left."

Predictably, Juliana came farther into the room, instead of leaving.

"How come you have snow all over you?" she asked.

Because there was a veritable Berkshire blizzard going on out there, maybe? "Forgot my coat, I guess," Meg said.

Juliana looked at her for a minute, then went over to the door. "Hey, Mark! Meg says it's snowing really hard now, so let's have a party here, instead."

"Got any beer?" he asked.

"Just a couple," Juliana said. "But call Harry and Simon, and maybe they can bring some more. Tell them to get something decent." She grinned at Meg. "So, this'll be fun. You can choose half the music, even."

What? Meg stiffened. "You don't think I'm *coming* to the party, do you?"

"Well, you're the co-hostess," Juliana said, "so, yeah."

Meg shook her head. "No, I—I really—"

"Change into something dry, and bring out some tunes," Juliana said, already on her way into her own room. "It won't be fun without you."

In her current mood, it wasn't going to be fun *with* her. But before she could figure out a good way to get out of the situation, Juliana had come back in with two Rolling Rocks, one of which she was drinking.

Meg waved the other bottle away. "Thanks, but—"

"Come on," Juliana said. "You don't seem that drunk."

Oh, yeah? Meg frowned at her. "Drunk enough to have had a *really bad* party make-out with some jerk named Jack Taylor."

"Whoa." Juliana looked impressed. "You were fooling around with him? He's supposed to be a complete asshole, but God, he's good-looking. Way to go!"

What? "No, it was really embarrassing," Meg said. Unpleasant, also. And she could now personally attest to the asshole characterization. "Everyone who was there is going to hear about it, and—"

Juliana shrugged. "Hey, aim high, that's what I always say." She opened the second bottle of beer and handed it to her. "So. How's he kiss, anyway?"

Well, as a matter of fact— "He, uh—" Meg grinned. "Actually, he kisses *great*."

"I'll drink to that," Juliana said.

What the hell—maybe she would, too.

She changed into sweatpants and an old Oxford shirt—her favorite kind of party garb—then picked out a few CDs, and told Jose, who was behind the security desk, that she would be in the common room for a while, trying not to make it obvious that she was already drunk—and planning to become more so. Mark, and some other guy—Ted? Tad?—who was in her Shakespeare class and lived over in Sage A, were already in there with Juliana, drinking beer, along with Mikey from the first floor, and Quentin and Khalid, from the second floor.

"Todd, Meg; Meg, Todd," Mark said, gesturing vaguely.

Todd. Okay. She nodded hello, and gave Juliana the CDs, which included, of course, Joan Jett.

Not that she was deeply mired in the past.

Possibly even her *grandparents'* past.

"All right," Juliana said, after examining them dubiously. "I'll make it work."

By the time Harry and Simon showed up with bags of chips and more beer, several other people from the entry, including Dirk, had joined the party, and everyone was in a pretty good mood.

Meg, included.

Simon looked very pleased to see her. "Hi," he said, taking off his snowy fatigue jacket. "I didn't know you were going to be here."

Meg shrugged. What could she say—her life was a social whirl.

The room was crowded enough now so that she was sitting on the floor, leaning her back against a milk carton crammed full of DVDs and CDs and indeterminate junk. Simon opened two bottles of Sam Adams and sat down next to her.

"Those both for you?" she asked.

"Nope," he said, and gave her one.

Okay. Why not. She was in college now. Time to walk on the wild side.

It was dark, except for a small study lamp in the corner, and some light coming in from the hall, and Meg found it very peaceful to drink beer, listen to music, and hang out with actual peers, even if she didn't know them all that well. The party size fluctuated, as people from all over the dorm came in and out, and she was surprised she didn't feel more shy.

Okay, mainly, all she felt was *drunk*.

Ripped.

Blasted.

Blitzed.

Simon—who she was now calling Skip, just for fun—was telling her long, involved stories about growing up in the Midwest, and Harry and Todd seemed to be swapping lurid and outrageous prep school tales, while Juliana sat on Mark's lap, and the two of them did a fair amount of kissing and whispering. Meg just drank beer, and nodded a lot.

At some point, Juliana got up and put a collection of old *Bob Newhart* episodes in the battered VCR/DVD combo machine.

"Want to play a couple of rounds?" she asked.

There seemed to be general excitement about this idea, although Meg had no idea why.

"It's a game," Simon said, putting his arm around her. "Every time someone says, 'Hi, Bob,' you have to drink. After that, we can do *Golden Girls*, and drink when they say 'St. Olaf,' and 'Sicily,' and eat cake in the middle of the night, and stuff."

Meg thought about that, since she had wasted hundreds upon hundreds of hours of her life slouching in front of Nick at Night, TV Land, and DVD compilations of long-ago canceled television shows with her brothers. "They say 'Hi, Bob' constantly."

Simon nodded. "That's why it's a great game."

Okay, what the hell. "The State of the Union is strong," Meg said, and drank.

Everyone else laughed, which surprised her.

"The President *wrecked* our game," some short guy with glasses—Jerry? Gerard?—from the first floor said, and almost everyone in the room nodded, and laughed again.

" 'Global community,' though," Andy, who lived on the second floor and was a very good-looking drama major from New York, said. "She was good with 'global community.' "

Whereupon, there was more nodding—and drinking.

So, they had all watched the speech. She had been curious, but never would have had the chutzpah to bring it up directly.

And even being drunk wouldn't make her brave enough to ask if they had all taken a drink every single time the First Family was shown.

The game was pretty hilarious—especially when three or four characters in a row said "Hi, Bob!"—and by the middle of the second episode, she was maybe a little smashed.

Bombed. Snockered. *Wasted.*

It would be very bad timing if the campus police suddenly burst in, and found a room full of mostly underage, intoxicated people. With luck, her agents would give them a heads-up, first.

When she finally staggered up to go to the bathroom—they were watching *M*A*S*H* now, and drinking every time someone's rank was mentioned: Corporal O'Reilly! Captain Pierce! Major Houlihan!—she almost fell, and Simon grabbed her and held her upright.

Which seemed very, very funny.

"Excuse me, Skippy," she said, extricated herself, and lurched out to the hall.

On the whole, she was noticing that alcohol worked almost as well as the painkillers the doctors so grudgingly doled out. Many more side effects, but so what? She knew better than most that life was short.

She was on her unsteady way back to the party, when Simon intercepted her on the landing. Big guy. Massive, even. Scarily so, if he weren't so clearly the sensitive type.

"You all right?" he asked.

How often had she been asked *that* in recent months? "Well, now, that's the real question, isn't it, Skip," she said.

He looked worried. "You aren't sick or anything, are you? Because, you know, you aren't very big, and well, maybe you've been drinking too much."

Maybe? She grinned, and tried to get past him. "Excuse me, while I go get my car keys, okay?"

He pulled her back. "Unh-unh. No way. Even if you hadn't been drinking, the snow is—"

Jesus. "They don't let me drive, Skip," she said, still grinning. A little. "I mean, come on. I don't get to do *anything* regular people do, I just—someone'll probably leak me getting drunk to the tabloids, know what I mean?" She reached up to pat his cheek. Or, anyway, his beard. "Relax."

"I really like you," he said, sounding very serious.

Had she inadvertently put on some kind of super-concentrated male-attraction scent tonight? This was just nuts. Pheromones run amok. She nodded politely. "Well, I like you, too, Skip."

"I mean it," he said. "A lot."

Christ. He didn't even know her. If someone was going to say that sort of thing, she would infinitely prefer that it was, in some way, based in reality. "Simon," she said, "I really don't want you to get the wrong—"

He kissed her, and like a very stupid and promiscuous drunk, she automatically returned it. Had she ever kissed anyone with a beard before? Then again, truth be known, she really hadn't kissed very many people, and they had all definitely been *boys*, as opposed to men. So, yeah, beards were new. It seemed fine. A little distracting, maybe. Slightly scratchy. But—fine. Just fine.

And, of course, she had *always* been a fan of tongues, and hands, and hips, and such. Except, why was she fooling around with someone in whom she had absolutely no romantic interest? Christ, she was as bad as Jack Taylor.

"Want to go to your room?" he whispered. "If you'd feel better, we could even just hold each other."

Which, given what a considerate guy he seemed to be, he probably *meant*.

She felt like letting him keep going, to see what might happen—why not?—but then she heard someone coming up the stairs.

Susan. Covered with snow, home from the Greylock party, holding Meg's bulletproof jacket in one hand.

"Hi," she said, and the inflection in her voice would probably have been hard to interpret even if Meg *hadn't* been drunk.

Noticing that her shirt was hanging open—when had that happened?—Meg flushed, moved Simon's hand off her chest, and held the two ends closed. "How was the party? I, uh, kind of lost track of you."

"I noticed, yeah," Susan said, and dropped Meg's jacket on the landing with a thud.

Curt. She sounded curt. Meg rubbed her forehead, aware for the first time that she had picked up a major headache somewhere along the line.

"It's getting pretty late," Susan said, and gestured towards the common room. "So, if people start complaining, you guys are going to have to keep it down."

Meg nodded.

"So, please do," Susan said, and started back down to the second floor.

Once she was gone, Simon moved closer, his arms going around her waist. "Don't worry," he said. "JAs have to act all strict, but it's not like they can get you in trouble. I mean, they're not your parents or anything."

No, but they could make a person feel awfully stupid and thoughtless.

Simon reached up, tentatively, to brush some hair away from her eyes. "So, uh—"

"Let's go back in, and see what everyone else is doing," Meg said, "okay?"

He looked crushed. "Is that what you want?"

She nodded. Emphatically.

18

THE PARTY BROKE up at four or five in the morning, and Meg was asleep—alone—almost before she managed to collapse onto her bed, the ceiling swirling around above her. When she woke up, she felt so terrible—much worse than New Year's Day—that groaning would have required too much energy. Her head hurt, the room was still spinning a little, and her mouth was so dry that she could barely swallow—an extremely frightening sensation.

She tried to go back to sleep, but it didn't work, and finally, she decided to go out to the bathroom and get a large drink of water. Take some ibuprofen, maybe.

When she opened her door, she saw Susan standing just down the hallway, talking to Jesslyn, and almost ducked back into her room, before realizing that that would only make her seem more immature than she had already proven herself to be. And besides, *nobody*—not a JA, not her father, not the Leader of the Free World—could tell her what to do, or not to do, even if her choices were self-destructive.

"Well, maybe they wouldn't mind as much if you only bet in increments of five or ten dollars," Susan was saying.

Jesslyn looked sulky. "If they have such terrible hands, they should just *fold*, instead of whining about it later."

So, she must have taken too much money from people during the regular Friday night poker game in one of the basement common rooms. Again. Meg had wondered how she could get away with winning—and losing—so much money on the Internet every day, but Juliana had told her that Jesslyn's father owned half of Denver, and so, it was essentially just pocket change for her.

Which probably upset the guys in the dorm who she regularly hosed all the more.

Then, Jesslyn caught sight of Meg, and broke into her grimacing version of a huge smile. "Cripes, were *you* wasted last night." She looked at Susan. "Did you *see* her? I mean, she was *fucked up*."

"I got back pretty late," Susan said, with a shrug.

A non-answer was certainly preferable to public criticism. Meg continued on to the bathroom, hearing them resume their poker conversation.

She was brushing her teeth, trying to get rid of the taste of stale beer, when Susan came into the bathroom, dressed in running tights, a couple of layers of fleece shirts, and her Nikes. Regardless of snow, sleet, ice, or rain, she seemed to run every day without fail.

"How you feeling?" she asked.

Unbelievably stinking lousy. "Positively super," Meg said, and spit out toothpaste in what was probably a most unattractive manner.

Susan nodded, and leaned back against the other sink, folding her arms.

Meg brushed, and spit, and brushed some more, hoping to scare her off, but Susan just kept standing there.

Okay. Fine. She rinsed out, then filled her Red Sox mug and drank the whole thing in three long swallows. "I think I acted like a dumb, little freshman, away from home for the first time."

Susan nodded again. "Sounds about right."

But, it wasn't the first time she'd been away from home, was it? And she wasn't too thrilled about the way she had behaved *then*, either.

Susan kept leaning, silently, against the sink.

Meg refilled her mug, fighting intense irritation. So she'd gotten drunk, so what? Big deal. This was college. If she felt like being a jerk, it was nobody else's business. "Look, I know you're supposed to advise and counsel, and all of that," she said, "but you don't have any real authority, right? I mean, I can screw up as much as I want."

Susan nodded.

It was infuriating when people didn't fight back. "Good. Because I *plan* to," Meg said. "Often."

Susan pushed away from the sink, stretching her hamstrings. "Your prerogative."

Damn right. She took two ibuprofen, then slammed her mug down so hard that it cracked. She looked down at the water seeping out of the bottom, wishing that she could throw it against the wall, over and over, until it shattered into a few thousand pieces.

"Just so you know, I didn't volunteer for this," Susan said, stretching some more.

Meaning? Meg frowned at her.

"I got *assigned*," Susan said.

To be the JA. *Her* JA. "Hey, any time you want out, all you have to do is ask," Meg said. "Rumor has it, I've got pull."

"Yeah," Susan said. "So I hear." She started for the door, then stopped. "I know you don't want to get into it, Meg, but for what it's worth, there's a difference between having fun, and being out of control, okay?"

Meg shrugged. "And I fully intend to explore that difference." *Regularly.*

Susan nodded, with very little expression on her face.

"Well," Meg said, and limped past her, heading back to her room—and back to bed.

SHE FELT TOO dizzy and wobbly to attempt going to the dining hall for lunch, but by dinnertime, she was starting to get hungry, so she made herself get up and put on some moderately presentable clothes.

At least six inches of snow had fallen since she had last been outside, and although most of the walkways had been shoveled, there was still plenty of ice, and it took her a very long time to make it down to Mission, even with her steel-tipped cane. Her agents were practically on top of her, apparently expecting to have to scoop her up from the ground at any second, but she pretended not to notice.

The dining hall was packed, and it was hard to find a place where she could sit by herself. She absolutely, in no way, felt like having a conversation. With anyone, about anything. Finally, she located a deserted spot by the windows and limped over with her tray. Except, of course, she had forgotten to get silverware, so she had to make another laborious trip up to the front. While she was there, to save time and effort, she poured herself a second cup of coffee, since caffeine might help restore her equilibrium. Kill whatever alcohol was still wreaking havoc in her system.

Her good hand was quivering so badly that she slopped most of the coffee over the edges of the cup, burning herself slightly. As she was reaching for some napkins to clean up the mess, she saw Jack Taylor walking by with a tray of his own. They stared at each other, and then she quickly looked down again.

He hesitated, and then came over to stand next to her. He looked pretty disheveled and hungover in his own right, and she decided that he wasn't nearly as handsome as she had thought. In fact, he seemed—seedy. Like he needed a shower. Maybe even *two*.

"Uh, look," he said.

She kept mopping at the spilled coffee.

"I feel really terrible about what happened last night," he said.

She shrugged, gathering up the damp pile of napkins.

He sighed. "Meg. I'm sorry. I didn't mean to—"

Now, she looked at him. "To what? I don't have a problem with it. Did you maybe get the impression that I can't take care of myself or something?"

He grinned for a second. "No. In fact—" He stopped. "Anyway, I just—"

"All right!" some guy on his way to the soda machine said. "Check it out, new couple!"

Oh, swell. As ever, she just loved being fodder for gossip. Public property.

"Bugger off, Roger," Jack said, scowling at him. "Who asked you?"

"Oooh," the guy said cheerfully, and moved past them to get himself a Coke.

Jack sighed again, and she found herself ever so briefly reevaluating his attractiveness. Without the cocky grin, he seemed much more interesting. Complicated, rather than shallow. A little bit intriguing. Maybe even—compelling.

Maybe not.

He let out his breath. "Look, I was out of line, okay? What I said, I mean. I should have thought first."

The rape crack. Meg nodded. "Yeah. You should have."

He nodded, too.

Meg wadded up the last of the coffee-soaked napkins and tossed them into the nearest garbage can.

"Well—I'm sorry," he said.

She shrugged, picking up her coffee and silverware, and heading for her table. "No problem."

"Uh, see you around," he said.

Not likely.

WHEN SHE GOT back to her room, there was a message from her parents, which she returned. She lied, at length, about what a very wonderful time she was having at college. Neal, for one, seemed to buy it. Steven—much to her annoyance—didn't even come on to say hello, although maybe it didn't matter, since she would have lied to him, too.

After that, she called Beth.

"So, um, I got completely trashed last night, and had party make-outs with two different guys," Meg said, a couple of minutes into the conversation, and then waited for—with luck—a very critical and disappointed response.

There was a pause on the other end of the line.

"Meg, you ignorant slut," Beth said, sounding outraged.

Okay, that was funny. Meg laughed.

"Good for you," Beth said, in her normal voice. "Was it fun?"

What? "Did you miss the part where I showed extremely poor judgment and my libido was a danger to myself and others?" Meg asked.

"No, I got that," Beth said. "But, I ask again. Was it fun?"

Well— "Um, yeah," Meg said. "It was."

She felt better when she hung up, but the central fact remained. Apparently, she just wasn't a person who could drink safely. At least, not without losing every shred of self-control. So, she just wouldn't. Ever again.

Which was, in all likelihood, going to severely limit her social life, but that might be for the best, too.

No matter how depressing the thought was.

She didn't feel like leaving her room at all the next day, but one of her agents called to say there was a delivery for her. She was tempted to ask if they could bring it upstairs—but they weren't her servants.

Or her employees. Or, God knows, her *friends*.

So, she pulled a sweatshirt on over her t-shirt and sweatpants, and slogged down to find a large florist's box on the security desk. She reached forward, and then hesitated.

"Have you checked it?" she asked.

The agent on duty, Ed, just looked at her.

Right. The Secret Service was notoriously fond of letting the First Family open unexamined packages. She lifted the cover of the box and saw two dozen long-stemmed red roses. The envelope had already been opened, of course—standard threat assessment—but at least that made it easier to take the card out with only one hand.

It said: *I apologize. Jack.*

Ed was trying to be discreet, but she could tell that he was extremely curious about what her reaction was going to be.

"Do you want them?" he asked.

Not really. But, roses were roses, and—what the hell. "Sure," she said, and tucked the box under her arm.

THE NEXT MORNING, after her psychology class ended and everyone was leaving the lecture hall, she somehow wasn't stunned to see a certain West Coast resident—and classmate—waiting around by the door for her to come out.

She stopped, gave it some thought, and then walked over to him. "Thank you," she said. "They were very pretty."

Jack nodded, his hands shoved deep in his pockets. "I'm glad you liked them."

They stood there.

"Well," she said.

He nodded. "Right."

Then, without looking at each other, they walked in different directions.

DURING THE NEXT few days, she settled into a new routine. Lots of studying, *meticulous* devotion to her physical therapy, and even the occasional well-balanced meal. An exciting evening was something along the lines of heating up instant coffee in the microwave and answering email.

Of course, she was completely freaking miserable, but—life was flawed. And, at least, it was a relatively familiar state of mind. She spent a lot of time watching CNN and C-Span, and thinking about how much she missed Vanessa, and wishing that she could hold her on her lap, and even get scratched a few times—just for the chance to hear that loud rumble of a purr.

During the weekend of the annual Winter Carnival, there seemed to be twice as many parties and social events as usual—all of which she skipped. Snow and ice sculpture contests, sledding excursions, fireworks, snowball fights, something called "Broomball," that sort of thing. But mainly, Winter Carnival seemed to be devoted to *skiing*. Going skiing, watching skiing, *celebrating* skiing. Listening to the distinctive sound of skis clacking together, and boots clunking, as people in her dorm packed up and headed off to the slopes was so depressing that, in the middle of reading *As You Like It*, she found herself crying. In fact, she felt so close to the edge emotionally that she didn't bother checking her email or answering her phone for almost three days—although she made herself call her parents once and try to sound happy, so that they wouldn't panic about not hearing from her. She also avoided the dining hall, avoided Goodrich, and avoided Sunday Snacks in the second-floor common room. In fact, she avoided doing much of anything whatsoever which involved leaving her room—or, more accurately, the *bed*.

Day after day, Juliana would pop in, full of ideas of fun things to do, and Meg would nod, and be polite, and refuse for what she suspected were nakedly-flimsy reasons. Susan and Dirk checked on her constantly, looking ever-more concerned and frustrated, and surprisingly, Mary Elizabeth showed up at her door once to ask if she wanted to go over to Bronfman and see a movie. Meg thanked her, but said that she needed to stay in and work on a lab report for her psychology class. Even Jesslyn stumped into her room to invite her to come join a hard-core

Texas Hold'Em game over in Morgan—another offer which she rebuffed as pleasantly as she could.

Jack Taylor and his long-haired buddy had stopped throwing the Frisbee at her, but whenever she saw him somewhere, he would hesitate, and then nod, or give her a slight wave. Most of the time, she would nod back, and they left it, uncomfortably, at that.

She was hunched over her desk one night, working on a philosophy paper, when Susan stopped by. *Again*. But, at least she wasn't going to get yelled at about food, for once, since she had grimly chewed her way through a full meal of beef stroganoff, noodles, and butternut squash earlier while sitting at the very same table with Susan, down at Mission. In fact, she even got some dessert from the sundae bar. Granted, she didn't finish it, but she *served* it to herself, at least.

"Hey," Susan said.

Meg nodded, using the mouse with her good hand.

"How's it going?" Susan asked.

It would be nice if these little encounters felt less—perfunctory. Meg turned in her chair. "Does Dirk hand this chore off to you? Or do you break your own rule—and *volunteer*?"

Susan looked tired.

"Anyway, I'm fine. Thanks for stopping by," Meg said, and turned back to her computer.

Susan watched her for a minute. "Are you going to spend the next four years this way?"

Quite probably. "I'm highly academically motivated," Meg said, typing a couple of notes about the section of Plato's *Republic* she had read earlier. "My studies mean a great deal to me."

"Since when?" Susan asked dubiously.

Since her drunken escapade. And, for that matter, since she'd had to listen to a JA's blunt lecture about it. Meg shrugged.

Susan sighed, and—since there weren't any other chairs in the room—sat down on the bottom of the bed. "I should never have said anything. You were just trying to fit in, and—I got in your way."

Yep.

"You *should* relax, and have fun, and do dumb things," Susan said. "I just—I really don't like Jack Taylor, so I got worried about you, and—I'm sorry, it was a bad call on my part."

Although she wouldn't have predicted it, Meg immediately felt defensive. "Jack's okay. He's just a little overwhelmed by having a penis."

Susan grinned wryly. "Aren't they all?"

Since the beginning of time.

"Just—I don't know," Susan said. "Try to find some middle ground. Okay?"

Yeah. Maybe she'd settle for a couple of A minuses, instead of straight A's.

During her brothers' February vacation, her security suddenly doubled, because her whole family was heading off to Europe, so that her mother could meet with the Member States of the International Atomic Energy Agency, and also make short hops to Berlin, Geneva, Brussels, and Madrid. Ramstein Air Base, Landstuhl, maybe Wiesbaden. An "if it's Tuesday, it must be Vienna" kind of trip. Behind closed doors, her mother referred to all meetings with European allies—with *any* allies, for that matter—as "cleaning up the mess," and the staff privately called them "America Is Your Buddy!" appearances. Her parents were very nervous about leaving her alone in the United States—which made *her* nervous—and so, they decided upon a huge expansion of her protective detail in their absence.

They had wanted her to join them, and she was tempted to say yes, since overseas Presidential trips were always interesting as hell, but if she went, she was pretty sure she wouldn't bother coming back to finish the semester when they returned. In fact, she had a feeling she might drop out of college altogether, given even the slightest excuse—and, as such, it would be the better part of wisdom to avoid anything which resembled an opportunity to do so.

But, she was very tense all week, and spent almost every free second glued to CNN, to follow the progress of the trip, and make sure that her family was safe, and appeared reasonably cheerful. For the most part, they looked okay, although she had to laugh when, right before starting to make a statement after a meeting at the IAEA Secretariat, her mother stopped, apologized, and went over to a very anxious-looking Neal, bent down, and spoke to him quietly. Then she glanced at Meg's father—whose radar was *good*, but not nearly as sharp as her mother's—and he came over to lead Neal off somewhere, presumably the nearest men's room.

Whereupon, her mother returned to the podium, entirely unruffled, gave her statement, took questions, and went back to the business of international affairs. The media seemed to be divided about whether it was wonderful, endearing footage—or whether her mother had been making a craven high-profile attempt to seem like an engaged parent. Apparently, they had missed the President's distinct, if subtle, attempt to make eye contact with Meg's father, or Linda, or one of her many aides, or *anyone* who could have quickly and easily interceded before she had to do it herself—and they were also, in Meg's opinion, perhaps lacking in senses of humor. Of course, one of the commentators routinely described the President as "The She-Devil" during many of his very biased round-table talk show appearances, so it was hard to take him seriously on any level.

Actually, right after her mother took office, some nut had self-published a book called *The She-Devil and Her Ruthless Plan for World Domination*, augmented by many author-planted five star reviews on Amazon. She and Beth had once spent an afternoon on the roof patio by the Solarium, reading it aloud and pretty much laughing themselves sick the entire time. It was easily the most hilarious book she had ever read, with the possible exception of a ranting diatribe titled *Dark Powers*, which included detailed accusations of satanic occult practices her mother was thought to embrace, complete with a photo of her holding their cat, Sidney—who looked sleepy, overweight, and deeply phlegmatic—and was described as one of the President's "familiars." Meg had even found a picture of herself in that epic tome, taken when she was about eight years old, dressed up for Halloween in a witch costume, smiling away with green makeup on her face. The caption was: "Grooming the next generation," which was funny all by itself, but made that much more so because the Evil-Being-To-Be was happily holding up a little orange cardboard UNICEF box in one hand.

It seemed to snow almost every day, which not only meant that she slipped and fell a lot, but served as a near-constant reminder that she was missing out on one of the best New England ski seasons in *years*. Maybe life would seem less bleak when, and if, the snow ever melted away. But, she just forced herself to keep getting up in the morning, going to classes, studying, heading over to physical therapy, and then studying some more. Trying to remember to eat, making a point of lying down at night even when she couldn't sleep, missing her cat, watching too much television. All of which was mind-numbingly dull, but at least she was probably going to get *really* good grades this semester.

Then, it was Friday, yet again, and she knew she was facing another long, empty weekend, which left her feeling so unhappy and out of sorts that when she got to her psychology class, she started to go inside the lecture hall—and then walked right back out again. Her agents exchanged glances—but, wisely, refrained from commenting. Paula was the first one to find the gumption to break the silence.

"Will you be needing a car?" she asked.

Meg shook her head. "Not until we have to go to god-damn physical therapy, no." What she probably needed was coffee, and maybe even something resembling breakfast.

So, after informing her agents accordingly, she decided to go down to the coffeehouse on Spring Street, and get a latte and a muffin or something.

The guy behind the counter was either unusually friendly—or, possibly, just flirtatious— and she was cordially aloof in return.

Which was, now that she thought about it, the character trait she *most* detested in her mother. It was always sort of disquieting to realize that the apple was making a regular habit of nestling itself directly underneath the tree.

Although a lot of people were coming in and out to get drinks or pastries to go, most of the tables were empty. She was looking for the most secluded place to sit down, when she noticed Hannah Goldman, her most recognizable journalistic shadow, slumping in a chair in the back room, with a cup of coffee, looking rather petulant and as though she *really* wanted a cigarette. She was still dressing as though she was expecting to be called into the White House Press Room for a vital briefing at any moment, and possibly then do an extensive live analysis on national television herself, but apparently, the reality of a foot and a half of snow had been enough to force her to abandon her high heels temporarily for a pair of impractical, but flashy, knee-high black leather boots.

Ms. Goldman looked up, saw her standing there, and instantly checked her watch.

It was scary to think about what an incredibly long list of people knew her daily schedule, down to the very minute. Meg shrugged at her, started to look for a seat as far away as possible—but then, changed her mind and limped over.

"Haven't seen you around lately. Happy to be back in town?" she asked.

Ms. Goldman nodded. "Mm-hmm."

Yeah. Sure. "Here for a gloriously exciting follow-up story?" Meg asked.

This time, Ms. Goldman's nod was more resigned.

Well, she wasn't planning to be helpful, but she could still have a chat. Maybe even try to cheer herself up, a little, by being *just* short of cooperative and revealing. Meg indicated the empty wooden chair across from her. "Mind if I sit down?"

Ms. Goldman looked delighted—and somewhat perplexed.

Meg eased herself down clumsily, managing to spill some of her latte—the largest size, with an extra shot of espresso—when an unexpected tremor of pain ran through her bad hand, intense enough to make her good hand shake, too.

When her lone napkin wasn't quite up to the task of wiping it up, Ms. Goldman pushed a couple more over to her. "How's your physical therapy going?" she asked.

Okay, this was a reporter. It wasn't as though they were going to sit here talking about how pretty the snow was, or the excitement of the Red Sox reporting to spring training, or anything. "I'm an inspiration to one and all," Meg said—and wanted to slug herself for making the grave mistake of being candid.

"You may well be," Ms. Goldman said, either overlooking—or missing—the sarcasm.

Oh, yeah. Totally. Meg motioned towards the cell phone resting on the table. "Don't you need to call in the fact that I'm skipping class? In case they want to use it as a Breaking News bulletin on the Web?"

Ms. Goldman blushed slightly, and tucked the cell phone into her blazer pocket, although she didn't—Meg noticed—turn it off. Not that, depending on her carrier, she was going to be able to count on getting a completely reliable signal, on a campus surrounded by mountains. Goddamn *snow*-covered mountains.

"Am I really that newsworthy?" she asked. "It doesn't seem particularly worthwhile to have so many of you still showing up here all the time."

"That's what I keep telling my editor," Ms. Goldman said, sounding gloomy.

Meg grinned. "So, this isn't what you'd consider a plum assignment?"

Ms. Goldman was obviously too polite to agree, but she had not been blessed—or, perhaps, cursed—with a decent poker face.

"Cheer up," Meg said. "Maybe you'll catch a break this afternoon, and someone'll—" She fired her forefinger in her direction— "take a pop at me."

Ms. Goldman stiffened, and Meg realized—too late—that she'd sounded considerably more malicious than she'd intended.

"I'm sorry," she said. "That was just meant to be a bad joke, not an indictment of your entire profession."

Ms. Goldman nodded.

Although it had almost certainly come across as a rather venomous insult. For lack of a better idea, Meg sipped some of her coffee. Not enough sugar, but she didn't feel like limping over to get more. "I really am sorry. It's—an innately adversarial process, that's all."

Ms. Goldman frowned at her. "Does your whole family *always* speak that way? Even when you're by yourselves?"

Christ, the country should eavesdrop on one of their contentious private dinners sometime. It would probably set off a whole new reality-show craze. An Evening with the Fractious First Family. "Yes," Meg said. "We do. In fact, my parents would be upset that I just slipped and used a couple of contractions."

Ms. Goldman smiled.

"I know you guys all want to be assigned to the regular press corps," Meg said, "but, it's really not such a great job." Which didn't seem to stop reporters from openly lusting for the opportunity. "I mean, it's pretty much just hurry up and wait all the time, except when Linda comes grumping out to give everyone a little spin and misdirection."

Ms. Goldman shrugged. "Maybe, but at least then you're in the thick of it. And, you're surrounded by actual *civilization*."

There were few things as glaring as city slickers who felt utterly out of place, despite being in the midst of tremendous pastoral beauty. "You know, this just might be the prettiest little town on the entire planet," Meg said.

Ms. Goldman nodded, glumly.

Right. "But you wish I'd picked Georgetown or Columbia or Harvard, or maybe even Stanford or Berkeley," Meg said.

Ms. Goldman's expression brightened. "Northwestern and UCLA would have been okay, too. Or Emory."

Cities, cities, cities. All big cities. Places where high heels and incessant ambition fit right in.

"Out of curiosity, why did you come over here?" Ms. Goldman asked.

Good question. Why the hell *had* she? It would have been easy enough to feign not seeing her, or just—if absolutely necessary—exchange unfriendly nods before going off to find someplace to drink her coffee in peace.

Let *both* of them drink their coffee in peace.

"I'm sorry, I probably disturbed you, didn't I," Meg said, feeling pretty stupid that it had taken this long for the thought to cross her mind. It wasn't as though they were friends, and enjoyed hanging out together. She started to stand up. "Maybe I should just—"

"I was only asking," Ms. Goldman said.

And it had been a legitimate question. Which meant that it probably deserved an answer. "To tell you the truth, I'm not sure why," Meg said. "I just did, for some reason."

Ms. Goldman nodded.

"I miss adults," Meg said. Except for her brothers, she usually pretty much spent all of her time around adults, and—she liked adults. Felt comfortable around them.

Ms. Goldman looked up alertly. A *reporter* look. "So, you find your fellow students immature?"

Oh, Christ, *that* was going to make a god-awful headline. "No," Meg said quickly. "Not at all." Damn. She'd better find her way the hell out of this, and fast. "I'm, uh—I'm making no pejorative implications about them whatsoever."

Luckily, Ms. Goldman's cell phone went off, so she was probably going to be able to escape from this one without creating too much more trouble for herself.

But Ms. Goldman just glanced at the number, shook her head, and turned it off. "I was only asking a question, Miss Powers. I'm not out to skewer you."

Which, if it were true, would probably be a first in the history of modern journalism. Of course, she'd walked right into this—okay, *limped*—and so, had no one to blame but herself.

And, it was rather telling that they weren't even on a first-name basis.

"I know it must seem that way, sometimes," Ms. Goldman went on, "but—"

Probably because it *was* that way. "Isn't that what you guys do?" Meg asked. "Wait for one of us to get tired, or distracted, and then try to make us say something as idiotic as possible?" The bigger the gaffe, the better the story.

"That's what *some* of us do," Ms. Goldman said. "But, the rest of us—" She stopped, and shook her head. "I'm sorry. You were trying to have a normal conversation with me, and I really blew it, didn't I?"

"We both did. Don't worry about it." Meg pulled on her jacket. "But, hey, I'd better go start getting ready for my next class. Take it easy, okay?"

"Yeah," Ms. Goldman said, visibly disappointed. "You, too."

19

SOMEHOW, PHYSICAL THERAPY felt even more grueling than usual that afternoon. Although by now, she probably should have figured out that she really didn't do very well when she tried to make it through a whole day on nothing but coffee. Going to the hospital tended to be stressful, anyway, because, inevitably, people would recognize her, and want to say hello, or have her stop so they could take her picture or something. And she couldn't exactly say no, when they were either injured or ill themselves, or visiting someone else who was. Her agents weren't thrilled about it, but she was pretty much damned if she did, and damned if she didn't, since everyone always seemed to get hurt or offended if she just nodded and kept going. So, most of the time, it was easier to be nice and pause for a few seconds.

There was a certain amount of schedule rotation, and usually a doctor or two somewhere in the general vicinity, but she mostly spent her sessions alone with the same two physical therapists—Vicky, who was a no-nonsense, but fairly jovial, older African-American woman, and Cheryl, who was a skinny, skittish Caucasian woman in her early thirties. Both of them were friendly, although Vicky was more inclined to chat. Meg was always very polite, and—well—*aloof*.

"Are you taking care of yourself?" Vicky asked, as they worked on her range-of-motion—which hurt like hell.

Meg opened her eyes, which, for some reason, made the pain feel much more intense. "How do you mean?"

Vicky shrugged. "Eating, sleeping, that sort of thing."

"Oh, absolutely," Meg said, and nodded to punctuate that. "You bet."

"Unh-hunh," Vicky said. "So, it's my imagination that you've lost about ten pounds since you've been coming here?"

No way. Meg looked down at herself. "*Two* pounds, maybe." Although, since she was wearing an oversized blue turtleneck and heavy black sweatpants, it was hard to tell, one way or the other.

"After we finish, I'd like to get a weight on you," Vicky said, blandly. "Keep your chart up-to-date."

Meg glanced at the water bottle resting nearby, wondering how much she would have to drink, before she got weighed, to make it seem as though—and Christ almighty, was that an anorectic thought, or what?

And Vicky was frowning at her. Damn. Caught in the act.

"What have you eaten today?" Vicky asked.

She could lie, but it wasn't going to be convincing. Meg sighed. "Today was unusual. It was—hectic." So terribly hectic, that after leaving the coffeehouse, she'd randomly skipped her Shakespeare class, too, and spent lunchtime in the library, reading a paperback mystery in the quietest enclosed carrel she could find down on the lower level.

Vicky nodded. "So, what, you had a couple of cups of coffee, and called that a meal?"

Yeah, so? "You have no way of knowing that," Meg said stiffly.

"You walked in here with a very large latte," Vicky said, "and your hands are shaking. It doesn't really take a rocket scientist to figure it out."

Suddenly very tired of physical therapy—and of being criticized—Meg yanked her leg free, which hurt so much that she had to fight off a gasp. "My hands are shaking, because every time I come here, it's *extremely* god-damn painful."

Vicky nodded. "I know. You want to take a break?"

Meg shook her head, aware that her good hand was tightly clenched. "No, I want to finish up already, so I can get the hell *out* of here."

That much of a growl would have been enough to scare Cheryl off for the rest of the afternoon, but Vicky just nodded and helped her resume the extension and flexion exercises. They worked in complete silence for a few minutes.

"I think it's to your credit that you don't throw your weight around," Vicky said.

Mostly because her father would hit the roof, if any of them behaved that way. Although there wasn't much he could do about ordinary crankiness, and general character flaws. Meg shrugged, not looking at her. "I'm probably too *thin* to throw it around."

Vicky's mouth moved as though she might be about to laugh, but she nodded again, and they kept working.

When they were finally finished—Meg's leg now quivering even more than her hands were—Vicky carefully packed her knee with ice.

"I think it would be a good idea if you started drinking some nutritional supplements," she said, "okay? At least two a day."

The very thought made Meg feel sick—sick*er*—to her stomach. When she was in the hospital, they constantly brought her what they cheerfully called "milkshakes" to choke down, to help her try and regain the weight she'd lost as the result of two full weeks of complete starvation and near-fatal dehydration. "You mean that gross stuff in the cans?" she asked.

"If you keep it in the refrigerator, it isn't that bad," Vicky said. "I assume you have one in your dorm room?"

Meg nodded.

Vicky looked pleased. "Okay, then. You should also keep yoghurt and fruit juice and things like that around. Bread, cheese, peanut butter. Skipping meals really isn't a good strategy, especially when your body's trying so hard to heal. You desperately need the protein and calories."

Except that stocking the refrigerator would involve planning, and shopping, and other tasks for which she had no energy. There were times, even when she knew she had several Cokes right there waiting for her, that she was too exhausted to bother getting up and taking one out. Too exhausted to pop the can *open*.

And, as far as she was concerned, her body wasn't healing at all.

Apparently deciding that she had bullied her enough for one day, Vicky gave her good knee a light pat. "All right, why don't you rest, and then I'll send Cheryl in."

Since she was only halfway through today's particular PT nightmare. Meg nodded, covering her eyes with one arm, in an attempt to get a little bit of privacy. She was probably alone for about twenty minutes, but it felt more like twenty *seconds* when she sensed Cheryl standing nearby, shifting her weight nervously from one practical plain white sneaker to the other. She lowered her arm—and saw that, indeed, that was exactly what her hand therapist was doing.

They exchanged pleasantries, and then Meg just followed instructions, without asking questions or commenting in any way.

Except that, she could feel tears in her eyes, and she swiftly wiped her good hand across them.

"No more with the thumb today, okay?" she said, trying to keep her voice steady. "I don't think I can stand it."

Cheryl hesitated, then nodded, and started working with the scarring and the fascia on her two slightly functional fingers, instead.

When the session was finally—*thank God*—over, Cheryl stayed around, looking more jittery than usual. All Meg wanted to do was go back to the dorm and sleep for the next ten or twelve hours, but she forced herself to smile.

"Is there something you want to ask me?" she said.

"Well, um—" Cheryl shifted her weight. "I have a friend."

Oh, swell. Some kind of god-damned White House–related favor. What was it going to be, an autographed photo of the President, or something? But, Meg confined herself to a relatively receptive nod.

"Upstairs," Cheryl elaborated.

If this was the beginning of some supposedly uplifting speech about God, Meg was pretty sure she was going to start screaming. But she nodded, more cautiously this time. Vicky had strolled over in their direction, and Meg had the strong impression that she might be about to intercede.

Cheryl bit her lip, looked away, and shifted her weight some more.

"I'm having trouble following the direction of this conversation," Meg said, keeping her voice as pleasant as possible.

Cheryl sighed. "My friend Olivia works in Pediatrics, and she—well, they all know you come here regularly, and—well—"

Okay. She wasn't in the mood, but it was manageable. "In other words," Meg said, "someone up there's pretty sick, and your friend was wondering if I would stop by to say hello." Although why in the hell anyone would want to *meet* her was a phenomenon Meg had yet to figure out. Regardless of how often it happened.

Cheryl looked at her unhappily. "More than one."

Right. This was a hospital. "Okay," Meg said, although the thought of having to go up there and be captivating and witty and encouraging made her feel more like bursting into tears than anything else.

Vicky frowned at Cheryl. "Today's sessions were a little grueling. Why don't we think about that for Monday, maybe?"

"Yes," Cheryl said, instantly. "Of course. Monday would be better. We can just—"

Meg shook her head, slowly taking off the ice packs, and strapping her splint and brace back on. "No, it's all right. Today is fine." She would just duck in, smile, shake a couple of hands, sign a cast or two, and then, she could leave. If she'd known in advance, she could have brought along a few of those little Air Force One boxes of M&M's or something to hand out, but—well, it probably didn't matter, since they wouldn't know what they were missing.

Vicky was still glaring at Cheryl, but the truth was, she could pretty much do a Pediatrics ward visit in her sleep. Been there, done that, for *years*.

Luckily. Or—unfortunately. Depending upon one's point of view. There were times, when she was little, that it felt as though accompanying her mother on public appearances was practically the only time she ever got to *see* her.

Not that she was still angry about it, years later. Hell, no.

She hoisted herself up onto her good leg, feeling dizzy enough to concede—to herself—that she should have gotten a damn sandwich or something at the Grab 'n' Go before coming over here.

Five minutes. Ten, at the most. No big deal.

She let a couple of her agents go ahead to decide whether her route out to the hall, into the elevator, and up to the ward would be sufficiently secure. While they waited, Cheryl got more and more contrite.

"You, um, you really don't have to do this today," she said. "Or *ever*, for that matter. I mean—"

Meg raised her good hand abruptly to cut off the rest of the sentence before it went any further, and Cheryl subsided.

She couldn't help hoping that the only patients up there would be rapidly recovering from minor things like tonsillectomies—but, she knew better. Wan, big-eyed children, quietly frantic parents, cheerful nurses with brightly colored scrubs and sad expressions—it was always the same. Only the names were different.

So, she was going to have to steel herself to do this. Figure out a way to look and act engaged, while making sure to keep herself inwardly detached. There'd been times, over the years, at hospices, and nursing homes, and hospitals—and animal shelters—when it had been a terrible struggle to keep from sobbing openly. Once, she had seen her mother start to completely lose it, because something about one *particular* brave young mother with terminal cancer hit her unexpectedly hard. She regained control immediately—as she always did—but later on, in the limousine, she'd covered her eyes with her hand. Most of the way back to the White House. She'd been in pretty rough shape after they'd made official visits to the sites of former concentration camps in Europe, too—to the degree that later, on Air Force One, the medical people thought she was having trouble getting her breath and clandestinely gave her some oxygen in the private Presidential suite.

Except that Meg had seen her react the exact same way, when she was ten years old and her grandfather died. She had loved him a lot, so it had been very sad, but her strongest memory from that day was her mother's silent, trembling grief, although she had never cried, and the long, heartfelt eulogy she had given had been flawless, and even made people laugh fondly here and there. When the family was finally alone, back at his rambling apartment on Fifth Avenue—which her parents sold a few months later, a hasty move they now sort of regretted—her mother had gone into the library without a word to any of them, closed the door, and didn't come out for several hours.

Brian came into the room and made a small "All clear" motion with his hand, and Meg nodded, took a few deep breaths, and lifted herself back up onto her cane.

Her mother, of course, had been gifted with the truly great politician's trifecta—a photographic memory for names and faces, the ability to make instant personal connections with total strangers, and the underrated skill of being able to convey genuine sincerity. Today, Meg figured she'd be doing well if she remembered to smile the whole time, and was able to hide the fact that she was mostly going through the motions.

Neal always liked talking to people he didn't know, but Steven hated philanthropic visits even more than she did—both of them were shy as hell, as a rule—and her father wasn't too crazy about making public appearances, either. He was just better at masking it. Her mother really seemed to enjoy doing it, most of the time, but—strangers were easy. It was only when her mother had to deal with people to whom she was actually *close*, that she—but Meg wasn't mad at her. Nope. No way. Never happen.

And not anything to dwell upon, at the moment.

She met a little boy with two broken legs, another boy who had burned his arm badly when he bumped against a wood stove, and a girl recovering from a bout of pneumonia. An incredibly sweet and very small girl with leukemia—Jesus—and a painfully thin bald boy about Steven's age, who also obviously had some form of cancer.

Which was about the time that her chest started feeling very tight, and her heart seemed to be beating much harder than it should be.

But, she kept going. Met a boy who had sickle-cell anemia, a girl who actually *had* had a tonsillectomy—and so many others that she had trouble remembering the various diagnoses—and names—once she had left a given room. The kids who were well enough were gathered together in a communal ward, and most of them were out of bed, playing with toys and puzzles, watching television, and so forth. The children who were more seriously ill or injured were in smaller single or double rooms. They were all shockingly pleased to see her, which was flattering—and disconcerting.

Vicky must have called ahead to warn the head nurse on the shift, Olivia, because she lingered close by, and kept asking whether she was too tired to continue. The answer was hell, *yes*, but Meg just smiled, and shook her head, and kept moving from bed to bed, and room to room, with a couple of her agents trailing nearby, but staying out in the corridors the entire time.

Some of the kids were asleep, but one mother actually insisted upon waking her son up, because he would be so disappointed not to have gotten a chance to see her in person.

And how strange was *that*? Meg, for one, found herself underwhelming, even on her best days.

She didn't get back to school until after the dining halls had stopped serving, but in the car, Ed had remarked that he was starving, and asked if she would mind if they took a quick detour to the pizza place at the shopping center. It was a transparent ploy, on his part, but she wasn't about to call him on it, and when he asked, casually, if he could order something for her, too, she thanked him and gave him enough money to get her a meatball grinder.

Which she was too tired to eat, but she stuck it in her refrigerator for later, and then went to bed without checking her email or voice-mail—or doing anything more than taking off her sneakers and dropping her jacket on the floor before she got under the covers.

Since it was Friday night, the dorm was even louder than usual, and she kept waking up every time music unexpectedly starting playing or someone shouted. She would do her best to doze back off—only to have some new noise wake her right back up again. A telephone ringing— her *own* telephone, two of the times; doors slamming; a bunch of people laughing. Benign sounds, which were getting on every single goddamned nerve she had.

In the morning, before she even opened her eyes, she could hear icy sleet against her window—and decided that there was no chance in hell that she was going to try walking down to the dining hall. So she heated up the meatball sandwich in the microwave, and had that for breakfast, along with a Coke.

She was bored, and feeling very lonely, so she turned on the television to watch C-Span for a while—nothing like watching Congress dither and argue and spout platitudes to brighten up the day. But, since it was the weekend, they were mostly only showing book stuff, and she lost interest almost immediately, and switched to CNN, instead. Somehow, the more homesick she felt, the more she felt a desperate need to get as much current events as possible. Among other things, she really missed reading her mother's non-classified daily news summaries, to say nothing of being able to request any newspaper or magazine she wanted, pretty much around the clock. Plus, at home, she could watch press briefings, or events in the Rose Garden or wherever, live, on closed-circuit television, which made it easy to keep up.

And, yeah, it made her feel better every time she caught a glimpse of her mother. Got to see how she looked, what she was doing. Knew for sure that she was *safe*, at least for the moment. Sometimes she got lucky and saw her father, too, generally with Preston standing a few feet away, looking dapper.

It was much less entertaining when she saw *herself*, but—Thank God for small mercies—that wasn't happening very often lately.

Her door was partway open, and Susan knocked on the doorjamb.

"How you doing?" she asked.

Time for the obligatory daily JA check-in. Christ. "Fine," Meg said. "You?"

Susan nodded.

They both glanced at the television, as the lead stories heading into the top of the hour were announced, more than one of them relating to the President, of course.

"It isn't weird for you to watch that?" Susan asked curiously.

Meg shook her head. "It's kind of comforting, actually."

Susan seemed to find that a little hard to fathom, but she nodded. Meg waved her into the room, and she sat down in the desk chair. They watched as there was a sound-clip of the President speaking about what the commentators were characterizing as "bold domestic policy initiatives." The one they were focusing on involved a detailed new health care reform plan, which already had the apparent, and somewhat surprising, backing of a good percentage of the AMA, although not the insurance companies. Yet. The Administration's legislative activities had been noticeably enterprising of late, although, as ever, the odds were very much against the prospect of the more humanistic ones succeeding.

"What do you see?" Susan asked. "When you look at that."

Unfortunately, she saw what she always saw—her mother was very tired and unhappy. Meg sighed. "I see a person who isn't getting much sleep." And who was worrying herself sick—possibly literally—about too many things. "What do *you* see?"

Susan shrugged. "Someone who actually wants the best for the country, and is trying to do something about it. For all I know, there's stuff going right over my head, but it sure doesn't come across that way."

"No, it's accurate," Meg said. "I mean, Christ knows she's a politician, but she can pretty much get away with it, because she doesn't have any kind of private agenda. I think it really all *is* for the greater good." And, on the occasions when she suspected otherwise, it usually only took one glance at her rigidly moral father to realize that the very fact that they were still together, however tenuously, was a strong indication that her mother was pretty close to being exactly who Meg hoped she was. Politically, anyway. On the other hand, her parents were so utterly private, that it was possible that, despite having lived with them her entire life, she had no idea whatsoever about what their marriage was *really* like.

"Do you think it'll actually get through Congress?" Susan asked.

Meg shook her head. "Not a chance." And the obvious reality of that was very annoying, now that she thought about it. Her mother should be too smart for this. "It's bad timing, and it's stupid. She's wasting a lot of perfectly good political capital, when she really just ought to pack her little bags on this one, and come back and fight another day. Aim lower, for now. I mean, you know what huge segments of the country are hearing practically every time she opens her mouth lately? They're hearing, 'Guess what, boys? As soon as I finish this, *I'm coming after your guns!*' "

"Sounds good to me," Susan said.

True enough. Despite being the ultimate pipe dream. "Yeah, but," Meg winked at her, "you're a Northeastern intellectual at a very exclusive college—what the hell do *you* know?"

Susan smiled. "Not a damned thing," she said.

But the actual political ramifications of what was going on suddenly made perfect sense—and Meg felt pretty dumb. Which was a relief. If her mother had suddenly lost her impeccable Washingtonian instincts, it would have been immeasurably disappointing. "Except, I'm wrong," she said. "By making these moves, she can't lose. Either there's some kind of miracle, and most of the stuff gets through somehow, and the country takes a remarkable, positive turn, and she has this wonderful place in history—or she blows herself out of the water, even though it *looks* as though she's just trying to push some ambitious new policies."

Susan looked confused. "But why would she want to—" She stopped. "Oh. The election."

Meg nodded. There was always a tremendous amount of pressure for any remotely successful incumbent—and, in her probably subjective opinion, her mother was considerably more than that—to run again, but if this specific incumbent's ambition exceeded her execution, then the Party might be more receptive to the notion of her gracefully stepping aside, in favor of a stronger, presumptively more conservative, candidate.

"It's a little Machiavellian," Susan said uneasily.

A *little*? Meg grinned. "Yeah, but in a real greater-good sort of way."

In fact, she liked it a lot. A *whole* lot.

"You know, I've never actually seen you look animated before," Susan said.

Meg flushed. Because, after all, she *hated* politics. With, you know, a fiery passion.

"I heard you telling Juliana that you're probably going to major in English," Susan said.

Meg nodded. "Yep. That's me."

Susan looked very amused. "Well, I'd bet my whole tuition that that isn't what you end up doing at all."

Political science? No way. Not in a million years.

Except—okay—maybe.

"But, I *am* going to be an English major," Meg said, without much conviction. Despite little details like the fact that she really wasn't enjoying her Shakespeare class at all. "Really."

Susan looked at her with tremendous amusement. "Yeah," she said. "Sure you are."

20

OTHER THAN THE weekly entry gathering for JA-provided snacks—which she almost always blew off, Sunday night was, relatively speaking, the quietest night of the week. So, naturally, *that* was when her subconscious decided it would be an ideal time to have the worst screaming nightmare she'd had in a couple of weeks. Martin was the upstairs agent on duty, and very mechanically, she let him check her room while she went down the hall to wash her face and try to calm down. Her hallmates must have gotten used to being rudely awakened by shrieking, because none of them rushed out to see what had happened anymore.

Once she was finished, she walked out to the hall with her head down, in case there was any visible evidence that she had been crying.

"I, uh—sorry about that," she said.

Martin, sitting back at his desk, just shook his head.

Meg looked around. It was very, very quiet. "At least I didn't wake up everyone else this time."

Martin shrugged. "Susan came up to check. I'm sure you could go knock on her door, if you wanted."

It was reassuring to know that Susan was pretty much *always* going to come upstairs and check—but humiliating to know how god-damned loud the screaming must be.

"Are you going to be able to get back to sleep?" he asked.

She didn't really know him at all, but Martin seemed like a very nice guy. For that matter, she didn't know *any* of them, beyond insignificant details, like the fact that Paula was from Atlanta, and Larry was a rabid New York Jets fan, and that sort of thing.

Martin lifted the large thermos of coffee, which he always kept on the left side of the desk during his shifts. "Want some?"

Did she? Okay. Meg went into her room, and brought out the

Williams mug she'd bought to replace the Red Sox one that had gotten broken.

"I hope you like lots of milk and sugar," he said. "I add it before I come here."

"Oh, I'm sure it's great," Meg said quickly. When it came to coffee, she was finding that she wasn't particularly picky. If it was hot—or even lukewarm, it was good.

He filled her cup, and she nodded her thanks.

"I usually have milk and stuff in my refrigerator," she said. Or, anyway, sometimes. "If, you know, you ever need anything."

He nodded. "I'm all set, but thanks."

Okay, then. She should go into her room, and watch CNN or ESPN, maybe.

"Want to stay out here for a while?" he asked, indicating the chair next to the desk.

Meg hesitated, and then sat down. She felt sad, and shaky, and it would be a relief to talk to someone, even a near-stranger. It was really pretty appalling that she knew so little about him. He was African-American, very light-skinned, probably in his late twenties, and pretty tall, with big shoulders. She wasn't sure if he wore contact lenses, but late at night, she often saw him with reading glasses on, and since he didn't have a wedding ring, he was probably single. Most of her agents were, and from what she had heard, a few of the others sometimes *acted* that way.

"Where'd you go to school?" she asked.

"Clemson," he said.

The only thing she really knew about Clemson was that it was in South Carolina. "Did you like it?"

He sipped some coffee. "It was okay. But I screwed up my knee playing football my sophomore year, and they took my scholarship away. I thought that was kind of lousy."

Definitely lousy. "So, what did you do?" she asked.

He shrugged. "Got my grades up. Took out some loans. Worked a couple of jobs. That kind of stuff."

Which instantly made her feel guilty—and obscenely, offensively rich. "I'm sorry," she said. "I don't always remember that I've been really lucky that way."

For the first time, he made direct eye contact with her. "I wouldn't trade places with you for a minute."

Christ, did it seem that awful? Oh, hell, it *was* that awful. "I'm sorry I don't talk to you guys more," she said. "I just—you must think I'm this unbelievable bitch."

He shook his head.

Yeah. Right. As protectees went, she was an absolute joy. She sighed. "What happened to Chet makes me sick." One of the two agents who had been shot—and died—that day in front of her high school. "He was my friend."

Martin nodded.

"And I don't blame you guys for Dennis," Meg said. The bastard who had sold her out—and also gotten killed for his trouble.

Martin looked grim. "*We* blame us for Dennis."

Yeah. They probably did. And, all things being equal, they probably should.

It was quiet. They were alone. No one else ever had to know that they had discussed this.

Meg swallowed. "If I ask you a serious question, will you give me an honest answer?"

"If I can," Martin said.

Okay. But the thought of even saying this aloud—a fear that, not infrequently, surfaced in some disguised form in her worst dreams—was scary. Terrifying, even. Meg took a deep breath. "If it happens again, are you guys going to kill me?"

Martin tilted his head. "I don't understand what you're asking."

The reality was that this answer might be so secret and covert—and inhumane—that even her mother hadn't been consulted. Because she sure as hell wouldn't have given her *approval.* Presumably. But it would be foolish to think that security and intelligence agencies revealed all of their secrets to anyone, even the President. They might justify it by spouting about national security concerns, and plausible deniability, and so forth, but it was really about power and corruption, and the simple reality that the combination of the two could sometimes lead to some very dark and evil activities. A person would have to be incredibly naive to believe otherwise.

Martin was still looking at her, clearly baffled. "Meg?"

She should have stayed with football, and college, and other friendly topics. She let out her breath. "If someone tries to kidnap me again, and it looks like they're going to pull it off, are you guys under orders to kill me, if you have to, to keep them from being successful?"

He stared at her. "What? Are you crazy?"

Yes, but that was another issue, entirely. "The country's security is a hell of a lot more important than *my* safety," Meg said. "If anyone managed to get away with it again, that would make us look—it would be a lot better just to wipe them out, even if it means taking me out, too."

His mouth had actually dropped open during all of this, and when he put his cup of coffee down, she was surprised to see his hand quiver. "Our only orders are to protect all of you, at all costs, even if it means giving up our own lives to do it," he said. "It's our *code.*"

Maybe Dennis had missed the training sessions on The Code.

"No one will *ever* get you again," he said, "but if, God forbid, they try, I can promise you that there isn't a man or woman on this detail who wouldn't instantly shoot anyone who drew down on you, even if it was one of our own people."

Christ, she hoped that was true.

Martin still looked very upset. "Meg, tell me that you haven't been spending a lot of time worrying about this. Because it's not ever going to happen."

She could only tell him that if she lied. "It's one of the nightmares I have," she said softly.

If he wasn't such a big, tough person, she might have been afraid that hearing all of this had made him feel like crying.

"The guy told me that it would have been over right then and there if you all had shot me." Except that no one, except for Beth and Preston, ever knew what she meant when she referred to "the guy." She sighed. "The kidnapper, I mean. The main one. He said he wasn't sure which way you were going to go, but that you should have killed me, to keep the government from being so completely humiliated. That the fallout from my being dead would have been much lower."

"Yeah, well, *fuck* him," Martin said, and then looked embarrassed. "I'm sorry. I shouldn't have used that word in front of you."

Since the kidnapping, she had started using it herself, regularly. One of the more unattractive aspects of her new personality.

Martin reached over to touch her sleeve apologetically, and then withdrew. "Did he tell you a lot of horrible stuff like that?"

And how. Meg nodded. "Oh, yeah. Big talker, that one."

"Yeah, well, I hope I'm the guy who runs him down someday," Martin said, the expression in his eyes noticeably darker.

Meg smiled a little. "You know what? I hope you're the one who gets him, too."

Somewhere over in Sage D, a door slammed, a couple of people laughed, and the door slammed again. Then, it went back to being quiet.

"I'm sure there were all kinds of back-channel discussions and overtures going on," Meg said. "But my mother really wasn't going to make any concessions." She had never had to be told, one way or the other, because she had been able to see it in her eyes ever since—and far too often, unnervingly, she recognized it in her father's eyes, too, when he was looking at her mother, and didn't that know she was watching. "I mean, she was willing to destroy herself, and sacrifice me, to live up to her oath, and serve the country's long-term interests. It was—" well— "pretty god-damned cold." *Ice* cold. "But, Christ, it was brave."

Martin had a "boy, am *I* in over my head" expression on his face.

"I mean, she'll never be able to forgive herself," Meg said, "but damn, it really was heroic. And I'm glad she did it."

She wasn't sure he was going to respond—because people just didn't talk about the President that way—but, to her surprise, he was nodding. "I was in the Marines for a while," he said. "Before I applied to join the Secret Service. And if you had an officer like that, you couldn't stand the son-of-a-bitch, but you followed him anywhere he told you to go, because—well, you knew you had a leader, and you felt lucky because of it."

The image of her mother, directing troops through the desert, or the jungle, or out of a helicopter, her uniform carefully tailored and her helmet perched at just the right angle, was kind of funny. Meg shook her head. "Yeah, but a lot of people must hate her for it. I mean, all over the country." Hell, all over the *world*.

"Probably," Martin agreed. "Especially anyone with children. But, the military, and law enforcement, and guys like me? She wasn't exactly a favorite. You know, rich New England lady? Walking around cracking wise and looking like a movie star? Not even a *jock*? Forget about it. But, damn, she *showed* us something. We might not have followed her before, but we sure will now."

Everyone always forgot that her mother had actually been born and raised as an Upper East Side New Yorker—but, it was still a perspective which never would have crossed her mind. Although she suddenly flashed back to watching a news clip with Preston a few months earlier, when her mother was on an aircraft carrier, and he had said something to the effect of, "My God, will you look at those salutes? Whole new ballgame." She hadn't asked him what he meant because, well, she was too tired at the time.

"*You* showed us something, too," Martin said.

Meg looked at him uncertainly. "Something good?"

He grinned. "Fuckin' A," he said.

THE NEXT MORNING, she rose above the temptation to skip her psychology class—mainly because they had a unit quiz coming up, and she should probably try to be somewhat prepared for it. She hadn't managed to wake up in time for breakfast—again, so she stopped at the Eco Café on the way to get some coffee and a couple of cookies. People weren't supposed to bring food or drinks into the amphitheater, but as long as she wasn't flagrant about it, with luck, her professor—who was inclined to be testy—wouldn't notice.

She was just taking her first bite when Jack Taylor came over, as though he had every intention of sitting next to her—even though there were *lots* of empty seats.

"You okay?" he asked. "I didn't see you in here on Friday."

Not that he'd been looking, right? Considering that they hadn't exchanged a single word recently. There hadn't even been many *nods*, of late. And, of course, she'd been down on Spring Street, anyway, which would have made her more difficult to find. Meg shrugged. "I was in the front row, taking notes like crazy."

"Right," Jack said, and smiled briefly. "I just wanted to be sure you weren't sick or anything, or—well, you know." He shook some snow off and unzipped his jacket. "Mind if I sit here?"

Yes, and no. "As long as you promise to pay *very* close attention if we cover erotomania today," Meg said.

Jack nodded. "Okay. If you explain the really hard words."

It wasn't quite a "touché"—but, it wasn't bad.

Despite the weather, all he was wearing under his jacket was an old flowered Hawaiian shirt, jeans, and high-tops. No gloves, a baseball cap which said "SM," with a scripted "SAMOHI" below the logo, black sunglasses. California boys didn't get cold, apparently.

The class started, which meant that they didn't have to sit there and try to make conversation. Which was just as well, but she found herself a little too aware of the fact that he was right next to her. For better or worse, he was exceedingly attractive. But she made a strong, if only minimally effective, effort to concentrate on the lecture.

"What's the cap?" she asked.

"My high school," he said. "Santa Monica."

Good to hear that it had nothing to do with sadomasochism.

"You have terrible handwriting," he said quietly at one point.

Yes. She did. She glanced over at his notebook and saw neat, very organized printing, with sections carefully lettered and numbered in outline form. Kind of a dramatic contrast to her jagged stream-of-consciousness scrawling.

"Security reasons," she said. "I'm sure you understand."

For at least a second, he fell for that, but then he grinned.

When the class ended, her plan was to stall until he gave up and went away, except that he was taking his own sweet time packing up, too.

"You going to lunch with anyone?" he asked.

It would be way too embarrassing to admit that she was going to go take a pre–physical therapy nap after her Shakespeare class. Meg shook her head. "I have an appointment later, and I need to get ready for it."

"Oh." He looked disappointed. "Well—you going to dinner with anyone?"

Dinner was likely to coincide with her *post*–physical therapy nap. "I'm sorry, I really can't," Meg said. "It's nice of you to ask, though."

"Aren't you even a little bit curious?" he asked, as she started to leave.

Christ, couldn't the guy take a hint already? After all, she'd just turned him down twice in less than a minute. Meg stopped, without turning to look at him. "About what?"

He walked around her so that they were facing each other. "About whether it was just alcohol, or whether we really *did* have that much chemistry. I mean, it was—I've never felt that way with anyone before. I can't stop thinking about it."

Well, actually, she couldn't, either. And even his bringing it up was, frankly, um, arousing. "Really? It's always like that for me," Meg said.

He grinned, and reached out to run his hand across hers.

Maybe, just possibly, she felt a tiny electric charge. A frisson, even. "Sorry," she said. "Didn't do a thing for me."

"Okay." He removed his hand from hers. "So, do I give up, or do I keep trying?"

It would be so easy just to get rid of him. *Too* easy. And maybe easy wasn't what she needed right now, despite its overall appeal as a lifestyle strategy.

"Keep trying," she said, and then limped away.

WHEN SHE GOT to physical therapy, Vicky was running late with her previous patient, so she started with Cheryl, and her hand.

"Do you think I'm going to have to have more surgery?" Meg asked, trying to distract herself from the pain by watching her fingers refuse to respond, over and over, as they attempted various exercises.

Cheryl hesitated—which was pretty much an answer in and of itself.

"So, all of this PT, trying to break up the scar tissue and the contractures, and get some movement back and all, will pretty much be canceled out," Meg said.

Cheryl hesitated again.

Swell.

"You're a very hard worker," Cheryl said. "And I'm really seeing some progress with your pinky."

Yeah. She could flick it, a little. Sometimes without even getting tears in her eyes.

When they were finished, Cheryl attached the TENS—Transcutaneous Electrical Nerve Stimulation—unit to Meg's hand. It was supposed to work wonders for pain management, and she even had a portable one to use in her dorm room, if she were so inclined—but, she really didn't think it had much effect at all, so she rarely bothered with it.

She had a short rest between sessions, and then Vicky came in to work with her knee. By the time they started doing the weight-bearing exercises, Meg was so worn out that she wanted to go back to lying down, covered with ice packs.

"I think that's going to be enough for today," Vicky said, watching her legs—even her good one—tremble as she tried to negotiate a barely moving treadmill.

"What about the Cybex?" Meg asked, although the thought of being strapped into the machine to do weight-resistance exercises was enough to make her feel like crying.

"We'll do that first on Wednesday," Vicky said, walking with her hand just below Meg's elbow, as though she might be going to crash to the floor at any second.

Did she really look that close to collapsing? Damn.

"I don't want to nag," Vicky said, setting her up with a fresh batch of ice packs.

Could have fooled her.

"But, what did you have for lunch?" she asked.

Should she tell the truth? Why not. *So* much easier than off-the-cuff lying. "A Coke and some M&Ms," Meg said.

Vicky pursed her lips.

"And, of course, my latte," Meg said, indicating her long-since empty cup. "Full of milk, for strong bones, and overall good health."

Vicky did not seem to be amused.

"The M&Ms really gave a boost to my fast-twitch muscles, I think," Meg said.

Now Vicky looked—faintly—amused. "You need to do better with your eating, Meg. I'm not kidding about this."

Yeah, yeah, yeah.

When she got back to the campus, she had her agents drive her as close to the dining hall as possible, so she would have to do less walking. She wasn't looking, of course—not even *peeking*, much—although if she had been, she might have been sad not to see Jack either in line, or at any of the tables. In fact, she didn't really see anyone she knew. But then, a couple of guys from her entry waved her over to their table, and she was relieved not to have to sit by herself.

Dinner was more relaxing than she expected—Andy was a really funny, high-energy African-American guy from New York, who had just gotten cast in a huge part in the next play the Theater Department was putting on, and she had already gotten to know Quentin a little, because he had a mild case of cerebral palsy and she saw him on the dorm elevator pretty frequently. He had something of a political science bent, too, and she had had an unexpectedly stimulating conversation about the pitfalls of free trade with him down in the laundry room once. So she couldn't exactly say they were her friends, but they were definitely moving out of the mere acquaintance category.

It was also, in all honesty, a relief to walk up the hill to the dorm, and not be the only one who moved slowly.

"I gotta get a sling," Andy said, watching Quentin swing back and forth on his metal crutches and Meg limp on her cane. "Then we'd all look really good together."

"Or an eye patch and a parrot," Meg said, and was pleased when they both laughed.

"Or a piccolo," Quentin said, and it was Meg's turn to laugh.

When she got off the elevator, there was a certain amount of emotional turmoil taking place on her floor. It turned out that Tammy's long-time high school boyfriend had broken up with her earlier that afternoon—by email, no less—and she had been crying in her room pretty much non-stop ever since, while Susan kept her company. Actually, Susan was so universally well-liked as a JA that a steady stream of people from all over the dorm—not just their entry—often shuffled into the JAs' suite to weep, or get gentle advice and sympathy about whatever was currently going wrong in their lives. Dirk handled some of it, but even the guys—Dirk included, probably—seemed to prefer confiding in Susan. If it hadn't been for the security issues, freshmen from other dorms—and maybe even other *campuses*—might well be showing up on a regular basis, too.

After filling her in, Juliana started shoving books into a knapsack and getting ready to escape to the library.

"I can wait for you," she said, "if you want to clear out for a while, too."

If she weren't so exhausted, it would have been a relief to tag along—even if it meant having to do some concentrated studying in exchange. Meg shook her head. "I'm sorry, I'm really tired. I'm just going to crash."

"Okay, your call," Juliana said. "Keep your head down, though."

Meg nodded. With luck, she'd be able to go get cleaned up, and then disappear into her room without anyone else even knowing that she was here.

But when she went into the bathroom, Mary Elizabeth was standing in front of the mirror, brushing her hair and putting on makeup, apparently getting ready for a date—or what she was hoping might turn *into* a date. "Juliana tell you?"

"Yeah," Meg said, using her arm to press the toothpaste tube against her right side so that she could open it. "By email. That really sucks."

"Sure does." Mary Elizabeth carefully applied some mascara. "My girlfriend pulled the same thing last October. Then she thought we were going to get back together during Christmas break. Oh, yeah, like *that* was going to happen."

"I'm sorry," Meg said. Wait, *girl*friend? Well, okay. What the hell. She squeezed out so much toothpaste, that a large blob landed on her clothes. Which happened more often than not, so she ignored it. "You must have been really upset."

Mary Elizabeth looked disgruntled. "That's your whole reaction?"

Meg stuck her toothbrush in her mouth, recapped the tube, and flicked most of the stray splotch from her shirt into the sink. "Why? Did you want something else?"

"I don't know." Mary Elizabeth put away the mascara rather sulkily. "I mean, I just came out to you. Couldn't you have cringed and asked if I was attracted to you, or planning to check you out in the shower, or something?"

Yeah, and purple cows could all fly. "You don't exactly hide the fact that you actively dislike me," Meg said. "So I can't say that I'm really plagued by the notion of your suddenly becoming besotted."

"Well, okay," Mary Elizabeth conceded. "I'm not crazy about your personality."

It was mutual.

"But even though you're not at all my type, objectively-speaking, you're damn attractive," Mary Elizabeth said, and looked her over critically. "Except for being such a slob. I mean, yuck."

Meg laughed. Yeah, she was a slob. Always had been. Even before becoming crippled and ungainly. So what? "I've *forgotten* more about sweatpants than most people will ever know."

"I'm sure you have," Mary Elizabeth said, but she was smiling now. "Straighter than a ruler, anyway, right?"

Meg nodded. So far, at least. "Enough to make a certain percentage of rulers very nervous."

Mary Elizabeth's smile broadened. "That was the vibe I got, yeah." She started to walk out, then paused. "You're not who I thought you'd be. Not even close."

Meg shrugged. "Who the hell is?"

"Well, yeah," Mary Elizabeth said, and then she did leave, the door swinging shut.

Meg finished brushing her teeth and turned off the faucet, resisting the urge to sit down on the cold, tile floor and fall asleep right there.

It had been a very god-damned long day.

21

TIRED AS SHE was, she couldn't convince herself to go to bed at eight o'clock at night. She thought about calling home, but then remembered that—according to an excited email she'd gotten from Neal earlier—her father and brothers were going to a Washington Capitals game, and her mother had been at the UN all day, and was still in New York, as far as she knew, at what was politely called "a dinner," but was actually a major fund-raiser.

Maybe she should have gone to the library with Juliana, after all.

She turned on C-Span, where a State Department spokesperson was giving a briefing, mostly about the Secretary, who was off grandstanding, as usual. India, this time. She watched for a few minutes, until the self-aggrandizement-by-proxy became too irritating, and flipped around the channels to see if anything interesting was on.

Unsurprisingly, there wasn't.

Of course, she *should* be studying. She should probably *always* be studying.

However.

Without giving herself time to think of all the reasons why she might regret it, she went out to the hall, and then, tentatively, down to the second floor. With the constant snow, she pretty much always had to use her cane outside, but when she was in the dorm, she usually tried to get along without it. As long as she stayed close to a wall, or hung on to the banister, so far, it seemed to work out okay.

She could hear a lot of laughing and talking inside the common room—and lost her nerve. Only, that was pretty stupid. So, she made herself open the door.

A bunch of the guys were in there, along with Debbie and Natalie from the fourth floor. Gerard, Quentin, Khalid, and—unexpectedly—one of her agents, Jose, were having an intense battle of what looked like some dumb sci-fi combat game, while Debbie, Mikey, Andy, Natalie, and Dirk hung out on the stained green couch and the beat-up futon, giving loud advice and making less than flattering comments.

Dirk saw her and gave her a wave with his Coke bottle. "Hey, Meg. You looking for Susan?"

She shook her head.

"Oh." He got up. "You looking for me?"

It felt sort of rude, but again, she shook her head.

"Oh," he said, and looked puzzled.

Jose had also noticed her, and put down his game controller, resulting in the almost immediate demise of one of the clunky robot warriors on the screen. "Do you need anything?" he asked.

Jesus. They couldn't exactly make it much more obvious that she wasn't inclined to come down here and mingle. But she just shook her head.

"Okay," he said, and gestured towards the game. "Sorry about that. I'm not actually—"

She nodded. "On duty yet. I know." It would be nice if everyone in the room didn't seem so uncomfortable. "I just thought I'd, you know, come down and see what's going on."

Everyone seemed to be making a point of *not* exchanging glances.

"So, sit down," Andy said, breaking the silence, and moved over on the futon to make room for her.

She nodded, but lost her balance a little, and Mikey, who was the closest, grabbed her right before she would have hit the cushion with most of her weight on her splint.

He was gripping her by the waist, and he quickly pulled his hands away. "Uh—sorry."

"No problem," she said. "I mean, thank you for catching me."

He nodded self-consciously, and as she lowered herself down, with him on her left, and Andy sitting on her right, she was all too aware the entire atmosphere of the room had changed, and that even the furiously competitive game seemed to have petered out.

Jesus, maybe she should just go back upstairs. "Keep playing," she said, "okay?" She looked at Jose. "You, too."

Jose nodded. In fact, *all* of them nodded, but it still felt very tense.

"Come on, Jose," she said. "Just play already. This really *is* one of those pretend-I'm-not-here times."

His nod was uncomfortable, but he returned to the group around the screen again.

"Uh, do you play?" Gerard asked politely.

She couldn't remember the name of it, but the game looked like one of the ones her brothers liked. Neal had talked her into trying out a few of their games during Christmas week, but—well, dexterity had been an issue. "I don't really know this one," she said. "But, thanks."

"You could give it a try," Khalid said. "We'll help you out."

From what little time she had spent with him so far, Khalid seemed like a good guy. Tall, medium-brown skin, and so preppy that he often wore loafers without socks even when it was snowing. For that matter, they *all* seemed pretty nice. Mikey was a big, broad-chested blond guy, who looked like a dumb jock, but was such a talented violinist that no one in the entry minded when he practiced at all hours of the day and night. Debbie was a hearty, cheerful Miss Porter's graduate who played field hockey, rugby, *and* lacrosse. Natalie, who was from Memphis and wrote for the *Williams Record*, was on the quiet side—and rumored to have a serious crush on happy, hyper Andy, who—according to Juliana—was entirely oblivious to this. And Juliana was convinced that Quentin had a big crush on *Natalie*—who was oblivious in her own right.

Oh, Christ, they were all waiting for her to answer. "I'm sorry, I'm not very good with a gamepad," she said, motioning in the general direction of her splint.

"So, buddy up with me," Khalid said, and then looked at Gerard. "Let's set up Slayer, and start her off with Ice Fields."

Gerard shook his head. "No, Danger Canyon's more fun. Mikey, go down and get your stuff, and then we can all play, if a couple other people buddy up, too."

Everyone seemed to be enthusiastic about this, and while Gerard started configuring a multiplayer scenario, the rest of them—except for Natalie, who had also never played before—explained the very complicated rules, the various weapons and vehicles, and so many different strategies and tips that she was lost within a matter of seconds.

But, it turned out to be fun. Totally confusing, but fun. There was a Red Team, and a Blue Team, and when Gerard asked her which one she wanted to be on, she said, "Which one do you *think*?," and he laughed, and put her on the Blue Team.

They played Slayer, and Rally, and Capture the Flag, and rode around in Warthogs and tanks and hovercrafts, and everyone fired their weapons at everything in sight, and got killed a lot. She and Khalid had some trouble making coordinated moves on their gamepad, but the first time they successfully blasted away a Red Team member—Dirk and Natalie, also buddying-up—with their flamethrower, she was more pleased with herself than it was probably politically correct to be.

If she thought about it, the violence of it all probably would have bothered her—but the one time she *did* think about it, her reactions slowed, and the Warthog they were in flipped over. Besides, it was cartoonish, and silly, and entirely *not* based in reality. Not at all worth having a flashback of any kind.

They played for a long time, and people—including Jose, who went on duty—came and went, and nobody except for Gerard was keeping score. When the game finally wound down, as people started worrying about studying and getting some sleep, she still thought video games were profoundly stupid—but in an undeniably entertaining way. And she felt less like an unwanted stranger, which was a very good thing.

When she finally got back up to her room, after midnight, her right hand was throbbing, even though she had gone out of her way not to use it. So she covered it with a gel ice-pack, and stretched out on her bed to read Plato for a while. Then, she switched over to her psychology book, and studied until she was so tired that she was sure she would fall asleep the second she turned the light off.

Except that she didn't.

No matter how hard she tried, she couldn't seem to do more than doze briefly, because she was having lots of stomach-turning nerve pain in her hand. Sickening pain. And her knee didn't feel so great, either—probably because she had done the stairs, instead of taking the elevator.

At about four, she gave up and went out to get some water, so she could take more ibuprofen. Maybe she could try to get Dr. Brooks to authorize a new prescription for something stronger. At the moment, she felt like *begging* for it.

The entry was very quiet now, everyone else asleep presumably, or, in some cases—most notably next door, judging from the sounds she kept hearing coming out of Juliana's room—locked in carnal embraces, and Martin was sitting behind the security table, with a thick book. He lowered it when he saw her, but she motioned for him to keep reading and limped to the bathroom.

Susan was already in there, one hand resting on either side of the sink on the left, staring down at a stream of running water swirling around the drain.

"Um, you all right?" Meg asked.

Susan looked up with a fatigue-dulled expression, then shook her head. "Yeah. I'm sorry, I'm just tired."

Neither Tammy nor Susan had ever appeared in the common room during the game marathon. "Have you been up here this whole time?" Meg asked.

Susan shrugged, instead of answering.

Jesus. "Long night," Meg said.

"Yeah." Susan glanced at the door. "Don't ever tell her, but I've got a paper due tomorrow, and now I don't think there's a chance in hell I'm going to be able to finish it."

The notion of which had probably never even crossed poor Tammy's mind. JAs were generally considered to be available to their freshmen, day in and day out, around the clock—and in Meg's experience, Susan never, ever indicated otherwise, no matter what else might be going on in her life.

About which, Meg realized, she didn't have a clue—and she was suddenly very curious. "You must get really sick of us sometimes," she said.

Susan smiled, and shook her head.

Yeah. Sure.

Susan splashed some more water on her face, and then turned off the faucet. "Are *you* okay? It's pretty late."

She wanted to whine a little about how much her hand was hurting, but she didn't. "I'm fine, just doing some studying," she said. "Go write your paper."

Susan nodded. "Yeah. Try to get some sleep, though, okay?"

Yes, ma'am. "Absolutely," Meg said.

And if she couldn't, well—thank God for twenty-four-hour cable news stations.

SHE ENDED UP being awake all night, but at least that meant that she didn't sleep through her classes. And, on the even more positive side, she didn't wake anyone up by screaming, either. When she saw Tammy, who was red-eyed and miserable, in the hall, she mumbled something about being sorry to hear it, whereupon Tammy shrugged and sniffled and sighed, and went back into her room and shut the door. Then, on her way outside, she ran into Susan, who looked like something of a zombie.

"You finish?" Meg asked.

"Eight pages of complete gibberish," Susan said. "My professor's going to think English is my second language." She frowned. "Possibly my third."

Still, to Meg's way of thinking, eight pages of gibberish were preferable to eight entirely *blank* pages.

Juliana dragged her off to dinner that night with Mark, the still gently, but stubbornly, flirtatious Simon, and an Asian-American girl named Greer from Sage B who Meg barely knew, other than seeing her among the crowd at a couple of dorm-wide get-togethers and occasionally down in the laundry room. She seemed nice enough, though—an ethereal, take-as-many-dance-classes-as-possible type from San Francisco. Tammy came along, too, silent and sad, but reasonably game.

"I wasn't sure if I should tell you about this," Juliana said, as the two of them left the dining hall together, with Tammy, "but—you know that there's all kinds of stuff about you on the Internet, right?"

"About me?" Meg asked. "Or Tammy?"

Tammy laughed, nervously.

Truth be told, though, she really didn't want to know if there were new creepy Web sites out there devoted to her. She had specifically requested not to be told about any of the details, *ever*, but she knew that the Secret Service and the FBI spent a pretty good chunk of time having Web sites taken down, and showing up on people's doorsteps to make sure that they very much appreciated the importance of permanently ceasing and desisting, and the dire consequences attached to failing to do so. But she was pretty sure that there were still plenty of doctored X-rated photos out there—her head pasted onto someone else's nude body and the like, as well as pages with long crazed rants about how it would have been better for everyone if the kidnappers had been successful in murdering her, complete with lurid details and hypothetical suggestions—and probably a fair amount of speculative and offensive fan fiction. She had a horrible feeling that there were many even *worse* sites about her mother, although she carefully never looked.

"I told your agents," Juliana assured her. "There's no *way* I'd see something like that, and not let them know right away."

Okay, but— "How did you come across it in the first place?" Meg asked. Christ, she hadn't gone and entered her name in a search engine or something, had she?

"Nothing weird," Juliana said defensively. "Don't look at me like that. I just, you know, read newsgroups, and sometimes these terrible rumors show up about you."

Ah, the plot thickened. Meg wasted quite a bit of time in newsgroups, and in various forums, herself. She relaxed. "Oh. You mean, you saw the one today about me not really going to college at all, but *actually* being hidden away at an unnamed drug rehab facility, in yet another attempt to save me from my many addictions?"

Juliana looked relieved. "Your agents already let you know about it?"

Meg shook her head. "No, I always read that newsgroup. It's pretty funny." Scurrilous gossip galore, mostly about household-name celebrities and their romantic interests and sexual proclivities. And, call her shallow, but she found gossip entertaining—when it wasn't about anyone she knew well, and sometimes, even when she *did* know the person. The group regularly endorsed the theory that her mother was almost certainly a raging lesbian—or possibly heterosexual, but insatiably promiscuous and prone to twisted fetishes—or maybe entirely asexual and prudish—and that, long ago, her father had accepted a huge lump sum payment from the Vaughn fortune, in order to participate in a sham marriage, so that her mother could retain her political viability. Which made her—and Steven, and Neal—what? *Beard* children?

And she just happened to know a little secret about that particular rehab post. "Besides, my friend Beth wrote that one," she said.

Juliana stared at her, and Tammy looked equally stunned. "You're *friends* with someone who would do that?" she asked.

"Doesn't sound like much of a friend to me," Tammy said primly.

Well, they just didn't know Beth. "She wrote the one last week about seeing me working at a brothel in Nevada, too," Meg said. "It's just her way of saying hello."

Juliana and Tammy exchanged disapproving glances.

The Secret Service wasn't thrilled about it, either, and more than once, they had appeared at her house to "interview" her, until Meg had finally gotten her mother to convince them to knock it off already, that it was only Beth.

Juliana frowned. "It's usually not the same user name."

Meg nodded. "I know. She changes it, for fun, but she leaves me a little clue in there." Some obscure, but unmistakable, reference to their past. "And you know how another post always pops up right away, saying something like, 'Yeah, I saw her there, too, that shameless hussy!' "

"Oh, no," Juliana said, catching on with admirable speed.

Tammy looked puzzled. " 'Oh, no' what?"

Meg grinned and pointed at herself.

"Oh, *no*," Tammy said. Gasped, actually. "That's awful. You *confirm* the rumors?"

Yep. And boy, did it ever piss off certain uptight White House and security types. Meg nodded cheerfully.

Juliana laughed. "Then, you're right—you are a shameless hussy."

They were on their way outside, when Paula listened intently to something in her earpiece, then raised a hand to stop her.

"Meg, would you mind diverting back inside?" she asked, her voice abrupt.

For a second, Meg was just confused, but then she was so scared that she wasn't sure if she was going to be able to get her breath. "Is it my mother? Is she all right?"

"She's fine," Paula said, sounding distracted as she listened to whatever report she was getting. "Please just go back inside for now."

Suddenly afraid that she might be about to faint, Meg had to lean against the side of the entrance for support. "Is it my father?" she asked, almost not recognizing her own voice. "Or my brothers? Are they okay?"

Kyle came over to take her arm and usher her into the building. "They're all fine. But we have a security concern at the dorm, and we'd like to keep you away from there until we can address it."

Oh, God. Someone must have shown up there to try and hurt her—and hurt someone *else*, instead. Oh, God. It was snowing pretty hard, but even from here, she could see bright lights, and what seemed to be a crowd of people gathering near the Frosh Quad. Oh, God.

"Meg," Kyle said, very firmly, as he tried to move her from where she was standing. "Please come with me. This has nothing to do with you at all. It's a situation involving Susan McAllister."

Which made no sense at all.

"Damn it," Juliana said, very quietly. "I knew this was going to happen."

Which made even less sense. Meg frowned. "What are you—"

"I meant Dowd," Kyle said impatiently. "Susan Dowd."

Meg stared at him. "They hurt *Susan*?" Oh, Jesus. Jesus Christ. Susan was smaller—and not crippled, but they both had brown hair, and some psycho must have mistaken her for—

"God, poor Susan," Juliana said, and hurried up the walkway, almost running, as she headed towards the crowd, Tammy right behind her.

"Meg," Kyle said, tightening his grip on her arm. "Go inside. Now."

The *hell* she would. "Juliana, wait up!" she yelled, twisting free and starting to limp after them. "I can't move as fast as you can."

"All right, all right, just come on," Juliana said, without slowing down.

"Meg," Kyle said, as he and Paula effortlessly kept pace with her. "I'm really going to have to insist that—"

She ignored him, limping as quickly as she could, and trying not to slip in the snow, which was close to impossible. As they got closer, she realized that the lights were television lights, and that most of the people in the crowd were reporters and photographers, although campus and local police officers were starting to join the group, too.

"What the hell's going on?" she asked Juliana, out of breath. "Is she—" Christ, she couldn't be, could she? "—having a press conference or something?"

Juliana scowled at her. "What, are you a complete idiot, Meg? This is the last thing she wanted. They never should have made her be your damned JA."

What? Why did everyone else seem to know what was going on? "What are you talking about?" Meg asked. "She's upset she got chosen, and so she's going public about it?" Christ, if she'd been asked to pick the person on campus who was the least likely ever to betray her, Susan would almost definitely have been her first guess.

"The *murders*, Meg," Juliana said. "Wake up, for Christ's sakes!"

Had she walked into some kind of psycho parallel universe or something? This made absolutely no sense. She looked over at Tammy, who was also glowering at her. "I'm sorry," she said. "I really don't understand."

Juliana whirled around as though she was *very seriously* considering decking her. "What the hell's your problem, Meg, you're supposed to be smart. That's Susan *McAllister*. The Boston Prep School Murders? Any of this ringing a damn bell yet?"

No. It wasn't. The Boston Prep School Murders had been a famous criminal case a few years earlier—right around the time of the Iowa Caucus and New Hampshire primary, actually. A group of rich kids at some ritzy private school over in Cambridge had flipped out on drugs, and a couple of other students—including the blond debutante valedictorian—had gotten killed. They would have gotten away with it, except that—oh, Jesus. The bell suddenly rang—clanged, banged, *slammed*—and Meg literally stumbled back a step or two.

"Oh my God," Meg said. Talk about being stupid. Susan had looked familiar when they first met, because she fucking *was* familiar. From television and newspapers. Jesus. "She's the friend." The valedictorian's best friend. "The one who—" Had gone after the murderers and damned near gotten killed herself in the process. The story had ruled the Boston—and national—tabloids for months—except that the Presidential candidacy of a certain Massachusetts senator was getting a hell of a lot of ink, too, and— "Oh, my God."

Juliana and Tammy were looking at her as though she was completely crazy.

"You mean—you didn't know?" Juliana asked.

Did they think she was some kind of selfish *monster*? Meg shook her head. "Christ, Juliana. You really think I would have let her keep being my JA, if I had? *Of course* it was going to come out." The only surprising part was that it had taken them this long to latch on to it.

They were close enough now so that Meg could see Susan surrounded by the reporters, looking overwhelmed—and scared—to the point of complete paralysis.

Which sent a wave of such blinding fury through her that she actually felt a white haze come over her vision, and a violent heat rise up into her face.

"Oh, those rotten sons-of-bitches," she said. Kyle and Paula—and Brian and Ed—were trying to guide her in the other direction, but she shook them off, slammed her cane onto the ground as hard as she could, and waded into the crowd without it. "What's going on?" she asked, making sure her voice projected enough to cut through the barrage of invasive questions they were throwing at Susan.

If the mood of the press had been eager and excited before, now it was downright *electric*, as though her timely appearance had promptly tripled the scope of the story.

"We're taking you both into the dorm now," Kyle said through his teeth. "Do *not* argue with me, just—"

"What, you want to help, Kyle?" she asked, so enraged that everything, and everyone, seemed blurry. "Fine. Start shooting the bastards."

Paula moved even closer than she had already been. "Meg, cameras," she hissed in her ear. "Filming."

"Good," Meg said. Okay, *snarled*. "That means, we can tape the carnage, and watch it over and over." Then, she saw Hannah Goldman standing near the back of the group, looking acutely uncomfortable, and felt—if such a thing were possible—twice as angry. "*You're* here?" she said directly to her. "What's the matter with you? If you have any damn sense at all, you'll walk away."

Ms. Goldman looked uneasy, uncertain—and embarrassed, especially when the rest of the press turned to focus on her.

"*Walk away*, Hannah," Meg said. "I might be a public figure, but she isn't. It isn't news. Walk away."

They looked at each other for a long minute, and then, Ms. Goldman suddenly nodded, turned around, and headed for the street. The rest of the reporters and camerapeople didn't seem to know how to react to this—but none of them made any attempt to leave.

In the meantime, Susan was just standing in the exact same spot, looking dazed.

"Jose! Brian!" Meg said—barked, really—to two of her agents, who were making their way towards her, trying to create a space through the surging crowd. "Take Susan and Juliana and Tammy inside. I'll be there in a minute."

Susan was apparently a little shell-shocked, because she was very slow to react when Brian gestured for her to follow him. Meg forced her way over there—some television guy damn near cracking her across the face with his camera as he swung around to film her; Kyle knocking him onto his back in the snow in response—and rested her good hand on Susan's arm.

"Susan, I am incredibly sorry about this," she said. "I don't think I'll ever be able to *express* how sorry I am. Go with Brian, okay?"

Susan snapped out of it then, nodded once, and let them hustle her into the dorm, along with Juliana and Tammy. Seconds later, Brian and Jose were back outside, along with Garth and Dave, clearing the way for her to go in, too. A fair number of students had stopped to see what was going on, and even more campus security and police officers were arriving, to help her agents try to control the scene.

"All right," Meg said, and despite the number of people swarming around, jostling for position, it got very quiet. Hushed, really. "Listen up. I'm going to give you a statement, and it's the only one I am ever going to make about this. So, *write it down*."

If nothing else, she definitely had their full attention. The college president's house was over on the other side of the student center, and he must have heard all of the commotion outside, because she could see him striding towards them, coatless despite the weather.

"I'm aware that, due to circumstances entirely beyond my control, I've become extremely well known," Meg said. God-damn *famous*. Infamous. Whatever. "And, although I find it very unpleasant, insofar as trying to lead any kind of normal life is concerned, I suppose the argument could be made that a moderate level of media coverage is justified. But, Susan Dowd—" No, not Dowd, apparently. "Susan McAllister is a private citizen. Every single student, and employee, on this *campus* is a private citizen. They won't be news today, they won't be news tomorrow, they won't *ever* be news, just because I happen to be a student here. I am completely disgusted that you all would feel the need to invade the privacy of any member of the Williams community, for any reason, forget a situation as sordid and exploitive as this one is."

Boy, it was quiet. She felt a little tremor of stage fright, and panic, and had to swallow.

"And I think I'll leave it at that." She looked at the college president. "I'll turn it over to you now, sir."

As he nodded, and started making some very similar, albeit probably more eloquent, remarks to the reporters, Meg walked, as steadily as possible, to the door of her entry and went inside.

Christ almighty.

What a nightmare.

22

WHEN THE DOOR had closed behind her, Garth and Brian posted themselves in front of it, blocking any possible view the cameras might have, and she sank down onto the stairs, noticing now that she was trembling horribly and that her knee hurt like hell. In fact, her knee was—*fuck*, it really hurt.

Kyle took a step in her direction, and she shook her head.

"Not now," she said, hearing her voice shake even more than her hands were.

He was obviously almost as furious as she was, but he nodded and stepped back.

"You don't look very good. Are you hurt?" Paula asked, bending down next to her. "Do you need to go to the hospital?"

She shook her head, even though she was dizzy, and nauseated, and her knee felt as though it was on the verge of exploding.

"Are you *sure*?" Garth asked, from the door. "We need a straight answer, Meg."

"I'm fine." She started to stand up, and then looked around. "Where's my cane?"

They all frowned at her.

"You threw it away, Meg," Paula said.

What? Why in the hell would she have done that? But, anyway, it seemed to be gone, so she grabbed the white metal banister with her left hand to pull herself to her feet. "Where's Susan?" she asked. "Is she all right?"

Brian pointed upstairs.

Which meant that she wasn't all right. Meg slowly started up the stairs, using her good leg to do most of the work. There seemed to be something pretty seriously wrong with her knee, but—well, maybe she damned well *deserved* it.

It seemed to take about an hour to trudge up to the second floor, and she had to stop a couple of times to rest, grip the banister, and concentrate on not passing out. The entry as a whole seemed unusually subdued, although she could here low voices here and there, and a couple of people were standing uncertainly in or near the stairwells. No one spoke to her, though.

The common room was empty, for once, and Dirk's door was open, while Susan's was closed. He saw her, and came out.

"Might not be such a good time, Meg," he said.

No doubt about that. She wanted to go upstairs and collapse on her bed, and maybe even sob hysterically, but she steeled herself and knocked on Susan's door.

After a few long seconds, Susan threw it open, not exactly crying, but damn close to it, her face red and her hair very much unbrushed. "*What?*" she asked, holding a cell phone.

"I—I'm really sorry," Meg said. "I didn't—"

Susan cut her off. "You're just about the last person in the world I want to talk to right now, all right? And—I'm on the phone."

Meg nodded, and Susan closed the door. *Hard.*

Okay, then. She glanced at Dirk, who shrugged ineffectually, as though he wasn't quite sure whose side he was on—except that it certainly wasn't *hers*.

So she went back out to the stairs, and dragged herself up to her floor, which was silent and seemed to be deserted. Larry was sitting at the security desk, and they nodded at each other without saying anything.

At first, she couldn't quite think what to do next, but then she saw that Juliana had just come out of her room and was leaning against the wall with her arms folded, looking as angry as Meg had ever seen her.

"Nice going," Juliana said.

Since it *was* her damn fault, inadvertently or not, Meg couldn't think of anything exculpatory to say. So she went into her own room, slamming the door. Then, she picked up the drop-line. Her mother wasn't going to be available—was she ever?—but to hell with it, they could god-damn well put her through, anyway.

And, indeed, the switchboard stuttered and fumbled about the President being certain to call her back at the first possible—

"Let me make myself really clear here," Meg said, having to fight to keep from shouting. "I don't give a damn if she's in the process of putting through nuclear missile launch codes at this very second. I need to god-damn well talk to her *right now*."

It still took a little while—Christ only knew what was being interrupted, and how nervous the underlings had been about passing along this particular message—but then, her mother came on the other end, sounding anxious in a very controlled way.

"What is it, Meg?" she asked. "Are you all right? Are you hurt?"

"You've got to get me the hell out of here," Meg said, too angry to feel guilty about scaring her. "I mean, *tonight*. It's bad enough that my life's completely wrecked—I can't fucking take someone else along with me."

Her mother didn't answer right away.

"Are you listening to me?" Meg asked, even more furious now. "I said, *tonight*. Do whatever you have to do to make it work."

"All right," her mother said, very calmly. "Anything you need, your father and I will arrange. Just—take a couple of deep breaths first, okay? Then, tell me what's happening."

Okay, maybe she didn't sound entirely rational. Meg pulled in one long breath, and then another. "Susan is Susan McAllister."

"I'm sorry," her mother said, after a few seconds, "but I have no idea what you're trying to tell me."

Yeah, right. Meg gritted her teeth. "Susan *Dowd* is Susan *McAllister*."

There was another silence, during which Meg heard several voices in the background, none of which she could fully distinguish, except that there was an urgency to the conversations.

"Meg, I'm having a slightly more complicated evening than usual," her mother said, "and I'm also getting ready to go up to Dover in a little while, so you'll forgive me, but I need for you to be very clear and, ideally, *concise*."

Oh. "Um, Dover?" Meg said. Which was the air force base where military casualties almost always arrived first when they returned to the United States. "What happened?"

Her mother sighed. "We lost a Super Stallion."

Which was a massive troop transport helicopter. Damn. "Hostile fire?" Meg asked.

"That's really not germane to this conversation, Meg," her mother said. "Please just tell me what's happening."

Maybe she should have been savvy enough either to have called her father, instead, or to have checked CNN before picking up the phone in a fury. "How many?" Meg asked.

"Nine," her mother said. "At least three more are likely."

A lot of funerals. And a lot of *caskets* to meet on the tarmac tonight. Meg let out her breath, and tried to sit down on her bed, except that her knee was so swollen that she couldn't make it bend. So, she leaned against the bookcase, instead. "I'm sorry," she said quietly. "I should have—I'll get them to switch me over to Dad, and you and I can talk tomorrow or something."

Her mother's sigh was the abrupt kind she usually made right before she lost her temper. "Let's pretend—for a moment—that I'm capable of multitasking, and give me the bare outlines, okay?"

Right. Meg tried to think of the fastest and most cogent way to explain it—especially since she still wasn't quite clear on what had happened herself. "There are reporters all over the place up here—I mean, *a lot* of reporters—going crazy, because it turns out my JA is the same Susan McAllister who was in the middle of those murders out in Cambridge a few years ago. You know, at Baldwin." Which was the name of the prep school.

She could almost *hear* the crackle of synapses firing during the half-second it took the President to absorb that. "How bad is it?" her mother asked.

"Total feeding frenzy," Meg said. "They've got their god-damn lights shining on my window right now." Although the bulletproof shade was all the way down, so at least they couldn't see—or shoot; in any sense—her.

"Oh, hell." Then her mother raised her voice and spoke to someone or other in the room with her. "Will you find Mr. Fielding, please? Tell him I need to see him right away." Then, she came back on. "Will you be okay if I hang up, and then either your father or I will call you back in a few minutes?"

There was only one appropriate way to answer that, under the very complicated circumstances. "Yeah," Meg said.

"One of us'll talk to you in a little while, I promise," her mother said. "Just sit tight. We're going to straighten this out, and it'll be fine, okay?"

Oh, yeah. Everything was going to be just *swell.*

She stared at the telephone for a few minutes, but it didn't ring. So she clicked on to one of the news sites she had bookmarked on her computer and scanned the headlines. The helicopter crash, cause undetermined, rebel insurgents claiming responsibility, nine Marines KIA, more than a dozen soldiers seriously wounded. A bombing in Tel Aviv, multiple civilian deaths, one of them an American citizen, numerous injuries. Three humanitarian relief workers in Africa ambushed and killed on their way to a refugee camp with food and medical supplies. A train derailment outside Dayton, resulting in a massive chemical spill and the evacuation of hundreds of local residents. And those were just the top four.

Okay, the President definitely had her hands full tonight.

She couldn't stand waiting for the phone to ring, so she made her way back downstairs to the JAs' suite, hesitating before she went in, because several scowling guys—including Andy and Quentin, damn it—were gathered in the stairwell just outside the common room. But she just stood there until they moved out of her way, and then limped past them and over to Susan's door.

"So, I wanted to give you a heads-up," Susan was saying. "In case they come after you, too."

Meg knocked a very small knock.

"Yeah, I know," Susan said, presumably to someone on the other end of the telephone. "I'm really sorry. It's just never fucking going to go away, is it?"

Then she opened the door, looked at Meg, and turned her back—but left the door ajar.

Not sure what to do, Meg stayed in the common room.

"Anyway," Susan said, into the telephone. "How's Derek?" She listened. "Good. Tell him I said hi."

Once she had hung up, Meg knew she should say something, but she didn't even know where to start. "I, um, I told my mother I wanted to transfer. I mean, you know, right away."

Susan's smile was unfriendly. "Funny thing, that's what I just told my mother, too." Then she blinked a few times. "That is, we were discussing it right up until our call got interrupted by an urgent message from the White House."

Oh, great. Not an ideal experience, when a person was trying to have an important, and very private, phone conversation. "I'm sorry, I didn't know they were going to do that," Meg said. "But I can be out of here tonight, if you want."

Susan sat down on her bed, still smiling the strange, unfriendly smile. "And that would accomplish what, exactly?"

The smile was scary. "Well—they'd lose interest," Meg said. "The story doesn't have legs that way."

"It'll *always* have legs," Susan said grimly. Then, she rubbed her temples, looking exhausted. "Close the door, okay?"

Right. Meg had only moved one step inside, but she retreated and started to shut the door.

Susan looked annoyed now. "Close it with *you* still in the room."

Oh. Meg reentered the room, and then closed the door behind her. She felt like such a complete intruder—which she was, of course—that she stayed back against it, instead of moving in any farther.

"I can't tell you how sorry I am," she said. "I had absolutely no idea. About any of it."

Susan studied her. "I have to admit, I've been wondering ever since you got here," she said finally. "I wasn't sure whether you honestly didn't know—or were just a self-obsessed asshole who doesn't care about anyone's problems other than her own."

So much for mincing words. Meg sighed. "Both, I suspect."

Susan's smile was still odd, but marginally more friendly.

"Whose bright idea *was* it?" Meg asked.

Susan shrugged. "I'm not even really sure. When it turned out that you were going to be coming here, they interviewed a bunch of the JAs, and started doing security screenings and all. And then—" the spooky smile came back— "Dirk and I got picked."

And had both regretted it bitterly every single day, ever since. Meg hunched over self-consciously, her good arm tight across her chest. "Couldn't you refuse? I mean, my parents didn't pressure you into it, did they?"

"I never talked to your parents," Susan said. "As far as I know, the whole thing went through the Dean, and then—I don't know—the White House, or the Secret Service or someone, must have approved it."

So her parents might—or might *not*—be culpable. "You could step down," Meg said. "Someone else could be assigned."

Susan nodded. "Oh, yeah, they'll be *lining up* for the chance."

No doubt. Even under the best of circumstances, it couldn't be much fun to be in charge of supervising a self-obsessed asshole. Even one of the non-notorious, danger-magnet, press-attracting variety.

"Sit down, instead of being a jerk," Susan said, indicating the desk chair. "Your knee looks as though it's about to give out."

Probably because it was. Meg made her way cautiously over to the chair, trying not to wobble. There were a lot of photographs around, on the desk and tacked to the bulletin board above it, but Meg found herself instantly drawn to the one of Susan and a taller, quite beautiful, blond girl, both of them about sixteen years old, standing on what appeared to be a New York City street, grinning at the camera. She hadn't exactly spent a lot of time in Susan's room, but she had never noticed it before. Not that she would have made the connection, if she had.

Colleen Spencer, murdered about three years ago now. Headlines across the country, and even a couple of made-for-television movies and quickie true-crime books. Christ, why hadn't anyone *told* her? Or, for that matter, why hadn't she been smart enough to put it together for herself? Except that, mostly, it was Colleen's name she remembered, and the murderer—who had been judged criminally insane, not the steadfast friend who had risked her life to find the killer. And here she was, sitting *across* from the friend.

Meg looked away from the photograph and directly at Susan. "I'm so terribly sorry."

Susan nodded indifferently. "Yeah, you said that already."

Meg shook her head.

"Oh." Now, Susan looked at the picture, too, and her eyes brightened. "Well. Thank you."

Meg couldn't even imagine what it would be like if Beth was suddenly—no, she wasn't going to let that thought into her head. Not ever.

"I'd give anything if I could have called *her* tonight," Susan said. "But, then," she blinked, and whisked the back of her hand across her eyes, "I pretty much feel that way every night."

Alone in a crowd.

And, even though she bloody well knew better, her first instinct was to want to ask questions. What it had been like, how it had felt, if she still had nightmares.

If she'd been scared.

If she'd ever *stopped* being scared.

"I wasn't trying to hide it from you or anything," Susan said. "All you had to do was ask. But I was damned if I was going to volunteer the story."

Meg nodded. "You've been dropping hints, though, haven't you." For weeks. "And waiting for me to have the good grace to pick *up* on one of them."

Susan nodded.

And, sadly, she had lacked the good grace. She'd noticed, more than once, that something was a little off in a few of their conversations—some extra hostility about the press, the "did it ever occur to you that maybe I know what I'm talking about" remarks, and that kind of thing—and had just never bothered following up on it. Which was pretty damned unforgivable—and self-obsessed.

And not something she was going to be able to rectify anytime soon.

"Why Dowd?" she asked.

Susan shrugged. "My mother's maiden name."

Meg nodded. "When'd you change it?"

"Right before my freshman year," Susan said, and indicated her hair. "After the trial was over, I started cutting this really short, too. My parents and I thought—well, there was still so much publicity going on then, and—it seemed like a good way to try and get a fresh start."

Made sense. "But, people like Juliana knew about it?" Meg asked.

Instead of being spooky, Susan's smile was sad this time. "All my friends here know. I might not want to advertise to the whole world, but it isn't some deep, dark secret, either. Why wouldn't I tell them?"

In direct contrast to people who *weren't* her friends.

"That didn't come out quite right," Susan said, and then sighed. "Or, I don't know, maybe it did. I only meant—"

Someone knocked, *loudly*, and they both jumped.

"Hey, Susan!" a female voice said, and then there was more knocking. "Are you in there?"

Susan got up to answer the door, and an African-American girl Meg had seen around the dorm before came rushing in. She might have been among the flurry of upperclassmen to whom Susan had introduced her that time at the Greylock party, too. Carla, or Kylie, or—Courtney, maybe.

"You okay?" the girl asked, looking very upset. "Fred told me what happened, and I was trying to call you, but the phone was—I decided I should just come over. You all right? God, this really *sucks*. Madison's coming, too." She glared at Meg. "Do you *mind*?"

Right. Meg got up, not looking at either of them.

Susan sighed, and followed her to the door. "Meg."

Meg just shook her head. "Let me know if there's anything you want me to do, okay? Because—I will."

"All right," Susan said. "Thank you." Then she said something else over her shoulder, in such a low voice that Meg didn't catch it.

"I don't know why you keep defending her," Susan's friend was answering, as she left. "I mean, I'm sorry about what happened to her and all, but why should *you* be the one to—"

Susan quickly closed the door, cutting off the rest of the sentence.

The friend, whoever she was, and regardless of her general lack of tact, had a point.

There were quite a few people in the common room now, and on the stairs leading up to the third floor, mostly from her entry, and Sage D and F, and they all stopped talking when they saw her. Tammy looked as though she might be about to say something, but then she glanced at Juliana—who wasn't hiding the fact that she was mad as hell—and subsided.

Well, terrific. This was just—terrific. Weeks of trying to make friends and feel like a part of the dorm, erased in a matter of seconds. There didn't seem to be any way to combat the situation at the moment, so Meg went into her room and shut the door, very softly and unobtrusively.

She spent most of the rest of the night on the telephone. First, with each of her parents, who were upset. Neal, who was happy he had just seen her on television. Steven, who seemed to find it all kind of funny, which bugged her. Her father again, at length. Then, Preston. Trudy, who was *un*happy to have seen her on television. Beth, who was in a near-panic, because a girl who lived on her floor had just come shouting down the hall, something about the President's daughter and shooting. Her father, Preston, and then finally, her mother, in one last, very-late-night, guilt-ridden call, which Meg was pretty sure left them both feeling even worse, rather than helping.

The upshot of the whole deal was that Preston, Ginette, and the head of the White House Presidential Protective Detail, Mr. Gabler, would be showing up in the morning, and in the meantime, the White House was doing what it could to convince—persuade—*strong-arm*—all of the more reliable news organizations into shutting down the story as fast as possible. What the less reputable media outlets and tabloids were going to do was still anyone's guess.

She knew she wasn't going to be able to sleep, but she didn't turn on the television. Neal might have enjoyed watching her, but she had a feeling that she wasn't going to find it nearly as pleasant.

It felt very wrong, but finally, at about four-thirty in the morning, she couldn't stop herself from going on the Internet and pulling up some of the archived news stories about the Boston Prep School Murders. After saying, "Wait, her last name is McAllister? *That* Susan McAllister?

Damn," Beth had filled her in a little more, since she remembered the case better than Meg did.

The details were ugly. A clique of rich kids, who had too much money and too much free time, and were using enough drugs so that at least one of them, the ringleader, pretty much went around the bend, and began dealing heavily—and killing anyone who got in his way. Another student at the school ended up dead, and apparently, Colleen Spencer had been unusually courageous and idealistic, because she'd been stubborn enough to try and find out on her own what had *really* happened.

And was found in front of the prep school, dead of a massive drug overdose herself, for her troubles. The initial news stories were uniformly vicious, describing her as a beautiful, spoiled, All-American debutante who'd been hiding a self-destructive, possibly suicidal, drug addiction—and those character assassinations must have been what had triggered Susan's involvement, all indications being that she turned out to be extremely god-damn courageous, idealistic, and stubborn herself. She had apparently managed to insinuate her way into the group, and gain their trust, which culminated in a near-fatal confrontation with the guy who'd lost his mind and thought he was smart enough to get away with murder. More than once.

Christ, if she were an ambitious, somewhat ethics-challenged television producer, Meg might have wanted to option the damn story, too.

Wealthy parents, expensive lawyers, cushy plea bargains, reduced sentences—it was all pretty sickening. She couldn't bring herself to do more than skim the articles, but given the absolute lack of direct quotes, Susan must never have given an interview or responded in any way to the media, despite the saturation coverage of the case. But when she came across a file photo of Susan, leaving a courthouse with two people who looked as though they must be her parents, she instantly clicked off. Even the briefest glance at the unhappy expression on her face was too much.

It seemed quiet out in the hall, and she decided it would be safe to venture out to the bathroom, and at least make a feeble attempt to get ready for bed.

Despite its being almost five-fifteen.

There had been a shift change while she was—well—*hiding*, and now, Martin was the one sitting at the security desk. They nodded at each other, and she repressed an urge to sink down into the chair next to him and cry for a while.

"Fielding's the brightest guy I know," Martin aid. "I'm glad he's coming up here."

She never thought of Preston as *Fielding*, or even *Mr.* Fielding. "Yeah." Meg looked around. God, it was quiet. Except now, she could see that Juliana's light was still on, although she sure as hell wasn't about to go knock on her door. She started towards the bathroom, then stopped. "You knew, right? I mean, with all of the security clearances and everything, you must have."

Martin nodded reluctantly.

Right.

"I just assumed you did, too," he said. "I mean, we're going out of our way to try and be as inconspicuous as possible, so I would never—" He paused. "I don't know, Meg. I thought women just naturally *talked* about things to each other."

Normal women, as opposed to self-obsessed ones. "Yeah," Meg said. "I guess they probably do."

She never did fall asleep—among other things, her knee was throbbing enough to make her feel feverish and sick to her stomach—but she went back out at about seven-thirty, to get ready for Preston and the others. At the very least, she desperately needed a shower. But, unfortunately, Juliana and Mary Elizabeth were already in there ahead of her. Juliana was wrapped in a large towel, while she wound another one around her wet hair.

"Uh, good morning," Meg said.

"Yeah, right," Juliana said, and banged the door on her way out.

Meg glanced at Mary Elizabeth, who was industriously flossing. It was hard to be sure, but she appeared to be both sympathetic—and a trifle amused by it all.

"Boy, you're sure unpopular around here today," Mary Elizabeth remarked.

Meaning that Juliana—who actually *liked* her, or had, at any rate, this time yesterday—was just the tip of the old iceberg.

"Your tough luck that they had to go after someone so completely beloved," Mary Elizabeth said.

Yeah. Meg sighed. "Think anyone's going to sneak up behind me, and give me a little shove down the stairs?"

"Well," Mary Elizabeth untwisted the cap from her mouthwash bottle, "if they try, your agents can just start shooting the bastards."

Meg winced. Christ, it sounded even worse being quoted back at her. "Right. There's always that." She didn't want to bring this up, but it was only fair. "Um, I don't want to borrow trouble, but are you out to everyone, or just people you know pretty well?"

For a split second, Mary Elizabeth looked petrified. "You think they'd do that?"

Yes.

Mary Elizabeth recovered herself. "Yeah, well, let them come after me, if they want. I don't care."

"I'm sorry," Meg said. "I know Preston's going to do everything he can to protect everyone's privacy."

"No big deal." Then, Mary Elizabeth closed her eyes. "Except, I haven't told my father yet."

So now she was on the verge of possibly screwing up yet another innocent person's life. "He should be able to head them off," Meg said. Yeah, since the mass media was *always* so cooperative and compassionate. "I didn't want to mention it, but I thought I should, just in case." So that at least she wouldn't be blindsided, the way Susan had been.

Mary Elizabeth's nod was resigned, but then she grinned. "Tammy's going to start worrying about having 'Coed Dumped by Slimeball Ex-Boyfriend's Cruel Email' headlines show up everywhere."

Yeah, she probably was. It wasn't funny—except, okay, maybe a little.

"Might as well laugh, instead of cry," Mary Elizabeth said.

Yeah. Meg managed a smile. "Might as well," she agreed.

23

AFTER SHE FINISHED showering and getting dressed—and received yet another worried, albeit not terribly productive, phone call from her father, she left her room to find all of her hallmates, as well as Susan, standing around near the stairs. That was strange, in and of itself, but it was also extraordinarily unusual for everyone—especially Jesslyn—to be up and about this early in the morning.

"They mostly seem to be on Park Street," Juliana was saying, obviously reporting back from a trip outside. "And there're a whole bunch more out near Spring Street. I guess campus security's booting them off college property for trespassing wherever they can."

Susan nodded, her hands tight fists in her pockets.

"Uh, hi," Meg said.

Juliana frowned, Jesslyn shrugged, Mary Elizabeth smiled slightly, Tammy looked ill at ease, and Susan just nodded, staring down at the floor.

"Are you going to classes today?" Meg asked her.

"With midterms coming up, I kind of need to, yeah," Susan said, without looking up.

"Are you?" Tammy asked.

And contribute to, or maybe even provoke, another media melee? Meg shook her head. "No. I'm just going to—I don't know—wait for Preston to get here, I guess." Keep the lowest possible profile.

"Fuck 'em," Mary Elizabeth said unexpectedly. "Fight back. Get some breakfast, go to classes, hang out at Goodrich, do your normal stuff. Don't let them change any of that."

It probably wasn't realistic—but, hey, it was plucky.

Juliana nodded. "We'll walk with you wherever you want to go, Susan. Hell, the whole entry wants to come along. Maybe even the whole dorm."

Good. Safety in numbers, one would like to think. Meg retreated back a couple of steps.

"Hey! Aren't you part of the entry?" Mary Elizabeth asked.

"Yeah, but, the *White House* is coming," Juliana said, before Meg could answer. "That's what's important. I mean, you know, to hell with Susan, let's get our priorities straight here."

Jesus, Juliana was holding a grudge—and Mary Elizabeth had become her loyal advocate. Maybe this was an alternate universe, after all.

Susan, who didn't seem to be paying attention to any of this, sat down on the top step, her arms folded tightly across her chest.

The rest of them just stood there, waiting for—well, Meg wasn't quite sure what. For someone, presumably Susan, to react. Take charge. And, surrounded by these random, hostile strangers who had been *so close* to maybe turning into friends, she suddenly felt more isolated than she ever had up here—which was pretty god-damn isolated. Unbearably so. When Preston got here—what the hell was taking him so long, anyway?—they were going to have to map out some respectable way for her to return to Washington, once and for all. She should never have—

"Stop being such an asshole, Susan," Jesslyn said.

Okay. This was now *officially* an alternate reality.

And it certainly got everyone's attention.

"She didn't know," Jesslyn said. "And even if she had, if you didn't see this coming, you're a much bigger asshole."

Susan frowned at her, but didn't respond in any other way.

"You could have said no," Jesslyn said. "I mean, shit, Angela did. And so did Lori. You could have, too. It's not like the frakkin' White House was going to *make* you do it. But, you said yes, and you're the JA, so just suck it up." She started towards her room, pausing only long enough to glower at Meg. "That doesn't mean that *you're* not an asshole, too. If you didn't know, you should have, but no, you're too busy being a fucking frail princess, and so, sorry if I don't cry big old tears for you, either. And the *President's* an asshole for thinking it was a good idea to send her fucked-up anorexic kid away to college in the first place." She turned to point at Susan. "You're the JA. *Act* like it." Then, she went into her room, slamming the door so hard that the sound seemed to echo repeatedly in the hallway.

Jesus. Meg was pretty sure she wasn't the only one who blinked.

"Look out, Internet gamblers," Mary Elizabeth said. "There's a tornado a comin'!"

And how. An astonishingly profane tornado, too.

Susan looked in the direction of Jesslyn's room, then nodded a few times. "Yeah. Okay. Yeah." She stood up slowly. "Look. We all got a little shook up last night, and yeah, I'm not handling it very well so far. But, it's no one's fault, particularly no one who lives on this floor." She looked pointedly at Juliana. "Okay?"

Juliana shrugged without making eye contact. "Okay, whatever. I got it."

Oh, yeah, she was *definitely* on board. Feeling tears come into her eyes, Meg abruptly turned away. "I, uh, I really am going to stay up here, I think—" Oh, Christ, was she actually going to start crying right in front of them? In broad daylight, as opposed to the dimly-lit and otherworldly aftermath of nightmares? "I'm sorry. Excuse me, please." She started towards her room, her knee so painful that it was an effort not to stagger.

Mikey leaped dramatically up to the landing. "Madame," he said to Susan, whipping off his Cardinals cap and bowing. "Your escorts await."

Susan smiled at him, looking like her regular easygoing self for a second. "Well, vanity being what it is, there's still some primping to be done here. Would the escorts be willing to give us another ten minutes?"

"Your wish," he said, "our command." He vaulted down the steps. "Fire the game back up, boys! We're not heading out yet."

Meg kept her face averted while she opened her door, mortified to be crying, but not sure whether she was going to be able to stop anytime soon.

"Oh, come here," Susan said, and—to Meg's shock—hugged her.

Meg tried to pull away. "No, I—"

"Shut up," Susan said, and kept hugging her. "And if you feel like crying, for God's sakes, go ahead and cry. Nobody's watching."

Meg laughed weakly.

"Okay, point taken," Susan said. "Several people are watching." She released her, then went past her inside the room, and sat down on the edge of the bed. Slumped, really.

Her knee hurt horribly, and she was very tired, so Meg sat down next to her, just as heavily, and reached for a Kleenex to wipe her eyes. "How much sleep have you had in the last couple of days?"

"Oh, I don't know," Susan said, and dragged her hands back through her hair. "About twenty seconds." She glanced at Juliana, who was standing in the doorway, with a black scowl on her face, Mary Elizabeth and Tammy waiting uncertainly behind her. "Juliana, you can help, or you can make things worse. Your call."

"I'm helping by being pissed off for you," Juliana said. "Since you're not doing it for yourself."

Susan just looked at her.

Juliana lifted her hands in defeat. "Fine. Whatever you want."

Yeah. That was convincing. Meg let out her breath, realizing that she had had almost no sleep herself for the past two days. Which might explain why she was having such a hard time thinking clearly. "If you've got something to say, Juliana, just say it to my face. No point in putting it off."

"Okay." Juliana put her hands on her hips. "Yeah, it probably would have come out eventually, but it never would have happened this way if you weren't so fucking impersonal all the time. I mean, maybe we don't know much about you, but you don't know anything about us, either. I don't even think you're *interested*. And now, Susan gets hurt because of it."

"That was—" Susan flashed her an extremely sarcastic "okay" signal— "really helpful, Juliana. Thank you."

It also had a distinct ring of truth. But, she probably wasn't impersonal, or even self-obsessed, so much as just plain dispassionate. And she knew damned well where she'd inherited *that* tendency. "I don't know," Meg said, meeting Juliana's eyes steadily. "Maybe I was afraid that if I opened up, and anything ever went wrong, one of you might—oh say—*turn* on me, in about half a second."

It got so quiet that Meg could actually hear every single one of them breathing.

"And, that was also very helpful," Susan said. "Thanks, Meg, I knew I could count on you to de-escalate the situation."

There was a longer, and uglier, silence.

"Maybe you should try the hugging again, Susan," Tammy suggested—and seemed to be perfectly serious. Either that, or fiendishly disingenuous. "That was working better."

They all stared at her.

"You could hug Meg," Tammy said, "and then, you could hug Juliana, and I could hug you, and—"

"God, is it just me, or is the estrogen getting incredibly thick in here?" Mary Elizabeth asked. "I've got to go find someone really butch to talk to. *Fast.*"

That shouldn't have broken the tension, but for some reason, it did, and they all laughed—even Tammy, who appeared rather flustered by the idea that someone would drop the word "butch" in casual conversation.

"Just promise me that you all aren't suddenly going to get your periods simultaneously," Mary Elizabeth said. "I don't think I could bear it."

"That actually happens, you know, when people live together," Tammy said. "Women, I mean. It's a scientific fact. They've done studies."

The rest of them laughed again—and Tammy looked offended.

"All right, all right." Susan stood up with an effort. "Let's go find our noble escorts, and we'll have some breakfast together."

Given the tenuous détente which had just been established, Meg wasn't about to argue, so she reached for her Kevlar jacket, her sunglasses, and her cane—which one of her agents had gone out and retrieved from the snow the night before.

Susan—apparently back to being a die-hard, dedicated JA again—focused on her knee at once. "Jesus Christ, Meg, do you have a basketball stuffed under there?"

Since she didn't want to irk Preston any more than he was already going to be, she wasn't wearing sweatpants, for once, and it was much harder to disguise the noticeable swelling under straight-legged Levis. "No," Meg said. "I'm just happy to see you."

Mary Elizabeth actually guffawed, and even Juliana smiled a little.

Susan, however, went straight out to the security desk. Damn near *marched*. "Martin, can you please make sure Mr. Fielding knows that Meg's going to have to get down to physical therapy early today so that she can have her knee checked out?"

Martin nodded, and made a note in his log.

"And you're not taking the stairs," Susan said to her, "so don't even try."

Swell. But, it was still the better part of wisdom just to keep her mouth shut and try to be cooperative, so Meg confined herself to a couple of vehement, but unspoken, expletives. As she limped towards the elevator, she saw Martin make a quick visual assessment of her knee, look alarmed, and then write himself another note, which he underlined twice.

"Enjoy your ringside seat to our girl-talk session?" she asked, not giving a damn if she sounded arch, and maybe even belligerent.

"Didn't hear a thing," he said quickly.

Yeah. Sure.

There was quite a large group of escorts waiting for them, a few of whom looked taken aback to see her, but they also seemed to be getting their cues from Susan, who got off the elevator with her quite chummily, and no one said anything.

But, before they went outside, Meg stopped.

"I'll catch up," she said to Susan. "Okay?"

Susan shook her head. "Nope. I'll wait."

Which meant that they would *all* be stuck waiting—giving them sufficient time to form still more negative opinions about her.

"It's going to take a few minutes," Meg said. "I'll be right there, though. You can hold a place for me in line."

Susan obviously didn't like it, but she nodded. "If you don't show up, I'm coming straight back here, which will *really* irritate the hell out of me."

An outcome very much worth avoiding. Meg nodded, and made her way up the very short flight of steps leading to the main security room, where Garth and a couple of other agents were conferring in the back by the windows, while Kyle sat at the desk, not looking thrilled to see her.

"Do you know if Hannah Goldman's still in town?" she asked.

Kyle nodded, and gestured in the general direction of the Williams Inn. "I think so. I saw her in the bar last night."

No surprise there. They'd all probably closed the place. "Pretty crowded?" she asked.

"Oh, yeah," he said, his jaw rigid. "And not a lot of camaraderie, either."

Presumably, there had been a bunch of media people stationed on one side of the room—and a gang of angry Secret Service agents on the other. As far as she knew, it was one of the places where her agents sometimes hung out when they were off-duty. "Still mad at me for completely ignoring your advice?" she asked. More precisely, his *orders*.

He nodded.

"I'd do the exact same thing if it happened again—but, I apologize," she said. "I know it made your job more difficult."

His nod seemed somewhat more mollified this time.

"Okay if I borrow your phone for a minute?" Meg asked. "I left my SATCOM upstairs."

He hesitated.

"I know," Meg said. "It's a really bad idea, and Preston's going to be just that much more annoyed when he gets here."

He nodded, but punched the numbers in and handed her the receiver. When the front desk picked up, she asked to be connected to Hannah Goldman's room.

"Hi, this is Meg Powers," Meg said, when she answered, sounding a little worse for the wear—indicating that it had, indeed, been a long night in the tavern. "Any interest in meeting me in front of Goodrich at—" she checked the clock on the wall— "nine-thirty?"

There was a brief pause. "Sure," Ms. Goldman said. "I can do that."

"Thought you might be able to clear room in your schedule, yeah," Meg said. "See you then."

As she hung up, Kyle's expression was nothing if not censorious.

"She was the only one who walked away, Kyle," she said. "That's worth something in my book."

He frowned. "None of my business, but you're *asking* for trouble."

No argument there.

When she got outside and started across the quad, a couple of dozen reporters and photographers hanging around on the street side of the cast iron gate all tried to move into more advantageous positions. They were asking questions, and snapping pictures, but Meg didn't even look at them, concentrating on getting down to Mission with as little interference as possible, her agents forming a tight, protective circle around her. Keeping her balance in the slush was something of a challenge, especially since her knee kept locking every few steps, and she hated the idea that this latest bout of infirmity was being captured on film and videotape for one and all to see, but there wasn't much she could do about it, other than try to limp less obviously.

In addition to more agents being on duty than usual, there were enough campus security people, Williamstown police officers, and even a few Massachusetts State Police troopers around to discourage them from following her—or attempting to barge onto college property.

Other than the fact that Juliana made a point of sitting as far away from her as possible, breakfast was uneventful. Susan registered her position just as blatantly, by frowning over at Juliana and taking a seat right next to her.

And so, the Sage E psychodrama continued.

For her part, Meg kept quiet, and ate a few mouthfuls of scrambled eggs, along with half a piece of bacon and a glass of orange juice. There were many more stares than usual being sent in her direction—some just curious, the rest of them openly unfriendly. Until this morning, Susan might well have had no idea how genuinely popular she was.

The people remaining at her table—several of them had already drifted off to go to various classes—seemed relieved when she finally made her polite excuses and got up to leave.

"See you later," Tammy said, sounding timid—but, she'd made the effort, which was in her favor.

Meg's mobility was becoming increasingly difficult, and it took all of her concentration to make her way across campus, towards Goodrich. If she could manage to be sufficiently verbally adroit, her meeting with

Hannah Goldman would be very short, and then maybe she'd have time to take a nap before Preston and the others showed up.

"Hey, Meg!" someone called as she was passing the student center. Someone male.

She didn't turn, or even pause, because it was such a predictable photographer's trick to get a full-face shot, and she was damned if she'd fall for it. Usually, they were dumb enough to call her "Meghan," so this one must have done some research, at least.

But then, Jack Taylor jogged up to her, with his jacket swinging open, wearing yet another one of his endless supply of Hawaiian shirts, jeans, and his Santa Monica cap, and she closed her eyes. She was *much* too tired to handle any flirtation—or foreplay, masked as banter—right now.

"So," he said. "What's new?"

Christ, was he oblivious, or did he think he was funny? She checked his expression. Okay, he thought he was funny.

"Not much," she said. "Just the same old boring stuff." Only, Christ, they were standing right out here in the open, which was a very bad strategy. "Could you do me a favor, though, and back off?"

His face fell, but then he nodded a tough-guy nod. A "fuck you" nod. "Yeah. Fine. Probably should have figured it out the *first* ten times you shot me down."

God, she was tired. "Jack, what I meant was, can you please *literally* back off," Meg said. "There are photographers coming out of the woodwork today, and I'm trying like hell not to give them anything they can use."

"Oh." He looked around, and then took several steps away from her. "How's this?"

It was a definite improvement from his standing right next to her, looking as though he might kiss her, if given even a minuscule sign of encouragement. She nodded. "Thanks."

He nodded, too. "God, Meg. You look—"

Awful. Yeah, she already knew.

"Uh, pretty," he said, catching himself. "Very pretty. I mean, gosh, you're a *fox*."

She ducked her head, so that she could smile, without even a telephoto lens being able to pick it up very well.

"Your knee doesn't look too good," he said.

Nope. Meg shrugged. "I think I just strained it." Or tore it, or ruptured it, or maybe even lost a solid six or eight months of rehabilitative progress. She noticed, then, that he was carrying a large black portfolio, in addition to his usual knapsack. It seemed out of character, for a shallow, cocksure Frisbee boy. "Are you an artist?"

"No," he said, too quickly. "I'm majoring in Economics."

Hmmm. "Are you an artist whose parents want him to go to business school, instead?" she asked.

He flushed, and didn't look at her. "No comment."

Yet another person about whom she knew almost nothing. Quite a disturbing trend. She put her cane under her arm so that she could pull her watch out of her pocket, and saw that it was just past nine-thirty, and she needed to get moving.

"Can I walk with you, at a distance?" he asked.

Not a good plan, with the bulk of the remaining press in town waiting eagerly right down there at the top of Spring Street. "No, I'm sorry, I have to meet someone over at Goodrich, so I'd better—" But it would only be fair to make sure he knew that she was Typhoid Meg. "You know, I have to be straight with you here. If there's anything in your life you'd like to keep private, and I mean *anything*, you'd be much better off avoiding me completely from now on."

He didn't look thrilled, but he didn't seem to be intimidated, either. "Well, I said something really terrible to a girl I was trying to impress at a party a few weeks ago, but—" he glanced at her— "as long as she keeps quiet about it, I don't think that one'll get out."

Unless said girl—woman—whatever—gave in to her occasional, and unfortunate, tendency to go off half-cocked. She looked at her watch again, and saw that she was now officially late. "Any chance you'd let me borrow the notes you take during psych class today?" she asked.

"Maybe," he said, and then winked at her. "Ask me again sometime."

Right.

BY THE TIME she got to Goodrich, she was about fifteen minutes late, and Hannah Goldman was standing on the sidewalk outside the building, where a cop was giving her a hard time.

"I know, but I'm waiting for someone," she was saying.

"Well, that's fine," the police officer said. "But if you don't have a campus ID, you're going to have to—"

Meg cleared her throat. "She's with me, ma'am."

The cop turned, looked surprised, and glanced at the nearest agent, Ed, for confirmation. When he nodded, the police officer nodded, too, and moved to intercept a couple of the journalists who were hurrying over to see what was going on.

She knew her agents were eager for her to head inside, but Meg was quite happy to stand on the sidewalk for another minute, and make it very clear that she was getting ready to talk to one reporter—and only one reporter. With luck, the unspoken message would be strong enough for even the most obtuse of the lot to understand.

"You're too young to play the game this well," Hannah said quietly.

Instead of answering, Meg just gave her a very small smile.

The *hell* she was.

24

ONCE THEY HAD gone inside and ordered coffee, they ended up finding an empty banquette on the mezzanine level, which was much less crowded than the main floor of the Great Room. Goodrich had originally been the college chapel, but after some major renovations, it had been turned into a student gathering place, with a coffee bar and everything.

They sat down, not speaking right away. Meg, for one, took the time to make sure that there was no one she knew anywhere nearby, and that, other than a curious glance or two, they weren't attracting much attention.

"My editor is *not* pleased with me," Hannah said finally. "Since I didn't come away with the story everyone else got. Or anything even close to it. He has this wacky idea that they're paying me for a reason."

Yeah, yeah, yeah. The predictable song and dance. "We both know how this works," Meg said. "You did something for me; I return the favor." She sipped some of her latte—two extra shots this time, plus some vanilla syrup. "So. What do you want?"

"Complete and total access, and every possible intimate detail," Hannah said instantly.

Right. "Got any parking tickets?" Meg asked. "Tax delinquencies? Maybe a bank loan you need approved?"

Hannah grinned, and looked around at the angled ceiling, the wooden beams, and the stained glass windows. Especially the stained glass windows.

Goldman. "It's okay," Meg said. "It's entirely secular in here now. You don't have to worry about encountering any Christian proselytism."

Hannah laughed. "I don't think I would have had to worry about that at *this* particular table, anyway."

Safe bet. They sometimes dragged off to church for appearances' sake, but the members of her family were nominal Protestants, at best. Which didn't thrill a goodly portion of the country, naturally, although Meg suspected that her parents weren't considered godless heathens, so much as being as adamantly if politely, private about their religious beliefs as they were about almost all personal matters.

Now, Hannah looked serious. "How did they react when they found out how smart you were? Do you think it threw them off?"

In this context, "they" could mean only one thing. And, obviously, the answer was yes. "My parents are on the brainy side," Meg said. "Presumably, they could have anticipated something of a genetic predisposition."

Hannah nodded. "That's a juicy quote. Thanks."

No, it wouldn't sell too many copies, would it? Meg frowned. "Completely off-the-record?"

The focus in Hannah's eyes seemed to sharpen, and she nodded. "Absolutely."

If she didn't honor her word, this would be—well. Damn the torpedoes. "It saved my life," Meg said. "He couldn't quite bring himself to kill me, because of it."

Hannah nodded. "Came pretty close," she said, after a pause.

About as close as anyone could get.

"*He*, not they," Hannah said.

Very much so. But, somehow, the latte no longer tasted as good as it had earlier. "Yeah," Meg said. Thinking about him suddenly gave her a second of such overwhelmingly intense terror that she actually got dizzy and had to reach out with her good hand to grip the edge of the table.

Hannah studied her reaction—well, she *was* a damn reporter, after all—and stopped leaning forward. "I'm really sorry they ambushed Susan McAllister like that. I thought it was lousy, too."

Thank God for a change of subject. A much-appreciated gesture. Meg took a deep breath, swallowed, and unclenched her hand. "It was like watching wild dogs fight over a piece of meat."

Hannah winced, but didn't contradict her.

"Anyway," Meg said, and moved her hand across her forehead, wishing she had thought to bring along some ibuprofen. She'd managed to suppress the terror pretty quickly this time, which probably counted as progress. Of a sort. "How'd you get up here so fast? You didn't *break* the story, did you?"

Hannah shook her head. "No. But it was in the wind, and since there was no way of knowing how it was going to play out, I guess everyone moved pretty quickly."

Which would have been her approximate guess. And her other guess was that Hannah's editor had been displeased to discover that she *hadn't* been the one to break it. Fairly sure that she had calmed herself down enough to repress any further flashbacks, for the time being, Meg picked up her coffee. "We can go back on the record."

Hannah shook her head.

Oh, great. Now what?

"How are you walking around?" Hannah asked.

What? "Well, if you've been paying attention," Meg indicated her cane, "I mostly *limp* around." Rarely more so than today.

Hannah ignored that. "It hasn't even been a year yet. If it were me, I'd probably be in a sanitarium or something."

"Really?" Meg said, pretending to be intrigued. Nay, *captivated.* "Can you recommend a good one?"

"Seriously," Hannah said.

Since she felt as though she was perpetually on the verge of a screaming nervous breakdown, that was hard to answer. She certainly wasn't going to be the Psychological Health Poster Child this year—although she liked her odds in the less-heralded Anhedonia Contest. "It seems different when you're actually in the middle of it," Meg said finally. "I mean, it's your reality, so you sort of have no choice, but to cope with it."

Hannah shrugged. "I'm not so sure. I think a lot of people would just fall apart and crawl into a hole to hide."

And she hadn't been doing just that for almost ten months now? "Depends on your definition, I guess." Meg looked over. "Still off?"

Hannah nodded.

"I hate it that people just assume I was raped," Meg said. "And that the White House covered it up. As though, because I happen to be female, there's no other possibility. If I had been, I'm sure I'd be doing a hell of a lot worse than I am, and—I don't know, it seems as though there's more of a titillation factor associated with it than anything else." Jack might have been the only one dumb enough to *say* it so far, but he was far from the first guy she had seen look her over with that little bit of extra-salacious curiosity.

Hannah didn't answer right away. "In some cases, maybe. But it's mostly probably just empathy, imagining how horrible it would be to be in such a vulnerable position."

"In other words, that's how you've been feeling," Meg said.

Hannah blushed slightly, but nodded.

Terrific.

"I'm really glad you weren't," Hannah said.

Meg nodded. Presumably, rape of the *soul* didn't count.

The formerly amicable atmosphere now felt so awkward and strained that they couldn't quite look at each other.

"The version of the story the press got," Hannah said, tentatively, "and, I guess, as a result, the one given to the rest of the country, is pretty obviously sanitized. And it's logical that that's the sort of thing that would be kept quiet."

There were moments, Meg knew, when even her parents weren't quite sure if she'd told them the complete truth, although she'd tried to convince them otherwise. She sighed. "He was a lot of things, but fortunately for me, rapist wasn't among them. He pretty much confined himself to punching, and threatening, and starving, and general terrorizing." And destroying her knee.

Along with her self-respect.

Hannah looked relieved, but also uncomfortable.

"It's a funny thing about punching," Meg said, touching the side of her nose without thinking about it. "When someone slugs you, they want to hurt you, and scare you, and show you how angry they are, but when they *kick* you, it's meant to make you feel worthless, and inferior." She moved her jaw. "Works pretty well, actually."

It was even more quiet than it had been before, if possible.

"And I'm sure there are plenty of people who believe I was actually ransomed, and rescued, and the whole escape story is just a PR sham to make it look as though my mother didn't capitulate to the demands," Meg said.

Hannah waited, intently, for her to go on.

Of course, the world was *also* full of nutjobs who didn't believe that the Holocaust or any one of a number of awful things had ever happened. So, why would her tiny, personal tragedy be any different?

"That theory makes your hand a little difficult to explain, though," Hannah said.

And, so it did. Meg nodded. "Well, I must have taken a hammer and smashed the bones into oblivion, to help sell the story. Or, maybe someone in the Administration—possibly the President herself—wielded it."

Hannah shuddered.

Yeah, that was a truly disturbing image. "God forbid she get credit for the sheer *heroism* of remembering that the responsibility of being the President goes way beyond anything else—even your obligations to your firstborn child," Meg said.

Hannah nodded. "That doesn't make it much fun to be the child, though, does it."

No, not much fun at all. "Well, it gets sort of complicated by the fact that I love her," Meg said quietly.

There was a pause, and then Hannah nodded again. "That's good," she said, just as quiet. "That has to help."

Yeah. And it helped even more that, deep down, she knew that the sentiment was very much returned. But, enough of the Confession Hour. "So," Meg said, trying to smile, "is it making you sick that you can't use any of this?"

Hannah shook her head vehemently.

Go figure. "Well, then, you might be in the wrong profession," Meg said.

Hannah looked sheepish. "I maybe have a *touch* of nausea."

Meg felt pretty sick herself, although it was for other reasons. Exhaustion. Tension. Things like that. She saw Ed trying to catch her eye, and nodded at him. The White House delegation must have arrived. Time to go. Then she focused on Hannah, who had also picked up on

Ed's non-verbal signal, and was already gathering up her coat and finishing the last of her coffee. "Out of respect to Preston, I'm going to have to talk to him about all of this, and he's probably going to want to sit in, if we follow up, okay?"

"*If* we follow up?" Hannah asked.

Right. "*When* we follow up," Meg said.

ON HER WAY back to the dorm, she saw Ginette standing on the crowded little traffic median, giving what sounded like a combination of a statement—and strict instructions and guidelines. There was an immediate flurry of interest when they all saw her, but Ginette snapped out one of her patented "Miss Powers will *not* be taking any questions" lines, and then, they were both ushered across the street by her agents and campus security.

Meg had yet to say anything more controversial than "Hello," but Ginette already seemed to be quite testy with her, which—with luck—was not a reflection of Preston's mood today.

"Um, how was your flight?" Meg asked.

"Fine," Ginette said, in a noticeably clipped voice.

How nifty. "I'm sorry you all had to come up here," Meg said. "I told my parents that it really wasn't—"

Ginette glared at her. "I don't think there's any question but that it was *very* necessary."

Well, for Susan's sake, maybe, but it wasn't as though she'd demanded that they show up. For that matter, Susan hadn't, either.

"The first thing we heard when we got here was that you'd taken off willy-nilly to meet with that shark Hannah Goldman," Ginette said, sounding very angry.

Okay, now the other shoe had landed neatly. Meg shrugged. "She's very nice. For a shark."

Ginette ignored that. "We were also told that you refused to seek the medical attention you obviously need, despite being strongly urged to do so."

Now, it was Meg's turn to scowl. "I'm never *not* in pain, Ginette. This actually isn't all that much worse than usual. And was I really supposed to take off to the hospital last night, when my good friend was reeling, because her best friend's murder was suddenly being thrown in her face, on camera, just because she has the bad luck to know *me*?"

Ginette looked guilty. "No. I guess not." She glanced over. "I guess I also didn't realize that you two had become friends."

Christ, she had just used the phrase "good friend" without thinking. "Well, we're not anymore," Meg said. "But, up until last night, we were headed in that direction." Maybe.

Her knee was throbbing crazily, and she paused to rest, and try to breathe the intensity of the pain down, so that when they finally got to the dorm, her eyes wouldn't be full of tears.

Ginette waited next to her, looking as though she was tempted to ask her agents to carry her the rest of the way to the dorm.

"I'm *fine*," Meg said. "I just have to pace myself."

Ginette nodded too hard, and too many times.

She wasn't ready to start walking again—but she did, anyway, since it was preferable to watching a press aide try not to fall to pieces.

"Preston wants me to escort Susan around, and be available for—well, as long as necessary," Ginette said. "I hope I'll be able to be of some assistance."

Meg just nodded, conserving her energy.

As they approached the entrance, Andy came out on his way to class—and then stopped. Judging from his expression, he was about as fond of her right now as Juliana was.

Another burgeoning friendship, dead in the water.

He was the first one to break the silence. "Did you *really* not know?"

Christ, did they all think she was an unrepentant liar, on top of everything else? "Of course I didn't," Meg said. "Come on."

He looked at her as though he was trying to decide whether to believe her, then nodded. "Okay. I'll spread the word. Because—people are pissed."

Yeah. She'd noticed.

When they went inside, Kyle was still at the front desk.

"Hi," Meg said. "Is he here, or—?"

Kyle pointed upstairs. "Follow the sound of female voices."

Ah, as usual, within moments, the typical fan club had formed around him. Sometimes she wondered whether Preston knew about the profound power he possessed—and milked it, or whether he was oblivious to its true dimensions.

When they got off the elevator, Preston was lounging in the chair by the upstairs security desk, surrounded by what appeared to be half of the girls who lived in the dorm, all of whom were laughing and nodding at whatever he had just said. Even Nellie, who must have come on duty to relieve Martin, had a fairly rapt, foolish smile on her face.

Preston saw her, and stood up with an easy motion. Hell, it was *feline-esque.* Even though he was, disappointingly, wearing a conservative grey suit, a plain white shirt, and a dark red tie.

"Ladies," he said formally, "it has, indeed, been a pleasure." Then he gave Meg a nod, and motioned towards her room with one jerk of his head.

No actual hello? *Very* bad sign.

It was crowded, but people were starting to drift away, now that the focus of their attention was no longer in view.

"He is so sexy," someone was saying, as she went down the stairs, and there seemed to be general agreement with that sentiment.

Susan was nowhere in sight, and Juliana had quickly ducked into her room, but Meg nodded at Tammy, who was lingering in the hall, seemingly hoping for one more glimpse of the First Gentleman's Chief of Staff.

"Hi," Meg said.

Tammy mouthed "he's *really* cute" at her, and Meg nodded, since—what the hell—he *was*, and went into her room to find him leaning against her desk. He indicated the door, and she closed it, then went over to her bed. Taking her weight off her knee was such a relief that it was a struggle not to burst into tears. But instead, she just closed her eyes for a second and then reached for a pillow to prop her leg up, while Preston watched her silently.

The man could communicate more without uttering a single syllable than anyone she had ever known.

"Start *shooting* the bastards?" he said finally.

The remark he had tactfully avoided mentioning during their phone conversations the night before. Meg sighed. "I lost my temper."

"Really," he said. "Gee whiz, I didn't pick up on that at all, Meg. You disguised it beautifully."

Christ, was she supposed to be perfect? It wasn't like she did any of this for a damn living. She was in *college*, for God's sakes.

"I liked the 'carnage' remark, too," he said, his gaze so intense that she was pretty sure he could see right through her to the wall. "Kudos, for the grace under pressure."

In all of these years, had Preston even given her anything more than a mild admonition, or a raised eyebrow? And he'd picked today to start being mean? Jesus, maybe there really *wasn't* anyone in her life who she could trust.

"And, if I may ask," he said, "have you been off favoring our friend Ms. Goldman with similarly irresistible sound bites?"

Meg didn't feel like answering him, so she just shrugged.

"Well." He straightened the crease in his pants, then brushed at what seemed to be a nonexistent piece of lint.

"God-damn peacock," Meg said stiffly.

He narrowed his eyes at her. In fact, they were actual *slits*. "Let's not push each other today, okay, Meg?"

"Right," Meg said. After all, it wasn't as though he'd started pushing *her* around, first. "It's funny. Here I am—on a bed—by myself in a small room, with an angry guy giving me abuse and trying to upset me." She frowned. "Hmmm. Why does this feel so familiar?"

Preston looked at her, then abruptly got up and walked out, shutting the door behind him.

Okay, she'd gone too far. About a thousand miles too far. In fact—

There was a knock on the door.

She swallowed, afraid to get up, but then there was another knock and she hesitantly limped over and opened it.

"Hi, Meg," Preston said, and gave her a quick hug. "God, it's good to see you. I heard you're having a tough time right now—anything I can do to help?"

She smiled, although—much as she would have preferred not to have this thought—the kidnapper had had a similar sense of humor.

"I'm sorry," he said.

That was one phrase which had never come out of the kidnapper's mouth. She nodded. "Me, too. I can be pretty rotten, when I want to be."

"Well—you have your moments," he said. "But then, I'm capable of being a complete prick, so there you go."

She was going to disagree, but right now, she was having no trouble imagining that whatsoever.

He indicated her desk chair. "Are you comfortable with my sitting there?"

Oh, for God's sakes. "Don't be an idiot, Preston," she said. "You know damn well I *adore* you. Just sit down."

He nodded, and took a seat.

The room was very quiet, but it was more of a tired silence, than an angry one.

"It's a poor excuse," he said, "but the only sleep I've gotten was for about an hour on the plane, and I guess I've also been building up a head of steam ever since your mother landed on me last night."

Which had, quite possibly, been a first for him. Much like the little scene they had just gone through themselves. Meg frowned. "The President lost her temper, too?"

"The President was on the *warpath*," he said. "I hadn't seen her like that—for a long time."

Since she was kidnapped, presumably. Meg still didn't know very many details, and possibly never would, about what it had *really* been like around the White House during those thirteen days—but it couldn't have been pretty.

He shook his head. "To tell you the truth, I actually thought she was going to throw something at me."

"She probably would have," Meg said, "if she had a better arm."

Preston grinned. "Well, you might be right about that."

One of the most closely-guarded secrets in the Administration was the degree to which the President dreaded April, and Opening Day for the major league baseball season, because she was required—often, at more than one stadium—to throw out the first ball, and was afraid of making a fool of herself. She and Steven would have several practice sessions during the month before, usually up at Camp David, where they would be mostly unobserved, but no matter how many times she was given advice and tips and even hands-on demonstrations, she still—well—threw like a girl.

Since Meg, personally, did not throw like a girl, she had always gotten a pretty big yuck out of the situation.

But even if her mother had a Hall of Fame pitching arm, Meg still couldn't picture her ever throwing something in anger. Considering her generally preternatural composure, even throwing a *fit* seemed like a stretch. "I don't get why she was mad at you. This wasn't your fault."

"The President feels that you and Susan, and by extension, your families, were very poorly served in this situation—by me, in particular," Preston said, with a rigid expression. "And, as it happens, I agree with her, so I offered my resignation."

Meg stared at him.

"Obviously, since I'm here right now, she didn't accept it," he said.

Even so. Jesus, he *had* had a bad night. And if her mother had allowed him to quit, she might well have never spoken to her again for the rest of their lives. "Do you even know Susan at all?" she asked. "I mean, other than meeting her when you guys dropped me off here."

He shook his head. "No, but I was certainly involved with coordinating the paperwork, and—I should have paid more attention to the possible ramifications of her personal history."

No question, but there was still something that wasn't quite tracking here. And while he might avoid giving her direct answers sometimes, she was almost sure that he would never outright lie to her. "So, you made the final call, entirely on your own," Meg said.

He hesitated.

Thereby upholding her suspicions. "At first, my mother couldn't even place the name 'Susan,' " Meg said. "Dowd *or* McAllister."

Which officially eliminated one of the two prime suspects.

"The Secret Service was *raving* about her," Preston said. "She passed all of the security checks with flying colors."

No, he couldn't fool her with a tangential issue. This whole thing had her father's well-meaning fingerprints all over it. "What in the hell was he thinking?" she asked.

Preston sighed. "He wasn't thinking, Meg. I don't think he *can* think clearly anymore, insofar as your welfare is concerned."

A loving, sweet—and selfish—instinct, on his part, then. And because of the first two reasons, she probably wouldn't take him to task for it. Not today, anyway.

"The fact that she's well on the way to getting a black belt didn't hurt," Preston said.

Yeah, if a band of armed terrorists—or possibly, suicide bombers—attacked her, Susan would immediately be pressed into service to karate chop them all and avert the crisis.

Preston sighed again. "Come on, Meg. I can't always read your mind."

That was probably for the best.

"He thought that she would have extra insight about me, because she's had a tough time herself," she said.

He nodded reluctantly.

"And even though it might end up screwing *her* up, it was a risk worth taking," she said.

"A calculated risk," he said.

Poorly calculated. But continuing to rake him over the coals wasn't going to accomplish much, other than annoying both of them more than they already were. "I still don't see how my mother can blame you," she said. Although actually, she might have made the conscious, safe choice to take most of it out on Preston, instead of waiting until she went back to the Residence later.

Preston shrugged. "She trusted me to be objective, and give good advice, but I wasn't, and I didn't."

She was glad he had trouble being objective about her—but, okay, it would be nice if he had been, on this one occasion.

"Gabler was telling me today that they were so hard on her during one of the last interviews that they all felt terrible, afterwards," he said. "But she didn't even flinch, and they really liked that. Liked *her*."

That didn't sound too good. "What do you mean, 'hard on her'?" Meg asked.

Preston looked tired. "Meg, they can't risk having anyone around you, especially in such close proximity, who they think, in any way, under any circumstances, could be *bought*."

Could sell her out to the highest terrorist bidder, the way Dennis had.

"And while they liked Dirk, and some of the other JAs, too, with Susan they were lucky enough to find someone who had already been tested in a terrible situation, where she never lost her dignity, never spoke to the press, and never showed anything resembling a hint of emotional instability," he said. "I mean, how could they resist? The problem is that everyone was so concerned about you, that no one really thought enough about how it might end up affecting *her*."

Hmmm.

"So, we blew it," he said.

They sure had.

25

A LUNCHTIME MEETING had been arranged at the college president's house, which included deans, Secret Service agents, campus security people, the college press office, the local police chief, and a few other campus officials whose exact purpose for attending Meg couldn't quite figure out. Naturally, Preston and Ginette were there, too, along with an uneasy Dirk, and a very quiet Susan.

Although Meg had been dreading the MRI and other medical exams which were likely to be in her immediate future, within about ten minutes, she decided that they would be preferable to sitting in this meeting. Everyone was being extremely nice to her—but, the MRI still seemed enticing, by comparison.

The upshot of the matter was that campus trespassing ordinances were going to be more stringently enforced, and that Susan was offered a choice between Meg's being assigned to another dorm and *definitely* getting another female JA, or that Susan herself could relocate elsewhere on the campus, as soon as this very afternoon, if she so desired.

Susan smiled, and nodded—and declined to accept either suggestion.

"Any or all of the students in your entry will naturally be given the same opportunity, if they feel they'd be happier with other living arrangements," one of the deans said.

"I'm not aware of there being any problems whatsoever, ma'am," Susan said, Dirk nodding in agreement, "but we'll certainly speak to each of them privately and make sure."

The discussion with Juliana was likely to be contentious, if not *blistering*.

Meg was also presented with similar options, but she just said that she'd do whatever would make life easier for everyone else, up to and including, transferring altogether—which everyone in the *room* dismissed, none more swiftly than Susan.

It was a great relief when the meeting—or, at least, the part in which she and Susan and Dirk had been required to participate—broke up. Susan was gone with only the barest nod, Ginette trudging along behind her.

"Maybe not a match made in heaven," Meg said to Preston, who grinned.

Before she could escape herself, Mr. Gabler came over to take her aside.

"Are you happy with everyone assigned to your current detail?" he asked. "Because if any of them are making you even the slightest bit uncomfortable, I'd like to replace them immediately."

Dennis had always made her very nervous, for no reason she could quite pin down, at the time, except maybe that he *watched* her so closely—and she'd been too stupid to tell anyone other than Beth and Josh, both of whom she knew still felt guilty that they hadn't told anyone else, either. Meg shook her head. "No, they're all really nice." Or, at least, the few with whom she'd had actual conversations seemed to be. Even short-fused Kyle. "But, if any of them don't like being assigned to me, my feelings aren't going to be hurt if you—"

"Not an issue," Mr. Gabler said abruptly.

She had her doubts—but, okay. Every so often, agents were rotated to new assignments automatically, but any atypical reassignments probably didn't look very good on their records. The theory was that if agents stayed with the same protectee for too long a period of time, nonprofessional attachments might form, which would hinder their ability to do their jobs effectively.

But, was she allowed to make a recommendation? At worst, Mr. Gabler would nod—and ignore her opinion. "When it's time for them to be reassigned, though, I'd *really* like to see Martin moved onto my mother's detail," she said. "Or, failing that, my father's. He always seems to be the one on duty when—well, lots of times lately, he's had the toughest job of any of them, and he's been great."

Mr. Gabler's eyebrows came together. "The toughest?"

She was supposed to believe that he wasn't monitoring the security logs regularly? Highly unlikely. "The nightmares," she said.

Mr. Gabler nodded now, so he must be fully up to speed on her tendency to wake everyone up in the middle of the night.

"He's handled it very delicately, and professionally—and I appreciate it," Meg said. Granted, all of her agents had been kind to her during the late-night—and, sometimes, mid-afternoon—encounters, but Martin was her favorite, by far. The most comforting one.

"Well, that's good to hear." Mr. Gabler made a quick note in a small leather-bound book, then returned it to his inside jacket pocket.

She wasn't sure she wanted to know the answer to this, but—"How's the, um, chatter lately?" she asked. Threats, intelligence, extremist groups bragging and preening.

Mr. Gabler didn't blink, but also didn't respond immediately. "I would characterize it as being within expected levels," he said.

Not terribly consolatory. Meg nodded. "You mean, the elevated number of crackpots and whack jobs we now take for granted since I turned into sort of a touchstone for terrorism?"

Mr. Gabler winced.

That could legitimately be described as a big yes.

"Everything is being very closely monitored, Meg, and I can assure you that we're not unduly concerned at the moment," he said.

Unduly. "Preston says you guys kind of like it when the press flocks around me, because it can actually help security," she said.

He nodded in his careful way. "On occasion, members of the media have voluntarily come to us with observations and information about some of our protectees, and we welcome their input."

She could only hope that that journalistic response would be the norm, and not the exception.

"Is there anything else you want to discuss with me?" he asked.

Yes, even though it was embarrassing. Meg glanced around to make sure that no one—not even Preston—was listening. "Have you run a full background check on Jack Taylor?"

"The Frisbee kid?" Mr. Gabler asked, and she nodded. "Several, actually. Why?"

That sounded ominous. She looked at him nervously. "Did he come through okay? I mean, is there anything I should know about?"

"Not from a security standpoint, no." Mr. Gabler was a very serious, all-business type, but he suddenly cracked a smile. "But—well—"

"What?" Meg asked, dreading the answer.

"He may be a cad, Meg," Mr. Gabler said.

Not exactly a shocking revelation. Meg grinned, too. "Figured that out by myself, sir."

"In which case, you're entirely on your own with this one," Mr. Gabler said.

The first good news she'd had all day.

She hadn't eaten anything at the lunch meeting, and Preston wanted to stop at Paresky and pick up something before they left, but she refused. The sooner they got to the hospital, the sooner she would find out how badly she'd injured herself. He frowned, but didn't argue.

"How much does it hurt?" he asked, once they were in the car.

Finally, she was alone with someone around whom she could be completely honest without a second thought. "It's god-damn *killing* me."

Preston nodded, and looked worried. "I was afraid that was going to be your answer."

The one possible upside was that she might get prescribed some slightly effective painkillers, at least for a week or two.

"It's terrible about the soldiers," she said.

He nodded.

The last she had heard, there were now ten KIA, and seventeen injured, most of them seriously. Terrorists were claiming responsibility, but the White House's public position was that the crash was a tragic accident and had been the result of unforeseen mechanical and weather-related difficulties. She had no idea whether this was true or not.

Her knee seemed to be locked in place again, and she absentmindedly slapped the side of her leg and shook it loose to try and get herself into a more comfortable—or, anyway, less excruciating—position.

"Your hand broke my heart," Preston said.

She frowned at him.

"There you are, storming around in the snow, not even noticing that you're *trashing* your knee, and the whole time," he demonstrated with his own hand, "you have your poor little hand cupped in front of you."

Swell. Meg set her jaw. "In other words, I looked pathetic."

"You *looked* like the Avenging Angel," Preston said. "Your hand just made me sad."

Well, it was sad. Especially, she assumed, for someone who had known her when she was still herself. "You know, you're the only one who can look me in the eye. You and Beth." She sighed. "And, strangely enough, Susan McAllister."

Preston nodded. "I noticed that about her."

His cell phone rang then, and it was her father, checking in. They were always cautious about the security of cellular transmissions, so they were both intentionally vague, on the off-chance that the conversation might be intercepted. But as far as she could tell, her mother was Not Happy, and he was still talking about the possibility of them both flying up to see her, even though they had all already agreed that it would only magnify the situation that much more, and should probably be avoided. She decided not to mention that, at the moment, she was Not Happy with him, either.

"How bad *are* the stories?" she asked, after she'd hung up. She had steadfastly avoided turning on her television, looking at a newspaper, or hitting her usual haunts on the Internet for about eighteen hours now—which might well be a personal record.

"Not as bad as they could have been," Preston said. "The New York and Boston tabloids really went to town, and apparently, Fleet Street is getting ready to have a field day, too. But we were able to get it buried reasonably well with most of the print media, and it didn't get too much play on the airwaves outside the Northeast and the Beltway. The blogs are working overtime, but that isn't anything new. You can pretty much count on seeing a fair number of 'where are they now's and features following up on the murders for the next week or two."

"And the same about me," Meg said, "only more so."

Preston's phone rang and he glanced at the number on the display, but didn't answer it. "Unfortunately, Meg, there's too much file footage of you out there to suppress it all. And—well, more and more, you just *look* and sound too damn much like her, so they can't resist, especially when something like last night comes along."

When she had thrown any political enemy her mother had a golden opportunity to make mischief and sow dissent. Christ, she needed some sleep. Meg closed her eyes. "How much damage did I do?"

"Not that much at all," he said. "I mean, yes, it's too bad that, seeing the gestures and hearing the inflections, anyone watching immediately gets a very vivid image of the *President* blowing her stack, but the media isn't exactly a much-loved institution, so not that many people are likely to be upset about your taking them to task. And, arguably, you may actually have done her some good."

Meg opened her eyes. Preston was a master of spin, but this one was going to be worth her full attention.

"Think about it," he said. "A lot of people out there are angry at her about what happened to you, but now they have some absolutely undeniable evidence that you're not only not off languishing somewhere, but that you might even be *thriving*."

Oh, yeah. Big-time thriving.

"It's true," Preston said. His cell phone rang again, but he turned it off without even checking the display this time. "Anyone who wants to assume the worst of her probably has a picture of you as a traumatized little victim, but what they *saw* last night was strength, and confidence, and total fearlessness. Which has to make them wonder how bad a parent she can be, if she has a daughter who bounces back from sheer hell so effortlessly."

"Effortlessly," Meg said.

Preston grinned. "Well, on camera, anyway."

Which, today, *did* matter more than reality. "It's going to make it much harder for Beth to spread her rumors, though," Meg said.

Now, Preston laughed. "See? There's always a silver lining."

Although she had a funny feeling that, even at this very moment, Beth was all over the Internet *thwarting* rumors.

"Do you think that son-of-a-bitch saw it somewhere?" she asked.

Preston didn't answer right away. "Odds are. Depends on how far underground he's gone."

Not very, was her guess—which did not, in her opinion, improve the chances that the FBI was ever going to find him. "How do you think it would have made him feel, seeing me like that?" she asked.

Preston frowned.

"Please tell me the truth," Meg said. "I *count* on you for that."

Preston nodded, but still took his time before responding. "I think part of him was probably kicking himself because he shouldn't have left you alive, but a bigger part felt a grudging respect."

A reasonable guess. "Maybe not so grudging," Meg said.

Preston looked at her thoughtfully. "Maybe not."

They were pulling up to the hospital now, and Meg forced her expression into some combination of nonchalance and impassiveness, since she could already see that there were a few reporters and photographers waiting around outside.

"Don't worry," Preston said. "I'll take care of them, and then come in and find you."

Good.

A group of doctors and nurses, along with Vicky and Cheryl, were waiting just inside the entrance, with a gurney. Surprisingly—or maybe not—one of the physicians was Dr. Steiner, her primary orthopedic surgeon from Washington.

Nice to know that her parents, and the White House, weren't overreacting or anything.

And now, the fairly large press contingent outside made more sense.

"Hi," she said, and then hopped up onto the gurney before anyone could help her—which made almost all of them gasp.

She had expected them just to look at her knee, and check the pulses in her leg and all, but after she was taken off for preliminary X-rays and had fluid aspirated from the joint and so forth, she ended up having a comprehensive physical, too.

"Oh, come on," she said impatiently, when they snapped one of those elastic tourniquets around her arm and started drawing blood. "I just twisted my *knee*, a little."

"Bob wants us to do a complete workup," Dr. Steiner said. Bob, being Dr. Brooks. "The President was very concerned to see that you've lost so much weight."

Which her mother had already expressed to her, at length, after seeing a copy of the full video feed from some network or other the night before. Meg had tried to convince her that the cameras had actually *taken away* ten pounds this time, instead of adding it, but the argument hadn't gone over very well.

"I am not pleased with the President right now," she said to Preston, who had come in to check on her between phone calls.

"Maybe the President's daughter should be sensible enough to wait and complain bitterly to the President herself later on," Preston said pleasantly.

Right. Meg nodded, and let them take four small tubes of blood without further comment.

The X-rays hadn't shown any evidence of new fractures—which hardly came as a shock, since she hadn't fallen down, and there apparently weren't any vascular problems, either, but Dr. Steiner seemed to be very worried about "noticeable instability in the joint," as well as the significant swelling and edema, and the possible need for surgical intervention, if one or more of her ligament grafts had failed. So, the MRI she had anticipated was going to be a reality.

There were a few other patients already waiting, and although she knew the doctors wanted to move her ahead in line, she refused and waited her turn, instead. Especially after two emergency cases arrived, following a car crash. Most of the time, Preston sat with her, but he was also taking and making calls, and he'd left to bring her back some lunch, and then another cup of coffee, too. She enjoyed the latter.

Vicky had been hovering about unobtrusively all afternoon, which made Meg wonder what *her* other patients were doing, but it was still nice to have a familiar, and calm, medical face around, while everyone else was busy fussing and fretting.

Preston was off yet again—Christ, he was *jittery* today—and Vicky came over to sit next to her. Meg had been forced to change into a hospital gown, but she had switched to a wheelchair, because she was damned if she was going to recline on a gurney the whole time. Also, if she did, the odds were too high that she might fall asleep.

They were sitting there quietly—Meg was too tired, and okay, too nervous, to concentrate on a magazine or anything—and then, Vicky broke the silence.

"You're going to ski, Meg," she said.

Yeah, *right.* Meg shook her head.

"No, you are," Vicky said. Insisted, really. "I'd never seen you move when you weren't consciously thinking about it, and—you must have been a really fine athlete."

She'd been a hell of a lot of things before—all of them significantly better than whatever she was now. The detritus that remained.

Vicky opened the small bag of potato chips Meg had ignored earlier and offered her some. It seemed impolite to refuse, so Meg took a couple.

"My husband said it was like watching an All-Pro running back move through that crowd," Vicky said, helping herself, too. "It was mobbed, it was snowing, you didn't have your cane, you were very upset, and you still kept your balance the whole time. You even dodged that camera that almost hit you without any hesitation."

And look where it had gotten her. "I'm about to go have an MRI, because I was *walking around in front of my dorm*, and my knee couldn't take the stress," Meg said grimly. "That's not a person who's going to be skiing."

Vicky smiled at her. "Meg, you're going to ski again, even if we have to figure out a way for you to do it standing on one foot. You won't be as good as you were before, but you'll still be a skier."

Meg gestured towards the hall. "There's a whole group of doctors out there who pretty much think that walking is going to be beyond me."

"The whole group of doctors doesn't know you very well," Vicky said.

Today, she was feeling as though no one knew anyone else even remotely. "Do you?" Meg asked, out of genuine curiosity.

Vicky shrugged. "I know that you're stubborn, and determined, and you can fight through pain. And now, I've got a real sense of your athleticism, which, believe me, is going to help you." She smiled again. "The temper isn't going to hurt, either. All you have to do is figure out how to harness it."

It would be nice to think that all, or even any, of that was true.

Vicky got up. "Stand on your good leg for a minute."

Meg checked the corridor, since she was supposed to be resting quietly, with her knee propped up in an immobilizing splint, until it was time for her MRI.

"Just for a minute," Vicky said.

Slowly, Meg stood up.

"Bend your right knee a little and lean forward," Vicky said. "Use the cane to keep yourself steady."

Dr. Steiner surely wasn't going to like this much—but, Meg did it.

Vicky nodded, and stood close enough to be able to catch her if she started to fall. "Okay. Hold that for a minute, and then I want you to roll from the inside of your right foot to the outside, a couple of times."

She had to tap the floor lightly with her cane during one of the weight shifts to keep upright, but other than that, it was pretty easy.

"Good," Vicky said. "Now—quick!—give me a skid stop."

Without thinking, Meg pivoted to the side on her right foot, flicking the cane up with one reflexive movement of her wrist. It felt—*whoa*. She blinked in genuine surprise and looked over at Vicky, who was smiling away.

"Congratulations, Meg," she said. "You just skied."

Son-of-a-bitch. She *had*.

AFTER THE MRI—which had, as usual, made her feel anxious and claustrophobic, the doctors gave every indication that they were going to spend the next couple of hours conferring and consulting with Washington, and just generally being cautious and conservative and careful. The wheelchair was an annoyance, but they didn't want her putting any weight on her leg until they had confirmed a diagnosis and decided upon a treatment plan. She had been hearing words like "joint effusion" and "meniscus" and "bucket handle tear" tossed about, which all sounded pretty depressing.

"I bet I'm going to spend spring break having surgery," she said to Preston, who was sitting next to her looking tense—and half-asleep.

He nodded.

"That sucks quite a lot," she said.

He nodded again.

She wasn't very good at sleeping while sitting up, but she had seen her mother, on numerous occasions, close her eyes in the backseat of a car, or even lean against a nearby wall, sleep for five or ten minutes, and wake up completely refreshed. Sometimes, she could even finish the sentence she had been speaking at the moment she'd dropped off. It was kind of scary.

Or, possibly, narcoleptic.

Apparently, though, she and Preston both finally dozed off, because a nurse had to wake them up to let them know that the doctors were waiting for them to come down to a small conference room, and Meg rubbed her good hand across her face, trying to get re-oriented. Preston looked very disheveled by his standards—which meant that he wasn't wearing his jacket and his tie was slightly crooked.

"Time to get the verdict, I guess," she said, and he nodded.

The initial diagnosis was that she had a Grade 2 tear of her medial collateral ligament—which she hoped was a fancy way of saying "bad sprain," and a torn medial meniscus. Surgery was a near-certainty, but not an emergency, and the orthopedists' general inclination was to keep her leg immobilized until the swelling went down, and continue evaluating her over the next few days. But they were very concerned about "the structural integrity of the joint" and Dr. Steiner's recommendation was that she remain in the wheelchair, for the time being, in order to avoid all weight-bearing activities.

"I have classes, and the dining hall, and—the wheelchair really isn't going to work for me," Meg said.

Dr. Steiner nodded. "Well, I'd rather see you fly back to Washington tonight, anyway, and—"

"I'm in *college*," Meg said, "in a place where it rains and snows a lot. And it's more important to me to try and make my life work, than to have my knee work."

The doctors all nodded, and mumbled—and exchanged glances.

"I'm also eighteen," Meg said, before anyone could suggest consulting any world leaders. "So, while I'll definitely talk this over with my parents, it's really my call. And what I'd like us to do is sit down and figure out the best way for me to get around between now and spring break—" which was only a week away— "while doing the least amount of damage to myself."

It was quiet, and they all seemed to be waiting for Preston to weigh in.

"You heard her," he said. "Let's make a plan."

To make them all a little less resistant to her treatment protocol notions, Meg agreed to have a conference call with her father and Dr. Brooks, at the White House. She knew that they would both kindly, and supportively, take her side, which they did.

In the end, she left the hospital wearing the immobilizing brace, using her cane, and allowing a wheelchair to be stuffed into the back of the trail car, just in case.

There were a few dogged reporters and photographers still outside, but Preston just said a cheery "Have a nice evening" to them, before following her into the car.

"Favorite day ever?" Meg asked, as they pulled away.

"You bet," he said.

26

NEITHER OF THEM could face the idea of going into a restaurant, but once they were back at the campus and Preston had seen her safely upstairs in the elevator, he went over to the deli on Spring Street to get some takeout. And, probably, to deal with any press people still hanging around out there.

Larry, who was at the third-floor security desk, told her that, as far as he knew, Susan was asleep, and had been for several hours. He didn't mention any of the others—and she didn't ask.

Before she even had a chance to check her voice-mail, her mother called.

"I am *not* that thin," Meg said, as soon as she heard her voice.

"Actually, you are," her mother said, "but we don't have to argue about it right now. I've been talking to your father and Bob, and I just wanted to see how you're doing."

She was tired, and cranky, and more than a little pissed off. "Excited, mostly, about getting to spend my vacation in the hospital," Meg said.

Her mother sighed. "I know. I'm sorry. Bob says it'll probably be for only one night, two at the most."

Whereupon she would spend the rest of her Spring Break dancing and leaping for joy, post-surgical complications be damned.

"How's Susan?" her mother asked.

Good question. "I don't know," Meg said. "She went to bed really early, I guess." Which reminded her of one of the main reasons she was angry at her mother right now. "Preston's been great, though."

"I know he would be," her mother said. "Even though he's probably going to be leaving his job soon, he's still the only person, other than Trudy, I would ever have trusted to send up there in our place."

Okay, now she was *more* than angry. Meg clenched the receiver so hard it made her fingers hurt. "If you're dumb enough to fire him, you should be impeached. In fact—I mean, I can't even believe that you'd *consider*—"

"I offered him Communications Director a few days ago, Meg," her mother said, sounding unruffled. "He's still thinking about it."

Oh. That was, um, actually a promotion. A *major* promotion. "I—didn't know that," Meg said.

Her mother laughed. "No. You didn't. But, at least you weren't quick to jump to conclusions."

Heaven forfend.

Her mother laughed again. "You're suddenly very quiet, Meg."

"I had a really hard day," Meg said. "And, you know, I'm awfully thin and frail. Maybe you should just be nice to me."

"Yes, maybe I should," her mother said, sounding much more gentle now.

They talked until Preston showed up with sandwiches, sodas, and a bag of groceries.

"Preston's back with the food," Meg said. "I'm going to hang up, so we can watch the game, okay?" College basketball, in this case. She looked at him. "Do you want to talk to the President?"

"Tell the President that I am, as ever, her humble servant," he said wryly.

But, of course. Especially the humble part. "Did you hear that?" Meg asked her mother.

"I did," her mother said. "Tell him to enjoy his supper and whatever it is that you're going to be watching. And—tell him I said thank you."

Right. When she'd hung up, she watched Preston put fresh milk, orange juice, apples, pears, carrots, and cheese into the refrigerator before unpacking their dinner.

"Mom says thank you." She raised an eyebrow at him. "Communications director?"

He took one of her reusable ice packs out of the tiny freezer and handed it to her. "I'm thinking about it."

Christ, it was an incredibly powerful position. A career-making position. "What's to think about?" she asked.

"You," he said. "Your father. Your brothers." He looked at her. "You, primarily."

Meg frowned, not sure where he was going with that.

"I'd be working about twenty-eight hours a day, Meg," he said. "So, I wouldn't be able to help. Not the way I can now, anyway."

Rachel, his ex-girlfriend, was the biggest fool in the world. A pox on her. Or, possibly, she was owed fervent thanks for not having had the good sense to snap him up once and for all. She slid the ice pack inside her brace and then looked back at him. "You've helped more than I could ever tell you. But, take the job, okay?"

Preston shrugged. "I'm thinking about it."

He was obdurate. "Think *hard*," Meg said.

He gave her a small salute, and then turned on the television, flipping channels on the remote until he found the game.

"Who's replacing you?" Meg asked, unwrapping her sandwich one-handed. Hot roast beef, cheese, lettuce, barbeque sauce. It looked good.

"Maureen," he said. "Today's been kind of a dry run for her."

She had to admit she was relieved to hear that it wouldn't be Ginette. "That's good. I like Maureen."

"Your father and I figured she'd be the best person for the job, yeah," he said, and moved her desk chair so that he would be able to see the television better. "Of course, I'm still only thinking about it."

She studied his grey suit, white shirt, and dark red tie. "Not exactly a carefree, freewheeling, East Wing sort of outfit you have going here."

"Let's watch the game," he said.

It was a poor substitute for baseball—and, in Preston's case, football, but the world was an imperfect place. And, luckily for her, April would arrive in the very near future.

She started to bite into her sandwich, and then stopped. "You sly dog."

Preston, already halfway through his, glanced over.

"You offered your resignation last night, because if you're going to move over to the West Wing, you need to establish new boundaries with her," Meg said.

"Or, also, because I happen to believe that I booted this one," he said.

That, too. She grinned at him. "Take the damn job, Preston."

He shrugged affirmatively, and then they watched basketball.

THE GAME WASN'T terribly interesting, but it was relaxing just to sit, and eat, and discuss nothing other than sports, and movies, and a few books they had each read recently when they were supposed to be busy doing other things. Both of their phones rang more than once, but they would just look at each other, shake their heads, and keep watching television.

Before he left, they decided to meet over at the Inn for breakfast, which Hannah Goldman either would, or wouldn't, attend. They also came to a mutual agreement that they would try to get something resembling a good night's sleep. Meg had every intention of following this edict, but with midterms coming up, she had to do some studying, first. Reading Plato made her drowsy, and she switched over to *Pericles*, which tired her out all the more. *Julius Caesar* and *Henry V* were the only two plays she'd enjoyed at all so far, despite being, of course, a devoted English major.

There was a tiny little tap on her door. She didn't feel like getting up, but she certainly wasn't about to ignore Susan, if she felt like talking—or yelling at her—or something. So, using her cane, she maneuvered her way over there, opening it to find—Juliana.

"You busy?" Juliana asked, sounding, and looking, atypically apprehensive.

Busy trying not to fall asleep. Meg shrugged. "Kind of. Why?"

Juliana hesitated. "Can I come in?"

Meg shrugged again, and limped back over to her bed. Juliana leaned against the desk, her eyes widening when she noticed the new, cumbersome brace.

"Are you all right?" she asked.

Meg shrugged, picking up *Pericles* and using her good thumb as a bookmark.

"I was really a jerk this morning," Juliana said.

Meg glanced down at the page she had been reading. "Whatever. Hadn't given it much thought."

Which was a total lie, of course.

"Seeing them go after Susan like that was just—" Juliana shivered. "I kind of wigged out. I mean, she looked so scared."

No argument there, considering Meg had pretty much wigged out herself.

There was a long silence.

"That it?" Meg asked.

"I don't know," Juliana said. "Depends on how good you are at accepting apologies."

"Okay." Meg returned to her book. "No big deal."

It was silent again.

"It *was* a lot less high-pressure around here last semester," Juliana said. "I wish I could tell you it wasn't, but—it was. I mean, it was just *college,* you know?"

Yeah, yeah, yeah. Meg nodded. "I know, I wrecked everything by coming here, and you wish I would just go away once and for all. Got the message loud and clear, okay?"

Juliana started to leave, but then shook her head and sat down in the desk chair. "You really want to spend the rest of the semester being mad at each other? On a floor *this* small? Why don't we try to straighten it out? Christ, Meg, people have fights, you know? It's not the end of the damned world."

Except that it was so much less work to keep her distance from people. Had been for a long time.

"Sometimes, it is the end of the world," Juliana said suddenly.

Meg looked up.

"My sister Tracy had this huge blowup with my parents last year, and I thought, okay, she'll get over it," Juliana said. "But, she stopped speaking to us, and didn't show up for Christmas or anything—it's really awful."

"I'm sorry," Meg said. "If that happened with either of my brothers, it would completely tear me apart." In fact, she couldn't bear to imagine such a thing. "Do you think it'll be okay?"

Juliana looked miserable. "I don't know. I was trying to run interference, but they all just ended up getting mad at me."

Tolstoy, and his unhappy families. "My mother and I are afraid of each other," Meg said. "It causes most of the tension in our family."

"Afraid of *each other*?" Juliana asked. "It goes both ways?"

"Much more so on her side, actually," Meg said.

Juliana thought about that, then grinned. "Well, you scare the shit out of me, so maybe I'm with her on this one."

All right, that was funny. Meg grinned back.

"So. We okay?" Juliana asked.

Meg nodded. "Yeah, we're fine." Then, she remembered something. "This morning, Jesslyn was saying something about a couple of people who turned down being my JA?"

Juliana shook her head. "Lori and Angela. No, they were freshmen. You know, here in the entry."

Oh. "Who didn't want to live near me," Meg said.

"Did you think these two rooms were just sitting here empty all last semester," Juliana asked, sounding very irritated, "in case you might decide to show up?"

Christ, she'd never really thought about it. "You mean, people got *kicked out*?" Meg said. Oh, hell. "Jesus, I never wanted anyone to—"

Juliana shrugged. "Lori decided to double up with Amber, over in Sage A, and someone in Mills decided not to come back this semester, so Angela was just as happy to go down there, since her boyfriend lives in Pratt."

Why hadn't something so obvious—the fact that she had *displaced* people—occurred to her long ago? "What about the security room downstairs?" Meg asked.

"It was just a common room before, so that wasn't too complicated," Juliana said. "Those guys always hang out in the JAs' common room, anyway."

Yeah, but still. Maybe she *was* a damn princess, after all. Accustomed to having trays of food magically appear, her sheets changed—which was hard as hell to do alone with one hand, and Susan had had to help her almost every time so far, her clothes washed and folded and put away, fresh flower arrangements everywhere, magazines and newspapers brought to her room—and every other conceivable convenience and luxury, regardless of whether she requested anything or not.

She let out her breath. "I *knew* there was something off about Susan, but I never once asked you, hey, what's Susan's deal, anyway?"

Juliana looked right at her. "No," she said. "You never did."

THERE WAS A heavy sleet falling the next morning, so her agents drove her to the Inn, even though it was just down the street. Despite taking two pain pills the night before—damaging her original plan to hoard the prescription as long as possible—she had slept badly, and her knee felt worse than ever.

A lot of the remaining media people must have been staying at the Inn, because the group standing in front of the main entrance smoking all put out their cigarettes as soon as they saw her. Meg just nodded, and limped past them. Most of the other reporters were in the dining room, having breakfast, and she was the focus of attention the second she came in.

Preston was sitting at the far end of the room, with Hannah Goldman, and four or five other reporters were also gathered around the table, holding cups of coffee. Today, he had gone with another tedious grey suit, a white shirt, and a blue and grey striped tie, although at least he had a snazzy pocket handkerchief to liven it up a *little*.

"How's the knee?" he asked, after walking over to meet her.

She shrugged, instead of answering, because she didn't really feel like complaining.

He indicated the small group of reporters with a slight movement of his eyes. "Up to giving them a few generalized remarks?"

No. "I thought it was just going to be Hannah," Meg said.

Preston nodded. "I know. But I have some carrot and stick action working here, and if you could hand them a couple of vague little carrots, I'd be very pleased."

She had to assume that he wouldn't ask, if it weren't important. "Okay. Do you want to take five minutes, and figure out a script for me, first?"

"Planning to swear at them?" he asked.

She shook her head.

"Then, I'm not going to worry about it," he said. "Just tell them how much you're going to appreciate it, if they give you some room to have a normal college experience, and that sort of thing. I'll let them have a couple of questions, too, okay?"

Well, she'd already agreed, so she could scarcely back out now. Meg nodded.

"Can you stand?" he asked. "Or would you rather sit?"

There were cameras, so she would definitely stand. She took off her sleet-covered Red Sox cap and moved her sunglasses up on top of her head, in the hope that it might make her hair look a little less unruly. "I didn't really dress for this," she said. Sweatpants, albeit reasonably well-fitting, because it had just been too hard to strap the new brace over anything else, a gold turtleneck, and a purple Williams sweatshirt with yellow lettering.

He looked her over quickly. "Lose the jacket, and you're fine. In fact, the sweatshirt's just right—it'll be an ideal reminder of the nice, normal coed thing."

She nodded, and put her coat down on a chair in the lobby, taking one fast second to grab some lip gloss from the side pocket and put it on while her back was turned. She hated makeup, but her mother had managed to convince her that it was worthwhile to carry lip gloss around for unexpected cameras. "What do I do with my hand?" she asked, tucking the tube away.

He smiled, but his eyes looked sad. "Absolutely anything you want, Meg. Just—whatever's the most comfortable."

It was at moments like this that she missed her sling. She leaned the base of the hand splint on top of her cane, without putting any pressure on it, and hoped that her good leg would compensate and keep her steady. But then, she got a better idea and moved over to one of the upholstered chairs by the fireplace, where—telegenically enough—a fire was burning. She perched against one of the chair arms, just enough to take the weight off her leg and make it possible to put the cane behind her, out of sight. Then she rested her bad hand on her lap. Ideally, the pose would look both casual and relaxed, while still in a dignified setting.

Preston waved at the reporters from the dining room, and the others who had come into the lobby from outside hurried to join them, which made Meg feel like the ball in the middle of a scrum. Civilian guests in the dining room, and checking out at the front desk, watched all of this with great curiosity.

"Good morning," she said, keeping her expression neutral, but affable. Genial, even.

She got a few responses, and a number of nods, back.

"Well. We few, we happy few," she said, purely for Preston's benefit.

Standing off to the side, near the entrance to the dining room, he grinned. And most of the reporters looked amused, too.

Would he enjoy it if she recited the entire speech? Probably not. Even if she did it with verve. Or maybe *especially* if she did it with verve. "I hope everyone's enjoying the weather up here," she said.

There were a lot of smiles.

Okay. Time to get down to business. "Obviously, I'm going to miss all of you terribly when you're gone," she said, "but I want to thank you in advance for doing whatever you can to help me be as ordinary a college freshman as possible. And I know that my fellow students will appreciate your efforts even more than I do, so I'll thank you on their behalf, also." She paused. "I'm starting to hear the siren call of—oh, I don't know—waffles and coffee, but I'll take a few questions, first."

"Can you update us on the status of your knee?" someone she didn't recognize asked, pointing towards her new brace.

"Well—" at the risk of possibly being too blithe— "I zigged, when I should have zagged," Meg said.

Most of them laughed.

"Is this going to be a major physical setback for you?" another reporter asked.

Meg shook her head. "No, I think I would characterize it as a blip. Or, at worst, a temporary glitch. I should be right back on track in a couple of weeks."

They all took notes about this.

"Can you describe your transition from life in the White House to this more secluded college atmosphere?" someone else asked. "Do you feel that you've made a smooth adjustment?"

"Absolutely," Meg said. "As you've been able to see during the last couple of days, I fly under the radar to a startling degree. My presence goes almost entirely unremarked."

Most of them looked amused, and uneasy. Preston, included.

"Which is not to say that I'm looking forward to the prospect of midterms with excitement and joy," she said.

One of the print people got a gleam in his eyes. "Have you found that your course load is too demanding?"

Few things bored her more than dealing with the humor-challenged. "On the contrary," Meg said, before Preston could step in. "I'm enjoying being in such an academically-rigorous environment. I feel privileged to be here." She glanced at Preston, who gave her a quick "wrap it up" twirl of his finger. "And on that note, I think I'd better address my craving for waffles, so that I can go do some studying. But, thank you again, for your consideration, now, and during the rest of my time here."

They seemed to be hoping for more, but after a little pause, they all started packing up and moving away—to Meg's extreme relief. Christ, a couple of minutes of banalities, and she was worn out. If she'd been *profound*, or even interesting, she'd probably have had to go to bed for two or three days in a row.

"That was nice, Meg," Preston said, once everyone was out of earshot, and motioned towards the fireplace. "Very Masterpiece-Theatre."

Next time, maybe she'd ask for pledge donations.

"You look exhausted," he said. "Why don't I postpone our friend Ms. Goldman?"

Which would be a tremendous relief, but then, it would just hang over her head. Meg sighed. "No, let's do it now. I'll just drink a bunch of coffee."

"How about some actual calories, too," he said mildly, "okay?"

Right. She'd been making all of those promises about waffles, hadn't she.

Once the three of them were at their table, several other reporters tried to sit down, too, but Preston rebuffed them, in a very cordial way.

"That's the stick part?" Meg asked, already halfway through her first cup of coffee.

Preston just grinned.

Hannah seemed to be on her best behavior, drinking coffee and eating an English muffin, but Meg caught a little extra sparkle in her eyes every single time Preston discouraged one of the other journalists from joining them.

"Enjoying this?" Meg asked.

"We're all professionals," Hannah said, and then paused. "Well, I guess *you* aren't—but that seems like a moot point, most of the time."

Increasingly, it was beginning to feel like the barest of technicalities.

There wasn't much conversation as she ate two-thirds of a waffle and a piece of bacon. Judging from his expression, that seemed to be enough calories to appease Preston, for the time being, and she pushed her plate to the side, nodding her thanks at the waitress who rushed over to take it away and refill all of their coffee cups.

"So. What are we going to talk about here?" Hannah asked.

Good question. "I guess I'm going to talk a little about the way my public and private lives have intersected," Meg said.

Hannah looked at her for a moment, and nodded. "Okay, then," she said, and opened her notebook.

27

THE INTERVIEW WENT fairly well. At first, they wasted some time going over ground rules and jockeying for position, mainly because Hannah's editor was so charged up about her coup that he wanted to bump it into the Sunday magazine section as a cover story. Naturally, that also meant that he wanted to set up a photo session with her, which Preston was flatly refusing to consider. The tenor of the conversation indicated that this was a rehash of several previous arguments on the subject.

"It won't take long," Hannah said, although her voice lacked conviction. "We'll just have our guy snap a few shots while she's in the middle of her everyday activities."

Preston nodded. "Yes, that's exactly what the White House wants—published photographs of Meg in habitual, easily identifiable locations."

Wait, that didn't sound too good. Meg had been trying to tune out, but now she looked up. "Hey, is even doing an *interview* risky?"

"No," Hannah said, sounding a little panicky.

"Not with a reporter who's willing to accommodate your security situation," Preston said, "and work with us to ensure your anonymity to whatever degree possible."

Maybe this wasn't such a great idea, though. God knows her father hadn't thought so, but she hadn't been very receptive about being told what to do.

Just for a change.

"We're aware of the need for extra care here," Hannah said, "but surely you can both see that we really need to have something new for the cover."

Preston nodded. "No doubt, but we're not signing off on pictures around the campus, or in the dorm, or near the hospital, or anywhere else up here. Just do a montage of file photos, or a representative sketch or something."

"Looking for a job as our Art Director?" Hannah asked drily.

Meg was going to make a joke about the new Communications Director, but then it crossed her mind that the news might not have leaked yet, and she was damned if *she* was going to be the one to blow it.

And Preston didn't actually kick her under the table, but she had the very distinct sense that he had given it some lightning-fast consideration.

They had to go off-the-record more than once, and a few times, Meg just shook her head at a particular question or conversational direction, and they moved on. Preston was almost certainly tempted to step in here and there, but he didn't—much to her relief.

At one point, she caught herself studying his fruit cup, which looked delicious, but without any other movement, Preston's eyes made the barest twitch, and she was reminded that eating from his plate—even though it was something she did routinely, or possibly *because* it was something she did routinely—might suggest a level of intimacy which probably shouldn't be displayed in front of a hyperalert reporter.

Not to mention her visibly sulking compatriots, who were still watching them.

So, she glanced around until she caught their waitress's attention—which took approximately three seconds.

"That looks very good," she said, indicating his dish. "May I have one, too, please?"

Whereupon, despite his utter immobility during all of this, she saw Preston relax.

When they were finally finished with the interview, and shook hands all around before Hannah left, she and Preston stayed at the table with her fourth, and what might well be his fifth or sixth, cup of coffee.

"Thank you for having the sense to order your own fruit salad," he said.

Meg grinned. "It was very good."

"Delectable," he agreed.

"Scrumptious," she said.

They sat there without talking, Meg wondering if he was as drained as she was.

"Is that how you really feel about the way your mother handled things, or were you doing some Presidential image rehabilitation?" he asked.

Meg shrugged. "Both."

He nodded slowly.

"Are you as angry at her as my father is?" she asked.

"I actually thought *you* were the only person in the world as angry about it as your father is," he said.

He hadn't answered her question, but she shook her head.

"Okay," he said. "I didn't know that. I mean, in some ways, it may make you eligible for canonization—but, good for you."

Except on very bad days, she could usually allow herself to see that her mother had had absolutely no maneuvering room. "What the hell else was she going to do?" Meg asked. "And at least I don't have to feel awful knowing that some of the country's future was mortgaged just so I'd have a chance to walk around still breathing."

He nodded, looking at her with unnerving concentration.

"Besides," Meg said, "I didn't say I wasn't a *little* steamed at her."

Preston grinned. "You could go as high as 'pretty god-damned steamed,' and I still wouldn't fault you."

Most of the time, that just about fit the bill, too. Meg added some more milk to her coffee. "I'm worried about them. My parents, I mean."

"They're worried about you," he said.

Meg shook her head. "You know that's not what I mean."

"Their marriage is unusually impenetrable, Meg," he said, "but I think we can both agree that your father loves all four of you fiercely."

So fiercely that it sometimes got in his way. Got in *everyone's* way, for that matter. Whether her parents could survive each other was an open question, but indeed, she had little doubt that they loved each other.

Preston leaned forward, folding his arms on the table. "My sense is that you have a visceral understanding of why she did what she did."

In other words, that she would have been capable of making the same untenable decision herself. "Yeah," Meg said. "Although I wish like hell I didn't." It made her—dangerous. The world could be ugly and complicated, and probably needed to have some people like that around, but she didn't want to *be* one of them.

Then again, she was quite possibly sitting with one of the others.

She met his gaze. "And I kind of think you understand it, too."

He nodded, and neither of them spoke for a couple of minutes.

"Is that why I remind you of him?" he asked.

Yes. "It's part of it, yeah," she said.

He looked so devastated that she immediately wished she hadn't told the truth.

"There were—" Christ, how was she ever going to explain it? Especially when she hadn't completely figured it out herself yet. "I don't know. Similar dynamics at work."

He nodded, unhappily.

The guy had been brilliant, and funny, and charming, and—even though it was inappropriate, and they didn't act upon it, she was almost positive that they had been wildly attracted to each other.

Which was probably more honesty than either she or Preston could handle this morning.

"It might have kept me alive," she said.

He looked up.

She had never quite thought of it this way, but— "Maybe I projected you onto him," she said, "as a way to make myself feel brave enough to be able to have conversations, and treat him like a normal person. And because of that, maybe he ended up seeing me as a human being, too, and killing me became a less appealing option."

"Or, you might just have been brave," Preston said very quietly.

Meg shook her head. "I was terrified." To the point of tears, a time or two, which had been mortifying. "Hell, I'm *still* terrified."

"But, here you are," he said.

More or less. "He enjoyed watching me be in pain. Like I was some kind of really fun science project." To torment, and maim, and study. "And *inflicting* it was even more fun for him." She glanced over. "Yesterday, in the hospital, you were so upset, you had trouble sitting still, or even talking to me."

Now, he looked worried. "I left you alone too much. I should have—"

"Preston, you couldn't watch, because you're thoughtful and empathetic, and you knew that there wasn't anything you could do to help me," she said. "You're nothing like him. You never will be."

He sighed. "God, I hope not, Meg. It would make me absolutely sick if I were."

It would make her pretty sick, too. "You know, I don't think you've called me 'kid' once the entire time you've been up here," she said. Not for months, now that she thought about it.

"No, I don't suppose I have." He sighed again. "It doesn't seem to suit you anymore."

Probably not. She looked down at her splint, and the metal pins protruding through her skin. "I'm pretty sure the kid died in the woods. And now you're all stuck with the fucked-up adult who came back in her place."

He smiled, and touched her splint for a second. "I don't think you're ever going to hear anyone complaining about having you home again. And—the adult turns out to be very compelling, so you're safe there, too."

Christ, he really was a lovely man. "How bad was it?" she asked. "When I was gone, I mean."

He ran his hand across his hair, which he always kept shaved very close to his head, before answering. "It was a complete nightmare. Your father was practically insane the entire time, and your mother was so calm and silent that, for a while there, I was genuinely starting to think that she *was* insane."

It was both hard, and easy, to picture those two reactions.

"As far as I know, she never cried. Not even once. She exploded a couple of times, but she never—I mean, it was—" He stopped. "Do you really need to know any of this?"

Yes. "It seemed like she cried for about a day and a half straight when I got to the hospital," Meg said. That is, when they were alone together; not in front of the general public.

He nodded. "I think people were relieved that she did. Before that, it was as though she was some kind of—" He broke off. "But then, you'd see her walk, or reach for something, and she moved so slowly and carefully that you knew she was in such bad shape that she wasn't sure if her hands and feet were going to work properly."

Often, there was *still* something of a deliberate quality to her mother's movements these days. Slightly stilted, and maybe half a beat late. "But, she ran the country," Meg said.

Preston nodded. "*Aggressively*. Kruger—" who was the Vice President—"was great, though. Never tried to push her aside, or overstep his bounds, but he was right there with her the whole time, and she was cognizant enough not to sign off on anything without getting a feel for whether it was a rational decision, first. The whole staff was terrific, but no one in the country's ever going to know how absolutely staunch Hank Kruger was."

Probably not, since Meg hadn't even known. She didn't run into the Vice President very often—other than in the Center Hall, sometimes, after her mother's kitchen cabinet meetings—but whenever she did, Mr. Kruger had always struck her as being a very considerate Southern gentleman, who never failed to stop, and smile, and ask how she was. "What about my brothers?"

"Almost as quiet as your mother, although Neal was—well, fragile would be the right word, I guess," Preston said. "Mainly, we just tried to keep them busy—played a lot of cards, turned on the Red Sox whenever there was a game, made sure they ate and slept on schedule, that kind of thing."

Meg nodded. "You and Dad, you mean."

He avoided her eyes. "Well, I guess I meant me, mostly. Felix, and a few of the others. And, of course, Trudy, before she had to fly back for Jimmy's operation."

Trudy's son had had a long-scheduled and, fortunately, successful kidney transplant right around then. Some of her parents' friends must have been around during the whole thing, but even if they were—especially if her father was pretty much out of commission—her brothers would have been inclined to depend on Preston. "Thirteen days is a long time," she said.

Preston laughed the same nervous laugh they all laughed whenever that basic reality was mentioned. "Very long."

It had been June when she got back, and now it was March. Summer, fall, winter, and the beginning of spring. "I guess I'd pretty much be a skeleton by now," Meg said.

Preston actually closed his eyes.

A thought that it might have been better to keep to herself. Meg looked down at her good hand. Thin, yeah, but unmistakably healthy and alive. Bones she could see when she moved her fingers, or clenched her fist, but all safely covered by skin and muscle and tendons and veins. "Except that I don't think they ever would have found me," she said. Nailed into that mine-shaft in the middle of nowhere, the whole area having been abandoned and condemned years before. The son-of-a-bitch had chosen his location well. "I just would have been—*gone*."

Preston nodded, also looking at her hand. *Both* of her hands.

It would have been horrible to discover her body, and have the last traces of hope destroyed, but surely, it would have been even worse never to find any trace of her at all. For weeks, and months, and years, to go by, with no resolution. "Do you think my parents would have survived that?" she asked.

"I don't think *any* of us would have survived it at all intact," he said.

For his sake, she elected not to point out that they hadn't, anyway. Also, there was one specific question which she had never, in all of these months, thought to ask. She looked around at the hotel dining room, seeing that, other than the hotel staff, and a few of her agents, they were just about the only people there. Presumably, breakfast service had ended, but it was still too early for lunch. "Why were you the one who took the call?" she asked.

He tilted his head.

"That day," she said. She'd been too weak and injured to stand, but she'd managed to prop herself against a counter in that Georgia family's bright clean kitchen and dial the White House, while the poor, stunned kid who'd let her inside just stared at her with his mouth hanging open. "It didn't make sense that neither of my parents came on right away."

Preston moved his jaw. "There had been a lot of crank calls. People who—well, pretty sick people."

No doubt, but— "On the *private* lines?" she asked.

He didn't look at her.

"It's okay," she said, although she could feel her heart beating a little faster from dread. "I want to know."

"They were afraid that the numbers might have been tortured out of you," he said. "So, the call could have been from anyone—and they didn't want to put your parents through that, unless they were absolutely sure."

Okay. That was logical. "I probably didn't sound like myself, either," she said.

He shook his head. "No. And, even if it was you—" He stopped again.

She gestured for him to go on.

Preston looked very tired. "They wanted to establish whether you were under duress, or—well, there was some concern that whoever had taken you might have been cruel enough to force you to call, and then make your mother listen to you be executed right over the phone."

Jesus. But if the guy had been wired that way, they probably would have filmed it, instead, and posted the tape on the Internet, where deeply disturbed and amoral types would have downloaded grainy copies, and emailed it to one another, with indescribably obscene fascination.

"I happen to think they made the wrong decision on that," he said. "If it actually had played out that way, it would have been absolutely unforgivable not to let one, or both, of them have a chance to speak to you."

Meg shook her head. "Yeah, but Jesus, it would have *destroyed* them."

His smile was extremely kind. "They would have done it willingly, Meg, with the hope that, during your last few seconds, it might have been a comfort to hear the voice of someone who loved you."

And there, surely, would be the personification of selflessness. With a prime example of it sitting right across the table from her. She looked back at him. "But none of them had any compunctions about possibly letting *you* listen to me be murdered."

He shook his head.

Very still waters, running very god-damned deep. And if she told him she was sorry, or even thank you, it would never come close to being enough. "You dear, sweet man," she said.

"Well," he said, self-consciously, and took a sip of what was now cold coffee.

It wasn't even lunchtime, and she felt as though it was the middle of the night. She would have expected him to change the subject now, or maybe take a glance at his long-silenced cell phone, but he just sat in his chair—slouched, really, staring at the remains of his coffee.

Which meant that there was still something—or maybe *several* somethings—haunting him.

"Whatever it is, please talk to me about it," she said.

He shook his head. "I can't, Meg. You're really the last person—"

"I'm probably the last person you should tell," she said, "but I might also be the *only* person you can tell."

He nodded, and then sucked in one slow breath before meeting her eyes. "It never leaves this table, right?"

She nodded.

He checked her expression, and then nodded in return. "They had me spend two weeks looking at morgue photos."

Okay. He'd already lost her. "I'm not, um—" She frowned. "What do you mean?"

"Someone had to look at the photos, Meg," he said.

Oh. Someone other than her parents, or Trudy.

"I had no idea how many unidentified bodies of thin, dark-haired Caucasian women turn up in this country, day after day—and, for that matter, all over the world," he said, and shuddered. "All of these anonymous young women, most of whom suffered *horribly* before some animal somewhere—my God, it was endless."

She had never considered that, either—and the concept was one that wasn't going to leave her anytime soon. "Yeah, but DNA, and dental records, and fingerprints, and—"

"Absolutely," he agreed. "And there were some, who, because of size, or age, or decomposition, they could rule out instantly. But even though they were going to be doing all of the testing, if they had any doubts at all, they thought it was easier, and much faster, to have someone who knows you well take a quick look. That way, they could get a potentially reliable identification in thirty seconds, instead of having it take, say, an hour or two."

Christ.

"Sometimes Bob Brooks would look, too," he said, "but they generally came to me, first."

And so, Preston—and Dr. Brooks—had been forced to go through the same ordeal over, and over, and *over.* For thirteen days. And nights, she assumed. It seemed cold in the dining room, and Meg repressed a shiver.

"A few of the times, I honestly wasn't sure. The build was right, and their faces had been—or there was other damage to the body, or—" He swallowed. "I'd have to go watch a live video feed, or have more photos faxed from whatever morgue or crime scene it was, and even then, I was about to fly to Texas one night before they thought to get a blood type from a body whose face and hands had been—Jesus. There are some truly evil people out there."

All of this was making her head hurt terribly, and she had to fight the urge to slump down and rest against her good arm. If she hadn't been worried about cameras out in the lobby, she *would* have.

"See, even people who'd never met you weren't really playing with a full deck," he said. "The whole situation was—I mean, most of the time, no one—the White House, the FBI, police officers, you name it—seemed to be in their right mind. And the phone would ring, or I'd hear my fax machine start, and—" He shook his head.

For months, she'd been leaning on him—and never really stopped to think about whether he might have some scars, too. Christ, what the hell was the matter with her? Susan had absolutely nailed it when she'd accused her of being self-obsessed. "I'm really sorry, Preston," she said. "I had no idea."

He smiled a tired smile at her. "Would you have done the same for me?"

"God, yes," she said. God *forbid.*

He shrugged. "All right, then. Let's leave it at that."

For now, maybe they should. Except that there was one small thing she could give him, which might help a little. "You're *nothing* like him," she said, and meant every word of it this time. "You never will be."

He looked at her for a long minute, and then, she saw the tension leave his shoulders.

"Thank you," he said.

28

PEOPLE HAD STARTED coming in for lunch, and what had been a good place to have a serious conversation no longer was. Since it seemed like a reasonable idea, they ordered some more food and resolutely began to talk about the Red Sox, and the chances of her mother's new fuel emissions standards bill passing, and whether it made any sense at all to take classes which met at eight-thirty in the morning when there were other, perfectly nice, courses offered at more appealing hours of the day.

Reporters were wandering over to the table again, and civilians kept stopping by, too. Very nice people, who mostly just wanted to say hello, and tell her how hard they had prayed, or how happy they had been when they found out that she was safe. A few asked to take a picture with her, or get a—scrawled—autograph, which was, as always, weird as hell, but she was careful to be friendly and cooperative and patient every single time.

"Ginette's going to be here through Monday, at least," Preston said, when they were waiting for the check, "but do you need me to stay, too?"

Wanting him to stay—just to have him around—and *needing* him to stay were two entirely different things. Meg shook her head. "I'm fine. Go back to Washington, you tired little fellow."

He grinned. "What, and report to my new boss?

Meg grinned, too. "Absolutely," she said.

Their good-bye was confined to a brisk handshake in the lobby, which felt strange, since they normally would have hugged, but that seemed like a really bad idea, given the number of people standing around watching them, especially since quite a few were taking extensive notes.

"Thank you," she said. "I mean it."

He winked at her. "See you in a week, pal."

Right. Spring break ever so rapidly approached.

Her agents drove her back to the dorm, where she knew she should immediately start studying for her midterms, but taking a nap sounded like an even better idea. As she passed the downstairs security desk, Larry indicated an envelope with her name on it.

Meg reached forward, then pulled back. "Is it from a stranger?"

He shook his head.

She leaned back against the banister, so that she could put her cane down and open it, finding a sheaf of Xeroxed psychology notes inside, with "*Hope you can read my disgustingly neat handwriting. Jack*" written across the top.

"Poetry?" Larry asked hopefully.

Christ, had her agents been sitting around taking bets on her romantic prospects or something? Meg laughed. "Just some class notes I missed. Sorry."

She was just pushing away from the banister when a football came flying in her direction. She managed to catch it, awkwardly, although she lost her balance and stumbled down a step or two in the process.

Khalid, who had just missed it—judging from the general noise level, most of her entrymates were in the middle of a pretty rowdy afternoon—looked guilty. "Hey, sorry about that. You should have ducked."

No, hurled footballs were—always—meant to be *caught*. Being crippled wasn't enough to change that. She shrugged and threw it back.

"Hey, pretty good spiral," a guy standing behind him, whose name she didn't know, although she was pretty sure he lived in Sage C, said. "Bet you can't do that twice."

She might not be able to catch it a second time, without falling, but she could sure as hell throw it with no problem. "Five dollars," Meg said.

"You're on," he said, took the ball from Andy, and flipped it down to her as a few other guys from the entry, including Dirk, came crowding out to watch.

She gave a split second's thought to performance anxiety, but made sure she had a halfway decent grip on the laces and whipped the ball up to him with a little extra zip—the spiral tight enough to win her a few yells of appreciation of the "Sage women *rule*!" variety. Then, she very slowly hauled herself up to the landing, stopping to hold her good hand out to the guy she didn't know.

He grinned sheepishly, dug into his pocket, and gave her five dollars.

"Thanks," she said, and stuck it in her jacket pocket.

"How about we go outside and see if you can throw it at least twenty-five yards?" he asked. "Double or nothing."

"Sorry," she said. "I'm saving my energy for the combine."

The jock types all laughed, and the ones who were less sports-inclined nodded wisely, although she was pretty sure that Gerard, and maybe Eric from the first floor, had no idea what she meant. Of course, if they began to talk about organic chemistry or developing software programs or Latin translations of obscure tomes, she would have been equally puzzled.

She could hear unfamiliar adult voices in the second-floor common room, and was suddenly afraid that some reporters—or terrorists—might have charmed their way past her agents and inside the dorm.

Only, how likely was *that*? It was probably just people from the Dean's office, or maybe the campus police or fire marshals checking up to make sure none of them had candles and burning incense and stuff like that in their rooms. But, as she was about to go into the second-floor hallway and take the elevator up to her floor—instead of fighting the stairs, she saw a tweedy man with greying hair, and a chic, but conservative-looking woman about the same age, and realized that it was only someone's parents. There was also a girl, who looked about thirteen, with long, brown hair and—oh, hell—very blue eyes.

Susan's family.

Great.

She thought about retreating—this might be a really good time to go outside and win herself ten dollars, after all—but the little sister had already seen her.

"Hey, wow!" she said. "You *do* look just like her. That is so cool."

All right. Too late now. Christ, Susan's parents must absolutely hate her for having made their daughter's life miserable.

"Uh, hi," Meg said. She should smile. Smiling was always nice. "You must be the McAllisters. It's very nice to meet you. I'm Meg Powers."

Which probably wasn't going to come as a great shock to them, but good manners still required the basic formalities.

While Mr. and Mrs. McAllister were introducing themselves, and the little sister, whose name was Wendy, Susan came out of her room.

"Mom, before we go, can Dad help me with the—" She stopped. "Oh. Hi." She took in Meg's new immobilizing brace with one very sharp glance, but just frowned, instead of saying anything about it. "I guess you've—?"

They all nodded.

"Okay, good," Susan said, and put her hands in her pockets, took them out again, and folded her arms across her chest. "That's good."

So, at least she wasn't the only one who thought this encounter was strained.

"Susan was just showing us the President's letter," Mrs. McAllister said.

Letter? But Meg smiled, inquisitively.

Susan shrugged. "The, um—your mother sent it up with Preston."

Good—both that she had taken the time to write a personal apology, and that she had made the choice not to advertise having done so. "Well, if you were so inclined, I'm sure you could do very nicely with it on eBay," Meg said.

Susan laughed. "That's exactly what Mary Elizabeth said."

No big surprise there. "Were there any spelling or grammatical errors?" Meg asked.

Wendy looked shocked. "The *President* has trouble *spelling*?"

Thirteen could be a gullible age. "Oh, yeah," Meg said. "It's a horror show to keep it covered up. Normally, I try to proofread everything, and do some revisions for her, but since I went away—well, she's really fallen upon hard times. Frankly, I often fear for the country."

"She's kidding," Wendy said to her mother, sounding almost sure, "right?"

Mrs. McAllister nodded.

"I knew that," Wendy said. "Yup. I did."

One of the many moments when she was reminded of how much she missed being able to goof around with—and sometimes, goof *on*—her brothers. "And there's also the little matter of her drinking problem," Meg said, mostly to herself.

Wendy's eyes widened, and she looked at her mother, who shook her head.

Susan came over and stood next to her. "I want to spend some time with my family," she said in a low voice. "So, call off your attack dog, okay?"

Meg stared at her. "Hannah Goldman's been coming around and bothering you?"

Susan looked confused. "Who's Hannah Goldman?"

Oh. Right. Hannah was a shark. *Ginette* must be the attack dog. "You mean, Ginette, then," Meg said. "Okay. But if you change your mind, all you have to do is—"

"If anyone bothers us, I'll just tell them that they're bastards, and your agents are going to shoot them," Susan said.

Always an effective strategy.

It developed that Mr. McAllister had some new software he wanted to install on Susan's computer, and while this was being discussed, and Wendy wandered towards Dirk's room—obviously, Susan's family had been here before, and they all knew one another—Meg took the opportunity to nod politely, mumble that it had been very nice to meet everyone, and resume her limp upstairs.

She was about to open the door to her floor when Susan's mother caught up to her.

"I wanted to invite you to come along with us to brunch tomorrow," Mrs. McAllister said. Although she was also quite small, Susan didn't really look very much like her, and seemed to take after her father's side of the family physically. The hair, the serious eyes, the general mien.

"Um, that's really nice of you, ma'am," Meg said, "but I don't think it's a very good idea. I mean, with everything that's been going on."

Mrs. McAllister flashed a smile, and now Meg *did* see a vivid resemblance to Susan. Friendly, but authoritative. No-nonsense. "We'd be delighted to have you come. Surely, you won't make me insist."

Hmm. A parent voice. Sort of a command-performance voice. "I have a lot of security, ma'am," Meg said. "It tends not to be—fun."

Mrs. McAllister shrugged that off. "It'll be fine, Meg. We'll just go over to the Inn, or down to Le Jardin or someplace."

Meg was going to argue, but— "This is what normal parents do when they come to visit their children at college, right? Invite their—" Could she say "friends?" It might be presumptuous—"dormmates out for a meal?"

Mrs. McAllister nodded.

Okay. She was a little foggy on the concept of conventional parental activities. "Then, thank you, ma'am," she said. "I'd like that." Getting to do something completely ordinary would be a treat. Of course, running it by Susan, first, to make sure she didn't mind, might be a good idea, too. "I'm *really* sorry about everything that's been going on for the last couple of days. I didn't know about what happened to Susan's friend, and—I'm sorry. I hate it that she had to be hurt that way."

Mrs. McAllister shook her head. "It's all right, don't worry about it. Unfortunately, it resurfaces fairly frequently, in various ways. But, Susan's very good at regaining her equilibrium."

So it seemed. "Did she always have—" What was the right word? "—gravitas?" Meg asked. "I mean, before."

"That's an interesting question," Mrs. McAllister said, and considered that momentarily. "No, I guess I would have described her as being happy-go-lucky in the same sort of way her sister is."

Impossible to imagine. Which was sad as hell.

"You have more than a touch of it yourself," Mrs. McAllister said.

Not bloody likely. "Loose cannon" was more accurate. And maybe she'd better do a little damage control, while she was at it. "I don't want you to think that I was going out of my way to be disrespectful to my mother," Meg said. "I was just—" Being injudicious. "Sometimes, I think I'm a lot funnier than I actually am."

Mrs. McAllister nodded solemnly, although Meg was left with the strong impression that she had found *that* funny.

Well, she'd gotten it on the record, anyway.

"Your mother seems like an extremely nice woman," Mrs. McAllister said, sounding a little surprised.

And therein, all too often, lay the tragedy. She was an extremely nice woman who was leading a life which somehow kept managing to swallow up everyone and everything around it.

"Yeah," Meg said quietly. "She is."

SHE SPENT THE rest of the afternoon and evening studying, although she agreed to accompany Juliana to the dining hall for dinner, since whatever friendship it was that they had still needed some repairs. They were a little stiff with each other, at first, but by the time Simon, and then Andy and Khalid, had seen them and come over to sit at their table, with trays piled high with pork loin and roasted potatoes, they had calmed down enough to have something very close to a normal conversation—mostly about the fact that they, in contrast to the others, were likely to enjoy protracted good health, due to their prudent choice of vegetarian entrees and near-daily embrace of the salad bar.

"Unh-hunh," Andy said, and went back up front to get himself a second piece of blueberry pie.

Hours of concentrated studying had only made her realize how far behind she was, and after supper, it was a terrific struggle not to give up, lie on her bed, and watch television for a while. Jack's psychology notes were excellent—much more comprehensive than hers tended to be, frankly—and after considering, and nervously rejecting, the notion of finding his number in the campus directory, and calling him up, she sent an email—using her Williams address, not any of the private ones—to thank him.

The dorm was unusually subdued, by Saturday night standards—she must not be the only freshman suddenly getting alarmed by the reality of midterms approaching. Among other things, she had to write a paper about presidential power and accountability within the confines of a democratic system for her political science class, and the whole assignment mainly just seemed *funny*, so it was hard to take it seriously. So far, her professor didn't really seem to be enjoying having her as a student, both because she didn't participate enough in class, and because sometimes, apparently, she grinned when he made certain pronouncements about aspects of the federal government and the executive branch. Or that's what he'd told her, when he had asked her to stop by his office one afternoon to discuss "her work"—or lack thereof. She tried to characterize any possible grins as nothing more than inappropriate affect, but he seemed to think that they fit into the category of outright smirking.

Whenever he mentioned any current political figure during lectures, someone in the class would inevitably look over and ask if she'd ever met the person—and, almost always, the answer was yes, although she usually shook her head, just to save time.

At about midnight, she took a break, which she used to answer email. One from each member of her family, except for Steven—who pretty much seemed to have forgotten that she existed, a friendly hello from Josh, who was having a great time at Stanford and possibly—if she was reading between the lines correctly—had a new girlfriend, an "*Everything okay? I'll be up late*" from Beth, and a single sentence from Preston, which simply read, "*We must do it again sometime.*"

In her campus account, along with some class-related and general announcement emails, there was also one from Jack, who had written, "*Goodrich? J.*" She wrote back, "*I'm way behind on everything, so have to study. But, thanks.*"

He must have been online, too, because his response was almost immediate—although not an instant message, because she found them intrusive, and always blocked that function on her computer. She wasn't wild about text messaging, either—to Neal's dismay. "*Meet you there in twenty minutes,*" his email said. "*Okay?*"

She really couldn't take the time, and besides, she was pretty sure there was a concert or a contradance or something over there tonight, for which she wasn't at all in the mood, even though it was probably starting to wind down by now. "*Too crowded,*" she wrote back, and then added, without stopping to decide whether it was a good idea, "*Snack Bar?*"

"*Leaving now,*" was his swift answer.

There was something gloriously lazy and liberating about the laconic informality of email. She logged off before giving herself a chance to change her mind, and got up to brush her teeth, straighten her hair, ease into a blue cashmere sweater, pop a painkiller, and put on just enough perfume and lip gloss to be able to pretend to herself, convincingly, that she had done no such thing.

By the time she'd made her slow, stumbling trek over to Paresky on her cane, Jack was already waiting out front, talking to a very slim and striking African-American girl who she recognized from their psychology class, although she didn't know her name. But, either way, the girl seemed to be standing much closer to him than was probably necessary, and kept touching his arm at approximately six-second intervals. She almost turned around and went right back to her room, except that it would be embarrassing to be so thoroughly rejected—and disgruntled about it, to boot—in front of her agents, so she kept limping forward.

"Hey," Jack said, when he saw her.

If this was going to be a threesome, count her out. "Hi," Meg said, and gave them each a nod. "How you doing?"

Jack looked amused, which displeased her. "You two know each other, right? Meg, Frances; Frances, Meg."

"Sure," Frances said, and, naturally, touched his arm again. "You're in our psychology class, aren't you?"

The two of them spent a great deal of time alone in class together, surrounded by lowly, admiring onlookers, of which she was thought to be one, apparently. Meg nodded. "I guess so, yeah. Nice to meet you."

They all stood there. It lacked congeniality.

"Well," Meg said. "I just came over to grab a cup of coffee before getting back to work, so I guess I'll see you all later."

To her annoyance, Jack laughed. "We were *meeting* here, Meg, remember that part?"

Better than he did, it seemed.

"I'll see you back at the dorm, Jack," Frances said, and nodded at Meg before walking away.

Jack watched her go, and then grinned. "You really think I was going to pull something like that right in front of you?"

Yeah, far better to do it in the privacy of their dorm. Meg shrugged, looking down at her cane. Frances was distressingly graceful.

"I figure it's a good sign if you're already jealous," he said, and then frowned. "Or else, a really *bad* sign."

Meg shrugged again.

"At least give me a chance to screw up, before you get mad at me," he said.

Yeah, that was probably a legitimate request. So, she nodded, and they stood there for another long, stilted minute.

"You want to call the whole thing off, or you want to say what the hell, and go inside for a while?" he asked.

The former, definitely. At this point, she'd just as soon stagger back up to her room, and sleep for as many hours as possible. But, he was waiting for her to answer, and it would be incredibly rude if she sighed deeply or looked resigned or any of the other similarly inhospitable reactions which came to mind.

"Let's give it a try," she said.

29

PEOPLE KEPT WALKING by, most of whom she didn't know, but they almost all said hi, anyway. It was possible that Jack was unusually well-liked; it was also possible that they were only saying hello because of who she was. Or, in the spirit of fairness, they might simply be friendly types.

"New knee brace," Jack said.

Meg nodded.

"Did you tear anything?" he asked.

She should actually speak, since this was supposed to be a social encounter. "Yeah. A ligament and some cartilage, they think. I guess they're going to go in there when I get back to Washington next weekend."

"So, you won't be able to spend Spring Break in the Caribbean with me," he said.

Meg grinned in spite of herself. Had that been a viable option? Maybe she had missed something. "Where are you actually going?"

He shrugged. "Home."

"Got anything interesting planned?" she asked. Better than surgery, say.

"Um, no," he said, without looking at her. "Not really."

She desperately needed more people in her life who bloody well made eye contact. "Jack, it's not a big deal if you're going to see an old girlfriend or something," she said. "I mean, if my friend Josh's break was at the same time as ours, I'm sure we'd go to a movie or get coffee."

Jack frowned. "I don't think any of my old girlfriends are still speaking to me."

Oh, swell. But, be that as it may. "So, what are you not telling me then?" Meg asked.

He looked guilty, and glanced at her brace. "I might go to Mammoth or Tahoe, and do some skiing. They've had a lot of spring snow."

"Sounds good," Meg said.

He just shrugged, uncomfortably.

"My family is so busy trying not to upset me that they haven't been going at all this season," Meg said. Although they didn't know that she knew that her father and brothers had gotten in one day at Innsbruck during the trip to Europe, because she'd seen a photo of them in a magazine someone left down in the laundry room. "Which is stupid, because they all *love* skiing. It's not like I'm going to hold it against anyone because they can do stuff I can't." Or, at the very least, she would probably have the decency to keep it to herself.

He held the door of the building open for her. "I just didn't want to, you know, flaunt it, or anything."

"It's no big deal," she said. Okay, it was a *huge* deal, but a tactful lie seemed to be indicated. "Thanks, though."

There were a bunch of people hanging out in the Great Hall talking, or lounging around on the couches or by the fireplace. The Snack Bar itself was about half full, and the line to order was pretty long, but almost everyone seemed to be picking up sandwiches and ice cream and that sort of thing to go.

Meg was only going to get coffee, but then decided to have a grilled honeybun, too. If she were a male heterosexual, women who never ate anything would make her nervous, so maybe it was worth pretending to have a hearty appetite. She probably should have ordered even more food, but she—big surprise—wasn't hungry.

They ended up sitting at one of the tables on the left side, away from most of the windows—which, no doubt, pleased her agents. It occurred to her, then, that she hadn't been on anything resembling a date since she and Josh had broken up—Christ, that meant that it had been a *year*—the notion of which made her so nervous that she wasn't sure if she'd even be able to manage a few sips of the coffee.

Of course, it was inevitable that she was going to start thinking about it, but drinking scotch with a terrorist had *not* been a god-damned date. She'd been a prisoner, trying to survive. Nothing more, nothing less. What she was doing right now—Saturday night, in the student center, with a guy her age—was absolutely normal. Downright humdrum.

Jack had even ordered a Chocolate Frost to go with his cheeseburger and french fries. How much more wholesome could a get-together *be*?

"Your coffee okay?" he asked.

She blinked, nodded, and took a sip. Her hand shook, which made her feel—well, even more feeble and aberrant than usual. This was a casual date. It wasn't as though they were going to get involved with each other—hell, he was probably just being polite, and counting the seconds until he could leave without hurting her feelings, so there was no reason to be having *quite* so much trouble swallowing, and getting her breath, and keeping her expression pleasantly blank.

And there was nothing quite as appealing to a prospective suitor as watching someone have an intense anxiety attack.

"Your JA doing okay?" he asked.

Was she? Probably not. "I hope so," Meg said. Could he tell that she was in a near-total panic? A veritable whirlwind of irrational fear? A couple of seconds from throwing up, fainting, bursting into tears, or racing out of the building as fast as her leg would allow? Or maybe even having all four unlovely reactions simultaneously? She sucked in a deep breath as subtly as possible. "But, her parents showed up today, so I don't know. I guess she's still pretty upset."

Jack nodded, most of his attention on his cheeseburger, and she wondered if he might be nervous, too.

"So, um, are you really an Economics major?" she asked.

He nodded, without much fervor. "My father wants me to go to business school."

Her parents would probably be overjoyed if she could manage to eat and sleep regularly. "At some point," she said, tentatively, "isn't it up to you?"

He shrugged. "He says college isn't cheap, so you shouldn't waste time with vanity and hobbies."

Pretty harsh. Although, somehow, she would have guessed that he came from money. "Well, sending their kids to private colleges is usually a huge financial sacrifice for people," she said. "And I really respect that."

Jack grinned a little. "No, they're definitely okay there. It's just what Dad tells me because—I mean, I'm not saying I don't love him and all—but he's one of those guys who thinks that if you like art, you might turn out to be gay or something."

Mr. Taylor couldn't be very observant, then, when it came to his son. "You are *so* not gay," Meg said.

Jack laughed. "I'll tell him you said so."

Well, maybe not. It would make a poor initial impression. She drank some coffee, ate a bite of her pastry, and put her hand back in her lap.

"Meg, I've already seen it shaking," he said. "Don't worry about it. And you've had a bad couple of days, right?"

No question. She brought her good hand back up, but wrapped it around her coffee cup to try and minimize the trembling. "It doesn't make you uncomfortable?" she asked, keeping her focus down. "I'd think it would be sort of—off-putting." To say nothing of the handcuff scars gracing her wrists.

"I'm probably pretty shallow," he said, "but aren't you kind of hoping I'm not *that* shallow?"

Yes.

"You don't have to hide the other one all the time, either," he said.

An ingrained habit, by now. She started to lift it up, then lost her nerve. "It's, um, more fun to be around people who aren't impaired." Frances, for instance.

Jack shrugged. "I don't know you well enough to know how impaired you are."

Nice try. "You're on a campus full of women in admirably good physical and psychological shape," she said. "Take advantage of it."

He looked irritated.

Maybe that had been too harsh. "Or," she said, "for that matter, a lot of extremely healthy *men*, in case this art foolishness really does go to your head."

That one got her a smile, at least.

Since they *already* weren't having fun, this might be a good time to do the standard double-check, and find out if he was another one of the status-conscious sycophants. Before things went any further, and she forgot and let lust turn into actual liking. Plus, she was out of practice, and might not pick up on the signs quickly enough, if she wasn't extra careful.

"Have you and your friends ever spent any time discussing me?" she asked. It was arrogant to bring the subject up, but it had happened too many god-damned times, particularly starting after her mother had won the Iowa Caucus. A mere Senator's daughter lacked the cachet of the potential Democratic presidential nominee's daughter, let alone the offspring of the full-fledged President. "About whether I'd, you know—" not to put too fine a point on it— "be inclined to put out, and that sort of thing?"

He nodded. "Absolutely."

A very rare case in which honesty just might be overrated.

"We talk about everyone," he said, "not just you. We've gone through the whole Face Book about a thousand times." Which she wasn't in, for security reasons. As if one more public photo would make any damned difference, insofar as her safety was concerned. "Your friend Juliana is in just about everybody's top three."

Terrific. "Well." Meg shoved her half-eaten pastry away. "If she breaks up with Mark, you'll have to make your move."

"Hey, you knew I was an asshole before we even sat down," he said.

She had, however, made the mistake of overlooking that fact briefly.

"If you don't want the answer," he said, "don't ask the question."

She didn't like it, but it was hard to refute that one.

Or the part about him being an asshole.

He picked up his cheeseburger, but then lowered it. "We don't really talk about you anymore, actually."

Maybe he would offer to sell her a secondhand car, next, which had never, ever been driven, except by a sweet, little old lady, who only used it to go to church on Sundays.

"Because guys don't, once it seems like maybe—" he shrugged— "well, you know, you actually like her. If they talked about you now, that'd just be *wrong*."

There might be a tiny ring of truth in that.

"So," he looked right at her, "I haven't told any of them that, lately, I pretty much can't concentrate on anything other than wanting to be inside you as soon as possible, for as long as possible."

Talk about an ill-timed moment to have lifted her coffee cup. She stared at the large splash of liquid now on the table, and then at him, suddenly so aroused that—damn. *Seriously* aroused.

"Jesus, Meg," he said, and leaned back, looking almost as stunned as she felt. "Do you know how much heat you just gave off?"

How utterly inadvertent. She could feel the heat rising up to her face now, instead—or, anyway, in addition—and decided to concentrate her energies on cleaning up the spilled coffee.

Jack frowned down at something below the edge of the table. "Well, shoot. I'm not going to be able to stand up in public any time soon."

If possible, her cheeks were now twice as hot as they had been a few seconds earlier. Then she thought of a pugnaciously ribald response, and had to work to keep a grin back.

"What?" he asked.

Oh, what the hell. He had started it, right? Meg decided not to fight off the grin. "I was going to say, 'Come on, get ahold of yourself, man,' but in this situation, that would only make things worse, wouldn't it?"

"No, it would actually *help*," he said, thoughtfully, "but it might take a couple of minutes, and this really isn't the place for it."

Jesus Christ. Someone had just snatched the safety net out from underneath her very high trapeze. She wanted to laugh—hard—but people might well be eavesdropping on them, and—catching a movement in her peripheral vision, she glanced towards the Snack Bar counter, and saw Simon, who must have come in to get some takeout, and was now staring at her with total consternation.

Oh, dear. She looked at Jack. "Are you still indisposed?"

He nodded vigorously.

"Okay." She reached for her cane. "I'll be right back."

Jack nodded, his face about as red as she suspected hers currently was.

When he saw her heading in his direction, Simon turned to leave.

"Simon, don't," she said. "You know it's going to hurt if I try to limp after you."

He scowled, but stopped, his hand clasping the take-out box so tightly that he was probably crushing whatever food was inside. He motioned accusingly towards the table. "Since *when*?"

It was going to hurt his feelings even more if he found out that tonight was technically their first date.

"You're practically having sex right there on the table," he said, sounding outraged.

A little bit, yeah. Meg sighed. "Simon, we're sitting quietly. We weren't even holding hands."

He just looked at her.

Okay, it must be pretty obvious that they had—at least, verbally—leaped way past holding hands. But this was a very sweet guy, and maybe even someone who was going to become an Actual College Friend, and the last thing she wanted to do was hurt his feelings. "Simon, I am a completely unreasonable pain to be around, on a pretty regular basis," she said. "And you're going to end up being very glad that you and I decided that we just wanted to be really good friends."

" 'We' didn't decide that," he said.

Meg nodded. "No, we did, Skip. I *swear* we did. We had a long conversation about it, and everything. Several, in fact. You just forgot, because you're stressed out about midterms."

Simon still looked upset, but he was starting to smile, too.

"And that means you also probably don't remember that we agreed we were maybe going to meet on Spring Street tomorrow afternoon and go drink too much coffee together," she said.

He studied her for a minute, then nodded. "I did forget that, yeah. What time did we say?"

Good. Potential platonic crisis averted. "Four o'clock," she said.

"Okay." He sent a quick scowl in Jack's direction—maybe just for general pride, and then looked at her seriously. "You do know that guy's an asshole, right?"

It seemed to be the general consensus. Meg nodded.

"All right. Just wanted to be sure." He headed for the exit with his food. "See you tomorrow."

She waited until he had left before she made her way back over to the table.

"What was that all about?" Jack asked, frowning.

Meg sat down. "My friend Skip. I was saying hi."

Jack frowned even more. "I thought his name was Simon."

Same difference.

"You looked pretty—friendly. How well do you know him?" Jack asked.

Shades of her recent Frances fixation. "It's probably a good sign if you're already jealous," she said. "Or else, a really *bad* sign."

He nodded wryly, and bit into what was left of his cheeseburger.

In the meantime, there were lots of french fries still on his plate, tragically going to waste. She helped herself to one, and then went back for a few more.

"Mind if I add about twice as much salt and pepper?" she asked.

He grinned and pushed the two shakers in her direction. "Knock yourself out," he said.

They sat there for a very long time, until Meg remembered that it had been one *hell* of a long day, and that she had promised to go to brunch with Susan's family in not too many hours.

They had yet to hold hands, or even do much more than stare across the table intensely—but any idle questions she might have had about the validity of the phrase "copulatory gaze" had been definitively answered.

"Um, this was very nice," she said, as they went outside, making a point of staying a couple of feet away from each other.

Which took some effort. On her part, anyway.

"Yeah," he said, and started to lean towards her, but then stopped. "Let me walk you home."

That was almost certainly a bad idea. "No, thanks. I mean—" she pointed at her dorm with her cane—"it's right there."

He nodded. "I know. But, I'm still going to do it."

Her dorm was very close, but it would mean walking several hundred feet, and—no. Okay, they had crossed a couple of rooms together, and passed each other here and there on campus, and that sort of thing, but he had never really seen her *walk* at length. Up close and personal.

And this was no time to start.

"What?" he asked.

Christ, did she really have to spell it out? Apparently so. "It takes me a really long time," she said, quietly, "and—I don't want you to see me that way."

Jack cocked his head, looking confused.

Christ. "I limp and stagger and lurch, and sometimes I even have to stop and rest for a while," she said.

He touched her good hand, which was wrapped around her cane. "It's how you get around, Meg."

She was, after all, a notorious campus cripple. Meg moved her hand, and the cane, out of his reach. "Yeah, well, trust me, it's worse when I have to go more than a few feet. So, I'd really rather not have you come with me, okay?"

Her agents had been keeping their distance all night, but now they suddenly seemed more obvious. In fact, Dave was shifting his weight, ominously, and Brian and Jose didn't look very happy, either—although Jack seemed to be oblivious to this.

"You want to know how I see you?" he asked.

Not really. Meg shook her head.

"This is how," he said, and moved forward to kiss her with great enthusiasm. Then, he stepped back. "Okay?"

Along with her agents, several people from her dorm had just walked by, and also managed to witness this. Meg was more than a little embarrassed, a feeling which seemed to be shared by everyone, except Jack, who looked quite pleased with himself.

"Uh, hi, Meg," Mikey said, on his way past them, and she nodded, too self-conscious to meet his eyes.

It seemed to take about three hours to make it to the entry door, even though she made a point of *not* stopping at all along the way, no matter how much she would have preferred to do so. Needed to do so, for that matter.

"You all right?" Jack asked, on two separate occasions, looking anxious, one hand poised to grab her if she fell.

Except for the part where she felt like crying, and was trying not to show how difficult every single inch was. So, she just shrugged and trudged. When they were finally standing just inside the main door, she was all the more aware of her agents—especially Casey, who was at the front desk—although they all seemed to be trying to disappear in plain sight again.

"I'll come up with you," Jack said.

Which would lead to many other things, and—no. Not yet. She was too tired. And maybe a little scared, too. Meg eased backwards on her good leg. "No, thank you. It's very nice of you, but, um, I'm fine from here."

"A gentleman always escorts a woman to her door," Jack said.

Most gentlemen probably didn't escort women accompanied by large coteries of armed guards. "And, this is my door," Meg said.

He shook his head. "No, I need to take you to your *actual* door. It's good manners."

Upon which, presumably, she would face a protracted and stressful "no, I'm sorry, you really *can't* come in for a while" tussle in front of her room.

Which wasn't the way their first date ought to end.

"I'm going to let you kick me out, once we get up there," he said. "I promise."

Famous last words.

"I *promise*," he said.

She didn't believe him for a minute, but she was worn out, and—to hell with it. She started to go up the first small flight of steps, but he put his hand on her back.

"There's an *elevator*, Meg," he said.

Yes. She was aware of that. And, after the past five or ten minutes, he *did* already know how extremely crippled she was. So she nodded, and made her way to the elevator, instead.

Since they rode up alone together, she expected him to immediately start trying to kiss her again, but he just stood politely next to her, with his hands in his pockets.

Maybe he really *was* only going to see her to her room.

But then, when they got off the elevator and she unlocked her door, he followed her inside before she thought to stop him. She would have expected him to look around and check things out—most notably, the photos of her family—but after a vague glance, his attention stayed on her.

Inescapably so.

She knew he was going to make a move, but she wasn't sure if she was ready to—surprising her, he pushed her hair to one side and gently kissed her forehead where the gun-butt scar ran through her eyebrow. Embarrassed, Meg brushed her hair back over to cover it.

"Christ, Meg, it's a badge of courage," he said.

Yeah, right. Meg instinctively checked to make sure that the scar was fully obscured now. "There's nothing brave about getting pistol-whipped." *Machine-gun*–whipped, in her case, but, regardless. "All you need is a little bad luck."

"Takes some guts to keep fighting back, afterwards, I figure," he said.

No, just more bad luck. It was late, and it would be very nice if he left now.

"Okay, never mind," he said, and reached out to touch one of her breasts, instead.

She looked down. "Who says romance is dead?"

"It's a *little* romantic," he said.

On the planet Neanderthal, maybe. "Did I miss the part where I gave you permission to do that?" she asked.

He shrugged, keeping his hand right where it was. "Well, you haven't said no, and you didn't start sobbing hysterically, and that's pretty much what I look for."

The World According to Jack Taylor. "But, my option to say no remains open," she said.

He nodded. "Absolutely, yes. The sobbing, too."

Good to know.

His hand felt warm, and affectionate, and as he flexed it, quite delightful, indeed. Then, he kissed her, which progressed from being friendly, to completely combustible, with remarkable speed, and his hands slid down to lift her up. She could feel him hesitate as he looked at her bed, but then he set her down on the edge of the desk, instead.

"I think we'd better close your door," he said against her mouth.

Carpe diem, or voice of reason and an inbred, lifelong tendency towards caution? Although it was somewhat challenging to retain complete intellectual clarity, given where his hands were, and what they were doing.

Voice of reason.

She sighed. "We need to spend a lot more time getting to know each other, Jack."

"Why?" he asked.

Now, how in the hell was she supposed to answer that? "Because," she said.

He frowned. "A *lot* more?"

She nodded.

"Right," he said, and took his hands away. "Okay. Right." He let out his breath, heavily. "Shit."

He probably didn't want to hear her "I don't know if I can trust you not to post on the Internet, or run off to the tabloids—or money-laden terrorists—with all of the intimate details" explanation.

Or the potentially more accurate "I'm very shy and maybe out of my depth here" spin.

"If I beg, will you look down on me?" he asked.

She must have been more exhausted than she realized, because for a second, she thought he was suggesting something else entirely.

He looked at her uneasily. "What?"

Okay, she had overreacted. Misinterpreted. "Yeah," she said. "I'll shun you."

There was some noise out in the corridor, and Meg turned to see Susan's little sister, holding a hand towel and a toothbrush, her expression both uncertain and terribly curious.

Meg quickly jumped off the desk, careful to land on her good leg—and a few feet away from Jack, as though they had not very recently been quite intertwined. "Hi."

"Uh, hi," Wendy said, sounding timid.

"Guess I'd better say good-night." Jack put his hand out—the left one; good for him—and shook Meg's hand firmly. Then he nodded in a friendly way at Wendy, started down the hall, and paused to look back at her. "Can I see you again, as soon as possible, for as long as possible, as *often* as possible?"

Wendy would have no way of knowing what he was actually asking, but Meg was still embarrassed. And then, considerably more so, when

Susan came through the stairwell door, presumably to check on her little sister. Was Ed watching, too, subtly, from the security desk? Yes. Great.

"Meg?" Jack asked, looking at her with fairly convincing little-boy innocence.

Everybody else seemed to be waiting for her answer, also, making the pause seem even more pregnant—damn, precisely the word she had *not* wanted to have come into her mind—than it might have otherwise.

What the hell. He'd know that she was at least half-kidding, anyway.

"You bet," she said.

30

BRUNCH THE NEXT morning was much nicer and more low-key than she expected, although she wanted to find a tactful excuse not to go when she found out that Susan's friend Courtney—she, of the "Do you *mind*?" remark—was joining them, too.

Ginette also came along, and Susan's parents insisted that she sit *with* them, rather than at a nearby table, watching alertly for media miscreants. On top of that, they actually drew her out, and Meg learned all sorts of things she had never known about Ginette's fondness for figure skating and bluegrass, as well as the fact that she'd spent time both at the Sorbonne *and* the London School of Economics. All of which indicated that they still didn't have much in common, but it was interesting to get a broader perspective.

At one point, there was a camera flash, and Ginette went stomping off—only to discover that it was another Williams parents-and-students group, celebrating someone's birthday and wanting to preserve the festivities for posterity.

Mr. and Mrs. McAllister also established that Courtney was looking forward to graduation, and would be starting an M.D./Ph.D. program at Yale in the fall; that Fred, another one of Susan's friends, was pretty sure that he was going to be spending the summer being an intern at a seedy regional theater; that Juliana hadn't decided whether she was going to major in American Studies or History or Linguistics or Classics or Comparative Literature or Romance Languages; that Meg was currently an English major, sort of, maybe, not really; and that Susan—who had been very quiet—was enjoying her omelet.

Wendy was full of a litany of chirpy questions about life in the White House and so forth, which were certainly preferable to the "so, did it *hurt* when you pulverized your hand?" line of inquiry. For the most part, Meg told the truth, although she couldn't resist a few disgraceful elaborations about the legions of devoted servants who, when she was in the Residence, came to her room very early each morning to sing her awake—in four-part a capella harmony—and then dress her, polish and buff her nails, put her through a full beauty regimen, and otherwise help her get ready for Her Day. Once they had assured themselves that her every need had been met, the lackeys would—in the unlikely event that they had any spare time left—go and minister to her mother in a similarly attentive fashion. But Meg made it clear that serving the Presidential children *always* took precedence over any invariably trivial and tedious request the President or the First Gentleman might make.

At some point during all of this, Meg had the distinct impression that Ginette was going to put her head down on the table for a while. Or, perhaps, directly into her plate.

"Is this what you're *like*?" Courtney asked finally, as though she just couldn't hold it back it any longer.

Susan and Juliana nodded—not necessarily with appreciative joy.

"You have to understand that, unlike the rest of my family, I *am* royalty," Meg said, "due to a certain illegitimacy factor that we, naturally, never discuss, in public or otherwise."

"Did you fill Hannah Goldman with this kind of garbage?" Ginette asked, seeming to put her hands on her hips, even though she was sitting down.

It would be tactless to remind her of Preston's approval—or, at any rate, tacit acceptance—of her style and overall political acumen. "No, I gave her a different, yet equally entertaining version of garbage altogether," Meg said. "The stuff where my mother keeps me on speakerphone during Cabinet meetings, so I can help guide them back on point if they go astray, or find themselves stymied by the ramifications of some of the more complex policy issues."

Wendy looked impish. "*Yesterday,* she told us the President has a drinking problem."

Ginette turned to glare at her.

"Don't worry," Meg said quickly. "I didn't breathe a word about the whole transsexual business."

Ginette closed her eyes.

Yes, it was a very pleasant brunch, indeed.

SHE WAS BACK in her room, with her knee propped up, watching one of the Sunday political shows she'd recorded—all things considered, she thought her mother's National Security Advisor was a little too self-important for his own good, and possibly the country's—when the phone rang.

"You made Page Six again," Beth said, as soon as she picked up.

The original plan had been for Beth to come up to Williams for a couple of days during *her* spring break, but her father had unexpectedly decided to marry his young paramour Jasmine—quite probably because she was now pregnant with twins—and Beth had flown off, grumpily, to be a bridesmaid in Brentwood, instead, returning to Columbia in a generally foul mood.

Christ, they couldn't have found out about Jack *already*, could they? And, really, how much was there to find out, anyway? "What did I do?" Meg asked uneasily.

"You and Dashing-Man-About-Washington Preston Fielding were spotted canoodling for hours Saturday morning in a hotel dining room at a cozy Berkshires hideaway," Beth said. "He was also seen leaving your dormitory in the wee hours on Friday night."

End quote, presumably. Meg frowned. "It wasn't wee—he took off after SportsCenter. And the hotel's right on Main Street. That doesn't sound all that hidden to me."

Beth laughed. "You mean, you *were* canoodling, but you were being open about it?"

Sadly, no. Meg turned off the television. "They also seem to have forgotten the part where there was a reporter from *The Washington Post* sitting with us most of the time."

"So, it was a ménage à trois," Beth said, and laughed again.

God, what a horrible image that particular combination was. "I have a feeling she's going to try to call you," Meg said. "For the interview."

Beth made a sound which would have been described as rude by almost any definition one might apply.

The appropriate response. "Well," Meg said, "Maureen can prep you, if you need to—"

"Maureen?" Beth asked.

"She's my father's new Chief of Staff," Meg said.

It was very quiet on the other end of the line.

"This is going to be a pretty long story," Beth said, "isn't it."

Yep.

After talking to Beth, she did, in fact, meet Simon for coffee—which was marred only by the hit-and-run appearance of a couple of paparazzi, who seemed to be convinced that they'd just captured the President's daughter's latest swain on film, and then she had dinner with Jack, Mary Elizabeth, Debbie, from the fourth floor, and Corey, one of Jack's Ultimate Frisbee–playing buddies—who rather predictably referred to each and every one of them as "Dude" at least once during the meal. Jack was clearly hoping to escort her back to the dorm—and her room, but she really *did* have to get some stuff done, and spent the night working, nervously, on a philosophy paper and studying for her Shakespeare midterm, instead.

At about nine-thirty, there was a knock on her door, and she was very surprised to look up and see Dirk, since he almost never specifically sought her out.

"Hi," she said, and motioned for him to come in, although she didn't really feel like hearing more about what a half-wit she was for not having known about Susan's past.

He hesitated. "I don't want to interrupt you, if you're working."

"I'm pretty bored, actually," she said.

Dirk nodded, and wandered into the room. As far as she knew, he was really into hiking and camping and that sort of thing, because he was always trying to organize dorm excursions revolving around the outdoors. Meg had never been much of a nature fan, but now, she pretty much hated the idea of being anyplace resembling a forest. Even the thought of sitting in a large, verdant backyard lacked charm. But, since hiking wasn't a realistic option for her anyway, these days, she had always been able to decline his invitations gracefully.

"So," he said. "How's it going?"

Maybe this was just a normal JA-wanting-to-touch-base-with-a-freshman-facing-midterms thing, then. Meg relaxed. "Okay. I mean, you know. Kind of a tough few days."

He nodded.

It was quiet.

He glanced at her door. "Would you mind if I closed that for a minute?"

Okay, so this wasn't standard checking-in. "I guess not," she said, wary now.

He closed the door, looked around uncertainly, then leaned against the windowsill. "This really isn't any of my business, but, well, some of the guys asked me to—" He stopped. "You know, Susan is a lot better at stuff like this, maybe I should—"

The nightmares, probably. "I'm sorry," Meg said. "I have trouble sleeping sometimes. But, if it's bothering any of them, they should make sure to tell me, and I'll—" Do *what*, exactly? Stay up around the clock? Never close her eyes again? "Well, I'll try to do better."

Dirk looked confused.

"I wake them up when I have nightmares," Meg said, "right? I'm really sorry about that."

Dirk grinned. "That's nothing. I mean, you ever heard the way Peyton *snores*?"

Actually, yes. It carried all the way up from the first floor. Unkind rumor had it, that people who lived over in North Adams, and other neighboring towns, were awakened by his snoring on a regular basis, and that it even sometimes caused fluctuations in the Richter scale along the Eastern seaboard.

"I should still maybe get Susan, though," Dirk said. "She's better at—"

Meg shook her head. "You're my JA, too. Go ahead and tell me."

"Um, Jack Taylor," he said. "I mean, there aren't a whole lot of secrets in a dorm, you know? And some of the guys kind of wanted me to talk to you."

Christ, was she going to be blamed for the fact that, on occasion—the previous night having been a notable example—Juliana and Mark were a little, um, *enthusiastic*? How totally embarrassing.

"He's got—not a great reputation," Dirk said.

Not a news flash. Luckily.

"And the guys were afraid that if you didn't know, you might be—well, that he might not treat you well, and they didn't want that," Dirk said.

Which was intrusive, maybe, but also sweet as hell. Meg grinned. "Exactly how much of a swath has the guy cut around this place?"

"Well—" Dirk's face reddened. "He's the kind who pretty much gets what he wants, then never calls her again. You know? And I really didn't want to see you—"

Oops, he'd forgotten to cloak himself in the protective coloring of "the guys."

"—get caught up in that," he said. "Because, um, well, I don't like to say it, but because of who you are, and you know, your situation, you'd seem like a, uh—well—"

Meg decided to rescue the poor guy. "An excellent trophy."

Dirk looked relieved. "Yeah, kind of."

"It's okay," Meg said. "Luckily, I stopped falling for that one a couple of years ago." She'd had to learn it the hard way, more than once, but she'd ultimately figured it out.

"Not that I don't think he wouldn't also like you for *yourself*," Dirk said quickly. "I just—that is, the guys—" He grinned self-consciously. "We thought it would be better if I talked to you about it."

Meg nodded. "Thank you. I appreciate your looking out for me."

He nodded, and straightened up from the windowsill.

She'd always envied people who had big brothers, because she figured they were privy to certain types of information which, for her, remained a mystery. "Is talking to a JA similar to attorney–client privilege?"

"If you mean, do we keep things confidential, yeah," he said. "Of course."

He probably found it insulting that she'd even asked. "I'm sorry," Meg said. "In my world, you have to be kind of formal about it, if you want to go off-the-record."

He nodded, and she had a feeling he was very glad not to be living in her world.

"I have to be extra-careful about—" Could she think of a good euphemism? No. She would have to use her mother's favorite. "The choices I make."

Dirk seemed to be lost, but he nodded gamely.

Okay, she was going to have to be more direct. Meg let out her breath. "I can't necessarily say yes, even when I *want* to say yes."

This time, she could tell from his nod that he understood where she was going.

"Do you think—" She stopped. This was too god-damned personal to ask a guy she didn't know all that well.

"I think everyone on the whole campus worries about stuff like that, one way or another," he said, when she didn't continue. "Because it's complicated as hell, even when people act like it isn't. Although, you know, about something like this, you should really probably talk to—well—"

Susan.

"But," he said, "if a guy's a good guy, he'd be okay with whatever *you're* okay with. You know?"

She sure hoped so.

SINCE SHE WAS supposed to keep her knee immobilized, she wasn't allowed to do any physical therapy the next day, but she still had to drag down to the hospital to have it checked. She had already blown through more of her pain prescription than she wanted to admit, but she was almost positive that they weren't going to give her more, and it would look bad if she asked. Far better to pretend that mere ibuprofen was doing the trick.

The doctors were upset that her knee was still more swollen than they thought it should be—and that she was running yet another pain-induced fever, and they decided to repeat several of the tests they had done on Friday—which she assumed was just a grotesque overreaction. Still, it made her tired, and short-tempered, and although she made an effort not to be rude, she also went out of her way to do as little talking as possible.

Vicky came by to see how she was doing, and while the orthopedists and radiologists were busy consulting with one another, she had an excruciating twenty-minute hand therapy session with Cheryl, during which she was polite, but essentially monosyllabic.

When she got back to the dorm, she wasn't in the mood to do much more than turn out the lights and lie down on her bed. It wasn't until nine o'clock that she could bring herself to check her messages, which included a "*Goodrich? As soon as possible?*" email from Jack.

With the proviso that they would, in fact, study, she decided to take him up on it—and, to her surprise, studying was almost exclusively what they did. They had a psychology unit quiz coming up on Friday, but since it was cumulative and expected to take up the entire class period, it was really a midterm, despite her professor's semantic choice to make it sound less daunting. They also had to hand in their lab reports on Wednesday, and she was severely behind in that aspect of the course.

On top of that, she had a philosophy paper to finish, her political science paper to *start*—about the damn Presidency; she had decided to focus upon the limits of executive powers—and more studying to do for her Shakespeare midterm. Jack had economics and Spanish midterms, and also had to hand in a fairly large portfolio of work for his art studio drawing course.

None of which seemed to be causing him the slightest bit of anxiety.

"Aren't you worried about *any* of this?" she asked, finally.

Jack looked up from a Spanish translation. "I do the reading, I go to class, I study. So, no big deal."

She was possibly a little weak in all three areas. "I slug down coffee, watch CNN, and look up at my ceiling a lot," Meg said.

He shrugged. "Not everyone needs to study all that much. But, I kind of do, so I have to make time for it."

She had always been inclined to coast. To do *just* well enough to keep her parents from noticing, but not so well that it would attract undue attention from any of her teachers—or the press, for that matter—but, despite the fact that she generally got A's, and had almost never, up until her Astronomy course, ended up with anything lower than an A-, as far back as she could remember, she had regularly received lectures, from all and sundry, about her flagrantly intentional propensity to underachieve.

"What?" Jack asked.

Poor old Josh had always spent a lot of time asking her what she was thinking, or why she had drifted off in the middle of a conversation—and she had rarely given him anything close to an accurate answer. She shook her head. "I'm sorry. I guess I was thinking for a minute."

It would be wrong to compare them, so she wouldn't—but, Josh would have been disheartened by that, and this guy just shrugged.

"Okay," he said, glanced at his textbook, and then amended something in his notebook.

"It doesn't bother you?" she asked.

He looked up. "What? That you *think*?"

Which made it sound all the more ridiculous, but she nodded.

"You're unbelievably fucking private," he said, "and, as far as I can tell, you've got—I don't know—" he grinned— "an active inner life."

That, she did.

"So, whatever," he said, and went back to his reading.

It was unusual, but kind of a relief, to have someone *not* captivated—or, more typically, alarmed—by her every exhalation.

They didn't leave until about two in the morning, and he must have been tired, too, because after only a knee-jerk "Are you *sure* you don't want me to come up and help you release some—tension?" suggestion near the first-floor command post, he kissed her good-night, politely, and headed off to his own dorm.

The next night, they studied together again, but they didn't even get started until past ten, because he had gone straight from an Ultimate Frisbee scrimmage to the studio to work on his portfolio for several hours. Which gave her plenty of time to go over to the library, do some research for her political science paper, and—well—take a nap.

In contrast to his normal sangfroid, he seemed restless, switching from one notebook to another, discarding a highlighter for a pen, and then a pencil, and going up to the coffee bar repeatedly to get various snacks, bringing her back fresh coffee each time.

"You're, um, not in the mood for this tonight?" she asked finally.

He looked up from a lengthy, neatly-printed Spanish vocabulary list. "No, it's not that, I—" He stopped. "Well, yeah, it kind of *is* that."

Great. "Well," she said, "my feelings aren't going to be hurt—" like hell—"if you want to take off, or whatever."

He grinned at her. "I bet a million dollars they *would* be hurt."

Very much so, but she shrugged in lieu of answering.

"I'm just—I don't know." He picked up one of the chocolate chip cookies he'd bought earlier and ate it in two bites. "I'm pretty sure my portfolio is, you know, stinkin' *lousy*, and—" He gulped down the last bit of his mocha freeze, then finished off another cookie. "Doesn't matter."

Yeah, it clearly wasn't bothering him at all. "You want to go back to the studio?" she asked.

He thought about that, then shook his head. "No. I'll start over-working everything, and—" He thought again. "No."

Which sounded more like a "Yes, I'm dying to," but, okay.

They sat there, not speaking—or studying.

"Can I draw your hands?" he asked suddenly.

She had been distracted enough to forget and let her splint rest on the table, while she took notes with her good hand, but now she moved them both to her lap.

He frowned. "I can't?"

"God, no." Hell, she didn't ever want him even to *see* her bad hand out of its splint, forget letting him stare at it with artistic intensity.

"How about just your left hand?" he asked.

It still felt—invasive. She shook her head.

He looked disappointed, but ate another cookie and returned to his Spanish list.

Then, a nervous thought crossed her mind. "You know, you can't *ever* draw me," she said. "Especially not—" Except, wait, there was still a very good chance that she would never even *be* fully unclothed in front of him. "Well, anyway, you really can't."

"Oh. Sorry. Didn't know that," he said, and pulled a sketch pad out of his knapsack, flipping it open about halfway through.

She looked across the table—and saw herself. Several small drawings, all on the same page. A profile. A three-quarters view of her sitting somewhere, holding a cup of coffee. A third of her looking watchful, even behind a pair of sunglasses. They were quick sketches—a few bold strokes; some shading—but clearly *her*.

The concept of someone drawing her, over and over, was kind of creepy, but it was also hard to overlook the fact that the sketches were damned *good*. Unusually so, and also disturbingly revealing. She looked—not imperious, exactly, but not friendly, either. Extremely self-contained. A little intimidating.

"I'm not like, *fixated*," he said. "I draw everyone."

She checked a few more pages, and saw that it was true. People in the dining hall, various scenes from what must be inside his dorm. Indistinct figures crossing the campus, bundled up against the snow and wind.

Some of the sketches were of people in their psychology class, immediately recognizable—Frances, of course; the skinny guy who sat up front, participated too much, and thought *everything* was Freudian; two flirtatious-looking girls who had obviously been trying to get Jack's attention, little realizing that they very much had it; a few rather eviscerating ones of their professor, Dr. Wilkins, with her typically pained expression; and then, a couple more of her, gripping a pen as though she might take a note or two, but appearing quite disengaged from whatever was being discussed that day.

"I don't look sexy," she said. Whereas the ones of *Frances* had a powerful come-hither quality.

Jack leaned over, looked at them, and nodded in agreement.

Swell. The person in the drawings had a very familiar untouchable quality. Meg frowned. "Do I really look that much like her?"

He nodded. "Especially when you're trying to make people back off."

How disquieting.

The next few pages were all couples. They weren't blatantly erotic—but they were clearly the creation of an artist who was very attuned to sexual tension and attraction. Lust. Desire. Disappointment. *Yearning*. Some, he must have drawn either during, or right after, a drunken party, because the couples all looked sort of sloppy—and predatory. Others seemed to be brief encounters he'd witnessed around the campus. A guy and a girl nestled together in a corner, maybe at the end of a hallway. A blank-faced pair at a table in the Snack Bar, possibly in the wake of some major argument. A girl leaning against a tree, while a guy faced her, one hand resting on the bark right next to her head, the other on her waist. A bearded male professor and a female student, on the steps outside Chapin, not touching, but also unmistakably involved in a non-academic relationship.

The most overtly sexual line drawing was two guys who were doing nothing more than playing pick-up basketball, but—whether they were aware of it or not—*definitely* had interests which went far beyond the game. The image was intriguing enough for her to spend some extra time studying it.

"Think they know?" she asked.

Jack checked to see which sketch she meant, then sat back. "No. The way I saw it, they just thought they were in athletic sync."

As opposed to sublimation. She pushed the sketchbook over to him. "You're very good. I mean, seriously good."

He shrugged, but also looked extremely pleased.

"Don't be a putz and major in Economics," she said.

He tucked the sketch pad away. "I could double-major, maybe."

As long as he didn't let the art go. "Do your parents know how good you are?" she asked.

"I don't know. I mean, I guess my mother does, because she always used to take me to museums, and sign me up for Saturday classes and everything. Although it started getting in the way of football, and Dad was—" He grinned. "Well, she ended up finding me a night class, instead."

He didn't look at all like a football player. "What position did you play?" she asked.

"Safety," he said. "Tight end, once in a while, if they wanted me on the other side of the ball."

Okay, he had the right build for that. "Did you play other sports?" she asked. Here at school, he was heavily into Ultimate Frisbee, and had spent the fall playing some pick-up rugby, too.

"In high school, you mean?" he asked, then nodded. "Baseball. Usually third base, sometimes outfield."

Yeah, she could picture that, too. And—call her one-dimensional—but it increased his attractiveness immediately. It was hard to relate to people who didn't like sports, even though Beth fell strongly into that category, serving as a rare—and major—exception to the rule.

"Do your parents want you to major in political science?" he asked.

Since he couldn't ask her any athletic questions. "I think my father would prefer that I picked anything *but* that," she said. Although he probably wouldn't mind at all if she went to law school. "And—" Hmmm. "You know, my mother and I have never really discussed it."

He stared at her. "*Never?*"

Not a single conversation was coming to mind. Not since last spring, anyway. Which—he was right—was weird. "I don't think so," she said. "I guess I mostly just pretend I'm going to major in English, and she pretends to believe me."

There was no question that he found that bizarre, but she was glad he didn't say so.

"I used to think—". She paused. No, the original ending of that sentence would sound arrogant. "I, um, I took tennis pretty seriously. I was hoping—to give it a try."

"Do you think you could have made it?" he asked.

Yes. Which didn't make it true. "Probably not," she said. "I mean, before I—got hurt, I was mostly playing against men—" Because her game had progressed enough so that she had a hard time finding female players who could give her a genuinely competitive match— "and beating them pretty often, so—I don't know. Probably not."

"But, you kind of think you could have," he said.

Yeah. She very definitely kind of did.

31

THEY REALLY DIDN'T get much work done, but it still seemed as though they had accomplished something. That they were no longer strangers to the same degree, maybe.

"Do I get to take you all the way up to your room?" he asked, when they were walking—very, very slowly, because her knee was so bad—to her dorm.

She nodded.

"Do I get to come inside for a while?" he asked.

She nodded, after only a very short hesitation.

"Cool," he said, and held the door for her.

She caught a glimpse of Garth on one of the phones inside the main security room, which seemed odd, since he technically wasn't on duty, but he had been working on the security plans for spring break, which were fairly complicated. As far as she knew, all of the agents on her regular detail were going to be given at least a little time off, as well as going up to Beltsville for some of their never-ending training sessions, which meant that there would be replacement agents stationed on the campus, as well as following her around Washington. So, there had been a lot more briefings and meetings than usual during the past day or two, arranging the transition.

"Do we get to do some serious making-out?" Jack asked in the elevator.

She glanced over at him. "Define 'serious.' "

"On your bed together, naked," he said.

He could not be faulted for a lack of ambition. "How about on my bed together, fully dressed," she said.

He grinned. "Okay. I can work with that."

Yes, she'd had a feeling that such might be the case.

———

IT WAS LATE when he left, and they were both in good moods.

And, okay, she had let him talk her, literally and figuratively, out of both her shirt, and her bra.

With really no argument whatsoever.

She didn't get much sleep—there seemed to be some extra activity going on out in the halls; looming midterms leading to dormwide insomnia, probably—but, when her alarm went off after what seemed like only about ten minutes, she still felt pretty cheerful.

Very cheerful, even.

It had, indeed, been serious making-out. More crucially, it had been *successful* making-out, despite the impediment of her brace and splint.

Totally *fun* making-out. And she hadn't had anything resembling fun since—it had been so long that she couldn't actually remember.

But, as nice as it would be to lie around ruminating about the details, she needed to get up, take a shower, double-check her psychology lab report, and maybe grab something to eat before class. She paused to check her email, and found one from Jack, which said, "*Same time, same place?*" and—to amuse herself—she wrote back, "*Wicked excellent*," before logging off.

When she came out of her room, Jose was in the hall, right by her door—so close that she had to stop short to keep from bumping into him—*and* Ed was at the security desk.

Weird. "What's going on?" she asked.

"Just testing out some new procedures," Jose said.

Well, okay. Whatever. She grinned at him. "So, my mother didn't jet off to other lands this morning without telling me?" Thereby unilaterally jacking up her protection.

He shook his head, giving her a slight smile back.

In the rush of people waiting their turns to get at the showers and head off to the dining hall or classes, she heard almost everyone else on the floor ask some type of "Did the President leave the country?" question, and receive the same "testing new procedures" response.

Ergo, they must be testing new procedures.

Jose rode down in the elevator with her, and when they got off, she saw Garth—who *absolutely* should not have still been on duty—talking to several agents she had never seen before, as well as Dave and Nellie and Casey and Brian, all of them crammed into the command post, along with what appeared to be a few police officers and FBI people, and she finally woke up enough to realize that there might actually be a problem.

So much for her nice, happy awakening, and hopes for a return to some version of a regular life.

She limped up to the doorway of the security room, and as soon as Garth saw her, he broke off whatever he had been about to tell the gathered agents, and said good morning to her, instead.

"New procedures?" she asked, stiffly.

Garth nodded.

Oh, like hell. She maneuvered her way into the room, agents practically scrambling over one another to let her by—and she saw that one of the police officers had a harnessed German shepherd close by her side.

Utterly and completely routine, no question.

Garth motioned for all of them to leave—which they appeared to be quite eager to do—and then, they were alone in the room.

"So," she said.

He sighed, his eyes heavy with fatigue. "There was a spike in your threat level overnight, on some of the Web sites we keep under regular surveillance, as well as some direct communications, and we're adjusting your protection accordingly."

Most of which, she'd figured out already. "Anything specific?" she asked.

"We're currently assessing that," he said.

Translation: yes.

"As a precaution, your classes are going to be relocated temporarily, and we may also recommend that you return to Washington earlier than planned," he said.

Relocated? Oh, great. "Am I endangering anyone else?" she asked.

He hesitated. "Obviously, we're going to make every possible effort to ensure the safety of the entire campus."

Another yes. God-damn it. And, with the cautious and rigid phraseology, he sounded as though he was parroting the exact party line, as, presumably, passed down from Mr. Gabler. Somehow, formal agent-speak sounder scarier coming out of a red-haired guy with freckles, whose mouth tended to turn up at the corners even when he was deadly serious.

Feeling very tired, she leaned back against the shelves where the security monitors were lined up. She scanned them, but didn't see anything out of the ordinary, beyond a few too many agents and law enforcement personnel, mingling among people hurrying off to class or the dining hall. "Do my parents know?"

He nodded. "The President received a full briefing within the last hour or so."

That would have been nice news to hear, first thing in the morning. It was strange that she hadn't called yet, but maybe she was trying to get as many details as possible—and not seem overly alarmed, until she knew more about what was potentially going on.

"I know this must be frightening, Meg," he said, "but I want to assure you that—"

She shook her head. "I'm not scared." And she *wasn't*, really, since every day for months now had seemed like one more than she ever expected to have. The exact method and timing of whatever horrible thing was ultimately going to happen might be a surprise, but the *likelihood* of its happening had a specter of inevitability. "I just—I don't want anyone else to get caught up in it."

"We're almost sure that this is because of all of the extra media exposure you've had during the past week," Garth said. "But we want to go out of our way to be *over*prepared."

Right. On the monitors, she could see that there was at least one other dog-handler team patrolling outside. "They planning to kidnap me, shoot me, blow me up, or what?" she asked.

Garth frowned. Mr. Gabler must not have given him clear instructions about how to answer such a direct question. "There've been a series of bomb threats, and one of them was chemical in nature."

For an instant, she felt absolutely sick to her stomach, but her second thought was that, if she had to choose, chemical was probably preferable to biological or nuclear.

And her third thought was that, at some level, only the first reaction fell into the category of being rational.

But, the thing to do was go back up to her room and call her parents, and find out whether going home early—thereby skipping out of her midterms—would be the best way to protect everyone else at the school. Which needed to be her top priority.

"Hey, did the President go abroad or something?" Quentin asked her, wearing a thick blue Highland Park Giants hooded sweatshirt, as he swung out of the elevator on his crutches.

He was a good guy, and she wanted him to be safe—but she couldn't tell him the truth until she knew exactly what the truth *was*. Meg nodded. "She defected, yeah. There's going to be quite a scandal."

He laughed, and headed outside, as she—and her new, very close shadow, Jose—got back on the elevator.

The drop-line was ringing when she walked into her room, and she picked it up to find—unsurprisingly—the President on the other end.

"I just talked to Garth," Meg said. "So, I already know."

Her mother sighed. "It's probably nothing, but obviously, your father and I are very concerned. I put Thomas on a plane, and they should be landing any time now."

Mr. Gabler. Meg sat down on the edge of the bed, exhausted by the thought of having to deal with all of this. "Maybe it's just because I became *interesting* again, after, you know, the stuff with Susan. And so, all the nuts are coming out of the woodwork."

"Probably," her mother agreed. "But, I gather that there's a specificity to it that—" She sighed again. "Maybe it would be better if you came home today."

But, probably not so good for her GPA—or her self-respect. "Is that really what you want me to do?" Meg asked.

"Your father's right here," her mother said, after a pause, "and—well, it goes without saying that your safety is paramount to both of us."

Okay, that meant that the President was torn—and the First Gentleman was not. "So, I should just cut and run," Meg said. "While the whole campus up here is still at risk."

There was a short silence. "Let me put him on for a minute," her mother said.

The First Gentleman must be taking a *very* hard line on this.

They spoke for a while, and while her father was calm and supportive, there was no doubt that he wanted her to return to Washington right away—or sooner, if possible. Then, her mother came back on.

"He's not happy," Meg said.

Her mother sighed.

"I'll wait until Mr. Gabler gets here and all," Meg said, "but if I have to make a decision, I really want to speak to you privately, first."

"Yes, I can see why that might be indicated," her mother said, obliquely. "I'll make sure to arrange that."

Good.

There wasn't much else to say, but the conversation limped on for another few minutes before they hung up with nothing whatsoever resolved.

Now what?

She couldn't think of anything to do, beyond making herself a cup of microwave coffee. Then, she sat down on the bed to drink it, and stare at one of her pictures of Vanessa.

There was a sharp knock on the door, and Susan came in without waiting for her to respond in any way.

"What's going on?" she asked. Demanded, really.

Naturally, Susan would be the one most likely to sense trouble—and to take immediate action. Meg sipped her coffee. "They're trying out new security procedures."

Susan looked annoyed. "Give me a break."

"That's the official word," Meg said, and took another sip.

Susan checked her watch—she was probably on the verge of being late to some midterm or other—and then shook her head. "I used to live in New York, Meg, I *know* what credible terrorist threats look like."

Well, then, so she would. Meg looked up. "You lived in New York?"

Susan nodded impatiently. "For most of high school." She gestured towards the hall. "So, what's the deal?"

Should she lie? She probably wasn't going to buy the defection story. "Some bomb threats," Meg said. "Possibly something chemical."

Susan took that in, and then nodded once. "Okay. Is the dorm in danger?"

Well, *yeah*. "They mostly just want to kill me," Meg said, "but no, I don't think they care if other people get hurt, too." Hell, they would probably *prefer* it. Whoever "they" were, in all of their various permutations, complete with twisted ideologies.

"Okay." Susan blinked a couple of times—nice to know that someone in the room wasn't completely immune from normal reactions—and then, swallowed. "I don't know what I'm supposed to do."

Run off and warn her *actual* friends, maybe? Meg shrugged. "Go to class, I guess." Or, alternatively, leave town. "And make sure to stay a safe distance away from me."

Susan bit her lip. "I'm sorry. I didn't mean to make it sound as though—I'm sorry." She glanced around the room, and then sat in the desk chair. "I think I meant to ask if you were scared."

Yeah. Sure. That's exactly what she'd had in mind. Meg drank some more instant coffee, which tasted pretty awful. "I'm really already supposed to be dead, so everything else pretty much just seems like *details*."

Susan started to say something, but then nodded.

Preaching to the converted, possibly.

Meg looked at her bulletproof—but definitely not, say, RPG-proof—window shade. "I'm trying to decide whether my going back home early negates the threat, or just means that *I'm*—" relatively—"safe, and the rest of you are still in the thick of it."

Susan frowned. "What do you think?"

She had no god-damn idea what she thought. "I don't know," Meg said. "But no matter what they say to try and make me leave, if I'm up here, security precautions are going to be a lot higher than if I'm *not*."

"But, if you're here, anyone who wants to pull something is going to be that much more motivated to try," Susan said.

Yep. Conundrum. So, which one was the lesser evil? Meg shrugged. "Better email my philosophy professor, see where he comes down on this."

"It's a strategy," Susan said, after a moment.

A weak one, as strategies went. Meg resisted the urge to duck back against the wall—and as far away from the window as possible. "The bomb threats could be misdirection. You know, talk about explosives, and then, when they're focused on that, climb up in a tree somewhere, or on top of a building, with a sniper's scope and shoot me."

"More than one damn plane," Susan said.

Yeah. Words it would be nice not to live by.

Be nice, also, if someone could explain to her why people she had never met would have any interest whatsoever in harming her.

The coffee was just too lousy to drink, even by her very low standards, and Meg set it aside. "If I take off today, as though I'm in a panic, and there's an intentional media splash about it to get the word out that I'm back in Washington and not limping around here, to try and prevent anything from happening, it's a *major* capitulation."

Susan moved her jaw. "Sounds better than a dorm full of dead and maimed freshmen."

Oh, and she wanted that to happen? Meg scowled at her. "Susan, I'm *always* dangerous to be around—this time, they just happened to get some potential warning, first."

Susan nodded, and looked unsure of herself again. "What do your, um, parents want you to do?"

Drop everything, grab a few valuables, and be whisked off to the airport. "They're trying to balance competing interests," Meg said. At least, one of them was.

"What's that mean?" Susan asked.

"They don't want me to get killed, but they don't want to flip out prematurely, either, in case it's only another hoax," Meg said.

Susan nodded, then folded her arms and slouched over them.

"Care for a specialty coffee?" Meg asked.

Susan shook her head.

Right.

"Do you have any midterms today?" Meg asked.

Susan didn't answer, but *did* maybe sneak a peek at her watch.

"So, don't be dumb, go to your midterm," Meg said. "I'm just going to be sitting around, waiting for Mr. Gabler."

Susan made no move whatsoever to get up. "No, I think I'd rather hang out here."

How very predictable. Duty, first. "That's really nice of you," Meg said, "but I'm fine. I don't need a babysitter."

Susan shrugged. "I'll still stay and keep you company for a while."

She had learned the hard way that trying to argue with Susan McAllister was generally nothing more than a waste of breath. So, Meg motioned towards the hall, and the unseen, but extensive, swarm of agents and police officers beyond. "Do you think people will figure it out?"

Susan sighed, running her hand across her forehead and then back through her hair, indicating that Meg wasn't the only one who currently had a terrible headache. "We're on a campus full of a statistically improbable percentage of former valedictorians. Odds are, there are a number of people around who are capable of making intuitive leaps."

" 'Yes' would have been an okay answer, too," Meg said.

Susan's smile was minuscule, but it was there.

Meg couldn't think of anything else to say, and Susan seemed to be deep in thought, so they spent the next few minutes in complete silence, Meg wishing that she could employ her usual tension-relieving trick of turning on CNN or C-Span.

"Leaving today *would* be a capitulation," Susan said, out of nowhere. "I mean, it would pretty much make a mockery out of—" She gestured towards Meg's hand.

Yeah.

It was quiet.

"Sucks to be you, doesn't it," Susan said.

That one caught her off-guard, and Meg laughed. "Yeah," she said. "Sometimes, it does."

MR. GABLER APPEARED ABOUT twenty minutes later, and Susan seemed to stay around just long enough to decide that everything was under competent control before she glanced at her watch, and hurried off without another word.

Mr. Gabler watched her go, looking a trifle anxious.

"You *know* she's not going to tell anyone, sir," Meg said, finding it rather irritating to have to point out the obvious.

"Of course not," Mr. Gabler said, although he looked less certain than he sounded.

Her phone rang, but it wasn't the drop-line, or even the medium-secure line, which meant that there was no pressing need to answer it. She could see from the caller ID that it was an unfamiliar cell phone number, anyway, so there was a good chance that it was a reporter, or some other unwelcome stranger.

On the other hand, it could also be a direct terrorist threat, and maybe shouldn't be ignored.

"Should I pick that up?" she asked.

Mr. Gabler shook his head firmly. "They're monitoring that line downstairs, for the time being. For now, we're prefer that you didn't take any calls at all, except on the drop-line."

That made sense—except it also raised a troubling question. "Do they listen in on my calls?" Meg asked. "Routinely?"

"Of course not," he said. "We keep a log of the numbers on your incoming calls, but, no, of course we don't, Meg."

Maybe. "Do you read my emails?" she asked.

He shook his head.

Maybe. But she was sure as hell going to check with her mother, and find out for sure.

And be even more careful than usual about trying never to say, or put in writing, anything which could come back to haunt her.

She had already missed psychology—and handing in her lab report, but she could still make it to the last half hour or so of her Shakespeare class, if she left right away. They were having their review for the midterm, and not being there was likely to have a significant, and negative, effect on her grade. Mr. Gabler nodded carefully when she asked if she could go, and while Garth and the other agents who accompanied her were hyperalert, she noticed that they seemed less tense than they had earlier—possibly because if anything went wrong, the buck now stopped with Mr. Gabler, not any of them.

Instead of their normal room, the class had been moved over to a different room, in another building entirely. When she opened the door, everyone stared at her, and she apologized for being late, then limped over to a seat in the corner, away from the windows.

When the class was over, and everyone was filing out, someone touched her on the arm, and—to her great embarrassment—she jumped about a foot and a half.

"Uh, sorry," the person said. Jill Something-or-other. A sophomore from Minnesota or someplace like that who seemed friendly enough, although they had never really spoken before.

"No, I'm sorry," Meg said quickly. "I just—" Panicked.

Anyway.

"Want the notes from the first half of class?" Jill asked. "We can stop by the library and Xerox them."

Was she allowed to go to the library? She glanced at Garth, who nodded. "Okay," Meg said. "Thanks." But, should she let this perfectly nice stranger walk right next to her? "Maybe, um, I should meet you over there."

Jill looked at her agents, too. "They let you leave the dorm, so how much worse can the library be than Griffin?"

So much for trying to keep everything quiet. "Did Professor Heldler tell everyone?" Meg asked. Since, she assumed, her professor would have been briefed, given the need to switch buildings at the last minute.

Jill shook her head. "The campus is *crawling* with security, and we got moved, and you didn't show up for the review. That's not really hard to put together."

Probably not. But, still. "Were you valedictorian at your high school?" Meg asked, out of genuine curiosity.

Jill looked surprised—and suspicious. "Yeah. Why?"

Score one for Susan. Meg grinned. "My JA said there were too many valedictorians around here for people not to be able to make intuitive leaps."

Jill grinned, too. "Susan, not Dirk, right?"

Now, it was Meg's turn to be suspicious. "You know who my JAs are?"

"It's a pretty small school," Jill said, frowning at her. "And that sounds like something Susan would say."

Hmmm. Maybe the two of them were friends, then. "Did she call ahead and tell you to keep an eye on me?" Meg asked.

"No," Jill said, and laughed. "But, I bet she would have, if she'd thought of it."

No doubt.

They were already halfway over to the library, and nothing seemed to be amiss, except that too many of the undercover people in jeans and sweatshirts looked much too old to be college students. She was able to copy the notes, without any violent incidents, during the approximately two minutes this process took. Then, she headed back to the dorm alone.

Jack was sitting on one of the picnic tables in the quad, and he got up when he saw her. "You blew off psych."

Perhaps not a valedictorian.

"You're not mad at me or anything," he said, "are you?"

Absolutely not a valedictorian. "Did psych meet somewhere else today?" she asked.

He nodded. "Yeah, didn't you see the sign on the door? They put us over in the dining hall at Greylock, because I guess they found what they thought might be asbestos, or something at Bronfman."

Not a bad cover story. "Did they keep you from going into the dorm?" she asked, motioning over her shoulder with her cane.

Jack nodded, looking hurt. "Yeah. Like, I don't know, you left orders, maybe."

As far as she could remember, the day really *had* started off well. Seemed like months ago. "So, our class got moved, I didn't show up, even though it was important for me to be there and I also probably wanted to see you, and now, it seems like my dorm is pretty much locked down." She paused. "Wouldn't it be weird if all of that was—connected?"

He processed that, then winced.

And, on further reflection, she felt like wincing, too, since he really hadn't done anything at all to deserve her being quite that bitchy.

"You all right?" he asked finally.

She shrugged. "So far." Other than maybe being a little more scared than she felt like telling anyone.

Or maybe a lot more.

"We allowed to go up to your room?" he asked.

She nodded.

"You *want* to?" he asked.

She nodded.

32

THERE WERE TOO many people around—and too strong a likelihood that one or both of her parents might call at any moment—for them to relax enough to do anything more than some low-key fooling around and curling up together on the bed, but it was good to have him there, regardless.

After a while, there was a knock on the door.

"We're studying very hard," she said.

Jack nodded, rolled to his feet, sat down at her desk, and opened a book. An utterly non-academic mystery, actually, but what the hell.

She opened the door to see Mr. Gabler.

"I wanted to let you know that the FBI has just made three arrests," he said.

She was so relieved that, for a second, her good leg felt as though it might collapse underneath her, and she had to lean as much weight as possible on her cane to keep herself steady.

At the desk, Jack turned to listen.

"Do you think you got them all?" she asked.

Mr. Gabler nodded.

It was going to be scary if he told her they had been captured right downstairs, attempting to storm the building. "Who are they?" she asked.

Mr. Gabler let out his breath. "Three tenth graders in Nebraska."

What? Meg stared at him.

Mr. Gabler nodded. "I know. That's almost exactly the way I feel about it, Meg."

Tenth graders. Jesus. Meg leaned back against the bureau, closing her eyes for a second. Then, she opened them. "Were they a genuine threat?"

He shook his head. "I gather they thought it would be funny."

They were mistaken. "Are they just little creeps, or are they incipient monsters?" she asked.

"I suspect they are primarily the former, but we fully intend to treat them like the latter," he said.

Good. "How's the First Gentleman taking it?" she asked.

Mr. Gabler paused. "I am very pleased to be spending the day in Massachusetts, Meg."

If that was the case, maybe she was, too.

After telling her that her security was going to remain somewhat elevated until she got back to Washington, but that she was otherwise free to go about her usual business, Mr. Gabler gave Jack a nod and left.

As she closed the door, Jack dropped the mystery and came over to rest his hands on either side of her waist.

"I'm glad they got them," he said.

She nodded, feeling unaccountably tired. "When you were in tenth grade, would you have thought that chemical bombs were funny?"

Jack shook his head. "I was a jerk, but not *that* much of a jerk."

She would have guessed as much, but it was still the right answer. She looked at his hands, and then up at his face. "I kind of have the feeling that your reputation for being a jerk is a little inflated."

He shrugged. "Got me on a good day, that's all."

Maybe.

He pulled her towards him. "If they're not going to come back up here anytime soon, maybe we should—"

She shook her head. "No, because the phone's about to—"

The drop-line rang.

It was, of course, her parents, on conference call, and they said encouraging, reassuring things to her, while she said confident, lighthearted things in return—and as far as she was concerned, all of their performances were unconvincing. Her father did suggest that she consider coming home early, anyway, a request which she deflected without giving him an answer.

Jack kept his distance during the conversation, glancing at the door every so often as though he thought he should probably leave.

"They're my *parents,*" she said, when she hung up. "We, you know, talk to each other. It's not that big a deal."

Jack nodded, not meeting her eyes.

She had been convinced that who she was didn't matter to him—but, it wouldn't be the first time she had been wrong. "You know, technically, if you're in a room when the President is speaking to someone, you're supposed to stand at attention," she said.

His eyes widened, and he actually straightened up.

Christ. "Too late," she said, picked up the drop-line, and asked to be connected to Mr. Fielding, to try and get a feel for what was *really* going on, as far as her parents were concerned.

The new director of communications told her that he was currently hiding under his desk with a blanket over his head, waiting for the wrath that was Hurricane Russell either to pass, or to burn itself out. He also said that, to the best of his knowledge, the President was hiding underneath *her* desk, too, although in lieu of a blanket, she had brought a briefing book along with her.

Which gave her a very clear picture of the scene at 1600 Pennsylvania Avenue. With luck, Steven was off at baseball practice, and Neal, being Neal, would probably just shrug and go play on his computer for the rest of the afternoon.

"You're all right, though?" Preston asked.

"Yeah," she said. "But, god-damn *tenth graders*."

He sighed. "I know. Not too many things out there nastier than teenaged boys, unfortunately."

"Speaking from personal experience?" she asked.

"Absolutely not," he said. "Beatrice Fielding insisted upon utter sweetness at all times."

Right.

"Our friend Ms. Goldman has been sniffing around all day," he said.

Well, no one had ever accused her of not being an aggressive reporter.

"Promise me you won't give her anything," he said, "okay?"

"No, Hannah, I can neither confirm nor deny," she said.

"How about you just refer her to me, or to Maureen and Anthony," he suggested.

That might be a serviceable plan, too. Anthony was her father's new press secretary—in his mid-twenties, openly and happily gay, and known to be terribly witty and blasé under stress, two character traits which were likely to come in handy in his line of work.

Today, for instance.

When she'd hung up, she and Jack stood there.

"It's *weird*, Meg," he said finally. "I'm not going to get used to it overnight."

She wanted to snap at him, but that wasn't going to get them anywhere. "What, the other people you've dated weren't the targets of chemical bomb hoaxes here and there?"

"When they were, they were smart enough to be a little shook up by it," he said quietly.

Oh, so now he was mad at her, for not running around screaming? But, she shrugged.

"Well," he said, and looked at her clock radio. "I should probably take off."

Probably.

She let him get as far as the door before she relented. "Jack."

He stopped.

"This is a stupid reason to have a fight," she said.

He nodded.

But, they were going to have one, anyway?

"I was *worried* about you, Meg," he said.

Oh.

"And then I have to listen to you going, 'I'm fine, Mom, no problem,' " he said, "and it's the *President* on the other end, and—it's weird for me. I mean, if you want, we can act like you aren't different, but you are."

All of which was probably legitimate, but still frustrating—and a very strong indication that this nascent attempt to be a nondescript college freshman who did conventional things like *date* probably wasn't going to work out.

"Anyway, I'm late for Ultimate," he said.

She nodded.

"That's it?" he asked.

More or less. "Have fun playing," she said, hoping she didn't sound as perfunctory as she felt.

His nod back was not particularly friendly, and he started to leave, but then stopped again. "You want me to lie to you, instead of telling you how I actually feel? Say what I figure you want to hear, since that'll make it that much easier to get you to sleep with me?" he asked. "Is that what you want? Because, I can do that. In fact, truth is, I'm really *good* at it."

"You want me to kill you?" the guy had asked, in the same sort of angry, conversational way. "You want me to kill you right now?" Staring at her, with the half-smile, pressing her up against a filthy concrete wall, his arm jammed against her throat, pointing a gun right at her face the entire time. The muzzle *touching* her face, just below her left eye.

"What?" Jack asked uneasily.

She looked at him, trying to remember what room she was in, and what room she *wasn't* in, and—it was hard to get her breath, and she had to swallow a couple of times.

"What is it?" he asked. "God, Meg, you look—what did I do?"

"Nothing," she said. "I just—never mind." She sat down on the bed. "Um, have a good game. Uh—practice, I mean."

"Is something wrong with your eye?" he asked.

She realized that she had brought her hand up to the spot where the gun had been, and dropped it. "No. It's fine."

"I really don't have to go play," he said. "It's not like I'm not out there almost every day, so I could—"

She shook her head. "No, you should go—" right away, if possible— "and I should make some calls, and find out if it's too late for me to do PT today."

"You sure you're okay?" he asked.

"Absolutely," she said.

He still hesitated by the door. "Am I going to see you tonight?"

Doubtful. "Well, I'm usually pretty wrecked after PT," she said, "so—well—"

He sighed. "Just tell me no, Meg. It's easier."

If that's what he wanted, then that's what she would do. "No," she said. "Probably not."

He didn't look happy to hear that, but he just nodded. "Okay, whatever." He went out to the hall, closing the door behind him as he left.

Once she was sure he was gone, she couldn't help touching her eye again. Jesus. That was one bout of terror she hadn't expected.

She had to sit there for a few minutes, taking deep breaths, before she felt ready to limp out to the security room and let her agents know that she wanted to go down to the hospital.

When she walked into physical therapy—after, as usual, being stopped a few times on her way through the hospital by people who wanted to say hello, shake her hand, or even have her sign "Get Well" cards they were bringing to a friend or loved one—she must not have looked very good, because the first thing Vicky did was take her blood pressure.

"We're not going to do any PT today," she said, when she was finished and had marked the numbers down on her chart.

"Is it high?" Meg asked, not wildly interested in the answer.

Vicky rolled up the cuff and put it away. "For blood pressure, no. For you, yes."

"Well, midterms," Meg said, and shrugged.

Vicky rolled her eyes. "Meg, the Secret Service and FBI have been around here most of the day."

Oh. Well, they would have been, wouldn't they.

Which didn't change the fact that Vicky summoned a couple of the doctors who had been waiting nearby, and she ended up having—what, her third? fourth?—comprehensive medical exam of the week. She seemed to pass muster—or, at any rate, no one suggested admitting her. But she felt pretty stupid when they asked her what she had had to eat so far that day, and she had no idea whatsoever.

Vicky scowled and left for a few minutes, returning with a chilled carton of vanilla-flavored nutritional supplement and a straw.

Meg sipped it, methodically, and while it didn't make her feel any less shaky, Vicky stopped frowning when she finished.

When she got back to the dorm, her posted security was still higher than she wanted it to be, but at least the feeling of urgency had diminished. There seemed to be an aura of fear in the air, but she suspected that it had more to do with a building full of people frantically cramming for their remaining exams than it did with anything to do with her personally. For once, no one even seemed to be playing video games in the common room, which she could almost never remember happening before.

Although she knew she should immediately start studying, she turned on CNN to see what the top stories were. The day seemed to have been relatively quiet, but in due course, the President was shown at a Rose Garden bill-signing ceremony—an expansion of health-care options for small business owners, sole proprietors, and freelancers; good for her—and Meg leaned forward to study the way she looked. Judging from the angle of the sun, the footage must have been from some time before noon—and there was no sign whatsoever that she was waiting to find out whether her daughter was on the verge of being caught in the middle of a terrorist chemical attack. In fact, she appeared so relaxed and warm and funny, that it was possibly a little psychotic.

But, Meg saw her stiffen ever so slightly as she glanced at something—or, more likely, some*one*—off to the side; then, she continued her remarks without any noticeable distress. So, the someone, probably Glen, her chief of staff, must have given her a signal, with an update of the situation. Or, all things being equal, he might have been letting her know about something *else* going on in the world today.

But it was still fairly amazing that there had been a potentially huge story about to break, and yet, the media seemed to have missed it entirely.

So far, at least. After all, Hannah the Shark might not be the only one who had been nosing around today.

She still felt too restless to study, so she took the elevator down to the basement to get a soda from the vending machine, and then rode up to the second floor, where the common room was still, strangely, deserted.

But Susan's door was open, and she tapped on it with her cane.

"Uh, hi," she said.

Susan, who was at her desk studying, looked up. "Hi."

"You got the word?" Meg asked.

Susan nodded. "Yeah. You okay?"

Depending upon one's definition. Mostly, she was tired. "Sure," Meg said. "I hope you didn't get in trouble about your midterm."

Susan shook her head, which was wrapped in a towel, so she must have just gotten out of the shower. "No, no problem. She just let me stay a while longer to finish."

"Well, that's good," Meg said, and nodded a few times too many. "I mean, I'm glad."

"Tenth graders," Susan said, sounding disgusted.

Yeah. God-damn cretins. Just thinking about it made her grit her teeth.

Susan clasped her hands behind her head and leaned back in her chair, which tipped onto the two rear legs. "If you're beating yourself up because you were spooked by the whole thing, that's dumb. Why wouldn't you have been?"

What, she looked scared? Meg stopped gritting her teeth. "I wasn't."

"*I* was," Susan said.

Yeah, cleaning up a dorm full of dead and maimed freshmen would have been a messy task.

Susan looked at her for a long minute, and then shifted her weight so that the front legs of her chair came banging back down onto the floor. "When you asked me if I wanted a specialty coffee, I wanted to deck you."

A change-up, when she'd expected a fastball. "It was polite," Meg said.

"It was *cavalier*," Susan said, "and it pissed me off."

Yeah, fine, she was an unbelievable loser for not letting herself give in to paralyzing terror and despair. It was *bad* to keep a stiff upper lip.

"For the record," Susan said.

She had a vague rule that—no matter how infuriating it was—if she received a similar criticism from more than one person, it might have some validity. Meg sighed. "I have to get through the day somehow, Susan."

Susan nodded, and rubbed her forehead for a second, so her headache must have come back. "I know. It's just hard to watch."

It was also hard to *do*. For the record. She could see that Susan had a lot of work piled up on her desk, and God knows she had plenty of her own, but the thought of going up to her room and closing the door was a lonely one. Of course, she could always leave it open partway, but it wasn't as though people were inclined to drop by to see her indiscriminately.

"So, um, how far did you run today?" she asked, to prolong the conversation.

"I don't know," Susan said. "Seven and a half, eight miles, I guess."

Wow. She'd never thought to ask before, but— "How far do you usually go?"

Susan shrugged. "Four or five."

So, she'd felt the need to run much harder, and farther, today. "You don't go out in the middle of nowhere, do you?" Meg asked. "I mean, you're careful, right?"

Susan smiled. "I usually stay pretty close to the campus, or head towards North Adams. But, if it's getting dark or anything, I make sure someone comes with me."

Okay, good. Meg nodded, slouching against the doorjamb. The friends of Susan's she had met—primarily drama majors—mostly struck her as being an unusually uncoordinated lot, but there must be another runner or two hidden in there somewhere.

Susan cocked her head to one side. "What?"

"Nothing," Meg said. "I just—" Could she bring herself to sit down and weep stormily, because she'd had a bad day—and because it had only been a few hours since she had experienced a tremendous romantic disappointment, and she wanted to indulge in a series of mordant, self-pitying remarks? No. In fact, she might not even subject *Beth* to this latest personal crisis. But, she would need to say something convincing, before Susan's bloodhound instincts kicked in. "I don't want to bother you or anything, but are you friends with a sophomore named Jill? I don't know her last name, but I think she's from Minnesota?"

"Blondish hair, wears it in a braid, looks like a jock?" Susan asked.

Meg nodded. Although actually, that description fit a fairly large percentage of the student body.

"Yeah, sure," Susan said. "Jill Kiley. She's from Wisconsin, though. Why?"

One small worry eliminated, then. Meg shrugged. "She's in my

Shakespeare class and she said she knew you. And—" She'd felt the need to double-check. "Small campus, that's all."

Susan nodded, but still looked curious.

"She's a valedictorian," Meg said.

Susan grinned. "Made an intuitive leap, did she?"

Precisely. She stood in the doorway for another moment, still not quite prepared to go up to her room and be by herself, but too shy to say so.

Susan looked at her, expectantly.

"I wasn't a valedictorian," Meg said.

Susan shrugged. "Neither was I."

That was a relief, since it would be demoralizing if she turned out to be one of the only non-valedictorians at the entire college. "You know, when you get right down to it, I didn't actually graduate from high school," Meg said, "and I guess I was thinking about that on the way back here."

Susan nodded.

"I missed the last couple of weeks of school—" And the prom, and graduation; the guy had mocked her, at length, about the former— "and they never made me take my finals, because—well, how could they, really? I mean, I didn't even get out of the hospital until *July*, and—" Too much information, maybe. So, Meg edged away from the door. "I'm sorry. I should let you study, and I should go do a bunch of stuff, too."

"Colleen died at the end of January," Susan said.

Meg stopped in her tracks, and then returned, tentatively, to lean against the doorjamb again.

Susan looked briefly at her bulletin board. "I wouldn't exactly say that I had a breakdown, but my grades pretty much went to hell for the rest of the my senior year. My teachers were nice about it, and mostly went ahead and gave me B's, but I didn't really deserve them."

Meg nodded.

"And, ironically, Colleen *would* have been our valedictorian," Susan said. "By a long shot. No one else in the class was even really close. So, the poor guy who ended up coming in first had no idea what to say in his speech. It was just sort of *there*, in the air all night." Susan shrugged. "I don't know. We're both probably doing too much thinking today."

Yes, that was the problem with brushes with mortality, regardless of how illusory they turned out to be.

"I think you would have been better off with a JA who didn't have quite so much baggage," Susan said.

A JA without significant baggage might not think to watch her like a hawk on a consistent basis. Dirk, for example.

Which still didn't mean that her father hadn't been completely wrong to allow Susan to be selected, in the first place. "I think it's kind of the other way around." Meg glanced over. "And, you know, it still isn't too late, if—especially after today—you want me to—"

"Don't finish that sentence," Susan said instantly. "You will annoy me."

But, if she were open to the idea, it would be easy enough to arrange—

"*Don't*," Susan said. "In fact, go study now."

It was always nice to be told what to do.

"Think there's a chance your grades are going to show up in the press?" Susan asked.

An excellent chance, since it happened more often than not. One of the most recent weekly celebrity tabloids had proclaimed, breathlessly, that she was having a scandalous affair with one of her Secret Service agents, the main proof for this being a photo some paparazzo creep had gotten of Jose catching her one afternoon when she slipped on the ice crossing Spring Street, and the article insisted that this was a view of the two of them in the aftermath of a torrid embrace. The writer had even quoted a psychologist—with the disclaimer that he had not actually treated the President's tragically troubled daughter professionally—who theorized that her sexual acting out was a desperate cry for help, and a poignant attempt to get the attention of her cold and unloving mother.

Of course, only the week before that, the very same tabloid had published the world-exclusive story that she was sleeping with her philosophy professor, as evidenced by a picture of him bending towards her when she asked him a question about a reading assignment on their way out of class one morning. This was thought to indicate that she was not only promiscuous, and frantic to get a passing grade at any cost, but that—given his age—she also might have unresolved feelings towards her father. Maybe even her *grandfather*. The fact that her professor was hard of hearing, and had leaned down because she hadn't spoken loudly enough when she first asked the question had not, apparently, been discovered by the crack reporters who penned the tale.

"Yeah," she said aloud, aware that she had drifted a little, since Susan was looking at her with some combination of amusement and irritation. "My grades usually get published."

"Do you want those brat tenth graders to think they scared you enough to screw up your midterms?" Susan asked.

Hell, no.

So, she went up to her room, and—after eating the last apple, a few baby carrots, and some of the cheese Preston had stocked inside her refrigerator—studied. Polished her political science paper, then finished her philosophy paper and began to edit it. She'd left her door open a few inches—and was gratified, and surprised, when Juliana, Mary Elizabeth, Khalid, and Andy *all* stopped by at various points to say hello—and maybe relieve their curiosity about whatever the hell had been going on with all of the extra agents and police officers hanging around earlier. Khalid, who missed his retriever/boxer mix terribly and even wore a custom-made t-shirt with her photo on it sometimes, was especially interested in—and wistful about—the dog teams.

At about eleven-thirty, when she heard movement out in the hall again, she turned, expecting that it would probably be Tammy—or maybe Susan, planning to hover, or criticize, but it was Jack, wearing a bright, flowered Hawaiian shirt and jeans, his hands jammed in his pockets.

"Same time, same place," he said.

Was it really as easy as that?

"You going to tell me what I did was wrong?" he asked. "I mean, I was here, and you seemed to be *glad* I was here, and then—well, you *weren't* glad."

Meg shrugged. "You happened to be in the room. That's all you did." And, okay, he'd kind of yelled at her, too.

"So," he said, "you go absolutely white, out of nowhere, whenever someone's in a room with you?"

If they triggered bad memories, yeah. She glanced at her computer, and clicked SAVE before she had a chance to forget, so that she wouldn't risk losing hours of work. "I really don't want to talk about it." No, that wasn't firm enough. "In fact, I'm definitely *not* going to talk about it, but it didn't have anything to do with you."

He half-smiled. "It's not you, Jack, it's *me*. Really."

Something like that, yeah.

He sighed. "Meg, I've said that to people when I was trying to break up with them, and didn't want to hurt their feelings."

How disappointing. "That's very boring," Meg said. "Do me a favor and promise that if you break up with me, you'll think of something more creative."

"Same to *you*," he said.

She nodded, and waited.

"Oh," he said.

She nodded.

"Can I come in for a while?" he asked.

She nodded.

33

HER MIDTERMS WENT reasonably well, and by one o'clock on Friday, she was packed and ready to go. Her parents had wanted to fly up to Albany International to meet her—her father had damn near *insisted*—and she had made an ineffective argument that she should just take a commercial flight, with a few of her agents, and not have everyone make such a fuss. The uneasy compromise was that a small military jet would pick her up at one of the tiny local airports, and then take her directly to Andrews Air Force Base, and home. It seemed like a significant waste of the taxpayers' money, but—as her mother pointed out—firing up Air Force One and having the President, essentially, play hooky for a good chunk of the day was not terribly frugal, either.

A fair number of people from the dorm, including Juliana and Mary Elizabeth, had already left, so it was pretty quiet. Susan, to no one's surprise, was planning to stay an extra day, in order to wait until the very last person in the entry was safely off on his or her journey home. Then, presumably, she would spend the next two weeks in a state of suspended animation, until she could get back to school, and resume being an authority figure again.

Jack, who was planning to take the afternoon bus to Boston to visit a friend at Tufts on his way to Los Angeles, carried her computer and leather Camp David duffel bag downstairs for her. They had exchanged phone numbers, although she wasn't sure if either of them would get up sufficient nerve to call the other—she was sure *she* wouldn't—since whatever it was that they were doing was still at such a delicate, early stage.

"So," he said, once they were outside, near the cast iron gates by the street.

"Yeah," she said.

They stood there.

Then, he leaned over to kiss her, and she heard a camera start clicking away—right across the road, telephoto lens, *great*—and dodged the kiss, moving so that her back would be to the photographer, but making sure that her expression stayed pleasant, in case she was still within range.

"Oh, sorry," Jack said, and jumped back, staying at a distance. Then, he frowned. "Except, is this some big secret? Like, so what if they see us?"

He had a point. "Just not a public display of affection," she said. "It'll be the difference between being buried somewhere inside, or showing up on the cover."

He grinned. "I *like* that phrase."

Well, America was a free country, and he had every legal right to be—predictable. Pedestrian. " 'Public display of affection'?" she asked. "Or 'showing up on the cover'?"

" 'Buried somewhere inside,' " he said.

On further reflection, that was even more predictable, but also kind of funny. Although still in the category of wishful thinking. Not that she couldn't feel herself blushing furiously. Nellie was the nearest agent, and Meg glanced over, hoping like hell that she hadn't overheard that one. Judging from her expression, she either hadn't, or wanted it to *seem* that way.

"I'm not going to see you for two weeks," he said. "I'd really like to kiss you good-bye."

And she wouldn't mind having him do so. She looked around until she caught Garth's eye. "I need a couple of minutes, okay?"

He nodded, and gestured to the nearby agents to adjust their protective positions accordingly. Brian and Ed were already on their way over to the photographer, in, she assumed, an attempt to discourage him from remaining in the area.

She limped back towards the dorm, with Jack following her. Once they were through the main door and out of camera view, he kissed her intensely enough so that it occurred to her that it might be nice if she could postpone her flight for a few hours. But, she couldn't, and he had his bus to catch, and—

"Hey, Taylor!" Andy said, coming down the stairs with a huge knapsack and his laptop. "You'd better be *nice* to her, dude."

"Well, yeah," Jack said. "I don't want her agents to start shooting me."

Right about now, she needed to be wearing her "The Queen Is Not Amused" sweatshirt.

Once Andy was gone—and the couple of agents who had come out of the security room had quickly turned around and gone back in there—they started kissing again, until they were both out of breath, and she was starting to think that two weeks was going to be a *really* long time.

"Jesus, get a room," a guy—who was known around the dorm as "Clyde the Clod"—said, passing them on his way outside.

They moved apart, although she didn't want to, and she could certainly feel that *he* didn't want to, either.

"We, um, I should go," she said.

Jack nodded, glanced down, and then untucked his shirt.

She checked the shirttails to make sure that everything was—obscured. "You need to stay in here for a few minutes, and maybe think about baseball?"

"Okay," he said, and thought. "No. Sorry. All I'm getting is us, in the dugout, and I'm on top of you."

But, of course. "Never mind," she said. "Maybe you should just think of England."

"Okay." He thought. "We're in England, in Trafalgar Square, and—oh, my God! I'm on top of you!"

Naturally.

He opened the dorm door, stepping aside to let her go first. "Now, we're walking through Piccadilly Circus, we're looking at the statue, and—oh, my God!"

Was he hilarious—or was he just a pain?

"Oh, no, *not* Westminster Abbey," he said sadly. "Right there, in the middle of the Sanctuary? That's just *wrong*."

"Please stop thinking of England," she said.

He grinned and walked her out to her car in a very gentlemanly way, keeping a couple of feet between them. It was quite a caravan, since so many of her regular agents were also going back to Washington, and there were also still some state and local police officers around, who had been handling extra protective-duty details since Wednesday.

"I'm thinking of playing baseball, in *England*," Jack said.

The agents and officers nearby who heard this looked baffled, but Meg laughed.

He shook her—left—hand in a dignified way, although his fingers stroked her palm so expertly that it made her shiver a little.

"Be careful," he said.

Yeah. She nodded, and returned the hand caress as subtly as possible. "You, too."

SECURITY AT THE airport seemed to be much higher than it needed to be, and she was wondering whether there might have been a new spate of threats when she recognized a couple of her father's agents standing around on the tarmac near a C-20 with "United States of America" markings.

For a second, she was offended that her parents didn't think she was strong enough to travel alone, but then again, maybe he was just *worried* about her.

Maybe he missed her, too.

She said hello to his agents, then made her way up—it was only about ten steps, but her knee was throbbing terribly and she was unsteady on her cane—into the small jet. One of the pilots was drinking a cup of coffee just outside the cockpit, and she scanned his rank and name tag—right before her mother took office, she and her brothers had spent a few hours with Preston studying military ranks and decorations for all of the branches of service, so that the three of them would be able to greet people properly and respectfully. It had been very discouraging when Steven and Neal instantly memorized even the most obscure details—while she had had to go over them repeatedly, and even use flash cards, before she stopped making embarrassing mistakes.

"Hello, Colonel Jefferson," she said.

He smiled. "Good afternoon, Miss Powers. Happy to have you aboard."

Her father was sitting in the private executive compartment, looking tense. He came out to give her a hug, clearly so happy to see her that she decided not to make any cranky remarks about overprotectiveness or anything of that nature.

Yet.

The stewards must have been given a comprehensive briefing, because the small sofa across the table from the two executive chairs had been set up with extra pillows and a wide, well-padded leg rest. The plane was only designed to hold twelve to fourteen passengers, at the most, so only Garth came aboard after her, taking a seat in the main cabin with a group of her father's agents, Barton, who was one of his personal aides, and Anthony, the new press secretary. The rest of her detail was going to be stuck traveling on a much less comfortable military plane, she assumed. Or else, flying commercial.

"A little clingy of me to show up?" her father asked.

More than a little. Meg grinned, in lieu of expressing her actual opinion.

His hug was gentle, but heartfelt, as though he really *needed* to see her in one piece.

"Are you as tired as you look?" he asked.

She nodded.

He hugged her more tightly. "But, you're okay?"

She nodded again.

"All right. Thank God for that." He kissed the top of her head, and then helped her onto the sofa.

It felt great to take her weight off her knee, and even though she wasn't cold, she didn't argue when he draped a small fleece blanket over her lap, and then got the steward on duty to bring her a Coke—to go along with the cheese, crackers, fruit, and cookies already set out on the small table.

Although if it weren't going to be such a relatively short flight, she might have given some serious consideration to taking a nap.

Her father looked worn out, too, and it occurred to her that she might have a pretty good idea why.

"Did you go to Nebraska?" she asked, once they were up in the air.

"No, my former chief of staff dissuaded me," he said, after a very long pause.

Indicating that his wife had not been able to do so effectively. "What did Mom think?" she asked.

"It really wasn't her call, Meg," he said, clenching his jaw.

Terrific. Just terrific. The wretched status quo continued at 1600 Pennsylvania Avenue, apparently. She might, just possibly, need to duck down and cover her head with her fleece blanket at any moment.

Then, her father sighed. "I think both of us would have given a great deal to be able to fly out there and give those punks absolute hell. But, at least Gabler says that his people and the FBI are putting the fear of God into them."

As well they should. She had no use for the FBI—but, giving credit where credit was due, they had done a decent job this time. Her stomach was starting to hurt, and she was surprised to find herself having trouble swallowing, so she put down the glass of Coke. "Have they figured out why three tenth graders hate me that much?"

Her father reached across the table to touch her arm. "I don't think they hate you, Meg. I suspect they weren't responding to anything more than your being someone they've seen on television."

Lots of people were on television, and didn't necessarily end up receiving bomb threats from fifteen-year-old boys in the Midwest.

"Meg," he started.

"I really don't want to talk about it," she said, "okay, Dad?"

He looked at her for a second, nodded, and then gave her arm a small squeeze before withdrawing.

During the rest of the flight, she sipped Coke, and told him that no, her knee wasn't too bad, yes, she'd been eating, yes, she was glad her midterms were over, and that sort of thing.

"I'm very sorry about the whole situation with Susan," he said.

Well, it was about time that the elephant crammed into the compartment with them got some attention. "Your former chief of staff tried *really* hard to take the fall," she said.

Her father nodded. "I know. And I truly am sorry that your friend got caught up in all of this."

"Susan and I aren't really friends," Meg said, "but, yeah, it screwed things up for her."

"Didn't do you much good, either," her father said.

Nope.

He looked at her for a minute. "And I apologize for making it seem as though we were all doing something behind your back."

Except that that's exactly what they *had* done.

"Meg?" he asked, when she didn't say anything.

She sighed. "It made me look like a helpless, incompetent, arrogant jerk." And, of course, a self-obsessed asshole.

"All of which is the last thing I *think*," he said.

Maybe. "Next time," she said, "if it involves me, I should be part of the decision."

Her father nodded.

But she definitely didn't want to spend her entire spring break fighting with him. Besides, fair was fair. "Although if you had," she said, "I might have just shrugged and said, 'yeah, whatever,' and not really listened." Which was how she had reacted to most of the many details revolving around the misbegotten decision to go away to school.

"Even so," he said.

Yeah.

But the compartment still seemed too small, and she was glad to see Anthony appear in the doorway with a couple of questions and updates for him, since they were going to land soon.

She had only met the guy a couple of times—he had been a deputy press aide over at State before coming over to work for her father, but based upon the way the two of them were interacting, as well as the efficient phone conversation she'd had with him after Ginette had gone back to Washington, he seemed to have been a smart choice for the job. Pretty *young*, and with a sense of humor that veered on the edge of being goofy, but he carried himself confidently, and so far, he didn't seem like the familiar Washingtonian type who went out of his way to curry favor, at the expense of competence.

Although he was a lot taller than she remembered—downright strapping, even—and since her father wasn't exactly tiny himself, it felt a little bit like being crammed into a football locker-room. Especially when Garth, and Ryan, the head of her father's detail, came in to go over a few logistical details, too.

Did her mother ever get tired of being surrounded? Yeah, there were a lot of women on the staff, but it was still a predominantly male atmosphere. But at this stage of her life, her mother might not even be aware of it anymore, although Meg had noticed that, while always elegant and dignified, she sometimes wore rather aggressive colors, especially on various world platforms, where there was inevitably a splash of red or bright blue or yellow in the midst of a row of dull grey suits, as though the President—who was not without vanity—wanted to make *very sure* that the focus of people's attention was precisely where she wanted it to be. There had actually been three female world leaders at a major summit meeting the previous year, and while watching a press availability, Meg had been left with the impression that, in a friendly sort of way, they were all making a strong effort to out-chic one another—and that her mother had won by a landslide.

"Are you really as exhausted as you look?" her father asked, once everyone else had stepped out and the two of them were alone again.

Which made her wonder exactly how exhausted she looked. "Rough week," she said. A rough *six* weeks.

Once they landed at Andrews, it felt like taking another midterm, as she had to greet—in rapid succession—the base commander, a first lieutenant, a senior airman, a technical sergeant, an airman first class, a master sergeant, a captain, another senior airman, a lieutenant colonel, a few more airmen, and a full colonel. And she almost got faked out by a Navy commander who ended up in the mix somehow.

"What?" she asked, aware that her father was smiling as they got into their car.

He shook his head. "You three are very cute when you do that. You're so *scrupulous.*"

She immediately flashed on Neal, during a campaign stop, saying, happily, "Hi there, Sailor!" —to a two-star Army general. Then, when he was gently corrected by someone, he snapped off a damn-near perfect salute, and said, "Hi there, Major General! Airborne, sir!" They had been at Fort Bragg at the time, and when everyone unsurprisingly cheered, she heard Linda mutter, "The walking vote machine strikes again," to one of her aides.

And when they pulled up in front of the South Portico, the walking vote machine himself was sitting on a black wrought iron bench near the stairs, throwing a tennis ball for Kirby to fetch while he waited for them. It was a little dislocating to see Maureen there with him, instead of Preston. Naturally, there were also plenty of agents, Marine guards, and White House staff people around, as well as some reporters and what appeared to be a few civilians waiting behind a rope line.

"Please don't help me out," she said in a low voice to her father, as he extended his hand. "I don't want them to photograph me that way."

He nodded, and she took a deep breath to force herself to concentrate on suppressing any pain grimaces, and then got out of the car, making a conscious point of smiling in the direction of the cameras.

Neal ran over to hug her, forceful enough to knock her off-balance. "Hi, Meggie!"

It was *good* to see him. Good to see Kirby. And even good to see the damn White House, and all that that involved. Kirby's greeting was equally rambunctious, and she had to lean extra-hard on her cane to keep from toppling over.

Which was going to look awful, on film.

She wanted to fall back on the dismissive wave-and-duck-inside strategy, and she knew her father would have preferred that she do just that, but they were already asking questions, and if she *didn't* pause, they might read too much into it.

So, she gave a few dull "yes, it's great to be home" responses, nodding slightly at Hannah Goldman, who was standing at the outskirts of the crowd. Maureen was right behind her the whole time, but didn't interfere otherwise, because they didn't know each other very well, and she was probably trying to read her body language and figure out whether to help her out—or keep her distance.

"What can you tell us about the threats you received this week?" someone asked.

Hannah looked very alert, and she felt Maureen's posture stiffen slightly.

She and her father maybe should have practiced for that one, on the plane. "I don't know," she said, and shrugged. "I was pretty busy with midterms, so the entire Eastern seaboard could have been consumed by locusts, and I probably wouldn't have heard about it."

Some of them laughed; some of them—including Hannah—heard her non-denial.

"Is it true?" Meg asked, and glanced towards the perfect green of the South Lawn. "About the locusts?"

A few more people laughed.

"How about your new boyfriend?" someone else asked.

Christ, she hadn't even really told her *parents* about Jack yet, beyond mentioning that a guy in her psychology class seemed to be kind of nice. "Which one?" she asked. "I have to keep checking the tabloids to get their names straight." Then she smiled, gave them a nod, and limped towards the entrance.

Her father had handed Neal her computer to carry, and she closed her eyes, knowing quite well that he was going to be uncoordinated enough to bang it into the side of the door as they went inside the Diplomatic Reception Room—which he promptly did.

"Why don't we head upstairs, and you can take it easy for a while," her father suggested, once they were in the Ground Floor Corridor.

God, that sounded good, especially knowing that Vanessa was up there. "I should probably, you know, go say hi, first," Meg said, and gestured towards the West Wing.

She was afraid he might argue, but he just nodded.

"We'll see you in a few minutes, then," he said.

She watched, as Neal banged her laptop into the side of the elevator as they got on. He would probably smash it two or three more times before getting to her room.

"The case looks pretty well-padded," Maureen said.

Meg nodded, although she had visions of her hard drive being utterly jumbled the next time she turned it on.

One of the military nurses, whose name she couldn't remember, had come out of the Medical Office area, and since she *really* didn't feel like having another god-damn checkup, Meg smiled pleasantly, but shook her head, and the nurse went back into the office.

"We haven't really talked about it yet," Maureen said, "but I think you prefer to be left alone to deal with the press, and not have anyone step in, unless you can't avoid it?"

Very much so. Meg nodded, and Maureen nodded back, and withdrew as discreetly as the nurse had.

As she made her slow way down towards the West Wing and out onto the colonnade, people seemed pleased—even ecstatic—to see her, and while she didn't have the energy to be effusive in return, she made a point of being cheerful and responsive, complimenting the two gardeners she passed about how beautiful the flowers looked, and that sort of thing.

Christ, when was the last time she'd been in the Oval Office? Jesus, *months*. Almost a year. The same way Neal always went straight to her father's East Wing office, and then over to see their mother when he got home from school every day, she had also usually made a habit of stopping by both places, if her parents were around, when she was on her way out to play tennis.

In fact, she now distinctly remembered walking—damn, *walking*—in there the day before she got kidnapped, lugging her tennis bag, before going out and—lucky for her—winning what had turned out to be the last match she was ever going to play.

She let Garth open one of the doors just off the Rose Garden, so she could give her full attention to negotiating the small steps leading up to it, and the various secretaries and aides in the outer office—as well as the Director of the OMB, who was either on his way into, or out of, a meeting with the President, and a policy undersecretary she recognized from C-Span—all looked over and smiled at her. She only knew some of them, but it was comforting to see Mrs. Berger, who had been her mother's personal secretary since she was first elected to the Senate—and so, had known her since she was about five.

"Welcome home, Meg," Mrs. Berger said, and stood up to give her a hug. "It's wonderful to see you."

Meg nodded, giving her a stiff, incompetent, one-armed hug in return. "Thank you. You, too." For some reason, she suddenly felt very nervous, and she clenched her hand around her cane. "I, um, I guess I haven't been over here—for a pretty long time."

"Well, we've missed you," Mrs. Berger said.

"Thank you." Meg glanced around the room, trying to put the image of herself, cocky and cheerful in tennis clothes, out of her mind. Back when she could still swagger. When her hands didn't shake. When she wasn't uneasy about the prospect of saying hello to her own mother on a sunny March afternoon. "Um, how busy is she?"

Mrs. Berger glanced automatically at the appointment schedule on the desk. "I'm sure they're winding down. You can go right in, Meg."

Meg hesitated. That meant that she was still in a meeting, and the idea of interrupting was—

Mrs. Berger winked at her. "She's been waiting for hours. If you value my job security, you'll go in there."

Okay, that must mean that her mother *wanted* to see her right away, no matter what else she was doing. She swallowed, nodded, and then moved forward as a military aide held one of the doors leading into the Oval Office for her.

Her mother looked up from her desk, where she was sitting with her arms folded and frowning slightly at Senator Malone, the Majority Leader, and a huge smile spread across her face. She was across the room in about two seconds, hugging her before Meg even had a chance to say hello.

"I am *not* that thin," Meg said against her shoulder.

"Actually, you are," her mother whispered back, "but we don't have to argue about it right now."

Shades of the old days, maybe, when bickering had kind of been a way of life for them. And, all things considered, her mother was pretty damn thin, too—and really didn't have much right to criticize.

Senator Malone came over to shake her hand—her right hand—and Meg leaned her cane against the back of the couch, then patted his forearm and moved to shake his left hand, instead.

"Oh. Of course," he said, and shook her left hand smoothly.

They exchanged pleasantries, and it was all very civil, even though she knew—and he *knew* that she knew—that he and her mother were not exactly the best of friends, and, in fact, could legitimately be described as bitter adversaries.

Regardless, it was obvious that his meeting with the President was over now, and after another minute or two, he politely excused himself.

"That was nice," her mother said, when he was gone. "You were reassuring and confident, without being provocative." She pantomimed the hand motions for herself, and nodded. "Very nice, indeed."

Meg shrugged. It wasn't as though she'd had the option of avoiding figuring out some sort of strategy for herself. "A lot of people seem to want to shake my hand these days."

"Well, it's good," her mother said. "Keep it in the repertoire."

Meg wasn't sure whether to laugh—or to be frustrated by the degree to which her mother was so unerringly pragmatic when she was in Presidential Mode.

Her mother's personal aide, Frank, glanced into the room, and her mother shook her head firmly. He nodded, stayed in the outer office, and closed the door.

"I'm sorry I wrecked your meeting," Meg said.

"You saved us," her mother said. "He didn't particularly want to be here, any more than I *wanted* him to be here."

Old news. She and Senator Malone had been knocking heads for about fifteen years now. Which had probably been less stressful back when he was the *Minority* Leader.

Her mother hugged her again, much harder. "I'm so glad you're home. Are you okay?"

Meg nodded.

"How about the knee?" her mother asked.

Her knee *sucked.* "It hurts a little," Meg said.

Her mother looked worried and indicated the nearest couch.

She did feel like sitting down, but it would be too hard to relax, knowing how many people were outside the various doors—maybe even staring through the peepholes at this very moment—waiting to see the President. "Do you have a lot going on this afternoon?" Meg asked.

"Ask me if I care," her mother said.

Okay, but personally, Meg didn't want to be the *reason* that the ship of state ran asunder. "Yeah, but I kind of want to go see Vanessa, too."

Her mother's eyebrows went up. "You came here first?"

Meg nodded.

Her mother looked very pleased in a shy sort of way, and then she grinned. "But, you had a little internal debate about it, right?"

Yep.

Her mother hugged her again, even more tightly. "I really am glad you're here."

She was kind of glad herself.

34

SHE ENDED UP leaving through the side door, and cutting through the private study and dining room, nodding hello to the Navy steward and cook on duty in the tiny kitchen as she passed them.

Her mother's chief of staff was striding down the hall from his office, but he stopped when he saw her.

"She must be in a better mood now," he said.

Glen was such a driven, workaholic guy that he was inclined to forget normal social graces. "Hi, Meg," she said. "Welcome home! You look *great.*"

He frowned. "You actually look really tired, and like you lost about ten pounds, and she's going to be worried as hell, and she won't be able to focus for the rest of the day."

As far as she knew, Glen never even bothered putting the cap on the bottle of liquid antacid he always kept on his desk. "School's just super," Meg said. "Thank you for asking. I'm *really*, really popular, and things couldn't be going better."

She had known Glen for a long time, but she was pretty sure that she had never made him laugh before—and she didn't manage it this time, either.

"Do you know what it's like around here when the President's head isn't in the game?" he asked. "How hard it is to get anything done?"

Which still shouldn't preclude his being able to say hello like a regular human being. "Is all that stuff I read in *The Post* this morning true?" she asked. "About the power-hungry cabal here in the West Wing and over in the OEOB trying to oust you?"

That had him going for a couple of seconds, but then he just shook his head. "I'll go see if I can get her back on track."

Typical. The surprise was not that Glen was currently in the process of getting divorced—but that he'd ever taken the time to get married in the first place.

He started down the hall, then paused. "Does it hurt?"

Everything hurt. "Does *what* hurt?" she asked.

He pointed at her immobilizing brace.

"Oh," she said, "you mean, the knee I blew out on national television while I was busy swearing at everyone, and driving her approval rating into the ground?"

He nodded.

"Yeah," she said. "It does."

"I'm sorry about that," he said, gruffly, and then continued on his way.

She wanted to go find her cat, but while she was over here, it would be stupid not to stop by and visit the director of communications.

He was on the telephone in his brand-new corner office on the second floor, surrounded by unpacked boxes, taking notes on a legal pad while he squinted at the three televisions across the room, two of them tuned to cable news stations, the third showing the White House closed-circuit feed. He saw her, and held up one finger to indicate that he needed to finish the call.

She sat down in his desk chair to wait, propping her leg up on one of the boxes. There was a large framed photo on his desk, next to a hammer and a picture hangar. She had never seen it before, but Preston looked about sixteen—tall, unbelievably lanky in a tight black turtleneck, his hair much longer than it had ever been during the time that she had known him, wearing a leather cap tilted to one side, shadowing part of his face. He was clearly in his family's kitchen, because his mother and all four of his sisters were either sitting at the table with him, or standing nearby, with brothers-in-law and nieces and nephews and cousins crowded around, too. It was probably either Thanksgiving or Christmas, because there were pans and casserole dishes and half-full platters on every spare space, and they all looked happy—and somewhat sleepy.

"Like that little slice of Americana?" he asked.

Meg grinned. "Look at you, Mr. Hip." A veritable beatnik, decades after it was in fashion.

Preston looked sheepish. "I think I read Kerouac and Malcolm X that year."

And had retained a great deal, it would seem. But now, here he was, in his crisp grey suit, in his West Wing office, juggling national policy and reporting directly to the President of the United States. "Beatrice Fielding's little boy has come a long way," she said.

Preston laughed. "That was her precise reaction."

Seemed like a reasonable response.

"How is it?" he asked, indicating the brace.

She just shook her head, although if she were by herself, she might burst into tears.

"I'm sorry," he said, and rested a light hand on her shoulder for a second. Then, he picked up the hammer, and carefully pounded the picture hangar into place on a blank space of wall. "You know, a funny thing happened. A few days ago, the President took a last-minute jaunt, which involved a stopover in Philadelphia, and unexpectedly had a visitor fly back with her, and even set up a little formal ceremony downstairs."

Preston was from Philadelphia, originally. "That was nice of her," Meg said.

Preston nodded. "Of course, later on, Mom ended up marching right out to the Metro and taking it to Union Station. I couldn't even get her into a cab, forget the plane ticket and car to the airport they'd set up for her."

A formidable woman, indeed.

Preston looked at her. "It *mattered*, though. In case it comes up in conversation."

"You know it won't," Meg said. And even if it did, her mother would instantly change the subject, or maybe even leave the room.

Preston nodded again. "I know. I guess I just wanted to be sure that *you* knew."

Duly noted.

He hung the photograph, and then stepped back to check its position. He frowned, straightened one side, checked again, and pushed it back to where it had been originally. "What do you think?"

Was he being so boyishly proud in front of everyone, or had she caught him at a weak moment? "Looks great," she said.

WHEN SHE FINALLY made it up to the family quarters, her father and Neal were nowhere in sight, but there seemed to be more noise than usual coming from the second-floor kitchen—which was unusual in the ever-silent White House. Some pot-banging and the like, which reminded her of the way the kitchen would sound when she came home from school back in Chestnut Hill.

She sometimes felt shy about interrupting the Cast of Thousands—since they were all far too eager to wait on her—but she peeked in, and saw Trudy, slamming cheerfully away at the stove, while Neal sat at the table with a plate of cookies and a large glass of milk.

"Hey, wow, you didn't tell me you were coming," Meg said.

Trudy turned, and beamed. "Well, look at you," she said, and came over to hug her.

"Was this a surprise for me?" Meg asked.

"Yes," Trudy said. "Are you surprised?"

Very pleasantly. Meg nodded.

Trudy looked her over with a critical frown. "Katharine's right—you're not eating at all up there, are you?"

It was impossible to lie to Trudy. "Mostly, I'm too tired," Meg said. "And other times, it feels like too many people are watching me."

"Well, then, we'll have to make up for that while you're home," Trudy said, and guided her over to the table.

Vanessa must have heard her voice, because she ambled in, sat several feet away, and stared at her with unblinking yellow eyes.

Two could play at that game. Instead of snapping her fingers and trying to coax her to come over, Meg just ate a cookie and ignored her completely.

Vanessa reacted with nearly audible outrage, and then, with some combination of resignation and great dudgeon, jumped up onto her lap and stuck a paw in her glass of milk.

"It's going to be gross if you drink that anyway," Neal said.

Then, he should prepare to be grossed out.

She was about to go down to her room and rest before dinner when Steven showed up, home from baseball practice, still wearing dirt- and grass-stained sweatpants, turf shoes, and a very old and beat-up red compression jersey.

"Hey," he said, briefly, when he saw her.

She waited for more, then realized that that was all she was going to get from him. "Hi," she said, just as briefly.

Trudy was frowning at him, and he paused on his way to the refrigerator.

"Uh, when you get back?" he asked.

Jesus, was that really the best he could do? "While ago," she said.

He nodded, and started filling his shoulder wrap bag with ice-packs. None of them had ever been completely sure whether he did that after pitching as a precaution, because he thought it was figuratively—and literally—cool, or because his arm hurt like hell. She and her parents suspected the latter, but he always vociferously denied it.

"Is your arm bothering you, Steven?" Trudy asked, her voice casual.

So, she must be suspicious, too.

He shook his head. "Nope. Just, you know, being careful." He used the Velcro straps to fasten the wrap in place, grabbed a couple of cookies, and headed for the door. "Later."

Okay. She wasn't going to take it personally.

Much.

"I think he's just tired, Meg," Trudy said. "And that his arm *does* hurt."

Yeah. Whatever. Meg sat for another minute, and then reached for her cane. "What time is dinner?"

"I'm planning for seven-thirty," Trudy said.

"Okay." She hoisted herself up, much to Vanessa's disgust. "I'm going to go take it easy for a while, then."

Trudy was maybe going to say something else, but she nodded, instead, and Meg limped out to the hall. Steven's door was firmly closed, and she made a point of shutting hers, too. *Firmly.*

Naturally, the minute she stretched out on her bed, she fell asleep, and her father had to come in and wake her up for supper. At first, she didn't recognize where she was, but then, when she figured out that it was her real room, and not her dorm room, she wasn't sure whether she was happy about that—or disappointed.

"Would you rather have a tray?" her father asked.

What, and live up to Steven's low expectations? She shook her head, and forced herself to sit up. "No, thanks. I'll be right there."

By the time she'd gulped some ibuprofen, washed her face, brushed her hair, and made it down to the dining room, everyone else was already at the table, and her brothers had started eating without her.

She wasn't even remotely hungry, but she told Trudy how good everything looked, and made an effort to appear to be eating heartily.

Trudy had just come back from a visit to Massachusetts, where she had seen a number of people they knew, and her parents asked questions about this and that, while Neal talked about how *fun* it would be if they could spend a bunch of time up there during the summer—and Steven plowed through about three helpings of everything, his conversational gambits erring on the side of being short, and mostly monosyllabic. And, of course, her mother left the room several times to take phone calls or speak to one of her seniors aides out in the West Sitting Hall.

For her part, she tried to walk the line between being agreeable—and unobtrusive. But then, about halfway through the meal, she felt so exhausted that she was afraid she might have to go down to her room and straight to bed for the rest of the night. And the thought of *not* being able to do so, without everyone getting overly concerned, was enough to set off a jolt of wild panic inside.

Her mother and Steven picked up on it almost instantly—and she could see them both go rigid in a "God, nothing's changed, and we're right back to where we were" way. Her father, Neal, and Trudy picked up on *that*, and then, the conversation which had been flowing along fairly easily slowed down—and ultimately stopped dead.

"Long day," her mother said.

God, yes. Meg nodded, trying to breathe through the dizzy spell which had predictably come to join the panic. Nausea would be next. "Is it okay if I—" Except that if she fled—limped—to her room, it was only going to confirm their worst suspicions. Reignite the family malaise. Make her, once again, the agent of their collective destruction.

Felix was coming in with more mashed potatoes, and she caught his eye.

"Could I please have a cup of coffee?" she asked.

He was back in less than a minute, pausing to refill her parents' cups on his tactful way out of the room.

"*You* don't like coffee," Neal said, accusingly.

The hell she didn't. Meg added more sugar than usual for the extra energy burst. "I do now."

It was very quiet, and she could tell that they were all busily overanalyzing the possible implications of that remark.

"Well, there's the sure sign of a college student," Trudy said, with a smile.

Which changed the atmosphere in the room, and she could almost literally see everyone else's brains process the concept of her as a *college student*, as opposed to a traumatized, housebound cripple, and calm down somewhat in response.

The conversation kicked back into—balky—gear again, with Neal carrying most of the load, as he asked her if she stayed up all night, every night; whether she had a whole bunch of new friends; and if she got to eat whatever she wanted, whenever she wanted. She had to fib, a little, with each of her answers, but none of them seemed to raise any red flags until she said that the food was *great*, and she saw her mother and Trudy exchange glances.

She managed to make it through the rest of the meal without falling apart—drinking two more cups of coffee along the way—and then, Trudy went into the kitchen to order the stewards to let her help clean up, her mother was on her way back downstairs because of the usual flurry of emergencies, large and small, and, since it was dark now and he wouldn't be bothered by anyone, her father took Kirby outside to walk around the South Lawn. Steven had disappeared right after dessert, but she didn't know where he had gone. Or why.

She also wasn't sure if she cared, at the moment.

"Will you watch a movie with me?" Neal asked.

She really just wanted to sleep, but she could tell that he was eager to have her join him—and expecting to be turned down. "Does it have soldiers in it?"

He looked perplexed. "You mean, they *make* movies without soldiers?"

Christ, what a one-track mind. But then, she saw him grinning. Okay. Maybe he was on the verge of becoming just as snarky as she and Steven had always been inclined to be. "All right, smart guy," she said. "Find a movie without any guns, and I'll be right up."

While he raced off, she went down to her room and splashed cold water on her face, since she was still so tired that if she got onto her bed, she knew she wouldn't even have enough energy to drag herself underneath the covers before she fell asleep again.

When she got up to the Solarium, she found him in there alone, perched on the couch, waiting for her with great anticipation.

"Dad and Steven aren't going to watch with us?" she asked.

Neal shrugged. "I think maybe Dad's going to come up in a while."

Which only answered half of her question. She wanted to ask him what the hell Steven's problem was, but he was fooling around with the remote, in an apparent attempt to avoid meeting her eyes.

Swell. It was her first night back, and Steven couldn't be bothered to—just swell. Would it kill him to *pretend* to be happy to see her?

She moved her jaw. "Is he in his room?"

Neal shrugged again. "Maybe. I don't know."

Terrific. "I'll be right back," she said, and motioned towards the little side kitchen, which had a refrigerator and a microwave and everything. "Why don't you make some popcorn and stuff, so we'll be ready to go?"

He nodded, but still wouldn't really look at her.

She found Steven lying on his bed, facing the headboard and bouncing a tennis ball off the wall—an activity guaranteed to make the White House curator, and presidential historians everywhere, blanch.

"Hey," she said.

He nodded, tossing and catching the ball.

"How you doing?" she asked.

He shrugged.

Mr. Communicative. "Neal and I are going to watch a movie," she said. "And we thought you might want to hang out, too."

He shrugged again, throwing the ball.

Mr. Enthusiasm, as well. She waited to see if he was going to say anything, and then sighed. "Well, okay. We'll be upstairs."

He shrugged.

Christ, could he make it any more clear that he liked it better when she was away? It wasn't as though she didn't already know that he hadn't missed her at all.

"Are Mom and Dad going to watch with us, since you're here?" he asked after her.

She paused, off-balance, and had to lean against the wall to catch herself when she didn't get her cane down in time. "What do you mean?"

He threw the ball, *hard*. "Fake like they don't hate each other. You know, so you don't get upset."

It would be a relief if it turned out that he was actually mad at them—and not at her. She made her way back into the room. "They haven't been faking it in front of you and Neal?"

Steven scowled. "They *think* they have. Or else, they think we're way dumber than you, and maybe can't tell the difference."

Her knee hurt, a lot, and she sat down at the bottom of the bed. "You mean, the stuff where they don't look at each other, and she leaves the table too soon, because she suddenly has a bunch of work she conveniently forgot she had to do?"

Steven nodded.

"Or," Meg said, "if you go into their room and she's reading, he's over on the couch, and if *he's* reading, she's at her desk?"

Steven nodded. "If they're both in there in the first place, which, like, they *aren't*, mostly."

Sometimes she wondered if her parents realized what a rapt little audience of three they had, during every waking hour. "That sucks," she said.

He nodded.

"Has Neal noticed?" she asked.

He looked at her with true scorn. "Neal notices *everything*. He only pretends not to, because it makes his stomach hurt."

Oh. Sometimes, Neal was sort of trapped in her mind as being younger than he actually was—and he would be quite justified if he found that insulting. "Is he doing okay?" she asked.

"I don't know, I guess." He threw the ball, and the wall actually shook this time. Somewhere, the head usher was cringing. "He still talks to that lady. Says he likes her."

After—everything, her parents had brought in various therapists for the three of them, although Neal was the only one who had been cooperative. In her case, a series of psychologists and psychiatrists had "stopped by to say hello," mostly while she was still in the hospital, or at physical therapy sessions, but also during and after interviews with the FBI, and twice when she was downstairs having checkups with Dr. Brooks. Each time, she had been disinterested to the point of nearly being impolite. She knew that Steven had been forced to go to at least one appointment, with three different psychologists so far, but had hated every second.

"What do you think they talk about?" she asked.

Steven snagged the ball one-handed, and then looked over at her. "You really asking, or you trying to figure out what *I* would maybe be talking about?"

Too often, Steven was so busy acting like a jock—or a jerk—that he didn't get enough credit for being unusually intelligent. "Both, I guess," Meg said. "Are you still going?"

He made a face. "I said, no way, but they say it seems like I'm maybe, you know, depressed, and that I have to go for a while, so it really sucks. I mean, *you* don't have to, and it *happened* to you. It's totally not fair."

Her parents weren't happy about her refusal to participate in any form of mental health rehabilitation, but the difference was, that she could get away with saying no—and Steven couldn't. "No, it isn't," she said. "But at least I abuse Beth and Preston's goodwill by talking to them a lot about stuff."

Steven shrugged and threw his ball.

"Steven, you don't even talk to me anymore," Meg said. Despite the fact that, for most of their lives, they had been nearly inseparable. "So, I kind of figure you're not saying much to Vinnie or Jim or anyone, either."

"We're not *supposed* to talk to you," Steven said, "because you might get upset, and like, cry or something."

And now, yet again, they found themselves mired on that hellish good intentions road. Meg shook her head. "You can always talk to me, about anything you want. And even if I got upset, what's the big deal? We *should* be upset, so we might as well quit acting like we aren't."

Steven shrugged, not looking at her.

Great. Half the time, it almost felt as though, privately, they all hated her for having had—bad luck. Like it was her damn fault or something. "I didn't do anything wrong," Meg said stiffly. "And I'm getting really tired of you—I don't know—*blaming* me for it. I'm sorry I got kidnapped, okay? I'm sorry I ended up crippled. I'm sorry it's been *inconvenient* for you, all right?"

Steven threw the ball so hard that it bounced all the way out into the room and crashed against his dresser.

Meg got up. "Fine. Just—do what you want. If you want to hate me, go right ahead. And—go to hell, while you're at it."

"You want to know what I think?" he asked, as she limped towards his door. "What I think is, fuck you for almost getting killed."

What? Like that was fair? She resisted the urge to slug him with her cane. Aim for his pitching arm, maybe, and see how he liked it. "Yeah, well, fuck you for being *mad* at me for almost getting killed."

She was furious, and he was probably even more pissed off and they stared at each other, but then, suddenly, they both laughed.

"Please pretend you're happy to see me, okay?" she asked. "And come up and watch a movie with us."

Steven nodded, but stayed on his bed, his shoulders slumping.

"Come on," she said.

He shrugged.

Talk about one step forward and two steps back. "What?" she asked.

He looked at her unhappily. "They almost got you again this week."

It hadn't even crossed her mind that he might know about the latest spate of threats—and maybe be obsessing about them. "I didn't know they told you guys about that," she said.

"Well, yeah," he said, looking at her as though she had an IQ of about twelve. "I mean, we suddenly have a whole bunch more agents with us, and we're not supposed to think something's going on? And Mom and Dad were all flippo, and we had to come home right after school, even though I had practice."

Was he mad that he'd had to miss practice, or had he been worried about her? "It was just some guys your age screwing around," she said. "It wasn't any big deal."

Steven scowled. "Turned *out* that way, that's all. It might not have."

Yeah, but there wasn't a single god-damn thing in the world she could do about that, one way or the other.

"Next time, it might be real," he said.

And the time after that, and the time after that, and the time after *that*. So, what else was new? "Yeah," she said. "Come up and watch a movie, anyway."

She thought he was going to get mad again, but he just sighed and stood up.

"It better not be the damn *Sound of Music*," he said.

What an excellent idea; she should have thought of it herself. "It will *definitely* be *The Sound of Music*," she said.

He groaned, but followed her out to the elevator, anyway.

THE MOVIE NEAL picked out was supposed to be a comedy, but mainly, it was profane and scatological. Her brothers *loved* it. Her father and Trudy both came up at different points, were disgusted, and left after about ten minutes of puerility each.

When the movie ended, Trudy appeared again to haul Neal downstairs to get ready for bed, and to warn Steven that he could only stay up for another hour and a half.

"I'm going to watch *The Sound of Music* now," Meg said, when Neal started complaining that it wasn't fair that he had to go to bed so soon.

"Yuck," he said, and followed Trudy without any further argument.

"How many times you seen this movie?" Steven asked, as it started.

A couple of hundred, maybe? "Not nearly enough times," she said.

He laughed, and went into the little kitchen to fix some more popcorn, also bringing back a Coke for her and some orange juice for himself.

While Maria was running into the abbey at top speed, disgracefully late for evening prayer or vespers or whatever it was that she had been missing while cavorting in the Alps, Meg glanced over at him.

"How's baseball?" she asked.

"Okay." He drank some orange juice. "We're kind of not as good as I thought we'd be."

Steven had won his first start, but they'd gotten blown out in their other scrimmage—by a notoriously weak team. She was pretty sure his ERA was in the 1.30 range—although if she asked, he'd be mad that she hadn't committed the exact number to memory. "Are they being okay about you playing?" she asked.

Steven shook his head. "They're all uptight and stuff. Like someone's going to show up and grab me right off the ballfield, or something. I mean, they might, you know, *shoot* me, but they might do that any time, so why's baseball any worse?"

Because, more often than not, he was standing out there all by himself on the mound, a perfect target. The Secret Service hated having to try and protect a large open field, especially at away games, where, no matter how much advance work they did, they just weren't as familiar with the surrounding area.

"I mean, you were coming home from school," he said. "And Mom was just, you know, going to some dumb speech. If something bad's going to happen, anyway, I'd way rather be playing ball and having fun and stuff, you know?"

Made sense to her. But, it still sucked beyond belief that a ninth grader had to spend time worrying about whether a maniac was going to kill him someday, just to make a political point.

"Dad says he's coming to all my games," Steven said, "and he was maybe going to come to the practices, too, but that was getting—it was screwing me up at the plate and all."

Meg nodded. They were so used to their parents *not* being able to show up for things regularly, that it seemed kind of unfamiliar when one of them did.

Steven glanced over at her tentatively. "I'm supposed to think he just wants to see me play. But he's figuring that like, if he's there, they'll decide to shoot *him*, instead of me."

Yes, that was the way her father's mind would be working. For that matter, it was also probably exactly how hate-crazed terrorists would react, if confronted with the situation. Knocking off the First Gentleman would be far more of a thrill than going after his son.

Steven looked guilty. "So, if something bad happens to him, it's going to be my fault."

Meg shook her head. "No way. If something bad happens, it'll be *their* fault. The terrorists, I mean—not Mom and Dad." Which maybe wasn't terribly helpful. "I mean, nothing's going to happen, but, at least if he comes, he gets to feel like he can protect you a little, and you get to have him at your games, so that's good."

"I guess," Steven said, without much conviction.

They were getting along so well that she hated to start trouble, but— "Do you, um, tell any of this stuff to the person they're having you talk to?" she asked.

Steven shook his head. "Hell, no. But, the guy they found this time, like, works with baseball players, when they're in slumps and everything. *Real* baseball players, I mean. You know, with visualization, and all."

Her parents were not fools; a professional sports psychologist was a clever choice. "That's cool," Meg said. "Has he ever done anything for the Red Sox?"

Steven nodded with actual enthusiasm. "Yeah. Even though he's not allowed to tell me their names or anything. Mostly, I guess, he hangs out near here, but he travels around, too. Like, at spring training, and during the off-season. I don't talk to him, you know, about our *family*, but the sports stuff is excellent." He grinned at her. "I might still be, you know, *sad*, but I swear I'm locating the ball better."

Well, okay, as long as he had his priorities straight. Meg grinned back at him.

"Do we *really* have to watch this stupid movie?" he asked.

"Yes," she said. "We do."

35

THE PLAN WAS for her to check into the hospital after lunch on Sunday, and have her operation first thing Monday morning. Or, operations, if they decided to do some more work on her hand. So, she was either going to feel terrible when the anesthesia wore off—or *really* terrible.

To her amazement, Neal and her parents, and Trudy, went off, bright and early, to mass at St. John's Church, across Lafayette Park, without even having brunch, first. She had assumed that they were only doing it to make Trudy happy—or, possibly, that the President was trying to play up her spiritual bona fides in an attempt to soothe the rarely-dormant uneasiness of a fairly large percentage of the voting public, but it turned out that about a month earlier, Neal had asked them if bad things would stop happening, if they started going more often. According to Steven—who had outright refused to participate in any form of religious exploration whatsoever—neither of her parents had had a satisfactory answer to that question, but had told Neal that the three of them could go together, whenever he wanted, presumably hoping that familiarity with the concept of God might, in this case, breed *less* contempt.

Not bloody likely, was Meg's feeling, but she was sensible enough to keep this opinion to herself.

After they were gone, she stayed in bed, watching the Sunday political shows, and napping on and off. Beth had called the night before, to wish her luck, and she was pleased—and slightly discomfitted—when Jack called, too. She was very drowsy, from having taken a pain pill, so the conversation was pretty short, but she hadn't really expected him to call at all during their break—and in this particular case, it was pleasant to be wrong.

She and her parents rode over to Bethesda on Marine One and transferred to a small motorcade for the ridiculously short trip from the helipad to the main entrance. There was a wheelchair waiting for her inside, along with the rear admiral who was the hospital commander, the deputy commander, and master chief commander; a bunch of doctors, nurses, and corpsmen—most of whom were in full uniform, except for a couple of the civilian surgeons; a good-sized group of agents and aides and assistants and advisors; and the White House press pool, complete with television cameras and boom mikes.

"Damn it, Kate," her father said in a low voice.

Her mother sighed. "Russ, she's so quotable that *I* want to interview her, too." She glanced at Meg. "By the way, start being a little less quotable, okay?"

Christ, were they all going to have a big fight on live television? "Don't you think that's going to backfire, and only make me want to be *more* quotable?" Meg asked.

Her mother frowned. "Yes, you make a good point."

"And I'm not riding in the wheelchair, either," Meg said.

She was sure they wanted to argue about that, too, but the hospital commander was coming over with a large entourage, and they all ended up clustered in the middle of the lobby, in front of the statue of the corpsman helping a wounded soldier. But, the good thing about shaking hands with people at a military hospital was that they were *accustomed* to amputees, and the like, and didn't hesitate to reach out for the nearest still-working limb, thereby avoiding any awkwardness. The lobby itself seemed more like an atrium than a hospital, with plants and huge windows, and a long row of flags—all of which made an excellent backdrop, for statements and impromptu press briefings.

The operative word for this one, though, *was* brief, because her mother did little more than smile, shake some hands, pose for a few stills with the hospital command structure, and make remarks about what a fine facility it was, and how pleased she was with the wonderful treatment she and her family had received there in the past, and that she had the utmost confidence in the surgeons who were going to be performing her daughter's surgery, and so forth.

When it was Meg's turn to say something, she went with nothing more than a modestly enigmatic, "Farewell to college joys, we sail at break of day." The allusion went past a few of the reporters—and some of the White House staff members—who all seemed to think that she was trying, and failing, to be profound, but everyone else in the lobby, especially the ones wearing uniforms, was very much—well—*on board.*

"I appreciate your resisting the urge to be at all colorful," her mother said, once they were on an elevator, on their way to the Presidential Suite.

Meg just shrugged, although she was quite amused by herself. And, really, if her mother hadn't taken an unsolicited poke at her earlier, she wouldn't have poked back.

Except, when was the last time her mother had criticized her—about *anything*? So, in a way, maybe it was a good sign that she'd felt as though she could do so. And if the elevator had been less crowded, she would almost certainly have said something to that effect.

Meg glanced up at her—since she had now been forced to sit in a wheelchair, on direct orders from Dr. Brooks and Dr. Steiner. "Are there people you need to visit here?"

Since being elected—and while she was in the Senate, for that matter, especially when she was one of the members of the Armed Services committee—the President had spent a couple of hours every week visiting veterans and active-duty soldiers at various hospitals. Sometimes, she just went to Walter Reed, but usually, she came over to the NNMC, too, especially when there were any newly-arrived injured soldiers from overseas incidents. As far as Meg knew, she had yet to miss a week, unless she was out of the country, or they were on one of their rare Massachusetts vacations. Also, it was safe to assume, there had been a notorious thirteen-day period in the not too distant past, during which everything non-essential had been suspended. But, as a rule, she went so often that the press had gotten bored long ago and stopped covering the visits extensively—much to her relief. Neal tagged along with her, more often than not, which probably had something to do with his intense interest in all things military.

"Unfortunately, yes," her mother said. "But, obviously, I won't do that until later, or maybe tomorrow."

When Meg had once asked her why the visits were such an unbreakable part of her ever-chaotic schedule, her mother's grim response had been, "*I'm* the one who put them on the ground." Or on the ship, or underwater, or up in the air, depending upon the situation, although predominantly, lately—luckily—it had been things like accidents during training exercises and routine humanitarian missions, for the most part. Which was still awful, but at least the recent casualties hadn't resulted from a full-fledged *war*. In any case, she made as many hospital visits as possible—and had gone to more than a few funerals, too.

Naturally, the same policy was in place for police officers and firefighters and EMTs and all of the other usual suspects.

"Who's here right now that you're planning to see?" Meg asked.

Her mother closed her eyes for the split second it generally took for her to retrieve her massive internal briefing book. "The kids from the CH-53. Some land-mine casualties. IEDs. The people who are still here from the engine room fire."

The usual depressing array. "Let's stop by a few rooms, then," Meg said.

Her father shook his head. "I don't think that's a good idea, Meg. I'd rather get you through your pre-op testing, and then have you settle in and rest."

How many damned times could doctors repeat the exact same tests in one week? "We'll just say hi." She looked at her mother uncertainly. "I mean, you know, if you think people wouldn't mind."

"That's not the issue at all. I'm sure they'd be very pleased to see you. Your father and I would just prefer that you—" Her mother stopped, and looked at her closely. "Is this something you think you should do, or something you *want* to do?"

Both answers had some validity. "I want to," Meg said.

"Okay, then." Her mother glanced at Frank, who was standing in the corner, behind a couple of agents. "Please tell Brannigan—" who was one of the official White House photographers— "that there are to be absolutely *no* photos of Meg, and none of me, either, unless someone specifically requests one for his or her family." Without waiting for an answer, she turned to the hospital commander. "As low key as possible, Admiral."

As he nodded, too, Meg noticed that her father had been *very* quiet during all of this. Much too quiet. And maybe he was mad at *her* this time, instead of just being angry at her mother.

"It's good not to feel like an invalid," she said to him.

He nodded. "I know. But, I just—you're *already* so worn out."

Yeah. She was. And it was incredibly discouraging to be someone who had no physical stamina anymore.

Nevertheless.

They ended up making about a dozen hit-and-run visits, and since it was Sunday afternoon, a lot of patients had visitors in their rooms already—all of whom were surprised as hell to have the President, and her tragically-troubled daughter—and far-too-subdued husband—pop in to say hello. In a couple of cases, there were medals or service promotions for her mother to present, but every single sailor or Marine they visited wanted a photo with the President—and most of them asked for Meg and her father to be in the picture, too.

Her mother had perfected a very crisp salute, but Meg was caught off-guard when some of them saluted *her*, too, and wasn't sure whether it was appropriate to respond with a clumsy movement of her splinted hand, or if she should just nod politely. In a subtle way, her parents kept an eye on her the entire time, but in her father's case, it was clearly because he was worried, while her mother's attention seemed to be more along the lines of a distinctly detached appraisal.

It was awkward when they got to a guy whose left hand was gone, because Meg didn't know what to shake—and he didn't, either. Finally, she bumped her left fist against the back of his right fist, and he grinned.

"Semper Fi, ma'am," he said, and she grinned back.

They ended up talking for a few minutes, mainly because the guy's mother was pretty much *grilling* her mother about whether her son's unit should have been sent off on such a dangerous peacekeeping mission in the first place, while her mother nodded, and listened—and then gave a sympathetic, but detailed, explanation of exactly why she felt the deployment had been necessary, and how indebted they all were to the young men and women who had participated in the operation on the country's behalf.

The guy was acutely embarrassed by this, but Meg just shook her head.

"Parents get pretty upset about their children," she said in a low voice.

He nodded as though he considered that the understatement of the millennium. Then he motioned in the direction of her hand. "You don't go and do that, I bet a whole bunch more of us'd be out there fighting somewhere."

God, what a thought. Although, yeah, her mother might have had to make some kind of military move, ultimately, in response to her daughter's violent disappearance, and unrecovered body. "She wouldn't put boots on the ground just because something bad happened to *me*," Meg said. Unless it had been state-supported, in which case she would have had to take action, and maybe—but it *hadn't* been, and—Jesus, what would it be like to be responsible for so many people's lives on a daily basis? For the welfare of an entire *country*? "I, um, I don't think she'd risk other people's children that way." Just her own children. She glanced over at her mother who seemed, improbably, to be winning over *his* mother. Or, at any rate, easing her mind a little. But she was, after all, notoriously good with strangers.

The guy lifted his stump. "Think it's going to matter? To girls?"

He looked like he *might* be nineteen. Barely out of high school. Quite possibly not a whole lot more experienced with the opposite sex than she was. She raised her splint. "Think it's going to matter to boys?" Was it going to matter to Jack, that there were—well—*things* she couldn't do as skillfully as she once might have?

The guy obviously thought of an instant response to that, but he lowered his head, instead.

"Go ahead." She checked to make sure that their parents were out of earshot. "I'm hard to offend."

"Well, um," he flushed, "*I'd* do you, in a minute."

Okay, she was a little bit offended, but it was also funny. "Me, too," she said. "For what it's worth."

And he looked pleased, so it had been the right response.

By the time they got to the Presidential Suite, she was so exhausted that all she wanted to do was sleep. Which probably proved that her father's original instincts had been correct.

Her mother looked at her, thoughtfully, while they waited for the pre-op doctors to finish setting up for her pre-op tests.

"What?" Meg asked.

"You were very good with them," her mother said.

Meg shrugged, tired enough to feel peckish. "Well, you've been running me out there since I was about *four.*"

That one must have stung, but after a tiny pause, her mother just nodded. "I daresay I have. But you were still good with them."

In the old days, her father would already have stepped in to tell her to be more respectful, but he looked away without commenting.

Meg was—maybe—going to apologize, or at least use being tired as an excuse, but the medical people were back now, and in the confusion of having blood-work done, and her knee examined, and everything, it was easier to pretend it hadn't happened.

Of course, by now, they were all experts at pretending that various things hadn't happened.

And that they weren't upset about them.

By the time the doctors were finished, and she had gotten into the bed in the main bedroom suite, Trudy showed up with Steven and Neal. If any of them noticed that she and her parents were being a touch more distant with one another than usual, no one said so. Besides, Steven hated hospitals so much that he was in a surly mood, and her father and Trudy immediately started running interference, by arranging to have snacks brought in, and tuning in a movie on the plasma television.

They got through the evening in relative, if not ebullient, harmony, and since they both had school the next day, Trudy took her brothers home fairly early. Her father went downstairs to see them off—or, more likely, make sure they got to the car without anyone shooting or assaulting them, and she and her mother were alone in the room together.

"Do you need anything?" her mother asked. "Are you hungry?"

Meg shook her head.

"How's the pain?" her mother asked. "Would you like them to bring you something?"

Meg shook her head.

Her mother nodded, refilled the water glass on her bedside table, and then, after a moment of mutual silence, went over to sit behind the executive desk across the room, scanning some of the messages and other papers her staff had been bringing in for the past few hours. She started to pick up the telephone, hesitated, and put it down.

"I'm sorry I tweaked you about being quotable," she said.

They were all angry about a hell of a lot more than that, but yeah, that crack had probably been today's Fort Sumter. Meg shrugged. "It wasn't a big deal."

"You just—you need to lower your profile, Meg," her mother said. "Not the other way around. This past week has been—well, that's all I meant."

What choice did she have? Anonymity would be *swell*. And, like it or not, the odds were against her ever having it again. "*I* didn't assign Susan McAllister to me," Meg said. For that matter, she hadn't made any chemical bomb threats to herself.

Hadn't run for President and put her whole god-damn family at risk, either.

Her mother nodded. "I know. I'm extremely sorry that that happened."

Good. She should be.

After another painfully quiet minute, her mother started returning phone calls, speaking in a very low voice, and taking rapid notes on a legal pad.

"How often do you go out in public without a bulletproof vest?" Meg asked, when she was between calls.

Her mother looked guilty.

She already knew the answer to this, but— "Did you wear one today?"

Her mother shook her head.

"Then, don't talk to *me* about looking for trouble," Meg said.

Her mother started to say something, but then shut her eyes for a few seconds, apparently reining herself in.

They were on the verge of a fight—a *colossal* one, which might be a good thing—but then, the door opened and her father came in, and she and her mother both—for no good reason—instantly smiled, as though they were just sitting there casually, passing the time of day.

"Everything okay?" he asked.

They both nodded.

"Are the boys all set for the night?" her mother asked.

"Should be," her father said. "Trudy said she'd come back over in the morning, after she gets them off to school."

Since her parents were planning to sleep in one of the guestrooms across the hall in the suite. Or, for all she knew, they were going to use *both* of the rooms, in lieu of staying together.

"All right, then." Her mother gathered her papers together and stood up. "I have some things I need to do, so I'll just step out to the conference room now, and—excuse me."

As she left, her father looked at her, and Meg just shook her head.

She could tell that he was trying to decide whether he should pursue it, but then he sat down in the chair by the bed.

"Want to watch SportsCenter?" he asked.

Christ, did she ever.

FROM MIDNIGHT ON, she had to begin her presurgical fasting—and by twelve forty-five, she was so desperately thirsty that she started to panic. Her father was dozing in the bedside chair, but her mother, who was back behind the desk, doing paperwork and glancing up every so often to check on her, saw that something was wrong and came right over.

"What is it?" she whispered. "Are you okay?"

Meg was too deep into the panic to do anything more than shoot a look at the empty water glass on her table.

"Oh." Her mother reached for a pitcher to fill it. "I'm sorry. I should have noticed that myself."

She couldn't seem to get her breath—or speak, so Meg shook her head, *vehemently*, and motioned towards the clock.

"Oh," her mother said, again, and actually looked a little panicked herself.

"I can't make it through a whole night," Meg said. "I *know* I can't."

Her mother stood, frozen, holding the pitcher, and seeing her look so indecisive and helpless made everything seem that much more terrifying.

She didn't want to cry—except that she had already started. "I *can't*, Mom," she said. "I really can't. Please don't make me."

Her mother stared at her, her own eyes filling with tears.

"I have to be able to have water," Meg said. "I *have* to."

Her father woke up, and stared at them staring at each other. Then he lurched to his feet, still half-asleep, banging into the side of the bed forcefully enough to jar her leg terribly—and she groaned, and then started crying even harder.

"Oh, God, Meg, I'm sorry," he said, and leaned down to kiss her forehead. "I didn't mean to do that. I'm so sorry."

Her mother just stood there, gripping the handle of the pitcher.

"*Kate*," her father said. "Take a deep breath. Okay?"

Her mother looked blank, and then nodded, sucking in her breath.

"It's okay, Meg," her father said, and brushed some of her hair back with his hand. "It was only another nightmare. Your mother and I are right here with you."

"It's not that," her mother said. "It's after midnight, and she's thirsty."

Now, he got it, and he nodded, very calmly, his hand still stroking her hair.

"Okay," he said. "It's okay." He walked over to the other side of the bed, and took the pitcher from her mother. "You're both okay," he said, quietly. He poured out about a third of a cup of water, put a straw in the glass, and then moved it over next to her mouth. "Here you go. Just take a few sips."

Didn't he know how dangerous that was? Was he trying to hurt her? "I *can't*, Dad," she said, recoiling away from it. "I have *surgery*."

"It's fine," he said. "They can always move it up a few hours. We can even wait a day, if you need an extra day. There's no pressure here. Everything's going to be fine."

She was still scared, but that made sense, so she let herself have a sip, and then another, and then finished what was left as fast as she could.

"Good," her father said, his voice extremely gentle. He set the empty glass down on the table. "Here's what we're going to do. Your mother will wait here and hold your hand, and I'll go find Bob, and we'll figure out a way to make this as easy as possible for you. Okay?" He looked at her mother, who still didn't quite seem steady yet. "Okay?"

Her mother nodded, avoiding their eyes, a self-conscious blush moving into her cheeks.

"You're *tired*, Kate," he said. "That's all. The three of us have had a long day, and—you're *allowed* to get tired sometimes."

Her mother's color deepened, but she nodded again.

"Okay." He gave Meg's hand a squeeze, and then kissed her mother's cheek. "I'll be right back."

As her father left the room, she and her mother stayed where they were, without speaking. Then, her mother picked up her hand, and tried to smile at her.

"Your father's right," she said. "We'll just—we'll fix this. Don't worry."

Meg was still scared—all the more so, because her mother had seemed so scared, too—and she hung on to her hand, able to feel that both of them were trembling. Had she ever seen her mother panic, about *anything*? Ever? Jesus.

But, she needed to stop crying, because her father was going to be bringing Dr. Brooks, and probably some other medical people, in, and it would be humiliating for them to see her having hysterics about something that would seem so minor to anyone normal.

Only, the more she thought about it, the more difficult it was to stop. Oh, hell.

Her mother seemed to be coming back to herself, finally, because she spilled some water onto a thick wad of Kleenex, reached down to sponge off her face, and then smoothed her hair away from her forehead, the same way her father had.

"Could I have some more water?" Meg asked, ashamed to hear how frightened her voice sounded. "Before they get here?"

Before they told her she *couldn't*. That it might be *fatal*.

Her mother filled the glass halfway and handed it to her, Meg gulping it down. Her throat still felt funny, but she couldn't bring herself to ask for a refill, so she shook her head when her mother raised the pitcher inquiringly.

"I—I don't want them to see me crying," she said.

Her mother smiled weakly. "I'd disagree with you, but I don't particularly want them to see me at the moment, either."

Meg nodded, and they looked at each other, her mother gripping her hand almost as tightly as she was gripping back. And they were both still shaking, too.

"So," her mother said. "How's your spring break so far?"

Well, it sure as hell wasn't comparable to wandering blithely around *England*. But Meg managed a small laugh. Very small.

Her mother started to say something else, but then the door opened, and she turned her back, whisking the wad of Kleenex across her own eyes before dropping it into a wastebasket.

Dr. Brooks and her father came in, along with a female Navy nurse. Dr. Brooks examined both of them with one penetrating glance, and then focused on her mother.

"Madam President, would you mind sitting down for a couple of minutes, while I take a look at Meg?" he asked.

Her mother nodded, and found a chair, her posture very erect, her face expressionless.

Now, Dr. Brooks smiled at her. "You know, Meg, if you'd feel better about it, we can certainly reschedule the surgery. In fact—"

Meg shook her head, because if it got postponed, people would wonder why, and if the real story ever leaked, she would feel— "No, I'm fine," she said, although she had to wipe her sleeve across her eyes. "I was, um, just thirsty, for a minute."

"Well, we don't have to decide right now," he said, checking her pulse, and then her blood pressure. "How's the pain tonight?"

Awful. She shrugged, not looking at any of them. "I'm okay."

"Even so, I think I'd like to give you something, to help make it easier for you to get some sleep," he said.

Meg glanced at her father, who nodded, so she nodded, too.

"I think it's a good idea," Dr. Brooks said, handing her a tiny plastic cup with two pills in it, and pouring her some more water. "And while we're at it, I'm going to have Lieutenant Benoit here start an IV for you, okay?"

Meg nodded, uneasily, and swallowed the pills with as little water as possible.

While the nurse began to set up the IV, Dr. Brooks motioned for her mother to push up her sleeve, and took her blood pressure, too. After listening through his stethoscope, he didn't say anything, but he left the cuff hanging loose on her arm instead of removing it, so he must not have liked whatever he had heard, and was planning to recheck it in a few minutes.

The IV needle hurt going in, but she didn't even let herself *blink*, let alone wince. Lieutenant Benoit got it on the first try, and then taped the tube down, so that it would be difficult to dislodge. Once the IV was safely in her arm, Dr. Brooks thanked the nurse, who nodded at all of them and left the room.

"I apologize for not ordering the IV earlier," Dr. Brooks said. "Normally, we do it as a matter of course, but I know how uncomfortable they can be, and—well, as I said, my mistake, Meg."

He was trying to send her a message, but she couldn't figure out what it was.

"The good thing about an IV," Dr. Brooks went on, very conversational, "is that while you're connected to it, you *know* you're staying fully hydrated, and if you have any doubts, you can always look right up there, and make sure that it's dripping properly."

Instinctively, she looked up at the bag, and saw that it was, indeed, dripping. Message received. "I'm sorry to be so much trouble, sir." She'd had other operations, without ever flipping out about having to fast overnight, so this didn't make sense. "I don't know why it's so scary this time."

Dr. Brooks patted her arm. "You're *healthier*, Meg. I was prescribing much higher dosages of painkillers for you back then, so you were generally pretty groggy the night before. I didn't, this time around, and so, you had a chance to think about it."

Or maybe she'd just been braver before the other operations.

"You've been walking around on that leg—much to my dismay,

I must add—" he winked at her— "for the past week, so there's really *no* pressing need to do the arthroscopy tomorrow."

A lifeline she *really* wanted to grab. "But, everyone would wonder why," she said.

He pulled a small penlight out of his jacket pocket. "Open your mouth for a second," he said, and then peered inside. "Well, now, it's possible you have a touch of strep, and if that were the case, I would be inclined to send you home, and have you come back in a few days."

She would still look like a jerk—and feel like a coward, so she shook her head.

"As long as you know the option is there." He tucked the flashlight away, and went over to take her mother's blood pressure again. He frowned, and then deflated the cuff. "Madam President, I strongly suggest that you go across the hall, and try to get a few hours of rest."

Her mother looked annoyed. "I'm perfectly fine, Bob. And I'd rather stay in here with my daughter, so—"

"Madam President, let me reiterate," he said, quite firm. "It is my *strong* medical recommendation that you kiss Meg good-night, and let me walk out with you."

On very rare occasions, her mother was capable of having "*I'm* the god-damn President, and there's no one on the planet who can tell me to do anything I don't want to do" moments, and Meg could tell from her expression—and the jutting jaw—that she was considering going that way.

Except that her father was giving her an extremely hard look.

"Very well," her mother said, after a few seconds. She came over to the bed, and bent to give Meg a hug, careful to avoid both her splint and the IV. "Will you be okay if your father and I take turns keeping you company?" she whispered.

Meg nodded.

"I'm really sorry," her mother said, even more softly. "Just know that we'll do whatever you need us to do."

Meg nodded again, and her mother straightened up.

"I'll see you all in a little while, then," she said, and left the room with Dr. Brooks, looking—well—*tired*. Wrecked, even.

Her father pulled the chair her mother had vacated closer to the bed, and then sat down, picking up her hand. He raised his eyebrows, as though asking whether she wanted to talk, and Meg shook her head. Then, he motioned towards the lamp, and she nodded. He nodded back, turned it off, and they sat there, in the dark, without speaking.

Her mother was right; she was having an absolutely *lousy* spring break.

36

HER FATHER HELD her hand until she fell asleep, which only took about half an hour. The pills Dr. Brooks had given her must have been pretty strong, because she didn't wake up until almost seven-thirty. Her father was still sitting by the bed, looking *really* tired, and when Dr. Brooks came in to see how she was, the First Gentleman went off to take a shower and change his clothes. And slug down about four cups of coffee, probably.

"How did you sleep?" Dr. Brooks asked.

Meg didn't look at him, ashamed all over again about having reacted so badly to the prospect of a few hours without water. "Fine, thank you. The, um, the pills helped."

"That's why we have them, Meg," he said.

It was still embarrassing to have *needed* them. "Is my mother okay?" she asked.

"Of course," he said. "She's in a meeting in the conference room right now, but I'm sure she'll be in shortly."

Odds were, her mother was feeling even more mortified than she was this morning.

Which was pretty god-damned mortified.

"So," Dr. Brooks said. "Do you want us to proceed with the operation, or—"

She nodded.

"Okay, then. I think that's the better plan," he said. "Do you have any questions?"

In fact, she did, but she needed to be quick about it, before either of her parents showed up. "Um, I wanted to ask you about amputation," she said.

He looked very unhappy. "Oh, honey, is *that* what you've been worrying about? This is just a routine arthroscopic procedure, and they're going to evaluate your hand, too. But, that's it, I promise."

"Actually," Meg swallowed, "I wanted to request one."

He shook his head. "I'm sorry, Meg. I don't think I understand what you mean."

"Look, we both know it isn't working out," she said, gesturing towards her leg. "And I thought—well—"

He looked so upset that she was hesitant to broach it any further.

"If you all went ahead and did it, we'd know where we were, and I could just, I don't know, start living my life again," she said.

"Do you want us to take your hand, too, while we're at it?" he asked.

She hadn't thought about that, but it wasn't necessarily a terrible idea. She frowned. "Well, maybe not on the same day. But, yeah, okay. If you think that would be good."

He sat down, heavily, and it occurred to her that that chair had been getting one hell of a workout during the past twelve hours or so.

"I don't know what the high-tech options are, but they could at least probably rig me up some sort of pincer appliance, right?" she said.

He stared at her.

Maybe she should have done some research on the Internet about the various types of prostheses before bringing any of this up. "Well, I mean, if I weren't a good candidate for that, either, they could just make me something, I don't know, cosmetic." Which would be a lot better than, say, a *hook*. She looked at him uncertainly. "Do you think it's a bad idea?"

He nodded.

The door opened, and when Dr. Brooks saw that it was her mother, he stood up—as, of course, everyone always did.

"Good morning," her mother said, but then slowed her pace, reading the mood in the room. "I'm sorry, am I interrupting you?"

Yes, but would Dr. Brooks be willing to say so? She definitely didn't want her mother to get involved with any of this, although he probably did. "Would it be okay if we had a few more minutes, Mom?" Meg asked. "We're kind of—I'd rather."

Her mother was caught off-guard by that, and she gave them both an anxious look, but then nodded, and left.

"Picture, if you will," Dr. Brooks said, "the conversation during which I told your parents that you'd made a unilateral decision to undergo an amputation—or even two amputations, and that I'd agreed to go along with it."

Ouch. It would be all kinds of ugly. Meg frowned. "It wouldn't bode well for your staying in this job."

"It wouldn't bode well for me remaining in this *profession*," he said. "And rightly so."

Great. As usual, the fact that she was an adult, and should be able to make decisions about her own life, was being ignored. She shouldn't even have bothered asking.

Dr. Brooks sighed, put his head in his hands briefly, then straightened back up. "I know you had a very bad night, Meg. Is that where this is coming from?"

"It's the soldiers," she said.

He looked confused. "I'm sorry, I don't understand. How so?"

"When we were making visits yesterday, there were some amputees," she said. "And a few of them were telling my mother stuff like that they were going to be learning how to ski again, and go running, and everything. One of them had already *competed* in a 5K, since he lost his leg."

He nodded.

"And because I still *have* my stupid leg, the best I can do is try to make it in and out of my dorm without tearing anything," she said.

He nodded again. Nodded several times, in fact.

What kind of fucked-up world did she live in, that she felt sorry for herself because she *wasn't* an amputee? "If you'd taken it off last summer, when everyone thought it might be getting, you know, necrotic, I would have been able to ski this winter," she said. "I'd probably be playing tennis a little, too." Maybe not very well, but playing.

Dr. Brooks sighed, looking older than usual. Elderly, even. "Yes, I see your point. In some ways, you might have been better off, but we just can't. It's a viable limb, and as long as there's a chance you're going to regain some function—well, it just isn't a realistic possibility."

She nodded, feeling—as always—tears come into her eyes.

"It's healthy to cry about it, Meg," he said, his voice very kind. "You've had some terrible things happen to you, and we don't have any easy solutions. I wish we did."

That made two of them.

He handed her some Kleenex, and she pressed it against her face. "I'm not going to lie to you," he said. "No matter how hard we try, I'm afraid we can't bring you back to the person you were. But, we're going to get you on skis again."

She looked up.

"Given the complication of your hand, it may take some creative thinking," he said, "but, at the very worst, we could put you in a mono-ski."

Those weren't skis; they were *sleds*. She had to cover her eyes again.

"Dr. Hammond—" one of her surgeons, who worked with the U.S. Ski Team— "and I have been discussing all of this a great deal during the past few months, and there are plenty of options," he said. "Three-track skis, outrigger poles—any one of a number of things. He's been gathering some material together, and—" He paused. "In fact, I think I'm going to have him come here this afternoon, and we can all discuss it."

Except, wait. "Isn't he in Utah?" she asked. Since this operation was supposed to be routine, he wasn't scrubbing in.

Dr. Brooks shrugged. "That's hardly insurmountable, Meg."

"Yeah, but I don't want him to have to drop everything, just because I'm kind of upset," she said.

Dr. Brooks smiled at her. "Which do you think is preferable? My calling and asking him to come here for a consultation, or the President *ordering* him to be on the next plane to Washington?"

"I don't think she'd do that," Meg said. Although, given her mother's apparent overall testiness and generally frayed temper of late, she probably *would*. "Could you maybe have him wait a few days, though? Since I probably won't be feeling very good tonight?"

"Sure. We'll arrange for it sometime at the Residence, later this week," Dr. Brooks said. "Is there anything else you'd like to talk about?"

There was plenty, but she was tired, and about to have surgery, so she shook her head.

Her parents came in, staying until it was time for her to be wheeled into the actual surgical suite. And even then, she could tell they weren't happy about not being able to accompany her the rest of the way. But they promised that they would see her as soon as the operation was over, and she was lethargic enough from the Valium or whatever it was she'd been given to do nothing more than nod vaguely and attempt to smile at them.

After that, they must have started the anesthesia, because she couldn't remember anything until she was suddenly aware of herself saying, "*Ow*," followed by "Fuck!," and then waking up just long enough to apologize before drifting off again.

The next time she opened her eyes, her knee hurt, her throat hurt, and her *hand* hurt. The lights were so bright that it made her head hurt, too, and she wasn't sure where she was. Back in her room, maybe? Still in the middle of the operation? In the Recovery Room? All she knew for sure was that she was in intense pain, and she groaned.

Her mother was by the bed, and she instantly got up.

Meg nodded at her, fighting the urge to go right back to sleep.

Her father was also in the room, because now he was coming over, too. They were asking how she was, and if she needed anything, but it took her a minute to make any sense of what they were saying, which gave her time to notice that she also felt very dizzy and nauseated.

A nurse was doing something to her IV, and when she smelled Old Spice, she realized that Dr. Brooks was there, too.

All of which was just too much activity to process.

More people seemed to be coming into the room, mostly wearing surgical scrubs, and she heard a series of numbers—blood pressure? her pulse?—and a jumble of voices saying things like "should expect that" and "we'll monitor the—" and "normal to feel—"

She closed her eyes again.

WHEN SHE WOKE up the next time, she still felt awful, and for a terrible minute or two, she thought she might be about to throw up. A nurse was ready with a basin, but by concentrating as hard as she could, and swallowing a few times, she managed to get her stomach under control, and then moved her head away from it, upon which, the nurse withdrew.

The lights were less glaring, and she looked around, finally figuring out that she was back in the Presidential Suite, and her father was next to the bed. There was a bunch of medical people standing around, too.

Her father said something, and there was a lot of movement, along with several voices, in response. Then, a minute or two later, the door opened, and her mother hurried into the room, holding her glasses in one hand and some papers and thick folders in the other, all of which she handed to Frank, before bending over to kiss her on the cheek.

"I have a catheter, right?" Meg whispered.

Her mother glanced down at the side of the bed, and then nodded.

Good. She wouldn't have to worry about a bedpan anytime soon, then.

Everyone seemed to be asking her how she felt, and given the negative slant to the answer, she decided to avoid saying anything at all, and just sipped the ginger ale her father was holding out, trying to regain some semblance of her mental and physical equilibrium.

After a while, she found enough energy to look at Dr. Brooks. "How'd it go?" she asked.

"Well—" His hesitations were always a bad sign. "You had done more damage to your knee than we'd hoped, but your hand has shown somc minor improvement, and they elected to remove the last of the external pins."

It was hard to tell, with the new splints and bandages. She tried moving her hand and wrist, which hurt so much that she didn't bother attempting to do the same with her leg.

"Am I, um," Christ, it was infuriating that her voice always shook, "hooked up to my morphine thing?"

Her father nodded, putting the little pump near her left hand.

She *wanted* to push it, and give herself a good strong dose, but there were too many people watching, so she sipped ginger ale, instead.

It was a great relief when they all finally cleared out, and she was alone with her parents—and could take advantage of the morphine without witnesses. Then, something or other happened—she was too tired to pay much attention, except the telephone kept ringing—and her mother had to go back to the White House for a while, instead of just working in the conference room. Regardless, it was nice to take a nap, while her father sat and read *The Washington Post.*

She didn't wake up again until about six-fifteen, when Trudy arrived with her brothers. They only stayed long enough to have a fast supper—none of which she ate, except for the vanilla pudding. She had used the pain medication pump more than once, although it didn't seem to be accomplishing much, beyond making her feel sleepy.

It was just before eight o'clock when there was a knock on the door and Garth came in, holding an impressive bouquet of roses and tulips. A lot of other arrangements had already been delivered, but almost all of them were from people who didn't know her personally, and were almost certainly just trying to curry favor with the President.

"Good evening, sir," he said, formally, and he and her father shook hands.

"You, um, you brought me flowers?" Meg asked. It was really thoughtful of him, but also unexpected. "Thank you."

Garth's already-ruddy face reddened more. "Well, no. I probably *should* have, maybe, but, uh—no."

"It would be crossing professional lines," Meg said, in an effort to bail him out.

"Yes." He nodded gratefully. "Yes, it would. Although—well, obviously, I hope you're feeling okay?"

She felt like the very devil, but no matter. "Yeah," Meg said. "Thanks."

None of which changed the fact that he was standing there, looking awkward and holding a bouquet of undetermined origin.

"I guess I'm *facilitating* a flower delivery from someone," he said, then set the vase down on her bedside table, and handed her a small card.

She opened it with some difficulty and found a note which read: *"Good-bye Piccadilly, Farewell Leicester Square! —Jack."* Not his handwriting, so he must have dictated it. "Oh," she said, and grinned, suddenly feeling a lot less like the devil.

After Garth left, her father leaned over to look at the card.

"I'm hoping that's not your philosophy professor," he said.

Meg just grinned.

SHE ADMIRED HER flowers for a while, and then let herself doze off again. When she woke up, the room was dark, except for a very small light on the desk, where her father was reading. Her knee was hurting even more than her hand now, and she looked at her pain-pump, but decided that she would rather not drug herself right back to sleep. Not yet, anyway.

Seeing that she was awake, her father closed his book, got up to pour her a cup of ice water, and then helped her drink it.

"Would you like some more?" he asked.

When she hesitated, he promptly fixed her another, and she finished it in a few gulps. Then, she looked around, feeling slightly more cogent.

"Mom hasn't come back yet?" she asked.

"She was in here before," he said, "but she didn't want to wake you up."

Meg nodded. "So, she's in the conference room?"

"She's downstairs," her father said. "She'll be up in a little while."

What would she be doing downstairs at this time of night? That didn't make any sense. Meg frowned. "Why? Are they having a ceremony, or a press conference or something?"

"Her stomach's been bothering her," her father said, "and since it's so quiet right now, they managed to talk her into having some tests."

Jesus. Solely within the privacy of the family, her mother was overwhelmingly medically phobic, and tended to get very queasy even thinking about the *possibility* of encountering doctors on her own behalf. "So, why are you sitting here?" Meg asked. "If she's having tests, you know how scared she must be."

Her father shook his head. "She's fine, Meg. Don't worry about it."

Was he trying to be nice—or was he being dismissive? "Or maybe you think her stomach *should* hurt, so you're not too concerned," Meg said, stiffly.

Her father looked so irritated that she was pretty sure that she'd guessed right. "Or maybe, your mother and I decided that the fact that our daughter had surgery today and is in terrible pain, had a higher priority."

Maybe. "So, she's down there because she's been *literally* eating herself up with guilt for months," Meg said.

Her father sighed.

Great. Just great. Meg scowled at him. "She didn't shoot herself, and she didn't kidnap me."

Her father's jaw clenched. "I'm aware of that, Meg."

Maybe her mother wasn't the sole genetic source for her dispassion, after all. Hell, maybe she wasn't even the main source. And, just possibly, she and her mother *weren't* the ones who were dragging the rest of the family down. "You going to let her off the hook someday, Dad?" she asked.

His jaw, if possible, tightened more. "I really don't think this is a good time to talk about it. Okay?"

Was there ever going to be a good time? Not bloody likely.

Someone knocked on the door, and then, a nurse came in to check on her. She wasn't happy about the interruption, but since she no longer had her catheter, she let the nurse help her into a wheelchair, so that she could use the bathroom. When she came out, her bed had been freshly made, someone had delivered a plate of cookies and graham crackers, along with some juice and a small carton of milk, and her father was back in the bedside chair, reading his book.

After the nurse left, neither of them spoke for a while. Her father stared at his book, without turning pages, and she looked at her snack, without eating or drinking anything.

"Do you want to watch television?" he asked finally.

She shook her head.

"Is there anything else I can have them bring you?" he asked.

She shook her head.

"It's getting late," he said. "Would you like me to turn the light out?"

She shook her head.

Given that sort of uncommunicative feedback, her mother would already have made some kind of excuse and left the room by now, but her father stayed where he was, still staring down at his book.

It would be very much easier to tell him that yes, she was tired, and maybe she should try to sleep some more—and not bring any of this up again. Easier on *both* of them.

"I would have done exactly what she did," Meg said.

Her father slapped the book shut. "Oh, the hell you would have," he said, sounding so angry that she couldn't help drawing back. "You don't have it in you."

Was that a compliment, or an insult? Or maybe he just didn't know her as well as she would have thought he did. Hoped he did. She let out her breath. "You would have, too."

He looked away from her, clearly so furious that he was afraid to answer right away.

"I've never known anyone more responsible, Dad," Meg said, "and the god-damn country *matters*. It would have killed you inside, but you would have done it."

He just shook his head.

"You going to let it kill her?" she asked.

"She's fine," he said tightly.

Yeah. She was super. And so was Steven. And Neal probably wasn't as god-damned well-adjusted as he seemed.

He reached up to rub his temples for a minute. "Let's not worry about any of this tonight, okay? Why don't you try to rest?"

In other words, it was an incendiary topic, and she was supposed to drop it.

As usual.

"How's the pain?" he asked.

It *sucked*, just the way it always did.

"Meg, I'm sorry, I just really don't want to talk about this right now," he said.

No kidding.

But, it had been a tough day, and he had been up for hours, and maybe she shouldn't push him anymore. "All right," she said. "But, will you please go check on her?"

He sighed.

"Please?" she said.

He looked at her, and then sighed again. "Okay," he said, and got up.

SHE HAD BEEN lying there for a while, staring up at the ceiling, when there was another knock on the door. Since she wasn't in the mood to see anyone, or force herself to be polite, she decided to ignore it.

"Okay if I come in?" Preston asked, from the hallway.

Preston was one of the few people she could probably tolerate right now. And if she felt lousy and asked him to leave, he wouldn't take it personally. "Sure," she said.

He opened the door, balancing two large Starbucks cups, as well as his briefcase.

"Oooh," she said, in a better mood immediately.

He nodded. "Thought you might have a little latte jones going by now."

Major jones, actually.

He handed her one of the cups. "Before you get too excited, it's decaf."

She frowned.

"But, it *is* mocha," he said.

She smiled. "Thank you."

He was wearing one of his West Wing conservative suits, and from the way he sat down, she could tell how tired he was, although he didn't loosen his tie, or even take his jacket off. Mr. Fielding, at hyperalert leisure.

"Are you just heading home from work now?" she asked.

He nodded wryly. "My predecessor did not see the need to leave the office shipshape."

Particularly since his departure had not been voluntary, in the wake of a minor ethics scandal, due to what had turned out to be his unfortunate propensity to do things like accept free golf vacations from lobbyists. To describe her mother as having been displeased by this turn of events would be putting it very, very mildly. But, the fallout hadn't been too bad, so far, because luckily, someone had tipped Glen off *before* it broke in the press, and the guy had already been fired by the time the story went public.

Which didn't change the fact that Preston looked tired as hell.

"Are you okay?" she asked.

He shook his head. "The important question is, are *you* okay?"

She wasn't, but there was no good reason to dwell on it, so she shrugged.

"I'm sorry," he said.

She shrugged again.

They focused on their cups of coffee, Preston slouching in his chair, in a way that managed to evoke the sixteen-year-old version of himself after Thanksgiving dinner.

"Did you run into Hurricane Russell on your way in here?" Meg asked.

"No," he said. "But they were still cleaning up debris out in the hall."

Not that her father ever raised his voice—but, he could most assuredly make an oppressive black cloud swirl in his wake, when he was out of sorts. "Mom's having a bunch of tests," she said. "They think there's something wrong with her stomach."

Preston glanced over. "Maybe she encounters stress in her workplace."

Just maybe. "Yeah, that must be it," Meg said. "Because we all know she has a happy home life."

Preston grinned, and helped himself to a graham cracker from her plate of snacks.

She wanted to complain about how lousy she felt, and the degree to which the morphine *wasn't* helping, and the fact that Dr. Steiner had indicated that she was almost definitely going to need to have more work done on her knee after the semester was over—and her wrist and thumb and forefinger, too, in all likelihood—but, he presumably had his own problems, and might be sick of hearing about hers.

"I'm sure she's fine, Meg," Preston said. "They're just going to remind her that she needs to take better care of herself."

Maybe. But, she nodded.

He looked sharply at her. "They may remind you, too."

Yeah, yeah, yeah. "Does that mean you want me to have some of the graham crackers?" she asked.

He nodded.

"But, you would never, ever tell me what to do," Meg said.

"Never in a million years," he said, and moved the plate closer so that she could reach it.

Subtle. She wasn't in the mood for crackers, but the cookies looked halfway decent, and she took one of the oatmeal ones. "Happy now?" she asked, eating it.

"Overjoyed," he said.

37

THEY HAD FINISHED their coffee—as well as most of the cookies, when her parents came in. Preston stood up right away, and after he'd said good-night to them, her father did the same, heading across the hall for some long-overdue sleep.

With the President back upstairs, there was a certain amount of traffic in and out of the room—a number of her aides and advisors showing up with thick folders and papers, and holding swift whispered conversations, and a steady stream of medical personnel, magically appearing to recheck every conceivable tube, chart, and medication, and also to bring in trays of fresh fruit, yoghurt, cottage cheese, chicken soup, and various other things that the Leader of the Free World was known to eat. Throughout all of this, her mother kept a close eye on her, and finally made a polite request for them to be left alone, if possible, for the next few hours, so that her daughter could get some rest.

"How was your barium?" Meg asked, when they were finally by themselves.

Her mother looked embarrassed. "I've had better."

"Are you okay?" Meg asked.

Her mother shrugged. "They're going to give me some medication to take. I'll be fine."

That didn't sound too good. Meg looked at her nervously. "So, you're *not* okay?"

"A little gastritis, maybe," her mother said. "Nothing to worry about."

And she might, or might not, be telling the truth.

"I'm sorry about last night," her mother said. "I should have—it won't happen again."

As far as she knew, it was the first time it had ever happened in the last eighteen years, so, odds were, that it had, indeed, been an aberration. "It wasn't your fault. I was stupid to overreact like that," Meg said.

Which probably *would* happen again, and not infrequently.

Her mother sighed. "Meg—"

Oh, Christ, she wasn't in the mood for this. "Could you help me get into my wheelchair, so I can go to the bathroom?" Meg asked.

"Of course," her mother said, and then waited by the door to assist her again on her way out.

Once she was back in bed, she let her mother turn her pillow, fix her blankets, and pour her some ice water.

"I need to do some work," her mother said. "Would you like me to stay in here, or go down to the conference room?"

Much as she wanted some privacy, she *really* didn't want to be alone. "In here is good," Meg said.

So, she lay in bed, dozing, the room dark except for the desk lamp. Her mother sat there, going through papers and making, or receiving, the occasional phone call. She tended to be a very quiet and serene worker, and it was soothing to listen to a page turning, a pen writing, a low voice on the telephone.

Meg was almost asleep when she heard her saying softly, "No, don't worry, it's not perforated. They gave me this gastric cocktail, and—really, I'm fine." Then, her mother listening, nodding in response to whatever the person on the other end was saying. "I know, I've been worried about that, but nothing's shown up in her tests. Apparently, she just isn't eating." She listened again. "I think about ten pounds, but it's hard to be sure."

Well, that certainly wasn't the President having a brisk, purely professional conversation. It would be interesting to listen, and get some idea of what her mother was thinking lately—but, it would also be sneaky, which had never been her style. So, she moved restlessly, coughed as though she was just waking up, and then lifted herself onto her good elbow, blinking.

Her mother's voice immediately became much more guarded. "Could I call you back tomorrow night?" She listened. "How late is really okay?" She listened some more. "All right. And, honestly, if there's *anything*—I know, I know. But, I can't not say it." She laughed, and then hung up.

"I'm sorry," Meg said. "I wasn't eavesdropping or anything."

Her mother nodded. "Thank you for letting me know that you weren't asleep, though."

Ah, so the beautiful awakening scene hadn't been convincing? The cough had been a shade too dramatic, maybe. "Was that Mrs. Peterson?" Meg asked.

Her mother nodded.

"How is she?" Meg asked.

Her mother shook her head. "I don't know. She *sounds* better, but—well." She crossed the room and poured fresh water into the glass on the bedside table.

Meg drank some without thinking, but it felt so Pavlovian that she put it back down.

Her mother looked at her desk—perhaps longingly, but then sat in the chair by the bed.

Which kind of bugged her, because shouldn't she be happy that her only daughter was home for the next couple of weeks, and take advantage of every opportunity to spend time with her? Not that they had to be attached at the hip, but Christ, the country wasn't expecting her to work twenty-four hours a day, right? And even if they did, that was *their* problem.

"What?" her mother asked.

Meg shook her head, and her mother subsided at once—which also got on her nerves. It would be such a relief to have her mother press *her* for an answer, instead of its always being the other way around. It wasn't as though she had problems being direct and authoritative with everyone *else* on the whole damned planet.

No wonder her father seemed to have lost patience to such a degree.

Her mother—who was, obviously, not a stupid woman, and was very good at taking the temperature of any given encounter—shifted uncomfortably in her chair. "I really am sorry about last night, Meg. I know I let you down."

To hell with that. "Can not, have not, and *will* not" had let her down. For starters.

And if her mother got up right now, and left the room, she just might not speak to her again for the rest of spring break.

Her mother glanced at the desk, glanced at the door, glanced at *her*, hesitated, and then, stayed where she was, folding her arms around herself.

They didn't get too many chances to be alone, relatively uninterrupted. Even in the family quarters, her father and brothers were there most of the time, and the phone rarely stopped ringing, so her mother could always find an easy way to escape, when she started feeling pressured. But right now, in the middle of the night, in a heavily guarded hospital room, with her father asleep, her brothers at home, and the staff under orders not to come in unless it was absolutely necessary, they had something resembling genuine privacy—and if she let an opportunity like this go by, there was no guarantee that she would get another chance anytime soon.

"Did you cry?" Meg asked. "When I was gone?"

Her mother looked startled. "I'm sorry, what?"

Had she developed a sudden hearing impairment? As a precaution, Meg counted to ten. "Did you?"

Her mother's posture had stiffened noticeably, and she was no longer even pretending to make eye contact. "I don't—that is, I'm not sure why you're asking."

Because she wanted to know the answer, maybe? Meg shrugged, slowly flexing and releasing her good hand. Somehow, seeing fingers work effortlessly was more surprising than watching fingers that *didn't* work anymore. "You don't have to tell me. I mean, I guess it isn't any of my business."

Her mother touched Meg's fist. "You can ask me absolutely anything you want."

Which was great and all, but she'd done just that—and look where it hadn't gotten her.

Her mother sighed. "Okay. Do you want the easy answer, or the complicated one?"

At this point, she really just wanted to turn the light out and try to go to sleep.

"No," her mother said. "I didn't cry until I got you back."

Terrific. Christ, maybe she really *wasn't* human. Or sane.

Her mother let out her breath. "I didn't have any safe place where I could even think of doing it. And I knew if I started—well, I couldn't, that's all."

No, there was no way that a President could risk being seen dissolving into tears, regardless of the provocation. "Usually, you only cry in front of Dad," Meg said.

Her mother nodded.

"But you didn't, this time," Meg said.

Her mother shook her head.

Not a promising reaction. "Are you guys in trouble?" Meg asked.

"Meg, I really don't—" Her mother stopped, apparently changing her mind about whatever she had been planning to say. "I'm not sure if that's something you and I can discuss. Or, at any rate, *should* discuss."

They were in trouble.

"Meg, it's not anything you need to worry about," her mother said.

Like hell it wasn't.

Her mother sighed. "All right, I'll give you this much. Your father and I are working on the fact that we not only weren't supportive of each other, during the most horrific event our family has ever experienced, but we were actually downright *destructive*. And, that's something we need to figure out."

"We," Meg said. "Not 'he?' "

"In a marriage, it's always 'we.' Don't ever trust anyone who pretends otherwise," her mother said, rather snappishly. "Anyway, we failed as spouses, and I failed as a parent. And that's—neither of us is taking it very well."

Really? She hadn't noticed.

"You wanted to cry, though, right?" Meg asked.

Her mother looked at her with an expression that went well beyond misery. "There aren't enough tears in the world, Meg."

No, probably not. She found herself wondering, out of nowhere, whether maybe it would have been easier for everyone if she hadn't made it back, instead of their having to deal with a daily reminder of how terrifying and random life could be, and how much damage—

"When they found your teeth, I thought I was going to lose my mind," her mother said, so softly that Meg had to lean over to hear her.

Jesus. How many ugly secrets were still hidden away? Could they all *be* any more damned repressed?

It had been dark in the back of the van, and the men had all been screaming and swearing at her, while one of them slammed a machine gun across her face a few times, and she had no idea what it was they'd been shoving in her mouth. Metal, was all she knew for sure. Pliers, maybe? Actual dental tools? Meg touched her jaw protectively. "Did they send them to you or something? To prove they had me?" Which seemed out of character for the guy—he'd been too careful to take chances like that.

"No. They abandoned the van they used initially, and our people found it that first night. And your teeth were—" Her mother's eyes brightened, but her voice was still perfectly controlled. "After I gave the order twice, they finally brought them over in these little plastic evidence bags, so that I could see them, and there were the roots, and tissue, and I knew it was *you*, possibly all I was ever going to *have* of you again, and—" Her voice was no longer steady. "My God, Meg, I can't imagine how much that must have hurt. It makes me sick every time I think—I am so sorry."

Here was one she could alleviate, at least. "I was only awake for the first part of it," Meg said. The tools slamming against her molars, and skidding off and cutting into her gums and tongue, as she tried to struggle away from the men, so scared that she couldn't breathe or speak. "He had them knock me out." Had it just been practical? A concern that she might scream too loudly, and people on the street or driving by would hear her? Or, had it been a moment of mercy? Either way, thank God for it. "I didn't even know what they'd done until I woke up in a puddle of blood."

Judging by the stricken look on her mother's face, the phrase "puddle of blood" had been a tactical error.

"Were the, um, teeth what you would have buried?" Meg asked. "I mean, if I hadn't—well, you know."

What little color had been in her mother's cheeks was now completely gone.

Okay. Much too blunt to say to an ulcer-ridden, *guilt*-ridden person.

Her mother picked up Meg's ice water, took a few methodical sips, and then put it down. "I don't want to put pressure on you," she said, her voice calm again, "but do you think there's any way you could bring yourself to start asking me the really *tough* questions?"

Humor. Rarely undesirable, even when tasteless. And despite her inability to throw baseballs effectively, it was comforting to remember that her mother *was* gifted at playing hardball, and therefore, nearly impossible to rattle. "I can try," Meg said. "Although I'm concerned about offending your delicate sensibilities."

Her mother smiled, slightly. "It's never going to be funny, Meg."

No. It never was.

She drank the rest of her water, not sure if she wanted to know the answer to the question she was going to ask next. "Did they find my clothes, too? In the van?"

Her mother nodded, reluctantly.

"Well," Meg said. How humiliating. "That must have given everyone a lot to think about."

Her mother just nodded.

So, an untold number of people—the FBI, the Secret Service, the higher-ranking members of the staff, probably some of the press corps, God only knew who else—had had some very vivid, if inaccurate, images of the specific conditions under which she was being held. Her parents. Trudy. *Preston.*

With luck, her brothers had never been told.

"I, uh, I assume they fondled me," Meg said. The thought of which was enough to induce violent nausea. And molested, or assaulted, were probably more accurate descriptions—but, she didn't want to use either of those words. Imagining them dressing her in that cheap sweatshirt and sweatpants, touching her the entire time, wasn't too entertaining, either. "I mean, he made it pretty clear that he'd—enjoyed the view, but I don't think they had time to—" God, she felt sick to her stomach. "I would have known, if they'd done something *terrible*, right? While I was unconscious?"

Her mother nodded. "You would have been in significant, probably severe, pain," she said, her voice so measured and gentle that Meg almost didn't notice how tightly her free hand was clutching the bed railing, "and I'm certain that you would have noticed quite a lot of blood. And if an attack had been, um—" she closed her eyes for a second, but still spoke evenly— "oral, you would have been aware of—you would have known."

Which was what she had always assumed—but, still.

Her mother was watching her, with some combination of urgency and quiet terror, and Meg shook her head. Her mother kept looking at her, and then sank back in the chair, breathing much harder than she had been, so pale that it was unnerving. Not sure what else to do, Meg touched her mother's now-trembling arm.

"Mom, it's okay," she said. "They *didn't.*"

Her mother nodded, took a deep breath, and then nodded again.

Jesus. "All these months," Meg said, "and this is the first time you've ever really believed me about that?"

This time, her mother's nod was more of a shudder. "I'm sorry. I just thought you might have—anyway. Thank God."

Yeah. But, there was still one thing that— "What if there are photos?" she asked, afraid to say it aloud, but realizing that, somewhere deep inside, she must have been worrying about it for a very long time. "I mean, when I was unconscious, they might have—" Not a scene she wanted to imagine. "What if they show up somewhere, and I'm—" Naked. Maybe even *posed* in some horrible, degrading way, or—she fumbled for a Kleenex.

Her mother opened her arms, and Meg not only sat up enough to hug her, but *hung on*.

"Do you have reason to believe that there might be?" her mother asked, still holding her. "Did they say anything, or maybe make jokes about it?"

Had he? God knows he'd made plenty of mean jokes at her expense, but she couldn't remember him even hinting about anything like that, so she shook her head.

"I have people scouring the Internet every day, looking for any references at all about you or your brothers," her mother said. "If anything surfaces, they'll find it."

Maybe.

"And if, God forbid, there *are* any out there, I don't think even the lowest of the tabloids would touch them," her mother said. "And they can be assured of very serious legal and criminal repercussions, if they do."

It was a small comfort, but better than nothing.

"Are they ever going to catch them?" Meg asked. Him, mainly, of course.

"They'd damned well *better*," her mother said.

NEITHER OF THEM got much sleep, although, after giving herself another pump of her pain medication, Meg was able to drift off, while her mother dozed in the chair.

At about five-thirty, she was aware of a small flurry of activity, after her mother took a couple of phone calls, and then various aides, including the national security advisor and the deputy chief of staff, came in for urgent, muttered conversations, and each time she finished one of the swift consultations, her mother would glance at the bed to see if she had woken up.

After Winifred, the deputy chief of staff, left for the second time, she watched sleepily as her mother frowned down at her desk, deep in thought, looking far more Presidential than parental.

"What's going on?" Meg asked.

"Riyadh continues to be a problem," her mother said, without elaborating.

Which could mean all sorts of things, none of them good.

It developed that her mother was going to be holding a high-level staff meeting down in the conference room at six-thirty, and then heading straight back to the White House, so, in short order, a nurse and two corpsmen appeared with coffee, juice, milk, cereal, fruit, yoghurt, muffins, pastries, and three different kinds of toast, all of which her mother ignored, except for the coffee and a piece of whole wheat bread. Then, her father came in, looking somewhat more rested than he had a few hours earlier, although after saying good morning, his first move was towards the coffee, too.

Her mother was long gone by the time Meg finally got discharged and was driven back to the White House with her father. There was a wheelchair waiting for her near the South Portico stairs, and even though there were some photographers around, everything hurt enough so that she let her father, Dr. Steiner, and one of the White House Medical Unit nurses help her into it.

Once they made it upstairs, she had an excellent excuse to go to her room and rest—and she took advantage of it. In fact, when Trudy came in at about five-thirty, and asked if she felt well enough to get up for dinner, she shook her head and also declined the offer of having a tray brought to her room.

She didn't bother looking at the tiny pile of phone messages on her desk, or checking her email. Didn't turn on the television, didn't read a book, didn't do *anything* other than pat Vanessa and sleep, waking up only long enough to take some Percocet every so often. She would have assumed that surgery would improve the way she felt, but she'd been in less pain staggering around on the torn cartilage for a week than she was now, and her hand was doing a lot of throbbing and twitching. She was also having even more nightmares then usual, which she assumed was because of the medication, but everything hurt too damn much for her to consider skipping any doses. And, in all honesty, she took an extra one, here and there, hoping that it might help.

Which it didn't.

To make matters worse, for the first time, Jack showed up in one of her dreams. He looked different—he had dark hair, for one thing—but, she could tell it was him. The guy was there, too, and they seemed to be very friendly, which meant—*Jesus Christ*. If they *knew* each other, that meant—she woke up, gasping and terrified, and then stared around the room to try and figure out where she was.

All right. Okay. Jack didn't know him; he'd been *cleared*, by all of the security checks.

Of course, Dennis had been cleared, too—for all the good it had done her.

Mostly, it was Trudy who bustled in and out of her room, with trays and ice packs and the occasional hug. Neal kept doing his tentative thing, where he would stand in the doorway and sort of shuffle back and forth, while he decided whether to come in, but Steven—other than a sullen "yeah, we lost again today, we *suck*" report—avoided her completely. Her mother hadn't come upstairs at all, for hours, and her father didn't seem to be around, either.

That is, he *was* probably around, but she assumed that he was angry at her about the conversation she'd tried to have with him in the hospital—or she was angry at him, for refusing to have it. It wasn't that they weren't speaking to each other, exactly, but it had been a very quiet drive home together, and an equally quiet afternoon and night, so far.

The next morning, she felt so sick from either the pills or the anesthesia—or her stinking, rotten, depressing spring break—that she made no effort to get up for breakfast, and then slept through lunch, too. A couple of the WHMU nurses checked on her more than once during the afternoon, and then, Dr. Brooks came upstairs, frowning and concerned. After having a long conversation with her father out by the Yellow Oval Room, he decided to change her pain prescription, which made her feel even *worse*, since he was now going to be giving her something that wasn't even half as strong.

In an attempt to get everyone to leave her the hell alone for the rest of the night, she forced herself to go down the hall and have dinner. Her leg felt as though it weighed about a hundred pounds, and even though Silvio had set up a padded footstool by her chair, it hurt too much for her to make herself eat more than some mashed potatoes and one of Trudy's biscuits before dragging herself back to bed.

She didn't see her mother at all until about ten-thirty, by which time she had already turned out the light. Her mother asked if she wanted anything; she said no; her mother went away. Then, about half an hour later, she and her father had a similarly unproductive exchange, and once he was gone, she took two of her new, weaker pain pills, wrapped her good arm around Vanessa—who scratched her—and tried to go to sleep.

At some point, she had a very vivid nightmare, improbably worse than usual.

It was hard to remember clearly, but she was pretty sure that she had been lying on her back in an overgrown field, or some underbrush, or something, with a lot of broken bones—legs, hips, ribs, arms—so she couldn't get up, or really even move. Her mother—oddly clothed in hunter's garb, complete with a camouflage bush jacket, bulky boots, and a bright orange cap—came out of what might have been a duck blind, as calm and friendly as ever, carrying a break-action shotgun. Meg *knew* she was going to fire the gun in her direction, which she did without hesitation, but it didn't go off for some reason.

"I'm sorry," her mother said, and checked the chamber for ammunition, smiled apologetically, loaded a fresh shell, and snapped the barrel shut. Then, she lifted the shotgun to her shoulder, smiled again, took aim, and—

Which was right around the time she woke up, crying so hard that it really could only be described as sobbing.

She waited for someone to come in and see if she was okay, but no one did, so she must not have screamed this time.

But, after a while, the door eased open, anyway.

The President. Exactly the person she *didn't* want to see right now.

With luck, she wasn't armed.

Meg turned over on her side and pretended that she was asleep, but there must have been just enough light coming in from the hall for her mother to see the tears, because after bending to check on her, she stopped short, instead of leaving the room.

"Meg?" she whispered. "Are you all right?"

Hardly.

"Is it okay if I turn on the light?" her mother asked.

Meg shook her head. "Please don't."

Her mother had already been reaching for the lamp, but she stopped, and sat down on the edge of the bed. "Is the pain worse?"

Yeah, but who really gave a damn? Old news. Meg shrugged.

"Bad dream?" her mother asked.

More old news. "Yeah," Meg said. "I guess."

Her mother rubbed her back gently. "Want to tell me about it?"

The parts she could remember weren't exactly flattering. "You were in it," Meg said. "I'm not sure what you were doing." Or, more important, *why* she was doing it.

Her mother's hand paused. "Whatever it was scared you, though."

Yes.

Her mother leaned down to kiss her forehead. "I'm sorry."

Christ, things were so fucked up that her mother felt compelled to apologize for something she had done in someone else's nightmare. But Meg was too tired, and afraid, and sad, to do anything other than try to stop crying.

"I know you don't like the idea," her mother said, after a while, "but you need to talk to someone."

Oh, yeah, that had been really successful the other times they'd tried to make her do it.

"I'd like you to start as soon as possible," her mother said, "but I'm willing to listen to an argument about why we should wait until the semester's over."

What, she'd had a bad day or two, and now she was around the bend? Meg didn't answer, concentrating on patting her cat.

"Meg?" her mother asked, when she didn't say anything.

All right, fine. Meg pulled in a deep breath. "I think what I need is to talk to *you*." About things that had happened, things she had done, and things he had said.

Her mother nodded, her expression both receptive—and cautious.

"*Both* of you," Meg said.

Her mother nodded again. "I think so, too," she said.

38

SHE FOLLOWED HER mother down to her parents' room, very clumsy on the modified, elbow-height metal crutch one of the nurses had brought up earlier, to help give her more support than her cane, but also much better mobility than the wheelchair. Her father, who had been reading in bed, surrounded by their other three cats, looked up, and then put his book aside.

She couldn't remember the last time she had been in their room, which was weird, because it had always been routine for her to sit with one or both of them late at night, watching the news, or some old black-and-white movie that would have bored Steven and Neal out of their skulls. But, for months now, her parents had always come to *her* room, when they wanted to see her, and mostly not together.

She wasn't even sure where to sit—they had never been the types to cuddle together in a big family clump, but they ended up on the couch, her father stacking some pillows on the undoubtedly priceless antique coffee table, and pulling it close enough so that she could ease her leg into a somewhat comfortable position.

They sat there, her parents on either side of her, none of them touching, each second of silence seeming more endless and profound than the preceding one. When she first came in, Kirby had wagged his tail and lumbered over so that she would pat him, but then he had gone back to sleep in his usual spot in front of the fireplace.

It was terrifying to think that they had *never* really talked about it. At least one of them—her father, more often than not—had always been with her during the countless grueling sessions when the FBI and other investigatory agencies debriefed her. Interrogated her, really. And sometimes, in the wake of nightmares or flashbacks, she had been able to gasp out whatever memory it was that had triggered the overwhelming terror, so they knew the basic story, and many of the specific details—but mostly, they all talked *around* it, and Preston and Beth were still the only people with whom she'd ever really tried to go any further.

She didn't know how to start. Where to start. Or even *if* she should start.

Her mother touched her sleeve—Meg was wearing a much-too-big, faded World Champion Boston Red Sox t-shirt—and her hand felt warm, and sure, through the cotton material. "What happened first?" she asked.

Yes. That was a good place. Okay. Meg pulled in a deep breath. "We were coming out the side door," she said. Her exits were always rotated, on an irregular schedule, and that had been a side-exit day, as opposed to, say, an underground parking lot day. "You know, up past the loading dock. And Dennis told me to stop and tie my shoe. Even though we were in transit."

Her parents nodded, and she could feel their absolute concentration on her.

An untied shoe. Jesus, that was all it took. A tiny little moment, just long enough to distract Chet—and whatever unknown backup security she'd had—and set the whole thing off. A split second during which she had no idea she was in the process of changing from the person she had always been—to some other, inferior creature. That everything that had made her *herself* was about to be gone forever.

It had been a hot day. The heels of her hands grazed the asphalt as she crouched down over her sneaker, and even now, when she thought about it, she was almost sure she could smell a whiff of steamy, sun-softened tar.

Which was the last thing she could remember, before all she smelled was cordite, and blood—she hadn't even known that blood *had* a scent—and then, the mens' terrible breath, and overpowering body odor. Once they had her inside the van, it was savage, and atavistic, and they were excited, and confused—and *primal*, in a way that—she was being punched and groped and pistol-whipped by men for whom rape would have been nothing more than an extra jolt of fun, on the best ride any of them had ever taken.

And the guy had let them enjoy it, for a few minutes—hell, he'd probably been aroused by the communal violent energy himself—before ordering them to focus on the task at hand, his voice entirely without affect. Commands not given out of sentiment, she suspected, but merely a desire for efficiency, and maybe a little less *noise*.

She looked at her mother, who did nothing more than motion for her to continue. Then, she looked at her father, who nodded.

So, she took another deep breath—and kept going. She didn't tell them everything—like about sharing Scotch with a terrorist—but she told them a lot. Things the FBI didn't know, and never would. A few things even *Beth* didn't know. Details. Nuances. *Inflections*. To her great shame, she cried a couple of times, because—well, she just couldn't help it. But her mother also had to cover her eyes, more than once. Especially when she talked about how it had felt to wait, alone in the dark, for them to come in and kill her, and how she'd worried about how bad it was going to be when they did. Whether it would be quick, or whether they would take their time. Whether it would *hurt*. And whether, when the moment came, she would beg to be spared—and die a coward.

Then, when she told them about what it had *really* been like in the mine-shaft, lying chained in the cold dirt, slowly dying of thirst, hour after hour, day after day, and about how utterly, gloriously happy she'd been when she realized that all she had to do to get away was destroy her hand, her father cried, too.

She wasn't sure if she could take herself—or them—through the days of crawling through the woods. A lot of it was kind of blurred in her mind, anyway. She closed her eyes, felt her mother's hand graze her cheek, and opened them again. "Did you think there was any chance I'd get back on my own?" she asked.

It was very clear that they didn't want to answer that, but finally, they both shook their heads.

Swell. She wanted to snap something like "Thanks for the vote of confidence," but she restrained the impulse. "So, what did you think was happening?"

Again, they avoided looking at her.

Then, her mother let out her breath. "I assumed that they were brutalizing you, but keeping you in relatively good shape, so that they could use you to manipulate me."

Her father made an abrupt and angry gesture with his hand, but didn't say anything.

"All right, manipulate *both* of us," her mother said, sounding as tense as her father looked.

That was a blatant lie, but Meg, for one, wasn't going to point that out.

"But then," her mother said, when neither of them responded in any way, "after a few days, when we weren't hearing anything, or coming up with any legitimate intelligence, I thought that—" She stopped for a second before going on. "I assumed that it was already over, and probably had been from the very first night."

Jesus. Meg glanced at her father, who nodded.

Another reminder that thirteen days could be a *really* long time.

And once again, her mother was the only one with the nerve to break the silence.

"When I saw the teeth, part of me hoped that you were dead," she said, quietly.

Jesus. Meg leaned away from her, although her mother was staring off into the indeterminate distance, and didn't even seem to notice. She looked at her father, whose face was so rigid and still that she had absolutely no idea what he might be thinking.

"It was almost the worst thing I could imagine, but I assumed that if they could do something that unspeakable to you, and casually leave the evidence behind, that they might—" Her mother moved her jaw. "I thought you might be in a situation where you would rather *not* be alive."

It was probably just as well that she was never going to know exactly what it was like to be inside her mother's head. And she could tell that her father felt pretty much the same way.

"He never crossed the line into unspeakable," Meg said finally.

Her mother looked directly at her, which was strange just by virtue of being notable. "I've always assumed that he was pure evil."

Meg shook her head. "He was very *controlled* evil." Mostly controlled, anyway. Except that she was never going to know how it might have played out, if he hadn't decided to end the whole thing abruptly, and just leave her to die on her own.

If he hadn't, frankly, chickened out.

"I, um, I don't think he would have let them decapitate me while I was still conscious," she said, which made her parents do something that looked very much like cringing. Although, obviously, they all knew that it would have almost been—predictable—if her body had been found that way. Terrorism, in its most grotesque, and hackneyed, form. "I mean, if they were going to film one of those—bad scenes, I think he would have stopped and made sure I was dead, first, before they got to that part." She *hoped* so, anyway. "Or, I don't know, maybe he just would have left the room, so he wouldn't have to watch it happen."

And gone far enough away so that he wouldn't have to *listen* to it happening, either.

The room was quiet enough so that the ticking of the grandfather clock—which had actually belonged to her grandfather—was almost painfully loud. Then, the phone rang, and they all jumped, and then looked over, as it rang again.

"I'm sorry," her mother said. "If I don't pick up, you know they're going to start knocking."

And maybe even break the door down.

Watching her effortlessly cross the room, Meg felt an intense combination of anger, envy, and resentment. It must be nice to get up and walk, without having to think about it and make plans, first. To be able to use both hands. To have hours, and maybe even whole days and weeks, when life didn't revolve around how much everything *hurt*.

God-damn her, anyway.

Her mother was listening intently to whoever was on the other end of the line, and then gave terse instructions, and authorized something or other. When she finished the call, she spoke somewhat crossly to the signal board operator, reiterating that she still didn't want any non-emergency communications put through for the time being, and then hung up.

"I'm sorry, Meg," she said.

Meg shrugged, staring down at her splint and trying to flex her middle and ring fingers, still feeling the resentment cocktail bubbling around somewhere inside.

Whatever conversational rhythm they'd managed to establish was gone now, and they sat there, about a foot apart from one another, in silence.

"I really do apologize," her mother said.

Yeah. Her mother was always sorry. Over and over and over again.

And had too damn many *reasons* to be. Time to take off the gloves. "What would you have done if they'd brought you a video, that showed them hurting me?" Meg asked.

Her mother shivered, instead of answering, and her father looked off in the other direction.

This time, for once, she wasn't going to back down, or be nice. She was *sick* of being nice. "If you knew," she said, "for a fact—saw it, with your own eyes—that I was being tortured beyond human capacity, and all they wanted was *one* small concession, what would you do?"

Her mother shook her head. "I don't know."

In other words, she wouldn't do a god-damned thing, no matter what. Mostly, she could keep all of it under control, duly and politely repressed—but, not right now. To hell with it. To hell with *her*. To hell with everything. "Yeah, well, fuck you," Meg said.

Both of her parents flinched, and her mother's shoulders hunched up.

Fuck both of them, for that matter. "Suppose the tape had sound," Meg said, hearing her voice shake. "And I'm screaming and crying and begging—I mean, *really screaming*, what would you do?"

Her mother shook her head, seeming to shrink right into herself, apparently unaware that she'd brought one hand over to hold her stomach.

But, fuck that, too. "Okay," Meg said, clenching her—still working—hand as hard as she could. "Let's make it even worse. There are *men* in the room with me. A bunch of them. And they're all—"

"Jesus Christ, Meg," her father said. Exploded, really. "Enough already! You're the one doing the torturing now."

Yes, she was, and with very specific intent. "We can tear her apart, Dad," Meg said, looking him dead in the eye. "Not just make her cry, but *shred* her. Eviscerate her, from halfway across the room. Maybe Steven and Neal can do it a little, too, but mostly, in the whole world, it's just you and me. Right, Dad? We can do it. Anytime we want."

The color in her father's face had darkened, and he stood up.

"Excuse me," he said, through his teeth, and then walked into the Presidential dressing room, slamming the door behind him.

Her mother hadn't spoken yet, but Meg could see her trembling, and breathing too hard, and, after the fact, felt completely awful.

"I'm sorry, Mom," she said. "I didn't mean to—"

Her mother smiled so bitterly that it was genuinely scary. "Nothing personal, Meg, but *fuck you* right back. Okay?"

Whoa. *That* was a first. And, oddly, it came as a tremendous relief. Broke a forbidden barrier. Made it seem as though she was sitting with an actual person, and not the god-damn robotic President. "Yeah," Meg said, and nodded. "Okay. I deserved that."

Now, her mother looked at her miserably. "No, you didn't. I'm sorry, I can't believe I just said that to you. I—Jesus Christ, we're all losing our minds."

The sad thing, was that they were all also sorry. Endlessly, constantly, perpetually sorry. And no matter how many times they told each other that, it never seemed to make any difference. Feeling incredibly lonely for some reason, Meg edged over until she was close enough to lean her head on her mother's shoulder.

Which felt very good.

A few seconds passed—long, damn seconds—and then her mother's arms came around her.

Which felt even better.

"They were supposed to protect you," her mother said softly. "And when they didn't do that, they were supposed to *find* you, and bring you home. Those sons of bitches would stand in front of my desk, kind of hanging their heads, and—" She shook her head. "I don't think they ever came within three states of you."

No, it didn't seem that way.

Her mother let out a shaky breath. "Meg, people vicious enough to make a concerted effort to torture an innocent seventeen-year-old, and force her parents to watch it, would never release her alive, no matter *what* I agreed to do."

No. They wouldn't. "I know," Meg said. "It's okay. I just needed to be pissed off about it for a few minutes."

Her mother nodded, and hugged her closer, but then suddenly stiffened. "My God, I said a very offensive thing to you, didn't I."

Well, *yeah*. Talk about showing up late for the party.

"I am so sorry," her mother said. "I don't know what I—I wouldn't even have thought that I was capable of that."

This, from the woman who could not, would not, and *did* not negotiate with terrorists, with her own child's life hanging in the balance. Meg had to grin. "It's all right. I said it first."

"Granted," her mother said, "but, let's not tell anyone, okay? Ever?"

"Our secret," Meg said, and her mother looked very relieved.

Kirby came wandering over, rested his head on her mother's knee, and wagged his tail. He was either very happy to see her—or possibly needed to go out. Or both.

"Hey, at least the dog likes you," Meg said.

Her mother nodded. "I'll have to have them start taking lonely, pensive pictures of me with him."

Preferably standing by the windows in the Oval Office, staring out at the Great Land for which she was responsible.

Her mother patted Kirby's head, and then brought her arms back around Meg.

"How much of the anger is something you need your father and me to help you with," she said, "and also have you talk to someone professionally, and how much is because, most of the time, you're in so much pain you can't see straight?"

Good question. Worth weighing. Meg thought it over. "I'd say sixty–forty, in favor of the pain."

Her mother nodded. "I'm going to talk to Bob. I think they're under-medicating you, and we need to bring the pain management people back over here, and come up with some new strategies."

Meg nodded, too. That would be nice. It was soothing to rest against her mother—whose heart, she could feel, had finally slowed down to a normal rhythm; which was a relief—and she let her eyes close. But then, she heard the dressing room door, and she opened them again.

Her father came out, and stared at them. "You're sitting there like *pals*."

Yeah, that's pretty much what they were doing. She and her mother both shrugged.

"Jesus Christ," he said, and went back into the dressing room.

They watched him go.

"This is not what that poor man had in mind when he chatted me up in Harvard Square that day," her mother said.

Which was how her parents had met, when her father was in law school, and her mother was at the JFK School of Government, having just dropped *out* of the law school.

And no, this couldn't have been anywhere in the realm of the way he'd imagined things would turn out.

Her mother's arms felt so warm and safe that she wished they could just sit like this, for hours.

"I didn't mean to swear at you, either," Meg said. "I'm sorry."

Her mother smiled. "Don't worry, we both know I earned it. In fact, I think it was probably long overdue."

Kind of, yeah. "We always used to fight a lot," Meg said. As far back as she could remember. "I mean, *always*."

"Well, mothers and daughters," her mother said, and shrugged.

Yeah. And they'd had a long night, so she should probably be quiet, and not push anymore, but— "Did it make it easier?" she asked.

Her mother looked confused. "Make what easier?"

Could she really ask this? What the hell. Torpedoes be damned. "Not negotiating," Meg said. "I mean, since I can be—hard to be around." And then some.

Her mother frowned at her. "Are you serious?"

Meg nodded.

"God, Meg," her mother said, sounding impatient, as opposed to defensive—the former being a far more comforting reaction, actually. "Do you think I sat there and did a cost-benefit analysis about you?"

Possibly.

Her mother held her hand up as though it were a microphone. "Madam President, when they disemboweled you, what hurt more—cutting out your stomach, or your liver?" She paused, pretending to listen.

"Oh. I see. Well, did it also hurt when they chopped your lungs in half? I see. *In*teresting."

Okay, she got the point.

"I'm guilty of many things, Meg," her mother said, "but not loving you with every fiber of my being isn't one of them."

Deep down, she knew that, but sometimes, it just plain had to be said aloud.

They sat on the couch, the clock ticking away.

"Could you have borne it?" her mother asked, her voice so soft that Meg had to move closer to hear her.

Rape. Torture. Some unendurable combination of the two. Meg couldn't help shuddering. "I don't know. I guess it would depend on how long it went on, and how sadistic they got."

Her mother slowly released her breath. "Yes, I suppose it would."

Not much else to say, beyond that.

The sun was coming up, which meant that the President wasn't going to be able to hold off the world much longer.

"How's the pain right now?" her mother asked.

They were being honest tonight. This morning. Whatever. "I feel like slaughtering a busload of nuns and orphans," Meg said. Maybe some puppies, too. Kittens. A nest full of newly-hatched robins.

Her mother nodded. "Just as well you took it out on us, then."

Yes, much less collateral damage that way. But, still. "If I had it all to do over," Meg said, "I think maybe I just would have come in here last night, and asked you to hold me like this until I fell asleep."

"Well," her mother kissed the top of her head, "we'll try that tonight, maybe."

Yeah.

39

AFTER A WHILE, her father came out again, and they all acted as though it was a normal morning—mostly because there was enough commotion out in the hall to indicate that her brothers were up and about, and probably already on their way into the dining room to eat breakfast. Her parents looked so wrung-out that she felt guilty, especially since they weren't going to have the luxury of going straight to bed after breakfast, if they felt like it.

Her mother gave her one last squeeze and then stood up, noticeably stiff, pausing to stretch her back slightly.

"Make sure they put some down-time in your schedule today," her father said.

Her mother shrugged. "A shower, and I'll be fine."

"*Kate*," he said, and her mother nodded impatiently.

Were they always this abrupt—and grumpy—in the morning? Now that she thought about it, she had no idea, because they almost never used marital shorthand in front of her.

Her father was wearing a flannel pajama shirt and old grey sweat-pants, and he frowned down at himself, then walked over to his dresser.

"You'll go this afternoon?" her mother asked. Steven's game, pre-sumably.

Her father nodded, as he pulled on a sweater and stepped into a pair of ancient loafers.

"Good," her mother said.

The first knock—the timing of which had been nervously debated by the staff, no doubt—on the door came, and Felix brought in coffee, English muffins, and a pile of morning newspapers. Then, Frank arrived with a stack of leather-bound folders, paperwork, and daily briefing re-ports, the phone started ringing off the hook—and the President, still dressed in yesterday's work clothes and unshowered, was back on the clock.

Her father reached out to ruffle Meg's hair. "I want you to get some sleep, but come have breakfast, first, okay?"

Meg nodded. Against all odds, she was pretty hungry, which seemed wrong, somehow. He gave her a hand up, and then held her crutch out for her. She had to stand very still to make sure that she had her balance, but then followed him to the hall.

He covered it up pretty well, but she pretty much *lurched* into the dining room, where Trudy was fussbudgeting around, while Steven and Neal sat at the table, eating pancakes and sausages.

"Well, don't you two look scruffy this morning," Trudy said.

Odds were, the President wasn't going to be at her most perky, either.

"Me, too, Dad?" Meg asked, as her father poured himself some coffee from the silver pot on the sideboard.

He brought over an extra cup, and she drank half of it before even remembering that it might have been nicer to add milk and sugar, first.

Her brothers didn't ask why her father wasn't wearing a suit, but she could tell that Steven was suspicious. And Neal seemed to notice Steven's reaction, because he looked worried, but neither of them said anything.

Her conversation with her parents had been private—but, that didn't mean that her brothers shouldn't know about it. In fact, arguably, they *should*. Except for the more gruesome, and personally unflattering, parts, of course. But she wasn't sure if she wanted to be the one to bring it up, although she was positive that her father had no intention of doing so, since he was drinking coffee and bent over *The Washington Post*. So, she decided just to let Trudy fix her a plate of breakfast and try to stay awake long enough to eat some of it.

After about fifteen minutes, her mother came in, all decked out in a royal blue designer suit and high heels, looking extremely soigné—except for one small detail, and Meg laughed.

"What?" her mother asked, pausing halfway to her chair.

"You, um, have a Mary Tyler Moore hair-bump," Meg said. As so aptly demonstrated in what might be her all-time favorite episode of the entire series—or any other television show, for that matter.

Her mother frowned. "Oh, I most certainly do not."

Her brothers and Trudy—and even her father—grinned.

"Well, of all things," her mother said, and bent to check her reflection in the side of the coffee pot.

Watching her try to fix her hair-bump—which kept popping stubbornly back up every single time she patted it down—made the atmosphere so wonderfully relaxed that it crossed Meg's mind that her mother had never once in her life left her bedroom without stopping for a long, critical examination of herself in the mirror, first.

"Does the President need a comb?" Meg's father asked.

"The President does, indeed," her mother said, and glanced at Neal. "Be a good kid?"

Neal laughed, and hustled out of the room, returning with a comb, and two different kinds of hairbrushes, all of which her mother employed, with questionable results.

This was an entirely intentional hair-bump, no two ways about it. The President, attempting to change the tone of family interaction, by providing unexpected comic relief.

"You should, perhaps, find this somewhat less amusing," her mother said to her, "given the fact that you have a significant hair-bump of your own."

Stop the presses. "Have I ever gotten through an entire day when I *didn't* have a hair-bump, at least part of the time?" Meg asked.

Her mother thought about that. "Sadly, no, but I think I might have preferred it if you hadn't reminded me of that troubling fact."

Felix appeared with more coffee, whole wheat toast, a bowl of fresh blueberries and cantaloupe, and a crystal parfait of yoghurt mixed with granola. Meg saw him register the President's hair-bump, with a second of indecisive consternation, but then continue serving her without missing a beat.

They were having a pleasant meal. Should she be smart, and leave it at that, or should she take advantage of the situation, and try to move things forward? She looked at her father, who shrugged in a resigned way, and then, at her mother, whose shrug was tentative, and maybe even had a touch of restrained panic in it.

Screw it, then. Back into the breach. She waited until Felix was gone, and then put down her fork. "Mom and Dad and I talked for a long time last night," she said.

Only to be greeted by complete, not terribly receptive, silence.

Noticing Trudy make a movement towards the door, as though she was about to make a tactful exit, Meg shook her head.

"You're part of the family," she said. And an ideal combination of peacemaker and strict disciplinarian—both of which they might need, to officiate. Referee. "Please stay."

Trudy glanced at her parents, then nodded, and settled back into her chair.

"I know everything's—" She should be careful here; Trudy hated profanity— "messed up, and we're all mad, and scared, and—" Okay, she was also in danger of doing some serious rambling. Maybe she should wait and bring this up on a morning when she'd actually had some sleep. Could think more clearly. "*I'm* scared, okay? All the time. And I'm just god-damned—" So much for avoiding swearing; she looked at Trudy— "uh, sorry—if I want to let them wreck our family like this. I want us to—Christ, I don't know. Try to be ourselves again. You know?"

"So, like, you mean, *all* of us trying to fix stuff?" Steven asked stiffly. "Or just you and me and Neal?"

Their father sighed. "She means all of us, Steven."

Steven's shoulders were even more stiff than his voice had been. "Yeah, well, at least Meg and Neal and me have been *trying*. You know, to act like we *like* each other."

Her parents didn't respond to that, but they also didn't contradict him.

"But, we do like each other," Neal said uneasily. "I mean, this is our, you know, our *family*. And everything."

Funny that her brothers couldn't quite bring themselves to look at their mother—but they weren't having any trouble sending glares at their father. Her mother's expression was blank to the point of being frightening; her father mainly looked worn out.

"You've all had a very hard time," Trudy said. "It's going to take a while for you to sort through things together, that's all."

Steven scowled at her. "It's *been* a while, Trudy. And they just, like—it keeps getting, you know, *worse,* not better."

Trudy smiled at him. "It's not a train, dear. You can't make it run on time."

A wise, and peaceful—and somewhat tiresome—remark.

"If it happens to me," Steven said, staring at their mother now, "or Neal, or Dad, or Meg again, you gonna negotiate or anything this time?"

Her mother's face was immobile—the shade of her skin seeming like some combination of green and grey—and then, she very gently shook her head. "No," she said, her voice almost inaudible. "I'm sorry."

Whereupon, the silence was so oppressive that it seemed *loud.* Deafening, really. Her father wouldn't look at anyone, but Meg saw his fists tighten.

"Yeah, well, *good,*" Steven said, unexpectedly. "Why should Meg be the only one who gets to be all heroic and stuff?"

Christ, could he be any more god-damned competitive? What a jerk. Meg shook her head.

"I'd break *both* hands," he said to her, in a challenging way. "You know, if I had to."

Oh, yeah, right. "The hell you would," Meg said. "After you broke the first one, it wouldn't work well enough anymore to hold the rock."

Steven frowned. "Then, I'd, you know, *stomp* on it."

Yeah, yeah, yeah. In his dreams.

Sitting up at the end of the table, her mother's mouth was trembling, but she closed her eyes and when she opened them again, she wasn't trembling anymore, but she looked about as sad as Meg had ever seen her—which was saying quite a lot.

"Mom," she started.

Her mother shook her head, pushing herself to her feet. "I'm sorry, I—I'd really better—" She turned her head enough so that it would be impossible to make eye contact with any of them. "I'm going to excuse myself now."

"If it happens to me, will it be scary?" Neal asked.

For a second, Meg thought her mother might actually pass out, and then she very carefully sat down again. Not that Neal seemed all that upset, since he had gone right back to drinking orange juice and dumping more maple syrup on his pancakes.

"Neal," their father said, "nothing's going to—"

Oh, enough already. Her parents trying so hard to shield them all the time had *caused* a lot of this. "Yeah," Meg said, cutting him off. "It would be scary."

Her parents, and Trudy, looked at her with absolute fury.

"I wasn't prepared," she said to them, collectively. "It would have been so much easier if I had been even a little bit prepared."

There was no question that they didn't like that much, but none of them said anything.

And her brothers were waiting for her to go on.

"You're both safe," she said to Neal, even though she knew Steven was listening just as intently, if not more so, "because of all the new precautions and procedures we have now, but if, God completely forbid, it ever happened, yeah, it would be scary. It'd be fast, and loud, and they'd be swearing like crazy—maybe in English, maybe not—and banging you around while they grabbed you. But, they would have gone to a lot of trouble, and they'd want to keep you alive, so you'd just have to stay really calm, and pay attention to whatever your instincts were telling you, because they would probably be right."

Neal nodded gravely.

"And do your best to be quiet, and polite, and try to do what they want," Meg said. "If you cooperate, mostly, it might go better. I kept bugging the guy—" maybe not such a bright move, in retrospect—"which probably made things even worse than they had to be."

"Yo, I so totally can't picture that," Steven said, to no one in particular.

Neal—no doubt to her parents' horror—laughed. "I bet she was telling him he was all stupid, and how mad she was and everything."

Well—yeah. More or less. Maybe her brothers knew her a little too well. "Why don't you guys shut up and eat your damn pancakes," Meg said, grinning. "I mean, I got back here—I must have done something right."

Her mother had a ten-thousand yard stare, her father was squeezing his temples, and Trudy looked as though she wished she could slump down and cover her head with her arms.

"Look," Meg said, "about six years from now, when we're all back in Massachusetts—" She stopped, not sure why her parents and Trudy had frowned at her again. Wait, she'd said *six*. Dr. Freud had apparently come leaping out of his dark, furtive corner, yet again. "Okay, I'm sorry. That's a different conversation, isn't it?"

The three of them nodded, still frowning.

Right. "Well, just think of me as the Iowa caucus," Meg said. "So, I'm either an aberration—or a *trend*."

She thought that might make them mad, but her mother smiled a tiny smile, and her father actually laughed. Trudy didn't seem to have committed to a position yet, and her brothers looked confused.

"You can be all of the southern states on Super Tuesday, Dad," she said.

Her father laughed again. "Thanks, Meg. That sounds about right."

The tension had eased enough for her mother to pick up her coffee and take a small, unsteady sip. "If you'd prefer," she said, dryly, "you can play the role of a vast right-wing conspiracy."

Meg grinned, visualizing a Broadway marque which read: "Russell James Powers: Appearing Now as *The Vast Right-Wing Conspiracy*! Two Terms Only!"

"Just promise that I get to be Texas, Katie," her father said. "That's all I really ask."

Meg still had the uneasy feeling that this conversation might swing wildly in either direction, any second now, and Trudy must have, too, because she got up and started bustling around, transferring glasses and dishes over to the sideboard.

On the other hand, he'd said "Katie." She couldn't even remember the last time he'd called her mother Katie. She looked at Steven to see if he'd picked up on that—and since he beamed at her, he must have.

"I think you're all so overtired that you're starting to get silly," Trudy said briskly. "Boys, why don't you go brush your teeth, so you can get to school."

Steven looked alarmed now. "But, we're totally late. I'm gonna need a note. If we don't have notes, they might say I can't play in the game today. And I'm *pitching*."

"Relax," their father said calmly. "We'll write you notes."

Saying *what*, exactly? That Steven and Neal were late, because the family had been carried away by a grueling, disturbing, psychological nightmare of an impromptu encounter session over breakfast and lost track of time? Meg shook her head, wondering what euphemisms they were going to use. Probably something along the lines of "Please excuse Steven's tardiness this morning, he was unavoidably delayed."

Or maybe the phrase "pressing national interests" could be employed.

"Can Mom write them?" Neal asked, sounding like his regular, happy self. "It's way fun when she writes them."

They all looked at her mother, who seemed to have retreated back into herself, looking a bit dazed—and very fragile.

"Kate," Meg's father said. "Notes. The boys need notes for school."

Her mother blinked. "What? Oh. Of course. Would you mind taking care of—" She stopped, studied Neal for a second as though he were unfamiliar, and then nodded. "Right. I'm sorry. Let me—go get some stationery."

Meg watched her walk, with cautious and deliberate steps—a little stilted, a little slow—out of the room—and felt guilty as hell. Why, after last night, had she thought it might be a good idea to spend breakfast inflicting even *more* stress on everyone? Christ, if anything major and unexpected happened in the country—or the world—today, they were all going to be in trouble.

Her father frowned, and stood up. "Excuse me," he said, and went after her.

The room got very quiet again, as they watched him go.

"So, who am I in your dumb game?" Steven asked, breaking the silence.

Right. The game. "You're the unexpectedly close call in New Hampshire," Meg said.

Steven made a sound that was something like a laugh, shook his head, and left the room.

"Who am I, Meggie?" Neal asked, smiling with great anticipation.

That was an easy one. "You're the dependable Democratic strongholds," Meg said.

Neal thought about that. "So, I'm like, New York? And maybe, Michigan and Illinois?"

Christ almighty, she was related to a little boy who understood the Electoral College. Maybe, if she was lucky, he would sit down sometime and explain cricket to her, too. The allure of effeminate male pop stars with no apparent musical talent. How, exactly, it made sense that people who were anti-choice seemed, almost invariably, to be *pro*–death penalty. And why, for God's sakes, Grady hadn't taken Pedro out of the game. "Yeah," Meg said. "Massachusetts, Rhode Island, Connecticut, California, Wisconsin, Maryland, New Jersey—and, if we play our cards right, Ohio and Pennsylvania, too."

Neal looked delighted. "I am some totally *cool* states. Big ones!"

Oh, yeah. Rhode Island, leading the pack.

"Young man, there is a toothbrush waiting somewhere with your name on it," Trudy said, sounding more stern than she looked.

Neal laughed, and went out to the West Sitting Hall.

Everyone was gone now, except for Trudy, and once again, silence hung over the room.

"All right, dear," Trudy said, as Felix and Pete—looking as though they were trying very hard to disappear into the woodwork—came in to start clearing away the breakfast dishes. "Who am I?"

Another easy one. "A completely non-partisan version of the Supreme Court incapable of ill-advised judicial activism," Meg said.

Trudy smiled. "Go get some sleep, Meg. You're a little punchy."

Only a *little*?

She limped down to her room, and pretty much fell onto her bed—which Vanessa found deeply offensive and inconsiderate. She was too tired to take the time to guide her leg underneath the covers, so she just stretched out on top of the spread. But she couldn't quite relax enough to close her eyes, so after a while, she picked up the phone and asked to be connected to the new communications director.

"Can you try to get them all to kind of take it easy on my mother today?" Meg asked, once the call had been put through. "She's really tired, and—well, I want to be sure she's okay."

"What in the hell went *on* up there last night?" Preston asked. "You're the third one to call so far."

She was very slow on the uptake, then, not to have thought of it sooner. "Who called? Trudy and Steven?"

"Your *father* and Trudy," Preston said.

Oh, well, that made more sense. And it was a relief to know that, despite everything, her father was still concerned about her mother's well-being. "Okay, that's good," Meg said. "I mean—" No need to drag Preston in any deeper than he already was. "Well, she didn't get much sleep—" or even, *any*— "so—"

Preston's sigh was absolutely long-suffering. "Yes, that piece of information is starting to sink in, Meg."

She couldn't help grinning. "Third time was the charm, then?"

"I'm hanging up now," he said, and did just that.

SHE THOUGHT SHE might sleep for several days straight, but when she woke up, it was barely past noon. She was going to close her eyes again, but she was so thirsty that she decided to get up, instead.

She was on her way to the kitchen when she saw Trudy on the couch in the West Sitting Hall, lighting a cigarette. Naturally, the Residence—hell, the entire *complex*—was supposed to be a smoke-free zone, but given her status within the family, no one was likely to confront her about it.

"You don't see me smoking," Trudy said.

"Nope, I sure don't," Meg said, and sat down in one of the easy chairs, propping up her leg.

Jorge came out to ask if she wanted anything, and she declined the offer of lunch, but was more than willing to accept a glass of lemonade, while he also brought a fresh pot of tea for Trudy.

"I really don't want you to skip any more meals," Trudy said.

Yeah, yeah, whatever. Meg nodded a perfunctory nod, and looked out the window, in the direction of the West Wing. Her mother sometimes went stir-crazy in the Oval Office, and held informal meetings out on the patio, or in chairs set up at the end of the Rose Garden, but today was an unlikely candidate for anything that relaxed.

"That woman never left her room with a hair out of place in her life," she said.

Trudy grinned. "No, I don't believe she has."

With luck, she'd regained her emotional wherewithal enough to repair the presumptively self-inflicted coiffure damage before going downstairs to the West Wing. If not, the press corps would have an unexpected Day of Joy. Meg drank some of her lemonade, hoping that she wouldn't finish it too quickly, since she would then immediately crave more. "I'm sorry breakfast ended up being—complicated."

"You're all doing better than you have any right to be," Trudy said.

Oh, yeah. Absolutely. Meg nodded. "Not at all uptight or repressed, right?"

Trudy smiled, and smoked. Although she had only one son, in his mid-thirties, Trudy's extended Irish family—her husband had died about sixteen years earlier—was large, and cheerful, and rambunctious, and prone to a great deal of hugging and shouting and laughing. And, while they might be geographically close, Brighton—the Boston neighborhood where she had always lived—was barely on the same planet as staid Chestnut Hill.

"Do you ever wish you'd gotten involved with a different family?" Meg asked.

"It's inconceivable at this point," Trudy said.

Hmmm. Not exactly a resounding "No! Of course not! How could you even *think* such a ridiculous thing?"

"Sean left me in very good shape financially," Trudy said, and looked unhappy for a few seconds, the way she always did, whenever she mentioned her late husband. "I really didn't need to work at all. Frankly, I wasn't even sure if I wanted to."

"Why did you?" Meg asked.

Trudy shrugged, her expression somewhat closed off—because, of course, even though she was often gregarious, she was *also* a born-and-bred New Englander. "After a while, I decided that I didn't want to spend the rest of my life rattling around an empty house."

Meg nodded, and let a respectful silence pass. "I can see that," she said, then, "but why would you want to get tied up with *my* parents?"

Trudy tapped some ashes from the end of her cigarette into a pristine glass ash tray dating back to, as far as Meg knew, the Johnson Administration. "We all knew it was a huge mistake within about five minutes of sitting down for coffee together." Trudy paused. "Which your mother had made, and wasn't tasty."

Not gifted at the stove, her mother—with the possible exception of a surprisingly good lemon-blueberry cake, which she baked every now and then for no readily apparent reason. Other than that, her culinary skills were exceptionally pedestrian.

"We were in the den," Trudy said, "and she was jittery and guilty about needing full-time help, even though she was commuting back and forth to Washington, and oh, about six months pregnant, and you were only three."

Pregnant with Steven.

"She was still in the House, then," Trudy said.

Meg nodded. Many of her very first memories involved things like being on the floor of the House and banging the Speaker's gavel after the session was over, and riding on the underground Congressional subway, and such.

"They were starting to look at her for the Senate seat that was going to be opening up," Trudy said, "but she was thinking that being Governor might be more compatible with raising children."

Yeah. Good plan. Meg laughed. After all, what could be a better career choice for a person who was hoping to be an aggressively hands-on parent than serving as the Governor of a state?

Trudy grinned, too. "And I thought, oh, dear."

Why she hadn't, instantly, run for the hills—or the beaches of Florida—was a complete mystery. Meg shook her head. "In some ways, she really doesn't have a clue, does she?"

"She never learned how, Meg," Trudy said.

No. Her mother had been only five when *her* mother died suddenly, and tragically, in a riding accident, and her well-meaning, workaholic father, a strict British nanny, and a couple of elderly aunts, had done their best, but as far as Meg could tell, they had produced a child who was missing a few crucial emotional pieces. "She just automatically assumes that we don't love her unconditionally," Meg said.

Trudy nodded.

Which pretty much *ensured* it, of course. And made them all behave accordingly.

"Your father was very quiet, over in the green chair," Trudy said, after a long minute.

He loved that chair. Sat there constantly, drinking long-necked Molsons or Rolling Rocks, doing paperwork from the firm, and listening to the Red Sox or laughing at feverishly impassioned sports call-in shows.

"Your mother was also defensive," Trudy went on, "because it should have been your nap time, but you were sitting on the rug, singing some little song and playing with a plastic container. Tupperware, I think."

She had been told, many times, that she had been the kind of child who always enjoyed the packing materials more than the toy itself. Her father insisted that he had once heard her mother on the phone, right before Christmas, talking to some mail order company, saying something to the effect of, "Yes, yes, I'm sure it's very nice, but please, could you tell me more about the *box* it comes in?"

"She was embarrassed that your hair was a mess, too," Trudy said, "but, as we now know, that's typical for you."

Probably even at this very second. Meg smoothed it down. "Tousled. I think 'tousled' is the word you wanted." Artfully so.

Trudy smiled, and stubbed out her cigarette.

"You, um, you really shouldn't smoke," Meg said. "It's bad for you."

"I know," Trudy said, and lit up another.

She'd said it once; there was no reason to repeat herself. "So, why'd you take the job?" she asked.

"Well, obviously, I wasn't going to," Trudy said. "We were all terribly uncomfortable, and I was gathering myself together so I could leave, but then I made a dreadful mistake."

That didn't sound very good.

"I *looked* at you," Trudy said, and touched Meg's shoulder affectionately. "And you gave me your little grin, and I was lost."

Which was nice as hell, and Meg smiled shyly at her before leaning away from her hand.

They both looked up as Jorge came out with a pitcher of lemonade, and topped off Meg's glass—for which, she was very grateful. Trudy also asked him if they could go ahead and have some lunch, suggesting a menu of grilled cheese sandwiches, soup, salad—and, well, much more than Meg had any interest in eating. But, she just stared out the window at the West Wing and the Old Executive Office Building, instead of saying so.

"Are you mad at her, too?" Meg asked, when they were alone again. "I mean, the way Dad is?"

Trudy didn't answer right away, fiddling around with her teacup. "We had some ugly words," she said finally. "During everything. And—I was very hard on *both* of them, Meg, and I regret not holding my tongue."

Her thirteen days had been no treat, but neither had anyone else's apparently. "What was it like around here?" she asked.

"I don't know if I can describe—" Trudy stopped to think. "It was like being trapped in a room full of wounded lions. Your parents, raging at each other in complete silence. And those poor stoic little boys." She shook her head. "I really *had* to go home, to be with Jimmy, during his operation—" her son, who had had his desperately-needed kidney transplant then— "but walking out of this building and leaving those two little boys behind was one of the hardest things I've ever had to do."

Christ, it must have been awful. The good news, being that Jimmy's surgery had been—and continued to be—a resounding success.

Wounded lions, though. What a thought. Except it was all too easy to imagine. Especially her father.

"Your friend was an absolute godsend," Trudy said.

Meg looked up. "Friend?"

"He was there, for all of them, every single second," Trudy said. "He never even seemed to need to sleep. And knowing that he would be doing his best to take care of your brothers made it possible for me to go."

Preston, then. "He's *everyone's* friend," Meg said. "Not just mine."

"Yes, of course," Trudy said, and smiled. "Anyway, he was wonderful. He's been wonderful through *all* of this, especially to you, and I'll forever be indebted to him for that."

Obviously, they'd often been together in the same room, but she had never really seen Trudy and Preston have any one-on-one conversations, so he probably had no idea that she felt that way.

"What?" Trudy asked.

Considering how jumbled up—and tired—she was right now, that was hard to answer. "It's important," Meg said. For better or worse. "What people do in the clutch."

"It most surely is," Trudy said.

40

LUNCH WAS, AS ever, immaculately prepared, and she made an effort to put a dent in her salad, before giving up and turning her attention to the grilled cheese sandwich, only managing to finish half of it.

"I'll go in and fix you anything you want," Trudy said.

Meg shook her head. "What I have here is great, thanks." Regardless of whether she felt like eating it.

They were just finishing when Dr. Brooks arrived to check her over, get a quick rundown on how she was feeling, discuss the concept of possibly setting up some acupuncture and biofeedback sessions, and hand her a prescription bottle of strong pain medication, Meg taking one of the pills before he had even gotten as far as the Center Hall. Then, she moved over to the couch, where Trudy was already sitting. Felix came out with a tray of coffee and petits fours, which looked too ornate and impressive to eat. But, she certainly wasn't sorry to see the coffee, and to appease Trudy, she put a chocolate-dipped petits four on her dessert plate.

"Before, you called Preston a godsend," she said.

Trudy nodded.

"Does it bother you that we aren't religious?" Meg asked. Neal's interest in Sunday excursions to St. John's, notwithstanding.

Trudy peered at her over her glasses. "In what sense?"

Oh, where to begin. "Every sense," Meg said.

Trudy shook her head. "It bothers me that you don't have the comfort. These terrible things have happened, and I think you all feel so very alone. So, I wish you had that."

She must be pretty far gone, since she couldn't fathom the idea of God being a *comfort*. More like an adversary. And a cruel one, at that.

"You know," Trudy said, when she didn't respond, "I've always had the feeling that you think religion is something reserved for people who aren't very bright."

Well, she definitely wasn't going to touch that one. Not even with a *thirty*-foot pole.

Especially since she knew that Trudy often felt self-conscious about not having gone to college, and the last thing she would *ever* want to do would be to hurt her feelings in any way.

But if she didn't come up with an answer, that, all by itself, would seem like a de facto endorsement of the sentiment. "No, of course not," she said. "Never."

Trudy nodded, but obviously didn't believe a single word of that.

Damn. All right, she was going to have to be somewhat more honest. "I think that maybe sometimes—" She stopped, to try and organize her thoughts. "Well, I guess it's possible that, in certain situations, there might be a tendency for, um, faith to negate reason."

To her surprise, Trudy laughed. "Meghan, you're even more cagey than she is."

Which wasn't exactly a compliment.

"Faith *isn't* reasonable," Trudy said. "That's the whole point, dear."

Granted, but she, personally, needed to have her life rest on much firmer ground than that. It just seemed too easy—and submissive—and, ultimately, futile to fall back on a knee-jerk "God will provide" and "it's out of our hands" outlook.

"Did you know that your mother's primary surgeon wasn't on duty the day she got shot?" Trudy asked.

Meg shrugged. There had maybe been some talk about that, but she hadn't paid much attention to it at the time, nor did she want to do so now.

"His wife had fallen off her bicycle and broken her ankle somewhere near the Tidal Basin, and he brought her over for X-rays, so the best cardiothoracic surgeon in the city happened to be standing in the Emergency Room when your mother came in," Trudy said.

Yeah, so? Meg shrugged.

Trudy sipped some coffee. "I don't know. Something like that happens, and I can't help wondering."

God, serendipity—or just plain dumb luck? "I bet someone else in Washington got shot that day," Meg said.

Trudy glanced over.

"And that person had a bad chest injury, too, but *wasn't* lucky enough to go to an ER where a gifted surgeon was waiting around, with nothing to do," Meg said.

Trudy nodded. "Maybe."

More like, definitely. "So, God decided to help my mother," Meg said, "and not *that* person, who was probably really nice, and had a family and everything, too?"

Trudy frowned. "I don't think it works that way. I don't think God chooses."

Like hell. "*I* do," Meg said. "If there's a God, then he or she is intervening sometimes—and not other times, and that isn't fair. I don't see any damn comfort in that."

Trudy looked at her thoughtfully. "You're something a great deal more than 'not religious,' aren't you?"

Yes. But, Trudy was deeply Catholic, and Meg didn't want to say anything unkind by accident, and it might be better to change the subject. At once.

Maybe they could try something non-controversial—like politics.

"Meg?" Trudy asked.

Well, okay, there was no easy way to avoid it, then. "I think we're on our own," Meg said. "At best."

At worst, there was no God at all, but just some malevolent higher power, toying with all of them like an unimaginably mean and mercurial cat.

Trudy nodded. "We might be. But, maybe God is wise enough to let people who want to be on their own do that, and to be more proactive with people who feel otherwise."

It was still picking and choosing. Which *sucked*. "What," Meg said, "you mean nothing bad ever happens to God-fearing true believers, and the rest of us are pretty much screwed?"

Trudy's eyes narrowed, and then she shook her head. "No. That's not what I meant."

And it had been a lousy thing to say, since she knew damn well how seriously Trudy took her faith—and also knew that, belief in God aside, plenty of awful things had happened to her over the years, too. Meg sighed. "I'm sorry. I really shouldn't have—"

"You've earned the right to be angry, Meghan," Trudy said. "I would never tell you otherwise."

Trudy was the only person she knew well who ever called her Meghan—and she only did it when she was at her most solemn. Strangers, of course, *routinely* referred to her as Meghan, thereby proving that they were, in fact, strangers.

"That doesn't mean that I don't consider it a great blessing that you're here," Trudy said.

Meg had been about to say something both apologetic and conciliatory, but now she was angry again. "I crawled through those mountains by myself." Broke her hand alone, fought the pain alone, fought the *terrorists* alone, did everything for thirteen straight fucking days completely alone. No revelations, no sense of peace, no intervention—or comfort.

"What made you keep crawling?" Trudy asked, sounding genuinely curious.

"*I* made me keep crawling," Meg said. Sheer god-damn exhausting force of will; nothing more.

Trudy nodded. "But, you could have quit."

Meg looked at her.

"No, I guess not," Trudy said, and smiled.

They sat there quietly, the petits fours still untouched.

"It would be easier not to believe in God, than to believe in a God who isn't kind," Meg said.

"Yes, it surely would be." Then, Trudy smiled again. "But, how can I not believe in God when I'm sitting here looking at one of his best efforts?"

Meg had an instant, cynical reaction to *that*, but it had been such a loving answer that she kept it to herself.

Trudy held her hand up. "And please don't tell me you think that means he needs more practice."

Pretty close to exactly what she'd had in mind. "How'd you guess I was going to say that?" Meg asked.

Trudy patted her good leg. "Because I've known you since you were three years old, and even after everything that's happened, you're still very much yourself."

The question being, was that a good thing, or a bad thing? "I feel like someone else," Meg said uneasily.

Trudy shook her head. "You aren't. You're just a little more complicated now."

Maybe. She was starting to remember how tired she was, and almost yawned. A nap would not be the world's worst idea.

Trudy lit up another cigarette, and then winked at her. "So. Is there a boy?"

Meg nodded, feeling herself blush.

"Is he nice?" Trudy asked.

A Great Unknown. "I'm not sure yet," Meg said. "Other people say no, but mostly, he's been really nice to me."

Trudy frowned and drew in on her cigarette. "Only mostly?"

"One extremely mean crack," Meg said. "But he sent me flowers the next day to apologize. Roses and everything."

"Well, good for him, then." Trudy settled herself comfortably against the cushions. "So, tell me all about it. Not just him, but everything you're doing up there."

The normalcy of the request was refreshing. Exhilarating, even. So, Meg told her about Jack, and her dorm, and her entrymates, and the mess with Susan—and even the nightmares. Her classes—about which she suspected she should make an effort to sound more interested, physical therapy, dealing with the press and paparazzi, dealing with hundreds of new people, dealing with ice and snow and mud and hills and flights of stairs, day after day after day.

"Am I boring you completely?" she asked, after a while.

"That *question* bores me," Trudy said.

Whenever they'd come home from school, Trudy had always wanted to hear chapter and verse, in great detail, from all three of them. She'd been inclined to quiz her parents, in depth, about their respective days, or weeks, at work, too, although maybe she regretted the impulse when her father would go into long explanations of taxation minutiae, or her mother said things like, "And *then*, after we vitiated the previous concurrent resolution, we incorporated it into an *alternate* resolution, which, despite the recalcitrance of the subcommittee, I thought was very promising, indeed."

They were still talking—or, okay, *Meg* was mostly talking—when her father came down the hall, wearing a dark suit, heading for her parents' bedroom. He looked surprised to see them, probably because he must have expected her still to be asleep.

"Are you going to Steven's game?" Meg asked.

Her father automatically looked at his watch, and nodded.

"Maybe I should come, too," she said. "I mean, he'd be glad."

Her father shook his head more adamantly than seemed to be necessary. "You look awfully tired. And besides, it's an away game."

Well, that didn't mean it was on another continent. And he was going, so how far away could it be? Meg shrugged. "That's okay. I mean, it's the only chance I'm going to get to see him play." Since her brothers' spring vacation started on Friday, and he wouldn't have any more games until after she'd gone back to school.

"The semester will be over in time for you to come to a couple at the end of the season, if you want," he said.

Yeah, but she was here *now*, and Steven was pitching today, and what was the big deal?

Her father sighed. "Meg, I really don't think this is the right away game for you to go see."

Which made very little sense, unless— "Oh, Christ," Meg said. "They're playing *us*? At home?"

Her father nodded.

With all of the private schools in the Beltway, they had to be playing her old school, on the one day when she was free to go to a game? Didn't that just bloody figure, although, in truth, the Mid-Atlantic Conference was small enough so that it really wasn't *that* improbable. And Christ, it was almost funny, in a wretched sort of way. "I think I should go," she said.

He shook his head. "I'm sorry, but I'd prefer that you didn't."

Had it slipped his mind that she hated being told what to do? "Fine," she said stiffly. "I'll ride over with my agents, and maybe I'll see you there."

Trudy made an extremely disapproving sound with her tongue.

Meg scowled at her. "He's treating me like I'm about ten years old." No, more like *five* years old, because Neal was probably happily en route to the game at this very moment.

"Possibly because you're acting that way," Trudy said.

Interestingly, she was quite willing to tell the President of the United States to fuck off—but she wouldn't ever be able to bring herself to say it to Trudy.

Her father yanked at the knot in his tie, either because he was trying to redirect some anger, or because it had started feeling as though it was choking him. "Meg," he said, sounding as though he might be about to *humor* her. "I really wasn't happy about your sitting down with the goddamn *Washington Post* a couple of weeks ago, and you didn't take my advice about *that* one, either."

Yeah, so he'd been against it; so, what else was new? Jesus, but he was a grudge-holder. Had he always been that way? "The story hasn't even come out yet," she said. "She might do a good job."

He nodded. "Yes, and won't she—and the rest of the mob—enjoy framing it around the scenario of your returning to the school for the first time."

Scenario. *Fuck*. One of her post-traumatic triggers. He wouldn't have been mean enough to choose that word intentionally, but she had a feeling that his subconscious might have done exactly that.

"Meg, why don't you go get cleaned up and decide whether you really do feel well enough to go out," Trudy said. "And, Russ, maybe you should give Maureen a call, so she can steer the press away, in case any of them pick up on the fact that you two might be heading someplace other than over to the hospital for a checkup."

The Wise Elder, trying to do her thing, with a hostile audience.

She thought about staying in her room for the rest of the afternoon—and maybe the evening, too, but then, brushed her distressingly unruly hair, put on a Williams sweatshirt, and limped back out to the hall. It would be nice if she could have called Preston, and invited him to come, too, and be a buffer, but that wasn't a viable option with him in the West Wing now. Anthony might tag along, but she barely knew the guy, so that wouldn't help much.

Her father was waiting by the private elevator, still in his suit. Normally, he would have changed into something more casual, and probably be wearing a Red Sox cap, but with the suit, the press would be less likely to guess that they were going to the game. Her brothers' schedules were tightly embargoed these days, but it wouldn't take the laziest reporter in town much time to look up the local interscholastic sports schedules and figure out whether Steven had a game this afternoon, and where it was being played.

It went without saying, of course, that terrorists could easily do the exact same thing.

Along with nasty little tenth graders in Nebraska.

There *was* a quick burst of "Hey, where are they going?!" activity outside the South Portico, but her father just smiled and said hello, and she did the same, except that when someone asked how her knee was, she added a "Fine, thank you."

Once they were in the car, and pulling away, they sat quite far apart, and other than her father asking whether her leg was comfortable, and her saying yes—even though it wasn't, neither of them spoke.

She could never remember feeling awkward in front of her father before. Somewhat estranged.

All right, *afraid*.

"Are you mad at me?" she asked.

"You're mad at me, Meg," he said.

That didn't mean that it didn't go both ways.

They were cruising past the gates, and for a second, she felt a retroactive panic attack coming on, but she gulped it down, because she was pretty sure that if her father caught on, he would have the cars turn right around and go back without a second thought.

"Are you all right?" he asked.

She nodded, looking out the window on her side. A number of tourists were standing around on Seventeenth Street, watching the small motorcade go by, most of them taking pictures of the cars, and presumably speculating about who might be behind the tinted windows.

"I was swinging at her last night," Meg said, "but I think I was aiming at *you*."

Her father nodded, unhappily. "I know that, Meg."

Which might explain his very long stay in the Presidential dressing room, and current inability to sit next to her without fidgeting. "Does Mom know, too?" she asked.

"Yes," he said. "In her way, she can be surprisingly bright."

Oh, good—humor. Things would be so much more bearable if they could all sometimes remember the concept of humor. She glanced at his agents up in the front seat, who, in typical Secret Service fashion, were going out of their way not to listen. There was an unspoken covenant that protectees had to be able to have otherwise private conversations, and try to live their lives, in front of their agents, who, as reluctant but necessary witnesses, were never supposed to reveal anything they might have overheard.

"It's ironic," her father said, "that, in essence, you're angry at me precisely *because* I put your well-being, and that of your brothers, above everything else."

With that particular spin, she felt rather petty. And yes, she could see the irony. "You spent about seventeen years running interference between the two of us," Meg said, "you know, trying to keep the peace and all, and when she finally actually did something really awful, I wasn't even very upset about it."

Her father nodded. "I know. It's a little infuriating."

Of this, she had no doubt. "Please don't be mad at me," she said, "okay?"

He shook his head. "I'm not, Meg. Stop worrying about it."

Yeah. It wasn't as though she had any good *reasons* to be worried. It made her sick to admit it, but— "Sometimes I'm scared of you now," she said.

He looked startled. "What?"

"You," she said. "Preston. My agents." Except for Paula and Nellie. "My god-damn political science professor, because he has dark hair and he's in his thirties." Although her political science professor probably *was* a threat, but only an academic one.

For the second time in less than twelve hours, she saw tears in her father's eyes.

"You'll never have any reason to be afraid of me, Meg," he said. "Not ever, under any circumstances."

She knew that, intellectually. She was safe with her father. And Preston. And, probably, her agents. Martin, for sure. Garth. Mr. Gabler.

Jack? Maybe.

She hoped so.

"I need to feel better about you," Meg said.

Her father tilted his head.

"Men, in general," Meg said. "I don't want to start seeing you as people who are mean to women."

Her father sighed. "If I may say so, women are generally mean right back to us."

Only when provoked—although she might be displaying a little gender favoritism there.

"And in my own defense," he said, "I haven't been in my thirties for quite some time now."

His hair wasn't all that dark anymore, either. In fact, during the past two years, it had turned frighteningly grey. Her mother had aged in office, but it was much more visible with her father. Alarmingly so.

She indicated her own hair. "How much of that is from me?"

Her father grinned wryly. "About a third. Your mother and Steven took care of the rest, although Mark's probably responsible for a big chunk."

Her too often ne'er-do-well ski-bum uncle. "None from Neal?" she asked.

"A patch as big as a dime," her father said.

Yeah, that sounded about right.

She looked at him, not completely sure what she was thinking, or how she felt. When she was little, her father had been the one person, other than Trudy, around whom she always felt protected. The person who was always *there*. In direct contrast to the person who, more often than not, wasn't.

"I know it may not seem that way," her father said, "but your mother and I are actually working very hard to—we're working extremely hard."

It sure as hell didn't *show*. She glanced at the two agents in the front seat, neither of whom appeared to be paying any attention to them whatsoever. Even so, she lowered her voice. "Do you think a woman could have gotten me to crawl?" she asked. She had told them, the night before, about having to drag herself down the hall to the filthy little room after her knee was dislocated, the guy watching, and smiling, every inch of the way. Amused. Triumphant, even. Although she hadn't really gone into depth about the fact that she had had to cry from the pain, handcuffed hands covering her face, in the unrealistic hope that he wouldn't be able to tell. "I mean, if she had a gun? Or was it because he was so much bigger, and we both knew he could turn it into rape, whenever he wanted?"

Her father's shoulders noticeably hunched. "I think a gun makes all the difference in the world."

Maybe, but physical size, and sexual menace, didn't hurt. "It was weak," she said.

"It was *sensible*," her father said.

But not exactly valiant.

He let out his breath. "As you pointed out to your brothers this morning, you had to use your instincts, Meg."

Unfortunately, her instincts generally sucked.

"I suspect there were moments when defiance helped you," he said, "but that there were many others when it only would have resulted in your being even more seriously injured, or him deciding that it would be less trouble just to go ahead and—" He stopped.

Kill her.

"You have a superb mind," he said, "and you had the good sense to use it."

One man's opinion. They were very close to the school now, and with unfailingly bad timing, she realized that he was right, and it was a terrible idea for her to have come, and that it was going to be too scary, and she might have to ask to be driven home, without even taking the risk of getting out of the car.

"He had to handcuff, starve, and *injure* you, repeatedly, with God knows how many armed accomplices for backup, to get you to cooperate at all," her father said with great intensity. "And despite stacking the deck in every way he could, how'd it play out?"

She really didn't like this conversation anymore. Or this entire *day*, for that matter.

"You beat the son of a bitch," her father said. "He's the one sitting around right now making excuses and second-guessing himself."

Or, possibly, sitting around and dreaming up a fiendish revenge plot.

"He had every possible advantage at his disposal," her father said, "and you beat him in front of the entire world, with a god-damn *rock*." He smiled unexpectedly, in a way that made him look very much like Neal. "Not to sound too much like your brothers, but it was *excellent*, Meg."

Her father never spoke that way—particularly not when he was in full formal First Gentleman regalia, and it was both jarring and amusing to hear such an adolescent sentiment come out of his mouth. "You need to go with '*wicked* excellent,' " she said, "to get the full effect."

Her father nodded, took a small leather pad with a Presidential Seal on it out of his pocket, and wrote a note to himself—which would have been much too goofy, if she hadn't known that he was kidding.

They were at the school now, pulling into the driveway in front of the administration building. It was too late to change her mind, and she followed her father out of the car, letting him support her elbow while she tried to get her crutch planted properly.

Her brothers had gotten there ahead of them, because she could see some of their agents, along with a couple of DC police cars, and people from the school security staff. Her old headmaster, the Upper School principal, and the academic dean all came outside to meet them, and she figured that the White House must have called ahead to—yeah, there was Anthony, standing next to the administration building.

She was dreading a "We are *so* sorry about what happened to you, it's all our fault" encounter, but they just told her how happy they were to see her, asked how she was liking college, and shook hands with her father. And they *did* seem really happy that she was there, actually.

Her father had wanted her to use a wheelchair, instead of staggering around on her crutch, but that was the *last* thing she wanted to do, in front of so many people from her past. It probably would have been a lot less painful than trying to walk, though.

He didn't say anything, but he looked very worried as she made her way across some fairly rough ground, heading towards the baseball field.

Josh, and Meg's friends Nathan and Zachary, had all been on the team, so she'd spent a lot of time on those rickety bleachers during her junior and senior years. Usually, she would go to the games with Alison, who had been her closest friend in Washington, and maybe Phyllis and Gail, or—Jesus *Christ*, but she'd lost touch with a lot of people.

The bleachers were up above the baseball field, not too far from the tennis courts—which she really should have given some consideration before deciding to come to the game. Not that she had to look over there. She could just watch the two baseball teams warm up, or look across the field at the girls' softball team over on the other side of the complex, which seemed to be practicing, as opposed to playing an official game today. Besides, she was only here to cheer Steven on, not to get caught up in some self-pity reverie.

Even though the sounds of *tennis*—balls hitting rackets, the swift noisy footwork of rubber-soled sneakers, the rattle of chain-link fences—were enough to make her feel like weeping

Neal was sitting on the grass right behind the visitor's side with Ahmed, and one of his other friends, Yancey, and he came bounding up the hill when he saw them, a big grin on his face.

"I thought you'd be all tired and stuff," he said to her.

She was, but she shrugged.

"Steven said no *way* you'd come," he said. "So, this is cool." Then he gave their father a big hug, since he either hadn't grown into finding public displays of familial affection embarrassing yet—or, quite possibly, given his amiable ways, he was *never* going to develop that particular character trait. "Hi, Dad! I'm going back down there, okay?" He headed towards his friends without waiting for an answer.

She probably knew at least half of the guys on her school's team pretty well, and some of the others looked familiar. They were all warming up on the sidelines, while Steven's team finished up batting practice, and Jamal, who must have taken over first base after Nathan graduated, saw her just as he was about to throw to another guy she knew named Christopher. He paused, and then waved tentatively.

She waved back, also feeling hesitant, and he stood there for a minute, then came around the backstop and up the hill.

"Hey," he said.

She felt stupid about being *quite* so impaired, but it was nice to see him, find out where he was hoping to go to school—his first choice was Cornell—and otherwise catch up.

Then, a lot of the other guys wandered over, in twos and threes, to say hi, with a certain amount of mumbling and shuffling of their feet.

"You gonna be mad when we score about thirty runs off him?" one of them asked, motioning towards Steven, who had just finished his warm-up tosses, put on a jacket and his Oakley Thump sunglasses, and gone to sit at the end of his team's bench, with his customary "don't even *think* of invading my space when I've got my head in the game" pre-pitching glower.

Mostly, she was going to be *amazed* if they scored thirty runs off him.

It was a relief when the game started, and she could try to concentrate on baseball, although various teachers began appearing, too—word must have gotten around pretty quickly. Interestingly, even teachers who had never been overly fond of her seemed to have embraced a revisionist history which resulted in their forgetting that small truth when they greeted her enthusiastically, asked about college, and told her how wonderful she looked and so forth. Her favorite English teacher, Mrs. Hayes, asked if she was going to be majoring in political science, and Meg shrugged shyly and said that she hadn't decided yet, but she was considering, um, English. Her father raised his eyebrows, but didn't contradict her.

Inevitably, the press started showing up, including Hannah Goldman, although Anthony went over to distract them, and so far, they were all keeping their distance. The presence of all of the agents and security people, and the fact that the school was private property, didn't hurt, either.

She had been going out of her way not to look at the tennis courts, assuming that it was only the boys' team practicing, but she glanced over by accident—and recognized Renee, who had been ranked number two when she was the top-seeded player on the girls' team.

As she came over to the fence to pick up a ball, Renee saw her, too, and straightened up, the ball dropping out of her hand. Meg felt like a jerk, and, for some reason, a *failure*, but she nodded in her direction, and Renee nodded back, then left the courts, coming towards the bleachers.

"How you doing?" Renee asked, avoiding looking at her sling and knee brace.

Tip-top. "Fine," Meg said. "How about you?"

Renee nodded, then looked down at the baseball field. "Your brother?"

"Yeah, he's pitching," Meg said.

Renee turned to check the scoreboard in deep right field. "Looks like he's doing okay."

So far. And he'd be doing even better, if his teammates were making fewer errors. He was also two for two, with an RBI. "How'd you guys do this season?" she asked.

Renee shrugged. "Our best player graduated."

More or less.

Renee glanced at her hand. "Are you, um, going to be able to play anymore?"

No. "I'm not sure," Meg said. "I hope so."

Renee nodded, sneaking another quick look at the splint.

It made perfect sense that people always did that; she should stop finding it so invasive.

When Renee had gone back—looking slightly hangdog—to finish her match, Meg wanted nothing more than to go lie down somewhere. Normally, baseball wasn't a nerve-racking experience, but she was going to have to reevaluate that analysis.

"Relaxing way to spend an afternoon," her father said, not without irony.

And how.

41

STEVEN WAS AVERAGING more than a strikeout per inning, but he'd also hit two batters, and brushed back a few more. In the bottom of the last inning, with his team hanging on to a 4–3 lead, he did it again, and the benches emptied, although mostly, they all just stood around. There were a few shoves, and scowls, and Meg could hear Steven shouting, "Hey, I'm just trying to establish the inside of the plate!" Finally, the umpire and coaches got everyone calmed down, and Steven was back on the mound, digging his cleats into the dirt in front of the rubber.

The bottom pretty much dropped out of his next pitch, and the batter—a guy she knew, Raymond—struck out with a flailing swing.

Her father frowned. "That damn kid just threw a splitter."

And a dandy one, at that. But Steven's coach must have noticed, too, because he was on his way to the mound. "Dad, he's trying to get *seniors* out," she said.

Her father nodded. "And by the time he's sixteen, he'll be having Tommy John surgery."

For Steven's sake, she hoped not.

After a fairly heated exchange, his coach went back to the bench, and Steven shrugged a few times, then stared in at the catcher to get the sign for the next pitch.

"You were a wonderful athlete, Meg," her father said, out of nowhere. "It was a pleasure to watch you play."

Nice of him to remind her that that was part of her past. She wanted to snarl something of that nature at him, but someone, among the spectators, was probably listening in, so she just stared down at the field.

"Which doesn't change the fact that your mother and I used to spend a lot of time worrying that you were going to waste far too much of your life playing some *sport* or other," he said.

What, and that would be the end of the world? Her getting to do the two things she loved best, one of them possibly even professionally? Meg nodded. "So, *I* was wasting my time, but it's okay for Steven to put everything he has into baseball?"

"No, we worry about that, too," her father said.

Just not as hard, apparently. She watched as Steven scrambled off the mound to field a bunt bare-handed, and threw it to first in time to get the runner by two steps.

"I don't meant that—" Her father let out a frustrated breath. "I'm not doing very well with you today, am I?"

Nope.

They watched as the next hitter popped up to the third baseman—who muffed it completely. Steven did a decent job of *not* looking pissed off, although Neal, who was hanging around down by the backstop, looked up at her uneasily. Meg shrugged, and Neal nodded and refocused on the game.

"What I meant," her father said, "is that you're extraordinarily gifted, in so many ways, and I'm not sure if there's anything you couldn't do if you put your mind to it."

Other than, say, *walk*.

Her father sighed. "Maybe what I meant is that you don't have to keep pretending that you're majoring in English. That's all."

Yeah, he just loved politics. And *politicians*. Christ, if they were having this much trouble getting along now, she couldn't even imagine what it would be like if she chose his least favorite thing as her career. So, she confined her response to a brisk shake of her head, and tried to pay attention to the game.

Steven came in high and tight to the next batter—her friend Jamal, as it happened—who stepped out of the box long enough to glare at him, before stepping back in. On the next pitch, he grounded to the shortstop, who overthrew the second baseman, and suddenly, there were men on second and third. Steven stayed very still on the mound, with no expression whatsoever, but his catcher came trotting out to talk to him. Calm him down, more likely.

"Not bad," Meg said to her father, who nodded.

Once, in Little League, Steven had yelled so furiously at a teammate who screwed up a crucial play that her parents had threatened to make him quit baseball altogether, if he couldn't be a better sport. Typically, it had been her father who did most of the lecturing on the subject, while her mother looked disappointed and took the more moderate position that lambasting a teammate simply wasn't done, and that he needed to learn how to keep his composure, because otherwise, it was very bad form.

"Come on, Steven!" Neal said, as the catcher trudged back to the plate and Steven scraped his cleats across the dirt. "Smoke 'im!"

Steven must have been paying attention, because he blew away the next—and final—batter on three straight pitches.

"Went right up the ladder," her father said, and Meg nodded, as Steven's team erupted into a small victory celebration, with the exception of the shortstop and third baseman, who looked somewhat shamefaced. But Steven gave them each a friendly smack with his glove, and the two guys relaxed and returned the slaps.

"I'll just head down there for a minute," her father said. "Do you want me to meet you in the car?"

Meg shook her head. "I'll wait for you here. Tell him I said he was really good."

Once he had finished shaking hands with everyone on both teams, Steven looked up at the bleachers until he was able to make eye contact with her. Meg gave him a left-handed salute, and he grinned back.

Some of the reporters, Hannah among them, took advantage of her father's departure to come traipsing over, and Anthony moved to intercept them. Normally, she might have told him not to bother, and wasted some time bantering around, but she was tired, and out of sorts, and her new pain medication had either worn off—or wasn't any damn good. So, she pretended that she hadn't even noticed that they were there, and some of their many agents, along with school security people and a few police officers, began escorting them away.

The guys from her school weren't too happy about having lost—or the fact that they thought her punk little brother had been headhunting—but they were friendly enough about it as they went slouching past the bleachers on their way to the locker-room, giving her nods and good-byes, and telling her to be sure and say hi to Josh and Nathan and Zachary the next time she spoke to any of them.

Which wasn't likely to be soon, much to her discredit.

Steven was going to ride back to school with his team, but he came up to say hello—and accept profuse compliments about his pitching prowess, which she gave him, at length. He was holding a plastic bottle of Gatorade, and she had to force herself not to look at it.

Steven, who had been about to gulp some, stopped. "I don't really want this. You feel like taking it for me, so I don't have to carry it around?"

Christ, had she been staring? Meg felt her face turning red. "No, I'm fine, Steven. And you were really great—made *them* look like freshmen."

"Yeah, kind of," he said, and grinned. "But, look, if you don't want it, I'm going to pour it out."

And he would, just to prove a point. Maybe he *was* a punk.

Steven sighed. "Meg, they have more down there. Like a whole cooler full. I'll just get another one."

Since it would be less stressful than arguing, she accepted the bottle, drinking more than half of it immediately, then feeling like an idiot and trying to give it back.

Steven shook his head. "What, with your germs all over it now? No way." He started back down the hill. "Thanks for coming and stuff. Later."

His father walked Neal and his friends to their minivan, waiting until they had pulled away. He seemed to be having a conversation with Ryan, the head of his detail, but she knew he was also going to stand there until Steven's bus left safely, too. Probably a fruitless exercise, but maybe it made him feel better. She hoped so, anyway.

By the time he came back, she had finished Steven's Gatorade, and was looking at the empty bottle, wishing that, moments after he'd won a big game, she hadn't managed to remind him of all of the bad aspects of their lives by the stupidity of a longing glance at the cold drink he'd more than *earned*.

Her father looked worried. "Are you thirsty? I'm sorry, I didn't think to bring anything along, but—"

And now, she was two for two, in the selfishness category. Christ. Meg shook her head, tucked the bottle into her sling so she would be able to throw it away later, and pulled herself up onto her crutch. "I'm fine. Thanks."

Her headmaster and principal were both standing nearby, to say good-bye, she assumed. She was incredibly tired, but odds were, it was going to be a very long time before she came back here again, and—well, she wasn't sure if she was quite ready to leave yet.

She turned towards her father. "Is it okay if I maybe look around for a few minutes?"

He didn't seem to like that idea, but he nodded. "Think it would help?"

Either that, or set off a massive post-traumatic flashback, and send her spiraling irretrievably into the depths of insanity. "Guess we'll find out," Meg said.

There were still some press people lingering around out on the sidewalk, but they were far enough away so she hoped that they wouldn't factor into any of this.

Except that she *knew* Hannah, and felt somewhat at ease with her, and it would be nice to have someone— "Do you think Hannah Goldman would keep it off-the-record, if I let her walk along with us?" she asked Anthony.

He shook his head. "I think she would try in good faith, but that there's no way she could keep it from coloring her writing."

Yeah. He was probably right. And it didn't matter that she was pretty much *surrounded* by men at the moment; it was fine. Many of them, very large men. She was used to that. The fact that most of her agents—including Nellie and Paula—and Martin—were either on vacation, or doing a training cycle at Beltsville this week, and that the people on her detail today were replacements didn't matter, either. Her father was here, and Garth, and—well, she *sort of* knew Anthony. So, they weren't all near-strangers.

Her father went over to her headmaster and said something in a low voice. Dr. Lyons nodded, clicked open his cell phone, and within about a minute, a woman she knew from the Human Resources Department came outside.

"Hi, Meg, how are you?" she said. "I was hoping I'd get a chance to see you before you left."

She was going to tell her father that she really didn't need to have any women around to do this—but, she couldn't help feeling better when, in short order, the female softball coach also joined them, and as they walked towards the Arts Center, she saw the head librarian walking towards them, too.

"Thank you," she said very softly to her father, and he smiled at her.

It was also good to see places where she had *happy* memories, first. The football field, where they used to come and watch Nathan and Zachary play, and where the track team was currently finishing up practice. An alcove where she remembered making out with Josh during more than one lunch or study period. The library. The wooden bench near the office, where they all used to hang out and make enough noise to annoy every adult within listening distance.

Her father was chatting with people about the baseball game, thereby relieving *her* of the pressure of having to make idle conversation—which had to be his exact intention.

As they walked around the main Upper School building and approached the place where it had happened, she caught herself holding her breath.

But, the reality was that it was just—an exit. A door. A driveway. A couple of tennis courts, where her matches had sometimes been specifically assigned, because the courts were more secluded than the ones in front of the school. A few more speed bumps than she remembered—which had maybe been constructed to slow down *other* careening vans, if a similar situation were ever—God forbid—to come up again. In fact, a good chunk of the area had been resurfaced, and she wondered whether there had been bloodstains to clean up. Probably.

She stood there, gripping her crutch, wanting very much to lean on her father, but not allowing herself to do so.

"Where were you?" he asked.

She looked back at the door, to try and set herself in space, then limped forward and to the right a couple of steps. "Here." She raised her crutch to point. "And then, Chet was—"

Something moved in her peripheral vision, and she lifted her elbow, ready to defend herself, but then saw that it was Anthony, looking taller and far more assertive than usual, for some reason. "Just use your voice, Meg," he said.

What the hell did that mean? She frowned at him.

"It's an irresistible visual," he said.

Christ, it was, wasn't it? And by standing that way, he was *blocking* her, from any possible cameras on the street. In fact, almost everyone in the group seemed to have moved to form a protective semicircle around her.

"Where was Chet?" her father asked.

Did she want to answer that question? Or would it be better just to get in the car and go home? Avoid reliving any of it. Of course, if she stood here without speaking, everyone would think she was too traumatized to function—and that would be bad.

She could see that all of the nearby agents were listening intently, and Garth and Ryan seemed to be getting ready to take notes. Christ, the Secret Service must have been *dreaming* of the opportunity to participate in an on-site debriefing for months, although no one had ever asked her to do anything other than identify locations in photographs or crime-scene sketches. But now, they had an actual eyewitness perspective, and she was the only non-terrorist alive to give it. Although however many backup agents she'd had must have been able to write relatively comprehensive reports, and since Josh had come running outside when he heard the shooting, he'd been forced to sit through repeated interviews with the Secret Service and the FBI, even though he'd admitted to her privately that it had been so smoky and chaotic—and he had been so scared—that he hadn't been able to tell them much of anything.

She glanced at Anthony, who nodded, so she must be safe from outside eyes at the moment.

"He was there," she said, gesturing with her chin, "ahead of me. And Dennis was over here, behind me."

And then, they had both been lying on the cement, bleeding to death.

With the resurfacing, no one who walked by would have any idea that two men had died in this very spot. Actually, *four* men, counting the two terrorists who had been killed, and there was another terrorist who had been wounded badly enough to be left behind by the others, although she had no idea where any of them had fallen. She also couldn't remember whether there had been other students, or teachers, around, but since it happened only about an hour after school ended, there must have been some.

She looked at Dr. Lyons. "Were there other people nearby, sir? During everything?"

He nodded. "Yes, but the ones who hadn't already ducked did when you yelled for them to get down."

She had no memory of doing that, but Josh had always insisted that she had—and that he was pretty sure that it was the only reason he hadn't gotten shot.

In fact, he felt *guilty* that he'd listened to her, because he was convinced that he should have done something—although, realistically, she couldn't imagine what—to try and rescue her.

"So, no one else got hurt," Meg said.

Dr. Lyons shook his head.

That was another thing she'd been told—but she was glad to hear that it was true; she had always had her doubts.

Ryan and Garth each had a few logistical and procedural questions, which she answered, but she wasn't sorry to see some of their other agents bringing the cars around, so that she would be able to escape soon.

As they pulled away from the school, one of her father's agents, Morty, was behind the wheel, and he drove very slowly and carefully, probably to make the ride seem as different as possible from being kidnapped. Even so, she felt as though she could almost hear the men shouting and swearing at her again. Laughing at her. Egging each other on. The way the punches sounded. The way the punches *felt*. The grimy fingers wrenching her mouth open, the metal tool banging against her teeth, the horror of having large, unfamiliar male hands grabbing at her body. The stench of—

"You okay?" her father asked.

She nodded, holding her sling against the front of her chest and gripping her right elbow with her good hand.

"Here, put this on," her father said, and tried to slip his suit jacket around her shoulders.

She shook her head. "Thanks, but I really don't need it."

"You're shivering, Meg," he said.

She was? She paid attention for a minute, and realized that her teeth were chattering. In an enclosed car, on a warm March day. "I, um, I must have gotten a chill," she said.

He was considerate enough to nod as he tucked the jacket around her.

When they got back to the White House, she spent approximately twenty seconds worrying about whether Steven would think less of her if she went straight to her room and stayed there for the rest of the night—and then decided that she was too god-damned tired to care either way.

Trudy brought her a tray, and clucked and fussed when she ate very little of the food, although she forced down a full glass of milk. Neal came in after supper to watch a couple of sitcoms with her, and Steven showed up long enough to say, "That looks *totally* dumb, you mutts," before leaving.

Once Neal had gone off to finish his homework, she just lay in bed, patting Vanessa, who purred non-stop, but also gave her a querulous swipe every so often.

At about eleven-fifteen, her mother came in, moving much more slowly than usual. Her hair, however, looked impeccable.

"Hey," Meg said, without sitting up.

Her mother nodded, then patted Vanessa, who hissed and flounced off to the bottom of the bed, more offended than was probably indicated for the minor offense of an unsolicited stroke on the head.

"How's the pain tonight?" her mother asked, instead of commenting on that.

Meg shrugged.

Her mother felt her forehead, then indicated the new prescription bottle on the bedside table. "When did you last take some?"

Meg felt sluggish enough for it to be hard to remember exactly. "Half an hour ago, maybe." Or, at any rate, recently enough so that there was still a slim chance it might kick in.

Her mother looked concerned. "Have you noticed a difference today?"

Meg shook her head. "Not really. I think they might be making me a little sick to my stomach."

"Do you want me to call Bob now," her mother asked, "or—?"

Meg shook her head again.

"Okay," her mother said. "But we'll talk to him tomorrow, and reassess things."

Another day, another medical appointment. Christ, what else was new?

Her mother sat down on the edge of the bed. "How was it, being over there again?"

So many conflicting emotions, so little time. "Stressful," Meg said finally.

Her mother nodded. "I wish you had waited longer. It was much too soon."

Probably, yeah. "Does it ever come back to you?" Meg asked. The shooting. "When you're outside somewhere?"

"Almost every time I see a rope line," her mother said, after a long pause. "And, whenever I get out of a car in public."

In other words, several times a *day*. Jesus. She looked at the way her mother was holding herself. "Does your arm still hurt?"

Her mother nodded, reflexively touching her bad shoulder.

"Always?" Meg asked.

Her mother shrugged. "More so, when I'm tired."

Which meant that today must have been very bad, painwise.

And—no thanks to her—probably in many other ways. "What about your chest?" Meg asked.

"I don't know," her mother said. "Mostly, it's fine."

She'd qualified it. Meg frowned. "Does it hurt to breathe?"

Her mother shook her head. "Not really. It just feels—different. I guess I lost some lung capacity."

Christ, they'd really taken some body blows, hadn't they. "I'm sorry," Meg said.

Her mother shrugged.

"The rest of the time I'm here, could we just watch movies, and maybe play Monopoly, and stuff?" Meg asked.

"God, could we ever," her mother said, leaned over to hug her, and then stood up. "Sleep well, okay?"

"You, too. One thing, though?" Meg asked.

Her mother paused, tensing.

"That was a counterfeit hair-bump," Meg said.

Her mother's smile came and went so quickly that Meg would have missed it, if she hadn't been waiting to see it.

"I'll never tell," her mother said, and left the room.

THE NEXT AFTERNOON, they went up to Camp David, for what she hoped was going to be a nice, low-key vacation. They watched movies—*lots* of movies, played air hockey and foosball and pinball, sat around the pool in lawn chairs, and stayed up too late. No tough conversations. No pressure. Almost no conflict. Neal was predictably cheerful, her father read non-stop, and Steven was somewhat less combative than usual. Whenever she could talk the Navy chefs into giving her free rein in the kitchen, Trudy cooked lowbrow stuff her brothers liked—meatloaf, tacos, spaghetti—and Meg noticed that her father put away more than his share, too.

She didn't do much herself, other than lie down almost constantly, call Beth several times, and talk to Jack and Josh once each. All of them seemed to be fine, although except for Beth, she kept the calls short. Which probably hurt Jack's feelings, but he sounded pretty awkward, too, since he was getting ready to go up to Tahoe to ski for several days.

Not that she was envious, of course.

She also got caught up on her email, finding—among other things—short "so, how was the surgery?" sorts of messages from Susan, Juliana, *and* Mary Elizabeth. As well as a couple of off-hand, if probing, ones from Hannah Goldman—whose article was supposed to run soon, but who still had lots of questions—which Meg politely deflected, forwarding both the originals and her responses on to Maureen and Anthony, just in case.

After vacillating for a while, she emailed Nathan at Duke, and Zachary at Penn, to tell them she'd gone to the game and seen their former teammates—and went ahead and wrote a similar one to Alison, at Bowdoin. She heard back from all of them within hours, so maybe she *did* still have a few high school friends. Nathan and Alison were both on break, too, but Nathan was heading off to some baseball tournament, and Alison was on her way to Cancun.

While checking *his* email one morning, Steven—whose home page was currently set to a disreputable, ever-updating celebrity gossip and scandal site—had come across a somewhat grainy photo of her standing near Paresky with Jack—and promptly dubbed him "Malibu Bobby." She found that insulting, on Jack's behalf, although when she pronounced the name aloud, the Bostonian in her was amused in spite of herself.

Her mother spent the entire weekend with them—interspersed with long meetings over in Laurel, and she was also able to come up for two of the four remaining nights. The second time, it was so late that Meg was the only one still awake, lying on the sun porch couch, watching C-Span, when she walked in from the helipad.

The stewards fixed her a late supper, and Meg kept her company while she ate. They didn't talk much—it seemed like the better part of wisdom, but after the stewards cleared the table and she had made, and received, a few phone calls, her mother saw the checkers board Neal had left out and brought it over. They played three increasingly competitive games—her mother taking two of them, and then switched to a quick round of Battleship, which Meg won swiftly and decisively.

"Two out of three?" her mother asked, poised to set up her ships again.

Meg shook her head. "It's better with us each winning an equal number of games."

Her mother nodded. "Yes, it probably is."

Definitely was.

So, they went back to the couch and watched *Bringing Up Baby*, instead, although neither of them was hungry enough to eat very much of the popcorn the stewards served. Her mother must have had a really long day, because she fell asleep during a noisy sequence of dueling leopard and loon calls, and didn't wake up again until the jail scene.

When the movie was over, her mother yawned. "Pretty late," she said.

Heading on to three. Which meant that the President really needed to get some sleep. But, once again, it was a perfect chance to have a thus-far neglected conversation. And this particular topic was pretty important. "I know you're tired," Meg said, "but, um, could I talk to you about something, first?"

A question which had to inspire dread, but her mother nodded.

"I think, um, I maybe need to see a doctor," Meg said.

Her mother was already on her feet.

"No, that's not what I meant," Meg said quickly. "I, uh—" She glanced around to make sure they were alone. "A gynecologist."

Her mother looked puzzled. "Didn't you see her a few months ago?"

Meg nodded. "Yeah. I just—I need to go again."

"Oh." Her mother took that in, also checked to establish that they were the only two in the room, and then sat back down. "I see. Of course. We'll have to—yes. That is what we'll do, then. For you, I mean."

Amazing how inarticulate the Leader of the Free World could be.

"Is there—a problem?" her mother asked.

Meg shook her head. It might be easier to go to the health center at school—Susan or Juliana would probably be willing to keep her company—but the odds of such a visit *not* leaking somehow, complete with embarrassing personal details, were minuscule.

"Are you—I mean, I know it's none of my—" Her mother stopped. "Gosh."

Well, now, this was a whole lot of fun, wasn't it. "Could I maybe go up here?" Meg asked. "So it can be private?"

Her mother nodded. "Of course. I'll arrange for her—" She and her mother shared the same gynecologist, a USAF Colonel— "to meet with you tomorrow, before you all come back to the city."

"Thanks," Meg said, and reached for her cane—Dr. Brooks had agreed that she could start trying to work her way up from the crutch—so she could go down to her room.

Her mother cleared her throat. "This is maybe something we should discuss?"

Ideally, no. Ideally, *never*. Meg shook her head. "I sort of just want to talk to Dr. Holtzman, if that's okay with you."

"Of course, but—I think it's what mothers and daughters do," her mother said, hesitantly.

Maybe. She'd have to ask around. Or, at least, ask Beth. "You mean, since we have a completely conventional relationship?" Meg asked.

A touch of pink came into her mother's cheeks, but she nodded.

Jesus. Talk about the blind leading the blind. Two people who had *no idea* how normal mothers might behave. The night she'd gotten her period for the first time, her mother had been down in Washington, and while they had—for lack of a better word—consulted, on the phone a couple of times, mainly, her father had had to handle it, because Trudy had already gone home for the night. He had been tactful and discreet, but they had both been pretty self-conscious about the whole thing.

It was very, very quiet in the room—in a way that it was *never* quiet in the White House, where there always seemed to be an underlying hum of energy, somehow.

Which was one of the nicer aspects of Camp David.

"Am I allowed to ask whether this is preemptive, or—" her mother hesitated again— "after-the-fact?"

"You're allowed to ask," Meg said.

And *that* hung in the air.

"You know," her mother said, after a minute. "There's no question that I'm not the easiest parent in the world, but on occasion, the argument could be made that you're not the easiest kid, either."

A year ago, that would have offended her; now, there was something calming about being criticized. But, Meg shrugged defensively, anyway.

Her mother folded her hands in her lap. "This young man Steven has been teasing you about is the same one who sent the flowers?"

That was a harmless enough question, so Meg nodded.

"The one in your psychology class?" her mother asked.

Meg nodded.

It was quiet again, and this time, the utter silence made her nervous.

"He's not even *from* Malibu," Meg said. "He's from Santa Monica."

Her mother nodded. "You're right, that's entirely different."

Well, okay, maybe not.

"Obviously, you already know this," her mother said, looking very uncomfortable, "but, even when you're using other forms of protection, condoms are still—"

"Got the memo on that, yeah," Meg said.

And then, there was more deadly, deadly silence.

"For what it's worth?" her mother said.

Meg looked over.

"Loving the person really does matter," her mother said.

This was in danger of getting *way* too personal.

There had been plenty of public rumors about her mother's sexual history over the years—at least ninety percent of which Meg assumed were false, especially the ones involving women, but she really had almost no concept of how many people her mother had dated, or—this topic could easily explode into more than either of them could bear.

But now, she was curious. "Um, did you? Love the person? Your first time, I mean?"

"Yes. Very much." Her mother smiled weakly. "But, I made the mistake of believing that it was mutual, and—well. I was not correct."

Ouch. "So, you, uh—" Christ, this was just no fun at all. "This was before Dad?" Meg asked.

"Well, obviously, that goes without saying." Her mother gave her an uneasy look. "I mean, that *is* obvious, isn't it?"

In hindsight, yes, so she nodded. The idea that either of her parents had ever had an affair was too horrible to contemplate—and highly unlikely, given the long-term inability of the rapacious press to find any convincing evidence of such a thing.

Not that they hadn't tried.

There was still a bunch of questions she wanted to ask—how old she had been, whether she thought she'd waited too long—or not long enough, whether she'd been—well—*disappointed* by the actuality of it, if the guy had been upset about her lack of experience the first time—but, if her mother was willing to tell her such revealing things, then it wouldn't be sporting for her to refuse to do the same, so— "I hate this conversation," she said.

Her mother nodded. "It's not my favorite, either. But, at least it's a *normal* bad conversation."

So it was.

42

THE GYNECOLOGIST ENDED up giving her three months of birth control pills, and a crisp professional rundown on potential side effects, sexually-transmitted diseases, and various risky practices she should avoid, and how to protect herself, if she chose not to do so. For the most part, Meg nodded, mumbled her assent where it seemed to be required, and avoided making eye contact as much as possible.

That night, when they were all back in Washington, her mother did nothing more than pause by her room to find out whether the appointment had been okay, and to assure her—although her eye contact was also less than stellar—that if she had questions, or needed advice about anything whatsoever, all she had to do was ask. Meg had no real intention of doing so, but it was nice to know that she probably *could*.

The next day, her brothers were even more hyper than usual, to the degree that right after lunch, her father excused himself and went into the Presidential bedroom and closed the door. Meg did some packing to get ready to go back to school, and then rested on the couch in the West Sitting Hall, drinking coffee and having a wide-ranging, if unfocused, conversation with Trudy. Her brothers were still bombing around, and wrestling a lot, and every so often—when an ominous sound came from one of their rooms—Trudy would yell, "Don't make me come in there, boys!" and it would, ever so briefly, be quiet again.

Her mother came upstairs in the middle of the afternoon, looking as though she wanted to go lie down for about a month and a half, but Steven and Neal decided that it would be *totally fun* to go into the kitchen and bake something with her. Her mother was dubious about this plan—and Meg and Trudy were even more so—but, in short order, there were several stewards standing uncertainly in the hall, until they pulled themselves together and went downstairs to the main kitchen. Xavier came back up twice, with premeasured cups of flour and sugar and all, and Meg knew he was only trying to be helpful, but it was kind of funny to think that the chefs were all afraid that the President was incapable of beating a couple of eggs by herself. The bowl of freshly washed blueberries and the dish of grated lemon rind made it clear that, as usual, her mother was making her one and only culinary specialty.

It sounded like the three of them were having fun in there, but Meg decided that it was nicer to lie on the couch, covered with strategically-placed ice packs, in something of a haze from her most recent dose of more-potent-than-usual painkillers.

"What are the odds that they burn it?" she asked Trudy.

Trudy peered at the row of stitches she had just completed on the afghan she was crocheting. "If I were a betting woman, I would say three-to-one."

Yeah, that was probably about right.

Glen came striding down the hall, but stopped short when he heard the commotion coming from the kitchen.

Meg shook her head at him.

"Steven, don't throw that," her mother was saying, while her brothers laughed like maniacs. "No, really, don't throw that."

There was a pause, then a small crash, and more evil laughter.

"That's great," her mother said, sounding very amused. "That's just great. You went ahead and threw it."

There was another mysterious crash, her brothers laughed, and Kirby barked.

"It's not funny," her mother said, and laughed, too.

Then, as Steven said, "Hey, he could have *ducked*, Mom," there was another crash, and a splat, upon which Neal said, "Whoa, there go the *eggs*!"

Glen listened to all of that, looked at his watch, nodded at Meg and Trudy, and left without a word.

"That was nice of him," Meg said, watching him head down the hall.

Trudy smiled at her. "Your family is not as alone as you sometimes think."

Maybe not.

A little while later, her father came out of the bedroom, looking sleepy and somewhat rumpled. He started to say something, then paused almost exactly the same way Glen had, took in the noise, and the fact that Trudy and Meg were on the couch, and that, therefore, Steven and Neal were goofing around with *someone else*.

After that slight hesitation, he sat down in the blue easy chair that had always been in the living room in Chestnut Hill. "I don't think it's very respectful," he said, rather cheerfully, "when children are so unruly that their father is not allowed to complete his nap."

Ordinary paternal humor. *Good*. Meg grinned.

"Do you want anything, Russ?" Trudy asked, poised to put down her crocheting.

He sniffed the air. "Someday, I want you to teach her how to bake something else."

Trudy smiled, and went back to her yarn.

In due course, Neal came out with plates of freshly-sliced, only slightly overbrowned cake for everyone, while Steven sat down at the mahogany table to finish what was left in the frosting bowl. *Purple* frosting. Then, her mother appeared with a large bowl of homemade vanilla ice cream that the chefs had sent upstairs, and served some to each of them, using a delicate silver spoon which had not, in any way, been designed for such a demanding task.

"Quite an impressive effort, Katharine," Meg's father said, looking down at his cake. "And so very colorful."

Her mother nodded. "I thought the frosting was ill-advised, but sadly, my lobbying efforts were ineffective."

"We could *completely* score with this on eBay," Steven said to Neal, who laughed.

The listing would probably get thousands of hits, along with many outrageously high sham bids, and read: "Cake! Baked and Sliced by the Cold and Unloving President Herself! RARE!"

Her mother put some ice cream onto Meg's plate. "Is it helping?" she asked, indicating the prescription bottle on the coffee table.

The only difference she'd noticed with this latest one was that while everything still hurt like hell, she didn't *mind* quite as much. "Fly me to the moon," Meg said.

Her mother smiled, but gave her father a worried look. "Then, don't take any more, okay? We'll have to try something else."

Meg shook her head and reached for the bottle, pretending to pour several pills into her mouth. "No, I'm sorry, your lobbying skills remain unimpressive."

Fortunately, her parents were amused. They might all be walking on eggshells, to some degree, but so far today, they were keeping their collective, intricate balance.

"You know, we could certainly arrange to have you fly back *tonight*, instead of tomorrow," her father said.

"And deprive yourselves of my joie-de-vivre?" Meg asked. "I so very much think not."

Her mother picked up the bottle and held it far enough away to be able to read the label, since she didn't have her glasses on. "What *is* this stuff? I think I want some, too."

"Okay, but save a few for me," her father said, and Meg laughed.

On the whole, it was quite a relaxing afternoon, although her mother did end up going back downstairs for a while, and then spent most of the evening holed up in the Treaty Room with various advisors, and part of her kitchen cabinet. In fact, it was pleasant enough for Meg to start having some major doubts about the wisdom of going back to school at all.

Hanging out and watching movies with her brothers was *nice*. Knowing that her parents were nearby felt safe. Being able to see Trudy and Preston was swell. Having physical therapy at home, instead of driving miles away, was so much easier. Hell, *everything* was easier.

And, it was less dangerous at home. Less scary. Even with radiation detection devices, bomb-sniffing dogs patrolling constantly, various sensors everywhere, regular lockdowns, fence jumpers, mysterious planes straying into protected airspace, occasionally being hustled down to the bunker, and the like.

By this time tomorrow, she would be alone again, surrounded by strangers, none of whom liked her very much. She would have to drag herself up and down stairs and sloping walkways constantly. She wouldn't have any privacy. She would have to *study*.

Christ, it was going to be awful.

She was sitting in her room, pretty much consumed by worry and dread, when her father knocked on the open door.

"Are you all set with your packing?" he asked.

She wasn't, but she nodded.

"Everything okay?" he asked.

She nodded.

"Do you need anything?" he asked.

She shook her head.

He started to leave the room, then paused. "Can't decide whether you're ready to go back tomorrow?"

Something like that. "Mostly, I think I want to stay here," she said.

He looked at her, and then nodded. "Today was a good day."

Yeah.

"Been a while since we've had one of those," he said.

Double yeah.

He came all the way in, and sat down in the rocking chair. "I think you've talked to your mother and Trudy, but you really haven't told *me* much about school."

Probably because the two of them had been too busy quarreling with each other.

"And I mean how you actually feel," he said, "as opposed to platitudes."

Which was going to limit her ability to communicate.

"Freshman year is difficult for people who *aren't* facing all of the extra challenges you are," he said.

Judging from the endless glum visits everyone in her entry made to Susan's room, day and night, he was right. Meg sighed. "I don't have any privacy, but it's also really lonely, a lot of the time."

Her father nodded.

"And—I don't know," she said. "I guess I thought college would be all good fellowship, and traditions, and everyone smiling and crammed into each other's rooms, and—" In other words, *movie* college.

Her father looked concerned. "But, you seem to be making friends."

Well, that was open to debate. Unless—Jesus, had her mother told him? He had been the one to drive her over to the infirmary, in one of the Camp David golf carts to see Dr. Holtzman, but she'd just said that she was having a checkup, and he hadn't seemed to suspect otherwise.

No. Her mother would never betray her confidence that way—she didn't *think*. And, even if she had, her father wouldn't be dumb enough to let her know about it.

"Should I allow you to use platitudes?" he asked.

It might be easier. "I think I *was* maybe starting to make friends," she said, "but then, after the whole mess with Susan, people got really mad at me, and—well, most of them stopped liking me anymore." Not that it had been perfect before that, but still.

"It'd be nice if a few more of the things that happen to you were actually your fault," he said.

She couldn't really blame the inability to maintain friendships on anyone other than herself. Enticing, though it might be. "Juliana—" She glanced at him to make sure the name was familiar; he nodded—"thinks I'm really impersonal, or—I don't know—aloof, I guess."

Her father sighed. "Why *wouldn't* you be aloof?"

Good point. Why, indeed?

"And, unfortunately, your two primary role models both have strong tendencies in that direction," he said.

So, what, she was genetically destined to be distant and reserved? Terrific.

"And you've also learned the hard way that you have to be very careful about trusting new people in your life," he said.

An idle remark, or *had* he and her mother been talking about her being involved with Jack? Time to redirect this topic, maybe. To find a clever diversion. "There's a girl in my political science class," Meg said, "who wears this 'I'm Glad She's Not *My* Mother' button, and shoots down everything I say—" on the rare occasions she actually spoke up— "even though *Vanessa* understands more about the machinations of government than she does."

Her father nodded. "I've always had the feeling that Vanessa knows a great deal more than she's telling."

Meg grinned, and patted her cat. She often had that same sneaking suspicion herself.

"But, that's a more unpleasant button than usual," he said.

Yeah. It almost went without saying that the same creep also sometimes came to class in a "Wicked Witch of the West Wing" sweatshirt.

Beth had once come to visit with a "But I thought the President was going to fix *everything*!" pin on her jacket, and her mother had been amused enough to ask if she would bring a few extra ones next time. She had a great t-shirt, too, with the slogan "No Boys Allowed" displayed across a picture of the White House, which Meg, quietly, coveted.

And, in the case of her obnoxious classmate, her general feeling was that she was also glad that the President was not her mother, since then, the two of them would be *sisters*—which would really suck.

"Are you physically well enough to go back?" her father asked.

Hell, no. "I wasn't well enough to go in the first place, Dad," she said.

He nodded, and she wondered whether her parents had any idea how lousy they were at hiding how very depressed she made them. It would be nice to be loved, *without* being pitied. But she didn't want to start another argument, because, for all she knew, her father's stomach hurt as much as her mother's did these days—and he just hadn't been able to bring himself to admit it to anyone yet.

"I'm worried about Steven," she said.

Her father nodded. "With good reason, I'm afraid. Your mother and I are, too. He's been having a very hard time adjusting to your being away."

Which made her wonder whether she really should stay home, instead of going back.

"When your mother got shot, I was horrified," he said, "but I wasn't *shocked*."

Privately, all of them—especially her mother—had probably anticipated that some coward or other would inevitably take a run at her while she was in office.

"But, with you, it was different," her father said. "Preston came into my office, shaking so hard that I thought he was going to fall down, and—I couldn't get my mind around it. It was even worse than the night I got the phone call about my parents."

Her grandparents had been killed in a car accident—by a nineteen-year-old drunk driver—a couple of months after her first birthday. The guy was already out of jail long before she turned three. Her aunt sometimes talked about it, but as far as she knew, her father never did.

He also never said anything about what it had been like to have his wife almost assassinated while he was standing right behind her, and then come very close to bleeding to death in his arms, while Secret Service agents fought to keep her alive during the frantic six-minute ride to the hospital.

"You've always been the one person your brother completely trusts," her father said, "so he was particularly devastated by what happened. And I don't think—" he glanced at her— "that either of you has been able to figure out how to handle the fact that you have a different relationship now."

Because she couldn't play sports. Because she never had any energy to do things. Because she was always so miserable, and scared.

Because he could no longer depend on her to be there, when he needed her.

Because she'd stopped being *funny*—the most unforgivable change of all.

She wanted to complain that she was doing her damned best, and why couldn't they give her a chance to try and get well, instead of pressuring her all the time, but what would that accomplish? Like it or not, all of their relationships with one another *were* different now. It would be absurd to argue otherwise.

With one exception. "How come it isn't like that with Neal?" she asked.

"Because, for reasons which still escape me, he never doubted for a second that you were coming back," he said. "The whole time, he kept saying things like that you were *way smart*, and you'd be fine until some of our commandos burst in and rescued you." Then, her father sighed.

"He was so optimistic, that, to my everlasting shame, there were moments when I found it difficult to be around him."

Which he would consider an unforgivable lapse of his parental responsibilities, and an indication that he suffered from a deep, heretofore unrecognized, character defect.

Not that any of them were hard on themselves.

"But, he didn't know about the teeth," Meg said quietly. Or her abandoned clothes.

"No," her father agreed. "And he was wrong about the commandos. But he apparently understood more about *you* than the rest of us did."

Maybe. "Or he got lucky," Meg said.

Her father managed something that resembled a smile. "Or that, yeah."

She looked down at the bottom of the bed, where her Camp David duffel bag was open, and much closer to being empty than full. It would be so nice just to hurl it into her closet, shut the door, and maybe give college another try in the fall. "Dr. Brooks and a couple of the surgeons could hold a press conference tomorrow, and say that the operations didn't go very well, and they need for me to stay here in Washington to have any chance for my rehabilitation to work," she said.

Her father's expression looked all the more haunted. "They really wouldn't be stretching the truth."

Nope.

"Your mother and I could make the arrangements in about thirty seconds," he said.

Yep.

He studied her. "Do you want us to?"

God, yes. And if she left school, it would take the pressure off Susan and everyone else in the dorm, too. They could all go back to leading ordinary college lives, with no security issues or media assaults, and she could go back to—total isolation and despair. Sitting alone in her room for hours on end. Everyone looking at her miserably. Nobody talking during meals. The staff treating her like a tiny glass sculpture they expected to see shatter right in front of them at any given moment.

Her father came over to sit next to her. "How about I give you a hand with the rest of your packing?"

As kicks out of the nest went, that was a very gentle one. Meg nodded. "That would be good, Dad," she said. "Thanks."

THE PLAN WAS for them to have a private family lunch the next day, before it was time for her to head out to Andrews. In the morning, to her father's barely-concealed annoyance, there was a coffee reception scheduled to be held downstairs in the Blue Room, with the French Ambassador and the First Lady of Mali included among the guests. One of those foreign policy encounters which appeared friendly and informal, but, in all likelihood, involved all sorts of unspoken geopolitical strategies and goals.

Neal was the only one who was enthusiastic about the get-together, and he spent about twenty minutes on a settee in the Center Hall, swinging his legs back and forth, and yapping happily to a very patient protocol aide about how he should behave when he went in to say hello. Of course, he liked meeting absolutely anyone anywhere at any time, and was famous for having long, intense "Do you like your job? Show me all the stuff you do!" chats with everyone who worked in—or visited—or, hell, *walked by*—the White House, but he especially enjoyed official functions. He had even voluntarily put on a tie.

Steven didn't want to have anything to do with any of it, but when her mother remarked that he always looked very handsome in his blue turtleneck, he came out of his room wearing it a few minutes later. Meg didn't feel like making an obligatory "Yes, I'm still sane, and vaguely mobile" appearance, but it would only be a few minutes out of her life, so what the hell—and her mother seemed both abashed, and very pleased, when she suggested doing so. Her father frowned, but made no actual comment.

She didn't have the energy even to consider getting dressed up, but in an attempt to look presentable, she changed into a red cashmere sweater and grey wool pants, fastening her surgical brace over the pants. She also put on her sling, so no one would forget and try to shake hands with her. Then she went to wait in the West Sitting Hall with Trudy and her brothers, until it would be time to go downstairs.

Neal had either taken notes during his meeting with the protocol aide, or gone off and spent ten minutes on the Internet, because he was full of unexpected tidbits, including the fact that Mali had celebrated its annual Democracy Day holiday recently, that the climate was hot and dry during most of the year, and that the country's motto was "One People, One Goal, One Faith." Trudy listened intently to all of this, asking several questions, and Meg *pretended* to listen, while Steven yawned and ate his fourth cinnamon roll of the day and read the Red Sox articles in the Sunday *Globe*.

When Frank came up, and signaled to her that it was time, she made her way to the elevator, her brothers trailing along behind her.

"I'm staying like, *two* seconds," Steven said grimly.

His father's child, although by now, she assumed he had steeled himself to face the inevitable, snapped into his First Gentleman persona, and was being warm and charming to one and all.

One of the social aides who had been assigned to the event met them at the elevator door, and escorted them across the hall. There were a lot of people around, including a few reporters and official White House photographers, all of whom perked up when they saw her, and she braced herself so that she wouldn't flinch when they were hit with the inevitable camera flashes.

"This *sucks*," Steven muttered, and the social aide looked uneasy.

"Hey, you're the one who went and put on your turtleneck," Meg said. "If you'd said no, they wouldn't have made you come."

Since they all knew that was true, and that his appearance was, therefore, entirely self-inflicted, Steven scowled. "Yeah, well—you're the favorite."

Always the ultimate trump card to pull on one another. They'd started having this exact same argument pretty much as soon as they learned how to speak. "I'm not the favorite," Meg said. "*Neal's* the favorite."

"*I'm* not the favorite," Neal said instantly.

More cameras swung in their direction, and they all smiled broad, friendly smiles.

As they went in to the reception, she tried not to limp too badly, but she must not have done a very good job, because people either stared or quickly averted their eyes.

Which made her feel like the god-damn Spirit of '76, but okay, fine, whatever. *She* didn't mind.

Also, like Steven, she would lose the moral high ground if she complained about being down here.

Neal waved at their father, who was over by the windows talking to some guests, and made a beeline for their mother, who was near the fireplace, surrounded by an even larger group, including the First Lady of Mali, and the French Ambassador and his wife. Her mother's French was superb, and the First Lady apparently spoke quite good English, but there were a couple of interpreters strategically posted a few feet away, just in case.

"*Bienvenue*, Madame Her Excellency *et* Monsieur Ambassadeur!" Neal said, as chipper as ever, and everyone standing within earshot grinned.

Christ, no matter what he claimed, the kid wasn't going to go to West Point; he was going to be the Secretary of State someday. Or, possibly, both.

Steven's entire appearance consisted of saying, "*Bonjour,*" and then, "*Excusez-moi,*" before he retreated from the room and went back upstairs.

Despite having studied it in both junior high and high school, Meg's French was pretty lousy, but she was able to produce a reasonably competent "*Bonjour, comment allez-vous? Il fait très beau de vous rencontrer.*" The First Lady and French Ambassador smiled, and responded in kind, but they spoke too quickly for her to be able to translate much of it, so she glanced at her mother, who mouthed, "They want to know how you are."

Okay, she could do that, too. "*Je suis très bien, merci,*" she said. "*Et vous?*"

She could tell that, although they were trying to hide it, the First Lady and the French ambassador's wife—and most of the other women in their vicinity—were watching the way she and her mother interacted in a subtle "So, what the hell kind of parent *is* she?" sort of way.

Which made her feel very self-conscious, and awkward, and couldn't have thrilled the President much, either.

Without giving it much thought, she leaned against the thin upholstered arm of the nearest gilded chair—probably not a great idea, since it was an irreplaceable antique, dating back to James Monroe—so that she could set her cane down without falling. Then, she reached into her pocket with her good hand, took out the watch she always carried, and passed it to her mother, who looked surprised, but then fastened it around Meg's left wrist, which she gave an affectionate tap when she was done. She also glanced at Meg's slightly too long fingernails on that hand—the only way she could do them herself was to drag her fingers back and forth across the nail file Cheryl had suggested that she tape down on her desk—and Meg nodded, her mother nodding back.

All of which took about fifteen seconds, but visibly put the other two women at ease.

The First Lady asked her a couple of questions in English about college, to which she responded, just as politely. Then, her mother rattled off something, and Meg picked up very few words other than "airplane." Possibly "vacation," too.

"*Oui, nous allons nous ennuyer d'elle beaucoup,*" her mother was saying. "*Elle est étée merveilleuse pour avoir sa maison.*"

After Neal answered the same sorts of questions about his school and they had both said a respectful good-bye to everyone, Meg leaned towards her mother.

"*Sacre bleu*, you have another hair-bump," she said, very softly, so that no one else would hear.

For a split second, her mother eyes widened and she started to lift her hand, then smiled and lowered it. Nevertheless, just for fun, right before leaving, Meg let her gaze drift up to the crown of her mother's head, and shuddered slightly. Her mother seemed determined not to fall for the same joke twice, but then, took a quick peek in the mirror above the fireplace—to Meg's great amusement.

When she and Neal got upstairs, Preston was in the West Sitting Hall, talking to Steven and Trudy, because he had promised to have lunch with all of them. Since it was Sunday, and a day of relative leisure, he wasn't wearing his jacket over his shirt and tie, although it was neatly draped over a nearby chair.

"Taking advantage of the chance to get some extra face time with the President?" she asked.

Preston nodded. "My ambition knows no bounds."

Which she had no doubt that a number of people down in the West Wing currently believed about the guy with the new corner office.

The chefs cooked enough for a group considerably larger than the seven people who ended up sitting at the table, but it all looked delicious. She was so nervous about going back that she didn't eat much, but as always, having Preston there kept the mood light, and they mostly talked about things like the fact that the next day, her mother would be off to the Nationals game to make her yearly inept throw for Opening Day, with a visit to Camden Yards planned for the Orioles' home opener later in the week.

After she and her father left for Andrews—he was going to accompany her *to* the plane, although not fly on it this time, her mother and Steven and Neal were maybe going to go outside and practice on Steven's pitching mound, which the gardeners had set up, long ago, on one of the most private sections of the South Lawn. With this in mind, the President had changed into tailored khaki pants, a perfectly starched white Oxford shirt, and Top-Siders—which, for her mother, was a very sloppy, even slovenly, outfit. The throwing session was probably going to be funny as hell, and Meg was sorry to be missing it.

After brunch, Dr. Brooks came upstairs and gave her one last checkup, complete with a new prescription and the strict instruction that she absolutely *was not* to spend the rest of the semester in more pain than she could handle, and to call him regularly so that he could adjust the dosage, or change her medication entirely, as seemed to be indicated.

Before it was time to go, she spent about half an hour in her room, patting Vanessa—who accepted this lengthy tribute as her due, but also kept looking warily at the packed duffel bag. After a while, her mother came in, holding a small manicure kit with the Air Force One seal imprinted on it.

Feeling very incompetent, Meg nodded, and her mother sat next to her on the bed—not to Vanessa's delight. She took out a small pair of scissors, put on her reading glasses, lifted Meg's hand into hers, and then very carefully cut the nails. Neither of them spoke during this procedure—Meg was too busy being embarrassed, and her mother was concentrating on what she was doing.

After using an emery board to file and shape each nail in turn, her mother glanced at her splint. "Would you like me to—?"

Meg shook her head, moving her good hand—okay, her entire left arm and half of her upper body—protectively in front of it.

Her mother nodded, lifting her own hands to make it clear that she wasn't going to go anywhere near the splint. As she replaced the manicure tools in the kit, her hair fell forward enough to obscure the side of her face, but Meg knew without looking how sad her expression must be.

They sat there, her mother's hands tense in her lap, and her shoulders drawn up, and Meg realized that she was sitting almost exactly the same way. She suddenly felt tearful, for no good reason—or, maybe, lots of good reasons—and had to swallow very hard a couple of times.

Her mother glanced over, then looked at her more closely. "What?"

Meg shook her head, avoiding her eyes.

They sat silently, for another minute.

"Meg," her mother said, sounding very serious.

Jesus, this wasn't the time for either of them to start anything. "I don't want to get into stuff," Meg said. "I'm about to leave, and—I'm about to leave, okay?"

Her mother nodded, then picked up her good hand and dropped a kiss near her wrist. More specifically, her watch.

It was good to have her blatant, public effort to jump loyally to the President's defense formally acknowledged—but she didn't want to talk about it. So she shrugged, her mother nodded, and they left it at that.

She and her father departed from the South Grounds, with a much smaller than usual contingent of reporters and staffers looking on, since it was Sunday. Neal and Trudy gave her big, uncomplicated hugs, while Steven stood there with his hands in his pockets, and said, "Later," sounding very disinterested. Her mother held her for a couple of seconds—stiff and reserved, as she almost always was when displaying affection in front of cameras, which probably didn't do much to change the minds of those who were of the "she's an unnatural woman who doesn't love her children" school of thought—and whispered, "Please take better care of yourself," Meg shrugging—stiffly—in response.

She and her father didn't say much on the way over to Andrews, mostly because she was trying to get control of how homesick and close to tears she felt, during the last few minutes of relative privacy she was going to have for the next month and a half.

"I'm sorry if it was, you know, difficult, while I was here," she said finally, as they drove through the main entrance of the air base. Sorry that she'd snarled almost every time he'd looked at her.

Her father smiled. "August twelfth will always be one of the three best days of my life."

Her birthday. "Do you still carry them?" she asked.

"Everywhere I go," he said, and took out his wallet to show her.

For as long as she could remember, he had kept baby pictures of the three of them in there, each taken on the days they were born, and she had never decided whether to be amused—or hurt—that in the one of her, while her father was clearly beside himself with joy, her mother looked very nervous, and maybe even overwhelmed. An "in retrospect, getting pregnant may *really* not have been a good idea" expression.

She knew the answer, but— "You always wanted children."

He nodded. "Absolutely. I couldn't wait."

She wasn't going to ask the obvious question about his spouse, because it would just start trouble. But, it begged another question which she would also probably never ask either of them—had her mother married him *because* he was so nurturing and eager to have a family, or in spite of it? Regardless, it was a relief to see that he also still had the photograph of her in her wedding gown in his wallet, her hair thick and somewhat wild, with such a charismatic grin on her face that it was highly unlikely that anyone who saw it would ever ask why he had decided to marry her. He watched her look at it, and she wondered what he was thinking.

"Russell James Powers never dreamed that one day, he would grow up to be the First Gentleman of the United States," she said. Which had been the opening line of the most breathless, and wildly inaccurate, biography published about her father so far.

He laughed. "Truer words have never been written, Meg."

No, probably not.

They were on the tarmac now, and the last-minute flight checks and so forth had been completed, and everyone was ready for her to board. Her father hugged her very close, and she knew he was maybe hoping that she would change her mind at the last second and ask him to come along for the ride. She had the sudden paralyzing thought that something bad might happen during the next six weeks, and that this would be the last time she ever saw anyone in her family again, but—well, there wasn't much she could do about that. Unfortunately.

"You're okay by yourself?" he asked, when he finally let go.

If he got on the plane with her, he would be back home by dinnertime, the press would never know the difference, and she would have someone to talk to on the way up. Someone she trusted. Someone who could make her feel safe, for a little while longer.

"I'll be fine," she said.

43

EIGHT OF HER agents came on the plane this time, and they spent most of the flight playing cards, although Martin sat with her long enough to ask how her vacation had been, Paula came over to compliment her sweater, and Garth took a few minutes to discuss some new procedures and security devices and code words and such which were going to be put into effect for the rest of the semester.

But, other than that, she kept her sunglasses on, stared out the window, and alternated sips of coffee and ice water. When they landed, she realized—with a sense of intense panic—that there was no way that she was going to be able to carry her bag and computer off the plane by herself. Even taking two trips and moving them one at a time would be a challenge, although it was the only realistic option, since it was against Secret Service guidelines—and not very dignified, to boot—for her to ask for help, so—okay. No problem. In fact, she would damn well make it look *easy*. She would—

"Meg, don't do that," Garth said. "We'll take care of it."

She hesitated, about to pick up her laptop. "I'm not ever supposed to ask you guys to—"

"We've got it," he said. "Just be careful on the steps, okay?"

Right. Starting with getting off the plane, she was now officially back to a life of constantly dealing with things like stairs. Steep, exhausting stairs. Sisyphean stairs.

It was a short drive to the campus, and all too quickly, they were pulling up in front of her dorm. There was a fair amount of activity going on—mostly, other people returning from their breaks, too, but also, a few reporters and paparazzi hanging around on the main road and Park Street.

Christ, she wasn't ready to put herself through this again. She closed her eyes, feeling sick to her stomach—and very much like crying.

"How overt do you want us to be?" Garth asked, from the passenger's side of the front seat. "It would be my *pleasure* to have them run off."

Her pleasure, too, but it would make for very bad visuals. "I'm fine, thanks," she said, picking up her cane. "They don't bother me."

Someone was holding the door for her—Ronald, maybe—and she took her time getting out, since the new brace was so cumbersome, and it would be far too easy to fall. She didn't think there were any tears in her eyes, but she adjusted her sunglasses to reassure herself that they were fully covered, and wished that she had thought to wear a cap, for extra protection. A photo of her sobbing helplessly in public would have to be worth a nice chunk of change, although only a tiny fraction of what a similar shot of her *mother* would get on the open market.

And she wasn't irrationally afraid of stepping away from the car, and back into very public college life, she was just—tired. Very, very tired.

"Hi, Meg," a voice said.

She looked up and saw Khalid, from her entry. Someone she had only just been starting to get to know before spring break, but so far, he seemed swell. Had grown up in Bloomfield Hills, was planning to major in chemistry, spent a lot of time playing intramural sports. "Hi. How was your break?" she asked.

He nodded, disheveled in baggy shorts and an old Detroit Tigers hoodie, and—judging from the shin pads stuffed inside his socks—on his way back from playing pick-up soccer. "Good. How was yours?"

"Fine, thanks," Meg said.

It was a relief to be able to fall into step—limp—with someone, although he paused when he heard cameras clicking.

"They'll probably get published somewhere," she said. "Do you care?"

He shook his head. "No. It's kind of funny, though."

The degree to which she was apparently dating every single man who had ever set foot in the Berkshires? Yeah, it was. She nodded. "Want a good laugh? Put your hand on my arm, and watch what happens."

He reached out to touch her elbow—and the sounds of clicking increased exponentially. "Jesus, that's a trip," he said, put his arm all the way around her, and grinned at the photographic response. "That son of a bitch Taylor's going to be pissed if these get printed."

With luck.

Once she was inside the dorm, she allowed herself thirty seconds to indulge in rampant self-pity and anxiety before getting on the elevator. Then, as she stepped out onto the third floor, she heard Susan saying, sounding very reassuring, "Well, yes, it's possible, but I really don't think you have to worry. It's probably just a statistical anomaly."

That was a conversation she was not at all sorry to have missed. And there was only one person on the floor with whom Susan could be having it.

"Hi," Susan said, when she saw her—and she was, in fact, talking to Jesslyn, over near the stairwell. "Welcome back."

"Yeah, you, too," Meg said, and nodded at Jesslyn, who looked very troubled by some numerical aberration or other. "Hi."

Jesslyn squinted at her, instead of answering.

Whatever. Let them return to math, then.

Juliana must have heard her unlocking her door, because she came out to the hall right away, grinned, and instantly burst into song—her voice much better and stronger than Meg would have guessed. "Anchors aweigh, my boys, anchors aweigh!"

Farewell to college joys, we sail at break of day. Meg grinned sheepishly. "You saw that?"

Juliana laughed. "Yeah. I mean, I didn't get it, but my father did, and he explained it to me."

"Was he in the Navy?" Meg asked.

"No," Juliana said cheerfully. "He's just smart." Then she went down the hall to pound on Mary Elizabeth's door. "Hey, sucker, pay up!"

Mary Elizabeth came out, looked at Meg, frowned, and then handed Juliana what looked like a ten-dollar bill.

She had probably just inadvertently forgotten to say a hearty—even overjoyed—hello. "Boy, it's so good to see you," Meg said. "I missed you *a lot.*"

Mary Elizabeth's nod lacked conviction. Or, even, interest.

Okay. Moving on now. "What was the bet?" Meg asked.

"That you'd find some plausible excuse not to come back," Juliana said, stuffing the money into her pocket. "But I said, not a chance."

"I should only have gone for five," Mary Elizabeth said, and went back into her room.

"Anyone else take you up on it?" Meg asked.

Juliana shook her head. "No, Tammy said ten was too much, Jesslyn said it was too small-time for her, and Susan said you'd drag yourself back here even if you were gushing blood from about five different arteries."

Typical, on all three counts.

She called her parents right away to let them know that she had arrived safely, but didn't talk very long, because she didn't want them to know how homesick she already was. She wanted to lie down, but knew she would fall asleep, so she set up her laptop, instead.

When she checked her voice-mail, she found three messages from Jack. In the first one, he wanted to know if she would meet him for dinner at 5:30, in the second, he suggested 5:45, and in the third, he suggested 6:00. Since it was now 6:13, she decided to wait until 6:15—which was when the phone rang.

"Hey," he said, sounding very pleased to hear her voice. "When'd you get back?"

Whoa, did she have a *boyfriend*? It was beginning to seem that way. "Just now," she said. "How about you?"

"This morning," he said.

He wanted to meet at the dining hall right away, but she talked him into holding off until quarter to seven, so she could wash her face and just generally pull herself together. Again, she had to resist the urge to stretch out on her bed, although she did allow herself to rest at her desk for a few minutes, leaning her head against her good arm and almost nodding off.

Now that it was almost dark, it was much colder outside than she expected it to be, but she wasn't about to haul herself back upstairs to get her coat, so her sweater would just have to suffice. Brian looked as though he might be about to offer her his jacket, but that was one of those awkward agent/protectee lines that none of them ever crossed. There was only one photographer still waiting around, out on the street past the cast iron gates leading into the quad, and he took a couple of pictures, but it seemed like more of a reflex action than anything else.

Jack was lounging around near the bike racks in front of Mission, and two girls—one of whom she recognized, although she didn't know her name—were busy flirting with him. She was very prepared to be jealous, but he jumped up, looking so happy to see her that it didn't seem to be necessary.

"Hi!" he said.

She wasn't sure she was ready to have them be a completely flagrant and open couple, so she backed away from his hug. But then, she was afraid that might have hurt his feelings, so she leaned into it for a second.

"Well, see you later, Jack," one of the girls said, giving Meg something of an "if you weren't famous, you wouldn't have a *shot* with him" look, while the other girl just seemed disappointed that Malibu Bobby was now going to be otherwise occupied.

"Yeah, okay, Connie," he said. "See you around, Gaylan."

As the two girls drifted, reluctantly, off, Jack grinned at her.

"How much tongue can I give you in public?" he asked.

He really was just an ambulatory penis, wasn't he. "I think maybe none," she said.

"Damn." Then, he moved much closer and kissed her, deeply. "Oops." He pulled away, and grinned at her again. "My bad."

She was amused—and aroused, but elected to keep these two facts to herself.

A lot of people said hello to him, while they were waiting in line on the stairs to get into the dining hall, and she was pleased when a few others—not just sycophantic strangers, but people she *knew*, from classes and the dorm—said hi to her, too.

She glanced at his ski jacket, which was hanging open, and noticed that the zipper was unadorned. "No lift tickets?"

Jack shrugged.

Wait a minute. "Did you cut off your lift tickets, so I wouldn't have to see them?" she asked.

He nodded.

That was *nice*. "Thanks," she said, and—because she bloody well felt like it—gave him a kiss.

Everyone standing nearby looked at them—in fact, some of them flat-out *gawked*—so, it was possible that the kiss had been a little on the deep side.

It was also possible that she completely didn't give a good goddamn.

Among other things, the dining hall was serving marinated steak, which looked pretty good, but she didn't take any, because her rocker knife was tucked inside her jacket pocket—back in her room, and she wouldn't be able to cut the meat by herself, otherwise. So, without being excited about the unavoidable compromise, she went with some vegetable jambalaya and a small helping of apple crisp, instead.

"Christ, Meg, is that all you're going to eat?" Jack asked, after they were both sitting down at a table with several people from his dorm, since it was too crowded for them to find one of their own.

She shrugged, already embarrassed that he'd had to carry her tray for her, because her balance on the surgical brace and her cane was so unsteady. "It looks good," she said, even though she was envious of his steak, two baked potatoes, onion rings, and double-sized serving of corn. In fact, if her leg didn't hurt so much, she might have gone back and gotten herself some onion rings, at least.

He frowned at her. "Are you a vegetarian?"

She didn't want to have anything resembling a personal discussion in front of people she didn't know. "Late lunch," she said, and reached for the pepper, a guy named Karl, who was sitting across from her, practically falling all over himself to hand it to her.

It felt as though everyone at the table was watching her eat—or, okay, mostly *not* eat, and she finally gave up and concentrated on her coffee, limping up twice for refills. Most of the conversation revolved around their dorm, Armstrong, so she just sat and listened, although they also talked a lot about what they had all done on their spring breaks.

"How was the skiing, man?" one of the guys, Ned, asked Jack.

He shrugged, not looking at her. "Okay, I guess. The weather wasn't so hot."

If that was a lie, she appreciated it. Hearing about perfect spring days and two feet of fresh powder would have been quite intolerable.

"What did you do?" someone asked.

Was that directed towards her? She looked up. "Oh." Should she tell them about her stay in the hospital, or just describe the many family encounters yanked straight out of *Who's Afraid of Virginia Woolf*? "Nothing special. Hung out. Watched movies. That kind of thing."

"See anything good?" the girl asked.

They weren't going to like her if she told them that all of the studios always made every single movie they were releasing available to the White House, and if any of them had an urge to see something in particular, old or new, it was just a question of someone on the staff picking up the phone, and it would be delivered with startling speed. "Not really," Meg said. "My brothers usually pick what we're going to see, and they have absolutely terrible taste."

Several people at the table laughed, which she didn't expect.

The story would be much more interesting, if she could add the part when her mother had lost her patience one night up at Camp David, and snapped, "Would it be even remotely possible for us to watch an actual *good* movie, or is that too much to ask?" The rest of the family had pretty much ignored her, since the film in question was, while very stupid, quite funny, but the staff members who overheard the outburst were disturbed to witness the President's vociferous frustration, and the fact that—although she at least stayed in the room, for once—she spent most of the rest of the movie sullenly flipping through briefing books.

Despite downplaying his ski trip, Jack was an active participant in the conversation, although he seemed to be getting increasingly tense, and she wasn't quite sure why. But it was upsetting, given the fact that he had been so glad to see her earlier. Christ, maybe this boyfriend business was going to be more trouble than it was worth.

The dining hall had stopped serving, so most of the tables were empty now. All but one of Jack's friends had taken off, and she wanted to leave herself, but he was still eating, and it would be rude.

"I can't *believe* you're not going to play Beirut with us tonight," his friend Ned said to him, standing up to go. Then, he nodded at Meg. "Uh, nice to meet you, Meghan."

Meg nodded back. "You, too, Ned." Then, once he was gone, she glanced at Jack. "Everything okay?"

He nodded, halfway through a massive heap of apple crisp.

"If you want to play with them, you should," she said, although it struck her as being pretty dumb to get wasted on everyone's first night back, with classes starting bright and early the next day.

He shrugged, eating.

What the hell was bothering him, anyway? "I'm sorry if I talked too much," she said.

He glanced up. "You only said about five words."

Okay. Maybe that's what had upset him. "Oh. I'm sorry," she said. "Since you all know each other, I felt intrusive, so—well, that's all. I mean, they seemed very nice."

He nodded. "They are, yeah. I mean, I could do without Mona, maybe—" who had something of a braying laugh, and, to make matters worse, seemed to find almost *everything* screamingly funny, as far as Meg could tell. "But, even she's okay, when she isn't showing off."

It had seemed pretty clear why Mona had felt the need to preen, noisily, during the meal, although it would be impolitic for her to say so. "Well, she probably likes one of you guys," Meg said, "and was trying to make a good impression."

Jack laughed. "She was showing off because you were sitting at the table. Like, if she said *just* the right thing, you two would end up being best buddies."

That had been her instinct, too. "I was a little surprised—" to put it mildly— "when she kind of grabbed my arm," Meg said. She hadn't yanked free, but she might have recoiled.

"Yeah," Jack said, and laughed again. "You didn't look too happy."

So, maybe *that* was it. "I'm sorry, I didn't mean to do that," Meg said. Christ, with all of the damn apologies, she was starting to sound like her mother. "I just don't like it when people I've never met are sure they already know me really well."

He nodded. "Must be weird, yeah."

Very much so. And the fact that they all, if so inclined, could have watched a large chunk of her spring break on television was unsettling, too.

She waited for him to say something else, but all he did was glance at her, and then bend over his tray again. Swell. She didn't want to fight with him, but if it was going to happen, she didn't want to put it off any longer, either. "Um, maybe it's my imagination," she said, "but it seemed as though you started getting angry at me during dinner."

He shrugged, finishing his dessert.

She was really worn out, and not at all in the mood for detective work. In fact, she wasn't in the mood to sit here anymore. Maybe she should date someone like Simon, after all. Being able to push him around too much would irk her, but it might be preferable to all of this sturm and drang. So, she hooked her cane over her shoulder and reached for her tray, hoping that she would be able to make it over to the dish-room without tearing anything new in her leg.

"*Look* how much you didn't eat," he said, accusingly.

Christ, was that the damn bee in his bonnet? And how in the hell was she going to explain it, without sounding self-pitying. So, she shrugged. "I guess I'm a little tired tonight."

"Yeah," he said, not without a trace of belligerence. "Normally, you eat so much, it's embarrassing to be seen with you."

Her appetite, or lack thereof, was really exclusively her own business.

"I mean, you go ahead and get racked up on caffeine," he said, "but that's about it."

It was tedious to be criticized constantly about something she bloody well couldn't help. She was tired, and she wasn't hungry. Nothing exactly earth-shattering about that.

During the first several days of her captivity, she had been ravenous to the point of near-incoherence, since starving her, intentionally, had been one of the many things the man found funny. It was hunger at a level she never would have been able to imagine. Hunger that made her dizzy, and sick, and incapable of thinking clearly. Hunger so severe that it *hurt*.

It had almost reached the point that if the guy had come in with a piece of pizza or something, grinned, and said, "It's all yours, if you do what I want," there was an excellent chance that she would have gotten down on her knees in front of him, or whatever other ugly demand he might have made. She liked to think that she would have told him that she would *never* be that hungry, but if—instead of being discarded in a mine-shaft, like a piece of worthless debris—she'd been forced to spend a few more days handcuffed in that dark, tiny room, she was pretty sure she would have been capable of agreeing to almost anything to get something to eat.

And also sure that, if she knew, even Beth would look down on her for being weak.

Jack sighed. "I'm not trying to tell you what to do, Meg, I just—"

Oh, the hell he wasn't. "No, I didn't think you were," Meg said, and looked at her watch—which made her homesick. "I need to go make a call, though, okay?"

He got up, lifting her tray on top of his. "Let me go get rid of these, and I'll come with you."

She wanted to go back to the dorm and be by herself, but she waited for him, wondering if she looked composed—or as impatient and irritated as she felt.

Of course, if she decided that she didn't need to have a hypercritical boyfriend, she could walk away from this. For good. Whenever she wanted. And he could move on to Frances, or Gaylan, or Connie, or some other female acolyte, in no time.

"Got a feeling I'm going to be playing Beirut tonight," he said, when he came back.

How perspicacious of him. But, she shrugged.

"Yeah, I figured," he said, and then shook his head.

She had neither the energy, nor the inclination, to pursue this post-break reunion any further, so maybe, if she made her way towards the exit, she could—

"Have to tell you, I've spent most of the last two weeks imagining what we might do the next time we were alone together," he said.

It had also maybe crossed her mind, more than once. And here they were, pretty much alone right this very second, except for a few people cleaning up the dining hall, and, of course, her damn security entourage. "Was standing in the middle of Mission being pissed off at each other part of what you imagined?" she asked.

"Well, I *did* picture us in here," he said, "but we weren't pissed off."

His probable train of thought was easy to predict. "Were you on top of me?" she asked.

"Other way around." He grinned for a second. "Lots of people watching."

Well, that was certainly vivid.

"Anyway, look," he said. "I'm not going to apologize if something makes me worry about you. I mean, it's just not going to happen. Okay?"

Fine. She shrugged. "I'm not going to apologize when I'm too tired to eat."

They looked at each other, and—well, she couldn't speak for him, but *she* was certainly still pissed off, albeit not entirely against the notion of being on top of him.

Just not tonight. And, of course, not here, in the dining hall.

Even though his dorm was part of the Mission Park complex, he insisted upon walking her back to Sage, and she didn't feel like getting into another fight, so she just nodded.

When they stepped outside, it was so cold that he offered her his coat, a suggestion she declined without a second thought. He frowned and took the jacket off anyway, even though all he was wearing underneath it was an In-N-Out Burger T-shirt. At least she had a sweater on. But, to hell with it. If he wanted to be even more doltish and stubborn than she was, that was his call.

They barely spoke along the way, and ended up standing outside the main door to her entry, not looking at each other. It was freezing, but since he wasn't shivering, she god-damn well made sure that she wasn't, either.

"Well," he said, rather sulkily, hands going into his pockets. "Guess I'll, I don't know, see you in Psych tomorrow, maybe."

Dating was supposed to be fun, wasn't it? Christ, she couldn't even describe this as a disaster-in-the-making, since it had already crashed and burned far beyond that. But she needed to remember that she actually *liked* this guy. Very much. "I wanted the steak," she said, as he started to walk away.

Jack stopped. "What, and you didn't get it, because you thought it might make you fat?"

He had no way of knowing how small and pathetic that made her feel, and the degree to which that tone of voice felt assaultive, so she shouldn't judge him for it.

Shouldn't being the operative word.

The wind was picking up, and she shivered for a couple of seconds, before remembering that she had had no intention of doing so.

"Well, trust me," he said. "You can afford the calories."

She didn't just feel small; she felt *tiny*. Insignificant. Like—debris, in fact. "Jack, I forgot to bring my stupid rocker knife with me, and I can't use a regular one by myself, so even if I'd rather eat something else, I have to pick foods that only need a fork," she said, gesturing with her splint. Or, alternatively, live in the god-damn White House, where unseen hands would artfully cut and chop everything up for her before sending it out of the kitchen.

His expression changed, every trace of anger disappearing. "I, uh, that didn't even cross my mind."

There was really no reason that it should have. "It's okay," she said. "I mean, it's not—I wouldn't have thought of it either, before."

"Did you think I wouldn't have helped you?" he asked. "I mean, God, Meg, you just had surgery, and—*of course* I would have helped you."

In front of a table of strangers, who had already watched him carry her tray, and pull out her chair, because she was too crippled to manage basic tasks by herself. Christ, that would have been a scene for one and all to remember.

"Meg?" he asked, when she didn't say anything.

A few people from her dorm walked by, including Dirk, who was carrying a large brown paper bag.

"Hi, Meg," he said cheerfully, and indicated the groceries. "Snacks in a while."

The weekly, unofficially-obligatory Sunday Snacks entry get-together—which she skipped, more often than not—although she nodded and smiled at him, as though she was incredibly eager to attend.

"Going to rush right up there?" Jack asked, when they were by themselves again.

She nodded. "You bet. When it comes to food, I'm a bottomless pit."

To her relief, he smiled, then looked at her for what seemed like a very long time. "Do I get to kiss you before I take off?" he asked.

"I'd like that very much," she said.

SINCE SHE HAD no intention of engaging in any further social interactions for the rest of the night, she took the elevator upstairs and ducked into her room as quickly as possible. She was already lying down before she remembered that she should have taken a couple of her not-cold-enough ice packs out of the mini-refrigerator, but the thought of getting up again was too daunting.

After a while, the phone—the private line, not the drop-line—rang, and she lifted her head just enough to be able to look at the Caller ID number. Beth. She wasn't sure if she felt like picking up, but right before it would have gone to her voice-mail, she did.

"Hey," Beth said.

"Hey," Meg said, in lieu of sighing heavily.

"That doesn't sound too good," Beth said.

It wasn't. Meg kept her sigh to one of only moderate depth. "I want to go home."

Beth laughed.

It was true, but yeah, it was also a little funny.

"Seen him yet?" Beth asked.

Meg nodded. "Yeah. We were at the dining hall, and it was great, and then he started giving me grief about not eating more."

It was quiet on the other end of the line. Too quiet.

"Please promise me that you aren't going to bug me about it, too," Meg said.

Beth took her time answering. "You're really thin, Meg," she said finally. "*Scary* thin."

Great.

"You're under a hundred pounds now, right?" Beth asked.

"I don't know," Meg said. Okay, *lied*, because she was a ninety-eight pound weakling, the last time she'd checked. Well—ninety-five pounds, without the surgical brace, if one wished to be precise.

Beth didn't say anything.

“Did I used to eat?” Meg asked. “I honestly have no idea.”

“Yeah, you put away almost as much as Steven,” Beth said. “Remember how Sarah was always bitching that you constantly stuffed your face, but never gained any weight?”

Only vaguely. “I think tennis gave me a pretty big appetite,” Meg said. Guessed, really, since she just couldn’t remember.

“Yeah, probably,” Beth said. “You were usually out there three, four hours a day.”

And, often, twice that much, on weekends.

“If he’d held on to me much longer, do you think I would have offered him sex, for food?” Meg asked, breaking the silence.

“No,” Beth said. “I think you would have let yourself starve to death, instead.”

Oh, she of too much faith. “I don’t,” Meg said.

Beth sighed. “Meg, you wouldn’t do it to save your *life,* so I really don’t think you would have given in for, I don’t know, a bag of potato chips or something.”

In theory.

“Besides, you were *getting* to him,” Beth said. “He was probably about to break down and bring you something on his own.”

Maybe. She swallowed, feeling nauseated suddenly. “He told me not to trust any food, because they would have done something to it, first.” The grotesque potential details of which she usually tried not to imagine.

“The bastard was just screwing with your head,” Beth said.

Yeah. Effectively so.

“None of this has anything to do with why you’re not eating, right?” Beth asked.

There were a lot of ways to answer that—most of which were mean. But, being mad at Jack—and the guy—and her parents—didn’t mean that she should yell at Beth. It might be cathartic, but, as her mother would say, it would be bad form. “The last time I remember being really hungry was in the mine-shaft,” Meg said.

“I know,” Beth said. “And I hate that. But I’d rather see Jack wanting you to eat more, than saying that if you’re not careful, you’re going to start packing it on.”

Which had been the precipitating remark in her breakup with Ramon, who had told her that after dinner one night—and managed to hit several of Beth's long-term, well-hidden insecurities in one fell swoop, despite the fact that she had had a striking, classic, hourglass figure since she was about twelve. Although when they were that age, they had both been confused, and unnerved, by the number of inappropriately graphic comments men made to Beth almost every time the two of them were out walking around somewhere.

"Ramon was a schmuck," Meg said.

"You got that right." Then, Beth laughed. "Nigel may be, too."

Her latest conquest, a graduate student from Oxford, who was studying abroad for a year.

"I'm sorry," Meg said. "I hope he isn't."

"Yeah, it'd be a nice change," Beth said, and paused. "Is Jack a schmuck?"

Was he? Meg thought about that. "I'm not sure yet. But it's kind of—high maintenance."

"So, you're already looking for an excuse to break up with him," Beth said.

The problem with having an extremely perceptive, highly intelligent best friend was that it was almost impossible to prevaricate. "I don't know," Meg said. "But, yeah, I might be."

Beth took a few seconds, apparently digesting that. "You want someone who can maybe keep up, or do you want to run the show?"

The very crux of the matter. "I have no idea," Meg said.

44

After they hung up, Meg studied her ceiling for a while—the slant was stupid; she did not like the slant—before summoning the required initiative to retrieve two ice-packs and a Coke, so she could gulp down another painkiller. While she was at it, she also took out the neatly wrapped package containing a hunk of lemon-blueberry cake, which Neal had insisted on sticking in her bag before she left.

She was lying on her bed, the Coke can empty and the gel ice-packs having long since warmed to body temperature, looking at the still-wrapped cake, when someone knocked on the barely ajar door.

"You skipped snacks again," Susan said.

Meg nodded, sitting up as though she hadn't spent the last hour or two lost in a morass of homesickness.

"I brought you a few leftovers," Susan said, and put a paper plate of what appeared to be homemade cookies on the desk.

"Thank you," Meg said. "I'll have some later."

Susan didn't seem convinced, but she nodded. "Okay. Good break?"

"You must be getting really tired of asking people that question," Meg said.

Susan smiled. "Well, some of you are better at answering it than others."

Some of them had probably had better spring breaks, too.

"How are you, really?" Susan asked. "You look—I don't know. Like someone who didn't just come back from a vacation."

And was feeling more so, with every passing second. "I'm okay," Meg said. "But, are you any good with tourniquets? Because a couple of my arteries are *really* bothering me."

Susan looked embarrassed.

"*Ow,*" Meg said, and held her stomach.

"I didn't think she was going to quote me," Susan said, still flushing, "but it was a compliment."

Yeah, okay, what the hell. Meg let go of her stomach. "How was your break?"

"Very nice," Susan said. "Thanks."

Was Susan lying, too? It was impossible to tell, one way or the other. Enigmatic, to the point of opacity. "How many miles did you run?" Meg asked.

Susan grinned. "You know, anyone who ever underestimates you would be making a mistake, Meg."

Which was cryptic, but also probably another compliment.

"Anyway," Susan said, and turned to go.

"If I show you something, will you promise not to tell anyone?" Meg asked.

Susan sat down in the desk chair, leaning forward, prepared—it seemed—for a profound confession.

It was going to seem silly, but Meg clumsily opened the package of cake with her good hand. "I brought this back with me."

That was maybe not the scope of secret Susan was expecting.

"My mother baked it yesterday," Meg said.

"Oh." Susan got up to examine it more closely, and blinked. "Well. How about that."

"The frosting was my brothers' idea," Meg said.

Susan glanced at the thick slice again, and possibly tried not to laugh aloud.

"Want some?" Meg asked.

Susan nodded. "Sure. That would be—pretty cool, frankly. But, be a sport and let me invite Juliana to come in here, too. She'll be completely into it."

And both hurt and disappointed if she ever found out that she'd been excluded, so Meg nodded.

Once Juliana had plopped down on the bottom of the bed, and vowed eternal silence, Meg used her rocker knife to cut the cake into three equal pieces and distributed them.

"It's very tasty," Juliana said, as they ate.

Meg glanced over to see whether she was being sarcastic, or sincere. There seemed to be components of both in her expression. "Well, except for the frosting, and maybe having been cooked too long—" Hmmm. "I mean, it isn't bad at all, considering how cold and unloving she is."

Susan and Juliana looked as though they assumed she was kidding, but weren't entirely positive.

"She *isn't*, actually," Meg said. "She just gets shy, when other people are around."

Susan and Juliana nodded, but not very convincingly.

It was tiresome not to be believed. "But, in all honesty, I'm not sure her time at Le Cordon Bleu was really money well spent," Meg said.

Susan and Juliana grinned.

"Is your father a good cook?" Juliana asked.

Meg shook her head. "Not really." He could put together a nice meatloaf, and basic stuff like that, but when Trudy wasn't around, and they'd already eaten everything she'd prepared and left behind in the refrigerator or freezer, they usually ended up ordering Chinese food or something. And on the very rare occasions she had stayed with her mother in Georgetown—when she was in the Senate, she and Steven and Neal had each gotten to go down alone and spend private time with her once in a while—they had either suffered through rubbery omelets and salads and the like, made a meal out of whatever was being served at embassy receptions or whatever, or gone out to the most funky and exotic ethnic restaurants they could find.

"Well, you probably always had people doing that stuff for you," Juliana said uncertainly.

"No, just Trudy," Meg said. Who, granted, was probably equivalent to a dedicated staff of ten all by herself. "And if there was some big dinner or garden party or whatever, they'd bring in caterers and all, but mostly, my parents just wanted our house to be our *house*, so they didn't do it much." Still didn't, in fact. To her mother's staff 's near-constant dismay, especially during campaigns. But, it would be too weird to get into all of that. "Are your parents good cooks?"

Juliana shrugged. "My mother doesn't like it much, but yeah, she's pretty good. And my father barbecues a lot. But they're really tired when they get home from work, so they like it when we help out and get things started for them."

She couldn't believe she didn't know this, but— "What do they do for a living?" Meg asked. "Your father's—a doctor?"

Juliana shook her head. "Financial advisor. And my mother runs a mutual fund."

She wouldn't have pictured Juliana coming from a family deeply involved in the business world, but it was disgraceful that she had never asked—or had forgotten, if she'd been told. She looked at Susan, trying to remember if she'd picked up on any personal information like that when her parents had invited her out to brunch that time. "Your father's in real estate?"

"Advertising," Susan said. "And my mother opened her own art gallery last year. And—sorry to tell you, but they're *both* really good cooks."

Okay. She was glad to have more information, but it was also glaring that she was only just finding it out. "I, um, I should already know things like that about your families," she said. That is, if the three of them were friends.

Susan and Juliana nodded.

Well, they didn't have to be that quick to agree. "And *you* guys should already know that she isn't cold and unloving," Meg said.

Juliana's nod was guilty, but Susan's was thoughtful.

"Yeah," Susan said, and nodded again. "We really should."

SHE WAS SO worn out that she slept very heavily that night—which had the benefit of minimizing any nightmares—and barely woke up in time to shower and stagger off to her psychology class, stopping along the way to get the largest possible cup of coffee from the Eco Café, even though, technically, they weren't supposed to bring any food or drinks into the lecture hall. Class had already started when she limped in, and her professor was noticeably ruffled by the disruption, even though she tried to be as unobtrusive as possible—and assumed her agents were doing the same—as she took a seat in the back.

Jack, who was sitting about a dozen rows up ahead of her, motioned to the seat next to his, and she shook her head, since there was no way she could make it down those steps without causing even more of a commotion. He motioned more emphatically, and she gestured towards Dr. Wilkins—who caught her doing it, and looked very peeved. *So* peeved, that a bunch of people turned around to try and see what she might have done to annoy her that much. Meg pretended not to notice, and lifted her coffee to take a discreet sip. But she must not have fastened the lid tightly enough after she had added milk and sugar, because it came loose, and she spilled about a third of it across her Red Sox sweatshirt, which made several people sitting nearby laugh. Loudly.

Their professor looked at all of them with beady "I thought I was teaching *college*, not kindergarten" eyes, and they subsided.

Before she had made her tardy appearance, their lab reports and midterms must have been handed back, because George, one of their TAs, came tromping up the stairs with hers. He was a wide, fairly untidy guy, and when he tripped right before he got to her, the papers went flying, more people laughed, and Meg had to cough to keep from joining in.

Dr. Wilkins waited, balefully silent, as George scrambled after the papers, and then laboriously continued up the stairs and gave them to her.

"Thanks," Meg said, very, very quietly.

"She *hates* it when people walk in late," he muttered.

Meg nodded—since she had gotten snippy every single time it had happened all semester, and most of the class had long since decided that if they weren't on time, it was better to skip it entirely, rather than show up and be castigated.

George tripped again on his way back down to the front—triggering more laughs, but managed to stay on his feet, and make it into his chair without further incident.

"Well," Dr. Wilkins said, in a clipped voice. "*If* I may continue."

No one suggested otherwise, and she resumed discussing their exams.

Meg was afraid to check her grades, and peeked at the lab report first, relieved to see an A-. And it turned out that she had gotten a 94 on the test, so that was okay, too. She pretended to follow along as Dr. Wilkins went over the correct answers, but she took some time to use the bottom of her already-sodden sweatshirt to wipe coffee residue from her splint. It was probably going to be hard as hell to get the stains out of the shirt—she would have to call Trudy, in case she knew some special trick—and since it was Opening Day, she was just superstitious enough to wonder whether it was a bad omen for the entire season, and whether she had inadvertently doomed the Red Sox to a year of mediocrity.

She spent most of the class thinking about baseball—*actual* baseball, as opposed to baseball in England—and took almost no notes, even though Dr. Wilkins outlined, in depth, what they were going to be doing for the rest of the semester. With her cane and brace, she was no longer capable of making a quick getaway, so when class was over, she had to make a calculated guess about whether she could make it out the door first, or if she should just keep a very low, slouching profile until Dr. Wilkins had left the amphitheater. But, a small group of students was already gathering down in the front, holding their exams, and it looked as though her professor would be occupied by people complaining about their grades for a while.

"Well, take *you* out to the ballgame," Jack said, grinning at her.

To celebrate the day, in addition to her now-soaked sweatshirt, she was wearing a Red Sox cap and actual red socks below her sweatpants.

Which probably didn't make today that different from most other days.

But, it was nice that there didn't seem to be any lingering tension from their verbal scuffle the night before. "Think I put the whammy on them?" she asked.

Jack nodded. "Definitely. It's going to be all your fault if they lose this year."

If they really *did* have a bad season, she would have to make sure that Steven never found out about her moment of carelessness, since he would not find it funny.

"What'd you get?" Jack asked, gesturing towards the cluster of grade complainers.

"Ninety-four," Meg said. "What about you?"

"Ninety-six," he said.

Oh. It would be petty to be jealous, so she would choose to see that as a fluke. One of Susan's statistical anomalies. "What about your lab report?" she asked.

He shrugged. "A."

That meant a straight A, then, not an A-.

Not that she cared.

At all.

God-damn it.

"You didn't study, Meg," he said.

The *hell* she didn't. "You sat right there in Goodrich and watched me," she said defensively. On more than one occasion.

He shook his head.

Oh, for Christ's sakes. She hated revisionist history. "I see. Were you in the midst of a fugue?" she asked.

He held the door for her. "No. *I* studied. You drank a bunch of coffee, and looked around the room, and thought about whatever the hell it is that you think about."

It still counted as studying. Sort of.

"Did you even do all of the reading?" he asked.

There might have been a few sections she had only skimmed. Hmmm.

"So, maybe it bothers *me* that I studied like hell, and you got an A without even half trying," he said.

She had no effective counter-argument to that, so she chose not to make one.

Once they were outside, the light was much brighter, and he grinned when he saw the extent of the damage to her sweatshirt.

"I'll swap shirts with you, if you want to put on something dry," he said.

A very nice offer, since she wouldn't have anywhere close to enough time to go all the way back up to her room for a fresh shirt, and still get to her Shakespeare class. Except that he was wearing a battered yellow t-shirt which read "I Are A Idiot," and she might be better off presenting mere coffee stains to the outside world. "Thanks," she said, "but I can't change out here, because I'm not wearing anything underneath."

It looked almost as though someone had lit a match behind his eyes. "What?" he asked.

They both bloody well knew that he'd heard her correctly the first time.

"Ow, wow," he said, and watched her chest intently as she limped along. "Oh, what a treat."

It was a thick, oversized sweatshirt; how could anything possibly show through that?

He stopped her then, putting his hands on her shoulders. "Want to skip out of your English class, and I'll blow off econ?"

Yeah, right. What a one-track mind.

"I mean it," he said.

Of this, she had no doubt. She grinned at him, and rapped the front of his t-shirt with the handle of her cane. "You *is* a idiot, Jack."

"But, still smart enough to get a ninety-six," he said.

When they had been up at Camp David, and she had handily won that game of Battleship, her mother had let a "how *dare* she beat me" expression escape, before smiling and suggesting that they play again. It had been funny, but not particularly attractive.

Although it was not her natural bent, either, around Jack, she should maybe make an effort to be attractive.

"What?" he asked.

"I'm trying to rise above myself," she said.

"Oh, yeah?" He draped his arm over her shoulders. "How's it working?"

"Kind of a strain," she said. "Since you ask."

It was a foregone conclusion that he was going to reach up under her sweatshirt to check for himself precisely what she was, or was not, wearing, so it wasn't a shock to feel his hand slide up her back.

"Do you have on underpants?" he asked.

She nodded.

"*Damn*," he said.

He was a putz and a half.

"I think I should maybe double-check," he said.

Where was a hefty dose of saltpeter, when she needed one?

Paula moved into her line of vision, which was unusual enough to be scary. Meg stopped, on instant full alert, but all Paula did was make a point of holding her gaze before stepping away and being unobtrusive again.

"Jack, there's a camera somewhere," she said.

He shrugged. "Yeah. So?"

"So, please don't put your hand anyplace controversial," she said.

"Oh." He removed his hand from the top of her waistband, and held it up in the air uncertainly.

She glanced at him sideways, trying not to turn her head, or make it obvious that she was examining the general vicinity of his fly. "Untuck your shirt, too, okay?"

He looked down, then flushed, and quickly yanked his t-shirt out.

She did a slow scan of the area, from behind her sunglasses, and didn't see anything other than a cell phone camera which a harmless-looking older woman was pointing at them from the corner of Spring Street—except, wait, *there* he was. An unshaven, shifty-eyed paparazzo in his late twenties whom she had seen quite a few times before, crouched down behind a car, his camera resting on the trunk.

"Meg, I really don't want anyone printing a picture of me with a massive erection," Jack said, very grim.

An entirely legitimate concern on his part. "Would you please carry my knapsack?" she asked.

He seemed to be on the verge of saying something churlish, but then he nodded, took the knapsack, and held it in front of his waist.

Almost every time they started to have fun together, something stupid happened to derail them. "I'm sorry. I wish they would just leave me alone, but they won't," she said. The fringe and tabloid press, anyway.

He nodded, not looking happy about it.

Maybe if she had a long talk with Maureen, there might be some way to—except, all the White House could really do was assign someone like Ginette to run constant interference for her, which would end up creating a whole different set of problems.

Possibly, it *wouldn't* be such a bad solution for her agents to start shooting them, at will.

They crossed Main Street, the jerk photographer snapping away, even though Brian and Jose were on their way over there—presumably to block his view, if not find a way to knock the camera out of his hands and try to make it seem like an accident.

And if she looked as vexed as she felt, the guy was going to be able to market them as shots of the President's daughter having an ugly breakup quarrel with her new blond male companion.

"Did they do this to you in high school, too?" Jack asked.

Meg shook her head. "Sometimes, but not that often." Partially because, before she turned eighteen, most of the press felt uncomfortable about invading the privacy of a minor—especially when it was against her parents' express wishes, partially because Preston had had a gift for keeping the media in line, and partially, of course, because at that point, she hadn't been considered nearly as newsworthy.

One exception having been when a very famous, and handsome, movie star showed up at one of her tennis matches a few days after she was introduced to him at a White House screening, and judging from the size of the media presence, his publicist had made dozens of calls to alert them about the "date" before it took place. The guy—for whom she felt sorry, because he was almost certainly very gay, and trying to use her as a way to stay in the closet—had sat in a chair on the sidelines, cheering her on with such a complete lack of discrimination that he actually clapped when she doubled-faulted at one point. It had gotten so chaotic that she had had to call Preston during one of the changeovers, and have him come over to bring things under control.

Even though it made her feel ill, she offered to forfeit the match to her opponent—a very tall serve-and-volleyer from Madeira, who was classy enough not to accept. A move she may have regretted when she ended up losing in straight sets.

"Well," Jack said, once they were in front of the building where her next class was. He hefted the knapsack. "You, uh, want me to carry this up for you?"

Meg shook her head. "Thanks, but I'm fine. And you're going to be late, as it is."

He glanced at his watch, and nodded, then shrugged.

Okay. It was going to be another awkward parting.

She needed to change the tone here, somehow. "So," she said, slinging the knapsack over her shoulder, balancing cautiously on her good leg. "Was it really *massive*?"

He grinned. "*Extremely* massive," he said.

45

SHE GOT AN A- on her Shakespeare midterm, and sat there staring at the marked blue book, wondering why in the hell she kept falling short of full-fledged A's—although maybe it was worth reminding herself that she had—well—only *skimmed* a couple of the less engaging plays.

And it helped, somewhat, when she was one of the people Dr. Heidler singled out for having written unusually good essay answers—in her case, a comparative analysis of *King Lear* and *Julius Caesar*.

Because the surgery had been only two weeks earlier, there wasn't much she could do at physical therapy, although an orthopedist and a hand surgeon both examined her, asking questions and jotting down lengthy observations, and it seemed that an acupuncturist was now going to join the local team, too. Dr. Brooks was up and getting alternative on her.

Vicky worked with her good leg for a while, helping her do some strengthening exercises, and she and Cheryl talked—without making any significant progress—about whether there were any new adaptive strategies she could use to cut her own food, if she was caught someplace without assistive utensils.

She and her father had packed a small supply of White House Easter souvenirs into her duffel bag, which she gave out to all of the patients on the Pediatrics floor, even though it was a week early. There were painted wooden eggs with her parents' facsimile signatures, pins, aprons, illustrated books, specially-designed M&M's and marshmallow peeps, and a few small posters which had gotten pretty badly bent inside the bag. The gifts seemed to be a big hit, and even though the Red Sox game had already started—it was on in a couple of the rooms—she concentrated on giving each child her undivided attention, and not allowing herself even to *wonder* what the score might be.

Much.

When she got back to her room and flipped on the television, it turned out that they were losing, 4–0 in the bottom of the fifth, but—no matter. It was only a game. She did *not* worship the very ground they regularly spat on.

They, not atypically, erupted for five runs in the sixth, and then, four more in the seventh, to take a 9–4 lead—before the bullpen coughed it up in the top of the eighth, and they ended up losing 10–9.

Luckily, it really was just a game—a mere diversionary piece of entertainment; *fluff*, even—so she wasn't furious that they had lost in such an idiotic and predictable way.

She also didn't have to fight a string of profanities after the last out, or the urge to hurl her cap at the screen.

Once she had finished the latest assigned readings in her psychology book, she knew she should make herself go to the dining hall, but she decided to lie down for a while, first—and didn't wake up for almost three hours. After making her way out to the bathroom to wash her face and try to shake off the urge to go right back to sleep, she propped her pillows up and slouched on the bed, knowing that she really ought to check her messages, or do some more studying, but turned on ESPN, instead.

As soon as she heard that the damned Yankees had won their opener, the percolating idea of going over to the Snack Bar and getting some takeout lost its already limited charms. But the clip they showed of the President throwing out the first pitch at the Washington game cheered her up somewhat. The ball was something of a dying quail, but it did reach home plate on the fly—to her mother's barely disguised relief, and the catcher didn't do a very good job of pretending not to be amused. Linda or someone had talked her into suiting up in a home team jacket—the better to hide the bulletproof vest the Secret Service would have insisted that she wear to protect herself from any possible loons in the crowd. She walked towards the plate to shake hands with the various players and officials gathered there, and said something which made almost all of them laugh. Then, one of the guys seemed to point at her chest, which Meg found rather offensive, until she realized that he must be commenting on the small Red Sox pin she could just barely make out on her mother's collar. Steven must have convinced her to put it on, to make up for the fact that she would, ever so briefly, be disloyally wearing another team's jacket.

It was just late enough so that she shouldn't call home to discuss the baseball events of the day, and her father and Steven were still probably spitting nails about the Boston bullpen, anyway, so it might be better to let them cool off overnight.

She heard movement in the hall, and saw Mary Elizabeth. "Hi."

"Hi," Mary Elizabeth said, wearing a plain white scoop neck t-shirt and black capri pants. "Are you in the middle of anything?"

Meg shook her head, and clicked off the television.

Mary Elizabeth nodded, and shifted her weight, not coming all the way into the room.

Oh, Christ, now what? Since she'd been out for most of the afternoon, and hadn't left her room since she got back, what were the odds that she could have done anything to bug her? "What's up?" Meg asked.

"I don't know if it's any of my business, but—look, I was wondering," Mary Elizabeth said. "Are you coming back next year?"

Sort of a menacing question. "I don't know," Meg said. "Why?"

Mary Elizabeth frowned. "You mean, you might not?"

She might not have a *choice*. "Well, something bad might happen," Meg said, "and then I wouldn't be able to."

"Okay," Mary Elizabeth said, "but something bad might *not* happen, too."

One could only hope.

"The room draw forms are due tomorrow," Mary Elizabeth said.

In order to be entered into the housing lottery for September. Now, the oblique approach made sense. Meg grinned. "What, you want to make sure you end up picking a room as far away from me as possible?"

Mary Elizabeth looked uncomfortable. "No, it's not that. I just—well—" She stopped. "Look. Are you signing up with anyone?"

Hell, no. "No," Meg said. "I mean, I guess I assumed people wouldn't want—" That sounded self-pitying. "I hadn't given it any thought. I just figured I'd—get put somewhere or other."

Mary Elizabeth nodded, and turned to go. "Okay. Never mind. I was thinking you might want to sign up with us."

What? Meg stared at her.

"Or not," Mary Elizabeth said.

How very bizarre. "But, you don't even like me, remember?" Meg said. "Run! While you still can."

Mary Elizabeth's face reddened. "Well, better the devil you know, and all of that."

Ah, sweet flattery. Always a clever strategy.

"I mean, if you don't want to, that's fine. I just—I don't know." Mary Elizabeth scowled. "I mean, maybe you think it'd be bad publicity hanging out with *me*."

Yeah, she—and her mother's administration, for that matter—were so famously homophobic. "No," Meg said. "I'm just afraid we might slug each other a lot."

"We might," Mary Elizabeth said, with a half-smile. "But, we could try for a suite, get a little more space that way." She gestured towards the hall. "Juliana wants you to come in with us, too, but she's not sure if—well, you know. She's worried about the way things were going before we went on break."

So, the third-floor Sage E soap opera was going to be the Morgan soap opera, or Bryant, or Mark Hopkins, or wherever in the hell they ended up. Jesslyn was out of the question, but— "Tammy hoping to sign on for another tour, too?" Meg asked.

"God, no," Mary Elizabeth said. "She's had it. I mean, I don't want that to sound—" She frowned. "Well, yeah, I guess she's mostly just had it."

Meg grinned. Fair enough.

"We were thinking Debbie would maybe come in with us," Mary Elizabeth said. "You know her pretty well, right?"

The jolly jock from the fourth floor. Meg motioned in the direction of the security room. "You sure she'd want to go through all of this again?"

"She's *really* relaxed about things," Mary Elizabeth said. "That's why Juliana and I figured she'd be good."

It was all sort of last-minute, and random—but, why not? Seemed like as good an idea as any.

She wasn't stunned when Mary Elizabeth didn't stick around to chat—or when Juliana stopped by about half an hour later, while she was sitting at her desk answering email. Among other things, Neal had written to tell her that their mother had been grouching around and wearing Steven's shoulder ice-wrap all night, because between her practice sessions on the private pitching mound on the South Lawn, and then behind the scenes at the stadium before the game, she had thrown her arm out, and needed it to recover in time to repeat her nervous public chore at Camden Yards on Friday. The staff was, she assumed, dithering about the dreadful possibility of a President with rotator cuff or labrum damage, and fetching and carrying twice as much as usual.

Juliana leaned in the doorway, holding a can of Red Bull. "Heard you and Mary Elizabeth talked. You know, about the housing stuff."

Meg nodded, sending a "Lunch tomorrow?" email to Jack before turning around.

"You cool with it?" Juliana asked.

"If you are," Meg said.

Juliana nodded, only somewhat tentatively, so Meg nodded, too.

"You *did* already put in your time," Meg said.

Juliana shrugged, and drank some Red Bull. "Glutton for punishment, I guess."

It was nifty, the way they were all so overjoyed about this. "If we end up with two doubles, Mary Elizabeth and I aren't the logical choice to be roommates," Meg said.

Juliana shook her head.

"I'm not sure if she thinks so, too," Meg said, "or—"

"Oh, she definitely thinks so," Juliana said.

Okay. "So, what are we going to do about that?" Meg asked.

Juliana rolled her eyes. "What do you *think* we're going to do about it? Come on already, Meg."

"Me with Debbie," Meg said, "right?"

Juliana laughed, and finished off her drink. "Yeah. That'll be perfect."

New email appeared in her in-box, and she glanced at the computer screen—it was from Jack—but didn't open it. Then, to make sure that she wouldn't succumb to rudeness and keep glancing at it, she got up and moved over to the bed, waving Juliana to the chair.

Juliana sat down, taking a quick look at the return email address. "Wow. You can actually bring yourself not to read that right away?"

Extraordinary self-discipline.

"Simon can't stand him," Juliana said.

Meg nodded. "I know. I feel terrible about all of that."

"No, you weren't going to be a good couple, anyway," Juliana said. "You would have pounded him into dust."

Not on purpose.

Juliana glanced at the computer. "He's nicer than everyone says, right?"

Meg nodded.

"He'd almost *have* to be," Juliana said.

So she gathered. But she was still too busy trying to figure out what she thought herself to be ready to talk about it to other people. "This room draw stuff is scary for me," she said.

Juliana shrugged. "We're going to get on each other's nerves sometimes, but we'll just try to be nice about it, when it happens."

Ideally, yes, but that wasn't what she meant. "No, I just—it feels like tempting fate, to make plans way in advance," Meg said.

Juliana swung her feet—black leather boots—up onto the desk. "Susan never talks about the future. I mean, not even what she's going to be doing this summer or anything. You ever notice that?"

Hmmm. She knew, for example, that Juliana was going to wait on tables, and then spend part of August at her family's lake house, Mary Elizabeth was going to be a gofer at an academic press, Tammy would be working as a camp counselor, Andy was staying in Williamstown because he was going to be an apprentice at the Theater Festival, Quentin was going to be in Madrid, taking a Spanish language immersion course, Khalid had gotten an internship at a laboratory where he would be helping research new protein rescue and ion transport therapies in the treatment of cystic fibrosis, and Dirk was planning to hike the Long Trail with a couple of friends. And Susan was—what? Going to run several miles every day? Spend time at the dojo? Beyond that, she couldn't even *guess* what her plans might be.

"And everyone's always going and telling *her* personal stuff all day long, so she can get away with it," Juliana said.

Well, that was true enough. "Maybe she only talks to people like Courtney, because she thinks we're dumb freshmen," Meg said.

"Maybe, but I don't think so." Then, Juliana grinned. "Even though she definitely thinks we're dumb freshmen a lot of the time."

Yeah. They probably were, at that.

"So." Juliana looked over at her. "What are *you* going to do this summer?"

She had absolutely no idea.

SINCE SHE ALREADY knew the guy didn't like her, she was dreading getting her political science paper back the next morning. After a somewhat curt "I hope all of you enjoyed your breaks" welcome, their professor walked around the room, handing out their papers and making general comments about the degree he had mostly been pleased, but thought some of them had done unnecessarily facile and superficial work.

Before he gave her hers, he frowned at her, but then moved on to the next person without saying anything.

Not a good sign. All around her, she could hear rustling, and see that he seemed to have made extensive markings in blue pen on more pages than not on people's papers, and then written a lengthy final comment on the back of the last page. There were some small sighs, and a few smaller smiles, as they all reacted to whatever grades they had been given.

For some reason, her paper looked—untouched. Pristine. As though he hadn't even bothered reading it. But, no, she could now see that he had corrected a small typo on the second page, so he had gotten that far, at least. It was disheartening, though, since he had apparently paid a great deal of attention to everyone *else's* efforts.

The only thing written on the back of hers was a blunt "*Please see me after class.*" Other than that, there were no comments, no criticisms—and no *grade*.

Terrific. God, if he disliked her enough so that she was actually going to flunk this class, the press would probably go wild with excitement and run with it all over the place.

Jesus, maybe she should just drop the course. She could explain—or, if necessary, have her father do it for her—that she had too many physical challenges to be able to carry a full academic load, and—yeah, that might work. It would be a major failure, in its own way, but much better than—oh, Christ, she was getting another frown. She hadn't been listening to a single thing the guy was saying, and now he would hold *that* against her, too.

When the class period was finally over, a couple of people bolted up to Dr. Richardson's desk, and it looked as though one of them was whining about his grade, while the other one—the girl who was so very glad that the President wasn't *her* mother—had apparently gotten an A, and was hoping to bask in further praise about her brilliance, and overall acumen, for a few minutes.

Meg was going to leave—after all, if she dropped the class, there wasn't much else he could do to her—but, she made herself stay in her seat, pretending that something had gone wrong with her splint, and that she needed time to adjust and reposition the straps properly.

Another class met in this same room immediately following theirs, and people started filing in, including one of the guys she'd met at dinner with Jack, and they exchanged nods.

"If possible, I'd like you to come over to my office with me, Miss Powers," Dr. Richardson said, standing in front of her desk. "I have some grave concerns I'd like to discuss with you."

She was startled enough to jump, which she instantly regretted. But, screw him—and his stupid dark hair, and unfriendly eyes. "I'm afraid I have another appointment right now, sir," she said. "I think I could stop by in about twenty minutes, if that would be convenient."

He didn't like it, but he nodded, and she nodded back, cocking her head just enough to let him know she had no other appointment at all, but that he didn't have a shot in hell of being able to prove otherwise, and she would damn well show up when she *felt* like showing up.

Because if he wanted fear, and immediate submission to authority, he could forget it.

She killed the time by going to get some coffee, and then wandered up to his office half an hour later. He was at his desk, reading a textbook, and when he saw her, he looked at his watch.

Yup. She had taken her own sweet time heading over here.

"Come in, please, Miss Powers," he said.

She limped over to the extra chair by the side of the desk and sat down, taking an ostentatious swig of her coffee. Yes, she had been late, and *yes*, that had not stopped her from going out of her way to walk down to Spring Street and purchase a beverage, first.

"I'm glad you could find the time to stop by," he said.

She nodded once, and waited.

"You probably noticed that you didn't receive a grade," he said.

Gosh, no. That trivial detail had escaped her scatter-brained attention.

"May I have it back, please?" he asked.

She unzipped her knapsack and removed the paper, which had gotten—oh, dear, what a disappointment—quite wrinkled and bent, by virtue of having been forcefully jammed in there.

"I appreciate that you're dealing with a unique set of circumstances," Dr. Richardson said, taking it from her. "But I can't tell you how disappointed I was by this."

What the hell was his problem? She hadn't thought it was the best paper ever written, but it wasn't *that* bad. She sipped some coffee.

"As I'm sure you know, we take the Honor Code very seriously here," he said.

Now she almost *dropped* her coffee. "Sir?"

He looked at her, unsmiling.

Jesus Christ. She could feel her heart beating faster. "Sir, I—" If she sounded frantic, that might suggest a guilty conscience. She took a deep breath. "Dr. Richardson, I really don't understand. I footnoted everything in sight." Which had made typing one-handed even more challenging than usual.

"That doesn't change the fact that it's pretty obvious you received a great deal of outside help," he said.

What was obvious about *that*? Unless he meant C-Span. She was starting to feel very hot, and wished she could drag her sleeve across her face, in case she was perspiring.

"It's partially my fault," he said. "I should have considered the fact that you have access to resources that the rest of the class doesn't, but it didn't occur to me that you would take advantage of—"

This was nuts. "What, do you think my *mother* wrote it, or something?" she asked. "During the incredible amount of spare time she has?"

"No," he conceded. "My assumption is that it was farmed out to a staff member, and—"

Oh, for God's sakes. "It isn't even that well-written, sir." She put her coffee down and leaned forward to point at a sentence in the second paragraph, which had bothered her terribly while she was writing it, but even though she tried several times, she hadn't been able to do a good job of improving it. "Look at that. That's very clunky."

"You may have done most of the writing yourself, but there's a political sophistication to the ideas that—" He sighed. "Miss Powers, students here are very bright, but I've read a lot of freshman papers, and this simply isn't one."

Jesus Christ, if she got brought up on honor code charges, it was going to be a disaster. Even the legitimate media would latch on to it. And, knowing how tired she always was and how much pressure she was under, no one—possibly even her own parents—was going to believe that she hadn't done anything wrong. Taken a few unethical, but human, shortcuts.

"I'm willing to try and work this out with you privately," Dr. Richardson said, "but we're really not going to get anywhere until you start being honest."

What was she supposed to say, that the mere concept of the assignment had been too much for her, and so she'd had it vetted by the best political minds in the country? Gotten the President to form a small task force, which met for several hours a day before spring break, devoted solely to ensuring her academic success?

"Miss Powers, let me be very frank. I don't want to bruise your feelings, but nothing I've heard you say in class comes even close to the acuity and focus in this paper," he said. "It's an entirely different voice."

What a self-righteous prick. Who clearly had a tin ear. Since insouciance seemed to irritate him, she picked up her coffee again and drank some. "Perhaps I feel ill at ease, sir, in a room where several people *regularly* take cheap shots at the current Administration, and the professor never steps in, no matter how specious their remarks are."

Dr. Richardson frowned.

"I don't mind the cheap shots," Meg said. Much. "But the lack of intellectual rigor behind them bothers me, sir, and it really ought to bother you, too." Except that it was easier for him to sit around and impugn *her* intelligence, instead. "You keep letting them descend into virulent partisanship, and it defeats the entire purpose of what should be an open and supportive academic environment."

His frown intensified.

"The voice starting to sound a little familiar to you?" she asked. "*Sir?*"

She would have expected that to make him very angry—maybe even *wanted* it to happen, but instead, he just leaned back and folded his hands across his stomach.

"Did you consult with *anyone* while you were writing it?" he asked.

She had many flaws, but cheating—in any form—had never been one of them. "Well, I went to the library a couple of times," she said. "But it's all right there in the bibliography." Because, yes, in addition to the footnotes, she had been conscientious enough to do a full bibliography, too. One night on the phone, she had mentioned the topic of the paper to her mother, who had laughed nervously, and said that she should try, if possible, to be kind—which was the extent of professional advice and counsel she had received.

But, they were still at an impasse here.

"Would it be easier for me just to drop the course?" she asked. "I mean, I don't think either of us is really enjoying my being in there, so—"

Dr. Richardson shook his head. "That's not the outcome I had in mind, Miss Powers."

Yeah, well, if he thought he was the one who could make the final call on that, he was in for a rude awakening.

"The section about the nature of threat raised my suspicions even more than the rest of the paper," he said. "It seemed—well, it was unusually savvy and provocative."

How could it be at all suspicious that she had spent a lot of time ruminating about the concept of the executive branch's response to *threats*?

Besides, why wouldn't she be politically savvy? Christ, the second time she had *walked*—not that it was any of his business—had been on the floor of the House. Apparently, crawling and scooting had bored the hell out of her, and her father had always said that she would try, over and over, to stand up on her own, and that every time she fell, she would be upset enough to slap the rug with her hands, and that it had been painful to witness. Her parents had been living in Georgetown, during that period of their marriage, although they commuted back to Boston on weekends, and one early evening, right after the sitter had gone home, she had taken several successful steps across the living room, only tumbling over once.

Her mother was so upset to have missed it—the House was in the middle of a late-running, very contentious session, getting ready to vote on a hotly disputed bill—that her father brought her over to the Capitol right away, and an enterprising photographer had been able to capture the huge grin on the Chief Deputy Minority Whip's face as her tiny daughter—also beaming—made her unwieldy way towards her. The backdrop of older male Representatives standing across the aisle, some of them frowning, the rest of them with bemused or nonplussed smiles, gave the photo—the original of which was now hanging in the Smithsonian—extra resonance, although her mother had commented, more than once over the years, that considering the degree to which the image had been disseminated, she really wished that her father had thought to brush her hair, first.

"I'd like to see another paper from you," Dr. Richardson said.

What a waste of time. "If you think I cheated on the first one, sir, what are the odds that I won't do it again?" she asked. "And you won't have any way of knowing for sure."

He looked so exasperated that it made her nervous, and she tilted back far enough to glance out at the hall and make sure that at least one of her agents was close by, just in case. And yes, there was Larry, looking like a long-in-the-tooth, slightly balding student in a Williams sweatshirt.

"I think it would be very interesting if you explored the threat concept in more depth," he said. "You'll get extra credit, naturally."

"I'm doing so badly I *need* extra credit?" she asked.

He let out a hard breath, smacking her paper down onto his desk, and she used her right leg to push her chair several inches away from him.

Out of easy punching range.

But he didn't seem to notice, picking up a pen, and making three quick slashes to write a large A at the bottom of the last page. "Very well," he said. "I guess we're finished here."

Had she earned this A—or was he only trying to get rid of her? She sure as hell didn't want a grade that wasn't rightfully hers. "No, thank you, sir," she said, giving it back again. "If I don't deserve a good grade, I don't want one."

He stared at her, and then his hands went up into his hair, as though he might actually tear some of it out. That was odd, and she looked up at his head, which made him realize what he was doing, and he brought his hands down again.

It also made her like him. A little.

"Why are you in college, Miss Powers?" he asked.

Implying, what, that she lacked the aptitude? The cognitive capacity? "Because I can't sing or dance," she said.

His smile was reluctant, but at least it was a smile. "I know that the college experience isn't all about academics, and sometimes, it isn't even *mostly* about academics. And I'm not going to insult you by pretending that, for a number of reasons, you can't spend the rest of your time here going through the motions, and *still* be able to walk into almost any career you choose. If you'd rather proceed that way, then it really isn't my place to urge you to do otherwise."

But.

"Just an observation," he said.

Variations of which she had been hearing since elementary school. *Très ennuyeux.*

"I apologize for jumping to an erroneous conclusion about your work," he said. "And I will also pay more attention to the tenor of some of our class discussions from now on."

She nodded. "Thank you."

The silence which followed was not a congenial one.

"Okay, then." She stood up, accepting the paper he handed her, and putting it—not quite neatly—into her knapsack. "I'd better get to my next class." Philosophy, where she hoped her professor would be nothing, if not generous, about the paper *he* was going to be giving back.

Dr. Richardson stood up, but didn't shake her hand, since it was wrapped around her cane. "Yes. Well. I'll see you in class on Thursday."

Maybe—or, maybe not.

46

SHE GOT AN A on her philosophy paper, and as far as she could tell, her professor's nearly illegible handwritten comments seemed to say something close to "Very well-reasoned. You have a splendid grasp of the material!"

So, okay, fine. Maybe she would just go ahead and major in philosophy.

And then, effortlessly, walk into her profession of choice, whatever it might be, esoteric educational background in hand. Piece of cake.

She met Jack for lunch, and he did a pretty good job of not seeming concerned about how much she ate—an attitude she encouraged by polishing off a hot turkey sandwich, french fries, some steamed carrots, and a couple of peanut butter cookies.

Once they had finished, he talked her into going up to his room—the first time she had been there—and after she admired some of his sketches and paintings, and sat down to look at photos of his family, and his equally blond golden retriever, they spent a good chunk of time on his bed, fooling around.

That is, until one of his suitemates walked in without knocking, stopped short, and backed out—although not before sneaking a couple of fast peeks. The whole thing was all the more mortifying because she had never met the guy before, and made that much worse by the fact that the extent of Jack's reaction had been to roll over lazily, flop his arm down over her exposed chest, and say, "Hi, Leo. This is Meg."

Once the door had closed again, she sat up to put on her bra—always challenging, one-handed—and shirt back on.

"Come on, Meg," Jack said. "He didn't see anything."

Meg shrugged into the bra, then threaded her splint through the right sleeve. "Except for the part where he stared at my *breasts*."

Jack shook his head. "No, he didn't. I covered you up."

Barely.

"Besides, you have really, really *nice* breasts," he said. "I bet it made his day."

Yes, that was her overriding goal in life—to make Leo's day.

"Anyway," he kissed her, "let's just pick up where we left off."

Yeah, it wasn't as though the mood had been at all interrupted. "It's almost time for Ultimate," she said.

He glanced at his clock radio, and shrugged. "I can be late."

"With the Yale Cup coming up?" she asked. A crucial tournament, which meant that he was going to be down in New Haven all weekend.

"Yeah, you're right, I guess," he said, sighed, and zipped his jeans—which he had originally told her he was opening "just to get the air." Then, he frowned. "Wait, that's not right at all." He unzipped them again, took the jeans off, stood up, and stepped out of his briefs, too.

And, yeah, she *watched*.

He had gone over to his dresser to take out a jock and a pair of shorts, but then noticed that he had an attentive audience, which led to an unsurprising physical response.

"Well, gosh," he said, grinned at her, and then was across the room in about a step and a half, pushing her down on the bed, cushioning the back of her head with one hand to make sure she landed gently.

He was even more excited than usual, which *she* found very exciting, and there was a frantic freight-train quality to it all, but then—much sooner than she would have liked—everything came to an abrupt halt.

"I'm sorry," he said, after a minute, turning his head enough to give her a clumsy, out-of-breath kiss. "That was really all about me, wasn't it?"

She nodded.

"Yeah." He looked at her, wiped his discarded t-shirt across his face, and then moved down, starting to ease her sweatpants and underwear over her hips.

Christ, what was he going to do? "Um, Jack?" she said.

He glanced up. "What?"

Given what had just happened, he couldn't have the notion of heretofore-unattempted intercourse in mind—at least, not in the very immediate future, but— "Well, I'm not sure if we—" She tried to push his hands away. "That is, I don't, uh—"

He frowned. "You don't think it should be all about *you*, for a while?"

It was an argument she could present on her own behalf, convincingly, but—this was all going too fast. And while she should be comfortable with leaping from zero to sixty—most other people seemed to be—she wasn't.

Which probably meant that there was something very wrong with her, but—she just wasn't.

An unspoken message he wasn't receiving at all.

"Jack." She lowered her hand again, touching his hair. "Please don't. Okay?"

"Oh." He looked confused, and then his eyes widened. "You mean—oh, wow. Really?"

Yes, really.

"*Never?*" he asked.

The fact had already been established. Was it necessary to belabor the point?

"Hunh." He sat up, blinking as though he had just woken up from a very deep, drugged sleep. He gave her another long, perplexed look, and then shifted his position so that he was sitting next to her, up near the top of the bed. "Not for nothing, Meg, but that guy Josh wasn't exactly a go-getter, was he?"

She was damned if she was going to trash Josh—or allow him to do so. "We never really got a chance to be *alone*. It—limited our options."

"Yeah, but—" He closed his eyes, maybe suppressing some critical remark or other, then opened them and nodded. "Yeah. Okay."

She had a feeling that he had a great deal more to say, but was glad that he decided to keep it to himself, since she was flustered enough already.

And yet, sitting next to a very naked guy seemed like the most natural thing in the world, somehow.

"They're all already down there, throwing around their silly little plastic discs without you," she said.

"Yeah." He kissed her, more gently than passionately. "Guess I've kind of spent the last ten minutes being an asshole. You mad at me?"

She shook her head.

"Good." He kissed her again, harder, then stood up.

While he was putting his jock and shorts on, she got ready to leave herself—and then saw the very large wet spot spread across the front of her sweatpants.

Great. "Do you have anything I could borrow to wear outside? There's, uh—" Was she evolved enough to say "semen" aloud in this context? Probably not. "A lot of—DNA—here."

He looked over. "Oh. Shit. Sorry about that." Then, he grinned. "*DNA?*"

It was technically an accurate description. Albeit very uptight.

He dug around inside a drawer, then tossed a pair of SAMOHI—Santa Monica High School—sweatpants on the bed. "These are kind of small for me, anyway, so you can keep them, if you want."

She unfastened her surgical brace, then took off her sweatpants, Jack lounging back against his desk to watch.

"Hey, you stared at *me* stripping," he said, when she frowned at him. "There's no way you can tell me I can't do it to you, too."

That was valid, so she continued without a pause, pulling on his sweatpants—which absolutely hung off her—and then going through the cumbersome task of refitting her brace to her leg, which always took a while to adjust properly.

"You need help?" he asked.

Since it was something she needed to be able to do by herself, she shook her head—even though it was so much easier when someone with two hands assisted her.

"You want me to wash the other pair for you?" he asked.

She shook her head, since she needed to do some laundry, anyway. Laundry, being another exhausting aspect of college life, since the machines were all the way down in the damn basement—and she'd maybe been spoiled by the degree to which everyday chores like that were magically completed in the White House before she even noticed that they needed to be done.

Back in February, Susan had arranged it so that she and Andy usually did their laundry together. That way, he could carry her bag and detergent for her, and—not that she was an expert—she could help keep him from using cups of bleach and washing and drying everything at the highest temperatures. According to Juliana, during first semester, he had shrunk so many of his clothes, and the colors had run so often, that he had had to take the shuttle over to the Berkshire Mall and buy a bunch of new stuff to replace them. Twice.

Jack walked her up to the Frosh Quad, and since there was no evidence of photographers nearby, there was no compelling reason not to kiss him good-bye with indecorous enthusiasm.

"So," he said, when they moved apart. "Going to over to the bio lab to do forensic analysis on the evidentiary sample?"

Meg nodded. "Yeah. Might as well find out where you've been."

He grinned at her. "Can't recommend that, actually, Meg."

Which was more than she wanted to know.

Juliana had decided that the two of them should have dinner with Mary Elizabeth and Debbie that night, and see what life as suitemates might be like. It was immediately obvious that Debbie was not only laid-back and cheerful, but also, innately diplomatic—which was probably going to come in handy.

On a regular basis.

The rest of the week felt fairly routine—which was a treat. An unexpected luxury, well worth savoring. It was also great to have the Red Sox up and running again—albeit, often right into double plays, although Jack had already made a couple of "wait, you don't *always* watch them, do you?" comments.

A question she couldn't quite bring herself to answer truthfully.

On Thursday morning, she waited until the very last minute to decide whether she was going to go to her political science class. In the end, she limped on over there, and slouched in the back row. But she was somewhat gratified when—after someone said, in the middle of yammering away, "Well, liberals *always*" do thus and so—Dr. Richardson asked, mildly, whether he had any empirical evidence to back that up, and the guy's high sense of smug dudgeon seemed to wither a little.

Along with something *else*, she was guessing—but that might just mean she was spending too much time with Jack these days.

After he left for New Haven on Friday, she was surprised to find herself feeling kind of bereft about the idea of not seeing him again until late Sunday afternoon, when the Ultimate team would be returning to the campus.

He had assured her, at lunch, that he had no intention of being his usual WUFO—Williams Ultimate Frisbee Organization—road trip self, getting trashed at whatever parties they went to, and trolling insatiably for likely female partners. He would, he said with great assurance, confine himself to quaffing many malt beverages.

Of course, until he brought it up, she hadn't thought to worry that he might take advantage of being away by looking for a one-night stand, but as soon as he promised he *wouldn't*, it became a small, but nagging, concern.

Her mood was not improved by the fact that when she got home from physical therapy, there were emails from both Maureen and Anthony, letting her know that one of the upcoming week's tabloids was going to be running an unusually unflattering photo of her on its cover, with the headline "The President's Daughter's Secret Anorexia Nightmare."

Which meant that all of the other tabloids and blogs, and maybe some of the mainstream media outlets, were likely to hit the theory hard for a while. Especially since Hannah Goldman—whose article was scheduled for the next Sunday edition—also emailed her with a "do you want to address it, or just let it go?" query.

Swell. Just fucking swell.

She forwarded the emails to Beth, with nothing more than a "*Goddamn it!*" comment, then went over to take some ibuprofen and lie down on her bed with an ice pack—which she put on her forehead, for a change of pace.

It would be productive to think about, say, the sociopolitical and historical ramifications of the nature of threat, or why, in fact, she *was* in college, but instead, she alternated between being generally disgruntled about her life and worrying about being thin. It wasn't like it was her fault—or her intent. And the President was pretty damn thin herself—wasn't there a decent chance that they were both just *built* that way?

She lifted the bottom of her shirt—an old yellow Oxford of her mother's—to look at her stomach.

Okay. There was a concavity, and her hips looked—not pretty. Sharp. Bony. As though they might crack under the slightest strain.

Which, judging from recent energetic, intimate activities, was not the case, but still.

"Is this a bad time?" Susan asked from the hallway.

When one planned to stare, critically, at oneself, it was probably a good idea to close the door first. "I *am* almost as thin as everyone keeps telling me I am," Meg said grimly.

Susan nodded. "Glad you finally noticed."

Meg frowned at her. "You know, you are, too, and I don't see anyone getting on your case."

"It's a different kind of thin." Susan raised her own shirt—a blue Lacoste—just high enough to expose her abdomen, which was slim, but also very muscular. "It's *fit* thin."

Running several miles and working out daily—or playing sports—wasn't a damn option for everyone, though, was it?

Mary Elizabeth, walking by on her way to her room, paused. "What the hell kind of distracting psychosis is *this*?"

"We have officially determined that Meg is too thin," Susan said.

Mary Elizabeth's expression indicated nothing, if not extreme distaste. "God, yes." Then, she checked out Susan's stomach. Extensively. "On the other hand, if *you* ever decide to switch teams, I'll be first in line to try and woo you."

Susan laughed, but also blushed and quickly lowered her shirt, tucking it into her jeans.

"Show's over, then?" Mary Elizabeth asked, and went on her way.

Meg smoothed her own shirt down, deciding that it would be foolish to be offended about having been deemed unattractive. Not that she didn't like her current team just fine—but, still.

"So, why the sudden realization?" Susan asked.

"There's a big story coming out about my secret anorexia nightmare," Meg said. "And that means there'll be a lot of coverage about my weight for a while."

Susan shrugged. "Start getting photographed with food."

What, some kind of women's magazine layout? Her standing happily in front of a State Dining Room table, gesturing towards a bounteous Easter feast? Meg looked at her blankly.

"They get you sometimes carrying huge cups of coffee around, but that's it," Susan said. "So, let them see you holding a piece of pizza or a doughnut or something."

Oh. Well, okay, maybe that was a decent idea.

"And you could always *eat* the food, too, if you wanted," Susan said.

Words spoken by someone a bit less experienced with being a paparazzi target. Meg shook her head. "You ever seen pictures of people chewing? *Not* a good look."

Which made her think of a carefully planned campaign stop in Philadelphia, where her mother had made short work of a cheesesteak—Whiz wit, naturally—holding it out in front of herself and leaning forward in the traditionally accepted manner, while a bunch of locals stood around grinning and doing the same.

She had actually been standing off to the side at the time, out of camera range, with a sandwich of her own—part of which she spilled on herself—and been appalled when Rob, one of the advance guys, watched her mother's deft gustatory attack and said appreciatively to Glen, "That was perfect. A little carnal, and a *lot* carnivorous." Glen had nodded, obviously well-pleased with the nominee's performance.

A little vignette she had never shared with her mother, who, afterwards, had mainly been glad that her new linen suit remained stain-free, and that it had been an excellent, if sloppy, sandwich, indeed.

There was a small, short whistle, and Meg looked up.

"Back now?" Susan asked.

Oh, right. There was someone else in the room.

"Come on," Susan said. "Let's grab some people, and go down to Spring Street, and get some ice cream."

She was really tired, but it was still light outside—so that any photographs would come out clearly, and—yeah.

What the hell.

SHE SPENT MOST of the weekend working on a more fleshed-out version of her political science paper, although she took off some time on Saturday night to go to a party some people Juliana knew were having over in Lehman, where she drank three beers, and rebuffed at least twice as many insincere passes.

The next morning was Easter. She had saved the two packages—one from her parents, and one from Trudy—she had gotten on Friday, and felt very homesick as she opened them, especially when she saw a short snippet on CNN of her family heading into St. John's for the early service. Somehow, they had talked Steven into coming along, because there he was, in a jacket and tie, with—something she had never seen him do off the ski slopes or baseball field—sunglasses on. Neither her father, nor Neal, had gone with dark glasses, but her father had a fresh flower in his lapel—a dapper enough touch to make her laugh.

The President herself was decked out in a bright yellow dress, with subtle white accents, topped by a wide-brimmed spring hat, complete with a striped ribbon and some impressively retro netting, which—along with her white gloves—gave the whole outfit some extra pizzaz. Despite not having the gift of making fashion statements herself, Meg enjoyed seeing the results when other people made the effort, and the CNN anchors seemed to share her sentiments, in this case.

In addition to the box, her parents had also sent her a very large bouquet of tulips, which she had put on her desk as soon as it arrived. The package itself—dispatched uneconomically by special White House courier—was stuffed with all kinds of candy, granola bars, microwave popcorn, and other food, a couple of new novels, and a blue silk t-shirt. Neal had written a card, although he signed it with Vanessa's name, and Steven's contribution was a computer printout of Jack, with his arm slung around her, near the dorm. He had written several exclamation points next to the Web page's excited revelation that the President's daughter was currently being romanced by a wealthy California Republican financier's playboy son, and underlined the word "Republican" twice. Her parents had also each enclosed cards, in which they had written long, encouraging, loving notes.

Trudy's package mostly contained well-wrapped homemade baked goods, along with a "Happy Easter, dear!" note, two bags of gumdrops, and one of orange marshmallow circus peanuts, which had always been a favorite of hers.

She was eating circus peanuts and watching one of the Sunday political shows when Preston called from his mother's house, where he had gone to visit his family overnight, to wish her a happy Easter. He was watching, too—although his snack of choice was a ham sandwich—and they swapped a few "Damn it, she just went *way* off message" remarks about the Attorney General, who was handling her rather standard grilling less adroitly than either of them would have liked. The Vice President was also making the rounds, but acquitting himself with far more skill and charm.

"The President has on an actual Easter bonnet today," Meg said, during the next commercial.

Preston laughed. "Are you wearing a frothy little holiday confection this morning, too?"

Meg looked down at herself, but sadly, there was nothing impressively chic to report. "I'd say it's closer to a 'Tennis, anyone?' look."

Which made her want to cry the second she heard it come out of her mouth.

"*Fuck*," she said.

"I know," Preston said. "I'm sorry."

While she was home on break, he'd come upstairs to drink coffee with her early one evening, on the small patio outside the Solarium, and he was still the only person she'd told about her request to Dr. Brooks for the amputations.

He had nodded, sighed, and covered her splint with his own hand briefly, before they returned to their coffee, and started talking about the NFL draft, instead, and how his Eagles, and her Patriots, were likely to fare.

"Anyway," Meg said, when the silence on the telephone had gone on a little too long, although they had also been distracted by the near frothing at the mouth of a supposedly objective, but wildly conservative, journalist about the prospect of a more equitable restructuring of corporate taxation. "Were *you* resplendent when you went to church this morning?" Since Beatrice Fielding would have insisted that her son attend the holiday mass with her.

"I'm here, outside the Beltway, among my people, Meg," he said. "You do the math."

The math added up to a spiffy combination of flash and style. "Some of your best plumage?" she asked.

"Well, don't tell the boys at 1600, but I fearlessly donned a pink dress shirt with my suit," he said.

Which meant that a magenta tie or pocket handkerchief was not out of the question. Something the girls at 1600 would not only take in stride, but *applaud*. "And ankle boots?" she asked. She just *loved* his pairs of ankle boots.

"Absolutely," he said. "The grey suede ones."

It was Preston's good fortune that his sleek feline qualities were balanced by a powerful enough aura of masculinity to keep from completely terrifying the members of the grey, very grey, and even greyer male fashion milieu in which he now found himself—but, he probably made more than a few of them extremely nervous. "A hat, too, I hope?" she asked.

"A very fine fedora," he said. "And you?"

"It's a rich navy blue wool blend, accented by a bright red embroidered B," Meg said.

Preston laughed. "Why, yes. I believe I can picture that perfectly."

They watched the rest of *Face the Nation* together—it was so much more entertaining to share a play-by-play with a kindred wonk, who found all of the same types of gaffes, portentous prognostications, and zealous punditry funny, and she felt happy and relaxed—and lonely—when they finally hung up.

But then, Neal called, and she talked to the whole family, although Steven pretty much just said hi, yup, and nope, and then, "We still *suck*," when she asked how baseball was going. Neal, however, chattered on at length about school, and the soccer league he had joined, and the fact that since the White House was getting ready to issue an official "Adopt a Pet Month" proclamation, they were maybe going to go to a DC animal shelter in the next week or so and get a puppy to keep Kirby company.

Or else, her mother had decided it would maybe be nice to have *two* friends in Washington.

When she came on the phone, Meg made a remark to that effect, and her mother agreed that it was an appealing notion, but then, when she was talking to her father, something he said made her realize that her parents might actually be thinking about getting another dog to try and cheer Steven up more than anything else.

A very worthy goal, in her opinion.

She also commented on the President's fancy choice of headgear, and her mother allowed as how the entire outfit had made her feel positively *dainty*, but that she would, perhaps, prefer not to be quoted about that, if possible.

All of which made her feel more homesick than ever.

She spent most of the rest of the day trying to catch up on the reading for all of her classes, and working on the damn political science paper, too. Since Jack still hadn't gotten back, she went to Sunday snacks, for once, and brought a couple of dozen of Trudy's brownies as a contribution. Juliana looked at them with eager anticipation, but Meg shook her head, since they had not been prepared by someone with the power to declare war—or peace—purely of her own volition.

Jack showed up on her floor at about ten that night, with an Ace bandage on his ankle, a bruise below his eye, and a big grin on his face, because they had placed second in the tournament, and come damn close to beating the heavily-favored, top-seeded team from Brown. He was also carrying a package of yellow marshmallow peeps, which he tossed her, and she flipped him a green wooden White House egg in return.

"Hey," he said, stopping when he saw her flowers. "Are you holding out on me about some other guy?"

Meg indicated the handwritten card tucked in among the stems.

"Oh," he said, when he read it, and did a decent job of not looking cowed.

"Are you sure you're okay?" she asked, watching him limp around.

His nod was closer to a shrug, which made her suspicious, but she decided not to press the issue.

"My friend Joel told me he saw you reject about ten guys at some party last night," he said.

He had spies, did he? "I think it was more like seven," she said. "How about you?"

He shrugged. "Made out with everyone female in sight."

If he turned out not to be kidding, she wasn't going to take it well.

But, regardless, it became almost immediately necessary to make very sure that her door was closed. The ground rule she suggested was that they both keep their underpants on, with everything else being fair game, but as rules went, it turned out to be quite—*elastic.*

"I want to stay here tonight," he whispered, after a while. "Okay?"

Yes, and no. "The bed's pretty small," she said. Narrow, anyway.

"I know. We'll have to snuggle *right up against each other*," he said, and kissed her. "But, I can stand it, if you can."

Point taken.

After she went out to brush her teeth and everything, he left for a few minutes, too, while she sat uncertainly on the edge of the bed, wearing a DIA t-shirt and a pair of maroon gym shorts from her high school.

He came back in, shut the door, stepped out of his jeans, and stood there in an "*I am a Diabolical Mastermind*" t-shirt, grinning at her. Then he limped over to join her on the bed, which made her start worrying about him again.

"Maybe you should come to PT with me tomorrow," she said. "See what Vicky thinks."

He pulled his t-shirt over his head. "No, I'm okay."

Except she could see how damn swollen his ankle was, even through the Ace bandage. "Will you go to the health center, at least, and get it checked out?"

He shook his head, taking her shirt off for her, pausing to kiss her here and there along the way.

"I mean it," she said.

He put his hand inside the waistband of her shorts to slide them off, too. "If I let a doctor or anyone see it, they might tell me I have to shut it down for the rest of the season, and—no way."

Dumb jock logic to which she could relate.

But, it was undeniably dumb.

The hem of her shorts got caught on her brace as he tried to tug it past the hinges, and she heard—but decided to overlook—a small tearing sound.

Jack froze. "Was that the brace?"

"No, it was an actual ligament," she said, but then relented when she saw how upset he looked. "It was my *shorts*, Jack. It's fine."

"Oh." He pulled them the rest of the way off. "I'm sorry. Are they wrecked?"

"It's okay," Meg said. "My mother will sew them for me."

His eyebrows went up. "Wow. Really?"

She shook her head.

"Oh," he said, sounding disappointed.

They sat there.

"What happens now?" she asked, very uneasy.

He put his arm around her. "A long, unforgettable night of fornication and debauchery."

She couldn't help tensing, although she tried very hard to seem nonchalant.

"I'm hoping you'll put on a little Catholic schoolgirl's outfit, too," he said.

She smiled. Tensely.

"Or, we could just turn out the light, do everything we think might be fun, and then, since it's pretty late, and we're both tired, we could, you know, *sleep*," he said. "Sound okay?"

It actually sounded great.

47

EXCEPT, SHE COULDN'T relax.

She did well with the everything-we-both-think-might-be-fun part, but falling asleep seemed to be beyond her. Jack dropped off almost immediately after they finished doing something he unquestionably found *very* fun, but she lay stiffly on her side, unable to find a comfortable position, wishing she had thought to take a couple of pain pills when he wasn't looking, and so hyperaware of him being there, just a couple of inches away, that she couldn't quite breathe normally. It just felt too *loud*, and so, she took tiny, shallow breaths, instead.

Which was not conducive to a sense of tranquility or well-being.

One of his hands was still resting inside her underwear, and she couldn't stop herself from moving forward against it. He woke up instantly—and they were off to the races again. Lying together, quietly, in the dark, made it easier to do some experimenting without second-guessing herself as much, and somewhere along the way—it had been about her, it had been about him, it had been about *both* of them—even he said, "*Jesus*," sounding a little stunned.

It was well past three, and finally, she was starting to have some trouble keeping her eyes open. He had already fallen asleep again, and after a while, she managed to doze off, too.

The next thing she was aware of, was fear. Terror, really. *Overwhelming* terror.

And noise. Banging. No, it was pounding on the door, and someone was shouting for her to open it. Meg blinked, trying to figure out where the hell she was—wait, there was someone *in* here with her on the bed, someone—Christ, was it the *guy*? Slipping in, while she was handcuffed, and asleep, waiting for her to be at her most vulnerable, getting ready to—

"Open up, Meg!" a male voice yelled again. "Or we're coming in!"

Agents. School. *Jack.* Oh, God. She started to stagger up, then realized that she wasn't wearing anything other than a pair of underpants. Underpants, her splint, and her brace. Fetching.

"Wait a minute," she said, her voice sounding much more tearful than she thought it would. "Please don't come in yet." There was a shirt crumpled at the bottom of the bed, and she yanked it on, hurting her hand in the process and fighting off a groan. There was the sound of a key in the lock, and she stumbled over to open the door before whatever agent it was burst in.

Ed entered the room so quickly that she lost her balance and fell back against the bookcase, slamming her *knee* this time, afraid, for a second, that she might pass out from the pain. Brian and Jose were right behind him, out of breath, since they must have just run up two flights of stairs. One of them turned on the light, and she had to shield her eyes from the brightness as they swarmed around Jack, who was in the corner of the room, shirtless and jumping into his jeans.

"I didn't do anything," he said. "Honest." To Meg's horror—and confusion—he actually raised his hands. "I didn't."

Ed grabbed him by the arm and jerked him towards the door. "Tell us about it out here."

Was this real? It couldn't be. "What do you guys think you're doing?" Meg asked. "Are you crazy? That's Jack. Leave him alone."

"Meg, you were yelling for him not to hurt you," Brian said. "You were *screaming.*"

What? She couldn't make sense of this.

Dirk came tearing down the hall, barefoot and wearing a pair of Groton shorts, with at least four other guys from her entry right behind him, all of them in various stages of undress.

Oh, Jesus. Suddenly noticing that, on top of everything else, she was wearing Jack's shirt, not her own, inside out, she sank down on the side of the bed, so humiliated that it was very hard not to cry. She was almost completely undressed, and she was surrounded by *men.* Very big, angry men. At least three of whom had weapons.

Now, Susan was in the doorway, in sweatpants and a "10K Race for the Cure" t-shirt, holding—for unknown reasons—a tennis racket. "What's going on?"

They stopped looking at Meg, and all stared at her, instead.

"Meg?" she asked, looking half-asleep, but sounding alert and gripping the racket with both hands.

"It's my fault," Meg said. Christ, was that a tear? In fact, more than one? Yeah. Damn it to hell. She rubbed her sleeve—Jack's sleeve—across her eyes. "I'm sorry, I must have had another nightmare. He didn't do anything. He wasn't even *awake*."

Susan nodded, leaned the tennis racket up against the doorjamb, then turned to glare at her agents. "All of you, get out of here right now."

"Susan," Jose said patiently. "We have to—"

"What you have to do, is get the hell out of here," Susan said, her jaw—and one fist—clenched now. "Unless you're getting your jollies out of invading her privacy while she isn't even *dressed*."

Ed sighed. "Susan, we have some procedures we have to follow here, okay? We're just going to take him out to the hall for a minute, and have a little conversation."

Susan glanced at Meg, glanced at Jack, and shook her head. "No, you abso-fucking-lutely are *not* going to do that. You're going to drop his arm, and you're going to leave the room."

"Susan," Ed started, "we appreciate your help, but this really isn't any of your—"

Susan grabbed the nearest book—Meg's psychology textbook, so it was *heavy*—and slammed it against the side of the bureau so forcefully that Meg wasn't the only one who flinched.

Brian was the first one to speak.

"Why don't all of us step out, and give Meg a chance to put something on," he said, sounding controlled—but angry. "And, Susan? I suggest you cool off. *Now*."

Susan gave him a very dark scowl back, and then put the book down with exaggerated care. "Meg, maybe you should pick up the phone, and call your mother," she said, calmly. "Seems as though it's starting to be the right time for that."

Nobody moved, and Meg couldn't help wondering if she *hadn't* woken up, and this was all still part of an unbelievably vivid nightmare.

"Or," Susan said, her eyes furious, "you three could just congratulate yourselves on a job badly done, and get out of here, which I think would be a *really* good idea."

Her agents didn't want to back down; Susan clearly wasn't going to back down; and Jack looked as though he wanted to run away as fast as possible, never to return under any circumstances.

Okay, someone had to break the standoff. "I'm fine," Meg said, even though—god-damn it—her voice trembled. "I had a bad dream. I have them a lot. You all *know* that." All except for Jack, who sure as hell knew it now. "I'm glad you were quick to check on me, but please give me some privacy."

And, fortunately, that worked.

As soon as Ed released his arm, Jack zipped up his jeans, then looked around for his shirt, and saw that she was wearing it.

"I'm sorry, Meg," he said. Mumbled, really. "I guess I should—"

Susan interrupted him. "Jack, this is one of those golden moments when you have a chance to find out a little about what kind of man you're going to be. Don't blow it."

Jack didn't respond right away. "Meg," he said finally. "I'm going to go out to the bathroom, and, uh, I don't know. Wash up. And then, um—" he hesitated— "I'll come back in here, and we can either talk, or say good-night, or, you know, whatever."

It was depressing that Susan had had to bully him into it, but Meg nodded.

As he left, Susan followed him partway out of the room, and now Meg saw that—yet again—she had woken up the entire floor, and that Juliana, Mark, Tammy, Mary Elizabeth and her new friend Audrey, and even Jesslyn had all joined Dirk and the rest of the guys in the hall. There were a few people from Sage D there, too.

"Stay here until he comes out, okay? Don't let any of them bother him, or even *talk* to him," Susan said, and they all nodded—Juliana, noticeably, glaring in the direction of the security room, and moving to stand in front of the bathroom with her arms folded, Dirk posting himself next to her, looking just as determined.

Then, Susan came back in, closing the door behind her.

"Not such a great idea to take on a bunch of pumped-up, heavily-armed men like that," Meg said quietly.

Susan just shook her head. "Ed and Brian are clearly *not* the ones who should be doing your overnights."

Yeah. She couldn't make a request for the poor guy to work permanent midnight shifts, normal rotation schedule be damned—but, Christ, this never would have happened if Martin had been the one out at the desk. Or Paula, or Nellie, for that matter. "Did I really scream?" she asked, putting on a pair of sweatpants, without taking the time to remove her brace, first. It seemed more important to be covered up, than to be comfortable.

Susan nodded, and then shivered. "You sounded like someone was trying to kill you. Completely scared the hell out of me."

So, at least her agents had had a viable reason to overreact.

"He *didn't* do anything to you," Susan said, "right?"

Meg smiled, in spite of everything. "You just defended him like a complete maniac—" putting the most ferocious of tigresses to shame—"and you weren't even sure he was innocent?"

Susan looked embarrassed. "Judgment call."

Good thing she'd guessed right, all things considered.

"And I maybe went out on a limb, a little, when I brought the President into it," Susan said.

"Gee," Meg said. "Ya *think*?"

Susan nodded, and ran her hand back through her hair, which was already sleep-tangled.

"Were you really going to try and help defend me from possible crazed killers with a tennis racket?" Meg asked.

"Well." Susan looked all the more embarrassed. "Your mother's a mean liberal who took my gun away."

Right. How could she have forgotten.

Susan sat next to her on the edge of the bed. "So, what happened? You half-woke up, and had some kind of flashback?"

Seemed like as good a guess as any other. Meg nodded. "I think so." One of her worst nightmares come to life. Waking up in the dark, and—the entire time, she'd tried never to let herself fall completely asleep, no matter how exhausted she got with each passing hour and day, so she could always listen for the key in the lock, and be ready, when the guy came in to—*if* he came in to—her heart was starting to pound again, and she closed her eyes long enough to ride through it. He wasn't here. She wasn't *there.* This time, anyway. "I think he might have put his arm around me while he was sleeping." It hadn't been threatening; it had been sweet. And look at the reaction he'd gotten. "Christ, he's never going to come near me again."

"Meg, you had a bad dream," Susan said. "If it turns out he can't handle that, then, to hell with him. I mean, when Patrick and I were still together, I used to—" She stopped abruptly, and shook her head.

Classic Susan McAllister—open the personal information door a tiny crack, and then slam it shut again.

And speaking of doors, she could hear the one leading to the bathroom swinging open.

"I hate to ask this," Susan said in a low voice, "but you *did* use protection, right?"

Jesus, she was never off-duty, was she? JA, to the tenth power. Meg frowned at her. "That isn't any of your god-damn business, Susan. Okay?"

Susan flushed. "Right. Yeah. Sorry." She stood up. "Right."

Jack came in, hands jammed in his pockets, his hair damp and much neater than it had been before, not making eye contact with either of them.

"Okay, then," Susan said, still blushing. "Good-night."

Meg trailed her to the door. Jose and Brian had made themselves scarce, and Ed was sitting at the security desk, expressionless. She waited until Susan was heading downstairs, Dirk and the other guys following her, and saw that Juliana, Mark, Mary Elizabeth, Tammy, and even Audrey, were staring at Ed, too. Pugnaciously. Jesslyn must have lost interest somewhere along the line, and gone back to bed. Or back on the Web. Ed shrugged a few times, without looking up from the security log.

"If you want to give me grief tomorrow, fine, but you guys had better not bother Susan, *ever*, about anything that happened tonight," Meg said. "Or Jack, either. Because if you do, I'll be on the phone to my mother in about two seconds." And her father. And Mr. Gabler. And anyone else who might be able to lay down the law for her.

"Me, too," Juliana said without any hesitation. "I would *immediately* call the President."

Yep, she probably would. And, hell, her mother would probably *take* it. She looked at Mark, Mary Elizabeth, Audrey, and Tammy. "You guys going to call the White House, too?"

"Absolutely," Mary Elizabeth said, with a slight grin, and Audrey nodded.

Mark nodded, too. "Count on it."

"Um, okay," Tammy said, and bit her lip.

Were all of that to come to pass, the President was going to need some advance warning. And, possibly, a couple of hours head start. "Excellent," Meg said. "Thank you. I'm very sorry I disturbed everyone again. Good night." She went back into her room, and shut the door.

Jack was sitting on the floor, tying his sneakers. Seeing her, he quickly jumped up, then winced, because of his ankle. "Uh, sorry. I was just—sorry."

"I apologize for having a nightmare in front of you," Meg said. "It—" She couldn't lie, and tell him it was unusual, could she? "It still happens pretty often. I should have warned you, but—I just forgot."

He nodded, stuffing his hands in his pockets.

Okay. He couldn't handle this, and who the hell could blame him? If she could avoid being around it herself, she would.

"Look, Meg, I think I should probably leave," he said, looking everywhere *but* at her. "Maybe we can talk tomorrow, or—or something."

Yeah. She'd be waiting by the phone.

"It's not your fault," he said. "I just need to—well, you know."

Yeah, she knew. She was damaged goods. Not worth the time, or trouble—not worth much of anything. She nodded. "Yeah. Okay. I guess you should turn your back, so I can change out of your shirt."

To her utter dismay, he *did*.

Great. He wasn't even attracted to her anymore. She was just—what? A deranged trauma victim. Frail, and cowardly, and unappealing. A *screamer*, in the worst possible way. She put her own shirt on, and then held out his. "Here."

He nodded, and tugged it over his head, without ever meeting her eyes.

If there was anything to say, she sure as hell couldn't think of it. She took a deep breath. "Look, I'm sor—"

He shook his head quickly. "Let's not, Meg, okay? I just—I don't want to talk about it."

Fine. "Well." She definitely was not going to cry in front of him. In fact, she wasn't even going to cry after he was gone. She wasn't *ever* going to cry over this guy. Or, with luck, about anything whatsoever. For the rest of her life. "Guess I'll see you around, then."

He nodded, still not looking at her. "Yeah. Uh—yeah." Then, he left, the door shutting behind him with a soft finality.

Okay, then. So much for that.

He may have discovered that she was much less of an admirable and attractive person than he might have hoped, but—for better or worse—tonight, they'd also both learned something about what kind of man he was probably going to be.

And she couldn't help wondering whether he was as disappointed as she was.

She couldn't risk falling asleep again, and doing any more screaming tonight, so she set two Cokes on her desk, then sat down to work on her political science paper. When that started to make her tired, she read some Aristotle, and then got through two acts of *Coriolanus*.

At about six-thirty, she decided to take an early shower, since that way, she stood an excellent chance of not running into anyone else. There was no way to avoid the security desk, so she decided just to keep her head down, and not even—except that it was Martin, sitting there with a thick novel. He saw her, and nodded.

Christ, why did her life have to make things so difficult for everyone *else*? "Oh, God," Meg said. "Did they wake you up in the middle of the night? I'm sorry."

He shrugged, closing the book. "I'm a night owl, anyway, so this works well for me."

Yeah. Sure. Damn it. He could claim to be the world's biggest insomniac, but he looked really tired. "I didn't ask anyone to call you," she said. "I would never do that."

"It would have been fine if you *had*, Meg," he said. "If anything we do makes you feel uncomfortable, you need to tell us right away, so we can change it."

How different everything would be if she'd let someone in authority know how uneasy Dennis had always made her, even if she had no idea why. All it would have taken was a couple of words to her parents, or Preston, or—but, Martin shouldn't have to take the hit for any of that.

"They feel terrible about what happened, if that helps," Martin said.

It didn't.

He indicated the chair by the side of the desk. "Want some coffee?"

She looked back at her room, not sure if she had the strength to go back and get a mug.

He opened one of the desk drawers and took out a fresh Styrofoam cup. "Here."

She nodded, and sat down. "Thank you."

They drank their coffee—and, *wow*, he did like it sweet, but she could certainly use the extra hit of energy.

"You can always talk to any of us," he said. "And I don't just mean about security."

Yeah, his compatriots had been so quick to be understanding and sensitive tonight. Like the swellest big brothers ever.

"Nightmares are normal," he said. "I have them myself."

She looked up. "Just in general?"

He shrugged. "Lots of things, I guess."

She wondered, then, if her parents had nightmares. Surely, they must. As far back as she could remember, they had always kept their bedroom door shut, and she and her brothers had been taught from a very early age to knock, first, *always*—a courtesy they invariably extended to each other, too.

But, when they had dozed in chairs in her hospital room, when she first got back, they were restless and anxious and grimaced a lot, and her father would seem particularly disoriented and upset if he woke up unexpectedly. She often suspected that her mother never slept deeply enough to *have* dreams—she had done far too good a job of training herself to move from sleep to complete cogency in a split second, and maybe that meant that she also never got any real rest.

But she *must* have had bad dreams after getting shot, right? She had definitely cried at least twice—Meg had been able to tell, afterwards—but never in front of them.

"My unit was in three firefights," Martin said.

Meg interrupted her train of thought to concentrate on listening.

He sipped some more coffee. "And we ran into IEDs constantly. It probably wasn't a lot of action, by war standards, but it sure stays with me."

These days, a Marine who managed to spend his or her entire hitch stateside, in secure areas, without being deployed to some global hot spot or other, had to be a pretty rare bird. "Did you ever get hurt?" she asked.

He shook his head, although she saw him reach briefly for his thigh, without seeming aware that he had done so. "No, nothing serious."

Maybe. "Purple Heart?" she asked.

He nodded.

This was a risky question, but— "Bronze Star, or anything?" she asked.

He looked self-conscious, but nodded again.

Somehow, that didn't surprise her at all. He seemed like a guy who would be brave and resilient under fire.

Lucky for her.

She glanced around to make sure that the hall was still deserted. "I hate it when people say I was heroic. Because all I did was save *myself*, and that doesn't count."

"If you ask me, you saved the President of the United States," he said.

Yeah, right.

"I don't see how she could have lived with it," he said. "There's too much love there."

Which seemed like an almost—impertinent—remark. Way too personal, anyway.

"We *notice* things," he said. "We can't help it."

No, probably not. They all spent too much time together, in close proximity, for agents to be able to avoid overhearing—and seeing—countless private interactions.

The only thing she knew for sure, insofar as outside opinions about her family were concerned, was that damn near *everyone* liked Neal.

It might have been interesting to find out what else he thought—if he turned out to be willing to volunteer the information—but she heard Mary Elizabeth's door opening, and knew that everyone was going to start coming out soon to take their showers and get ready for classes, or head over to breakfast.

"Nightmares are normal, Meg," he said, very quietly.

Maybe.

When she went downstairs, Garth came out of the main security post to meet her at the elevator door, looking very concerned.

"I'm sorry about last night," he said. "You should have called me right away."

Meg shrugged, afraid that Bruce, from the first floor, who was walking by, might have been listening. "It was no big deal. Just a misunderstanding."

Garth glanced at Bruce, too, who nodded uneasily and went outside.

"Please leave Susan and Jack out of it, though, okay?" Meg asked. "They were just caught in the middle."

Garth nodded, although she couldn't tell whether he was in full agreement.

"I'm not kidding," she said.

He nodded again, more firmly. "You have my word."

Good.

"I'm also going to rotate a few people back to Washington," he said.

Oh, great. She shook her head.

"It's not even a close call, Meg," he said.

And then, all of her *other* agents would hate her for it, and assume that she'd thrown a spoiled-brat First Daughter fit, and demanded that they be removed, for interfering with her assignation.

"What did you want them to do, Garth?" she asked. "Just sit there while I scream that someone's hurting me? Their only mistake was not leaving when Susan tried to talk some sense into them. Just—I don't know—have them apologize to her—" And Jack, if he ever turned up again— "and leave it at that, okay?" Then, she thought of something else. "And *please* don't let it get back to my parents."

Garth frowned.

"I've already have my privacy invaded enough, without having them weigh in, too," Meg said.

"Well, why don't you think about it, and we'll talk later," he said. "At the very least, I'm going to make some changes to the overnight desk assignment."

Fine with her. In the meantime, she was running late—her plan had been to time her trip over to her psychology class so that she could duck into the back at the last minute, without actually being late.

She made it with about three seconds to spare, trying so hard not to be noticed that—it went without saying—she dropped her textbook on the floor while she was taking it out of her knapsack. Jack, who was sitting down near the front, had looked up when she came in, but glanced away as soon as they made eye contact, and hunched over his notebook.

So, he was either angry at her, or repulsed—or both.

Whatever. She no longer gave a damn.

As soon as the class ended, she moved as quickly as she could to the exit, not giving him a chance to come over and talk to her—although he probably wouldn't have, anyway.

She didn't want to risk running into him again, so she avoided the dining hall and Paresky, and went up to her room to rest before going over to the hospital. There were no voice-mails or text messages or emails from him, and—well, she hadn't expected any, so it didn't matter. He was part of her past now, and—good riddance.

The minimal amount of physical therapy she could manage hurt a lot more than usual, and she felt increasingly short-tempered with each passing minute, but maintained a polite, if unresponsive, silence the entire time—including when a red-haired woman named Felicia came in and stuck a bunch of thin, disposable acupuncture needles into various illogical spots on her body.

She had to lie there for about forty-five minutes, with the little needles waving around whenever she moved, and it seemed like an utter waste of time. But, when Felicia returned to remove the needles, and asked her if the treatment had helped, Meg smiled and nodded, mentally counting the *seconds* until she could escape.

When Felicia went over to the corner of the room to deposit the used needles into a red sharps container, Meg got off the table—and had such a violent dizzy spell that she was afraid she might be about to—except, she *must* have fallen, because suddenly she was on the floor, and her entire right forearm hurt like hell.

Felicia spun around, gasping when she saw her, and there was a rush of activity as people came hurrying into the treatment room, everyone talking all at once and gathering around, which made her feel even *more* dizzy and confused. So, she ignored them and tried to concentrate on sitting up.

"No, don't move!" someone ordered, and someone else was asking Felicia, accusingly, why she hadn't been keeping an eye on her, and Felicia was insisting that she had only looked away for a few seconds.

Oh, Christ. This was about to get totally out of control. Meg grabbed the edge of the table with her good hand, and pulled herself up, still feeling dizzy, but having no god-damn intention of letting it *show*. "I'm fine," she said. "Really. I just slipped when I forgot and tried to stand up on my bad leg, that's all."

People were trying to help her onto the table, and she shook the various hands off impatiently.

"I'm *fine,*" she said, and felt around for her cane. "I tripped. It's no big deal."

"All right," one of the physical therapy supervisors—whose name she couldn't remember, at the moment—said. "But, we're going to take you down to the ER, and do a few—"

The *hell* they were. Meg shook her head. "No, that really isn't necessary. I just slipped." She smiled and indicated her knee. "I fall down *a lot*. It's nothing to worry about."

It took another ten infuriating minutes before she could talk them out of running extensive tests, and calling the White House, but she did have to agree to let one of the doctors do a quick neurological exam—which she apparently passed—and listen to her heart with his stethoscope, while she sat on the treatment table, tapping the fingers on her good hand. Just to shut everyone up, she also allowed him to take her blood pressure, and palpate the elbow she'd landed on, and so forth.

"Are we about done here, sir?" she asked. "Because I have a lot of work to do, and I really need to get back to school."

The doctor—his last name was Flaherty—frowned. "Well, I'd still like to—"

"If I had to go through a billion tests every single time I lost my balance, I would do nothing *but* have tests," she said, trying to keep her voice very friendly. "I promise I'll be more careful next time, okay?"

She finally managed to get rid of all of them—except for Vicky, who hadn't been saying much, but had been watching her very closely.

"Did you land on your hand?" she asked.

Sort of, but Meg shook her head, to save time.

Vicky looked suspicious. "Okay. What have you had to eat today?"

Oh, she was just *not* in any god-damn mood for this. "I don't know, nothing special," Meg said, getting off the table more slowly this time, to make sure that the dizziness had passed—which, mostly, it had. "A turkey wrap, some potato chips. Orange juice. A couple of cups of coffee." All of which was a complete lie, of course—except for the half cup of coffee she'd had with Martin. She shrugged. "I wasn't really keeping track."

Vicky sighed. "We can't help you, Meg, if you don't let us."

All things being equal, she didn't *want* to be helped. Not today, anyway. "Look, I appreciate everyone's concern, but I'm fine," Meg said, and limped—carefully—towards the door. "I'll see you Wednesday, okay?"

Even though none of them had seen what had happened, her agents also seemed upset, but she gave them the same sort of bland assurances, instead of getting testy and telling them to back off and let her breathe, already. Naturally, of course, during all of this, an older man on his way into the hospital recognized her and wanted to shake her hand and tell her that he was happy to see her doing so well, and someone else snapped a cell phone picture, so while she was very polite, it was a tremendous relief when she was finally sitting in the car, on the way back to Williamstown.

She wanted to go straight to bed for the rest of the night, but she made herself stop by the JAs' suite, first. She said hi to Dirk and Mikey, who were throwing a Nerf football back and forth, and then found a mopey-looking Gerard on his way out of Susan's room. He and Tammy—who had been throwing a fair amount of her caution to the winds, since breaking up with her boyfriend—had ignored an unwritten cardinal rule over the weekend by engaging in a drunken, intra-entry, one-night stand, and while Tammy had shrugged the whole thing off the next day, it had been all too obvious that Gerard was crushed by the rejection. And was *still* crushed, three days later.

Something she might find mildly funny, if she weren't feeling the exact same way herself.

Susan, who was just picking up the phone, saw her and lowered it.

And smiled, ready to greet her next patient.

"I just wanted to make sure Garth and the others didn't bother you today," Meg said.

Susan shook her head. "No. They're just sorry the whole thing happened."

So Garth had kept his promise, at least.

"You don't look so hot. How you doing?" Susan asked.

Meg shrugged. "Tired. Embarrassed. The usual." And then some.

"They made it into a much bigger deal than it had to be. *You're* not the one who should be embarrassed," Susan said, and then hesitated. "Did you see him today?"

"In psychology," Meg said.

Susan nodded. "Did that go okay?"

No. But, Meg just shrugged.

It was quiet.

"You want to talk about it?" Susan asked.

Very definitely *not.*

After she had made her excuses and went up to her room, she couldn't resist checking her messages, and her email—only to find that he still hadn't bothered trying to get in touch with her.

Christ, would it have *killed* him to send an "I'm sorry it didn't work out, but I still think you're a nice person" email? To say that it wasn't her, it was *him*. To show some sort of common decency, or at least, courtesy?

But, fine. Whatever. No great loss.

She wrote Beth an "It's no big deal, but Jack and I broke up last night. Do me a favor, and don't mention him anymore, okay?" email, and a similar one to her father, assuming that he would pass some form of the information along to the rest of her family. Her mother was off on an overnight West Coast swing, touting some economic initiatives and appearing at a North American environmental conference addressing global warming, and such, so she didn't expect to hear from her, anyway, until she got back to Washington.

It was obscenely early, but she got ready for bed. When she put on a clean t-shirt, she saw that her right elbow was covered with a dark, puffy bruise and was so swollen that she couldn't straighten it all the way, but decided that she was probably okay. Her hand and knee hurt like hell, of course, but when *didn't* they?

As a rule, taking two pain pills was usually enough to make her very drowsy, so she took *three*, just to guarantee that she would have no trouble dropping off.

The sooner this day was over—in fact, the sooner the entire *semester* was over, the better.

48

SHE FELL ASLEEP right away, but had long, confusing nightmares—mostly about terrible things happening to her brothers and Vanessa—and would wake up, trembling and gasping, before crashing out again. The drop-line rang a couple of times, and so did her medium-secure phone, but she neither answered the calls—nor checked her messages. Hell, she didn't even bother turning on the *light*.

In the morning, she still couldn't bring herself to go to the dining hall, but when she tried to get out of bed, she had another intense dizzy spell, and had to quickly sit back down and take deep breaths until it passed.

So, she ate one of the granola bars from her Easter package, and a somewhat stale brownie, since she wasn't completely sure when she had eaten last, and that might be why she felt so terrible—and had a monster headache, to boot. The pain pills didn't seem to have worn off completely yet, to the degree that she almost felt hungover, so she took a couple of ibuprofen with the dregs of the open bottle of flat Coke on her desk.

Before leaving for her classes, she checked her email yet again—nothing, of course, from *him*, but a few from her family, and Beth, and so forth. She zapped her father an "Everything's fine, on my way to class, more later" reply, along with a similar one to Beth—whose two emails seemed more concerned about her than her pathetic romantic failure probably warranted. When she retrieved her voice-mail from the medium-secure line, it was, indeed, Beth who had left the two messages, the first one telling her she was sorry to hear about Jack, and to call her as late as she wanted, and the second one asking, more anxiously, if she could *please* call her back, and let her know that everything was okay.

Which she wouldn't have time to do before her political science class started, so she would just have to take care of it later.

After her classes were over, she was going to go into Paresky, and grab something to eat, but she saw Jack crossing the Chapin Lawn, apparently about to do the same thing, so she retreated to the library, instead. Did a little more research for her political science rewrite, skimmed and took notes on a couple of the articles her English professor had put on reserve, as supplementary reading material, and got through twenty-five more pages of Aristotle.

By then, she was so tired that she was starting to get dizzy again, and it was obviously time to go back to her room, and take a nap. A *long* nap.

Although, considering how truly wretched and miserable she felt, she just might spend some time crying, first.

When she got off the elevator, she could have sworn that she heard a very familiar voice, but decided that it had to be her imagination. Wishful thinking. She started down the hall towards her room—and saw Beth, sitting in the chair by the security desk, talking to Dave.

Meg stopped short, and stared at her. "Hey. What are you doing here?"

Beth shrugged. "Took the bus up."

Oh. It was a somewhat dislocating surprise, but also, a good surprise. An excellent surprise. "Okay," Meg said. "I mean, hi."

Beth nodded, looking her over slowly, and then frowning.

Which was—weird. Unfriendly. Something else seemed different, and it took her a minute to figure out what it was. That is, other than the fact that she was wearing old jeans—*torn* jeans—and a black turtleneck, instead of something fun. "Your hair's brown," she said.

"Dyed it back last night," Beth said.

They had never been inclined towards demonstrative greetings, but there was a strange energy in the air, and—hmmm. "Well—it looks good," Meg said, warily.

Beth shrugged again.

Now, she was a *lot* wary. "I'm sorry I hadn't gotten a chance to call you back yet," Meg said. Since she definitely would have made sure to head her off, before she came up here, if she had. "But, I was working on a paper, and—I'm sorry."

"Yeah." Beth stood up, carrying a faded orange Newton South Lions bag from their old high school. "See you later, Dave, it was nice talking to you."

Afraid that she might look too frail and unsteady, Meg tried to unlock her door *without* fumbling around or dropping the keys.

"What's wrong with your arm?" Beth asked.

Which she still couldn't really straighten, but she hadn't realized that it was obvious. "It's fine," Meg said. "Just post-surgical junk." She pushed the door open. "It's really good to see you, but I wish you had—" Called first. "I mean, don't you have a midterm or something tomorrow?"

"Yeah, whatever," Beth said.

Christ, was she really so pissed off about not having been called back, that she thought it was worth coming all the way up here? Except, maybe something was wrong with *her*, like another pregnancy scare. "Are you okay?" Meg asked. "Did something bad happen?"

Beth shook her head and put her bag on the floor next to the bed, then looked around the room. "So, this is it, hunh?"

Meg shrugged, knowing full well that she could have made more of an effort to decorate. Or, any effort at all, beyond the few photos she'd set out the very first day she'd arrived.

"What happened with Jack?" Beth asked.

If she'd dropped everything and rushed up here because of a stupid breakup with a jerk of a guy, it had been a complete waste of time. "No big deal." Meg eased herself down onto the bed. "He just—he turned out to be a schmuck."

Beth frowned.

"He didn't do anything awful—" exactly— "We just—I don't know," Meg said. "I don't really feel like dating anyone right now, anyway. Too much other stuff going on."

Beth folded her arms. "So, you're not upset at all."

"No," Meg said. "But, I'm sorry if I made it seem that way." Time to change the subject. "Um, how's Nigel?"

Beth looked annoyed and shook her head, which Meg interpreted to mean that he was still a schmuck in his own right.

So, maybe she had just wanted to get out of town for a couple of days, and had, therefore, manufactured an excuse to do it. And, after all, they hadn't seen each other since right after New Year's. Although that didn't explain why this all felt so horribly strained. Or what the hell it was that was simmering below the surface.

"You look awful," Beth said.

Nice. Meg nodded. "Thank you. It took some effort, to look this bad, but—"

"I'm not kidding," Beth said.

"Well." Meg touched the bridge of her nose, feeling the crooked part. "I—"

Beth shook her head. "You know that's not what I mean. I mean, you look *awful*."

Oh. Not anything she wanted to hear—although she pretty much always looked awful now, so it didn't fall into the category of new information. "I didn't sleep very well last night," Meg said, "and I guess maybe—"

"Christ, don't be an idiot," Beth said. "Okay?"

Great. Now she was an idiot, in addition to looking ugly.

"And what the hell's the matter with your parents?" Beth asked. "Why did they let you come back here, looking like this?"

Now, she was starting in on her *family*? What the hell was going on here?

Beth leaned over, unzipped her bag, and took out a few magazines. "You're a lollipop girl, Meg," she said.

What? Now she was *really* confused.

Beth pointed at the glossy tabloid on the top of the pile. "I saw this on a newsstand last night, and then you didn't answer your phone, or your email, and—" She tossed the magazine onto Meg's lap. "So, I went down to Port Authority this morning, and got on the fucking bus."

The cover showed all of the usual—predominantly too blond and too thin—celebrity types, plus a photo of her in the top right corner, with the headline "Wasting Away." Meg shoved the magazines aside. "So what? They just want people to cough up a few dollars and buy the damn thing, so they try to create news."

"Look at the picture," Beth said.

It wasn't worth a second glance, but Meg humored her, and gave it one. Sunglasses, purple cap with a gold W, gripping her cane—because God forbid they *not* print a photo with her looking as crippled as possible. It was hard to be sure, but it might have been taken the previous Monday, when she was on her way to PT.

"You look like one of those skeletal, fucked-up starlets," Beth said.

Albeit lacking a wildly overpriced designer bag—or a jittery, equally expensive, little dog of some kind.

Or the smug satisfaction of having had a whopping opening weekend at the box office.

But Beth was staring at her, accusingly.

This was ridiculous. "You know they go out of their way to find the worst possible pictures," Meg said. "And then, they Photoshop the hell out of them, or whatever, until the person doesn't even look human anymore."

"You *do* look like that, Meg," Beth said.

Maybe, maybe not. And, frankly, she didn't care much.

Beth reached over and yanked her left sweatshirt sleeve up partway. "Is that what a normal wrist looks like?"

Jesus *Christ*, but she was getting tired of hearing this from everyone. And, so what if her wrist was a little skinny? Since it was her good hand, she couldn't pull her sleeve back down, and had to press her arm against her headboard, and hook the cuff to the corner, to do it.

Beth sighed. "Meg, all I'm saying is—"

"If you just came up here to yell at me," Meg said, "I really don't feel like hearing it."

"Tough," Beth said. "You *have* to start hearing it."

Well, no, as a matter of fact, she didn't. She could hear any damn thing she pleased—or not, whenever she pleased—or not. She folded her good arm across her chest, and they glared at each other. During their entire friendship, they had never done more than a little minor snapping at each other, and Meg was afraid to push it any further than that—because it suddenly seemed as though one of them might go too far. Irrevocably so.

Beth was usually as good at stare-downs as she was—maybe even better, but she was the first one to sigh, and look away this time.

Good. Maybe this wasn't going to get worse, after all. Maybe they could relax now, and slip back into their normal—

"You're letting him win," Beth said quietly.

Oh, she was not. "Jesus, Beth, I only went out with the guy for about twenty seconds," Meg said. "I'm already over it." Sort of. "Hell, I wasn't even that *into* it." Sort of.

"Not Jack," Beth said.

Oh. And no, she *wasn't* letting him win. No way in hell. And *fuck her* for even thinking such a thing.

"You are, Meg," Beth said. "Every time the guy sees a new picture of you, he must laugh his head off. Maybe he didn't have the guts to do it himself, but he's getting to watch *you* do the job for him."

She didn't believe that for a second—except that, the very idea made her feel as though she couldn't move, or breathe—or think.

Beth put the magazines back on her lap. "Look at the pictures," she said, her voice very gentle. "Really *look* at them. Objectively. And then, tell me what you think."

Meg shook her head, feeling very panicky. "I don't want to look at the pictures."

"Look at them anyway," Beth said.

Except, the truth was, she didn't *have* to look at the pictures. Because—she already knew.

But, she wasn't going to cry. Not a chance.

Or, anyway, not much.

Beth sat down on the bed next to her. "Look. I didn't come up here to upset you, I just—Jesus, Meg. I'm *worried* about you."

And probably should be. "It's not anorexia," Meg said. "It really isn't."

Beth nodded. "I know. I think it's mostly depression."

Yeah. And fear. And shame. And embarrassment. And shattered confidence, and all of the other garbage that ruled her life now.

Christ, she was tired. It was hard to believe that there had ever been a time in her life when she wasn't tired.

Beth sighed. "And yeah, you're right, I *do* have an exam tomorrow."

What, and now that was her fault, too? "So, go back," Meg said. "I don't want you to screw up your classes."

Beth shook her head. "No, it's okay. I emailed my professor and told him I had a family emergency."

Which was stupid, because if she got caught lying, she would get in trouble. "It's not an emergency," Meg said.

"Well, I actually think it is," Beth said, "but either way, it's *definitely* family, for me."

Oh.

"You want to know something else?" Beth asked.

Jesus, after the last twenty minutes or so? She'd heard just about as much as she could handle. "Nothing personal," Meg said, "but, *no,* not really."

Beth laughed, and luckily, it was a normal laugh. A friendly laugh. "I think there isn't a single chance in the world that you're *actually* going to let the son of a bitch win."

God, she hoped that was true.

"And even if it didn't work out, the fact that you dated Jack at all means you're a million times better than you were the last time I saw you," Beth said.

Then, considering how she felt now, she must have been in *indescribably* bad shape back at Christmas. "I liked Jack," Meg said. "I really liked him a lot."

Beth shrugged, and moved to sit at the bottom of the bed, so they were facing each other, the way they had always sat together—since they were five damn years old. "So, tell me about it."

Hmmm. "Only if you tell me all of *your* dirt, too," Meg said.

Beth laughed again. "Deal," she said.

After that, they both relaxed enough to talk about regular, everyday things which—other than Jack or Nigel—weren't stressful, or upsetting.

Depending, that is, upon how one felt about Boston's current four-game losing streak.

"So," Beth said finally. "Are we going to eat here, or do you want to take off somewhere?"

The possibility of doing anything other than trudging over to one of the dining halls hadn't occurred to her. And, okay, she wasn't actually hungry, even though she wouldn't *dare* admit it right now. "Take off?" Meg said uncertainly.

Beth nodded. "Yeah. Someplace where we don't know anyone, full of cranky New Englanders who won't give a damn even if they *do* recognize you."

Which sounded enticing enough for her to call Garth, and ask if her agents knew of any places like that, and if so, could they go there. The answer to both questions was, of course, yes, and they ended up being driven to some diner in a little town off Route 7A, up well past Bennington. She had tucked most of her hair under a Patriots cap, and put on one of her pairs of clear glasses, but, as it turned out, there were only about half a dozen other customers, none of whom gave them a second glance, and as a further recommendation for the place, the television in the corner was tuned to the Red Sox game.

Paula and Larry had come in ahead of them, and were sitting in a nearby booth, giving no indication that they knew her, looking like an ordinary couple going out for a quick supper. Of course, they had their earpieces on, but, surprisingly often, civilians assumed that they were wearing hearing aids, and would go out of their way not to stare. The rest of her security was outside, although Garth came in and got a couple of cups of coffee to go.

"I think the pastrami might be frightening here," Beth said, looking at the menu.

Safe bet. "Ask for it with mayonnaise," Meg said, "and you might be able to pass."

"What's scary," Beth said, "is that I think you people actually *like* it that way."

She would never admit it—or order it with anything other than mustard—but, yeah, she kind of *did*. The same way that, if left entirely to her own devices, she could thoroughly enjoy a large wedge of iceberg lettuce covered with bottled Thousand Island dressing as a salad course.

When the waitress meandered over, Meg asked for a grilled cheese sandwich, a large order of french fries, and coffee, while Beth looked around to see what all of the locals were eating, and then ordered the chicken croquettes special, which came with rolls, peas and carrots, mashed potatoes and gravy, and either Jell-O or chocolate pudding with whipped cream for dessert.

They talked some more about Nigel—who, alas, *was* a terrible schmuck, and then, about Jack briefly, but for most of the meal, they were pretty quiet, Meg leaning back to check the game every so often, having to lower the tortoiseshell-frame glasses to read the score clearly. It was one of those grinding, lead-changing affairs, moving from 2–1, to 3–2, to 5–3, to 6–5, in a matter of a couple of innings.

"Should we have tried to go to the same school?" she asked, shaking pepper onto her fries.

"I don't know," Beth said. "Sometimes, I think yes, and sometimes I think we'd get in each other's way, and should wait and go to the same law school together, instead."

Meg tucked the ketchup bottle under her right arm and unscrewed the cap with her good hand. "I'm not going to law school."

Beth laughed.

Why did everyone always do that? Meg poured some of the ketchup onto her plate. "Okay, fine, maybe I am. But, *you're* not going to law school."

Beth looked embarrassed. "Don't tell anyone, but I love my constitutional law class. I sit in the library sometimes, and read case law on my own, even."

Had she ever heard Beth, despite being a top student, say something positive about academia? Going all the way back to elementary school? "Seriously?" Meg said.

"Hey, you're writing an extra-credit paper," Beth said. "I don't want to hear anything from *you*."

She should never have told anyone—not even Beth—about that moment of weakness. Or competitiveness. Or whatever the hell it was. "Well, I *have* to do well in political science," she said. "It would look terrible, otherwise."

Beth laughed again.

The diner wasn't very busy, so the two waitresses hung out at the front counter, flipping through magazines and newspapers, and talking to a stocky man with grey stubble who was wearing an ancient Red Sox cap, eating chicken croquettes, and kept covering his face whenever Toronto scored another run. Every so often, someone else they all seemed to know would come in, and sit down on one of the green stools, or maybe just get takeout, and there would be some conversation, which managed to be both animated and desultory.

Their waitress drifted over every so often to see how they were doing, refill Meg's coffee, and ultimately bring Beth a thick white mug, too, along with her dish of chocolate pudding. And, for the hell of it, Meg ordered some apple pie. Jose and Kyle came in and were seated in a booth, and Paula and Larry paid their check and went outside, to take over their posts, Meg assumed. If she and Beth were still in here an hour or so from now, Garth and Ed would probably take the next turn.

"I'm supposed to be dead," Meg said, once they were just sitting there with coffee.

Beth nodded. "I know."

Yeah. Ten thousand times over, she knew. "So, how come I'm here?" Meg asked.

"Because that's what happened," Beth said.

It couldn't be that simple, but maybe it was. But it seemed so—random. Arbitrary. *Terrifying.*

"Do you think God is just an artificial construct created to help nervous people make it through the day?" she asked.

Beth choked on her coffee. "I don't know," she said, once she'd stopped coughing. "Probably. Is that where you are these days?"

Meg shook her head. "No, I'm still pretty sure the vengeful, malicious puppet-master version is the accurate one."

Their waitress was heading over with more coffee and Beth politely waved her away.

"How much time do you think your mother spends wondering about what would have happened if the bullets had hit her two inches over?" she asked.

"A lot," Meg said. Possibly every night before she went to sleep. And, for all Meg knew, she *did* have nightmares—and plenty of them.

Beth looked at her. "Honest opinion?"

What, like Beth was capable of anything else? Meg shrugged, but found herself gripping the edge of the table, not sure if she was prepared to hear it.

"I think they might have gone after you, anyway," Beth said. "I guess you still would have had some protection, until you turned eighteen, but you wouldn't've had as much, and Mr. Kruger's kids are all grown up, and probably not as tempting as targets, so maybe they would have thought—I mean, imagine how people would have reacted if they grabbed the orphaned daughter of the dead President, and made a big violent splash doing it. It would have shocked the hell out of everyone, and—I don't know—been cruel in a whole different way."

Jesus, this couldn't just be coming off the top of her head; Beth had to have *thought* about this before. At length. Which was disturbing.

"And, considering the circumstances, Mr. Kruger would almost have had to negotiate," Beth said, "while your mother could say, 'nope, my kid, *my* call, not a chance,' and there was no one around with the moral authority to stop her."

Except for her father, who had failed in whatever efforts he had made. "Jesus," Meg said. "Maybe you need a damn hobby or something." Should spend more of her time reading about *Miranda* and *Griswold*, and such.

"You don't think that the extra-vicious spin on it would have appealed to the guy?" Beth asked. "Put the new President in a situation where he had to make decisions about an even more sympathetic hostage than you already were?"

That was a line of reasoning she would have to think over, because right now, she wasn't necessarily buying it. "And what," Meg said, "he still wouldn't have had the sense to kill me, and it would have played out the same way?"

Beth shrugged. "I don't know. Too many variables. And maybe some money would have changed hands, behind the scenes, and you would have ended up being dumped by the side of the road somewhere."

Alive, or dead? More to the point, maimed, or mostly intact? Besides, the guy had told her that he'd been paid in full up front, and had insisted on working with total autonomy, so any negotiations wouldn't have involved him—or probably even *interested* him, one way or the other. On top of which, Mr. Kruger would probably have taken just as hard a line against terrorist demands as her mother had, because even if he liked her personally, and felt very sorry for her father and brothers, she *wasn't* his child, and he would have been able to keep some objectivity—and make the right choice for the country, the same way her mother had. It was what Presidents *did*, or they god-damn well didn't have any business setting foot in the Oval Office.

Arguably, they shouldn't have children, either, but that was a subsidiary issue.

"I guess I'm still trying to say that it all already happened, no matter how many ways you try to change it in your head, and you'll make yourself crazy if you keep trying to force any of it to turn out differently," Beth said.

Like she wasn't already less than sane? Her head was starting to hurt, and she reached into the front pocket of her sweatshirt to see if there might be a painkiller or two floating around loose in there. One ibuprofen, which would have to do. "If they'd come after me up in Chestnut Hill," Meg said, taking it with what was left of her coffee, "there's a pretty good chance you would have been *with* me, at the time." Since they'd been together, more often than not, especially at school.

Beth nodded. "A really good chance."

So she'd run through that version mentally, too. And maybe she wouldn't have been able to duck in time, the way Josh had. Maybe—

"It's theoretical, Meg," Beth said impatiently. "The only thing either of us knows for sure is that no matter who took you, or when, or where, you would have fought back like a rabid demon the whole time."

Except during the parts when she capitulated. And cowered, and cried, and all of that good stuff. Meg shook her head. "You can fight like crazy, and still only win because you got lucky."

"Doesn't make the fight any less worthwhile," Beth said. "I mean—" She hesitated. "There are supposed to be a lot more Shulmans and Morgenthals walking around the world, you know? But there *aren't*, and I don't have an answer for that one, either."

Both sides of Beth's family had lost numerous relatives during the Holocaust, and Meg had a very vivid memory of seeing a row of blue numbers on one of Beth's grandmother's arms, back when she was about nine and had been invited to a seder. She'd managed to figure out that she wasn't supposed to say anything about it, but asked Trudy what they meant as soon as she got home. It was one of the very few times she could ever remember Trudy having difficulty explaining something to her, and later that night, when her father came in to say good-night to her, he hadn't done much better.

Some people survived tragedies, and some people didn't, for no logical reason—and how in the hell did anyone ever come to terms with that, or make sense of it?

"More honesty?" Beth said.

Christ, maybe it was *good* that they went to school a couple of hundred miles apart. But, Meg nodded.

"What if the rock hadn't worked?" Beth asked. "I mean, if you smashed the crap out of your hand, and it stayed jammed inside that god-damn cuff, anyway. And you never got out of there. Or you *did* get out, but the fucking forest was too much, and none of us ever knew what—" She stopped, but then just squeezed her eyes shut for a few seconds, and opened them again. "The outcome isn't what made it important, the *fight* was what mattered."

One ibuprofen wasn't going to be enough to handle this discussion. *Twenty* might not do the trick. She was starting to feel close to the edge of her temper again, or maybe just on the verge of tears, and she took the damn fake glasses off, because they were making her headache worse.

"And now, maybe I should say I'm really sorry I've been giving you such a hard time today, and shut up already," Beth said.

It was an idea.

They both sat back as the waitress came over to refill their coffee and water. Meg forgot that she still had her glasses off and that her splinted hand was resting on the table, and saw the waitress glance at it, glance at her cane—and then look at her face more closely.

Well, she'd made it a *little* while without being recognized, at least.

She ducked her head, slipping the glasses back on and lowering the brim of her cap, which probably only confirmed the woman's suspicions.

"Anything else?" the waitress asked, after a pause.

"Just the check, please," Beth said.

The waitress nodded, made a point of *not* looking at Meg, and headed up to the front counter to total up their bill.

"Got to be anonymous for about an hour and a half," Beth said.

Meg nodded. Much longer than usual. She glanced at the television, where the Red Sox were now down by five runs in the eighth. And the waitress must have whispered something to her co-worker, who was showing her a tabloid from the stack of newspapers and magazines, which appeared to be the Secret Anorexia Nightmare issue.

"At least they saw you eat," Beth said.

And hadn't witnessed her racing off to the restroom in a potential bulimic frenzy, either. Since her cover was already blown, she took off the glasses for good, picked up her cane, and went over to Kyle and Jose's table to let them know that she and Beth were almost ready to leave, and that Garth and Ed should come in and order some takeout, if they were hungry.

After finding out that she had an overnight guest, Dirk—outdoors guy, that he was—not only rounded up a sleeping bag for Beth to use, but located an air mattress, too. Various people from her entry stopped by to say hello—and Tammy actually said, "Wait, *you're* the one who writes the terrible Internet stuff about her?" —but Beth seemed to be even more tired than she was, and so, atypically, by midnight, they were both lying down with the door closed, and the light out.

"I'm glad you came up here," Meg said. "But I'm sorry you felt like you had to. Sometimes it seems like all you ever *do* is try to pick me up when I fall down." Even literally, these days.

Beth lifted herself up onto one elbow. "Is that what you think?"

Considering that it was smack in the middle of the *completely self-evident* category, yeah.

"Walter Reed," Beth said.

Meg shook her head. "That doesn't count. I didn't do anything."

"But, you *would* have," Beth said. "I was freaking out, and it took you maybe thirty seconds to come up with a plan to solve it, and I thought, okay, even if I am pregnant, Meg's going to help me, and—well, I wasn't afraid anymore."

Meg turned on her side so that she could look right at her. "I don't ever want anything bad to happen to you, but if it did, I would *always* help you. No matter what."

"I know that," Beth said. "Hell, I knew that in kindergarten."

They had been the only two in the class who were already reading chapter books, so they got thrown together pretty much from the very first day. Fortunately for both of them, they had hit it off.

"Remember the way teachers used to treat me?" Beth asked.

Very much so. "Yeah," Meg said. "They were unbelievably mean." The thought of which, even years after the fact, still infuriated her. For some reason—probably because she had always been astute and observant—and vocal about it, most of their teachers had been inclined to dislike Beth, and slap her with detentions, and extra homework, at every possible opportunity.

Beth laughed. "And when they'd stop during class and yell, 'Miss Shulman!,' you'd almost always raise your hand and say, 'No, ma'am, it was me.' "

Meg shrugged. "Sometimes it *was*."

Beth laughed again. "Yeah, but mostly, it wasn't, and you'd still try to take the hit for me."

It felt weird to be reminded of that period in their lives. "Well, you were, you know, having a rough time," Meg said. Beth's parents' divorce had been so drawn out, and openly vicious, that Beth, as the only child, had been dragged into the middle of it for what seemed like *years*.

"Remember how I'd call you up constantly, and give you a bunch of grief?" Beth asked.

Meg nodded. When Beth got angry, it was generally because she actually felt like crying—and she'd been angry a lot, for a while there.

"I had dinner at your house and spent the night, what," Beth said, "about seven hundred times?"

Give or take a hundred.

"And we'd hang out," Beth said, "and bug Trudy, or your father would drive us to the movies, and—you were pretty much the only person I could talk to about things."

Yeah.

"You still are," Beth said. "I mean, okay, we're both making friends, and all, but *you're* who I call."

It went without saying that Beth was who *she* called.

She wasn't sure which one of them fell asleep first, but she woke up again a couple of hours later, tired and confused from a nightmare she couldn't remember. Beth was still on the floor, breathing evenly, so it must have been a silent one, and gradually, she dozed off again.

The pattern repeated itself, at about four in the morning, but this time, Beth must have been awake, because when she stopped crying, Beth said, very quietly, "You okay?" She said yeah, but the room was too still for a while, and she knew that they were both wide awake, and likely to remain so.

"After he kicked my knee out, I cried for several *hours,*" Meg said. Most of it unwitnessed, but not all of it.

"Well, your knee was torn to pieces," Beth said.

Yeah.

"He was a monster," Beth said.

Yes, indeed.

Trying to escape had *seemed* like a good idea. The odds of success were low—and that was even before she knew about the armed guards posted everywhere, but she hadn't wanted the guy to think less of her, so she took a chance. Hoped he would respect her for it. But he hadn't—and it had cost her a working leg. *Almost* cost her her life.

"He was, he was *so* angry," she said. "He—" Beth probably couldn't see, because it was dark, but she caught herself gesturing towards her face, holding her hand as though it were a gun.

And the guy had meant it that time. Not just trying to scare her, but a finger-twitch away from killing her. Planning to destroy her *brain.* He had been too crazed with fury to speak, but she was almost sure she could remember one of the other men behind him saying, over and over, "Do it, man. Fucking kill the bitch! *Do* it." And the guy just stared at her, gripping the gun with violently-shaking hands, trying to make up his mind—while she did nothing at all, other than stare back at him.

The first kick had been pure anger, and she hadn't seen it coming. But, after that, it had been different. "He walked around me, the second time," she said. And the third time. And even the time he slammed her leg into the door-frame. "You know, back and forth, really slowly, looking at me, trying to figure out the best angle for the next kick." The one which would do the most harm. "Making me *wait* for it." Giving himself the extra thrill of putting her through the terror of anticipation, his eyes crinkling with the exact same deep amusement she saw whenever she said something funny to him, the tilted grin on his face. She hadn't been able to keep herself from crying, but she only screamed the first time—because the kick had been so unexpected.

And so excruciating. And so brutal.

"When they came in, though, that last day, and I was sure they were about to kill me, I didn't cry," she said. Had been god-damned *determined* not to give him the satisfaction. "I *swear* I didn't. Not even when he told the really big guy to hold me down."

The only response Beth made was to let out a very shaky breath.

"I tried to hit back," she said. Panic-stricken, flailing punches, with her unhandcuffed arm, none of which seemed to have any effect on the men. "I lost the fight, though."

"Yeah," Beth said. "But you're going to win the *war*."

Maybe.

"You *are*," Beth said.

She was god-damned well going to *try*, at least.

"Most of that, you never told me before," Beth said.

Really? It was often hard to remember what she thought, and what she actually said aloud.

"You know what I think?" Beth asked.

Well, if nothing else, her response was going to be entirely honest.

"I think, fuck him, and the horse he rode in on," Beth said.

Yup. Meg didn't expect to laugh, but did. "And fuck his family, and *their* horses, and everyone who ever *met* them—or met their horses."

Beth laughed, too. "And how," she said.

49

BETH HAD A paper due, *and* her exam to make-up, so Meg talked her into taking the first bus out in the morning, instead of waiting until the afternoon one. The bus stop was in front of the Inn, so they went there for an early breakfast, Meg not at all sorry to have her agents drive them the short distance. When the bus pulled up, they went outside with a group of five or six other people going back to the city, and Beth dug her ticket out of her bag.

"How's your sense of humor?" she asked.

Well, that was really for others to say, wasn't it. Meg shrugged. "Okay, I guess."

Beth nodded, and pulled a folded t-shirt out of the bag, too. "I got you this a few weeks ago, but I wasn't sure if I should give it to you."

Meg shook it out with her good hand, and saw that there was a picture of the White House on the front, along with the boldly printed slogan, "If Lost or Stolen, Please Return to 1600 Pennsylvania Avenue."

Which was funny as hell.

When she laughed, Beth relaxed. "Good. I was afraid it might be pushing it."

"No, it's perfect," Meg said, and put it on over her Williams shirt. "Thanks."

"The tabloids are going to love it," Beth said.

Meg nodded. "Fuck them, and their horses."

They both grinned, and then looked at each other.

"*Thanks,*" Meg said.

Beth shrugged an embarrassed shrug. "See ya," she said, and got on the bus.

BY THE TIME the bus left, her psychology class was almost over, but she made it to her Shakespeare class—and after that, doggedly ate some lunch over at Driscoll, a dining hall where freshmen didn't go very often. Naturally, she wasn't hungry, but—well—she was just going to have to try to figure out a way to work around that. If she could.

Then, when she went down to physical therapy, she was cooperative, and even a little bit communicative. A different acupuncturist came this time—and never left the room, so apparently, they were all worried about a repeat of what had happened on Monday.

But, as soon as she got a chance to be alone with Vicky, right after their knee session, she cleared her throat.

"Um, I was thinking," she said.

Vicky looked up from the post-exercise ice packs she was arranging around her knee.

"Maybe you should start weighing me sometimes," Meg said. "See how I'm doing."

Vicky was obviously caught off-guard by that, but then, she smiled. "That sounds like a very good idea," she said.

When she returned to the dorm, she studied for a while, but then went down to Susan's room, where—as ever, the door was open, and the Doctor was In.

"Hi," Susan said. "Your friend head back to the city?"

Meg nodded.

"Did you guys have a good time?" Susan asked.

Well, that wasn't *exactly* how she would describe it, but she nodded. "Yeah, it was great to see her. But, um, my agents still haven't bothered you, right?"

"No," Susan said. "I mean, Garth wishes I'd called him first, but—no. Other than that, it's all fine."

So, if they'd had a tussle, it had been a minor one. Which was good. Meg nodded.

Susan looked at her curiously. "Is there something else you want to ask me?"

Well—yeah. "It's not important," Meg said. In fact, it was *stupid*. "But, um—could I hold your tennis racket?"

"Sure," Susan said, and bent over to pull it out from underneath her bed.

She hadn't touched a racket—any racket—since the day before she was kidnapped. When she'd spent several hours serving, and practicing, and beating a guy from Reuters in two straight sets. At her express request, all of her skiing and tennis equipment had been packed away before she was released from the hospital, so that she wouldn't have to look at any of it. *Ever.*

She leaned her cane against the wall, tested her balance to make sure her leg would hold up well enough, and then took the racket. It was a much lesser model than she would have selected—adequate playability, at best, but the handle fit easily, comfortably, into her hand. In fact, she had a sense of utter familiarity and calm, followed, of course, by despair. The grip was a little small—she liked to tape hers up, for the perfect fit—but, it still felt good. A couple of the strings needed adjusting and she automatically brought her right hand over, and then looked, stupidly, at her splint and worthless fingers. Anyway, it was Susan's racket, and maybe she liked having her strings a little off-kilter, for whatever reason, so it wasn't her place to rearrange them to her own standards.

"Long time?" Susan asked.

Meg nodded, switching from a forehand to a backhand to her favorite service grip, before returning to the forehand. She checked to make sure that she wasn't going to knock over the bedside lamp or whack the computer or anything, and then swung it slowly. Topspin forehand, down the line. Lots of touch and precision, restrained power.

And if she swung again, she was probably going to start crying.

She started to give it back, but Susan shook her head. So, she gripped it, tightly. "You, uh, you should always keep a cover on it." A proper tennis bag would be better, of course. "Protect the strings and the head and all."

"I don't really worry about it," Susan said. "I mostly just hack around."

Meg nodded, thinking about what it felt like to whip a two-handed backhand cross-court, flick a little drop shot barely over the net, smash an ace past a demoralized and befuddled—preferably male—opponent. Jesus, the muscles in her back and shoulders were *crying out* to serve, and swing, and serve some more. "So, um—" the very notion was anathema—"you don't play seriously?"

Susan shook her head. "I'm not that big on competing with anyone. I used to do some gymnastics in high school, but only for the hell of it."

It was hard to fathom not being obsessed by sports. By *winning*. And it was weird that ordinary little life details like that were the sort of thing she and Susan rarely discussed.

The things friends discussed.

"How good were you?" Susan asked.

One of the Big Questions, to which she was never going to know the answer. Meg shrugged, her hand clenching on the racket. "Jocks who get hurt *always* assume that they were a lot better than they actually were. It's part of the ethos." Albeit, of limited consolation.

"How good were you?" Susan asked, again.

Very good. Excellent, even. And she'd had fantasies of developing into being world-class. "I could play a little," Meg said.

Susan grinned, apparently hearing the unspoken braggadocio.

But that was all long gone now, so there was no point in standing here feeling sorry for herself about it. "Well," Meg said, and dropped the racket on the bed. "Thanks."

"Sure," Susan said. "Anytime."

No, reliving her not-so-glorious glory days, repeatedly, would lack dignity. She started to leave, but then realized that there had been a tiny discord in part of their conversation. Something that didn't quite fit. "Wait a minute," she said. "You called Martin directly the other night?"

Susan shrugged. "Yeah. I wasn't about to wait around for the end of the shift."

In the middle of the night? It would have made far more sense for her to approach Garth, first thing in the morning, or—Meg frowned. "So, you have Martin's number?"

"Of course," Susan said. "I mean, sometimes—" She stopped. "Well, there are procedural things, and—" She thought about that, and then nodded— "yeah, procedural matters, to discuss, and so, uh, I have to call him, and—yeah." She nodded too hard. "That's all."

Christ, she had *Martin's number*. His private number. And didn't hesitate to use it, even thought it was very late. And Martin came racing over, at her request. Hmmm.

"It's purely routine, of course. I would never—that is, *he* would never—" Susan sighed. "Oh, hell. I'm not selling this at all, am I?"

Not even remotely.

Susan had a tendency to blush, anyway, but this one went straight up into her hairline. "We just—talk, sometimes. And, well, that's the whole story."

Okey-doke. Meg grinned.

"Obviously, he's a complete professional," Susan said, blushing away, "and nothing untoward would ever—" She stopped. "Oh, shit. Never mind."

Holy Christ, how had she missed all of this, anyway? Had it been going on for weeks? Did everyone else know? And now, something else clicked into place. "You *run* with him," Meg said.

"Yes, well, weren't you the one who was telling me it was dangerous to run by myself when it was getting dark?" Susan asked stiffly.

So, she had only started going around with him after that? Yeah. Sure. Meg grinned.

Susan blushed some more. "You could maybe leave now, okay?"

Good advice, since she was going to laugh pretty hard if she didn't. Meg picked up her cane. "Did he get shot in the leg? When he was in the Marines?"

"No, it was shrapnel," Susan said, and indicated her right thigh. "The scar's about a foot—" She broke off abruptly. "Well, I have no idea. Just, you know, what shows when he has running shorts on."

Except that she had gestured right up past her hip there, for a second.

Meaning that she had seen him *naked.*

Wow.

"Please go away now, and never mention this again," Susan said, her blush practically *purple* this time.

Right.

She went upstairs in a much-improved mood. In fact, she was tempted to call Beth right away, to share the gossip—but Juliana's door was open, and Meg saw her sitting at her desk, studying, although she was also singing along to the very loud music which was playing, drinking Red Bull, and eating microwave popcorn. To be polite, she knocked.

"Susan and *Martin*?" Meg asked, after making sure that no one else could hear her.

"Hell, yeah," Juliana said. "Where've you been?"

Out to lunch, it would seem. As usual. "How long?" she asked.

"I'm not sure," Juliana said. "But she was wearing this big old Clemson shirt about a month ago, and she was all embarrassed when I asked her about it."

And she hadn't mentioned that guy Keith, who she supposedly liked, for *weeks* now. "Are they—I mean, do you think—" She didn't want to be crass. "Well, you know."

Juliana frowned. "Hard to say. But I saw them down near the Log one time, when they were coming back from running, and they looked—well, you could tell they were *really* into each other. I mean, they looked all happy and stuff."

She had possibly never seen Martin *or* Susan without worried expressions on their faces—or looking anything close to being off-duty. So, it was nice to imagine that there might be something going on which made them both happy. "Does anyone else know?" she asked.

Juliana crunched some more popcorn. "Not much gets past Mary Elizabeth. And, you have to figure Dirk would catch on. But, other than that, no, I don't think so."

She had no idea what the protocol was, about agents dating, but Susan was almost twenty-one, and Martin really wasn't that much older, and she wasn't a protectee—so it didn't seem as though there would be anything wrong with it. "And *we're* never going to tell anyone."

"Hell, no," Juliana said.

A LITTLE WHILE later, a bunch of people from her entry headed down to the dining hall for supper, and she tagged along with them. She *still* wasn't hungry, but at least Beth wouldn't be able to say that she wasn't trying. To her relief, she didn't see Jack there, although she ran into Mona near the coffee machine, and his Frisbee buddy Corey by the salad bar. In both cases, though, she just said hello, and left it at that.

But she couldn't spend the rest of the semester arranging her life around trying to avoid him, so after dinner, she packed up some books and notebooks, and went over to the library, where she finished off *Coriolanus*, and did some final, minor bits of research for her political science revision.

She stuck it out until past ten-thirty, then headed outside into the dark with her security shadows. It was going to be nice to lie down. To be alone. To *sleep*. She was so tired that she had to lean on her cane more than usual, and for some reason, her hand seemed to be having its own idiosyncratic little convulsion. Kind of unnerving.

There was a guy lying on his back on one of the picnic tables in the quad, his hands folded behind his head, and she probably would have limped by without even looking over, except that she caught Nellie glancing at her.

Jack.

Nifty.

She was *still* considering going inside without a pause, but he was sitting up now.

"Hey," he said.

Hard to accomplish anything incognito when surrounded by agents. She nodded once, instead of answering.

"How you doing?" he asked.

"Just super," she said. "Hope you are, too."

"Yeah," he said. It was dark, so she couldn't see his expression, but he didn't sound happy. "Very super."

Neither of them spoke. She could hear voices coming out of dorm windows, and from people walking nearby, as well as music, cars out on Main Street, and even a few crickets.

"Well, I, uh—" she moved towards the dorm— "kind of need to go get some more studying done. Good to see you, though."

He sighed. "Come on, Meg. Sit down for a minute, okay?"

The thought of which made her feel so exhausted that, for a second, she thought she might burst into tears.

"I really can't," she said, keeping her voice as blasé as she could, so tense that her hand was cramping around the cane. "I'm very—it was a long day."

"Just for a minute," he said.

What was the worst thing that could happen if she walked away without another word? He'd think she was a cold, arrogant jerk? That might be preferable to being seen as a *thin*, deeply-disturbed person who screamed and cried a lot.

"What do you have to lose?" he asked.

The tiny, remaining fragments of her dignity? As well as the result that he might get the bright idea to share all of this with the media at some point. In graphic detail. But, at least if she went through the motions of officially breaking up with him—such as it had been—she wouldn't have to worry about him bothering her anymore. So, she sat down at the picnic table, facing out, with her back to him.

"You one of those people who looks at stars?" he asked.

She was not now; nor had she ever been. More emphatically so, though, after the dark terror of the nights in the forest, when she'd been too scared to do anything other than try to concentrate on clutching whatever rock or stick she had grabbed to use as a potential weapon, in case anything, or any*one*, came unexpectedly lunging out at her.

And if they were going to sit here talking about nature, she might just possibly have a nervous breakdown.

"A lot of fucking help I would have been," he said.

Okay, she was lost.

"I froze," he said. "You were scared out of your mind, and I stood there like—well, like some kind of felon. And, in the meantime, your tiny little friend shows up, ready to take on the world."

Susan was, indeed, small. Meg sighed, and rubbed her sleeve across her eyes to keep them from closing. And maybe—just maybe—to make sure they were going to stay dry.

"Might have been nice if I'd told you it was okay, instead of taking off," he said.

Yeah. Extremely nice.

"Is that how scared you are?" he asked. "Just, you know, on a regular day?"

She had no interest in answering either question, so she shrugged.

It was quiet again. Crickets, voices, laughter here and there, music. A few more cars.

"*Fuck*," he said.

He sounded angry enough for her to look quickly at Nellie, who took a step closer.

"I mean, it's way more than—" Jack stopped. "This just isn't what I'm looking for, Meg."

Did he *have* to be so god-damn honest?

"I just, you know, want to screw around," he said.

No kidding.

"Literally, but also—well, if there's anything *difficult*, I don't want to—" He stopped again, and shook his head. "This really isn't—I'm sorry. I don't think I can do it."

Once again, he was living up to her worst expectations. "Well, lucky for you, your long national nightmare is over," Meg said. "You can go off and find someone shallow, and uncomplicated, and promiscuous as hell. Play your cards right, and I bet you'll score before morning."

He stared at her. "You know, I may be an immature asshole, but you can be an absolutely *glacial* bitch."

Glacial. Oooh.

"Is she anywhere close to being as mean as you are?" he asked.

What, was he an idiot? "Well, *yeah*," Meg said, and laughed, except that it made her throat hurt. "I mean, she pretty much gave the terrorists *permission* to kill me." Practically put the guns in their hands. "Where would you score that on the Mean Scale?"

"Pretty high," he said.

Yeah. Pretty fucking high all right.

She reached back to use the table for support, and slowly eased up onto her good leg.

"I had a really crappy time in New Haven," he said.

She was overflowing with sympathy.

"It was mostly okay while I was actually playing," he said, "but other than that, I was down there, and you were way the hell up *here*, and I missed you."

She shrugged. "Probably should have found someone to make out with, then."

He shook his head. "I missed the stuff you say, and how you think all the time, and the way you look at me when you forget you aren't sure whether you actually *like* me."

Oh.

"But then, when you walked into Psych, you wouldn't even come *near* me," he said. "And today, you didn't show up at all."

This came as a surprise, somehow? Besides, he had been the one who stayed away from her, hadn't he?

She didn't want to forgive him. Didn't want to take the time, or make the effort, and try to work this out. Didn't even, really, want to get to know him better. It just took up too god-damned much energy.

A couple of dismissive words, and she could end this right now. Be off the hook. Try to meet someone who would never dream of pressuring her, and would spend a lot of time making remarks like, "Of course, Meg, you're right. You're always right" and "Sure, whatever you want, Meg."

"Josh ducked," she said.

Which, judging from his expression, must have seemed like a complete non-sequitur.

"He came running out when it happened, and they were shooting everywhere," she said, "so I yelled at him to get down—and he did."

Jack nodded. "And feels all emasculated now, because he didn't save you."

Unfortunately. "Yeah," Meg said. "But they would have killed him. They shot my agents without thinking twice."

Jack—probably involuntarily—glanced around, as though a wild flurry of machine-gun fire might break out at any second. "You must have really loved him, if you thought of him right in the middle of all hell breaking loose for *you*."

Yes. She shrugged. "It was a reflex, mostly. But, yeah, I loved him." Which the guy had figured out right away, because he'd spent a lot of time trying to knock her further off balance by telling her that Josh had been shot repeatedly—and had died. She had believed it right up until her mother had had someone bring him to her bedside to see her in the hospital.

"Still sort of fits into the whole hero zeitgeist," he said.

Christ, hearing the word "hero" *once* was already two thousand times too many, especially when the sentiment was so very misplaced. But, she made a point of not correcting him, since that would just prolong the issue. "Don't tell your beach dude friends that you like to use the word 'zeitgeist,' " she said.

"Yeah, you're probably right," he agreed.

Well, it was nice to be right.

They looked at each other.

"I'm really sorry about my agents," she said. "I think it was an honest mistake, but they shouldn't have treated you that way."

He shrugged. "Everyone around you's scared all the time."

Serious understatement. "Yeah, but I should have warned you that it might happen. But, we had been—" No point in embarrassing both of them—and whichever agents might be within earshot—with a play-by-play. "I was distracted," she said.

He nodded.

"I've, um," she lowered her voice, "never slept with anyone before."

"Well, no kidding, Meg," he said. "I already know that."

And now, in all likelihood, Nellie, and possibly Ronald, knew, too, since they were standing the closest. She carefully didn't look at them, hoping that they were tactful enough not to be listening. "I meant *literally*," she said. "And so, I didn't stop to think about whether I was going to wake up screaming."

"It's okay," he said. "I just got scared, and—I really thought I *might* have hurt you somehow, by accident."

Made sense. She shook her head. "You didn't. I'm just—I don't know—still trying to find my way back. And, I have to be honest, I don't know how long it's going to take, or even if—well, I might not ever be able to get there."

Strangely enough, he didn't disagree.

Which left them, where?

"I've never made love with anyone," he said.

Could have fooled her. But she looked around to make sure that her agents were all a safe distance away, which seemed to be the case.

"What I do, is *have sex*," he said. "A girl says yes, I say, 'Yay!,' and away we go."

Which wasn't likely to happen here. It wasn't any secret that she was going to need a hell of a lot more from him than that.

"I don't even know if I know how," he said. "And if I try, I'm going to do stuff wrong, and you're going to get your feelings hurt sometimes, and I'm going to get *my* feelings hurt, and—well, I don't know."

"So, we both feel like running away," she said.

He nodded.

This entire conversation was making her feel even more tired than usual.

"Does your mother give your father that 'I'm not sure if you're even worth the effort' look?" he asked.

An expression she could picture all too easily on her own face. "No," Meg said. "He gives it to *her*." As a rule.

Because her mother had gone out of her way to pick an equal, instead of someone who would let her completely run the show.

"I hate that look," Jack said.

Yeah. Josh had hated it, too. So, she nodded. "Well, maybe you can study up on the making love business, and I'll work on the trying to do a better job of letting you in part."

Jack grinned at her. "Works for me," he said.

50

HE HELPED HER up from the picnic bench, and she was shaky enough so that she leaned against his arm for a minute, until she was sure she could stand on her own. Then, he kissed her good-night, they looked at each other, he kissed her again—and they left it at that.

For the time being.

Although she *did* call Beth—who was very pleased—the second she got upstairs.

She had dinner with him the next night, and they went out for a very long session of coffee and pastries down on Spring Street the following day. Spent a fair amount of talking on the phone, and sending lots of cryptic, flirtatious emails and instant messages, too.

Both Maureen and Hannah emailed her advance copies of *The Washington Post* profile, and while it seemed to be very well done, she felt uncomfortable reading about herself, and stopped after the first couple of paragraphs. Regardless, she arranged to have flowers sent, with a "*Great job! Thanks— Meg*" note attached.

Jack's ankle was still pretty bad, and he probably had no business being out on the field, but the team was playing at home on Saturday, and she and Juliana and Mark went to watch. He seemed to *love* having her as an audience, and did quite a lot of showing off, but also made some sparkling plays along this way.

If it hadn't been a required uniform, and he had been able to take his shirt off, it would have been a nearly perfect afternoon.

They spent most of that night alone in her room, closing the door for the first time since the nightmare. She was pretty sure that he was trying to take it slow—but that didn't last long, and she knew that she was getting very much closer to saying *yes*, and probably would once she was sure the birth control pills she'd finally started taking had really and truly kicked in.

Right before midnight, he used his cell phone to order some pizza, and she ended up eating three pieces, while they watched a replay of that afternoon's Red Sox victory on NESN, and took time to fool around at odd moments. It was erotic, and entertaining, and just a hell of a lot of fun.

They hadn't discussed whether he was going to spend the night, but it was getting late, and they were both drowsy, and it seemed to be inevitable. Plus, Martin was out there on overnight duty, in his staunch way, which made her feel less anxious about what might happen, if things didn't go well.

Once the light was out, and they were lying together, she got the nerve to bring up something which had been bothering her.

"Are you a Republican?" she asked.

Jack laughed. "What?"

"Are you?" she asked.

"Well, I think, lots of times, entitlement programs cause more problems than they solve," he said.

What? She sat up. "You do?"

"Yeah." He shrugged. "Don't you?"

Oh, dear. Although her mother was a devotee of Moynihan's works, and entitlement strategies sometimes seemed to lead to a certain infantilization, and large bureaucracies didn't tend to breed efficiency, but it was still potentially troubling. "Gun control, freedom of choice, estate taxes, states' rights, big government, gay marriage, medical malpractice, affirmative action, the separation of church and state," she said.

"I don't know." He sat up, too. "Yes, yes, no, mostly, no, sure, out of control, sometimes, and maybe." Then, he frowned. "Is this a *litmus* test?"

She nodded.

"Oh." He frowned. "Jesus, hope I didn't get them out of order. Did I pass?"

Hmmm. "You got an incomplete," she said.

"The *President's* kind of centrist," he said, sounding very annoyed. "Why can't I be, too?"

She herself was also closer to the middle than the left, in many cases, but— "Separation of church and state," she said.

He folded his arms. "What's the big deal if someone wants to put up a damn Christmas tree? If someone else comes along, and says, hey, can I add a menorah or something here, why can't *they* do that, too? I mean, what the hell. A person feels like saying, 'God bless America,' it doesn't wreck my day."

"Okay," she said, and tilted her head to look up at him, squinting to see in the very dim light. "Gay marriage is fine?"

He shrugged. "People loving each other and getting married? Sure. Besides, my brother's gay, and what if he wants to have a family or something?"

She would have to give him a full passing grade, simply for apparently not being at all bothered by the fact that his brother was gay. "Is your father upset about it?"

"Pretends he doesn't know," Jack said. "But his partner, Bucky, stayed with us during the holidays and everything, and he can't be *that* dense. I don't think."

Interesting. "What do your parents think about my mother?" she asked.

Jack shrugged again. "Mom likes her, mostly. Dad says at least she turned out to be an Iron Lady, so the country will probably still be here once we get someone good back in office again."

Not a rave, but not a disaster, either.

He grinned. "My brother says it was like getting to vote for Emma Peel."

She grinned, too. "Gay brother, or straight brother?"

"Greg," he said. "So, gay brother. But, Phillip started calling her that, too."

Jack, and his unexpectedly Anglophilic family. Hell, when she'd visited his dorm room, she'd even seen a whole sketchbook devoted to little line drawings of London and the English countryside.

"I think it's why she won," he said seriously. "I mean, yeah, she's incredibly smart and all, but she also charmed the hell out of everyone."

"It didn't hurt that the other guy was so smug," Meg said. And wishy-washy. And seemingly perpetually angry, in an off-putting smiley way.

"No," he agreed, "but in the debates, and with the press and all, the harder they went after her, the more sparkly she got, and it was fun to watch. Like you really wouldn't mind having her all over the place for four years. Wouldn't get sick of seeing her. And Greg'd be sitting there, pumping his fist and pissing my father off, saying, 'You go, Mrs. Peel!' "

Something she would definitely have to run by the President, who was probably going to be very pleased by the comparison, regardless of whether she admitted it.

"That's who the country voted for, and that's who they want back," he said, very seriously.

Because the President was no longer—jaunty—in the same way. No longer necessarily fun to watch go through her day. "Maybe she'd rather do theater," Meg said.

He laughed, and then reached out to touch her cheek, his fingers moving up and across the scar on her forehead lightly. "How long did it take?"

To split her eyebrow with a smack of a machine gun? Oh, say, *two seconds*?

"They had you with them, what, three, four days?" he said.

She stiffened. He had never asked her *anything* specific about the kidnapping. Why start now, when they were having such a nice time? "Something like that, yeah," she said, her throat feeling tight.

"So, how long before you wised off to them?" he asked.

"I didn't," Meg said stiffly. "I was afraid." When she woke up in the dark room, and the man came slamming in for the first time—a big muscular guy, looming over her in a stocking mask—she had trembled so hard that the damn metal bed actually shook. And, he'd laughed, with a soft contempt she could still hear somewhere inside her head.

Jack nodded. "Yeah, I'm sure you were, but I still bet it didn't even take you an hour to pop off for the first time."

More like five minutes. But—the guy had been so cocky that it made her mad, and well, what was she supposed to do, just sit there and let him think he'd already beaten her? Even though he *had*?

And still *might*, long-term.

"Shit," Jack said. "It wasn't even close to an hour, was it."

No. None of which changed anything, but—no. "Um, can we talk about something else?" she asked.

He nodded, and eased her down so that they were lying next to each other again, and she was resting on his chest. She couldn't relax at all, but he massaged his hand up and down her back, and after a few silent minutes, she finally felt herself release something resembling a normal breath.

He pulled her closer, his arms feeling heavy now, as though he was starting to fall asleep. "When Greg emails me lately, he always asks, 'and how's Little Emma?' "

The Taylor boys were goofy. "My brother calls *you* Malibu Bobby," Meg said.

"Yikes," he said. "I'm not sure I like that one."

Then he was going to be even more upset if he ever found out that Steven's agents must have mentioned it to her agents, because she had heard the nickname bandied about more than once of late.

She would have sworn that she never fell asleep, but suddenly it was light out, and she was being kissed awake by someone who tasted like pepperoni.

"Hi," he said. "Sleep okay?"

It seemed entirely improbable, but— "Yeah," she said, and kissed him back. "I think I did."

FOR THE NEXT week or so, she tried to ease back into—well, whatever it was that her life was. On Monday afternoon, she dropped her new political science paper in Professor Richardson's box, and without a word, but smiling—he handed it back to her the next day, with an A+, and a succinct and interesting half-page of handwritten comments. Which pleased her enough so that she actually spoke up during one of her classmates' diatribes, and spouted out a little riff about the dangers of the tyranny of the majority, and the probable intent of the framers of the Constitution, and while her professor didn't entirely agree with her analysis, she could tell that he was glad to see her make the effort.

Other people in her classes had either decided she didn't make them nervous anymore—or picked up on her somewhat increased comfort level, and she ended up having lunch or coffee with a couple of them. Maybe she actually *could* start making friends.

Her mother took a three-day trip to London, Edinburgh, Cardiff, and Dublin, which meant that her security was jacked up during that time period, and presumably her brothers' and father's details were expanded, too, but none of them—including her mother—mentioned this state of affairs during telephone conversations or in emails. There were, as always, a number of angry anti-American protests held wherever her mother went while she was abroad, and when Meg saw film of the President walking over to engage some of the people in conversation—an infuriating, but not shocking move on her part, made that much more irritating when many of the protestors looked pleased, and even laughed in response to whatever it was she said to them—she found herself wishing that there was a brick nearby, so she could throw it through the goddamn screen. The only mitigating factor was that her mother was wearing a chic raincoat during the spontaneous stroll, so there was a *chance* that it had a bulletproof liner—but Meg still felt like slugging her for taking stupid chances. Yet again.

Jack went away the next weekend to play in the sectionals tournament, which was being held at Middlebury—and called her several times, including from a noisy party on Saturday night, at which he was clearly very drunk, somewhat maudlin, and more than a little preoccupied by the idea of sex and what she might be wearing, or, ideally, *not* wearing. He also said that his teammates were kind of pissed off at him, because they thought his game focus sucked, especially in the red zone, and that they'd lost to UMass that afternoon, and he'd had to leave the game with a yellow card, because he'd gotten into a fight with some guy who asked how she was in the sack, but that she shouldn't worry, because while it bled a lot all over his shirt, his nose wasn't broken.

"So, anyway," he said, after some more drunken rambling. "*What* are you wearing?"

Just to get him going, she told him that he should picture Mrs. Peel's outfit in the "A Touch of Brimstone" episode, except with a much bigger snake.

Which might have erred on the side of being too provocative, because she was treated to some lengthy stream-of-consciousness questions and suggestions, most of which were funny, but also quite X-rated. But then, suddenly, he said, "Oh, wait, there's that UMass son of a bitch now, I gotta go," and hung up.

The next morning, she watched the Sunday political shows, which were pretty uneventful, except that the Attorney General—who was appearing on one of them, in an attempt to rectify her poor performances a few weeks earlier—managed to boot it again. Meg had met her a number of times, and knew that she was a very intelligent, articulate, and reasonably pleasant person, but live television was apparently not her bailiwick.

When she called home right after the show went off the air, the President was extremely annoyed about the situation, and said something snide to the effect that that was what a Yale education did for a person, and it seemed quite possible that the Department of Justice would be under new leadership sooner, rather than later.

The weather was absolutely beautiful—a perfect spring day, and even though the Red Sox were on, and playing well, she felt restless. She had plenty of work to do, including a psychology lab report and a philosophy paper, but she wasn't about to pick doing *that* over baseball.

But, even the Beloved Team wasn't holding her attention today.

The dorm was so quiet that it seemed as though the building might be empty. Was everyone off frolicking in the sunshine? Or, more likely, out playing some damn *sport* or other? Off in the library, studying industriously? Or just in their rooms, taking naps?

She considered doing the latter herself, but the thought was pretty depressing. Sometimes, it felt as though she was napping her whole life away.

She had on her "If Lost or Stolen" shirt, sweatpants, and air pump sneakers, which would all work quite nicely as afternoon sleepwear, but were designed, of course, for athletics. Activity. *Fun*. Not for lying around with splints and braces and canes and ice packs.

Christ, and it was such a nice day out.

Oh, the hell with it.

She made sure that her sneakers were tightly fastened with their elastic laces, and reached for her cane.

Time to go play sports already.

WHEN SHE WENT down to the second floor, Susan was just getting back from running, looking healthy and energetic and only slightly overheated.

"Hi," Susan said, not at all out of breath, although she had probably sprinted up the stairs, since that's what she always did when she was by herself.

Meg nodded. "Hi. Good run?"

"Not bad." Susan opened her door. "What's up?"

Nothing whatsoever. Who was she kidding? She could barely stand on her damn cane. The only thing she should do this afternoon was go back upstairs and lie down, and watch the rest of the Red Sox game. "Not much," Meg said. "Um, how far did you go?"

Susan picked up a towel to wipe off her face. "I don't know. Five and a half, something like that."

How weird was it to go running, and not even keep track of the distance? "How fast did you go?" Meg asked.

Susan shrugged. "Six and a half minutes, maybe. I don't know, I was a little tired today."

It made no sense to be good at something—and not care, one way or the other. Meg looked at her curiously. "How fast could you go, if you went all out?"

"I don't know." Susan tossed the towel at the laundry bag in the corner, and then drank some water from the CUPPS cup—the reusable coffee travel cups students were issued, although most of them, Meg included, usually forgot to carry them around—on her desk. "Pretty fast, probably."

Christ. Jill Kiley, from her Shakespeare class, had told her at Brunch Night one time that the cross-country coach had seen Susan out running during their freshman year, and had tried, for *weeks*, to recruit her for the team, never getting more than a "No, thank you, but it was very nice of you to ask me" from her. What a waste of talent. Jill, who was on both the field hockey and softball teams, didn't get it, either.

"So," Susan said. "What's going on?"

Should she pretend she had been doing nothing more than coincidentally walking by, and had just stopped to say a friendly hello?

"Meg?" Susan asked.

Jesus, was she that damn transparent? It wasn't like she had some sort of *agenda*. As such. Not exactly like that, anyway. Meg took a deep breath. "Could I borrow your tennis racket?"

"Sure," Susan said, and pulled it out from underneath the bed. "You know, if you wanted, you could keep it upstairs. I almost never use it."

Meg shook her head. "No, I'll bring it back in about an hour. I was just, you know, going to—go hit for a while." All right, she'd said it aloud. Now she was committed to doing it.

Susan's eyebrows went up, but she just handed her the racket. "Okay. Who you playing with?"

Well, she hadn't thought it out quite that far, so Meg shrugged.

"Do you have any tennis balls?" Susan asked.

Hadn't thought that part out, either. Meg shook her head.

"Okay." Susan dug around until she found a can of balls, too. "I can't play with you, though."

It was foolish to be disappointed—maybe even a little crushed—by that, but she was. "Well, no," Meg said. "I mean, you just got back from running, so—"

"I gave you my *racket*," Susan said.

Oh. Right. Yes, trying to hit without one would present some challenges. Meg frowned.

"Let's go find Tammy," Susan said. "She was on her team in high school."

Really? "Is she good?" Meg asked.

Susan shrugged. "She'll be a damn sight better than I am."

Tammy was in her room, studying for a biology quiz, eating Cap'n Crunch out of the box, and looking bored, so she seemed happy enough about the idea of going to play tennis for a while, although she looked at Meg's brace and cane dubiously. Then, on their way downstairs, they ran into Juliana and Mark and Andy, all of whom wanted to come along to watch, Meg deciding not to point out that she might end up taking one swing, yelping in pain, and then having to be helped back to the dorm—or maybe straight to the nearest emergency room.

However, her agents all looked nervous enough to indicate that that probability had occurred to them.

"Maybe I should carry the racket," Juliana said. "If anyone's out there, and they see *you* with it, they'll want to take a bunch of pictures."

Sadly, that was likely to be true.

"But if they think she's going to go watch other people play, they might want to take pictures of her looking *wistful*," Tammy said.

Andy frowned. "Maybe we should stagger our exits. Juliana and Tammy could be going off to play, and the rest of us can leave after that, like we're going to the Snack Bar or something."

They were all becoming amazingly, and appallingly, media-savvy.

This was also already turning into much too big a deal, so Meg stayed out of the debate, but in rapid course, the rest of them decided that they would all walk together, but *Susan* would carry the racket, because Juliana's flip-flops did not look sufficiently jock-like.

And there was a photographer hanging around on Park Street—possibly two, although the second person might just have been a tourist—so, maybe it was just as well that she didn't appear to be doing anything unusual. The guy looked bored, snapping a few cursory shots, but mainly, looked bored.

Just walking—limping—across the campus to the tennis courts was enough to wear her out, but she was damned if she was going to admit it.

"You sure you still want to play?" Susan asked.

Sometimes, it would be nice if she were less god-damned attentive. "Yup," Meg said.

Most of the courts were full, but there was an open one in the middle. Which meant that everyone else playing would have an excellent view of this disaster-in-the-making, but, okay. Too late now. They were already here.

"Um, do you just want to rally?" Tammy asked.

No, she wanted to leap into an intense, competitive, no-holds-barred match. Meg nodded. "That would be good, thank you."

"Okay," Tammy said, looked at Susan for reassurance, and then trotted over to the far side of the court.

Meg swallowed and bent over to tighten the straps on her brace. This was a mistake. A very big mistake.

On the other hand, the worst that could happen was that she would walk out there, fall down, and shred her knee again. Or she might land on her splint, and rebreak some of the bones in her hand. Both possibilities would *suck*, but wouldn't be the end of the world. The end of her summer, and most of next semester, maybe, but not the world.

All of the other people playing had noticed that she was there, but most of them were too cool to stare, and continued with whatever they were doing on their own courts, although they gave her stray glances.

Tammy was waiting patiently, bouncing a ball on top of her racket. The way she moved indicated that she was probably an average player, but not an excellent one.

"Go take a couple of swings," Susan said.

Meg nodded, using her right arm to pin the racket against her side so that she could move the strings into better alignment with her good hand. Her stomach was starting to hurt, and she swallowed again.

"Ah, I bet you're a crappy player, anyway," Juliana said. "Tammy can probably beat the pants off you."

Which was just the right mean joke to make. Meg grinned, and made her way over to the baseline. She tested her weight on her bad leg, able to feel at once that there was a better than even chance that it would give out, and that her already limited recovery was going to rest upon a combination of sheer luck, not falling—or even tripping, and the brace holding firm.

"Do you want me to hit it right to you?" Tammy asked.

No, she should hit it as far away as possible, and make her *run* to get it. But, Meg just nodded.

Tammy hesitated, bounced the ball a couple more times, and then hit a slow, looping shot towards her. The ball was coming to her backhand, and Meg panicked, because she couldn't think of a way to hit it without using her left leg. And she'd always had a two-handed backhand, except when she was on the run and couldn't get to a ball in time, so she had no idea how to—she swung late, and mis-hit the ball badly enough to send it flying into the next court.

Fuck.

She thought she might burst into tears right there, especially when the guy playing next to her retrieved the ball and brought it directly to her, instead of casually hitting it in her direction.

"I'm sorry," Meg said. "I—haven't played for a while."

The guy shrugged. He looked vaguely familiar—maybe she'd seen him hanging out in Goodrich, or something. "No problem," he said, and then nodded in the direction of the grassy slope, where Susan, Juliana, Mark, and Andy were sitting. "Hey, Susan, how's it going?"

"Hi, Burt," Susan said.

She should no longer be surprised that Susan seemed to know everyone on the entire campus.

"Should I hit you another?" Tammy asked.

Meg stuck the ball into the pocket of her sweatpants, and nodded.

The second shot also came to her backhand, and she didn't want to risk missing it again, so she let it go by.

"Sorry," Tammy said, looking flustered. "I forgot you're left-handed, and—I'm not very good at aiming."

Meg shook her head. "No, it's okay. I just—it's fine."

This time, the ball came to her forehand, but it was couple of inches out of reach, and she was afraid to move towards it, so she had to watch it go past her and bang up against the fence. Again.

Okay. The experiment was a complete and total failure.

She could feel tears in her eyes, but managed to blink them back as she limped over to pick up the two balls and leave the court, her good leg almost as weak and shaky as her bad one was.

"Hit it to her," Susan said quietly, from her spot on the grass.

What did it look like she was *trying* to do? Meg shook her head.

"Just hit a ball back to her," Susan said. "Like she double-faulted, and needs one so she can serve again."

People were pretending not to watch, but she could hear—from the increasing lack of nearby ball- and sneaker-sounds—that most of them had stopped playing, so she was attracting some attention.

Way too much attention.

What a stupid, demoralizing, and *depressing* idea this had been.

"Okay. Just hit them back to her, so she can pack them into the can," Susan said.

What, like Tammy couldn't walk over, and do that on their way off the court?

"Or, you could hit the ball at Susan's head," Juliana said. "Since she's completely pissing you off right now."

That one sounded like a pretty good idea. She balanced a ball on her racket, flipped it up in the air, and then swung, hitting a clean forehand over the net.

Tammy looked surprised, but hit it back. Meg had to let it bounce twice to be able to reach it without hurting herself, but was able to return the ball fairly smoothly.

They put together a few abortive rallies, during which Meg had to keep watching balls go by, and Tammy got increasingly frustrated because she couldn't control her shots better.

"I can't do this, Meg," she said. "It's too much pressure."

Right. Meg nodded, and turned to leave the court.

A girl from the court on their other side—who had been hitting methodical, steady ground-strokes and serves the entire time they had been there—walked over to intercept her.

"Want to hit for a few minutes?" she asked. She was quite tall, and wearing a Prince visor, with light brown hair tied back in a neat, perky ponytail.

With a complete stranger? Hell, no. Besides, she was tired. God-damn worn out, in fact. "Thank you, but," Meg shook her head, "I really don't have much range."

"I'll groove them," the girl said. "Just stay deep, so I can work the baseline."

Well, hell. That sounded like a *player*. Meg glanced at Tammy, who nodded. "Um, okay," she said. "Thanks."

The girl nodded, and then frowned. "*That's* your racket?"

"No, all my sports stuff is in storage." Meg gestured towards the grass, where Tammy was already on her way over to join the others. "I borrowed this from my JA."

The girl looked past her, and then waved. "Hi, Susan."

"Hi, Nancy," Susan said, and waved back.

Nancy. Hmmm. Possibly the same Nancy who was ranked number one on the tennis team, and had been picked to the All-NESCAC first team this season. Not that she'd been able to bring herself to follow the fortunes of the women's team, but sometimes, she maybe glanced at the sports articles in *The Record*, or checked out the tennis pages on the Williams Web site.

Obsessively, even.

"That's an incredibly crummy racket," Nancy said.

Susan shrugged. "I like it just fine. You two are arrogant, persnickety jocks, that's all."

Nancy grinned, went over to her bulky tennis bag, and pulled out two other rackets. She hefted each of them, picked one, and then brought it back over. "Here. Try this."

Meg swung, tentatively, and then nodded. Now, that was more like it. The grip was a shade too big for her hand, but not enough to be a problem. Babolat strings, with VS natural gut on the mains, and Pro Hurricane Tour on the crosses. Which had been one of her favorite hybrid combos, too, when she was practicing. She braced the racket under her right arm, and felt the strings lightly with her good hand to check the tension.

"Sixty-four?" she asked. Possibly 62.

Nancy nodded, looking at her with more respect. "Yeah. Is that what you played with?"

No, it would have been too hard on her elbow. Besides, she had never minded sacrificing a little bit of control to improve her power. "I usually went with sixty," she said.

Nancy nodded, then motioned towards the court. "So, you want to give it a try?"

Yes.

51

WHILE NANCY TOOK her position on the other side of the net, Meg limped to the baseline, trying to concentrate and feel what her leg was, and wasn't, going to tolerate.

It was pretty clear that it still wasn't going to let her do much of anything, but if she was careful, and made sure to have her right leg do most of the work, she could put more weight on it than she had been so far. Not much more, but some.

Nancy hit her a perfectly-placed forehand, and she returned it to the exact same location on the opposite side of the court—and they both grinned, continuing with fluid, easy swings, and Meg immediately remembered how soothing a metronomic rally could be.

"Holy shit," she heard Andy saying behind her. "Look at *that.*"

There were a couple of out-of-range balls she didn't attempt to go after, and she was so rusty that she netted a few shots, but for the most part, they just hit back and forth, Meg feeling as though she could breathe freely for the first time in almost a year.

The people nearby had stopped pretending not to stare, and in this particular situation, Meg didn't mind having an audience at all. In fact, the bigger, the better, as far as she was concerned. Her agents were watching, too, and they all looked pretty happy. In fact, she almost wouldn't have recognized them with such big smiles on their faces.

"Can you hit a backhand?" Nancy asked, as she was retrieving a couple of balls up by the net.

"I'm not sure," Meg said. "I don't know where to put my leg."

Nancy frowned, and tried it out for herself, as though her knee had been injured. "You could pivot, I guess, but God, don't stride on the bad one. Just drag the toe a little, maybe."

Meg nodded, and waited until she hit her a backhand, with a room-service hop, and then cautiously pivoted to return it. A one-handed backhand really did feel foreign, and the ball sailed enough so that Nancy had to turn to see where it landed.

"How far out?" Meg asked.

Nancy shook her head. "You caught the corner."

Oh. Really? *Cool.*

They hit for another few minutes, mostly forehands, with some backhands sprinkled in, and she knew she was starting to get very tired—especially when her accuracy began to drop, but she never wanted to stop, even though her good leg was trembling uncontrollably and she came so close to falling once that she had to drop the racket and throw her good hand out to catch herself against the fence.

"Call it quits," Susan said in a low voice, when she limped back to pick up a ball.

Not a chance. Meg shook her head.

"You're *stumbling*, Meg," Susan said, and then paused. "Pack your little bags, and come back and fight another day. Okay?"

Well, she could scarcely question the wisdom of *those* words.

"She's right," Juliana said. "Stop while it's still a victory."

The sad part was that they were making sense. Much as she hated to do it, Meg nodded and made her way up to the net.

"This is completely excellent," she said, "but my stamina really sucks."

Nancy nodded. "I figured. The last few, you started losing the top-spin."

Yeah. It was disappointing, but not as disappointing as having her *good* leg collapse underneath her would be. "Thanks for hitting with me, though," Meg said. "It was—I can't tell you how great it was."

"Anytime," Nancy said.

Even if she didn't mean that, it was kind of her to offer, and Meg nodded. "Thanks." She handed the racket back, resisting the urge to fondle it, first. "Thanks for letting me borrow this, too."

"Well, that other piece of crap," Nancy said, and shuddered.

Yeah.

"Uh, look," Nancy said, as Meg was about to limp away. "It's not really my place to say, but—you were the real thing, weren't you?"

She could be modest—or she could be forthright. "Yeah," Meg said. "I think I was."

Nancy nodded. "I do, too. I mean, I always figured it was hype. Like, let's write up that the First Daughter's a great player to make the President feel good."

The President, who would never have told her that she couldn't play as often as she wanted, but in hindsight, would much rather have seen her expend her energy on academics, or good works, not on a *game*. Meg shrugged, not sure how to answer.

"You could learn to work around having a bad hand," Nancy said, "but not a knee that won't hold you up. Is it going to get better?"

This time, she could either go with honesty, or optimism. Meg shook her head. "No, not really. I don't think I could ever get back to even mediocre club-level." The finality of that was fairly mind-numbing—but, there it was.

And it must be hard to be a strong, uninjured athlete, standing across the net from a prematurely disabled one.

"I guess we would have spent this whole year fighting for the number one ranking," Nancy said, breaking the silence.

Or maybe Nancy would have had to accept the number two rank, graciously, after being soundly vanquished. But, Meg nodded.

Nancy looked at her, not without a touch of competitive fire lurking somewhere in her eyes. "You think you would have beaten me, don't you?"

Yep. Meg shrugged.

Nancy gave her a cocky grin. "Keep telling yourself that, freshman."

In all truth, she probably *would*.

Walking back to the dorm was almost more than she could handle, and she had to stop twice to rest, first on a bench, and then on the Chapin steps. She'd bought a bottle of sports drink from the machine by the courts, so at least she could *pretend* that she was only pausing to quench her thirst, not to prevent herself from toppling over. Tammy had already gone on ahead, and after a while, picking up on the fact that she needed some quiet time to recover, Juliana, Mark, and Andy headed off, too.

Susan sat next to her on the steps, twirling the racket idly.

"Um, Nancy seems nice." Meg said.

Susan nodded.

"You know her pretty well?" Meg asked.

"Sure," Susan said. "We've been in a few of the same classes together."

"Does she want to be a pro?" Meg asked.

Susan shook her head. "No, I think she wants to be a history professor."

When she could possibly play tennis, instead? Jesus. Or it might just be mature. Sensible. All of those good things—which she, alas, had never been. "To be a pro, you pretty much have to start when you're about six, put all your energy into it, and have absolutely nothing else in your life," Meg said.

Susan nodded. "Probably wouldn't leave a lot of time for lying around watching *Meet the Press*."

Or, someday, *being* on *Meet the Press*, now and again.

Which, frankly, held more appeal than showing up on ESPN. Not that lounging on her bed *watching* ESPN wasn't nice, sometimes.

"If I'd been really serious about it," Meg said, "I probably would have been begging my parents to let me go to one of those full-time tennis academies in Florida or something, instead of applying to hard-core colleges."

Susan nodded.

What the hell *had* tennis been for her? A misguided compulsion? A distraction? A hobby? A fantasy? Meg looked at her sports drink, feeling, for some reason, no driving need to finish it right away. "I was probably just going to be a *really* good NCAA-level player. I mean, when you get right down to it, I bet that was the extent of my talent."

"Nothing wrong with that," Susan said.

Wasn't there? But then, she remembered something, and frowned. "I wasn't actually worried about tennis."

Susan looked very alert, without anything in her posture or expression seeming to change.

"When he—um, you know, the kidnapper, the main one—kicked my leg out, I was mad because I wasn't going to be able to *ski* anymore,"

Meg said. Had growled something like that to him, right before he slammed his third, and most painful, kick into the already dislocated joint. "And in the ambulance, and at the hospital, I always asked about skiing, first."

And during her first confused moments after surgery, and at physical therapy, and—Christ, she considered herself a tennis player, but maybe what had really broken her heart was the idea of not being able to ski again. Was there a quantifiable difference between loving tennis—and *adoring* skiing?

The steps were a popular spot on campus, known as Chapin Beach, and people kept walking by, almost all of whom said, "Hi, Susan." After which, some of them would nod at Meg, while others tried to pretend that they hadn't noticed or recognized her. And hell, maybe some of them *hadn't*.

"Would you have tried out for the ski team here?" Susan asked.

Meg shook her head, not even having to think about that one. "Hell, no. Skiing is just—" Fun. And tennis was—work. Work she had loved, but still *work*. "This is strange," she said slowly, "but I never even raced Steven or my mother. Like, one of us might say, 'Bet I can beat you to the bottom!,' and we'd ski down like maniacs, but that wasn't racing, that was—" Fun.

Skiing was fun. One of the only times her family ever *had* fun. Normal, relaxed, noncompetitive fun.

"You looked like you were having a great time out there on the court," Susan said.

No question about that, so Meg nodded. "Yeah, we were just hitting, and I wasn't trying to beat her, so it was—fun." Hmmm.

"Figuring out a way to have fun might be a more manageable goal than trying to be the best player there ever was," Susan said.

No doubt. Although that didn't mean that she didn't want her damn leg back. Meg glanced over at her. "How about you? The having fun part, I mean."

Susan shrugged, and looked away.

Nothing new under the sun. "You can't *always* not answer questions, Susan," Meg said. "It's not fair."

Susan twirled the racket to the left, and then to the right.

"It's a pretty good goal," Meg said. "Having fun."

Susan nodded.

It was quiet, and Meg took a sip of her drink, which tasted fine, considering that it was an off-putting shade of blue.

"Karate is rewarding," Susan said, thoughtfully, "but running is *fun*. A lot of fun. Especially when it's raining."

Susan McAllister, expressing a clear opinion. Sounding *enthusiastic*, even. Of all things.

"Hey," Susan said, "it's a start, right?"

Meg grinned at her. That, it was.

JULIANA AND MARK came wandering back, along with Simon and Harry, and Meg went to the dining hall with all of them, even though her knee was beginning to throb so much that she felt kind of ill. Afterwards, she was in enough pain so that she didn't even consider the idea of venturing down to the Common Room for Sunday Snacks—and neither Susan nor Dirk pushed her to do so, this time.

Her knee had swollen so much that it barely fit inside the brace, so she loosened it, wondering whether she was going to need to ask her agents to take her to the hospital. But, that might mean someone having to carry her, or maybe even being strapped onto a gurney, neither of which held any appeal whatsoever. So, she propped her leg up on a pillow she had folded in half, took two painkillers, and tried to read Plato.

It was just past nine when Jack appeared at her door, very hungover, cranky because the team had placed fourth and barely managed to qualify for the Regionals, limping from his still-balky ankle, and sporting a fat lip, in addition to a bruised nose. The other guy, he assured her, looked much, much worse, and was, he was almost sure, a sheep shagger, to boot.

An insult she had never heard before, but did not really want him to define.

"Hey, are you all right?" he asked, suddenly looking at her.

This might be a good time to try letting him be her boyfriend. "No," she said. "I kind of hurt my knee today, and I might have to cry soon."

He sat on the bed, resting his hand on her stomach. "What happened, did you fall?"

The guy had put his hand on her exactly the same way, more than once, possessively, and suggestively. Some combination of arousal and intimidation. Jack was being possessive, too, but there was also affection there, and concern, and—it wasn't fair to mix up anything happening here with—

"Meg?" Jack said, anxiously.

Jesus, she had to stop drifting off like that. She felt muddled, anyway, since she'd broken down and taken an extra painkiller, about twenty minutes earlier, but that wasn't much of an excuse. "I'm sorry." She shook her head, reminding herself that this was an entirely different person with—as far as she knew—no ulterior motives. "Could you hold my hand, instead?"

"Sure." He took her hand. "Does your stomach hurt?"

It would be so uncomplicated if she just nodded. "The man touched me like that a few times," she said. "And—I'm sorry. I never know when I'm going to have a flashback until I'm actually in the middle of it."

Jack absorbed that, his hand loosening on hers.

"It's not at all your fault," she said quickly. "You're just—" Male.

Fortunately, and unfortunately.

He let go of her hand and changed his position so that he was still on the bed, but sitting much farther away from her.

Damn. She should have lied.

"Do I *act* like him?" he asked.

She shook her head.

"I must," he said. "I've seen you go all pale like that before."

Since she didn't understand it herself, other than the fact that it seemed to happen more often when she was extremely attracted to a person, she couldn't explain it. "Would you think it was funny if you hurt me?" she asked.

He stared at her.

"And then, would you do it *again*, to try and figure out how far you had to go to break me?" she asked. "Sit there enjoying the hell out of it, if you somehow managed to make me cry?"

He got off the bed, looking very sulky. "Jesus, Meg, I put my hand there because your knee is all screwed up, and I wanted to make you feel better."

It was hard to talk to a guy whose feelings were so easily wounded. "I know," she said. "That was, you know, my *point.*"

He shrugged and jammed his Santa Monica cap on his head, turning away as though he might be about to leave. "Did he do more than just touch your stomach?" he asked, keeping his back to her.

Maybe the painkillers were confusing her, but that made no damn sense at all. "Well, yeah," she said, and automatically touched her nose. "Didn't you see the movie?"

Which had aired during February sweeps, and was only the first of three film projects she'd heard about so far. The second one, in fact, was scheduled to be shown in a couple of weeks—May sweeps, this time, and was being told from the point of view of an entirely fictional crack FBI agent, working around the clock to solve the case, trying desperately to find the President's fragile, sheltered daughter before it was too late.

A tale which was bound to be something of a lead balloon, given the fact that the god-damn thing *still* hadn't been solved.

"I did watch it, yeah," he said, facing away from her.

What an ignominious admission. She had been tempted, but made herself keep her television turned off that entire night, although Beth reported to her later that, among other things, the starlet who had been cast in the role had fluttered her eyes constantly and spent a lot of time begging the swarthy, bearded terrorists not to hurt her, and promising that her mother would do anything—*anything*—to get her back alive. Also, her—overdyed—brown hair had remained remarkably clean and tidy throughout the entire ordeal, which Steven—who, much to her horror, had also tuned in—thought was really funny.

The director and screenwriter had both discussed, proudly, in numerous interviews the incredibly comprehensive and detailed research they had done about the kidnapping, the White House, and poor, brave Meghan—which, perhaps, made it all the more puzzling that the terrorists spoke in broken English, and that words like "imperialist" and "infidel" were flung about at will. Beth also told her that there had been a long and unconvincingly poignant late-night scene during which the busty, tremulous actress who was playing the President wept bitterly, and quite loudly, in the Oval Office, *in front of people*, her bee-stung lips quivering the entire time. Her makeup, however, remained gloriously intact, despite the stream of stormy, yet pretty, tears.

"They made it seem like I got raped," she said.

He nodded, not looking at her.

Steven obviously wouldn't have mentioned that, but Beth, after much coaxing, and then a sharp demand or two, had finally conceded that there had been an interlude during which two of the terrorists came into the room where the terrified young girl was artistically tied and gagged on top of a bed, gave her lascivious smiles, and shut the door, as the camera faded to black—and then, cut to a commercial.

And if she had to guess, she would predict that Preston had had to talk her father out of raising hell about that, or maybe even filing a large civil suit.

"I know you think I would, but if you tell me that's what happened, I'm not going to run away," Jack said.

Perhaps he was underestimating her ability to make up a vivid, scary story, then. "It wasn't his style," she said. He had been far more subtle than that.

He glanced at her. "But he touched you."

Yes, and no. "It wasn't that simple," she said. "I mean, okay, I'm sure he would have liked—" Under most circumstances, of course, she didn't mind using the most obvious word to describe what the guy would have done to her, but only as an all-purpose expletive, *never* as a demeaning sexual reference. "—forcing himself on me." But, that wasn't right, either. "Or, no, forcing *me* to—" Closer, but still not there.

Jack's arms were folded, but he seemed more upset than hostile.

"People who throw around the phrase 'mind fuck' have no idea what it's like to *undergo* one," she said finally.

Yeah. That might be as close as she had ever gotten. But, his expression was so strange that she was afraid he might be about to get sick, so she should probably stop now.

And maybe he was kidding himself about not running away, because he sure as hell seemed to be on the verge of doing that, too.

Okay. Enough for one night. "By the way, as far as I know, none of them were Middle Eastern," she said.

Jack turned around now, looking startled. "Really?"

At least there was *one* secret the law-enforcement community had done a good job of keeping—and that the media hadn't managed to ferret out yet. "They were Americans. Spoke perfect English," she said. The minions' version of which had been obscenity-laden, but still grammatically correct. "He looked—I don't know—WASPy." Preppy, even.

Jack sat down in the desk chair, frowning.

No specific information, or physical descriptions, had ever been officially released about the kidnappers, but people had found it remarkably easy to jump to their own conclusions. For her safety, and also to increase the chances of catching the son of a bitch, the White House had never issued any sort of statement to indicate otherwise. Which bothered her, but not quite as much as it probably should.

Her knee hurt. A lot.

"Can I see your hand?" he asked.

What? Where had *that* come from? "I, um, I don't—" She swallowed. "Why?"

"Because you've never let me," he said.

Which was her prerogative, surely.

He got up and sat next to her on the bed. "Either you think I'm going to hurt you, or you don't," he said.

That wasn't playing fair.

She didn't move for a while, but neither did he.

Crap. He wasn't going to let her out of this, was he.

But, Christ, if he *did* hurt her, when her knee was already in bad shape, she would end up in the Emergency Room tonight, after all.

She took as much time as possible unstrapping her splint, raising her right shoulder to block his view—and any sudden moves he might make. Then, she set the splint aside and used her left hand to move her injured one onto her thigh, where it would be supported.

He slid his hand next to hers, palm up. "Can I hold it for a minute?"

No.

"Meg," he said.

She didn't need this. She really didn't. But she picked it up with her left hand, and set it on top of his open hand, blinking in case she was going to burst into anticipatory tears, and trying not to hold her breath.

Then, she waited.

He raised both their hands, so that he could look at hers more closely. He didn't say anything, and she couldn't tell whether it was the artist studying the deformed anatomy, or the boyfriend, who was shaken to see the extent of the damage. The entire time, she could feel her hand trembling—except that it wasn't just *her* hand; he must be petrified, too.

"You probably had the best surgeons in the world," he said.

One of the few fringe benefits of being the President's daughter.

"And they still really couldn't put it back together again," he said.

No. Not even close.

He ran his thumb very gently across some of the scars, and she held her breath. It didn't hurt, exactly, but the sensation made her shiver, anyway.

"Were you scared?" he asked.

She had been *happy*. "Only that enough bones wouldn't break," she said.

He nodded, although she felt his hand tense underneath hers.

They stayed in the same positions, Meg pretty sure that she was going to jump out of her skin.

"You should put the splint back on," he said. "Make sure it's protected."

God, yes. She nodded gratefully, and transferred her hand into it as quickly as she could, not relaxing until all of the straps had been attached, and it was resting on her lap where she could guard herself from anything unexpected.

"Probably shouldn't have put you through that," he said.

Too late now.

Her silence must have seemed more damning than a response, because he was fidgeting, and looked at the door once or twice.

"You know what you could do which would really help a lot?" she asked.

He looked tentatively eager.

She pointed at the warm gel packs resting on top of her knee. "You could try to find me some damn *ice* somewhere."

He was on his feet in about half a second. "You bet," he said confidently. "Can do."

Which struck her as being awfully American, but also charming.

He was gone longer than she expected, but returned lugging three full plastic bags of ice and, much to her delight, a large latte.

"Yeah," he said, nodding, as she reached for the coffee. "Knew you'd go for that, first."

Well, one had to have one's priorities.

When he saw how swollen her knee really was, he tried to talk her into having her agents drive her to the hospital, after all, but she just sipped the latte and enjoyed the luxury of having *lots* of ice to surround her leg, for once, while he fretted about what would be the best way to arrange it, so that she would be as comfortable as possible. By now, the painkillers had her feeling drugged enough so that she didn't hurt as much, and she was able to watch what he was doing with more detachment than interest.

"Is there a way we can make out really intensely without moving my leg?" she asked.

He grinned, and gave her a kiss before turning his attention back to the ice, some of which had melted and was starting to leak onto her quilt. "Probably not, but let me put my little thinking cap on, okay?"

If she found herself in possession of a thinking cap, she would want it to be very, very *big*—but everyone was different.

Whenever they fooled around, her hand had always been something of an impediment, but her knee—even when it wasn't the approximate size of Kentucky—was an outright albatross. There were too many things that it was hard to do, although Jack had such an intuitively accurate sense of the way people's bodies worked, that he was generally good at adjusting their positions without making her feel quite so crippled. In fact, at one point, a few days earlier, he had picked her up and moved over to the desk, which he employed in a way that would never have occurred to her—but, it was a creative, and effective, use of space.

"How'd you hurt it, anyway?" he asked, putting Scotch tape on a hole in one of the plastic bags.

Duct tape might work; Scotch tape wasn't going to do the trick. "I played tennis," she said.

"No, really, what happened?" he asked.

The bag continued to leak, but she was too benevolent to make any remarks about this, or criticize his efforts in any way. "I borrowed Susan's racket, and went over to the courts to try and play with Tammy, but I ended up hitting with this person who's on the tennis team, instead, and it was *great*," she said. "Even though I guess it was a pretty dumb thing to do."

This was enough to distract him from the dripping water. "Wait, you're serious," he said. "You really played *tennis*?"

By some definitions. She shrugged. "Well, I hit forehands for a while, and maybe eight backhands."

He sat back, grinning at her. "That's totally cool, Meg. I'm—I'm *gobsmacked*."

Well, okay. Why not. "Are you chuffed, too?" she asked.

He nodded. "I am. Totally and completely chuffed."

He was often an odd fellow, if sweet. "I have to ask," she said. "Why are you such an Anglophile?"

"Well, I mean, my *mother's* British," he said.

Really? News to her.

"That's the way she talks," he said, "so I guess I do it sometimes, too."

In the photos she had seen, his mother appeared to be just as classically Californian as the rest of his family, so she was going to have to adjust her internal image to fit the new details. "So, that makes you half British," she said.

He looked at her curiously, and maybe glanced at her bottle of pain pills, too. "I don't really think of it that way, but yeah, I guess so."

Was she, just possibly, about to achieve one of her lifelong Holy Grails? "Does that mean you know something about cricket?" she asked.

"Yeah," he said. "My uncles are really into it, so they always have us out there playing when we visit. I'm not the greatest bowler, but I'm a pretty decent batsman."

Ergo, he really *understood* cricket—and she was on the verge of a great personal victory. "Can you explain it to me?" she asked. "In depth?"

He laughed. "Sure," he said.

Yay!

WHEN SHE WENT to physical therapy the next afternoon, Vicky was pleased that she had attempted something bold, but disturbed by the degree to which her knee had continued to swell overnight. Orthopedists were promptly summoned, and she ended up back inside her home away from home, the MRI machine, as well as having a creepily large amount of fluid aspirated from the joint. There didn't seem to be any new ligament tears, but she had to sit through three different lectures about why she needed to be more careful, and what she had to do in order to maximize her chances for healing. Her lone accomplishment of the afternoon was convincing them *not* to call her parents.

Except that when she got back to the dorm, there were two messages from her father, and one from her mother, so while the doctors might not have talked to her parents directly, they had apparently had no qualms when it came to alerting Dr. Brooks about this latest damn setback.

When she caught him between appearances, she told her father, several times, that she was fine, and that he definitely didn't have to rush off and get on a plane, and once she and her mother finally spoke, she gave her the same assurances, although her feelings got hurt when her mother immediately suggested that maybe her father should fly up, as opposed to offering to come herself.

Not that she wanted either of them to race to her side because of her—admittedly extreme—version of a garden-variety sprain, but it might have been nice if her mother had barely been able to restrain herself from doing so.

Regardless, she changed the subject, and answered questions about her classes, and whether she was eating enough, and how she was sleeping, and that sort of thing, instead.

Right before they hung up, her mother coughed.

"I hesitate to bring this up, but did you grope your strikingly handsome wealthy blond Republican boyfriend at a crowded party, to the shock of nearby onlookers?" she asked.

Ouch. More merry fun for the tabloids, it would seem. And she was pretty sure exactly which party it must have been, since they maybe *had* been a tad indiscreet at a beer-sodden brawl some of the guys on the Ultimate team had thrown one night. "You know, someone on your staff has way too much free time," Meg said.

"I happen to agree, and shared that opinion with him quite strongly," her mother said, "but I'm still not hearing the outraged and offended denial I'm expecting."

She was going to have a long wait for *that* one. Meg tried to think of a reasonably adroit way out of this. "I wouldn't say they were shocked, exactly." Or that more than a couple of people had even noticed. Although someone had apparently felt the need to report it, and probably got paid a chunk of change for doing so, which posed a significant security breach to consider. "I mean, most of them were pretty drunk, and— " No. That was an unfortunate detour. "Juliana said she was maybe a little taken aback."

There was a long silence on the other end.

"I might be wrong," her mother said, "but from what you've told me about her, I would think that it takes a great deal to startle Juliana."

Yeah.

Her mother sighed. "I don't want to tell you what to do—"

But.

"But," her mother went on, "would it be too much to ask for you to confine yourself to groping him when the two of you are alone together?"

A far less demanding request than she would have predicted. "Okay," Meg said. "I can do that." No point in mentioning that he'd mostly been groping *her*, not the other way around.

There was more silence.

"Would you be upset if we didn't pursue this conversational thread any further?" her mother asked.

Delighted would be a better description. "Not in the slightest," Meg said.

SHE DID HER best to take it easy, but every time she put any weight on her leg, her knee seemed to puff right up again. On Wednesday, she considered skipping physical therapy altogether, because she really didn't feel like having a surgeon stick a huge needle into her joint again, while other doctors hovered around with strained expressions. But if she didn't go, her father and Dr. Brooks would probably jump on a plane, so she was going to have to haul herself down there.

As a result, she was in a pretty foul mood, and also really tired. She napped in the car on the way, and Paula had to wake her up once they arrived, so she felt sluggish and logy before the appointments even started.

Afterwards, she was all the more exhausted, and it took a great effort to put on a big smile and pose for a photo when some people stopped her in the main lobby as she was trying to leave. But, the man's son was on crutches, and she would have been a complete jerk if she said no, so she did her best to look enchanted by the opportunity to have her picture taken yet another time with a total stranger.

Then, once she stepped outside, a grey-haired woman wearing a beige raincoat approached her, holding an envelope and what looked like a Raggedy Ann doll. It could also probably be a Raggedy Andy—she really wasn't up on her dolls. As far as she was concerned, they were all sort of spooky-looking, and best avoided whenever possible.

"Would you mind signing this for my granddaughter?" the woman asked, indicating the card inside the envelope.

God-damn it, she felt too lousy to be friendly and polite. Nevertheless, Meg smiled as though nothing would please her more, and accepted the pen she was holding out. "Sure. What's her name?"

"Gladys," the woman said.

Hmmm. Either she was even more sleepy than she thought, or that was a hard one to spell. "Um, okay," Meg said. "That's G, L—?"

"—A, D, Y, S," the woman said.

Right. Okay. Meg nodded, trying to repeat the letters silently to herself, since she would look like an imbecile if she had to ask twice. "Thanks. As you can see, I've been getting a *really* good education."

The woman smiled widely, although there seemed to be a bit of a disconnect there, somehow.

But, okay. Whatever. Maybe she really *wasn't* as damned funny as she thought she was. Meg balanced the "Get Well" card on her right arm, above her splint, and tried to sign it as neatly as possible.

"Your mother kills babies," the woman said, still smiling away.

For a second or two, Meg couldn't quite process that, but just as she realized that there was something very wrong, the woman was already reaching into her raincoat pocket, yanking out something metal, and lunging towards her.

She tried to leap back out of the way, but her knee buckled, and as she fell, she was aware of movement and noise all around her. She heard a strange hissing sound and then, a lot of shouting and swearing—followed by a gunshot somewhere close to her head. Or, maybe, more than one. There seemed to be a red mist in the air, and—Jesus Christ, it was happening again. How could this be happening again?

Oh, God.

Oh, no.

Oh, help.

52

THE GREY-HAIRED woman seemed to be screaming louder than anyone—hatred and anger and blood and death—and Meg tried to get up, or at least scramble away from her, but then, suddenly, hands were grabbing and lifting her off the ground—except that she god-damned well wasn't going to go without a fight this time. No fucking way were they going to get her twice, not a single chance in—and Christ, there were people *everywhere*, standing and staring and—

"Get down!" she yelled. "They have guns!"

More hands were grabbing her now, and she was being propelled backwards—to another van? A truck? Maybe just a car, this time? Oh, God, there was no way she could do this again. Not a single chance in hell.

"Don't fight with your bad hand, Meg," a voice said harshly in her ear. "*Protect* it."

Garth. Christ almighty, they had managed to buy off *Garth*? And Kyle, and Jose, and *Paula*? At first, the concept of that was so terrifying and overwhelming, that she couldn't move at all, but then she started fighting twice as hard, swearing and struggling and trying to punch her way free.

Doors. Glass. Bright lights. A hallway. A room. A desk, with a woman ducking down behind it, her eyes terrified.

They were going to bring an innocent civilian into it, too? *Bastards*. They were unbelievable, cowardly, bastards. She fumbled around on the desktop, trying to find something—anything—she might be able to use as a weapon. She was going to do some *damage* this time, serious damage, even if—Garth still had his gun in one hand, and was speaking into his wrist receiver, as he did a full visual sweep of the room, and there seemed to be lots of people out in the hall and just inside the door, also holding guns.

"Get her pants off!" someone was yelling. "*Fast*."

"That's a lot of blood," someone else said, sounding scared, while a third voice shouted, "Is it *hers*? Where's she hit?"

There were hands on her legs, pulling at her sweatpants, and she heard a jumble of urgent conversation with scattered words like "acid" and "corrosive" and "butyric," and a male voice was saying, "No, no, it doesn't smell right," while another man said, "Jesus, we've got to stop the bleeding, someone get some pressure on her." There were too many people speaking for her to focus on what the hell they were talking about, and her ears were ringing for some reason, which made it hard for her to hear clearly, but when she felt her sweatpants being ripped down past her hips, and someone else tugging at her shirt, she twisted away from them, kicking out with her good leg, hearing a grunt when she connected.

The door to the hall was blocked, but maybe there was another door, or a window, or—

"It's *not* blood!" someone yelled. "Okay? Get on the damn perimeter!"

Was that Garth? It sounded like Garth.

A male hand ran across her bare thigh, and she kicked at whoever the person was, yanked her sweatpants back up, then stumbled over to the desk, still looking for a weapon.

"I said, back off!" the same man ordered. "I want this whole place contained!"

She grabbed the sharpest object she saw, then spun around on her good leg, ready to defend herself. But, the room seemed to be clearing out, although the hallway was crowded, and there was still a lot of shouting. Dave and Jose were posted on either side of the door, with their guns, and the only other man in the room was Garth.

Meg stared at him. "Are you kidnapping me?"

Garth looked startled, then shook his head, spitting sharp orders into his wrist receiver.

But she still seemed to be trapped in an unfamiliar place. Isolated. In danger. "Am I a hostage?" she asked.

"*No*," he said.

Christ, did that mean they were just going to kill her? Some sort of savage, public execution, and—except he was still giving a long string of commands, and—what the hell was happening here? She shook her head to try and make the ringing in her ears stop. "Don't!" she said, as the woman behind the desk started to stand up. "It's not safe!"

The woman looked at her uncertainly, then crouched down again.

"Put that back, Meg, okay?" Garth said. "You're not going to need it. I promise."

Meg looked, stupidly, at her good hand and saw a stainless steel letter opener clenched in her fist.

"Meg," he said, and reached out to take it from her.

She gripped the handle more tightly. "What are you going to do to me?"

For the first time, he really *looked* at her. "Nothing, sweetie," he said, and reholstered his weapon, his voice very gentle. "Take it easy, okay? You're going to be fine."

Out in the hall, she could still hear a lot of commotion, and words like "secure" and "police" and her code name and such. Normal Secret Service stuff.

The desk. She was in an office. A *stranger's* office. A very frightened and confused middle-aged stranger. She stared down at the letter opener, trying to remember where she had gotten it.

"You aren't kidnapping me?" she asked again, just to be sure.

Garth shook his head.

Oh. She tried to stick the letter opener into a mug full of pens and pencils, but her hand must have been shaking, because instead, she knocked the whole thing over, which was loud enough to hurt her ears, and the woman behind the desk cringed away from the sound. Garth might have ducked, too. She tried to pick the pens up, but couldn't seem to control her good hand well enough to keep from dropping them again.

Her heart was beating crazily, and she thought she might be having an attack, but then she saw that her legs and torso seemed to be covered with bright red sticky liquid, and the room went grey for a minute.

"*Yes,* I want a doctor," Garth said to someone in the hall. "How many damn times do I have to tell you I want a doctor in here?"

The blood had a strong, familiar smell—a sickening smell—and she realized that she must have been shot, that—

"It's only paint, Meg," Garth said. "You're okay."

Paint? But she smelled chemicals. She was sure she smelled chemicals. Jesus, were they burning her skin? She felt her stomach, and then her legs, but everything seemed to be—maybe she was—

"I'd like to check you over, if that's okay, Miss Powers," a man said.

A man she had never seen before. Dark, thinning hair, a neatly-trimmed mustache, maybe in his forties. She shook her head, taking a couple of backwards hops on her good leg, moving to keep the desk in-between them.

"I'm Doctor—" he started.

"Nope," she said abruptly. "Sorry."

He looked confused.

"I don't know you," she said. "Please leave, sir."

He glanced over at Garth for guidance.

"Please leave *right now*, sir," Meg said. Which was maybe the only good idea she'd had all afternoon. "Garth, I need some privacy, okay?"

"Well," he said, "I'd feel better if a doctor—"

She shook her head. "It wasn't really a request, Garth."

He frowned at her for a minute, and then nodded.

She indicated the telephone on the desk. "Is this secure?"

"More so than most," he said.

If this was a predesignated fallback room, then that's the sort of detail which would have been handled long ago. She hoped. At least it was a land-line, not a cell. "Okay, thank you." Jesus, if they didn't all leave her alone *very soon*, she might scream. Or hit someone. She turned to the still-unidentified woman who was standing nearby. "Would it be all right if I borrowed your office for just a few more minutes? I need to make a phone call."

When the woman nodded, Meg looked around for her cane—which seemed to be long gone, and so, had to use the desk to support herself as she moved to sit down in the office chair.

Her heart was pounding away, and she wasn't sure she was going to be able to stand it if they all didn't just *go* already.

When she was finally alone, with the door closed, Garth and God only knew who else posted out in the still-frantic corridor, she picked up the phone and tried to dial, but it didn't work for some reason. She set down the receiver, stared at it, and then felt around for her satellite phone, which also seemed to be missing.

Swell. Just fucking swell.

She wasn't about to ask anyone to come back in and help her, so she slouched forward with her head on her good arm, trying to think. Trying *not* to cry.

The way her heart was beating was genuinely alarming, and she felt her chest, worried that maybe she had been shot, after all. But, as far as she could tell, there were no open wounds, although there *did* seem to be something wrong with her heart. Something bad.

Fuck. And double-fuck.

She looked at the phone again, and then remembered the concept of dialing nine to get an outside line. So she tried that, and this time, the call went through. It only took a minute or so for her to get connected to the communications director, although her heart did more crazy jumping around the entire time.

"I'm sorry to bother you," she said, when he came on.

"No bother," Preston said, although she could hear a buzz of people in his office, and the sound of more than one television newscast in the background.

"Is it okay if I talk to you for a minute?" she asked, and checked to make sure that the door was still shut and no one could hear her. "I'm scared."

There was a barest of pauses on the other end.

"Absolutely," he said, and then raised his voice. "We'll have to finish this up later, okay, everyone? And—no calls for a while, Janice. Thanks."

Meg waited, aware that she was holding her breath—and probably shouldn't be.

"Are you all right?" he asked, when he came back on. "Are you hurt?"

Two tough questions. *Christ*, impossible questions.

"Meg?" he asked, sounding tense.

"Are Mom and Dad back yet?" she asked. It had been Kansas City today, or St. Louis, or Houston, maybe. She couldn't remember.

"About twenty minutes ago," Preston said. "What's going on?"

She took a deep breath. "I'm not really hurt, but Mr. Gabler's either already in there, or on his way over to talk to her."

There was another short pause on the other end. "Tell me again that you're all right," he said, "and then tell me what happened."

She should be calm. Cool. *Succinct.* "I don't know what happened," she said. "I don't—nothing makes sense."

"Okay," he said, his voice very soothing. "Tell me where you are."

Jesus, where was she? She looked around the office. "I don't know."

"Okay," he said, although she could hear a strong edge of anxiety in his voice now. "That's okay. Is anyone else there with you?"

"No," she said. Only, that wasn't quite right. "I mean, they're all out in the hall. We're at the hospital."

"Are you *hurt*?" he asked.

Oh, Christ, the poor guy. She laughed weakly. "Am I going to make you crazy if I say 'I don't know?' "

"Yes," he said. "You are."

Right.

"Why don't we get your father on here," he said. "Okay?"

Yeah, God forbid anyone ask the *President* to pick up the phone in the middle of the day. "What, you don't think my mother would want to talk to me?" Meg asked.

"I think she may need a couple of minutes to calm down, first," Preston said, and then laughed a laugh even more shaky than hers had been. "Might take thirty seconds myself, too."

Now she felt guilty for upsetting him, but relieved that it *mattered* to him.

"I'm all right," she said, when her father came on, and heard him let out a very long breath.

"They told me you were, but—" He stopped. "Okay. Thank God." He stopped again, presumably taking thirty seconds of his own. "What's happening? The only thing I've gotten so far is a 'Shots fired' report."

The Secret Service wasn't exactly quick off of the starting blocks, then, were they? She remembered that it had been just past four-thirty after she had finished letting that man take her picture with his son, and she glanced at a clock on the wall, shocked to see that it wasn't quite quarter to five yet. She would have said that a couple of hours had gone by. "I don't know," she said aloud. "I was signing a 'Get Well' card for this lady, but then she came after me, and—I don't know." She had heard at least one gunshot, though; she was *sure* of that.

They had barely started talking when her mother clicked on.

"Are you hurt, Meg?" she asked, sounding as though Preston either hadn't gotten down there in time—or that nothing he'd told her had had any effect whatsoever. "You didn't get cut, did you?"

Cut? What the hell kind of information sources did the President have? "She threw *paint* at me, Mom," Meg said, more than moderately annoyed.

"Actually, my understanding is that there was a can of red spray paint inside her horrid little doll," her mother said.

Oh. That explained the hissing sound. "I think she had a gun, too," Meg said, although she was increasingly less sure of anything at all.

"No, that was one of your agents bringing her down," her mother said. "And one of the others got the knife away from her."

Knife? What fucking knife? How come she had *been* there—and her mother was the one who knew all of the correct details? "Did they, um, you know, kill her?" Meg asked.

"No," her mother said, and Meg heard the unspoken "unfortunately." "I gather it's a leg wound, or—I'm not entirely sure."

The President, expressing *doubt*? Any foreign intelligence agents who were currently listening in had probably just fallen off their chairs. But Meg still felt as though she was about ten minutes behind. "So, wait. You hate dolls?"

There was a split second of utter silence.

"*What?*" her mother asked.

Maybe she, personally, had no problem with dolls whatsoever, but had been raised—more or less—by someone who *despised* them, and had ended up absorbing the prejudice by osmosis.

"I really don't know what you're talking about," her mother said, "but my God, Meg, exactly what is it going to take for you to figure out that you simply *can't* stop in transit? Ever."

Wait, she was being blamed, because a lunatic assaulted her?

"You don't have a lot of credibility there, Kate," her father said grimly.

He was god-damn right about *that*. "Yeah, really," Meg said. "I'm not the one who went prancing over to a mob of Edinburgh hooligans last week."

The sound of the long-distance connection seemed acutely loud—or else, her stupid ears were still screwed up.

"Well, that's neither here nor there," her mother said in a stiff voice. "We're talking about *you* right now, and the fact that you have to grow up and start being more careful."

Like any of this was her fault? *Any* of it? And since when did being attacked by crazy people translate to a lack of maturity? Meg thought of about a dozen mean responses to hurl back at her, but couldn't decide which one would be the most effectively vindictive. And, ideally, hurtful.

"In any case," her mother said, "we're going to fly up tonight and bring you back."

The hell they were. Meg gripped the phone, wondering whether she should just slam it down. "Yeah, well, good luck with that, because I'm not coming."

"Yeah, well," her mother said, hitting her inflections with insulting accuracy, "guess what? *You* don't have a vote here."

Fuck her, and her horses. "I'm eighteen," Meg said. "I not only have a vote, I have the deciding one. All you've got is an *opinion*." And a stupid one, at that.

Her mother expelled a hard breath. "Well, I'm afraid that you're very much mistaken about that, Meg. In fact—"

"All right," her father said, sounding furious. "That's enough. I think you'd better hang up now, and count to ten—or do whatever the hell it is that you do—before we continue this conversation."

It was very quiet. Excruciatingly quiet.

"Um, Dad, are you talking to Mom, or me?" Meg asked.

Her father laughed. "I'm talking to your mother, Meg."

There was more silence, and she assumed that her mother's mood was rapidly moving from violent simmering to outright boiling-over.

"Are you really okay?" her mother asked quietly.

"I don't know," Meg said. Her heart still felt funny, and she was bruised everywhere, and her hand was throbbing horribly, and it was hard to hear, and— "I was scared."

"Well, I'm scared, too," her mother said, and took a deep breath. "I'm very sorry to have gotten so upset. I didn't mean to yell at you."

Apology accepted. Meg nodded. "Okay. But I really want to stay here. At school, I mean."

Her mother sighed. "Yes, I can appreciate that. But, your father and I are going to need to come up to see you, and—I don't know—hug you, or something of that nature."

A not entirely unappealing concept. "You can't blow off the Cinco de Mayo dinner," Meg said. Which was scheduled to be held that night, and would garner a fair amount of press coverage—especially if the President didn't bother showing up.

"Well, as it happens, I *can*," her mother said. "Especially under the circumstances."

It still seemed like a bad idea. Meg frowned. "But, doesn't that mean Psycho Lady gets what she wants?"

Once again, it was quiet.

"Not letting them run our lives is another way of letting them run our lives," her mother said.

Hmmm. Was that circular logic, or a good argument?

"We're your parents, Meg," her father said. "And we love you, and—give us a little room to work here, okay?"

Yes, that was only fair. "I just—if you come racing up here, won't it embolden more nuts, and make them think it's open season on me?" she asked.

Neither of her parents responded.

Oh. Right. It was *already* open season on her.

"I think we're all too upset to think clearly right now," her mother said finally. "But what I'd like to have happen first is to have a doctor look you over, and make sure you're all right. And then, the three of us can talk some more, and decide what we want to do next. Okay?"

Since that seemed like a good strategy, neither she nor her father disagreed, and she promised to call back as soon as she had been examined. She was pretty sure her father would have preferred keeping the line open the entire time, but she needed a little space to decompress, and she was *sure* her mother needed some.

And there was also the minor detail of her Cabinet meeting having been interrupted.

No female FBI agents had arrived from the nearest field office yet, but a female police officer, as well as a woman from the local district attorney's office, stayed in the room to maintain the chain of custody and collect her paint-stained clothes and surgical brace for evidence. Meg thought about refusing, but someone had the sense to go find Vicky, who stood by the examining table with her hand on her shoulder, and that made her feel somewhat more safe. And while two of the three doctors were male, at least she had met all of them before.

She was afraid to admit that she had been worried about the way her heart was beating, but they listened to her chest with a stethoscope and took her blood pressure, without her having to ask, and when she was offered a small dose of Valium, she didn't turn it down.

Her knee had *already* been banged up from the tennis-induced sprain, and the two orthopedists didn't think it seemed much worse, but all three doctors were very concerned about a new displaced boxer's fracture of the fifth metacarpal on her bad hand, as well as a large crack in her fourth proximal phalange—she sort of remembered slamming into something very hard, like a *wall*, when she was trying to punch her way free—and her wrist seemed to be swollen, too. The X-rays and so forth were being faxed or emailed or something to her Washington doctors, and they all seemed to agree that after a closed reduction was performed, she should be put in a cast to immobilize the area completely and protect it, until more studies were done, and then they would decide whether to continue to treat it conservatively, do a more complex form of closed reduction, or resort to an open reduction with internal fixation or some other surgical correction.

It had started to improve somewhat, but she told them about the ringing in her ears, and an ENT was immediately brought in. Apparently, it was a normal auditory response when a gun was fired *right next to a person's damn head,* and the specialist didn't think she'd sustained any permanent hearing damage, although—big surprise—she was going to have to undergo some comprehensive tests, to be sure.

There was a land-line in the room, and her parents called several times during all of this. Increasingly, her father was the one making short-tempered "we could already *be* there by now" remarks, while her mother said evenhanded, reasonable things, and tried to keep the peace.

Obviously, they meant well, but the constant phone calls were very stressful, and she could feel her own temper fraying. She'd lost all track of time but surely the Cinco de Mayo dinner had started by now. "What, do you guys keep running out of the room?" she asked. "Aren't your guests starting to get upset?"

"In all honesty, should it come to that, I feel strangely sanguine about the prospects of our winning a war against Mexico," her mother said, and then paused. "Are we on speaker-phone?"

Christ, that would be all they needed. But, even if they had been, the doctors were busy conferring in the corner, and Vicky had gone out to find her a snack. "No," Meg said.

"Ah. Good," her mother said. "It would have been unfortunate if someone had overheard that."

No question. But the fact that she had spoken without weighing the possibilities first indicated that her mother's energy was flagging, too. Meg shook her head. "You'd better go drink some coffee, Mom." Either that, or risk mis-speaking her way into an international incident.

"Yes, you may have a point," her mother said. "Russ, she's right about people being offended, too. Would you mind going back out there for a while, and we'll take turns?"

An idea her father did not adore, but he agreed, and then, for the first time since all of this had started, she was alone on the phone with her mother.

"All right, it's just the two of us now," her mother said softly. "Tell me what you really want us to do."

Because they both knew that she wouldn't feel comfortable being quite as brutally honest if her father was still on the line. Meg gritted her teeth. "Mostly, I want you to *know* what I want you to do, without me having to walk you through it."

Her mother didn't quite groan, but she didn't seem pleased, either. "Okay. I assume you want us to drop everything and come up there, but you're so wrung out that you'd like to get some sleep first."

Not bad. "Very close," Meg said.

"Do you want us to come up tonight, then?" her mother asked.

"Very *far*," Meg said.

Her mother made an exasperated sound. "Meg, I'm going to feel like a perfect fool if you make me stand here and guess."

Tough.

"I really don't—" Then, her mother's voice changed, the annoyance instantly departing. "Yes. Just put it on the desk, please."

Someone on the other end said something unintelligible.

"No, black is fine, thank you," her mother said.

Coffee, then.

"All right," her mother said, back on the telephone. "Presumably, you want *me* to drop everything and fly up first thing in the morning."

Bull's-eye. "Yeah," Meg said. "And then, Dad can come in a few days, after you both go to the Correspondents' Dinner—" which was scheduled for Saturday night— "and are funny as hell there, to prove nothing's wrong, and that way, I'll get two visits, without it seeming like such a big deal."

Her mother sighed. "I really wouldn't mind if you were a little less of a politico, Meg."

When it was all said and done, what was wrong with being a politico, as long as one tried to serve the public interest? "He's been here twice," Meg said, "and you've never come to see me."

Not that she was pissed off about that, or anything.

Her mother seemed to be weighing her answer—unless, of course, she had just paused to gulp some coffee. "Are you sure that's what you want?" she asked.

"*Very* sure," Meg said.

53

BY THE TIME the doctors released her, Garth had arranged for her to be taken out through a back exit, to avoid what she gathered was a good-sized crowd. She had no idea whether that meant primarily civilians—or mostly the media, but she wasn't interested enough to ask. Vicky had found a pair of clean sweatpants and a Mount Greylock Mounties t-shirt somewhere, so she changed out of her hospital gown and wore those, along with her brand-new, paint-free brace and cane.

She would have preferred to put on her sunglasses, but they—goddamn it—had disappeared during all of the confusion, too. Security was extremely tight as she was hustled outside, and while she had the sense that lots of people were around, all she could really see were agents and police officers.

Once they were in the car, surrounded by extra lead and follow vehicles, she found her satellite phone near the seat belt, and thought about checking her messages, but set it aside, instead. She was too damn tired to bother.

She started to close her eyes, but then forced them back open. "Thank you," she said. "I can't remember if I told you guys that, but I should have."

Dave, who was driving, and Garth, who was in the passenger's seat, both shrugged, but Dave looked pleased. Garth seemed too edgy and focused to tune into much of anything other than the goal of getting her back to her dorm, and safely inside her room.

There was also a chance that he was as embarrassed about the whole letter opener business as she was.

"Is everyone okay?" she asked. Another thing which hadn't even entered her mind until now—and certainly should have.

Dave started to say something, but Garth interrupted him.

"We're all fine," he said. "I'm sorry we had to manhandle you that way."

She never wanted to know who had had his hand on her thigh, even though intellectually, she knew it had been with the sole purpose of checking her for injuries. "It's okay. I didn't mean to get so scared."

Garth laughed without any humor whatsoever. "You *should* have been scared. We didn't—well, I'm really sorry."

If he was already second-guessing himself to such a degree, she could only imagine what the formal debriefing meetings were going to be like. But something about the way Dave was stolidly looking straight ahead made her suspicious. "Are all of you really okay?" she asked.

"Yes," Garth said.

Somehow, she didn't believe him.

"Paula took a few stitches," he said. "But she's fine. She'll be on light duty for a few days."

Stitches? Realizing what that meant, she felt even more exhausted. "She grabbed the knife, then."

Garth and David nodded.

"But, she's okay," Meg said.

They nodded.

God, she hoped so. She didn't really want to hear the answer to this, but— "How big was it?"

It was obvious that Dave wasn't going to answer, and Garth looked reluctant, too.

"About ten inches," he said finally. "It was a hunting knife."

Jesus. A knife that big would have gone—well—pretty far inside her body. Could easily have *killed* her. Ripped her organs apart. She touched her stomach and lower rib cage, wondering what it would have felt like to have someone—Jesus. Time to think about something else. "Was she lying about the granddaughter?" she asked.

"No. It was even the right name. That's why we—" Garth shook his head. "I'm sorry. We thought we'd checked her out sufficiently."

But they were stuck with a protectee who was dumb enough to respond whenever anyone so much as waved or said hello. "She didn't exactly fit the assassin profile," Meg said.

"No," Garth conceded.

Because nice grandmother ladies weren't supposed to have any interest in doing things like murdering people.

"That damn raincoat," he said. "I should have—I'm sorry."

A raincoat, on a sunny day. "I'm not supposed to stop in transit," Meg said. As her mother had so pointedly reminded her.

Garth turned around to look at her. "You're eighteen years old, Meg. What you're not supposed to have to do is *think* about things like that."

It would be nice, yeah. "Who shot her?" she asked.

"Kyle," he said.

Which made sense, since he probably had the quickest reactions of anyone on her detail. Meg brought her left hand up to her ear, which was still ringing faintly. "Is she going to be all right?"

Garth nodded.

"Is *Kyle* all right?" she asked.

Again, he nodded.

She really had no choice right now, but to believe him, so she nodded, too. For the time being, that was more than enough specific details, and she closed her eyes.

She had anticipated that the police presence—and press contingent—near her dorm would both be very large, and she was correct. Although it was highly unlikely that any of them were even aware that the President herself would be appearing within a matter of hours.

"Please don't talk to them," Garth said. "Okay?"

Would that it were that easy. She used her good hand to straighten her hair, wishing that she were the kind of person who routinely thought to carry around a brush and comb.

"Meg?" Garth said, more insistently.

She shook her head, taking off her new sling and tucking it into the pocket of her sweatpants. With luck, no one would notice that she now had a cast, instead of her splint. "She needs to know that she accomplished absolutely *nothing*. I'll be quick, though."

He didn't like it, but started transmitting an efficient set of instructions about where he wanted people to deploy, as Jose came over and opened the door.

Knowing that the cameras would be on her from the first second she stepped out of the car, she reminded herself to be as controlled as possible, and mentally tried to prepare her eyes for the barrage of flashes which were about to hit them.

There was more than enough security to keep the press from getting any close physical access, but she walked over in their general direction, noticing that her knee was even more swollen and painful than it had been earlier.

"Did someone in the dorm do something notable?" she asked, and a few of the people laughed.

A lot of questions came at her at once, but she would be okay as long as she remembered that she could hear what she wanted to hear, and answer what she wanted to answer. Mostly, of course, they all wanted to know how she felt about someone trying, and failing, to kill her. Again.

"Well," she said, with enough of a drawl to give them all time to shut up and listen. "All I have to say, is that performance art just isn't what it used to be."

There were more laughs, but most of them sounded uneasy.

"Anyway," she said. "I have a paper due tomorrow—" which was, alas, true— "so I'd better hustle inside and get to work. Have a good night, everyone, okay?"

They were still asking questions, but she nodded at them in a friendly way and headed for the entry door, giving herself an A for striking the right, lighthearted tone, and a C+ for the quality of the humor.

Once she was inside, she put her sling back on, and leaned against the wall, trying to gather enough energy to go upstairs. The main checkpoint was very crowded, with a mix of Secret Service and FBI agents, and she assumed that Mr. Gabler was already on his way up from Washington, and they were all trying to get ready for him.

And, of course, the President.

"Are Paula and Kyle here?" she asked Garth.

He shook his head. "I don't think they'll be back for a few more hours."

Meaning that she wasn't going to be able to thank them personally any time soon, then.

When she got off the elevator, Mary Elizabeth, who was just coming out of the bathroom, saw her first.

"Of all the dorms, in all the towns, in all the world," she said.

Well, that was *sort* of like saying hello. Meg nodded. "Hi."

"Look who's back," Mary Elizabeth said, more loudly.

Juliana rushed out to the hall, looking very tense, and some of the guys from the second floor came up to see what was going on.

"I guess you heard what happened," Meg said.

They all looked at her as though she was an absolute idiot.

"Has it been on the news?" she asked.

"This really small local access station maybe kind of *mentioned* it," Andy said, and most of the guys laughed.

More people were coming out, including Tammy, Debbie, Natalie, and Jesslyn. She could also see Dirk, and Susan, and three more guys on their way up. The sound of all the cars outside when she and her small army got back, and the sudden flashing of cameras and television lights, would have to have been pretty obvious to anyone in the dorm, especially people whose windows faced the street.

"I'm really sorry about all of the commotion," she said. And now, just to be *sure* they were all upset about having the campus being taken over— "But, it's going to be worse tomorrow, because, um, my mother's coming up here."

There was such a mix of expressions that she couldn't interpret the general reaction to that.

"She won't be staying all that long," Meg said. "She just—" Hmmm.

"Wants to see you," Mary Elizabeth said.

Yes. That was a good description, of a rather conventional situation, so Meg nodded.

Everyone hung around in the stairwell for a while, asking her "so, you're okay, right?" kinds of questions, and it was a relief when they gradually started drifting off to go back to whatever they had been doing, leaving her alone with Juliana, Mary Elizabeth, and—nominally—Susan, who was leaning against the banister, about half a flight below them.

"Have you seen Jack yet?" Juliana asked. "He's been by here about three times."

Oh, damn. *Jack*. She hadn't thought to call him, or Beth, or—oops. Christ, she hadn't even talked to her brothers yet.

"What happened to your hand?" Mary Elizabeth asked.

Right. The cast. Meg shrugged. "I kind of broke it in one place, and cracked it in another." News her parents had not been thrilled to hear. "Or the metacarpal was maybe *already* broken, and I've been walking around with it." News which had displeased her parents all the more.

"Already broken," Susan said.

"I don't know," Meg said defensively. "It always hurts, so it's hard to—I don't know." Not that it mattered, since broken was broken, regardless of when it had taken place.

Susan nodded. "Just a detail, right?"

Well—yeah. If she wanted to put it that way.

"Do you need anything?" Susan asked, retreating down a few more steps, away from them.

With body language like *that*? Meg shook her head.

"Well, if you do," Susan said, and went down to the second floor.

Meg frowned. "What's wrong with her? Is she worried about the reporters? Because, after tomorrow, they won't be sticking around."

"God, you're a cretin, Meg," Juliana said.

Probably, but that didn't explain why Susan had seemed so—cold. Distant. Unfriendly. "Is she okay?" Meg asked. "I mean, is she sick or something?"

Juliana and Mary Elizabeth exchanged glances.

"You called it right," Mary Elizabeth said. "Complete cretin."

Juliana nodded.

Yeah, fine, whatever. She was incredibly stiff and achy and wanted to go lie down, but sat on the steps and took out her phone to call Jack and let him know that she was back now.

Juliana sat next to her. "Nobody likes it when their friends almost get killed," she said, "but maybe it bothers Susan more than other people."

Oh. Meg paused, not hitting the automatic-dial button.

Mary Elizabeth took a seat on her other side. "The films are really bad. It looked—well, they're upsetting."

"Films, as in plural?" Meg asked.

Juliana and Mary Elizabeth nodded.

She had no recollection of any reporters being there, not even a stringer or a paparazzo. "I didn't see anyone taking pictures."

"I guess there were people with cell phones or digital cameras or something," Juliana said. "One of them got pretty good video, and the sounds were really clear on the other one."

So, if she had behaved like a coward—which she suspected was what had happened—it was going to be very hard to erase the image from people's minds.

"Did she think you were there for an abortion?" Juliana asked.

Maybe. But, three times a week, *every* week? Meg shrugged. "I don't know. Was that what she was saying?"

"It was hard to hear, with all of the other noise," Mary Elizabeth said. "But she seemed to be going on about dead babies."

And what better way to demonstrate one's reverence for life than to try and stab someone? She stared down at the cast, which was still only partially dry. She was supposed to be very careful of it, and keep her hand elevated as much as possible, although mainly, she just wanted to lie down and take another Valium—they had sent her home with five more pills. "I must have looked like I was in hysterics," she said, dreading having them agree.

"A lot of it was all jumpy and out of focus, but as far as I could tell, you looked pissed off," Juliana said. "And you definitely *sounded* pissed."

Oh, no. Meg glanced at her. "I didn't swear, did I?"

Juliana thought. "Maybe 'god-damn it.' Mostly, it seemed like you were yelling for people to get down."

She remembered telling the woman in her office to stay down, but that was all. "I was probably trying to get my agents to *put* me down."

Mary Elizabeth shook her head. "No, you were pointing at all of the people who were standing in the parking lot watching." Then, she grinned. "And you *did* look pissed."

It continued to make no sense whatsoever that despite having been there, right in the middle of it, people who were miles away had a better sense of what had gone on. Of course, maybe they were only being nice, and she had looked terrified and addled. "What about my agents?" she asked.

"It was really hard to see," Juliana said, "but, wow, Paula got in there so fast that it looked like Kyle almost shot *her*."

Which would have to have scared the hell out of both of them—and probably explained why, despite being at such close range, he had only hit the crazy lady in the leg.

When he had fired the gun *right next to her damn head.*

God, she was tired.

"I should probably go down there, hunh?" she asked, using her chin to indicate the second floor.

Juliana and Mary Elizabeth nodded.

Right.

So she got up—let Mary Elizabeth give her a hand up, actually—and limped very slowly down the stairs. Dirk was in the Common Room with Bruce, Debbie, and Gerard, all of them focused on the television screen, playing some video game.

They asked her again if she was okay, and she nodded, then looked into Susan's room to see her on the floor, doing abdominal crunches.

"Too dark to go running," Meg said, as the others returned to their game.

Susan nodded, holding her upper body off the floor for about ten seconds, and then slowly lowering it.

"You could probably burn off more energy if you did push-ups, instead," Meg said.

Susan nodded, lifting herself up again. "I tried that, but I could only manage thirty-four before my arms got tired."

Thirty-four was a pretty decent number. "Modified, or full-out?" Meg asked.

"Full ones," Susan said, not even out of breath as she maintained the abdominal hold.

But, of course.

"So." Susan started lowering herself to the floor. "You need something?"

A JA who was less of an asshole. For starters. "Looking forward to the semester ending?" Meg asked.

Susan nodded. "Pretty much, yeah."

No doubt. In fact, she probably had a countdown clock hidden in her room somewhere. "If I see you in the dining hall or something next year, do I say hello," Meg asked, "or do I turn and go the other way?"

"I don't know. Maybe you could wave at me, from a distance," Susan said, lifting into another crunch.

Yeah, that would work. Even though the notion really hurt her feelings.

Susan glanced at her. "I'm kidding, Meg."

In which case, how very hilarious. Or maybe just thoughtless.

"All I was doing was trying to walk to the damn car," Meg said. "I didn't exactly figure it would be dangerous to sign someone's granddaughter's card." Since, ordinarily, that would be considered a low-risk activity.

Susan nodded, lowered herself to the floor, took a deep breath, and lifted up again.

"I have a higher than average chance of getting knocked off, any day of the week," Meg said. "I wish like hell I didn't, but—well, there isn't much I can do about it. If that's enough to make you not want to be friends with me, that's your call, I guess."

Susan abandoned the crunches and sat up all the way, wrapping her arms around her knees. "Meg, I'm dating a guy whose *job* it is to get knocked off. And the combination of the two of you—" She shook her head. "I need to go run about ten miles, that's all. Then I'll be okay again."

Meg was going to say something sympathetic, but laughed, instead. "Hey, that's the first time you've ever confirmed it."

"Don't tell your mother," Susan said quickly.

Like her mother couldn't find out on her own, if she were so inclined? Except that, of course, she wouldn't be. Bigger fish to fry, one assumed.

Susan blushed. "Anyway. It's none of my business, but try being a little less Jane Wayne next time, too, okay?"

Which would accomplish *what*, exactly? But Susan was one of the rare people—along with Beth—who would tell her the truth. Meg checked to make sure that Dirk and the others were mesmerized by their video game. "Did I, um, look bad? Like I was panicking?"

Susan shook her head. "You looked really *thin*, next to Garth and everyone. But, mainly, as far as I could tell, you were mad as hell."

There seemed to be a commonality of opinion about that, so maybe she was going to have to believe it. "Did *that* look bad?" Meg asked. "Like I was losing it or something?"

"You did her credit, if that's what you're worrying about," Susan said.

Well, yeah. Only Susan didn't know the whole story. "I, um—" Christ, if this got out, it would be terrible, so she threw another glance at the Common Room— "might have had a—" for lack of a better phrase— "psychotic break."

Which got Susan's full attention. "What do you mean?" she asked.

"I thought I was being kidnapped again," Meg said, and shivered. "I mean, I *really* thought so. Then, they had me in this room, where I'd never been, and they all had their guns out, and I *still* thought so."

Susan shook her head. "That's not a psychotic break, that's just a normal reaction. Besides, even if you'd had a huge flashback, that would have been normal, too."

It all seemed sort of blurry now—but, then, it had seemed blurry at the time, too. "They pulled my pants down," Meg said. "I guess they were afraid she'd thrown acid on me or something, but I thought they were about to—well, you know."

Susan scowled. "What a bunch of clods. If they had more women, that kind of thing would—Christ, maybe I *should* let them recruit me."

News to her. "They're trying to recruit you?" Meg asked.

Susan nodded. "I keep getting visits from three-letter agencies, too."

She was pretty small, but demonstrably brave, and in *excellent* shape, and currently on the DC radar, and—it made perfect sense, really. A natural fit. Meg looked at her curiously. "Are you interested?"

"I don't know," Susan said, but, frankly, sounded pretty interested.

"For now, I hear them out. In fact—" She hesitated. "Well, if I had a place to stay in Washington, I might come down for a few days this summer, and go talk to some of them again."

Aha. The plot took an unexpected twist. "You have a boyfriend in Washington," Meg said. Martin had to live within reasonable commuting distance, anyway.

Susan shook her head. "It might be too soon. I'd rather—we're not there yet."

Okay. "Too bad you don't know anyone else who lives in the city, who has *stacks* of spare rooms going to waste," Meg said.

Susan nodded. "It's a damn shame," she said, and they both grinned.

ON HER WAY up to her room, she called Jack, who was very upset and told her he was on his way over, hanging up almost before she had time to say "Hello." So she called Beth, instead, who was also upset, but somewhat less so, because she had managed to get through to Preston earlier, and had heard most of the accurate details already, including the fact that the President her very own self was flying up in the morning—information which had yet to be released officially.

"Want to hear the sad part?" Meg asked.

Beth laughed nervously. "All of it seems pretty sad, so far."

True enough. "The bone I cracked is actually one I *didn't* break the first time around," Meg said. One of the very few.

Beth's laugh was more normal this time. "That *is* sad."

Yeah. It was. Hurt like a bitch, too.

Right after they finished talking, the medium-secure line rang. She wasn't going to pick up, but the caller ID showed Trudy's number.

"Are you all right, Meghan?" Trudy asked, when she answered.

"Mostly, yeah, thank you," Meg said. Although she'd be better after she took a couple of pain pills, and possibly another Valium. "But, Mom and Dad flipped."

"Can you blame them?" Trudy asked.

Not really. "Mom's flying up here tomorrow," Meg said.

"Yes, your father told me," Trudy said approvingly. "That's as it should be."

Months overdue, even. "How long do you think Dad'll be able to hold off until he shows up, too?" Meg asked.

"Tomorrow afternoon, I expect," Trudy said.

Probably, yeah. Meg let out her breath. "She looked like a nice, safe grandmother lady."

"I know, that's one of the reasons I called," Trudy said, sounding unhappy. "I'm sorry."

Well, hell, it wasn't *her* fault that one of her peers had gone around the bend. And if the lady turned out to claim to be some twisted version of a Catholic, *that* wouldn't be her fault, either.

"I'm going to come visit you on Saturday," Trudy said.

Which was very thoughtful, but not necessary. Meg shook her head. "You don't have to do that. I mean, it's really nice of you, but—"

Trudy cut her off. "I already have my reservations, dear. I'll be there in the afternoon, and if you want, we can have supper together, unless you and your friends already have plans."

Of *course* she wanted. "I think C-Span'll be showing the White House Correspondents' Dinner," Meg said.

"Well," Trudy said, and Meg could almost hear the smile in her voice. "Then, we'll have to order room service or takeout, won't we."

Yep.

She was just about to check her voice-mail when Jack rushed through the half-open door, breathing hard.

"Did you run the whole way?" she asked.

He nodded, panting. "Except for the part when I was being sly, so that reporters wouldn't notice me." He took off the baseball cap which had been pulled down to cover most of his face, and she was offended to see that it was a Yankee's cap.

"What's that?" she asked, even though she knew perfectly well what it was.

He flicked the hat out into the hallway, where she hoped it landed in the most undignified way possible. "Wore it on purpose, Meg, so they'd figure there was *no way* I was someone you were dating."

Oh. "That *was* sly," she said.

He nodded, looking very pleased with himself.

Not the method she would have picked, but it had been effective, in its skin-crawling way.

He sat down on the bed and kissed her so hard that they didn't talk for a while.

"You all right?" he asked finally.

She nodded. "Yeah. Not my ideal day, maybe."

"Not mine, either," he said.

No, probably not.

"Saw some guys outside on my way over here, looked like they were sealing up a mailbox," he said against her mouth.

Meaning that people from the advance team, and her mother's security detail, and the White House Communications Agency, and so forth, were starting to arrive, and the complicated logistical dance of preparing for the President's imminent arrival was under way.

"We having company tomorrow?" he asked.

An intuitive leap; how nice. "We are," she said.

He nodded. "So, there's not a chance in hell I'm going to get to spend the night here tonight."

Alas, no. Among other things, the WHCA people were going to appear at her door soon, to sweep her room, and install new high-tech super-secure phone lines, and that sort of thing. But, it was still pretty funny that that had been his first thought.

They had barely started kissing again when the drop-line rang, and they both looked at it.

"Aw, crap," he said, sighed, and took his hands off her breasts.

While she talked to each member of her family in turn—Steven's sole contribution was a muttered "Sorry you got hurt again and stuff," Jack picked up her psychology book and started going through the chapter they were supposed to have completed by Friday. He used a blue pen to underline various phrases and sentences as he read, which was an unexpected bonus, since it meant that she might be able to get away with just skimming those specific parts later on.

"I really need her to do this," she said quietly, when she was talking to her father, since she was worried that his feelings might be hurt.

"I know, Meg," he answered. "It'll be good for both of you."

"But, I'm guessing you're coming in the afternoon, right?" she asked.

"Yes," he said.

When she hung up the phone, she was amused to see that Jack felt compelled to finish the section he was reading and neatly close the book before he kissed her again.

Except, maybe they should hold off for another minute. "Hang on, okay?" she said, picked up the drop-line again, and asked to be connected to Steven directly.

"*What?*" he said impatiently, when he came on the phone. "I already talked to you and everything."

"I'm *okay*, Steven," she said. "I really am. And my agents were excellent. Fast as hell."

There was a heavy silence on the other end.

"So, what's the deal?" he asked. "Now, we've gotta be afraid of *old ladies*?"

"No, she was just a nut," Meg said. "It's not going to be, you know, a trend."

"Man, it better not be," he said grimly.

Yeah. As of today, Secret Service profiling guidelines had become much more complex. "I just wanted to be sure you and Neal are okay," she said.

He made an extremely offensive noise, and she decided to take that as a yes.

They talked for another few minutes, and she got him relaxed enough to tell her more about the new dog her family had, in fact, adopted over the weekend—a shepherd/collie mix they had named Sam, who had only had two accidents in the house so far, and was mostly sleeping on Steven's bed at night, and when they finally hung up, she felt a lot better—and hoped that he did, too.

Jack closed her psychology book for the second time. "More making out now?"

Hell, yeah. Ideally, *a lot* more.

They were in grave danger of getting too carried away for her to be capable of answering the door, when the inevitable knocks from WHCA and everyone started to come, so she pulled away from him, and patted the side of his face lightly. He nodded, took a few deep breaths, zipped himself back up, and then moved so that they were sitting next to each other at the top of the bed, with his arm around her.

"So, we're not going to do it tonight?" he asked.

Could he maybe *try* to be less phallocentric? She shook her head.

"That way," he said, "when I meet her, I could be thinking, 'Hey, lady, you may run the world, but *I* nailed your daughter last night.' "

Jesus. Could he possibly think that was funny? She didn't look at him, because she was afraid to see whatever expression might be on his face.

"We kid, because we love," he said.

It was a joke. Okay. A person could make an inappropriate joke, without being a sociopathic—

He cleared his throat. "And I meant the part about the, uh, love."

Christ, if she was going to spend the rest of her life associating any kind of remotely barbed male humor with—she realized what he had just said, and stared at him. In fact, it was entirely possible that her mouth fell open.

Jack flushed slightly. "Okay, so not only did I say it *first,* which'll get me drummed out of the Guy Corps, but I just said it to someone who I'm pretty sure isn't going to say it back."

She was still staring at him—*frowning* at him, more accurately—when she realized that he was waiting for her to respond.

Which she didn't.

He looked disappointed. Crushed, in fact. "Jesus, you really aren't going to say it, are you."

Either he was someone she could talk to honestly—or he *wasn't.* "No, I think I am," she said. "But, I'm going to need a few minutes to get there, okay?" Get her nerve up, more precisely.

He nodded, but his jaw was clenched.

Damn. "Could I—" She stopped. In certain ways, this was almost worse than facing a raving, knife-wielding maniac. Very dangerous territory. "Would it be okay if I told you about today, first, and how completely, freaking terrified I was?"

His body relaxed, and then, he tightened his arm around her shoulders. "Sounds like a good idea."

She looked at him. "I *won't* kid, because I love."

"Sounds even better," he said.

54

THE PRESIDENT WAS very prompt.

At any rate, she arrived at the campus on time, and appeared to have only the briefest of press conferences, followed by an exchange of handshakes with college officials, outside. But even though there were agents and aides everywhere, indicating that she was in the building, it seemed to take a very long time for her to show up on the third floor, and Meg limped down the hall to try and figure out where the hell she was.

Then, the elevator opened, and the President appeared, unabashedly elegant in a jazzy red ensemble, albeit sans chapeau. She and her mother both had to stop short, to keep from bumping into each other, Meg almost losing her balance, and an already potentially stressful encounter seemed that much more so, especially given the fact that there were so many people clustered in the stairwell and hallway, watching every move they made.

She wasn't sure where the designated holding room was—the basement Common Room was her best guess—but maybe they should have arranged to meet there alone, first, instead of being forced to exchange greetings in front of such a large group.

Her mother glanced at her cast so swiftly that Meg was almost positive that no one else in the very crowded corridor had caught the deep anguish in her expression. But then, it was gone, and she was already working the hall, introducing herself to people with a dignified, but approachable, "Hello, I'm Meg's mother."

Tammy was clearly dazzled—to the degree that she actually *curtsied*, and Juliana and Mary Elizabeth, and most of the other people from the entry, were all so busy trying to be cool, that it was obvious that they were pretty impressed, while Susan was standing off to the side, looking, in her polite way, suspicious, and maybe even downright judgmental.

For whatever damn reason.

Jack had come over early, kindly bringing coffee along with him, and while he hadn't dressed up, his Hawaiian shirt was tucked in neatly, and fastened one button higher than usual. He stumbled a little, both over his feet, and his words, when the President shook his hand, and Meg wasn't sure whether to feel sorry for him—or laugh.

It was frustrating that her mother had yet to give her anything resembling full eye contact—or any real physical contact, even—but at least she seemed to be making a good impression on almost everyone else, with only Susan's reserved frown to mar an otherwise clean sweep of her entrymates.

"You're eating a little more?" her mother asked in a low voice.

Oh. Wait. Was that actual, undivided attention? Meg nodded. "I'm trying."

Her mother touched her arm for a second, right above the sling. "Okay, I'm glad."

Which was about much more than her recent caloric intake, of course, and Meg caught on to the fact that they were both unbelievably upset about the attack—and entirely unable to show it, in front of so many witnesses, and that was why they couldn't look at each other, or even say a satisfactory hello. She was about to suggest that they go into her room for a minute, by themselves, but Winifred came sidling over and murmured something to her mother, who listened, and then shook her head. Winifred nodded, and stepped away, already lifting her phone to her ear before she had even made it all the way out to the landing.

It was a typical interlude in their lives, but for some reason, it seemed to throw her mother off that much more, and even though this was the person who had given *birth* to her, Meg couldn't think of anything to say to her, either. Which made her feel a tiny twinge of panic, to go along with the general discomfort, and awkwardness, and—

"You played tennis," her mother said.

Something she had only mentioned in passing, a few days earlier, and, at the time, her mother had seemed either not to be listening—or not to be sufficiently impressed by the information.

Or it might just have made her nervous, because of the negative repercussions for her knee.

"How'd you hit?" her mother asked.

Meg couldn't not grin, feeling—well, okay—proud as hell of herself, even though she wasn't likely to be out there again anytime soon. *Shouldn't* be, anyway. "The ball pretty much has to come right to me, but I wasn't bad. Especially the forehand. I mean, I got really tired after about fifteen minutes, but I played."

Her mother smiled at her. "When you come home, you'll have to show me."

Yeah.

And just like that, it seemed so good to have her here—looking incredibly goddamn confident, and powerful, and hell, *presidential*—that, if there hadn't been so many people around, Meg was almost sure that she might lean her head on her mother's shoulder. Or maybe even—perish the thought—*hug* her.

Which her mother must have picked up on, because she moved a step closer. "I can't tell you how happy I am to see you," she whispered.

At the end of the hall, some of the hostility went out of Susan's posture, and she nodded, seemingly to herself.

"Maybe the two of us should—" her mother started.

Upon which, Winifred reappeared, and her mother inclined her head to listen to whatever she was being told, and then nodded once.

"I'm sorry, you all will have to excuse me for a moment," she said, and went into Meg's room, Winifred right behind her.

"Is everything okay, or is it some kind of national emergency?" Jack asked.

Hard to tell. "Either," Meg said, and shrugged. "Or both. I don't know."

"Hmmm," he said. "Kind of makes me nervous."

It probably *should*, given the panoply of dire crises which could be arising, even as they all stood here casually in a college dormitory corridor on a partly cloudy Thursday morning. "Can you do me a favor?" she asked. "I need to spend some time with her, but I'll call you if she's going to be here long enough to have coffee or something?"

"Sure." He glanced at his watch. "I'll go catch the rest of Art History."

Unquestionably a swell, if astoundingly academic, guy.

Once it was apparent that the President was going to be engaged for an unknown length of time, everyone else started to wander away, too, but she caught Susan's eye and motioned towards the restroom. Susan shook her head, but Meg motioned again, and, after frowning, Susan nodded and changed her direction to walk in there, instead. Meg followed her in, gesturing for the Secret Service agent who was posted just inside—a woman she didn't know—to step out momentarily, while Susan leaned against one of the sinks, folding her arms.

"You were expecting Medea?" Meg asked, when they were alone.

Susan looked worried. "I don't know. Maybe."

Oh, for Christ's sakes.

"How'd you *hit,*" Susan said, with undisguised disgust.

What was wrong with that? Meg shrugged. "Seemed like a fair question to me." A perfectly legitimate question. The obvious question, even.

"She's your *mother,*" Susan said. "She's supposed to say, 'Hooray!,' 'Wow!,' 'Good for you, you spunky little thing!' "

If any of that were to take place, she, personally, would hide behind the nearest large object until, with luck, the President came to her senses again.

"She was supposed to hug you," Susan said.

Well, that was a more valid criticism, if still presumptuous. But, in all fairness— "I was probably supposed to hug *her,*" Meg said.

Susan nodded. "Yeah."

When, and if, she met the McAllisters again, she was going to have to remind herself to be openly, cruelly critical about them, afterwards, regardless of whether the reaction was warranted. Meg shrugged. "She's just private. It's totally different, when nobody's looking."

And her best guess was, that a few minutes from now, her mother was going to hug her like crazy—and then make some sort of bitchy remark about her "If Lost or Stolen" shirt.

"That's a little scary, then, because in public, you always seem like a polite, perfect family," Susan said.

Meg shrugged again. "When we're alone, we're a polite, *imperfect* family."

"Well, okay, so are we," Susan said, sounding somewhat quelled.

Since families could mostly only choose between being polite and imperfect—or *impolite* and imperfect.

"We should really just leave it at that," Susan said, "right?"

Yup.

When they went out to the hallway, her mother was opening her door to see where she was, and Winifred was walking away, back on her cell phone.

"It was very nice to meet you, Madam President," Susan said.

"You, too, Susan," her mother said, and shook her hand. "I can't thank you enough for everything you've done to help my daughter."

Susan blushed, shrugged, and made a fairly quick exit to the stairs.

Once she and her mother were finally alone in her room, her mother gave her a nearly ferocious hug.

"Are you all right?" she asked.

Meg nodded.

"Are you *sure*?" her mother asked.

Meg nodded, even though she really wasn't sure at all.

"My God, Meg, your hand," her mother said, her voice shaking. "I can't believe you broke your *hand*."

Did she mean yesterday—or ever?

"I am so sorry," her mother said, hanging on to her. "I don't even know what to—they're going to prosecute that monstrous woman into oblivion."

"She's probably insane," Meg said, slouching into the hug, without really having the energy to return it, but happy to be a recipient.

"She's *indisputably* insane," her mother said, "but I don't ever want her walking free again."

Hard to make an argument for a lesser punishment, when a large hunting knife was involved—and had been used. She had finally seen Paula earlier, in passing, and it turned out that she had needed thirty-two stitches, and her arm was thickly bandaged, but she assured Meg that it was just a scratch, and that there was no need whatsoever to thank her, although Meg did so, regardless. Profusely.

Her mother touched her cheek. "You look so tired. Were you able to sleep at all?"

Barely. Jack had left around midnight, his exit duly recorded by the press, and she'd felt lonely and afraid, and stayed awake for hours, her hand and knee aching intensely, even though she'd propped them up on pillows and several folded sweatshirts. So, Meg shook her head. "Not really."

"Do you want to come back to Washington?" her mother asked. "You could just take a few days at home, and—"

With the semester winding down? No way. "I'll be fine," Meg said. In the small picture, anyway. "Don't worry." To force them onto another topic, she moved back to examine her mother's outfit. "It's nice and all, but you look sort of—I don't know—*French*."

Her mother nodded. "I know, but it's cut so beautifully that I couldn't resist."

Which was the sort of flimsy excuse the President always used when she occasionally caught flack for wearing something designed by anyone other than an American. "Well, it might keep me from voting for you, but *c'est très charmant*, regardless," Meg said.

Her mother smiled, and picked up the huge unfinished cup of take-out coffee that was on the desk. "I confess that I helped myself to some of this already. I assumed you wouldn't mind."

Not to go too Clouseau on her, but— "I don't mind," Meg said, and waited for her to start to drink some. "Of course, it's not mine."

Her mother stopped, mid-gulp.

"It was Jack's," Meg said.

"Oh." Her mother frowned down at the cup. "Presumably, *he* won't mind?"

"No," Meg said, and gave her time to lift it up again. "But, it's decaf."

Her mother nearly recoiled, and set the cup down. "Yes, of course. I sensed that it was a bit off, at once."

Yeah. Sure.

"He's a handsome devil, by the way," her mother said.

Indubitably.

There was a knock on the door, and her mother opened it, listening to the Deputy Chief of Staff tell her something Meg couldn't hear, and then frowned.

"Winnie, I'm sorry, but that did not even remotely pass the test of being important enough to interrupt us," her mother said.

The fact that the President had a *refined* bark didn't make it any less of a bark.

"Anything bad going on today?" Meg asked, when her mother was sitting in the desk chair again, looking nettled.

Her mother shook her head. "Some minor huffing and puffing. It'll be fine." She looked at the decaf coffee some more, then shrugged and resumed drinking it. "I must say, I don't think your friend Susan is very taken by me."

Didn't seem that way, no. " 'How'd you hit?' bugged her," Meg said.

Her mother nodded. "I heard that come out of my mouth, and I thought, Christ almighty, Kate, can't you just tell the kid you're proud of her?"

It wouldn't have been the world's worst idea.

"I am, by the way," her mother said. "Immeasurably so."

Which was nice to hear.

"But I suspect that what's really bothering her is 'Can not, have not, and *will* not,' " her mother said.

Meg didn't have the heart to agree.

Her mother stared at her purloined cup of coffee, then put it down, where it would be out of reach. "It's the Susan McAllisters of the world I'm never going to get back."

It was difficult to see that much pain in someone's eyes.

"More importantly, I don't think I'm ever going to get the four of you back," her mother said softly. "Or, at any rate, the *three* of you. I suppose Neal is in his own category."

If Neal ever figured out the extent of his capacity for power and influence, he would have to work very hard to resist the temptation to become unbearable.

"Well," her mother said, and glanced at the door as though she might be hoping that Winifred would make a timely return.

"You have to start forgiving yourself," Meg said. "Because, as far as I'm concerned, it's *completely* getting in the way."

Her mother's laugh was harsh. "You can say this the very day after you bore the brunt of the fact that I happen to believe that women have an inviolable right to make private medical decisions about their own bodies?"

Meg nodded.

"I can't protect you," her mother said. "I have more power than any one person has a right to—" She shook her head, instead of finishing the sentence. "But it's all superfluous in the end, because *I can't protect you*. Any of you."

Granted, this was an extreme case, but had a parent ever lived who had found it humanly possible to protect his or her children completely? Not anything she felt like pointing out right now—but, still.

There was another knock on the door, and it was admirable that her mother *didn't* swear, before she went over to answer it. But this time, it was Dr. Brooks, along with her primary hand and knee surgeons from Washington.

"Oh, good," her mother said, and let them in.

So, she was examined and prodded and questioned, while her mother paid very close attention, even though Winifred and Linda and Saunderson, the deputy National Security Advisor, each came in and out more than once, with various updates and requests.

Then Frank stood in the doorway, and nodded.

Her mother nodded back, and got up. "Thank you," she said. "I know it's inconvenient, but can you have each of them hold in place for a few minutes, and I'll come right down?"

As he left to arrange that, Meg raised her eyebrows.

"I can't not thank them in person," her mother said.

"Kyle and Paula?" Meg asked.

"And your friend who doesn't like me very much," her mother said, giving her a fast kiss on the top of the head. "I'll be back momentarily."

Her father—who was just about to leave the White House and head out to Andrews—called while her mother was still downstairs, and it was far more pleasant to spend time on the phone with him, than it was to listen to Dr. Brooks and the others talk to one another about possible rotational malalignment, the dorsal midline, whether they should proceed with percutaneous k-wire fixation, how they felt about the AP and oblique views they had seen, and if she should have a tomogram, and maybe a CT scan, too.

If she spent too much more god-damn time with doctors, she was going to be informally qualified to practice medicine herself.

When her mother came back upstairs, her only comment was that her conversations had been confidential, and that if any of them wanted Meg to know the details, she was sure that they would share them later on.

There was some debate about whether they should go to the hospital so that the doctors could do more precise tests and radiographic studies, and the general feeling seemed to be that her North Adams doctors could drive down and meet the Presidential party at the hospital in Pittsfield—which, Meg assumed, was designed to spare her from having to revisit the scene of the attack.

But, god-damn it, she really didn't need to be coddled that way. She would prefer not to have more tests, but if she needed them, she wanted to be someplace where she knew people, and since all area medical facilities were put on alert whenever the President left the White House, there was no need to ask whether it would be secure enough.

Meg looked at her mother. "I think you should see where I've been going all these months, and meet Vicky and Cheryl and everyone, too."

Her mother picked up a brush from the dresser and started running it through her hair, which seemed affectionate, but was also probably designed to fix whatever mess was there, as opposed to complaining about it later. "I'm not sure if I'm comfortable having you go back so soon."

Meg pointed towards the hallway, where Dr. Brooks and the surgeons were waiting. "You know they're dying to go do that tomography or whatever."

Her mother sighed. "I don't know if I want you to go through *that* today, either."

She wasn't excited by the concept herself, but if she had to do it, she would rather get it out of the way—accompanied by at least one of her parents, instead of having to spend the weekend dreading the prospect. "I think we should just go," she said. "And afterwards, you can stand out front and give a nice little statement, and make that lady twice as crazy by not even *mentioning* yesterday."

Her mother shook her head, but she was also smiling. "There are moments, Meg, when I think you are a woman after Nero's heart."

Yeah, yeah, yeah. A woman after *Linda's* heart, more likely.

"And if I haven't mentioned it yet," her mother said, "I really dislike your shirt."

Christ, it had taken her long enough to say so. Meg grinned. "Beth gave it to me."

"Well, as you know, I love Beth, but I despise the shirt," her mother said.

Odds were, her father was going to hate it twice as much as her mother did. Meg took a purple and white pinstriped Oxford shirt from her closet, and after she shrugged into it, she let her mother button it up for her, and help her put the sling back on.

"Are you sure about this?" her mother asked, looking at her intently. "Bob and the others could come back here on Monday, and do the tests, then."

No doubt. "If you have enough time, I'd rather go today," Meg said.

"Okay, then," her mother said, and held out her cane for her. "Let's take a ride."

THE SEATS IN the Presidential limo were so comfortable that she was tempted to curl up and take a nap. Her mother looked exhausted, too, and maybe the best decision would have been not to bother going to the hospital at all, and just have the motorcade drive around aimlessly while they both sacked out for a couple of hours.

"Did *you* sleep okay last night?" Meg asked.

Her mother smiled faintly. "I don't think I can remember the last time I slept well, Meg."

Odds were, she hadn't had a night of *uninterrupted* sleep since the Inauguration, and maybe not since before the campaign. Her staff was under orders not to disturb them during this drive, unless it was an emergency, but, of course, that was no guarantee that the phone wouldn't start ringing.

"What?" Meg asked, aware that her mother was sitting there, staring at nothing.

Her mother shook her head. "I'm sorry. I was just thinking."

Dark thoughts, no doubt. "Sunshine and daisies and little bunnies gamboling about?" Meg asked.

"Naturally," her mother said, but her smile was still weak.

Did she want to pursue that—or just let it drop? "What?" Meg asked.

Her mother shook her head again, and reached for the top folder on the nearest stack of briefing materials.

Perpetual avoidance got tiresome. "*What?*" Meg asked, less patiently.

It didn't seem as though her mother was going to answer, but then she let out her breath. "A lot of what you've been told about my mother isn't true," she said.

That was out of left field. Meg frowned. "What do you mean?"

Her mother flipped the folder open. "Nothing. I'm sorry. I was thinking aloud."

Swell. Then, why bring it up? "You've never told me much of anything," Meg said. "Other than what happened to her." Whoa, was there some hidden, unsavory secret there? Except, how likely was that, in a world where journalists and bloggers managed to find out damned near everything about people, no matter how personal or obscure the information was? "A riding accident *is* what happened to her, right?"

Her mother nodded, using a silver pen to make a note in the margin of one of the pages.

"You always never think aloud," Meg said. Too damned cautious for that.

"Well, I just—" Her mother stopped. "She wasn't—I'm sorry. Forget I mentioned it."

Fine. Whatever. Nothing new there. Meg looked at her cast, noticing that her hand had started throbbing. Badly.

Her mother sighed. "You're right. That isn't fair." She closed her eyes for a minute, then opened them and put her pen away. "I don't know. From what I gather, apparently the novelty of having me wore off pretty quickly. I mean, I don't want to sound—for all I know, that would have changed, with time. She was very young."

Twenty-six, when she died. Possibly twenty-seven. And it was beyond strange that she didn't actually know which answer was right. That none of this had ever been discussed.

And all the more unnerving to see her mother looking so unsure of herself. Vulnerable. Her face very pale, in comparison to her bright red suit. "It was an accident," Meg said cautiously. "She didn't mean for it to happen."

Her mother nodded. "No, of course not. After all, I was *there*. She fell right in front of me."

Which had to have done some serious damage to the sweet, happy five-year-old she'd seen in photographs, who looked so different from the thin, forlorn child of only a year later—and for that matter, the rather remote, sad-eyed adult.

"She was a reckless person," her mother said. "Reckless with her possessions, reckless with me, reckless with the damn horse. Too often, I think I was a plaything, whom it was easier to leave with Maud, when there was something more interesting to do."

Maud, being her very British nanny. Governess, to be precise. "But, you loved her," Meg said. Or, so she had always heard.

Her mother nodded. "I adored her. And my father did, too. But—well, I gather that she was a certain kind of Upper East Side woman. Too rich, too spoiled, and too bored."

So far, this conversation felt utterly bewildering. Or maybe she was just tired, and not following the connections properly. Hell, maybe they were both too drained to make sense.

Her mother swallowed. "I'm not saying that she didn't love me. I'm sure she did. But, on the whole, she wanted to live her life, and I could be so very inconvenient, I suppose. And she had the luxury of being able to hand me off to someone else, at the slightest whim, so that she could go away and do what she wanted to do."

Finally. A little bit of illumination. "That's not who you are," Meg said quietly.

Her mother looked right at her. "Isn't it? I'll grant you that it may manifest differently, but in the end, it's really very much the same thing. Misplaced priorities, and an inexcusable self-absorption."

Maybe. Meg returned the steady gaze. "How many people would you, personally, have been willing to kill to get me back?"

"How high can you count?" her mother asked.

Meg shook her head. "I don't mean cruise missiles, or calling up the 82nd Airborne, or something. I mean, *you*, personally."

"How high can you count?" her mother asked, never breaking eye contact for a second.

Jesus. It was maybe more than she wanted to know, but it was also something that only a person who loved her desperately would say. Meg looked down at her cast and tried to move the one finger which still had never been broken, feeling a searing shock of pain go through her, shooting all the way up to her shoulder and neck. She didn't need to be told the answer to this question, but— "Can a person who isn't ruthless win the Presidency?"

The cold "can not, have not, and will not" expression moved across her face, and then her mother shook her head. "No, I don't think so," she said. "And even if it were possible, he or she wouldn't be strong enough for the job."

Exactly what she had already assumed, so Meg just nodded.

"Do you want to know something I've never even told your father?" her mother asked.

Hard to believe that there could be any secrets *left*.

"It *was* easier because it was you," her mother said. "As opposed to Steven or Neal."

Well, great. The truth finally came out. Parents weren't supposed to havc favorites, and now her mother was admitting that she did. She had always suspected it; now, she knew for sure.

Her mother reached out to touch her shoulder. "Which is not to say that it was in any way easy, but simply that it was easier."

Meg nodded, and shrugged the hand away. "Because of my being more difficult to be around."

Her mother shook her head. "Because of your being so much more likely to survive."

Or less likely to be *missed*.

"You're even tougher than I am, Meg, and I'm so tough that I frighten myself," her mother said.

Well, God knows her mother scared *her* on a regular basis. "I'm not that tough," Meg said stiffly.

Instead of contradicting that, her mother brought her hand back over to rest just above the cast.

If they were swinging for the fences today, *fine*. No point in hiding her own big secret anymore. "I gave serious thought to trading sex for freedom," Meg said.

Her mother nodded. "I thought you might have."

Which was the last reaction she had expected, and Meg stared at her, horrified by the idea that her mother had known that she was a coward for all these months, and never said so.

"Did he talk you into it?" her mother asked.

Jesus Christ, *that* was what she had assumed for the past year? Meg scowled at her. "What in the hell kind of question is that?"

Her mother moved her hand up to cup her cheek. "I'm sorry. But—all rumors to the contrary—I know you pretty well, and there has to be some reason why you're so very angry at yourself."

It might be better if her mother were a little less perceptive.

"And," her mother said, when she didn't answer, "it's really your own private business, isn't it."

That was for god-damned sure.

But, if she didn't respond, her mother would end up with some very incorrect assumptions. "He talked me *out* of it," Meg said through her teeth.

Her mother's hand tensed for a second. "Ah," she said, then. "A few things suddenly make a great deal more sense."

The reality of her not being brave enough, for example.

Her mother put her arm around her. "Sometimes, there aren't any good decisions available, and you still have to make one, anyway."

When it came to that, she was certainly sitting next to an expert.

Her mother sighed. "Meg, do you honestly think I didn't come *very* close to negotiating? I was pretty sure I wouldn't be able to bring myself to do it, but that doesn't mean that I didn't weigh my options, every single minute of every single hour, for thirteen days."

Was that really an apt comparison? The political, as opposed to the personal.

Her mother brought her other arm over, and held her the exact same way she had the time they'd stayed up all night. "And there's nothing wrong with having mixed feelings about him, either," she said gently. "I'm *grateful* if there were moments when he showed humanity."

The moments had been few and far between, but they had been there. "I feel like a coward," Meg said.

"And I feel like an absolute failure," her mother said. "But, that doesn't make either of us right."

Meg leaned against her, wishing that the hospital was much farther away, and that they weren't going to have to get out and face the world soon.

"I can't remember the last thing I said to you," her mother whispered.

How unsettling. "Well," Meg edged away from her slightly. "We were talking about whether I should feel like a—"

Her mother shook her head impatiently.

Oh.

Her mother looked at her with great intensity. "I go over it, and over it, and I can't remember that morning at all."

Whereas she remembered the entire thing, almost verbatim.

"I remember that you didn't really eat anything," her mother said unhappily. "And I kept thinking about how hungry you must be."

An area where the man had entirely *lacked* humanity.

"I can't bear it that we sent you off that way," her mother said.

Which was kind of silly. "I've almost never had a good breakfast," Meg said. "I mean, you guys let me go to school like that for years."

Her mother nodded, guiltily, then looked at her with distinct urgency. "Was I unkind to you that day? I think I remember being cross."

Again, a run-of-the-mill family breakfast. "Well, yeah," Meg said. "Sort of. You guys didn't approve of what I was wearing, and Neal and I had a little scuffle, and you didn't like it that I ate cereal right out of the box, and you also wanted me to maybe go somewhere else and do homework and stop bugging you."

All of which, from the look on her mother's face, was even worse than she'd imagined.

"That's every morning, Mom," Meg said. Or, anyway, before, it was. “You also laughed at some of the stuff I was saying, and you and Dad both wanted to know if I was staying after school, or if I was coming home to play tennis, and I said yes, and yes, but I didn’t hug either of you good-bye, because I was too cool for that.”

Her mother’s shoulders slumped. “I just wish I’d sent you off with a reminder of how deeply I love you. That maybe it would have been something you could hold on to during—that you would have had the strength of that behind you.”

“I did have it, Mom,” Meg said. Which was actually the truth. “I also had it yesterday.”

And *today*, too, if either of them happened to be keeping score.

“God, I hope so,” her mother said.

They were very close to the hospital now, and people on the sidewalks, and strip mall parking lots, were all stopping to stare at the motorcade as it passed them.

“I don’t want to spend the whole damn summer going to doctors’ appointments and physical therapy,” Meg said.

Her mother nodded. “I know. Maybe we could set something up for you over at Brookings—” which was a mostly non-partisan, but also very open-minded, think tank— “or, perhaps—”

“I want you to help me put together something humanitarian,” Meg said. “Not just, you know, a goodwill appearance, but me really trying to accomplish something.”

Her mother frowned. “You know how strongly your father and I feel about lowering your profile as much as possible.”

And what a fine, sturdy barn they were building to house their long-gone horses. “Technically,” Meg said, keeping her voice as non-confrontational as possible, “given the fact that I’m an adult, I could decide to decline my Secret Service protection, go out and find full corporate or NGO sponsorship, and head out on any god-damn trip I want.”

Her mother took that one without much more than a small twitch at the side of her jaw. “Well,” she said, sounding just as reasonable, “ideally, you’re considerably more intelligent than that.”

Ideally—but not necessarily.

"Do you have any specific humanitarian effort in mind?" her mother asked.

Well, there were certainly lots of social problems out there to be tackled. Poverty. Prejudice. Disease-stricken children. Illiteracy. Landmine victims. AIDS orphans. Subjugated women. Religious intolerance. "Your world hunger initiatives," Meg said.

"No war-torn lands," her mother said instantly.

Hmmm. Given the nature of hunger, that could be limiting. Meg thought that over. "Define 'war.' "

Her mother looked very tired.

"Okay. But it has to be a hell of a lot more than some lame afternoon photo-op at a soup kitchen in downtown Washington," Meg said. And more than sitting in a tiny cubicle somewhere doing policy research.

That left a lot of middle ground, and her mother gave her a careful nod. "I'm willing to have our people explore the logistics, and maybe come up with some possible itineraries, but if your father isn't going to accompany you the entire time, the whole idea goes off the table. It can't come at the expense of your physical recovery, either." She paused. "And you have to gain ten pounds."

Wait a minute, how had that last one gotten in there?

"Meg, you can't go out there and talk about world hunger, when you look like you're *suffering* from it," her mother said.

Oh. Okay, she had a point. And there was a workable compromise to be found somewhere in all of that, so Meg nodded, and her mother nodded back.

They were pulling up to the main entrance now, surrounded by the flashing lights of police cars, as well as her mother's massive security contingent.

Even though this was an impromptu, unpublicized visit, a small clump of protestors was already waiting, waving signs, and standing behind a police-line in the parking lot. Christ, did they carry posters around in the trunks of their cars—or, more likely, inside the cargo holds of their stupid, gas-guzzling SUVs—on the off-chance that the President of the

United States might happen by, on a given day, and they would have the opportunity to fling invective and verbal abuse in her direction?

She considered being afraid, but really, what was the point? So, she nudged her mother's arm with her cast and gestured towards the seedy little crew. "Pissed off any wacko fringe groups today?"

"Oh, no doubt," her mother said, sounding simultaneously wry and resigned.

Meg nodded. "Okay. When the car door opens, you go left, and I'll go right. It might confuse them, if they have to choose, and maybe it'll improve our odds."

Her mother looked at her—directly *at* her, which was good—for a very long minute.

"It's never going to be funny, Meg," she said finally.

"No, it isn't," Meg said, and—what the hell—laughed, anyway.

Thank you for reading

this FEIWEL AND FRIENDS book.

The Friends who made

LONG MAY SHE REIGN

possible are:

JEAN FEIWEL
publisher

LIZ SZABLA
editor-in-chief

RICH DEAS
creative director

ELIZABETH FITHIAN
marketing director

ELIZABETH USURIELLO
assistant to the publisher

DAVE BARRETT
managing editor

NICOLE LIEBOWITZ MOULAISON
production manager

JESSICA TEDDER
editorial assistant

CHRISTINE TADLER
marketing/design assistant